Deadly Endings first published as an eBook in the USA March 2013 and in London as a paperback in November 2013.

This second Paperback edition published in the UK in August 2014

Published by Random Harvest Publishing, London and Barcelona.
Randomharvestpublishing@yahoo.co.uk

A CIP catalogue record for this book is available from the British Library.

ISBN 9780953390113
Also available as an eBook ISBN 9781626754478

For Wilma and Gigi

My thanks to dear friends,
Anne-Marie Herrmann and Joana Ocaña
Garcia, two women of Barcelona who lived
under Franco's rule.

I also owe my gratitude to the staff of Tower
Bridge, who gave me unparalleled access
and the people of Richmond, Paris and
Barcelona.

Deadly Endings
By Raymond Russell

Chapter 1
Piombino, Italy, Easter 1907

Wide, brown leather straps with small, brass buckles
ensnared the young boy's wrists and ankles against a thick,
circular piece of wood. His body sprawled out like Leonardo
da Vinci's Vitruvian Man. He couldn't move an inch in any
direction and what's more, he didn't want to. The wooden
board felt unstable beneath him and although the arena was
large, it was also pitch black, except for a powerful spotlight
trained on his entire body, like a full moon reflected in a
puddle. The target squinted his serpentine-green eyes shut
against the glare. The people present were silent, watching,
anticipating disaster or even hoping for it.

The first knife was a shock to the seven year old boy,
the deadly sharp, metal blade exactly twelve inches long,
moved through the air at incredible velocity, slicing into the
wood with a sharp thud. He couldn't see anything, except
the blinding pool of light filling his eyelids, and then the boy
heard the whoosh of steel when it passed his head, missing
by a couple inches. He was more prepared for the second
blade; it arrived with another whiz and thud in the oak
panel. This time the angle was different; after the tip entered
the wood, the blade vibrated wildly and nicked the child's
left ear.

A small trickle of blood erupted from his lobe and
dribbled leisurely down his neck. Each of the damascened
ancient blades was a rare antique, languishing in the Turk's
family for generations, beautifully crafted, and inlaid with
solid gold images of wild animals. The continual thud of the
other metal shafts hitting the circular wooden panel behind
him, became faster and faster.

Now the oak disk started to move, a girl was
spinning it around so that Zamo's body turned upside down
as rapidly as a record on a tilted gramophone. The faster he
turned on the board the more rapidly the antique blades
arrived: Eighteen – nineteen – twenty!

The formally silent circus crowd roared and clapped
with joy and admiration.

1

The tent's lights went up, the brass band broke its silence, the powerful limelight moved to the centre of the sawdust ring, following the Great Scallini, billed as the greatest knife thrower in Europe, he bowed and waved to the adoring crowd.

The Turk looked magnificent in his maharaja's costume of red, green and gold, crowned with a pointed turban, crested with a foot long ostrich feather. His voluptuous, odalisque assistant was dressed in baggy, transparent, eastern trousers that hung low on her flat stomach. Above she wore a short décolleté top that had long transparent sleeves in matching green and gold, exposing her slim waist down to her supple hips. Zahra, the young Eastern Russian, joined the Turk in the limelight to the delight of the men in the audience who clapped and cheered her every move.

Little Zamo, now released from the turntable was dressed as an Auguste clown. He sported an all-in-one, navy blue and gold, baggy silk suit, with a pointed red hat, topped with a huge yellow pompom.

It was tied under his chin with a red ribbon, his oversized boots were tightly strapped around his unusually muscular child's legs and his white painted face wore a false, red-button nose with a matching, cheerless mouth. Yet no other clown's make-up; he didn't have the right to a registered clown's face, until he qualified. And that was no easy task.

Young Zamo joined the Great Scallini and exotic Zahra, to the delight of the cheering crowd, by bounding over chairs, doing somersaults and cartwheels until he arrived in the limelight again, scattering the sawdust in the ring by tearing towards the knife-throwers at full pelt, and sliding on his knees to a halt between them. The Master of Ceremonies entered and took centre stage, cracking his whip, bowing to the audience, lifting his tall, shiny black hat and crying out in a recitative voice in heavily accented Italian and French.

'My lords, ladies and gentlemen,' He exclaimed, walking around the ring with long exaggerated strides in his knee-length riding boots.

'Now for the highlight of the evening, the greatest flying act the world has ever seen, the *Uccelli Che Volano!*' The audience cheered and clapped excitedly.

'For the first time in *Italia*, the fastest, soaring trapeze artist in the world, the great, the only, the most beautiful flyer in the Universe; *Jullietta Fratellini!*' The Ringmaster cracked his whip into the dust and the audience went insane, clapping, cheering, standing up on their seats and craning their necks to see the famous beauty. She flew onto the ring swiftly, wearing a clinging, feathered and bejewelled costume, acrobatically bouncing around the sawdust stage, basking in the adoring glow from the enthusiastic audience. A young girl from the horse troop ran onto the circus's stage with a small bunch of flowers for the star, as she raced around on her tip-toes, a magnificent swan about to take flight from the sawdust lake.

'And now, I present to you, the celebrated, the magnificent, the extraordinarily talented flyer; *Gustavo Fratellini!*'

The crowd went crazy again; after all, they hadn't seen anyone from outside of their little port town for years. The only entertainment the peasants experienced was the colourful mass on Sundays, except for a few travelling tradesmen and two years ago; there was a visit from a freak show that doubled up as acrobats. Therefore, to get these great stars from an international circus that had travelled the world was phenomenal. When the Fratellinis absorbed their fill of the admiration and applause that was their raison d'étra, the Ringmaster cracked his whip in the air to get the spectators' attention.

'And now my dear friends, I introduce to you a young man with arms of steel, the catcher for the great *Uccelli Che Volano,* the Flying Birds; András Pascalli!*'

The crowd again clapped and cheered, albeit with a little more reserve, because the catcher never got the plaudits of the flyers, even though without him the act would be impossible.

András ran over to the thick twine with a perfect smile, thick eyebrows, a mop of wavy hair and a quick salute to a group of infatuated schoolgirls in the front row.

He then scaled the hemp snake to his station at the top of the tent. Another crack of the whip from the Ringmaster, dressed in a long red jacket with gold military epaulets and matching buttons. He now used his unique trick of shouting to the spectators so that they could hear him at the back, yet with the exceptional talent of speaking in a conspiratorial whisper. 'My Lords, ladies and gentlemen, I can now announce, that for the first time in Italy, the great *Uccelli Che Volano,* will perform exclusively for you tonight, a feat not seen anywhere in Europe for over five years. The impossible, the unbelievable, the death-defying, flying triple somersault; without a *safety net*!'

The audience went wild with excitement and anticipation. The showman whip-lashed the warm air again and pointed his solid, gold-topped, lion-head walking stick to the spotlights, which followed the two flyers to their lofty nest. They were scampering up the ropes using only their muscular arms, with their crossed legs jack-knifed out in front of them, to ascend to the trapezes, fifty feet above the heads of the audience. Again, the spectators were ecstatic; they had seen the colourful posters on every available space around the minor port town for a week now. The Circo de Grimaldi boasted some of the best acts in Europe. The troupe included a knife-thrower, a fire-eater, some sharp-shooters, tightrope walkers, clowns, acrobats, a pair of ferocious lions, half a dozen white show horses, two giraffes, one baby Indian elephant, a crazy family of chimpanzees, a strong-man, a fortune teller, a ten piece brass band and a side-show of freaks: although without doubt, the king and queen of the show were the couple risking their lives at the top of the tent. The flyers - the trapeze artists.

The whole town and even people from outlying villages, lined the streets to see the vibrant and exotic strangers, who could lay claim to fifteen different nationalities. Some people even undertook the journey across the Golfo di Follonica on the ferry and in fishing boats, from the island of Elba.

The kids wanted to see the wild animals and the clowns, the fathers wanted to ogle the gorgeous girls in their skimpy costumes; because most of the village women wore long black dresses and not much less in the marital bedroom. However, the whole family wanted to witness the trapeze act. The posters inferred that the flying act was so dangerous, they would more than likely witness the famous couple fall to their deaths. On both nights of the weekend show! Zamo, the young trainee clown, ran from the dusty ring, up the shaky wooden steps, until he arrived behind most of the audience at the highest seats on the back row. He mused that his mother looked so beautiful that evening; wearing her magnificent costume that hung in their painted caravan under a gauze dustsheet each night, after the performance.

Bejewelled with semi-precious stones and sea pearls, the tight-fitting corset sported long, trailing feathers to make Jullietta, with her tiny waist, voluptuous bust, jewelled green eyes and long, raven black hair, resemble an exotic bird of paradise as she soared through the air.

The orchestra played their dramatic music, the drums rolled their thunderous beat and the artists started to swing across the Big Tops' artificial sky. Vendors walked among the crowd peddling cakes, fruit and sticky sweets, calling out; 'Zucchero filato!' waving the new pink-cloud creation from America that children adored.

Above the audience, there were the two flyers, Jullietta, her elder brother Gustavo and one catcher, András. The good-looking young man needed his muscular shoulders and arms with a vice-like grip for the task ahead. He was part Romanian, part Hungarian, from Jullietta's point of view; he was just her latest lover. She looked so young and robust when she was on the trapeze, flying far above the ground over the tilted heads of the spectators. Conversely, in her caravan at night, when yet another show was over, after she had taken off her costume, the hairpieces and the thick grease paint, she looked her forty-four years. Not that Zamo noticed, to him, his mother was the most beautiful woman in the world.

All he wanted was for her to notice him from time to time.

Since twenty-two year old András arrived last

month, Zamo needed to find somewhere else to sleep, the colourful gipsy caravan was far too diminutive at the best of times, particularly with Zamo's pet snake taking up half his narrow cot. And, when Jullietta acquired yet another 'Uncle' who was staying overnight, or a few months, he needed to find a bed somewhere in the circus compound.

When Zamo was a toddler, Jullietta would place him with the chimps. The apes were great foster parents and taught him how to swing from the cage's bars, climb on the dead piece of tree and to eat termites with a stick, nevertheless now that he was older, he found them too rough and noisy. So, he usually ended up in the iron caged trailer with Aleser and Jansher, the old lions, they never bothered him, apart from the occasional lick on the face they usually just slept and snored noisily after the tiring show. Therefore, on that night, Zamo slumbered on the soft straw next to the great cats, with his pet snake Stephan curled up in his deep, clown's pocket.

Jullietta was brutally honest and always told her fourth son, that he was a mistake and an unwelcome inconvenience. Like his Czechoslovakian father, who she had only known for a month in Prague. The tall handsome professor from the university, Univerzita Karlova v Praze was infatuated with Jullietta, and pestered the performer to stay in the city with him. Nevertheless, when the circus steamed out of town, she evaporated with it.

After Zamo's three half-brothers were grown up, his mother didn't want any more children. François, the eldest, was born when Jullietta was fifteen: the son of her Parisian lover, a crazy and passionate artist from Montmartre.

Albert was born in Moscow, an issue from her Russian lover, a handsome and moody poet. Paul, the youngest, was the offspring of her Italian lover, 'the best chef in Naples.' Well, that's what he claimed, 'but Italian men are like that,' she thought.

Most of her lovers were physically puny and wore glasses; she loved men in glasses.

Unlike Jullietta whose body was sculptured in polished steel, some of her former men insinuated that her heart was equally tensile. Nevertheless, the flying bird knew that she needed to protect herself from the emotions that once wounded her so deeply, when she was young and innocent.

Young Jullietta was an incredibly beautiful child and developed at an early age into an exotic and voluptuous teenager, many men wanted her and most women hated her. The Victorian circus business was hard on all of the performers, though to be the star, a female star at that, alone, without a man to fight your battles, you needed to defend off any weakness, like a lone leopard. Make your babies with the best man you can find, keep your heart locked up tightly, then move on, and when the kids could fend for themselves, chase them off as well. One day, even they would try to take your place at the top. After all, for Jullietta, nothing was more important than being the best flyer in the world.

The elder children were now fully grown men and successful registered clowns. Jullietta didn't have much contact with them, even though the siblings worked in circuses, clowns worked in the basement, yet trapeze artists worked the penthouse. Besides, she reflected often, grown up children only reminded her that she was getting older, and what's more, the possibility of her not being able to fly one day. The four children, well in fact, all of the circus performers were polyglottal, speaking a circus slang that included over ten languages. It was almost impossible for an outsider to converse with them, unless they decided to speak in one language at a time, like the Ringmaster when he made his announcements in each of the countries on their tour. The circus travelled constantly, as habitually as Gnus searching for rich pastures from the azure Mediterranean to snow-white Russia. As the excitement of the night grew in intensity when the three trapeze artists reached the top of their climb, Jullietta and Gustavo stood on the springboards.

These were narrow pieces of wood attached to the ropes for the flyers to use as a base. The couple checked the canvas aprons, attached the ropes, which helped catch them when they landed at high speed, and then they made sure that the risers were a good height.

These extra bars were slotted at two different heights above the planks and allowed the flyers to take off from a higher point, to increase speed for some of the tricks.

The circus royalty were waving to the spectators and showing off, balancing on tiptoe and spinning around the ropes horizontally. Jullietta's choreography included bending into beautiful balletic shapes, doing the classic pirouette, arabesque and plié. Masking the fact that she was checking her rigging and the grips, which were a type of thick bandage around the hands and wrists, covered in chalk.

All of a sudden, the band started to play the famous circus music, *Entrance of the Gladiators*.

Without warning, Jullietta leaped into the open space in front of her, diving through the air at speed and the crowd gasped, expertly she caught the bar twenty feet below, sent by her brother at the appropriate moment. She clenched the cold metal firmly in her strong grip and warmed up with a few classic cutaways and reverse knee-hangs. The long feathers flowed in the wind when she was swinging at over twenty miles an hour through the open space. She did a force-out to gain height, which involves opening and closing the legs at the right moment. Then she started to calculate the first single somersault. Gripping the bar, she dived into a hollow and then a sweep, Gustavo called out. *'Listo!'* Signalling that he was ready, the two flyers swept towards each other and just as their bodies almost collided in the middle of the void, Jullietta let go of her bar and somersaulted over his head, the audience were up on their feet swooning, until she finished her spin and caught the third bar sent by the catcher, which was falling away from her at high speed.

Both flyers landed on opposite boards waving their arms triumphantly and the crowd cheered in admiration and disbelief. Gustavo then started to swing to the music wafting up from the band below and the crowd joined in singing:

'*The Man On The Flying Trapeze...*'

His rippling muscles blew up as fat as an inflated dingy, because G-forces put tremendous pressure on his arms, back and shoulders. Ten minutes elapsed and the siblings executed increasingly more dangerous passes, when they suddenly came to a halt on their boards and the band became silent. The limelights left them to recover; panting in the shadows, below clowns ran out onto the sawdust ring and started to remove the safety net; making jokes, juggling and fooling around at the same time.

Zamo's elder brother François played the trumpet while walking on a tightrope. The spectators moved to the edges of their seats, and when there was nothing between the flyers and the deadly hard ground below, the drums started their thunderous roll.

All the illuminations were dimmed, except for the beam of three limelights, which rose up to the canvas sky, and the only thing visible in the darkness, were the *Uccelli Che Volano,* still breathless from their efforts on the boards. The music built to a crescendo and the siblings looked at each other, realising that it was time for the climax of the evening show; the death-defying, triple somersault.

Earlier that day, Zamo was looking for his mother, he was hungry as usual, Jullietta didn't cook and rarely seemed to eat herself, therefore, Zamo normally had to beg for food from the other performers or even steal from the animals, who at least were fed once a day.

Zamo knew that his mother had the character of a cuckoo, she knew where he was, yet relied on the circus to foster him. Finally, he saw her at the rear of the big top, having a furious argument with the Ringmaster and owner of the circus.

Joseph Grimaldi rarely removed the fat cigar from his mouth; it had become a fixed extension of his face like a saucepan handle.

The Cuban leaves usually sat motionless on his lips or between his heavily stained fingers, although now he was puffing furiously, as swiftly as a steam locomotive at full speed.

Joseph was always nervous on the anniversary of his famous father's death, even though it was sixty-five years earlier; he had lived in the great man's shadow when he was alive and even more so after his demise.

The adversaries were arguing mostly in French and Italian, yet Jullietta kept cursing in Russian, which Zamo knew from his own experience, meant that she was particularly angry. They stood in front of the Indian elephant Rindi, who was becoming stressed by the altercation so close to his makeshift pen. Therefore, he started to swing his huge head rhythmically from side to side like an Indian Odissi dancer.

Zamo decided to run around the back of Rindi's pen so that he could get closer to the couple and hear what was going on. When he found a spot about ten feet away, behind a bale of hay, he heard his mother screaming. She said that she was exhausted at the moment and it was too dangerous to perform the act without a net. András was a new, young catcher, who had only practised the dangerous manoeuvre for a few days last week, for the first time in his short professional life. Nevertheless, the owner, who Jullietta thought was a misogynist, complained that the takings were down and followed with an aggressively rude remark in guttural Hungarian, which Zamo translated roughly in his head as. *'If you are happy to screw him, you should be happy he could catch you!'*

The young clown realised that it must have been even worse than that, because his mother smashed the Ringmaster in the face with a clenched fist, using all the force of her muscular arms. Despite the fact that he was a substantial man, he fell back on the ground dazed as she stormed off.

In the circus tent that night, when the young boy looked at his treasured mother, sparkling in the limelights, flying from the shiny bars, she looked fantastic.

She was swinging exceptionally high, she seemed strong with legs like steel cables and each exchange with András resulted in a clean, firm *slap!*

Jullietta was taught how to fly by her favourite lover, the world famous Frenchman from Toulouse, called Jules Léotard. Who not only invented the flying trapeze act, using five separate trapezes, he also created a tight fitting costume to help him be more aerodynamic, which has borne his renowned name ever since. The couple were together for merely two years, because the great man died when he was only twenty-eight years old: not due to the incredibly dangerous profession, but because he caught smallpox.

Jullietta Fratellini was now considered in the circus world as being the best female flyer in Europe, and her fourth son Zamo couldn't have been more proud of the mother he adored.

The excitement in the Big Top now reached a fever pitch, the drums rolled, Jullietta oscillated higher and higher. András swung with every once of his strength and skill, to get maximum height and speed.

He was more nervous now than he had ever been in his life, as he felt that his lover didn't have confidence in him for this stunt.

His palms started to sweat through the bandaged grips and the chalk became damp. Fifty feet below, he could see the sawdust swaying side to side in the shadows, while he hung upside-down from the long trapeze. He felt sick with fear, yet he knew that failing was not an option. András's experienced partner had taught him a great deal about life, love and her profession, she showed the eastern European how to have a clock in his head, as she has. She had taught him as she had her four children, how to look at her and count the seconds, so that his hands arrived at the same moment as hers. Jullietta called out to her lover when she passed on the third sweep. 'Listo!'

'Oh my God!' András thought, kissing the tiny gold crucifix around his neck. 'This is it, she's going to swing up to maximum height, dive into the valley, let go of the bar, swoop through the air, squeeze her beautiful body into a tiny foetal ball, somersault three times, using the energy and force of the fall.

Then throw her arms and legs out to full height, with hands outstretched, those beautiful, skilful hands that caressed his muscular body every night. Hands that hold his face when he's afraid. Hands of a mother that he never had. Hands of an experienced lover who showed him what true love and passion really is; and he, András, who worships this woman more than life itself, has to catch those wonderful hands when they pass him for a split second at more than forty miles per hour.'

Zamo perched apprehensively on his favourite corner seat at the back of the audience, he found the highest seats were the best place to see his adored mother fly above the spectators. A few rows below sat the new boy and his parents, the Glowaki family. He had met sixteen-year-old Aleksander Glowaki for the first time earlier that day, when the Ringmaster told him to show the stranger around.

'What's your act?' Zamo asked the Polish boy enthusiastically, walking by the stables.

'I-I... J-Juggler and artist.' He said in almost unrecognisable Italian, which was the only language they found in common. Not that it was easy for the little clown to understand the strange boy, his brother's first language came naturally to him, unfortunately the Pole found the rhythmic flow of Italian difficult to pronounce, and to make it worse, the lofty lad suffered from a stammer.

Zamo thought he would be able to speak Italian better if he used his face and hands when he spoke, yet he was so emotionless and static. Aleksander was incredibly tall for his age and stooped his long back as curved as a banana, to make himself look smaller.

He wore a thin face, with the hooded golf-ball eyes of a chameleon and looked as though he was about to throw out a long tongue to whiplash a passing insect.

His head balanced on an elongated neck with a protruding Adam's Apple, added to his angular nose and lifting gate, he made Zamo think of a wading bird, he once saw on a poster for African holidays.

'And what about your parents?' Zamo asked the new boy inquisitively.

'My...f-f-father is greatest strongman and lion...t-ta-tamer in whole world, he can lift lion in air and k-k-kill with hands, so.' Aleksander twisted the imaginary neck of a huge lion. And my mother, most b-be-beautiful woman in all circus, very intelligent, can say future.'

Zamo was beginning to get annoyed with this tall teenager, everyone knew that *his* mother was the most beautiful woman in this circus, well any circus, and she didn't just sit in a little tent reading palms and glass balls, she flew through the air at twenty miles an hour. Zamo thought that it would be better not to say anything, as he didn't want to hurt the new boy's feelings and thought; how nice it would be to have a friend in the circus, as it could be a lonely life for kids with so many busy adults.

'Oh that's wonderful, I'm looking forward to meeting them.' Zamo said kindly.

'They much b-bu-busy, such greatness, no speak with b-ba-baby clown.' He stuttered, with dark beady eyes darting with the urgency of a busy wasp, in all directions, except towards Zamo.

The young boy thought that he should leave, when he heard someone calling in the distance, as he turned around, two of the smallest midgets he had ever seen, carrying two tiny Chihuahuas in their arms were waving and calling Aleksander's name. The lofty bird scuttled over to the couple grouching down on his knees, kissing them repeatedly on the cheeks and stroking the tiny dogs. Zamo walked over slowly and was fascinated to see such a diminutive man, albeit with huge muscles and a baldhead, wearing a leopard skin, strongman's Léotard. He held the hand of a tiny lady who was dressed as a Romanian gipsy, but looked like a china doll with a large head, altered by the Crazy-Mirrors the circus had erected in the freak-show tent. Zamo walked over and introduced himself politely to Helena and Jerzy Glowacki, who both spoke half a dozen languages perfectly.

Helena stretched up on her toes, kissed the seven year old on both cheeks, and was full of praise for his mother and uncle. Zamo thought the couple were so charming, he wondered how their son had become so obstreperous.

After a few minutes of casual chitchat, Helena looked up at the seven year old and took his hand, ushering him to one side saying: 'My husband and I are so pleased Alex has made a friend, he finds it difficult you see, because he has a complex about his height. When he was a child we lived with some other dwarfs and he felt, so out of place. I hope you will become good friends, he likes people smaller than himself.' She said kind-heartedly.

'Oh yes, of course, he's very nice,' Zamo lied; overwhelmed by the wonderful people who were not much more than two feet tall. 'Are you coming to see the *Uccelli*

Che Volano tonight?' He asked excitedly.

'Of course Zamo, we are really looking forward to seeing your beautiful mother, she's so brave,'

Helena said sincerely.

'Yes she is and she loves me so much you know.'

'I'm sure she does, but Zamo, you must be careful in this strange world,' Helena warned with a worried glint in her hooded eyes. 'The first day we arrived at the circus I consulted my crystal ball. I saw two terrible accidents: a grown man who looked just like you, he was old and afraid of something,' She said in low sibylline tones. 'He was being chased by someone and was hanging from a wire, like a thick tightrope over a restless sea in the dead of night. I didn't understand it then, but now that I've seen you closely. I'm sure he had your unusual green eyes...' She said, with more unspoken words still dancing on her lips.

'In that case Helena, I won't go near any tightropes close to the sea when I get older!' He laughed. Helena laughed with him sympathetically, yet her piecing eyes didn't join in with the joke, she knew that the curse of her life was that her premonitions were never wrong, and she should never had mentioned the other vision.

'Bye-bye for now Zamo, and thank you for your friendship to our son.' She said worriedly.

Zamo watched the three people walk to their little caravan holding hands, the one in the centre over six feet tall bent in half, and he was reminded why he loved the circus so much, and now he was determined to make Aleksander his friend.

That evening the three Glowackis were sitting three rows in front of Zamo, chatting enthusiastically to the Great Scallini and his girlfriend Zahra. Next to them was the usually silent, fire juggler and eater from Mexico called Montezuma; tall and dark, he wore the most incredible costumes and jewellery and claimed to be descended from a great Aztec king. When Zamo gazed around the vast tent, he noticed that the entire circus troupe were unusually out of their caravans, mingling with the spectators. Zamo knew the normally blasé performers were there to see the triple-somersault without the net, because no one had tried this trick since Grimaldi had left Russia five years before.

Jullietta, the great trapeze artist soared high into the top of the tent; swung her legs forward, to get full speed and maximum height, descended backwards through the air, jack-knifing her muscular body, sharply pointing her dainty, perfectly painted toes into the air, her plumage almost touching the canvas roof behind her.

Despite the darkened tent and the limelight concentrated on her, from that height she could see the whole circus below, the three different types of clown, the other acts, the spectators, her brother and her catcher.

They moved as scholarly as Goldfish around the edge of a magnified goldfish bowl, in the middle there was no water, just an empty gaping void, ready to swallow her whole.

The artist left the trapeze bar and leaped into mid-air; the clock started ticking noisily in her head, she dived with arms outstretched, then balled tightly with her elbows in, somersaulted three times at tremendous velocity, instantly she unravelled her body and flew as gracefully as a dove with her back arched, a human boomerang in the imitation sky.

To the thousands of spectators below she seemed to float in the empty space, static, yet airborne. The huge crowd got to their feet in complete silence, their faces titled upwards like sunflowers honouring the sun. Then Jullietta bowed her head towards them and plummeted through the tented universe, her taut body aimed like a feathered dart to a bull's eye, pointing her small hands towards her lover.

András missed them.

Chapter 2
Paris, Autumn, 1963

The cross hairs of the telescopic rifle-sight languorously caressed the beautiful girl's naked body, while the assassin watched her rest against the ancient window. Streetlights brushed the contours of her flesh with a blue-grey hue, reminiscent of an impressionist nude. The stucco frame around this masterpiece, hung on the old building in Place des Vosges. She clutched a handle-less bowl of coffee in one hand and a crumbling golden croissant in the other, which she dunked absentmindedly into the steaming dark liquid. Her chocolate eyes were surrounded by lead-toned mascara, akin to a stained-glass window, gazing down into the square from her candle-lit room.

The marksman, sitting on the roof of the building opposite, guessed she could be in her early twenties, her *oscuro* stare, shoulder-length, jet-black hair, suggested that she originated from the south of France or perhaps she was a Pied-Noir. The young girl wore a soft tan, obviously acquired confidently on long, warm days, with scant concern for modesty.

His mind wondered back to the years spent on the deserted beaches in the Var. The pine trees and vineyards blocking access to the pale, golden sands of the Plage de Pampelonne; except for a few narrow tracks, from the tiny villages of Saint-Tropez and Ramatuelle, with their little cheap restaurants and suspicious Provençaux. They didn't want to share their lives with strangers, since the invading Germans and liberating American soldiers had departed a few years before. He started to think: if this job went smoothly - maybe he would take his wife down there again this year.

The room was only lit by a brass, office light with an opaque, green, glass shade, glowing hauntingly on Jacques Dupré's battered face. He appeared to be tied to an old Victorian oak chair, with a thick, gold coloured curtain cord.

The place was expensively furnished with heavy

antiques, although it looked like it hadn't been lived in for a long time. A smell of burnt wood and stale dust filled the air. The windows were frosted with grime, cloaked by thick, maroon velvet curtains and topped by matching, deep pleated pelmets, with grey faded edges. Most of the furniture had been covered with whitish dustsheets and spiders had spun their intricate, silky traps in every advantageous corner.

If Miss Havisham sat in one of the old chairs, she wouldn't have looked out of place. One of the dustsheets thrown to the side, revealed a large, mahogany Kriesler Radiogram, where a scratchy recording blared out a version of Verdi's Rigoletto.

On this rendering, the Duke of Mantua was played by the unmistakeable, raw genius of Enrico Caruso. The cotton cloth under Jacques Dupré looked more like an abstract painting than a cover, drizzled with his dark red blood, artistically staining the improbable canvas.

The Italian bull of a man standing over the slight figure, managed to squeeze himself into a fashionable silver-grey Tonic suit. The buttons performing an adamantly structural service, as stressed as a knot on an expanding balloon. His shiny trousers were so snug around his massive thighs; they resembled a woman's dance tights. His round greasy face looked tired when he leaned over the thrashed Parisian, yet again.

'Jacques, parle avec moi!' The Fat-man voiced huskily, with a strong, southern Italian accent. When the faultlessly dressed banker didn't reply, a flabby fist, littered with chunky gold rings smashed into his heavily bloodstained face, for the umpteenth time during the long night.

'You fool!' Angelo Massoni shouted from a chair in front of the long window - his strong Sicilian accent grating on the Italian's nerves.

'We don't want to finish him yet, you tub of lard.' He threw his arms in the air with incredulity, and shook his head.

'Come on Jacques,' The Fat-man continued in heavily accented French, whispering close to the bloodstained ear, 'Tell us where the money is and I promise to kill you real nice, no pain – *finito.*' The Italian mimed a knife with his thumb, slicing from ear to ear.

The assistant manager Jacques Dupré had worked at two branches of the Credit National Banque for the past two decades. At forty-one years old, he hoped to be the manager long ago. Le Director, that's the title he craved, the extra money for a new car and a better home, the powerful authority, and the respect. Ah yes, the respect given to a Director of a bank like CNB; that was what he really needed. He also craved something else, something magical, but he didn't think he could get one without the other. For the last two years, Jacques dreamed constantly about his nubile young colleague, the junior clerk, Mademoiselle Magali Thomass, with her dark rebellious hair and innocent hazel eyes. He could just imagine her bouncing into the manager's office after his promotion. He in a new designer suit from Daniel Hechter, sitting behind the imposing oak desk, her in the usual fashionable *mini jupe* and little flat Gucci loafers, with a gold chain over the instep. Wearing her gleaming Colgate smile that danced all over her beautiful face whenever she spoke.

'*Je m'excuse Monsieur Le Director - Monsieur Jacques - Jacques my darling...*'

He longed to hear these words on her lips, such wonderful soft, pink lips. Unfortunately, he had been passed-over twice in the last five years by his superiors and recently realised that he may never become the Director. Jacques' life could have been so wonderful if head-office would only recognise his abilities. The French banker enjoyed being a meticulously organised man. His account books at the CNB were faultless.

His desk pristine, and despite the fact that he never had the opportunity of going to university, because he worked seven days a week on his parent's impoverished farm. He still passed all of his exams, studying at home every night for three years before he started his career.

He called himself, '*More qualified than most Bachelor of Arts students who attended posh universities.*' His impecunious, yet painstakingly organised wardrobe of four suits, one dark grey, one dark blue and two black, were sponged and pressed each time he wore them.

He ironed his six shirts, in varying degrees of aging white cotton, until they were crisp. Moreover, his three ties, which were all roughly the same pattern in a dull mixture of the national Tricolour, were spruced up at weekends in a one-hour cleaning ritual: along with his two pairs of deteriorating, wrinkly black shoes.

The functionary could be accused of being a man of habit. He went to the same restaurant on the Avenue Émile Zola at exactly twelve thirty everyday, since starting at this branch in the position of a junior clerk, nearly fifteen years ago. Jacques always followed the same ritual. Madam Breton's, Les Trois Mousquetaires, bar-restaurant, the corner window-table for one. Because the metal pillar supporting the ancient ceiling wouldn't allow other seats, which suited him perfectly, because he didn't want to sit with anyone else. The plat de jour, a glass of house rouge from Bordeaux, a sweet dessert followed by a small black coffee, with two packets of fine white sugar; no tip. 'Well it's called prix fix.' He would always say defensively to anyone who asked. 'And she is the owner with her grumpy old father, who chain-smokes while he cooks in the kitchen!'

After the lunch, he would take a short walk, passing the metro station, where he purchased Le Figaro newspaper. Then, turn into the Rue du Théâtre, sneak through the magnificent grounds of the Temple de la Résurrection and onto the Rue Cambronne. Where once again, he would continue his life-sentence, being an inmate of the financial institution.

Jacques returned following lunch, to the Credit National Banque Monday to Friday, at exactly five minutes before two o'clock.

After a few minutes in the cloakroom, carefully washing his hands and combing his thick dark hair, he would apply a tiny ration of Ice Blue Aqua Velva, from a small bottle he had bought for himself on his Birthday the previous year. *'La lotion après rasage'* is what the street posters announced. The banker liked to think he resembled the confident, good-looking male model wearing the smoking jacket and a black bow tie, whilst holding the young, exquisite girl in the photograph in such an intimate embrace. After checking his appearance by ducking and diving in front of the small, cracked toilet mirror, he would go directly to the assistant manager's cubicle in the main hall of the bank, where his impeccably tidy desk demanded his presence. Hour after hour, day after day, and year after year, except for the two-week holiday in August. When the bank closed and the masses left stuffy Paris as panicky as rats from a sinking ship. Unfortunately, he and his family couldn't afford to go anywhere.

Nevertheless, it did give him a chance to clean up the garden and do all of the chores around the house - forgotten in the previous twelve months.

Despite the fact that his dear wife nagged him constantly to complete a list of her preferential 'Must dos'. His dream of whisking petite Magali off to Cannes for a passionate weekend, became more compelling each month. Jacques felt agonizingly infatuated by her slim calves, her tiny waist, all of her little clinging tops from Galeries Lafayette on Boulevard Haussmann; wrapping her small, firm breasts into a delicate sculpture that would surely grace any museum in Paris. Genevieve owned firm breasts once - before the two children. Though recently she had let herself go. All she could talk about of late were the garden, the kids and he not being promoted or earning enough money.

She would nag: 'Monsieur Bertrand Warin (their neighbour), became a company director, la-la-la, he had just purchased a new Peugeot estate car, and his wife Monique, always bought her clothes from boutiques on the Rue du Faubourg St-Honoré, la-la-la.'

She went to the hairdresser weekly – and had a manicure!' This appeared to be his wife's customary chant. The rich neighbours, their new possessions, where they shopped, and the designers' clothes they wore. Yet poor Genevieve, plump Genevieve, grey-haired Genevieve, wrinkly Genevieve, always moaning Genevieve; did her own hair, gave herself a manicure, clipped her own toenails and bought her boring clothes from the local market.

Quelle horreur!

Living in Banlieue seemed like a good idea when they were first married. Éyry nestled in the green and peaceful suburbs, and was a refreshing relief from the sixth arrondissement on the Left Bank of Paris. Populated by longhaired bohemians; queues of traffic, noisy students from the Sorbonne, horrible, highly qualified, pompous students, attaining their degrees in accountancy and banking. Originally, living in this up-and-coming neighbourhood satisfied Jacques' long-term, meticulous plan. After a few years, they could sell their small house and move up to an apartment in fashionable Neuilly! Their neighbours would be the best people; they could have cocktails with the upper classes and the nouveau riche. Maybe he could even join Paris's most prestigious golf club in Boulogne.

Unfortunately, after fifteen years of saving every centime, they still couldn't move, due to the lack of promotion. He enthusiastically fell in love with his pretty, young classmate Genevieve, from the moment that she kissed him, stretched up on her tiptoes in the local park after school. Jacques then eighteen years old and she fifteen, the whole village said she seemed: '*Far too good for him,*' and, '*How lucky a boy like that would be to get her,*' because he came from a small pig farm just outside of the village.

'*How did he get a girl of such quality? Her father owned a Maître's detached house and was a retired, senior civil servant - who wore an official képi.*'

Nevertheless, it seemed inevitable to the young couple at least, that they would eventually marry and have a suburban house near the capital. Including a new Citroën 2CV, two kids and perhaps a small dog.

Finally, after all of these years, Jacques' life had become so boring, he felt trapped on a carousel of *metro-boulot-dodo*. Each morning he fell into the same boring train carriage, saw the same grey-faced passengers with their fake politeness of '*Bonjour and Au revoir*', their non-stop smoking, the folding and refolding of newspapers, relentlessly for all the time he worked at the CNB. And it drove him crazy.

All Jacques could think of recently were Magali,

mignon Magali and a visit to the Croisette of Cannes. He constantly imagined the feel of her naked body, lying next to him on crisp clean sheets. The newspapers said that some girls on the Côte d'Azur are sunbathing topless nowadays! 'Oh, la, la, Magali topless…'

Splash! Jacques' eyes opened in shock the moment the freezing water drizzled down his face. Marco Sotori, the third man, dropped the dripping bucket and looked closely at the groggy, bank employee. His previously impeccable pressed navy suit, white shirt and patterned blue and red tie, were now a bloody mess.

'Hey Monsieur, listen to me, we made a deal, no?' Marco lit a cigarette slowly examining his captive carefully. 'We meet in the horrible little restaurant you go to everyday?' He said in French, revealing an educated northern Italian accent. 'We give you the Italian Lire in cash and you give us some nice French Francs, all clean and legal, no? You understand, we like to keep an eye on our friends and business partners, and what happened?' Marco waved an envelope from a travel agent with an advert on the cover for Air France. 'You go off to the travel agent and buy two, one-way airline tickets for Nice, dated the day before our meeting, now tell me Monsieur, were you being nice to us?' Marco's broad smile evaporated without ever reaching his eyes and Jacques started to mumble deliriously through his broken jaw and teeth.

'Hotel Carlton - I just wanted to take her…' He coughed up some more blood onto his shirt. 'She'd fall in love with me there, I-I know she would.'

Marco grabbed the dying man angrily by the throat and squeezed tightly, 'Where have you hidden the money?' He said, in a voice of quiet menace.

'I love her,' Jacques choked. 'I love her…'

'What are you saying you crazy *bastardo*, just tell me, where's our money?'

Jacques began to gag and his eyes glazed over, he could still see the Croisette in Cannes, from all of the brochures he had collected over the last few years. With its beautiful palm trees and grand hotels, and of course, lying on the beach, topless, in front of the famous Palais, where all of the movie stars would go for the *Palme d'Or, Festival de Film*; there would be his star, his dream girl. Magali.

Marco dropped him back on the chair and walked away wiping his hands on an expensive handkerchief. Tall, vain and very handsome; women fell for him instantly, when Marco wanted a woman, he knew what to say and how to say it.

He had always possessed this flair from a child, the dark eyes, with thick, curly lashes most women wanted for themselves, square jaw, wavy jet-black hair and that brilliant smile. For some crazy reason that even he never really understood, most people believed whatever he said: especially young girls. The Fat-man rushed over at amazing speed, considering his size, and said angrily, 'I'll make him talk if I have to kill the bastard,' and swiped a broken chair leg into Jacques' nose. The great Italian tenor grooved into the black seventy-eight record, singing his heart out in the background, and the cracking of his facial bones, were the last sounds that the ambitious, assistant bank-manager would ever hear.

'Well, is he talking?' Angelo bawled across the room, having heard the cracking skeleton.

'I think it's too late patron' Marco, the athletic type, told the mafia boss, walking back to the chair, peering closely at Jacques and taking his pulse.

'Balena!' Angelo screeched, turning to the Fat-man, 'I don't know why I keep you on the payroll, when I want a stupid bank-manager finished, I'll tell you, you fat pig!'

Angelo fuming, walked over to the old desk, took a cigarette from his pocket and lit a match at the end. He carefully laced some papers and a small Bernardelli pistol in his briefcase.

'Marco, talk to your friend from Napoli ugh! He don't understand nothing.' He continued a little more calmly. 'I needed a surgeon and you brought me a butcher.' The Fat-man lifted his huge shoulders in resignation, still holding the chair leg, now dripping with Jacques' blood. Marco pushed him away from the messy corpse. 'You crazy *balena.*' He complained quietly 'You do everything real slow except eating, drinking and killing people – Uh?'

Angelo Massoni loosened his tie and took off his designer jacket; he caught his own reflection in the gilded, ornate mirror and saw a very tired man looking back. The open curved fingers of his left hand roughly ploughed a small amount of his thinning, grey hair from his face, and then he walked over to the window and looked down into the ancient square in the centre of the Marais. Angelo looked back into the room and said thoughtfully to the two Italians, 'Now we will have to find his pretty, little girlfriend from the bank. I'm sure Fatso here will have some fun getting the information from her, when she sees him naked and jumping on top of her, she'll give up her own mother!' He said maliciously.

Little Angelo Massoni, 'The Angel' to all of his immediate family, sprang to life in Caltagirone, Sicily in 1893, just thirty-three years after the island united with Italy. Unmistakably a poverty-stricken and lawless place, run by a number of families including the one headed by little Angel's grandfather, on his mother's side.
Don Cesare Calvino managed the largest dynastic family outside of the capital Palermo.

The Calvinos controlled all of the land, fruit, vegetables and wine from the town of Gela in the southwest, to Augusta in the southeast. These Mafias were the nearest things that most of Sicily could call a government at the time. This illegal society worked well for many years, assuming everyone did exactly what the Mafia Dons told them to do. Angelo enjoyed a fantastic childhood, the sixth and last child born to his parents, Carlo and Angelica. He had always been totally spoilt by his five elder sisters, parents and grandparents.

'At last Carlo.' Grandfather announced to his son-in-law when Angelo came screaming into the world. 'After all of these beautiful girls, we didn't think you could make a baby boy!' He laughed.

On Sundays after mass, Don Cesare would sit like a Roman Emperor at the head of one of the numerous long tables in his courtyard. They were covered with brilliant white tablecloths, surrounded by his large family, his soldiers and invited guests. The men usually wore the

Sicilian Mafiosi uniform of a Coppola cap, a collarless shirt, an unbuttoned waistcoat and a shouldered shotgun on a leather strap. They played cards, draughts and talked business, all of the Don's men were *uomini d'onore*, these honoured-men also benefited from *raccomandazioni*, their preferments; they received a system of privileges and rights from the Don to control certain markets. Therefore, these made-men and their families were tied to the Calvinos by blood or business. Angelo and the other male children, played ballgames together, and the women and girls did all of the cooking and served the huge lunch.

There would be jugs of local wine, endless bowls of different shaped, hand-made pastas, fresh fish, whole *cinghiale* on a spit, roasted goat, hot bread straight from the oven, and every fruit and vegetable that could be grown on the island by the Don's farmers and suppliers. In contrast, many of the island's peasants were starving; while the Mafia bosses, their friends and families lived like kings. The family, all faithfully attended the ritual of Sunday lunch.

To refuse would be an insult to the Godfather, such rudeness could only mean one thing, a lack of respect and loyalty; one person less for lunch, may become one less person alive on the island.

As a young boy, Angelo didn't understand the politics or violence of his family, on the warm and comfortable island of Sicily; he only knew that his life couldn't be any better. From an early age, he discovered that he could get almost anything he wanted. If his mother refused him an extra piece of apple pie, one of his five adoring elder sisters would get it for him. He was richer than most of his school friends and with all of the loving care and good food; he looked bigger and stronger than any boy in southern Sicily of a similar age.

Young Angelo loved the early morning; he would run to the top of the hill near his parent's villa to see the blazing sun come up over the Straights of Messina. After climbing a metre or so into the pale blue sky, its scorching heat would slap the young Sicilian in the face and light up his world.

He enjoyed such fond memories from his childhood

with his extended family, well the whole village really, because most people he knew were his close relatives or at least distant cousins.

At the weekends, he would fish and hunt with the huge shotgun bought for his twelfth birthday. Weekdays Angel would run barefoot to the local school with half a dozen other kids, and was delighted to see his teacher, Signorina Clara, or Zietta Clara that she liked to be called when school finished at lunchtime. Angel's aunty or more than likely a distant cousin; was certainly the most beautiful girl on the island, with unusually pale skin and radiant blue eyes. He always knew that he would marry her when he grew up, after all, he mused, she was only eight years older than him. When he becomes twenty one - she will only be twenty nine, when he reaches thirty five - she will only be forty three, after a few years he will catch her up; no *problema!*

Teenage Angelo thought that life couldn't be easier at that time, everybody liked everybody else; certainly, he had heard rumours that occasionally grandfather would need to dispose of someone or at least teach them a lesson. There weren't really any local police during this epoch, and so grandfather and his men kept law and order. Life was great in the village.

'How did it all change?' Angelo said aloud without realising it.

The Sicilian took a deep breath and looked up from the Parisian square, early morning light started to define the skyline over Paris.

His eyes narrowed and his face hardened, when he turned around and gazed at the scene in the huge room. The over-weight minder from Naples seemed to be a stupid punk, he thought. *'All he wanted was a slice of easy money, a few whores and lots to eat, mamma-mia, he eats enough for a whole village. All of those kids from Naples ate a lot, it's something to do with so many of them starving during the war. Look at him!'* The Godfather shook his head; Fatso couldn't even wrap up the stupid banker properly.

'Hey, why don't you use more dustsheets, it's not complicated, didn't you ever wrap a Christmas present?'

Angelo spoke gently now, because his thoughts were still influenced by the warm memories of his childhood in Sicily. In years past, he only dealt with Sicilians, who knew him and his reputation; after all, he had known most of them and their families all of his life. Angelo reflected. *'It's only when you start to work with foreigners like these mainland-Italians and this French bastardo Jacques, the clerk, who would have died with nothing, working at that bank, if I hadn't tried to help him with this money changing deal. It could've been an easy transaction, unfortunately like all the French, he was a backstabbing greedy merdoso, who should be cooking in a restaurant; they're no good for anything else. Conversely, that Marco...'* He said to himself. *'He's a different kettle of fish, very smart - too smart. He's the one who approached all of the southern families and asked them to join forces with the northern Mafias.*

He's got what it takes to be a leader, a vicious killer, not like the hot-headed Fatso here, this young Milanése is as cold as ice in a butcher's storeroom, and he's a planner.'

Angelo realised that he must be careful of Marco; he was ambitious and very dangerous.

They say that before the war he became a young fascist in the *Partito Nazionale Fascista;* Mussolini's PNF; evidently he joined at just thirteen and acquired 'special talents' that soon saw him promoted to the position of one of the youngest commanders in El Duce's unique campaign. There were rumours about him getting the Nazis to break Benito Mussolini out of jail, then, when the dictator lost national support Marco joined with the Northern Partisans, and they finally shot the *bastardo.* *'This man changes his allegiances like he changes his pants. What's it those fascists used to cry? Molti nemici. Molto onore.* Now, this clever punk is fairly rich, he belongs to some right wing religious group in Spain called the Fondazione Nazionale di Cristo. Recently he has made contact with Spaniards and Americans, saying he can bring us more business. He claims he wants to be one of us, part of the family, a Made-Man. But the question is; Angelo's man, or his own?'

Jacques was now wrapped tighter than an Egyptian mummy; using half a dozen dustsheets with no trace of any blood seeping through, and so the Italians were busily packing their bags.

The old Don continued to reflect back to his past and thought about the events on the road from his small, happy little village, to the huge empire he now controlled. It only seemed like a few years ago that he sat with Aunty Clara one weekend, on a hilltop above the beautiful golden beaches of the east coast of Sicily. Looking out to the emerald Ionian Sea and Italy beyond, they could've been so happy together, his life was beautiful then, until the handsome Father Benadicto came to Caltagirone from the mainland.

That summer, the Mediterranean sun, baked the island as quickly as a fresh Focaccia, daily for over five months. Without a drop of rain, it was difficult to go outside in the stifling heat after midday and yet fifteen-year-old Angel felt too bored to take a siesta like the grown-up villagers. The little old church was usually empty and the coolest place in the dusty village. Therefore, many of the local kids would often hang around the shady, tree-covered grounds until their mothers readied dinner.

Unusually, on that afternoon Angelo seemed to be the only teenager there. Father Benadicto had arrived at the village church just a couple of months before. He wasn't a Sicilian and said that he had been the clergy at the church, in the beautiful seaside village of Amalfi on the mainland. The year previously in Naples, and before that he worked on the exotic island of Capri. It sounded as though the bishop tended to move him around quite a lot over the last few years.

Nonetheless, the good-looking young priest explained that he liked visiting different churches and villages and he always appeared to be so charming and kind, especially to the children. Therefore, most of the locals took to him straight away.

After all, he was the messenger of God.

Angelo sat on the sun-dappled altar of the church; playing with some cicadas he had imprisoned in a small wooden box, when he heard a gentle voice behind him.

'Hello my son'. The priest said, on a Tuesday, at three-forty-six, on that airless, oppressively hot afternoon. 'Would you like some nice cool wine to drink, I have some in the vestry.' He continued, flashing his dazzling smile, lighting up the dim church.

The ancient, holy building stayed cool and quiet, Angelo felt very grown up chatting with Father Benadicto and drinking wine. The young priest told him some amusing stories about Naples and what an exciting life he had experienced in the big city.

'You shouldn't tell your family I gave you some wine...' He whispered conspiratorially, his lips touching the young boy's ear. 'This afternoon will be our little secret.' He laughed.

'I think my mother would kill me!' Angelo giggled. The wine flowed, the boy easily became drunk, the stories moved on and Angelo's clothes were pulled off. It wasn't difficult for the priest to overpower the *ragazzo*; something he had practised many times before. The struggling, screaming and occasionally crying, added to the pleasure of the sexual act for him, each time the man of cloth engaged in it.

Unfortunately, for the priest, he found this young Sicilian very strong for his age, even after the alcohol had softened him up, and so he needed to be particularly violent with Angel, yet it just made the undertaking even more sexually arousing.

Angel's virginity was sacrificed over a black marble altar, like an Old Testament offering. The young boy cried out in agony and shame, as he was rhythmically pounded against the cold stone, with his forehead almost touching an ornate crucifix. The priest knew how painful it was for the child, although for him the mixture of the sexual act and the sadistic pain he inflicted was the experience his insatiable desire needed. Normally, about thirty minutes after the priest had finished his rapes, he felt repentant and wanted to confess his sins. He prayed to his God, rubbed away his tears and hated the good-looking image he saw in the mirror.

29

Despite these feelings of remorse, after a while, the desire came back as fervently as ever, and his irresistible urge returned with all thoughts of guilt, evaporating as smoothly as garlands of smoky incense from a church thurible. Half an hour later, young Angelo, still dizzy from the wine and the attack, got up from the church yard where he had been thrown, and scrambled along the dirt track unsteadily, with tears in his eyes and blood on his face, and legs, desperately searching for his family's small house just outside the village.

Halfway along the dusty path he saw someone he recognised in the distance, yet kept running in a blind, hysterical stupor.

'Angel – Angel – Angelo, stop – STOP! It's me Clara.' The schoolteacher threw out her arms and grabbed the boy around the shoulders in a rugby tackle.

'What's wrong? What's happened?' She pleaded, looking down at his condition, perplexed and shocked.

Young Angelo couldn't speak; tears erupted from his eyes like lava from Mount Etna and avalanched down his cheeks.

They strolled slowly, holding each other closely, without saying a word, until they reached the Massoni family home.

The couple walked through the back garden gate and entered the kitchen to find Angelo's mother, wearing the usual floral apron and old brown slippers, with her greying hair scrunch-up in a bun. The aroma of olive oil, garlic and basil filled the room. She cooked hand made pasta in a large pan on the old wood-fired stove. The kitchen was a myriad of Catholic effigies, paintings and faded photos, akin to a tourist's shop in Lourdes. When she turned and saw the state of her baby boy; she screamed, she cried, she prayed to all the saints and pleaded with her beloved son to divulge the circumstances behind his injuries.

Except, he was voiceless.

Signóra Angelica Massoni was a simple and undemanding woman in her fifties, even though she looked much older. Since a child, she knew that men were superior to women and ruled the world. It had always been a woman's place to cook, sow and clean, and of course obey her husband and father. She suffered being slapped around quite a few times over the years, still; she accepted her role and the occasional black eye, because it was normal in her village. In fact, it was normal in most of Sicily in the early nineteenth century. Angelica thought little of selfish things. She felt content with her simple life and wasn't interested in fancy furniture or in clothes for herself. Nevertheless, she loved spoiling her six children and getting possessions for them, particularly for her baby boy Angelo.

A son, who the Virgin Mary decided to send her a little late in life, after twenty-two years of praying and about twenty-two thousand candles lit in sacrifice at the village church: therefore this masculine miracle was very precious to her.

Two of Angelo's sisters came running into the house, when they heard the noise and were dispatched immediately to tell their father Carlo and grandfather Cesare Calvino, that someone or something had inflicted harm on their boy. While Angelica, with tears in her eyes, took him upstairs, bathed his intimate wounds, gave him some warm pasta and hot bread, which he ate alone and in silence on his bed.

At eight o'clock that evening, the whole family were assembled at grandfather's massive house. Villagers and farmers living in the area congregated outside, because news of the emergency gathering had spread as rapidly as a tsunami. The last time the Godfather had called such a meeting, was when Sicily became part of Italy, forty-nine years before.

The fierce sun slowly melted behind the hills in the west. Nevertheless, the sky still clung onto the last light and the lanterns and torches illuminating the substantial house and grounds were only just earning their keep.

The three houses were blended into one, creating an extensive dwelling.

The former farm with two outbuildings were fused together, in the style of a walled panopticon; viewed from grandfather's bedroom balcony, all of which had been built-up into a semi-fortress over the years.

31

From the distance, the whole place looked small and insignificant. Partly due to a miniature forest of pine trees camouflaging three sides of the residence that nestled in the prickly valley.

Bordering the forth side, a rivulet flowed slowly by, its power sapped by the summer heat. A trickle of fresh water tumbled through a deep gorge, because the winter rains had chiselled their mark over the years, when the stream gushed down from the mountains at full strength. At the front of the house, the sturdy oak doors were about three metres high and six wide, covered by an ornamental stone arch, with casemates on either side, continuing into the substantial surrounding walls. A sinewy path from a narrow stone bridge formed the only access to the entrance, after crossing the river.

On the night of the gathering, the sheet of heat united with a blanket of humidity. Outside the entrance there were a large number of sweating horses attached to a long, purpose built, black metal, forged railing. Blocking the narrow bridge road were several traps, and three black horseless carriages on spindly wheels. Once through the open doors one could see how substantial the whole place really was.

The ample stone walls sat heavily on top of their ancestors and encased seven bedrooms upstairs, spread around a double height gallery exposing the roof's rafters, used for storage in the original grain barn. A large, white tiled bathroom constructed ten years before, was famously the only one for a fifty-mile radius. At the back of the house there hid, a small wood-panelled office without windows, where grandfather dealt with people on private matters.

Downstairs, a huge outside dinning space filled the front courtyard for the famous Sunday lunches, with long tables and over a hundred chairs stacked up in a half-open outhouse. This area, with a partly covered terrace, clothed in grapevines, formed a tunnel towards the *casa campagna*. The elaborate floor tiles continued into the interior dining room suitable for another fifty seated people.

The cooler north side of the complex, with the ground floor annex, had been divided into a large kitchen with two storerooms. They contained enough food and drink to keep a small army in a comfortable siege for several months. The rest of the ground floor benefited from three, half-panelled drawing rooms, looking onto a beautiful garden speckled with olive trees. Highly polished, double, wooden doors separated these rooms.

On special occasions; weddings, birthdays and the annual regional meeting for all of the island's unofficial leaders, the three sets of doors were completely opened, allowing the fairly large rooms to become an elongated stateroom. On that stuffy Tuesday night, all of the doors were pushed back and the whole house and the areas outside were full to bursting, with men, women, children and babies in arms.

The made-men kept their minders with them, who were all heavily armed. Most of them wore revolvers, stuffed into pockets and belts holding up loose-fitting trousers. Other men carried shotguns, casually slung over their shoulders.

And, outside, mounted on the balconies and the roof, there stood militia with *mitragliatrici*. These machineguns were either hand-held or fixed to small tripods.

The noise inside and out became deafening, with a cacophony of women crying, babies crying, even some of the men were crying. There were arguments throughout the compound, people gesticulating with their hands, swinging their arms and shouting; some men were banging their fists on the furniture to embellish their opinions.

The women were dressed mostly in black, some with veils. They held rosaries, crucifixes, holy statues, faded religious photos or paintings, which they kissed and held up to the heavens or used to cross themselves during the altercations. Angelica Massoni hadn't spoken to anyone except her husband and father. Therefore there were plenty of rumours circulating about what could've happened to little Angel, until one of the Godfather's workers returned to report that he went to see the priest as instructed, with two other men.

He explained to the Godfather the details, as silence

fell around the house and grounds.

'Don Calvino...' The young mafia soldier started respectfully. 'We went to the church, but no one was there, then we saw old Paulo, you know him from the market. He told us to speak to the Sisters who were in the street laundry. When we arrived, Sister Concepcion and her cousin Sister Teresa were there.' These two old women were the only nuns in the village for the last forty-two years. 'They told us that Father Benadicto left quickly with all of his possessions a few hours ago, after he heard that the meeting had been called. We went to the other villages, but no one has seen him.'

Godfather Calvino immediately sent ten more of his men to search further a field for the holy-man at other villages and the ports, with instructions to bring him back in one piece, to the compound.

'We looked around the church and found these stuffed behind some cushions.' He held up Angel's trousers, underpants and shoes, the packed household gasped at the incriminating evidence.

The huge assembly now tasted two names on their lips, two names in their arguments and two names in their vivid imaginations.

The first was little Angel, fifteen-year-old Signorino Angelo Massoni, grandson of the second most powerful Godfather in Sicily, a prince of the fiefdom. One of their local children, who they all knew since his birth, since his christening and confirmation in front of God, in the local church.

These events were always followed by a huge, generous party given by Don Cesare Calvino, at this very house in *their* village.

The other name, was that of the newcomer to their community, the Foreigner, the Italian, the Mainlander, the priest of just two months, who they realised, nobody really knew, and had apparently fled.

The nine-hundred and fifty-six people gathered in and around the country house, found it hard to verbalise the terrible things, which they all fictionalised in their minds.

For hours, the crowd discussed every single

scenario of what could've happened to little Angel.

His mother begged all of heaven to make Angelo speak. Aunty Clara held her pupil in her arms for hours and tried to reason with the boy. His father threatened to beat his son with a belt if he didn't tell all.

Finally, old Doctor Paluchi, who loved the child and delivered him in the very same house fifteen years before, administered a sedative and used his best bedside manner to extract any kind of explanation he could from his much loved Godson.

Still, the teenager said nothing. Despite the fact that he still hadn't said one word, since he appeared in front of the much-loved schoolteacher Clara, earlier that afternoon. She described, repeatedly to grandfather Calvino, how she found Angelo running along the road from the church, naked, except for his cotton shirt held against his crutch, crying and hysterical, with bloody injuries. The whole family pleaded with him, simply to describe

The ornamental metal hands hesitated at ten minutes past eight on the porcelain face of the antique hall clock. Suddenly, the crowd stopped speaking because Angelica, dressed in uniform, black blouse and skirt, white lace handkerchief in hand: brought her only son out of one of the bedrooms onto the gallery floor, over-looking the large hall. Nearly two thousand eyes squinted in silence, to and from young Angelo and the Mafia boss; like nervous spectators watching the final of a tennis match. The young man kept his eyes to the floor, until he slowly walked down the circular stairs with his mother, towards his old grandfather, sitting on his throne-shaped chair, fifty metres away at the end of the third room, behind his richly carved desk. The only other sounds heard when mother and child ambled through the three long chambers, were the small bats fluttering their tiny wings above the house and the tapping sound of Angelo's Sunday best, church shoes on the hardwood floor.

The gathering waited in silence while the young boy's chest heaved and his legs quivered before the old man, who he had loved, feared and respected all of his life. The wisely boss was physically frail; his face and body reduced to skin and bone as thin as transparent cling-film stretched tightly over a scrawny chicken.

When the Don finally spoke, his weak, high-pitched voice carried over the heads of the gathering, and they all held their breath, waiting for little Angel to reply.

'Who hurt you Angelo?'

Grandfather never called him Angel, even when he was a baby.

He had made big plans for his only grandson over the years, and these strategies were for a powerful man called Angelo Massoni, who would someday inherit an empire. There was a little plaque over the Don's desk; the words crafted into it were an apothegm for his family and all of Sicily.

Il Sangue Non é Acqua

The large chronometer's second hand usually throbbed inaudibly, muffled by the normal sounds of daily life in a busy Sicilian household. Now, the sound of the clock's chimes and the tick-tick-tick of the second hand seemed to fill the whole house.

Eight ticks resonated around the rooms before the boy spoke. Angelo's voice was croaky from crying, fear and embarrassment, yet he knew that he needed to pull himself together. His grandfather wouldn't accept anything less, and to defy his grandfather would be unthinkable. Angelo looked straight into the Mafia Godfather's shrouded eyes and said with all the force he could muster.

'Father Benedicto.'

A collective gasp filled the room while the boy's small, yet clear voice rang-out throughout the enormous house. Even though rumours mentioned the Priest's name, a thousand times during the afternoon as he had apparently run off. In the hearts and minds of these simple, devout Catholics, the idea that a man of God could do harm to this young boy, seemed to be inconceivable. Nevertheless, hearing young Angel verbalise the name of his assailant, to his grandfather; the head of the village and virtually the whole south of Sicily, to a man that *no one* would dream of lying to, made the worst nightmares in the imaginations of the villagers; a shocking reality.

'What did he do to you?'

The room went silent again; the morbid curiosity of the crowd could be felt like a wave of hot air from a furnace.

Angel's face went deep red and tears flooded into his eyes. For the first time his stare left his grandfather and he looked around at the huge audience, his mouth opened, yet only a squeaky gasp came out.

His grandfather beckoned the boy to approach him and said.

'Whisper in my ear.'

The *ragazzo* sobbed his embarrassing story, leaning his head on the patriarch's shoulder.

As he spoke the old man didn't seem to react at all, but his made-men knew the vicious ruler well, and saw him fondle his left ear lobe with blue veined fingers and long nails. Whenever this had happened before, someone usually died soon after. Before the boy finished whispering the story of his ordeal, he collapsed sobbing onto his knees.

'Angelica! Come, take the boy, I've heard enough, we have work to do.' The Godfather commanded.

The Mafia boss gave a slight nod to a senior band of armed men standing close to him, who quickly left the room. A few moments later, the sound of their horses' hoofs crossing the little stone bridge, galloping off at high speed, echoed around the house.

Several of the Godfather's older made-men, including Angelo's father, walked over in a cluster. The old boss got up from behind the desk and walked through the rooms using a straight walking stick, his council followed him towards the private room upstairs.

On the way, he nodded to several members of his close family and some of the known faces, only stopping to console his daughter Angelica, who now suffocated her favourite child in a loving, protective embrace.

Her father told her to serve the food. 'It might be a long wait.' He explained. Women of all ages helped in the kitchen and carried the food and drinks that were prepared several hours before.

Family members pulled out further supplies from the storerooms, and so more cooking started, to feed the hundreds of villages who were all starving and desperate for some wine.

Many of them had been waiting since the late afternoon. Each thirty minutes or so messengers ran up to the inner sanctum to give the Don progress reports on the possible whereabouts of the boy's attacker. Sometime after two o'clock at night the Godfather came out of his room onto the balcony, accompanied by his council of *uomini d'onore* standing close behind him, and announced:

'Everyone should go home, it's getting late, you will hear what's happening when there's some news.' The Godfather spoke with an even and friendly voice, as though he needed to explain to some schoolchildren that a football match had been cancelled.

In verisimilitude, a deadly manhunt had begun over the island; the Don's tentacles spread out as vicious as a toxic, giant squid. Even outside his jurisdiction in the north of Sicily. This was dangerous for him; he left this region until last, because he didn't want to owe any favours to the other Godfathers.

Nevertheless, these political complications were not reflected in his pleasant tone. An hour later, the numerous tables and chairs were stacked away, pots, pans, plates and cutlery washed up. The small legion of females, who had gathered with their families since the previous afternoon, meticulously cleaned the kitchen and dining areas, while the men discussed the emergency and became drunk.

The following noon felt stifling hot and eerily quiet, because the school and market stalls were ordered closed by the Don. Therefore, very few men could be seen in the fields or on the streets, even the birds respected the silence. The hot day seemed endless. Just before eleven o'clock in the evening, the night was as motionless as an ancient coffin and the heat of the day continued to hang heavily in the air.

The Don's house rested in darkness, when eight men arrived on horseback pulling a pack-mule. They dismounted wearily and one of them pulled the metal lever ringing the old rusty bell outside the tall entrance doors. A few lights cut through the darkness around the house and grounds, when several men on the inside gathered up their arms and torches and ran down to let the visitors in.

The horses were left outside, one of the older men with a grizzled face, who they all called Pappy, led the mule into the courtyard, after a few rolled cigarettes and mumbled exchanges between the guards and the newly arrived posse, four made-men rushed out of the house determinedly, followed slowly by the Godfather.

Old Pappy went over to his patron and said, after he bent and kissed his hand respectfully. 'We found him getting on a boat at the port of Augusta, near the Spanish Gates, Don Calvino.'

The grizzled face turned to the mule, pulled back a blanket, grabbed a clump of thick black hair and held up the head of the sweating priest.

'Bring him inside,' Commanded the Godfather in a spiteful voice. 'And Giorgio,' He gestured to one of the younger men.

'Go and get Angelo and bring him to my room, tell him to bring the gun I bought for his Birthday, but no one else, *capisci*? No women.'

The Don turned thoughtfully and entered the house.

The priest was untied and taken off the mule; at first he collapsed exhausted onto the ground.

Pappy helped him up and the young man slowly started to recover from the painful journey. Devoid of his usual dog collar and black cassock, he wore some dark brown work clothes with open sandals.

Six men roughly escorted him into the house and up to the Godfather's private room. When the priest entered, he pulled himself together quickly, squinted at the lights, pushed his hair back, and contrived a facial mask of pious tranquillity. The Kafkaesque, bricked up chamber smelled of lavender, cigarettes and, the priest thought; death.

'Don Calvino, my-my son...' He stuttered, holding his palms together, closing his eyes tightly as though ready for prayer.

'I'm so glad you're here, I thought that I would be attacked by these - these, ruffians....' He explained nervously. 'I believed that they were trying to rob me - rob the church! I was just going to visit my sister, and…'

Angelo's father, Carlo, lunged at the priest flicking open a large fishing knife. His father-in-law stopped him in his tracks, using his high-pitched voice, as violently as a slamming door.

'Stop Carlo!'

'I'm going to cut the devil into a thousand pieces!' He screamed, resisting two of the Don's soldiers who leapt upon him.

'Stay calm Carlo, the man wants to tell me an interesting story.' The Don said passively, he had years of experience dealing with enemies and had honed the art to perfection.

'It's a nice village Augusta, did you have a chance to visit the Castello Svevo, Signóre?'

The priest appeared confused; his eyes flickered to and from the Don, who looked so impotent, whilst Carlo, the boy's father, acted like a raging bull, about to gouge a wounded matador. He had only met the village elder briefly once before, when he first arrived at the diocese. His close friend, the Bishop of Naples, advised the young priest to pay his respects when he arrived in Caltagirone, because: 'That's how things are done in these small villages, the people there are just uneducated peasants and very simple, sometimes you have to pacify them. You know,' he laughed, 'treat them like children.'

The Don seemed like a rational man, the priest thought, not the monster that some people suggested he could be. Perhaps, with the help of God, he would be able to reason with the simple old peasant; after all, didn't the boy edge him on.

'I-I thought that I would visit the convent there…' He stuttered with a dry throat and an increasingly clammy body. 'I-I didn't know what time the boats would leave for the mainland and-and…I…'

The pious priest came to a sudden stop, because a loud knock on the door made the assembly look up.

The Godfather, almost imperceptibly moved his eyebrows, as calmly as an experienced bidder at an auction.

One of the soldiers, holding Carlos, let him go carefully, unsure if he if he would stay still, turned and opened the door, revealing Giorgio and little Angel standing in the frame. Giorgio carried Angelo's powerful Birthday present over his shoulder. At first the accused appeared to shrivel up, his shoulders drooped, his face distorted into a fearful grimace, finally he gained his composure and turned to Angelo with pleading eyes, saying desperately.

'Angel, my child, now what have you been telling your family? I hope you didn't say anything about you stealing the wine from the church? Because I told you that I would pray for you... and I'm sure that if there's any misunderstanding, we can explain everything to the Don and your father... God will forgive you...I...it seemed so very hot in the church yesterday, and...'

'One moment please.' The Godfather interrupted lifting his hand. 'Angelo would you please wind up the gramophone and put that record on.' Grandfather said in a social voice, pointing to the brown paper record sleeve with a drawing of a terrier dog, listening to the horn of a gramophone.

'Do you like Enrico Caruso Signóre?'
The disciple of the Catholic Church opened his mouth, yet no words came out; he watched the young boy he had attacked the previous afternoon, pass him without acknowledgment. Then he deftly wound the little handle on the side of the record player, carefully lowered the heavy arm holding the needle close to the large, slightly warped record, and tried not to let the spike scratch the grooved surface. When the great Caruso started to sing, the Mafia boss asked the men to leave the room. 'Except Angelo and our guest.' He said, signalling to two of the largest soldiers, to stand on either side of the priest.

When the group departed, the Godfather closed his eyes and cocked his head listening intently to the tenor, after a few moments the Don spoke to his prisoner resembling a psychiatrist comforting the insane.

'You may know Signóre, that we have a saying in Sicily. *'Where vice is, vengeance follows.'*
It seems to me that you have a vice Signóre? Or

would you prefer me to call you father?'

The Don didn't wait for an answer.

'And so now I want to tell you about the Birthday present I bought for my grandson. It's a Neumann Brothers, double barrelled, twelve-gauge shotgun, from Belgium.' He picked up the heavy shotgun and examined it carefully. The weapon sent a silent, telepathic message to the priest and he started to panic.

'You see it has two triggers and hammers. Normally it can only be used for a long distance target.' He pointed into an imaginary void. 'The problem with this gun is that if you use it on a prey too close, it blows a big hole in it!' The Godfather smiled and made a circle with his hands.

The priest attempted to move forward to the edge of his seat, except the two large men placed their hands on his shoulders and he fell back into the winged chair.

'Well, I can't really say that I'm grateful to you, although we are, where we are.' He paused and looked kindly at his grandson.

'I have decided that I shall use the experience of the last forty-eight hours or so, to turn my little grandson into a real man. Omertà, we call it; I have been searching for a way of explaining to him the responsibilities he will have when he gets a little older. He's experienced a very easy life up until now, and to be honest with you, he's been rather spoilt by my daughter and the whole family.'

The Don leaned over, opened one of the drawers in his desk and found a yellow cardboard box containing bullets. 'Angelo...' He said softly. 'Open this box and insert two of the shells in your gun please.'

Angelo hesitated at first; nevertheless, grandfather pushed the box towards him giving that famous stare, which had controlled many a man over the years. Using slightly unsteady hands Angelo loaded the gun.

This time the priest launched himself towards the door with the desperation and force of a cornered rat.

Unfortunately, for the man of God, the two fit soldiers were more than a match for him, in both weight and speed.

As quickly as he leapt up, he was thrown back down

42

into the large chair.

The man of the cloth's eyes darted from side to side looking for a way out, his face erupted into a volcanic red that could have heated an oven. The panelled room was clearly made for privacy and confinement; when he realised his hopeless fate, he started to sob into his hands. Cesare Calvino ignored his hysteria, turned to his grandson and calmly explained.

'Angelo, listen to me, this is called '*Primo Sangue*' you must get all of the hatred that you feel for this man, and turn it into a strength, not a weakness, and not an anger; people who get angry make mistakes.'

The frail Mafia boss stood up, faced the boy, resting a spindly hand on his shoulder, and for the first time, spoke with a passion that Angelo had never seen or heard before from the old man. 'Listen, to me Angelo, you must also use this experience, not only to make *you* stronger, but to remind those who will hear about this night, that you are part of *my* dynasty, and no one should be in any doubt on this island or even in Italy, that the blood of the Calvino family can *never* be spilt by anyone, without the ultimate consequence.' He paused.

'*Vendetta.*'

The Mafia Don spat out the last word with all of the venom of a rattlesnake. Then he turned to stare at the priest, directly in his eyes. The holy man dropped his head, sobbing violently and his trousers were wet around the crutch.

The head of the family turned to the boy and spoke gently. 'Now do exactly what I tell you, don't ask any questions.'

Angelo looked frightened, yet determined and pointed the rifle a few inches from the head of the trembling priest.

'No Angelo, first both barrels in the groin, let him look at the wound while you reload. After that, look into his eyes Angelo, remember what they are like.
Understand his fear and your power, and then, and only then, give him the other two barrels in the head.'

Don Calvino went over to the record player, because the singer started to slow-down, he gently gave the little handle a few turns until the rhythm became just right. He heard the first discharge and the man's ear-piercing cry at the hole, where his genitals existed a few moments before. Then he heard Angelo fumble with the other two shells using trembling hands. The shotgun clicked as the chamber shut, after a short pause, the second blast, and a terrible, death-scream.

The Godfather turned up the volume on Caruso with a wry smile on his face, and without turning around said to his men.

'Take the boy home and hang the body on the church gates, leave it until we get a new priest, who knows, the next one might show the correct respect.'

The following morning when the young Sicilian jumped out of bed with the first avian chorus of the morning; he looked into his little bedroom mirror and instead of seeing the usual image of little Angel; he met for the first time, a young man called Angelo Massoni.

Enrico Caruso still sang in the grand apartment in Paris, Angelo had avidly followed the great tenor ever since that night in Sicily, his soulful and passionate voice felt so soothing and yet powerful. By now Angelo's back hurt and he was tired of this job in Paris, he closed his eyes and sank into the chair in front of the radiogram. 'Boss-boss, are you alright?' The Fat-man asked in his husky voice.

'Sure-sure no *problema*.' The Godfather replied weakly, stopping the music and replacing the record back in its brown paper cover and then carefully into his bag.

'Let's go and get the French girl, huh?' He said lifting his spirits, closing the locked suitcase with a flourish.

The marksmen across the street saw the shadow move in the window, and peered into his rifle's magnifying lens at the Sicilian Godfather's balding cranium. The red, juvenile, morning light, haemorrhaging across the old man's silhouette, showed that the years of violence had gouged a devastating story on his face.

Despite the wrinkles he still looked strong. His eyes were dark and hard. Still holding the rifle at his cheek, the masked man glanced at the photo he had been given of the 'mark' once again. Certainly there was no doubt about this

Sicilian murderer. The gunman had followed him for days, noted his every move, witnessed him, and his men, eating in Paris's best Italian restaurants, visiting a famous brothel in Rue de Saint Denis, buying fashionable clothes in the finest boutiques. Then the Mafia three, picked up Jacques Dupré outside the Credit National Banque yesterday evening.

The sniper planned to terminate the mark before the banker was killed; unfortunately he couldn't get the shot. He now carefully aimed his old faithful, Japanese Arizona Type 99 rifle.

The sight's cross hairs fell between the eyes of aging Angelo as he turned to the street, and the assassin started to squeeze the trigger, just as he had done so many times before; when he felt a hand gently touch his arm.

'Wait.' the familiar, soft voice said.

'Why?' He asked, without lifting his head from the sight.

'Look at the next window.' His accomplice whispered. The marksman looked up and saw a black and white cat jump from the adjacent ledge onto the windowsill in front of his victim, the two masked individuals looked at each other and then at the cat.

'We love cats, but that pussy could stay there for hours...' He whispered.

'I saw you looking at the girl.' His collaborator accused teasingly.

'What girl?'

'You still look at girls, particularly cute ones like her, come on - you know you do.' The other assassin chortled gently.

'Hey, back to work, the cat's moved on.'

The sniper went back to his rifle, gave a quick glance to the Provençale beauty's window, though she must have gone to bed, his watch read 05.30 in the morning, and most of Le Marais was fast asleep, like the rest of Paris.

Nonetheless, the other apartment still seemed busy and Angelo came back into view again.

'Come on you two, we *gotta* get out of here and find the *sacchi*, we can't lose fifty million lire just because my fat-friend here can't keep calm!' Angelo complained.

'Don't worry patron, I'll go and get the Alfa and we'll bundle the Frenchi in the boot.' Marco added.

'Fatso, you start to drag him downstairs, it looks quiet outside…' Angelo said, now motivated again, checking the square through the large window.

'Alright Marco it's all clear, gra…'

CRACK!

Angelo stopped speaking and looked at his two henchmen with surprise. He touched the tiny hole in his bleeding forehead, laughed and studied his hand dripping red liquid. A small cavity in the huge window appeared, allowing the early morning breeze to whistle its song.

'What's this?' He said, crashing heavily to the oak floor.

'Mamma mia!' The Fat-man cried, rushing over to the Don, checking his pulse. 'He's dead Marco, he's dead!'

'Get down you idiot it's a hit!' Marco said looking through the glass.

'Whatta-you-mean?' He said in stupefaction. 'Who'd want to kill Angelo?'

'Are you really so *stupido*?' Marco answered crouching on the floor. 'Who doesn't want to kill Italy's most powerful gangster? He's been killing people for the last sixty years. No!'

'Yeah, I know, only bad guys though, like the bank manager here.'

He said looking over at the dustsheet mummy. Marco stayed behind the curtains and searched the street.

'They say he's killed six priests and two bishops with his own hands. The first a famous bishop in Naples, when he was only seventeen years old!
He used to be crazy when he was young, what could all these priests have done, robbed some change from the church plates on Sundays?'

Marco crawled over to the other window and peered through a crack in the curtains; he aimed his Bernardelli B-76 pistol along the rooftops opposite, and passed all of the windows, the square looked dark, and then he saw movement. A black Mini drove slowly out of Place de Vosges.

Marco glanced at the Fat-man and said 'Look at the English car over there, it must be the hitter, let's get after him, fast!'

The two men picked up their belongings and ran down the white marble stairs, when they reached the heavy street door, the Fat-man asked:

'Hey Marco, what about the bodies in the apartment?

'Run!' Marco pushed his friend out of the door and started to dash towards the Alfa Romeo, his gun still in hand. When they reached the car, he explained:

'Let's get the hit-man first, there might even be two or more, then we'll pile up the whole lot and dump them in the Seine tonight, with the little French girl from the bank, after we have partied with her for a while, and got the money, *capisci?*' He explained excitedly.

The Mini drove slowly out of the beautiful square, passed the former house of Victor Hugo, and turned right onto Rue de Rivoli.

The wide cobble-stoned boulevard looked as empty as a church on Saturday night and the two assassins pulled off their hoods checking the two, inside rear-view mirrors.

The rifleman in the passenger seat arranged his bags, and his accomplice brushed her shoulder length, blonde hair, whilst driving slowly and inconspicuously along the wide boulevard.

The man said, 'We'd better warn the young girl in the bank, what's her name?'

She's called Magali.' The driver said, lighting a cigarette. 'I bet that she'll be surprised, I doubt if she knows what Jacques was up to. I got the impression when we did the surveillance, that she wasn't at all interested in him; it seemed to be all one sided.'

The hit man looked up and said urgently.

'Check your mirror, we've got company, and it's coming fast.' The red Alfa Romeo, Guilia Sprint GT, drifted sideways, with its tyres smoking and screeching vociferously, skidding onto the unstable cobblestones of Rue de Rivoli. The blonde driver changed gear, flooring the accelerator and the Cooper S Special leapt forward, just as it famously did in all of the rallies. Nonetheless, the Guilia used a new twin cam engine and was no slouch, it soon came powering behind them.

'They're too fast on the straight.' The sharpshooter calculated, shouting over the screaming engine, while looking in the second rear-view mirror.

'We'll have to visit our friend, the fishing cat. Take the next left over the Pont Neuf.'

The Mini careered at the last second to the left. The driver moved the gear-stick at speed, using her right foot to heel and toe, with her left foot on the clutch. The rev-counter lived in the red zone. They past an early morning; olive green, corrugated, Citroën delivery van, at death-defying alacrity, to the shock and horror of the sleepy chauffeur. Unfortunately for the English couple, Marco was also a great driver and he repeated the action in the Alfa, even though the grip wasn't of the Mini's standard, they still made the turn, albeit bouncing on the pavement. The nose of the Alpha pursued the Mini as greedily as a hungry tiger, its engine growling angrily. The Citroën van now screeched to a halt, the driver in shock. He felt as though he had just made a wrong turn that morning and ended up in the Le Mans Race.

'Okay my dear.' The passenger shouted while the Mini's wheels left the ground at the high point in the centre of the bridge. 'Take a left at the end of the bridge onto the Quai de Conti.'

'Isn't that a one-way darling, in the opposite direction?' She laughed.'

'Try not to run over any stray dogs.'
The Alfa nearly caught them on the bridge, but the gangsters received a surprise losing a couple of seconds when the woman turned left. The red Alfa followed suit, chipped some paint, when it smashed into the central island. Yet, the Italians kept going faster.

'Hard right onto the Pont Notre Dame!' Suddenly, the couple's faces flashed intermittent yellow, when a refuge collection truck turned ahead of them, blocking their route.

The Mini lurched hard to the left; the driver

executed a handbrake turn.

The smell of burning rubber filled the air, and smoke surrounded the car in its spin, although it came up perfectly behind the truck. Then they screeched to the left, and dashed over the bridge passing the magnificent, illuminated cathedral of Notre Dame.

'Wow! That was close.' The passenger in the Mini said. 'Down to the bottom of the bridge, sharp right and then our friend, the cat, will be on the left.' The Mini bounced in the air aquaplaning over the cobblestones. 'I think we can say goodbye to that rather *wide* Alfa.' He said hopefully.

The Italians slowed a little, because Marco had trouble getting past the refuge truck, now the handsome killer was gritting his teeth, smashing his foot on the throttle, until the Mini was in sight again.

The girl ahead of him didn't drive the car, it was instinctive; her movements were as smooth and mechanical as the engine itself.

'I've never seen a woman drive like that before...' He shouted to the Fat-man, while he wrestled with the steering wheel.

'Maybe it's a guy, one of these new rock stars from London with long hair?'

The Mini turned right onto the Quai de Saint-Michel, closely followed by the Italian saloon. Suddenly the little black car dipped forward, violently braking.

The tyres complained bitterly, and the small car turned sharply to the left into Paris's narrowest street.

It looked more like a crack in the stone buildings than a proper road. At only five feet nine inches wide, Rue du Chat-qui-Pêche was impossible for most cars. Despite that, the Mini measured only four feet seven and a half inches wide.

The blonde driver squeezed the car along its thirty yards, at high speed, the stone walls flashing inches from its windows, like trains in the Metro tunnels under Paris. A manoeuvre she'd practised many times before.

The occupants of the Mini scanned their mirrors and sped to the end of the renowned narrow road. Their pursuers turned quickly in the Mini's wake. Although the Alfa didn't make it, crashing noisily into the restricted width of the stone walls at high speed and was crushed on both sides. The first explosion was small, quickly followed by the crack of breaking glass, and then petrol came gushing out of the bottom. The Mini squealed to a halt, the couple got out and looked back over their shoulders at the huge blast, through a pane of smoke and flame. Another cracking noise like a shot rang out; followed by a huge explosion. The firestorm soared up twenty feet in the air, due to the vacuum created in such a restricted space.

'I don't think anyone will be getting out of that furnace,' said the Englishman.

'No, mind you...' His female accomplice replied seriously, 'At least the young girl will be safe now.'

The Mini purred out of the tiny street as quietly as a cat and drove into the centre of Paris slowly. The driver blew clouds of cigarette smoke out of her window.

Chapter 3
Kent, England, May 1907

Zamo and his elder half-brother François, walked along the English country lane under a fast moving cloudy sky, eating a breakfast of peanuts that they had bought from a street vendor at the train station. Fluffy shadows blew across the fields as swiftly as sweeping birds. On each boundary, posh cedar trees stood to attention like palace sentinels, proudly guarding the wealthy properties behind them.

The circus brothers were a strange sight, striding through the tall, leafy Kentish tunnel side by side. Their clothes were ill fitting; François had straw-coloured hair that stuck out from under a pointed grey hat, his bulbous nose supported arched, bushy eyebrows on a thin face with large rubbery lips. Zamo had a tight grey suit, several sizes too small and battered leather boots that he wore with string laces over bare feet. They both had the distinctive rolling walk of fit men. François and his brothers had gained a huge reputation over the last few years in the circus world, for being great clowns. This meant that he owned a registered, face make-up, which could never be copied by anyone else and confirmed that he had passed all of the exhaustive exams. François was a qualified acrobat, juggler, prestidigitator, fire-eater and tightrope walker; he spoke numerous languages fluently and the European circus slang. He was also excellent on the trapeze, although not to the standard of the great flyers.

Like all circus children, Zamo was also unusually fit and strong for his age. Unlike most kids of seven years old, who usually had pipe-cleaner limbs and little shoulders, the same width as the rest of their bodies. Zamo had the arms, agility and grip of the chimps he was brought up with; he rode and did tricks on horses bare-back, everyday of his life from the age of two. He was also well on the way to being a good acrobat, juggler, conjurer, knife-thrower, tightrope walker and flyer, as was everyone else in the Grimaldi Big Top.

To his great regret, Zamo's family and the circus

thought that he would be better off leaving after the accident. 'Just a temporary measure for a year or so.' They said firmly. Because no one could look after him, he'd never been to school and couldn't read or write, and the owner and ringmaster complained:

'The circus couldn't afford to carry anyone.' Everyone must have a qualified and professional act to make money for the Grimaldis.

Zamo pleaded his case strongly, he could work the lions, that he'd known and loved all of his life. Nevertheless, they said no, he wasn't officially qualified. He beseeched them to recognise that he was a great flyer. He was, incredible for his age, yet far too small and weak to fly with adults. He listed all of his other skills and everyone agreed that in a few years he would be a great asset to the Grimaldi Circus, though until then, they couldn't afford to pay for him, and besides, the problem with András loomed in the background.

The catcher didn't want to get a twelve-inch knife in his back one dark night when the boy grew up.

Many blood feuds had been settled fatally in circuses, there were just too many opportunities for an, accident.

Zamo was very upset for a long time after András dropped his mother, and no one could be sure how the young boy really felt, he ignored the catcher most of the time; if it were unavoidable he would nod his head or make some other social gesture. Everyone at the circus knew that he was in complete awe of his mother, she was everything to him, he had never seen his Czech father, and his half brothers, who were all very kind to the boy, were so much older, more like uncles. Moreover, they lived their own lives and had careers to worry about. The love-lives of clowns was legendary, for some reason women found them irresistible and so because they travelled constantly, like sailors, they often knew a girl in every town from Asia to southern Europe.

François always spoke to his young half-brother in French, although they often switched to other languages and circus slang without realising.

After walking in silence from the train station, they arrived at the small village of Otford. The job that was advertised in the newspaper said:

'Stable boy, for Somerleyton Manor, located in Otford, Kent, England. Fourteen to twenty years old, preferably from a family in service.'

When they were just outside the village, Zamo said that he was nervous. François had answered the advertisement, enclosed a reference from the horse trainer, leaving out Zamo's age and that they were in a circus. The clown consoled the boy and told his half brother not to worry.

'They will never find anyone as good as you with horses, just tell them that you are small for your age.'

At the time, Zamo was still fighting his corner, he complained that he didn't speak English and knew nothing about English people.

However, nobody saw that as a problem, circuses went all over Europe and somehow conversed and entertained the foreign audiences without difficulty.

They arrived at the village square and François entered the only public house, telling Zamo to wait outside. He entered the small saloon and walked towards the bar when the crowded room suddenly stopped speaking and drinking, including the Landlord. The silence was palpable.

'We don't serve no gypsies in 'ere.' The balding innkeeper said through a massive beard and moustache. He wore a striped stiff-collard shirt and leather braces, and waved his arm aggressively to emphasise the point. François didn't understand the words exactly though he understood the tone, he was a very confident man and so he walked over to the bar and took out the advertisement from Somerleyton Manor from his pocket.

Two of the local farm boys left their ales on the table and stepped up standing on either side of the great clown.

The one with muscular arms said, poking François in the shoulder with his index finger.

'You 'eard what the landlord said, no gypos right!'

François ignored him and spread out the paper on the bar, looked directly at the landlord saying, in his strong international accent and pointing to the letterhead.

'Where is?'

'What does a gypsy like you want up at the Manor?' The landlord asked, talking to the whole bar, like a music-hall entertainer.

'Going up there to steal horses are you?'

The patrons all laughed, nudging each other in collusion.

'Where is?' François asked again calmly, still unafraid.

'He's a pushy bastard, this one, isn't he?' The muscular farmhand joined in aggressively.

François decided that he would need to go somewhere else and turned to walk out, after the first step the two young men grabbed him from behind by his arms and tried to pull him to the floor. The acrobat was too fast for them, using their forearms arms as a springboard he pressed down and did a forward somersault leap, landing four feet ahead of the two men, in front of the door, leaving them scrambling on the floor from the force of the standard acrobat's move. He opened the door and looked back, the farm hands were still staggering around and were happy to let him leave.

Outside on the porch, François almost bumped into a pretty, young girl who was delivering a large basket of bread to the inn, covered with a red and white checked cloth. She smiled kindly at him, and so he asked, unfolding the piece of paper crumpled in his hand.

'Where is?'

The young girl looked at the address, and then at the clown's smiling rubber face, took his arm affectionately steering him onto the narrow road, and pointed the unusual stranger in the right direction.

'It's not far, about one mile down the road...' She said with a strong Kentish accent. 'You'll see a big double metal gateway, don't go in there...' She wagged her finger for emphasis. 'It's not for the likes of us, go to the next door; it's a small wooden one for the staff. Have you got a job there then?' She asked flirting.

François understood roughly what she was saying, though more importantly he realised that she was a nice girl. He pointed to his little half brother and said.

'Stable boy.'

'Oh, lovely, mind you he's a bit young, isn't he?'

'He good boy.' François looked at the cute girl exposing her straight teeth while squiggling her attractive eyes at him; and made a mental note to learn some more English. He waved goodbye with both hands and walked off with Zamo on his heels.

The circus brothers soon found the impressive wrought iron gates to Somerleyton Manor.

They peered through and saw a long gravel driveway with closely planted oak trees pretending to be an impenetrable brick wall, curving to higher ground on the east side of the estate and camouflaging the Manor house.

A green carpet of perfectly groomed grass covered the land in all directions.

A few feet ahead, they saw the more modest trade and staff, pine entrance gate, the status of which was explained on a small brass plaque. François tried the little door and it opened, complaining in a squeaky voice, onto a copse with a well-worn path snaking off into a shadowy distance.

'This is as far as I go my little brother.' He spoke in French, yet used the friendly Spanish word, *guapo,* for beautiful boy. Zamo's eyes spoke a thousand words of fear and reluctance.

'Listen to me. The moment you walk through this gate your life will change forever. There will be good days and bad days.' He said in Czech. *'Bude dobré dny a špatné dny.'*

Because the language was more expressive for sad prepositions and his face communicated the emotion, as only a clown's could.

'You must learn their language and customs; they are strange people, always laughing, even when they hate you, they don't have passion, if there weren't so many of them, I would think that they don't have sex!' He squeezed his cheerful, rubbery face until his eyes disappeared and they both laughed together.

'If you have a problem Zamo, you must ask yourself this one thing. What would circus people do now? '*Capisci*?' François hugged his little half brother placing the advertisement and a little brown box, tied with string in his hand, then at the speed of a cat, lifted the boy up above his head. Zamo knew what to do immediately and stood up on the clown's shoulders with the ease of a trained acrobat, so that he was nine feet tall. Suddenly without saying a word, they both tumbled and somersaulted forward completing the roll by jumping up in unison.

Zamo found himself on the path to the house laughing with joy, when he looked back, the gate had closed silently behind him, and François had left as quickly as a dry leaf in an autumn breeze...

Chapter 4
London, October 1963

The autumn light dealt a hand of gold across the windows along Kings Road, Chelsea. Britain was getting an Indian summer that inspired the population to resurrect their summer clothes again and stand outside pubs with pints of beer, and for the trendy types, glasses of dark red Italian Chianti, whose straw covered, empty bottles supported a candle and decorated most bistro tables in Swinging London.

Sundays were always quiet in the capital; most shops had been closed since midday on Saturday, so that hardworking shop and office workers could recuperate before the dreaded Monday morning, when it inevitably rained. It was time for the tradition of going to the pub for a few pints before a Sunday, roast beef lunch.

Unlike the rest of Europe, British drinking establishments were only open for a few hours a day. Usually from noon, for two and a half hours when the landlord called time and closed, to the annoyance of the British population. Then they reopened from six thirty for another three hours. Nevertheless, in some parts of London, local laws allowed certain areas, such as Knightsbridge to stay open until eleven. These erratic restrictions were due to a law passed in August 1914, called the Defence of the Realm Act. Many ordinary people thought that these laws were merely a way of controlling the masses, enabling the upper classes to keep the working man sober and ready for work, in their factories or to fight in the fields and ditches of battle. Despite these stringent regulations British workingmen were resourceful, and most people knew a pub landlord where they could find a lock-in. The pub looked closed from the outside, yet a special knock on the glass door or an open rear door, succeeded in extending the opening hours.

'Oh shit!' Charlotte cursed, falling from bed and staggering into the bathroom.

'What's wrong babe?' Justin managed to spurt out,

still half-asleep, stretched on the other side of the narrow divan.

'It's *eleven o'clock* Justin...' Charlotte said in her public school, sulky tone. 'And you *know* that we've got to be at my grandpapa's place for lunch by half past twelve.'

She peered through the open bathroom door, sitting naked on the toilet doing a pee, waving a reprimanding finger at her sleepy boyfriend.

'I thought we're going down to the Chelsea Potter for a quick drink first?'

'No way, I don't want to upset granddaddy and Ya-Ya by being late, and besides, hippie Pippa's going for lunch too - with that twit parking warden, so she'll be fleecing him before I get there.'

'You mean you want to squeeze some money out of your grandfather, before your sister does? You're so spoilt Charlotte.' He said with a bored yawn.

'I just need a little help *this* month, Justin, because I still haven't been paid for the modelling job I did for the Chelsea Girl shops, six weeks ago.'

'I thought the agency would advance you the fees, if the clients don't pay quickly?'

'They *do* darling, though Gavin already charges twenty per cent commission, so if you ask for an advance, he takes twenty *five* per cent. By the time I pay for my Z-card and the test shots I did with Lichfield's assistant last month, it's almost not worth modelling!'

Justin felt wide-awake now, his head propped up on his arm. He looked over mischievously at the indentation Charlotte's body had left in the bed, picked up her hairpiece that had fallen off in the night, spreading it out artistically on her pillow, then he turned over the spidery false eyelashes, left next to him and pressed them onto the sheet.

After that, he held up her bra, stuffed his socks into the cups and arranged them all in the right order.

'You know what?' He said chuckling, with his Thames valley accent. 'You've got so many false bits, if I turned the lights out, I would think that you're still lying here.'

'Piss off! You poufy hairdresser...' She said

affectionately from the bathroom, and then in a childish voice, 'May I have a ciggy, Justin darling?'

'I thought you were having a shower!' Justin said, throwing her the packet of Senor Service without a filter tip.

'I hate these, they're for navies and old age pensioners.' She said lighting the cigarette and stepping in the shower.'

'If you hate them so much why don't you buy your own!' Justin replied; looking at his last damp cigarette from the packet, she'd thrown back. Charlotte rented a one bedroom, third-floor flat above a wine shop, in the former Wright's Dairy block. The Victorian Building had been constructed in red brick and proudly displayed a bovine head, which enjoyed a view of beautiful Markham Square opposite.

Affording the beast a great aspect into the private gardens, and a clear vantage point to see the trendy crowd, hanging-out in front of the famous pub of the same name.

The flat boasted a corner bedroom with no cupboards, which meant that you had to walk on top of the young model's clothes to reach the bed, since the string that she had tied between the bedpost and the doorknob had broken. Again.

The flat had a large living room under a lofty ceiling with detailed Victorian cornicing. The two windows overlooking Chelsea's most famous street, took up most of one wall. On the other, a fabulous marble fireplace was wrapped around an ugly, modern gas heater, that had an umbilical pipe to the coin operated meter.

The slot only took shillings or sixpences, which Charlotte usually managed to squeeze out of Justin from his tips. On one end of the room, the landlord had constructed a corner kitchen.

It was furnished with an old fridge, and a small sink over a couple of wonky cupboards, served by a gas water-heater, that also fed the bathroom, via a lead pipe that clung precariously onto the wall and crossed the room like a dance-studio ballet bar.

Charlotte was nineteen years old. A tall, very attractive, leggy blonde, well blondish, with a tad from

Clairol's *'Miss Clairol Hair Colour'*, having done the: *'Does she...or doesn't she?'* advertising campaign last year.

She delighted in the fact that she had earned a fee of two hundred pounds, (less agent's commission) a trip to Paris, albeit only for the day, taking the overnight boat-train, and a free, one year supply of the smelly white liquid, that streaked her hair a sun-kissed flaxen. Charlotte also managed to get some good tear-sheets from the photo-shoots that were so important for her portfolio. She had been a part-time model at Gavin Robinson's agency in Bond Street, for the last twelve months, which is how she met Justin. She might have been a full-time model if she could get out of bed in the mornings and took the whole thing seriously.

At Charlotte's first interview with Gavin, he told her to stand in front of him and his assistant booker, wearing only her underwear for the appraisal. They had an Edwardian screen in the corner of the office where models could change their clothes if they were rushing from one job to the next. Charlotte left her jeans, t-shirt and trendy military jacket there, which she'd bought the week before in the Chelsea Antique Market.

'Well I adore the raw material sweetie, a lovely English rose with a kind of sex appeal, great. And those eyes! Wow! I've never seen eyes that shade of green before; they're electric.

But you do need work luv, look at those nails, they look like a builder's! And those pubes darling, have got to come right off!' He said pointing to her crutch. Your long hair is great, yet it looks like you've just stepped out of Roedean.'

'I have.' She said, as though there weren't any other schools.

'Don't worry darling, Mary-Jane will arrange for you to become a house-model at Vidal's.'

'Oh great, how much do they pay?'

'Pay! Oh my God, you dolly-birds only think of money these days, listen sweetie, they're the most expensive hairdressers in Europe, well apart for that old queen, Alexandre de Paris, but we won't do my sordid past just yet.' Gavin proffered, gazing up to the ceiling and elbowing

Mary-Jane knowingly.

'The way it works Charlotte...' Mary-Jane started to explain, when Gavin interrupted.

'That's another thing, how are we going to market you? We can't call you Charlotte darling, it's too; middle class, for the cockney snappers and crimpers.'

'Snappers and crimpers?' Charlotte bit the lips of her full mouth to look cute, which is what she always did when she had no idea what people were saying: men loved it. Several phones chirped away on the first floor, Bond Street office. Gavin had two other bookers, Christian, an ex-model and Gavin's ex-boyfriend, who shared a desk with Sarah, a former bookkeeper from a firm of stuffy solicitors. They were both glued to the phones, busily negotiating fees, castings, go-sees, photo-shoots and fashion shows, for their assigned models.

Despite the outrageous personality, blond and bronzed Gavin was a shrewd businessman, with an intimate knowledge of the industry. He also owned an associated company for staging fashion shows.

Originally, specialist teams would co-ordinate the choreography, lighting, music and staging for London's top designers. This whole process could be very expensive for the designers who wanted to make an impact for the press and buyers. Therefore, Gavin came up with the idea of doing package deals. He produced a professional show of similar format for department stores, such as Harrods and Selfridges or for large manufacturers who weren't at the top-end of the market with a star designer.

The income afforded him a large collection of china frogs and a Victorian house in a cul-de-sac in Chelsea, albeit at the wrong end of Kings Road.

'It's like this...' Mary-Jane continued, lighting a long Rothman 100 cigarette,

'We arrange for you to go to one of the top hair salons, you know, Vidal Sassoon, Leonard or Evansky, except old man Evansky is absolutely awful, something straight out of a Dickensian Novel, what was he called?'

'Fagan.' Gavin chipped in. 'Oh yes that's him, well don't worry, his wife Rose does all the photo-sessions.'

'I've got it!' Gavin interrupted again. 'Charlie!' From now on you'll be called Charlie, with an 'i-e', I love it, it will look great on your new Z-card.' He said, pleased with himself.

'Wow that's fab,' Mary-Jane added enthusiastically, 'He's so good at tags, Gavin, even if most of the girls end up with boys names, except Scottish Wilma, she refused to be called Willy.' Mary-Jane got the giggles. 'Anyway, all I wanted to say was, you get your hair and nails done free of charge by one of the top hairdressers and in exchange, they use you without paying, when they do pix for their salon; get it?'

'Pix?' Charlotte now tried her other trick of putting her index finger in her mouth, she thought it looked cute in the long mirror in front of her; yet, it appeared to be wasted on the two experienced agents.

At that point, a group of five models wondered in, jabbering away excitedly about a fashion show they had just finished; there were two young men and three cute girls. The men, very tall and very good-looking, collapsed on the sofa in the reception area, throwing their leather portfolios on the coffee table, near to where Gavin and Mary-Jane were doing their appraisal.

Without taking a breath the three talkative girls walked over to their agents in the inner sanctum and kissed them on the cheeks with an exaggerated, Mwah - Mwah.

Charlotte now felt really self-conscious, standing in her skimpy underwear, and tried to cover her crutch and her tiny, blue and gold tattoo of a leopard, with a copy of Vogue magazine that was on the desk.

Not only because her bra and pants looked somewhat see-through, but also because these girls were also really expensively dressed, with coiffed hair and *so* made up. She thought that next to them she resembled a scruffy, country schoolgirl.

'Well boys and girls how did the Mary Quant show go?'

The agent asked extravagantly. 'Were you all fab?' He queried, looking over and flirting with the boys in the reception area, who were smoking feverishly.

The two boys ambled into the small room ignoring Charlotte. She now wanted to disappear into the floor, then, to make things worse.

Gavin introduced her to the new arrivals, which all casually did the Mwah – Mwah thing, close to her blushing cheeks, somewhere an inch or so in the space left and right of her head. Charlotte thought that none of the boys looked Gay, but wondered why they didn't seem to notice that she was standing virtually naked in front of them?

'Let me introduce you all to my latest discovery, Charlie!' He then went on to list the names of the glamorous group, however, Charlotte couldn't concentrate on who they all were, especially as Freddie, Henri and Pieta, all seemed to be the girls. After Charlie had been in the business for a few months she realised that male models were constantly surrounded by virtually naked girls at photo shoots and behind the scenes at fashion shows and so they were usually more impressed by the latest designer clothes, than bare flesh.

Charlotte stepped out of the steamy shower in her scruffy flat, patting her long dripping hair with Justin's T-shirt left next to the loo the night before, because as usual, all of her towels were dirty. She grabbed a piece of dried toast from yesterday's brunch, which she found under her pink knickers, as Justin had pulled them off in a hurry and thrown the lacy triangle on the floor, as soon as they had arrived home.

'How can you eat that Charlotte? It's got fluff on it.' Justin cringed, jumping out of bed naked.

'I'm hungry…' She mumbled, her mouth full of crumbling stale toast. 'I hardly ate anything this week, because my booker Mary-Jane told me I'm putting on weight and I've got the shows starting next Friday, if I can't squeeze into the designer's stuff, they'll get some new skinny bitch straight from school, who can't afford to eat.'

'You can't afford to eat either.' He laughed, pulling her damp, nude body close to his.

'Naff-off Justin.' She said giggling and chewing.

'We must leave in a few minutes and I've still got to iron something from that pile of clothes.' She explained, pointing to the rag mountain on the floor.

'Come on Charlie-girl, let's have a quick shag and a joint before we go...' He whispered, licking her ear. 'It'll set us up for your boring old granny's lunch.' He gently nibbled her neck because he'd learnt that she loved the tingling sensation.

'Don't Justin, you know that drives me mad.' She said, throwing her head back in ecstasy. Justin pulled her down onto the pile of clothes covering the floor and kissed the leopard on the inside of her right thigh.

'No! No! Justin.' She cried unconvincingly, wrapping her long skinny legs around his back, stroking his naked body with her blood red, Chanel painted toes. 'I said don't touch me with that thing,' She squealed. 'I can't remember if I took the pill recently!'

Justin leapt up shocked. '*What*!'

Charlotte fell into hysterics and cried. 'April fool.' She rolled over on her stomach, pulled a pillow over her head and smothered her face in her hands, trying to hide her laughing.

'You little minx.' He said in a husky voice crouching over her on the floor, he pulled the blonde up on her knees and made love to her urgently.

At five past twelve, Charlotte and Justin tumbled out of the flat and crossed Kings Road, they almost bumped into a Chelsea Pensioner pottering along in his red uniform jacket, black trousers and shiny peaked cap.

Three medals proudly decorated his chest; Pip, Squeak and Wilfred as they were affectionately called amongst the men in their Sloane Square barracks, or on formal occasions, the 1914-15 Star, the British War Medal and the Victory Medal, the old soldier looked up at both of them in amazement when they passed by in the latest fashions, *their* decorations were steeped in fashion, not history.

Charlotte wore a black and white silky mini dress, that Justin had complained barely covered her bottom, with an op-art shoulder bag designed in black and white stripes, that could have been painted by Bridget Riley. She had pulled her hair up into a schoolgirl ponytail and skipped along in short white plastic boots, designed by André Courrèges, to have a cut-out in the front that finished in a folded square bow. A red, E-Type Jaguar with chrome spoked wheels slowed down parallel to them, the two young men in the matching red leather bucket seats, attracted by Charlotte's speciosity, gave loud wolf-whistles, before they accelerated past.

Justin made a rude sign with two fingers in their direction. He wore black Chelsea boots, low hipster trousers, held up with a very wide, white belt, both of which came from Carnaby Street's trendy Donis boutique and above that, he sported a psychedelic shirt, with an enormous pointed collar, partly covered by his shoulder-length, dark hair.

They past the shop widows with a swagger, looking at their reflections and walked into Markham Square towards the young model's aging, orange Mini 650cc.

She had parked the night before on a resident's parking bay, and the car had now been awarded two parking tickets, neatly folded in a plastic bag and slid beneath one of the windscreen wipers.

'Oh bugger!' She said annoyed, pulling the plastic bag from the screen and stuffing it into the door's plastic side pocket, to join the growing wad.

'Why do they always pick on me?' She complained.

'Wait until I see that little shit Harold, it wouldn't surprise me if he hadn't driven over here from Battersea and wallpapered my windscreen with all of these dam tickets; I mean what sort of person would want a job like that anyway?'

At that moment a middle-aged women walked up to them smiling and said with a friendly Manchurian accent.

'Hello Justin - how are you?'

'Oh, hello Mrs Smythe, are you coming in on Tuesday for your highlights?'

'I'll be there Justin…' And looking at Charlotte. 'Nice legs love, I had a pair like that once!' She gave a little wave and walked off towards the shops.

'That's Andy Capp's mum.' Justin said delightedly.

'What are you talking about Justin, is she one of

your Essex neighbours?' Charlotte responded, still upset with her latest parking fines.

'You're such a snobby bitch sometimes, she's one of my favourite clients, Mrs Smythe, her husband Reg writes the famous cartoon, Andy Capp, haven't you seen it in the newspapers? They've made a fortune.'

'You know I never read newspapers Justin; they're so boring, I suppose I might, if I were on the fashion pages. Anyway, I can't concentrate on anything, I'm still in the middle of hating Harold and all of his parking warden brotherhood.'

'I thought you said he seemed kind of smart...' Justin quizzed.

'He's not smart, well he *thinks* he is, the idiot's always reading crime fiction novels and coming up with complicated conspiracy theories about everything. I mean he's either reading crime fiction or talking about it, he drives me crazy, such a horrid little nerd.'

They slipped into the car and drove around the Square coming out onto Kings Road.

'So what does Pippa see in him?'

'Well she *is* a somewhat intellectual, or at least really well educated, apart from being some sort of guitar-playing-hippy-Communist, she keeps taking useless degrees and they both follow some chap called Gurdjieff.'

'Isn't he that new German fashion designer, who we saw in Queen magazine last month?'

'Oh Justin, you're just as dozy as I am sometimes, she knows nothing about fashion darling, grandpapa says he's some kind of philosopher or mystic. Pippa's also a Vegan...'

'What's that, a new religion?'

'You know what Vegetarians are like? Well Vegans make them look like cavemen.'

'So what does she eat?'

'Nothing, that's why she's so skinny, I'd hate her if she wasn't the best sister anyone could have.'

They turned right and drove west down the Kings Road when Justin said excitedly. 'Hey look! There's a big crowd in the Potters, let's stop and have a quick drink before it closes.'

'Wow! It looks groovy today, but no way Justin, it's getting so late and we'll never get to my grandparent's place on time.' She said swerving to miss an elderly woman crossing the road.

'I thought you said that their house is in Ham, we'll be there in ten minutes.'

'We could be, on your Vesper, with all of its flashy chrome mirrors, my favourite sexy crimper...' She chided him.

'Listen in this traffic it'll take longer, besides, their place is on a private island in the Thames, so we have to get their little boat across, and it all takes absolutely ages - I hope you know how to row, town boy?'

The Orange Mini meandered passed World's End, with the two trendies looking at the shops and the fashionable people smooching around the cafés and pubs. After a few minutes they crossed Putney Bridge, turned right along the south side of the Thames to cut through London's habitat for wild Deer in beautiful Richmond Park.

At the first roundabout a large car pulled out suddenly in front of the couple and drove slowly through the common.

Charlotte used the easy drive to freshen up her make-up and pulled Max Factor mascara out of her bag.

She spat on the little black square and spread the paste on her false eyelashes with the spiky brush, blinking and pulling faces in the car's rear-view mirror.

Unexpectedly Justin bawled. 'Look out!' Charlotte came to a screeching stop, bashing into the Silver Cloud, Rolls Royce in front of her.

A breakaway herd of Roe deer nervously darted across the narrow road in fits and starts ahead of the traffic. The first dozen or so passed at high speed forcing the line of cars to brake hard in front of the Mini.

The rest of the herd hovered nervously on the edge, pretending to graze, then without warning, made a mad dash for the other side of the Great Park and the whole herd raced off into the distance.

An impeccably presented chauffer, of Guinness

Book of Records proportions, in a dark grey suit, crisp white shirt and a thin, plain black tie, jumped out of the driver's seat, walked around to the back of the car and examined the rear bumper of the Rolls. Charlotte looked over nervously at Justin who said casually.

'Don't worry babes, it wasn't that hard, your insurance will pay.'

The blonde model started doing the sexy thing with her pinked-up lips and said. 'Insurance?'

'Charlotte; are you telling me that you don't have any car insurance.'

'Well... I've all of the papers, the quote thing? I just haven't sent it off yet.'

'Why Charlotte? Don't tell me you forgot!'

'Of course I didn't forget Justin, it's because I need a cheque, and I'm *so* overdrawn at The National Provincial Bank, I didn't think that I should write any more; well that's what that horrible Mr Pike said in his awful letter last week.

That's one of the other things I was hoping to talk to granddaddy about.' She said, as sulky as a mischievous child, who had just eaten her last sweet and wanted another.

The colossal man was now tapping on the car's glass with a gaudy gold signature ring on his pinkie.

He had an immense skull that filled the Mini's window frame, with a deep scar running from his forehead through his eyelid and onto his left cheek, the eye above the indentation appeared to be made of glass.

Actually, Charlotte thought that it resembled something manufactured badly in a Japanese toy factory, like a marble or a plastic eyeball for a cheap doll. Charlotte pressed the little black clip and slid the window forward, saying cheerfully in an exaggerated upper class accent.

'Hello; how are you?'

Justin gave a deep sigh, thinking that she could've come up with something better, nevertheless, he wasn't sure what to say either, he was just praying that she wouldn't blunder out anything about the insurance. A few cars started to hoot behind them, since it was so difficult to pass on the narrow lane.

'Miss...' The driver said in a thick, eastern

European accent, taking off his black cap with its shiny peak, exposing his globe-like head.

'You *hiet* car you *giffe* money now.' He pronounced each word deliberately, as though they weren't part of the same sentence.

'Well, yes, except we must discuss this problem.' She stuttered nervously.

'We go car *pork,* get *detols*. Yes?' He pointed further along the road.

'Details?' Charlotte replied, biting her lower lip in the most provocative manner that she could muster.

'Yes, give *detols*, phone *nombers*.'

The skeletal head pronounced in staccato style. Without waiting for a response, he returned to the luxurious car, having received dirty looks from a number of drivers when they passed the limo. One young man in an old, green Morris van leaned out of his window and said, with a cockney accent.

'Why don't you pull over on the grass? You rich prick!' The chauffeur turned aggressively towards him, who, seeing the distorted face on the massive cranium, stepped on the accelerator rapidly. The Rolls Royce indicated and slowly glided off with a whoosh.

Charlotte who was now really nervous, and had trouble putting the Mini into gear. The box complained loudly with a grating noise and the engine supported it by jerking along with a stutter.

'Keep calm…' Justin consulted her.

'What am I going to say to this monster Justin, when he asks for the insurance papers? He's nearly ten feet tall!' She panicked, lighting the last cigarette from Justin's pack.

'Look, we'll just say that we don't have all the papers with us now, but we can swap telephone numbers and we'll sort it out next week...'

The Rolls turned into the gravely, public car park, the Mini followed and Justin continued. 'That'll give us a chance to arrange something after the weekend, you know, just be calm and polite and don't do that nervous giggling thing you do when you want to borrow money.'

In the car park Justin and Charlotte got out and looked at the damage to the cars. The Mini's useless front bumper was squashed like a roll of aluminium cooking foil, as was the flimsy grill; on the contrary, there was hardly a mark on the sturdy chrome bumper fitted across the rear of the luxurious limousine.

Charlotte fruitlessly attempted to pull down the mini dress over her bottom when she walked over to the limo, trying to look sanguine.

She nearly jumped out of her trendy boots when the rear, tinted-glass window smoothly slid down and a foreign voice from inside called out. 'Good afternoon young lady.'

The sound of classical music blended with a strong smell of cigar smoke and cognac, wafting through the window frame. The chauffeur wearing his hat again, clambered out of the front seat and opened the rear door for his employer.

A short, rotund, theatrically dressed man of about sixty years old, sidled down from the large car and blatantly scrutinized Charlotte from head to toe, as meticulously as a scanner analysing a complicated document.

He offered his gloved hand, giving a jerky little bow of his head and said profligately.

'I am *zer* Count Sergei Belevsky-Zhukovsky.' He kissed her pale hand slowly, holding it up as though examining a precious antique; at the same time he took a deep breath, akin to a sommelier sampling a fine wine.

'Oh!' She uttered, virtually speechless, the tall model looked down at him, because the top of his greying head was barely level with her shoulders. 'I'm sorry about the little bash.' She spurted out childishly, lifting her shoulders and tilting her head on one side.

The Count wore a grey goatee beard with matching moustache and had a small, white, Dandie Dinmont Terrier under his arm, which was yapping constantly. It wore a bejewelled, pink suede collar and looked as though it was used to getting its own way.

'I'm sure my dear child, that my chauffeur, Boris, was in some way, partly to blame.' The oozing charm evaporated from his face, as he glared up at his grotesque servant standing next to the silver limo. The dog stared at him as well and growled with undisguised hatred for the giant.

'I'm sorry about Milyi making all *zer* noise.'

'No problem, I love dogs, is it a bitch?'

'Sometimes yes.' He laughed hysterically. 'Oh excuse me, I love to make *zer* little jokes - etcetera-etcetera.'

Charlotte smiled and looked over at Justin confused.

The Count kneeled down and placed the small dog on the ground at Charlotte's feet, as he used his walking stick to help himself up he glanced at the model's long legs and noticed the tail of her feline tattoo.

'Boris tells me that you don't appear to have *zer* appropriate documentation, perhaps you could join me for lunch...' He said excitedly, thinking about Charlotte's inky leopard.

'I'm just on my way to *zer* Inn at Bray on *zer* river, it's a wonderful place with one of *zer* best cellars in Europe.' He described the cellar by throwing his arm in the air, whilst his watery eyes continued the detailed study of Charlotte's porcelain face.

'Hello, Count was it? I'm Justin, Justin de Vere, Charlotte's boyfriend.' The young, handsome hairdresser squeezed in between the Count and the model, with a huge smile on his face and a very firm handshake, verging on being the first part of a Judo throw.

Justin thought. Here we go again. It was just the same as the nights in London's discothèques. The moment he turned his back to acknowledge someone he knew, or when he queued up for a couple of drinks at the crowded bars, the vultures were on her.

Not that she helped much, because whatever they said, no matter how bad the chat-up line was, she was off. Giggling, touching their arms, poking them in the ribs, pointing her toes together copying a five year old, sticking her finger in her mouth, looking coy. And, oh yes, what's the other one that makes every bloke wobbly? Biting the fleshy edges of her wide mouth and then sliding her tongue slowly across her teeth and pouting her moistened pink lips. Just as she does for the camera, at least she gets paid for that. Justin reflected. The trouble with Charlotte was, that apart from the period blues and the grumpy mornings, she was always *on*. Always in character, even *she* didn't know when she was flirting.

Justin's best friend Alex at the salon, who was Gay, had noticed the same thing. He said to Justin that the thing about Charlotte was: *'She's dumb enough to seem dumb, but smart enough to keep it up!'*

'Ah! Yes of course, Charlotte's boyfriend, a beautiful young lady like this!' The Count waved as though he was conducting a huge orchestra. 'Would have a handsome boyfriend just like you. Justin, of course – of course, I assume that you have many admirers, Charlotte.'

He turned to concentrate his attention on Charlotte as clearly as a powerful spotlight on an opera singer, standing alone on an empty, darkened stage.

'Lots of admirers Count-mate, yet only one boyfriend; me.'

Justin decided to turn up the pressure a little, because the Count didn't seem to be at all fazed by Justin's presence, in fact he appeared to accept it as a challenge or part of some unknown game, where he was the only one who knew the rules, and that the Count, no doubt, had played successfully many times before.

'Wonderful – Wonderful, you have a gallant protector at your side Charlotte.' He smiled ingratiatingly.

Boris Stadnyk, noticing the change of tone, quietly walked around the back of Justin, pushing out the prognathic half of his face while towering over the slim hairdresser.

The chauffeur was born in Ukraine and at six feet nine inches tall; he was the shortest of three brothers.

'Unfortunately my own protector's not as charming as young Justin here…'

The Russian said, making the couple aware of the malevolent presence hovering menacingly inches behind them. Boris was now panting like a predatory animal about to be released into the wild.

'He does have his uses sometimes, mind you, little Milyi doesn't care for him.' He smiled benevolently at

Justin, his threat heavily cloaked in Russian charm, yet more than a match for the young lad from Gants Hill.

'Anyway, what was I was saying? You are of course *both* invited for lunch.' The Count placed his arm confidently around Charlotte's waist, which he could reach easily as it was level with his shoulders. 'And I'm sure my dear if there're any problems with your insurance company, your young protector here will pay for you.' The charisma never left him, however, Justin sensed that this guy was going to be difficult and he should be careful now.

'That would be great, ah, Count, but...' Charlotte stuttered, running out of cute mannerisms.

'Please, my dear – new – friends; call me Sergei!'

'Oh! Okay, Sir-Gay...' She said, confused by his weird name.

'Well, ah, we have to go to my grandfather's place for lunch and we're already running late.'

'I understand completely, you couldn't have known that we would bump into each other today; bump into each other, do you get it?'

The Count chuckled at his own humour enjoying every moment. 'Yes, you must go, give your telephone number, etcetera – etcetera to Boris, by the way, which agency are you with, I assume that you're modelling? Yes?'

Charlotte nodded and explained, 'I've been with Gavin's for about a year now.'

'Ah yes, dear, cute Gavin Robinson, I know him well, actually I know all of *zer* model agencies, casting agencies, etcetera-etcetera. And what about you dear boy, are you a model too?'

'No, I'm a stylist at Vidal Sassoon's.' Justin said proudly.

'Marvellous, a marriage made in heaven, a handsome hairdresser and a beautiful model.'

Despite all of the crazy theatrical chitchat and the waving of his gloved hands, the Count made sure that Boris had obtained all of the details Charlotte could eventually find in her messy car, under a pile of underwear, clothes, make-up, leftover snacks and the contentious wad of parking tickets. Then, as abruptly as he had jumped out of

73

his car a few minutes earlier, he disappeared back into it, shouting at Boris in some foreign tongue.

'Au revoir mes amis!' He said out of the rear window with a flurry and a cloud of leaves blowing up behind the car, camouflaging his rapid exit.

Chapter 5
Somerleyton Manor, June 1907

The gravel path twisted and turned through the dense forest, where pinprick shafts of light managed to penetrate the green mosaic of innumerable leaves. It was hard for Zamo to realise that he was really there, only a few minutes before he was strolling with his half-brother who had been his closest friend all of his short life, and now he was completely alone in this strange country. To the young clown it felt as if his body was walking through this English forest, yet he, the real Zamo was floating above on a cordless trapeze, looking down on a small lost boy, crawling like an insignificant beetle across the forest floor. He could see in his mind's eye the surroundings of the circus tent. The brass band thumping its huge bass drum, overpowering all other instruments, beating out a rhythm that the vast crowds loved to clap along to.

He could see the clown's antics, pretending to throw a bucket of cold water on the audience that turned out to be confetti. The screams of delight from the children, when the baby animals entered the sawdust ring. The bells and glitter from the beautiful, white Lipizzaner stallions that danced their equestrian ballet, raising their statuesque heads and marching their powerful front legs in perfect musical harmony, as nobly as ceremonial soldiers changing the guard. When the Grimaldi Circus arrived in Calais last week, there seemed to be a cold atmosphere, Zamo said his goodbyes to his stepbrothers, to the animals, who were as much his family as the adult clowns. A few of his fellow performers casually wished him luck, they were used to acts coming and going, it was their way of life. The train journey past by without reality, even crossing the wild sea to England made no impression on the young clown. His thoughts then turned back sadly to his mother, flying like a majestic bird under a canvas sky. Zamo abruptly squinted when the brilliant sunlight flooded the clearing in front of him, a summer's breath warming his face. He had reached the end of the leafy path and the end of his imaginary flight over the small boy. Now he felt the painful realisation that he is that small boy, and he is standing a hundred yards from an enormous ancient house, that may in some way, be part of his destiny.

A robust middle-aged man was working next to a horseless wagon that had a monochrome collie using it as a bed. The farmhand was swinging a heavy pick into the ground with the ease and fluidity of a conductor's baton; it looked as though he was extending a gulley at the side of the track. Shep jumped up from his sleepy nest and lowered his head poignantly, having noticed the sheep-looking boy meandering in the distance.

When Zamo was in sniffing range, he wagged his thick, furry tail and decided that no herding was needed and perhaps he had found a new friend.

The man didn't make such a rapid decision or stop work when Zamo arrived next to the cart, holding the advertisement, François had told him to show at the house.

'Stable boy?' He said in English, pointing to himself with both palms.

The muscular, middle-aged farmhand stopped his mechanical rhythm, leaned on the handle and looked at Zamo peculiarly; he took a dirty, colourful handkerchief from his overall's side pocket and wiped his glowing brow. He spoke with a huge smile and a chuckle to the seven-year-old. 'Just going to look after the Shetland pony I assume?' He teased in a strong Kentish accent. Zamo was stroking Shep automatically and remembered his brother's advice about the English always laughing, even when they're angry; therefore, he wasn't sure what to do.

He unravelled the little piece of paper offering it to the big man, and copied the clown saying, 'Where is?' The bulky man looked down his sweating nose at the piece of paper and smiled again curiously. He climbed out of the deep ditch with a groan, stretched his aching back and towered over Zamo, brushing some mud from his shirtsleeves he said.

'Looks like you're an ambitious young'un - come on then, I've been thinking about taking a break.' He started to walk in the direction of the Manor, followed by the faithful dog on an invisible lead and so Zamo jumped in step behind them.

'Problem is…' He started casually as though he had known the boy for years. 'You've come on a bad day see, 'cos the General and the family are all up at the church…' He paused to see if Zamo appreciated the predicament. 'At the Memorial service for the young Master, Peter.'

'Peter?' Zamo understood nothing, although he did recognise the name Peter.

'You'd better come up to the kitchen and see Mrs Jarvis, she's a nice old girl, if you get on her good side, she might let you have an apple.'

Zamo didn't comprehend anything he said, except he felt that this could be a good man and if he was the ringmaster of the house, he might already have the job.

He decided to just smile and follow the Englishman to the Manor; maybe he would find some food, because he was starving.

They crossed the cobblestone mews and arrived at the back door that lead into the large kitchen, a rickety chair sunbathed by the entrance, the minion used it to take the weight off his throbbing feet and removed his muddy boots. He opened the door entering in thick wool socks, both exposing matching big toes. Shep dropped on the grass, but Zamo was on the big man's heels; however, the peon quickly looked over his shoulder and said urgently warning the boy with his index finger. 'Don't go in with those boots on or we'll both be in trouble.'

When Zamo looked confused, the labourer pointed to his feet and said louder this time. 'Boots off!'

Zamo followed the advice, even though he had dirty, bare feet, so he tried to wipe them on the back of his three quarter length, grey trousers.

'Who's that?' A woman's voice cried from the next room.

'Just me Mrs Jarvis.' The peon called back.

The door was flung open by a small, round women of forty years old, obviously in a hurry, she wore an immaculately clean, broidery anglaise, white hat, used by cooks and servants to keep their hair back, with an ankle-length black dress under a full-length white apron matching the lacy headpiece.

'Hello Bill.' She said cheerfully, her cheeks reddening while lifting a large sack of flour onto the table, not noticing the boy. 'I expect you'd be ready for a sandwich and a cup of t...Oh my God! What on earth's that!' She said, standing in front of Zamo with her hands on her hips.

'I found him on the lane, looks like a gypo kid, but he reckons he's the new stable boy?'

'Mr Jarvis said they were advertising for someone, but he's absolutely filthy, he can't stand in my kitchen like that, he'll have to be fumigated!'

'He more than likely could do with a bite to eat, I'd say.' Bill said thoughtfully.

'Does the master know he's here? She asked. 'He looks too young to be a stable boy, that new horse will eat him for breakfast.'

'Don't ask me Mrs Jarvis, he don't seem to speak no English.'

Mrs Bessie Jarvis grabbed hold of Zamo and pulled him into the scullery, he held back at first, then allowed himself to be pushed into the room with a huge white enamel sink.

She pulled off his grey suit jacket, that hadn't fitted him for the last few years, rolled up the sleeves on his beige and cream striped shirt and shoved a large bar of yellow carbolic soap in his hand. The housekeeper ran the tap and said 'Wash!'

Zamo reluctantly obeyed and Mrs Jarvis returned to the kitchen.

'You can go next Bill.' Mrs Jarvis commanded, nodding to his grubby hands.

When Zamo came back into the kitchen the housekeeper had set three places at a long wooden table.

She pointed to one of the chairs, which Zamo hoped was an invitation, quickly taking the place. By the time Bill had returned with slightly cleaner hands, the table was piling up with a warm cottage loaf, straight out of the oven, a plate of Cheddar cheese, a bowl of onions and a small jug of beer.

Three flowery patterned plates with a sharp knife were set in front of the chairs. Bill helped himself to the beer, while Mrs Jarvis cut some bread and cheese, which she placed in the centre of the long table and helped herself to a small portion. Then as an afterthought, she got some lemonade from the cool scullery and filled a glass for Zamo.

Bill with his mouth full said. 'Thanks very much Mrs J, I've been thinking about this for the last hour or so.'

After several mouthfuls, in between telling Bill about the family leaving that morning for the church's Memorial service, she explained that her husband Joe had risen at five thirty with the cockcrow.

He cleaned the General's Sociable coach until it glistened and then spent some time dressing in his best dark suit with a striped waistcoat and a black tie. She suddenly stopped speaking and looked over at Zamo, who hadn't touched his food. Bill looked up from his plate at Mrs Jarvis and followed her stare to the young boy.

'Well go on then.' She said. 'It's for you.' She mimed for Zamo to put some food in his mouth. He looked slightly embarrassed and then felt in his trouser pockets and took out four coins of the realm, tuppence ha'penny and a thruppenny bit, which was all the money François had given him, and placed it on the table.

The two servants looked at each other in silent amazement, when the housekeeper said. 'Well I never, if this is a gypsy boy, he's the first I've seen who won't eat food till he's paid for it!'

The woman got up and looked at Zamo properly for the first time. She walked around the table, picked up his money placing it on his palm, folding his little fingers into a fist.

'It's alright son.' She said kindly. 'Travellers eat one meal free of charge, mind you, you might have to work hard for the next one.'

Zamo needed no more encouragement, because he hadn't eaten anything except peanuts, since he left the circus thirty-six hours earlier. Bessie Jarvis filled his plate four times, which he scoffed at speed and washed down with three glasses of cool lemonade.

The housekeeper winked at Bill, because they hadn't seen an appetite as ferocious as that for quite some time. He finally looked up and burped loudly, the three hearty consumers all laughed together.

Chapter 6
Ham, October 1963

It wasn't long before Charlotte and Justin arrived in Ham, strangely rather psyched-up by the unusual encounter with Count Sergei and his freaky chauffeur, they couldn't help speak excitedly about the accident, all the way to the grandparent's house.

Charlotte was giggling about the difference between the heights of big-Boris, as she now called him, and short-Sergei: they soon found themselves on the little road opposite Duck's Island.

'Here we are!' Charlotte announced to her boyfriend bumping into a short wooden post defining Thames path. She reversed away from the post and parked the car on the grass verge reserved for walkers, and tottered over to the small timber pier where a wooden rowing skiff was tied to the end.

On an aged plank at the front of the jetty, someone had hand-painted a little sign that read 'Duck's Island', a drawing of a green hashish leaf by way of emblem told the history of the island's hippy commune past. Charlotte skipped onto the back seat as she had done most of her life, while Justin lowered himself gingerly onto the swaying rowing bench and grabbed the oars unsteadily.

'Justin, you're not facing me.' She told him.

'You said it's only a couple of minutes across the river...' He called playfully over his right shoulder. 'Surely you can cope without seeing my handsome face for a few minutes.'

'Justin darling, before you row a boat you have to do two things; one, untie the rope and two, face the back!' Charlotte pronounced, enjoying teasing him.

The landlubber boyfriend followed the instructions awkwardly and tried to look adept while he struggled with the oars, after an enormous effort that seemed to Justin comparable with the annual Oxford and Cambridge boat race, they eventually managed to crash into the little jetty on Duck's Island.

Justin looked around relieved to be on dry land, yet could only see trees and hedges; the little island appeared to be deserted apart from the wall of green plants. Charlotte jumped up, slipped the rope and they walked along the tree-lined path towards the diminutive wooden gate marked 'Rose Cottage'.

'This looks like a really cute little house.' Justin chirped politely, trying to recover his composure after the uneasy crossing. 'It's a strange place'. She answered dreamily. 'It rambles all over the island, you'd better stick close to me when we get through the gate, just in case the dogs are running around.'

'Why, what are they going to do, lick me to death?' He joked.

'Actually both Neme and Heli are really groovy with the family…' She said in a serious tone. 'At times they get nervous around strangers.'

'I promise to do my best not to frighten them…' Justin joked sarcastically. 'What are they pedigree Poodles?'

They walked into the beautiful rose garden on the crunchy, gravel surface, with climbing flowers rambling over a pergola the length of the path.

'Actually they are long-haired, attack-trained Alsatians.' She laughed.

'Very funny Charlotte.' Justin said, hoping that she was kidding.

They arrived at the open front door and walked in, Charlotte called out to her grandparents with Justin now close on her heels, looking over his shoulder for Neme and Heli. A distant stereo system played The Lark Ascending and the retired couple came out of the kitchen wearing professional style aprons. They walked over to Charlotte with outstretched arms, covering her with hugs and kisses. Charlotte turned to Justin and said.

'This is my Greek Ya-Ya…' holding her grandmother closely. 'And here's my trendy coiffure and sexy lover, Justin.' She joked to the couple.

'It's a great pleasure to meet you Justin, please call me Phaedra.' She said warmly.

'Hi Phaedra, I can't believe that you're anyone's

grandmother, you look so young.' He said with his confident hairdresser's charm.

'That's kind of you, I'm Sam's second wife and so I've a few years on him.' She explained, with an imperceptible international accent. The grandfather cuddled the young girl he had brought up since she was a toddler.

'And this is my favourite and most *generous* grandfather, you can call him Sam.'

'That sounds like another expensive compliment.' Sam joked.

'Hello Sam, great place you have here.' Justin joined in.

'You are both very welcome; I hope you were alright with the skiff Justin? It's rather tricky the first time.' He said sympathetically.

'Oh sure...' Justin bragged. 'A piece of cake - I go on boats all the time.'

'Charlotte, why don't you take Justin through to the garden, we've got some drinks and tapas laid out, so just help yourselves, the dogs are on the boat so don't let Justin worry about them.' Sam smiled, pointing them towards the back doors.

Charlotte asked Phaedra for one of her cocktail cigarettes that she lit eagerly and took her boyfriend's arm. They crossed the spacious drawing room and past a York-stone fireplace that was high enough for an average man to walk into.

On another wall, there was a forest of wooden bookshelves housing hundreds of volumes. The back wall leading to the garden was mostly modern glass, they sauntered outside where Charlotte kicked of her trendy boots and squelched her bare toes in the perfect lawn.

The property appeared to Justin to take up the whole island, running down to the river on the north side of the land, where a large motorboat was moored.

Over to the east, they had a tennis court and swimming pool. The whole place had been carefully planted with a ring of massive trees and climbing flowers creating the effect of being isolated from the mainland.

Although there seemed to be another small house on

the west side of their island estate.

'When you spoke about your grandparents, I imagined a little old man bent over, wearing an old cardigan and a pair of carpet slippers, and a frail lady with thick glasses.'

'I know, people say he resembles that actor, Cary Grant and she looks like Melina Mercouri. Ya-Ya has the same sexy voice because of all those cigarettes she smokes. Although they are both very healthy for their age, Grandpapa enjoys climbing and sailing, they both go in for marathons, Ya-Ya is very competitive, she thrashes Pip and me at tennis.'

'I think my parents look older than them, my dad has a big beer belly and my mum has put on a lot of weight ever since she put her back out, I don't think they've ever played tennis in their lives!'

'Well you're not very sporty either Justin, you can't even take my rubbish bag out when you leave at night.'

'That's because you wear me out in bed.' He said kissing her passionately.

'Stop it Justin, I don't want my grandparents thinking we do it.'

'Don't be stupid, everyone's doing it, it's the Sixties!' Who lives over there?' Justin asked, pointing to the cottage, his other arm around Charlotte's waist.

'Nanny J. She's been our nanny and housekeeper for as long as I can remember, you'll meet her in a while, she helped bring us up after our parents were killed, now she's over ninety or more, no one knows, so she doesn't really do anything, Sam and Phaedra just look after her really.'

'Wow, that's really nice of them, some people would have just let her go.'

'I know, you'll soon find out that they're a really wonderful couple, so kind and gentle, they adore people and animals, and won't even kill spiders. They're also in love with each other. I know that sounds strange, but when Pip and I were kids, they always seemed to be close, you know like lovers.'

'Well I just wouldn't want to think about my

parents having it off. Let alone my grandparents, I thought people gave it up when they were forty!' They both giggled.

'Including the dogs, they look after two, stray black cats, Molly and Mickey, four swans and at the moment, half a dozen baby ducklings who've lost their mother.'

'Um! What about Neme and Heli, why are they kept locked up?'

'Well, it's a long story darling, Helius and Nemesis, were named by my grandmother after Greek gods, not that I would know. Anyway, they were both trained by a kind of special-forces unit. Unfortunately for some reason they became really nervous of their handlers and so they were going to put them down. Then, grandpapa said that because Heli became pregnant, he would take them both. And they've lived here ever since.'

'So when do they come out and kill us all?' Justin chided.

'After lunch! Charlotte joked. 'Now let me introduce you to my dear sister and...' She whispered. 'The ticket twit.'

The stylish couple walked over to a large marquee, erected near the house, the surrounding curtains were pulled back on three sides with chunky ropes. The roof of the tent supported two high points and the canvas was in red and yellow stripes, at the summit, the roof housed an enormous chandelier. In the centre, a circular table looked like a carousel with gold figures of horses painted around the edges.

The chandelier was studded with a hundreds of candles on ten layers.

Large cushions covered in animal print fabrics were thrown on the grass edges of the marquee. The table was set for eight using eastern black and gold, papier-mâché place mats and ornaments.

'Wow!' Justin said, 'This is fabulous.'

'I know, grandpapa is kind of childish, he's always doing crazy things.'

When Charlotte and Justin walked under the canvas giggling with each other, they found Pippa and Harold sitting on some of the cushions in studied silence. Harold clasped a drink in one hand and a book in the other; Pippa in an Indian tunic was strumming an acoustic guitar. Justin thought she played well, but he didn't recognise the song.

'Pip darling, how are you!' Charlotte said sincerely.

Pippa jumped up kissing and cuddling her younger, taller sister saying. 'Where have you been Lottie? I've left so many messages on that stupid machine of yours.'

'I'm so sorry Pip darling, I've been doing everything I can to earn some cash recently because...' She glared down at Harold, who still hadn't looked up from his book. 'I've got so many dam parking tickets, from those fascists bastards.'

'Now don't start again on poor Harold...'

'We aren't fascist Charlotte, quite the opposite...'

He sniggered in a strong, singsong Welsh accent, looking up from the book for the first time. 'We are mostly brother Communist, who are trying to equal out the imbalance of rich, spoilt young women, living in expensive Chelsea flats, with private cars, illegally blocking the streets, so that poor hard-working comrades can't get onto public transport to work, their usual one hundred hours a week, for a mere pittance!' A small amount of spit landed on the grass as he spat out the last word. Charlotte pushed past her elder sister ready for an argument, when Sam silently came up behind her, and with muscularly arms, swiftly picked her up, spun her around and pinched her cheeks playfully.

'Charlotte, Pippa, Harold and our new friend Justin...' He said extravagantly.

'I want to introduce you to my dear friend Maurice, who I met in Korea some time ago and has been one of my closest friends ever since.'

Harold got up reluctantly and joined the back of the queue to greet and shake hands with the handsome, fair-headed lunch guest, who turned to a voluptuous, raven-haired young woman with an eye-catching cleavage, introducing Lucila Fernandez-Gonzalez, the Spanish love of his life, who he described as Barcelona's latest starlet.

'Actually don't listen to this old Captain...' He said loudly with a cockney accent. 'I've changed my name a while back, to Michael, yet this grey-haired bastard keeps on calling me Maurice just to piss me off!' He laughed and everyone laughed with him, he was naturally charming, they couldn't help but like him.

'I don't understand why you've change your name...' Sam declared. 'Private Micklewhite, served you very well in the army...' The former RAF Captain teased, saluting professionally. 'I suppose now that you're becoming such a famous actor and meeting such beautiful *joven guapas*, like Lucila here...' Sam flirted, taking the arm of the beautiful Latin girl. 'You might need a different name in Hollywood dear boy, but I'll continue to call you Maurice, just to keep your feet on the ground. In preparation for the day when you get your first big role and the millions that go with it!' He mocked. Everyone laughed, including Phaedra, who joined the group carrying a Methuselah bottle of vintage Champagne.

'*¿Hablas español Sam?*' The young girl purred in a sexy Andalusian accent when she sidled up to him.

'*Si*' Sam smiled back.

'Now don't let him start that flirting with you Lucila...' Michael joked, taking Lucila's hand as a precaution. 'He speaks every bloody language when there're young girls around.' Everyone laughed.

'This is very true Michael.' Phaedra confirmed, poking Sam in the ribs. 'When there're beautiful chicas in sight, he forgets that he's in his sixties.' She goaded, with a tinge of jealousy in her voice.

'So what about you Justin?' Michael asked. 'I hear you're called De Vere, that's a posh name mate.' He teased. 'Are you part of the Gstaad De Vere's?'

'To tell you the truth Michael.' Justin said conspiratorially. 'My real name is Micky Jacobs, I'm part of the Gant's Hill Jacobs's.' They both laughed together.

'Why don't we all take our places at the table?' Sam said, thinking that Justin seemed like a nice boy.

Phaedra and her two step-granddaughters served an enormous, luxurious lunch.

Justin made sure that he sat next to Lucila, and was chatting to her about her long dark hair. He said he wanted to stamp one of Vidal Sassoon's iconic haircuts on her.

'It'll be great on you babe,' He flirted naturally, as he did everyday in the salon. 'Really short, cut over your ear on this side.' He demonstrated by running his fingers around her lobes. 'And a long Bob on the other side.' He said playing with her tresses.

Michael shouted down the table. 'Oi! Keep your bloody hands off her hair, I love women with long hair running down their backs, it's really sexy on their bare shoulders, what do you think Harold?' He asked flippantly.

Harold was in a serious conversation with Pippa and looked up to see the whole table turn and study him in expectant silence, waiting for an amusing response to Michael's banter.

'Oh, I'm not really interested in such things, you know.' He offered in his rolling Welsh accent, trying to collect his thoughts. 'I mean with so many people in the world starving...' He recovered. 'We shouldn't be talking about such trivia, isn't. I mean five pounds for a haircut at these top salons, it's ridiculous, you could feed a whole village in Africa for that boyo!' He said raising his voice.

A brief moment of uncomfortable hush engulfed the table, when Michael finally responded. 'You know you're absolutely right Harold.' He paused. 'And if you've finished with that bowl of Beluga caviar could you pass it over?' Michael took off his black-framed glasses and his puffy eyes were smiling ironically. Harold was suddenly conscious of the blini in his hand, piled high with the extravagant black eggs, which he quickly stuffed into his bulging mouth.

'Ah Nanny J' Phaedra said warmly, when the elderly lady shuffled into the tent. 'Let me take those glasses from you, come and sit down over here.'

Sam noticed that Justin rushed over and pulled out the vacant chair helping her to settle in.

'You all know Nanny J everyone.' Phaedra said loudly, as Nanny's hearing wasn't what it used to be; the whole table smiled and greeted her affectionately.

She ignored everyone, sat bolt upright, knocked back a large glass of red wine and enthusiastically piled a mountain of food on her plate as though she hadn't eaten for a month. Nanny J suffered from a limp; due to her right foot being twisted inwards, which seemed to be painful for her. Justin had the impression that she was in a great deal of discomfort yet with an iron will, ignored it.

She wore a simple black dress with her long grey hair pulled back tightly over her head ending in a neat bun. Nanny's forehead seemed to be uneven, as though it was slightly dented on one side. Her small face was a mass of wrinkles like screwed up paper, and she seemed to have an inner strength, walking surprisingly quickly for such an old woman. She carried an ebony walking stick, topped by an ornate, gold coloured animal head. Justin noticed that she still benefited from amazingly clear, green eyes.

The rest of the lunch past smoothly and was dominated by Michael and Sam telling funny stories from their period in Korea together, plus some of Michael's tales of life, treading the theatrical boards. When the lunch neared its end Michael turned to Pippa: 'What about one of your songs Pippa?' The young girl looked shy and said that she was still working on one but it wasn't finished. Phaedra turned to Lucila and praised her eldest granddaughter, saying she had a real talent for song writing.

'You are very proud of her Phaedra.' Lucila said smiling.

'I'm proud of both my girls, they each have their own qualities; we Greeks are passionate about out families, I think it's the same in Spain. It must be the Mediterranean air.' She laughed taking Lucila's hand affectionately.

'Well, I'll try one of Bob Dylan's, but I'm not very good.' She said with a modesty inherited from her mother.

The lunch crowd settled back in their chairs and Pippa sang softly. The diners joined in for the chorus and the grandparents were so pleased that everyone seemed to enjoy Pippa's singing.

Everyone clapped enthusiastically, Pippa went red and started taking plates into the kitchen.

After three and a half hours the actor and his striking girlfriend got up to leave, everyone kissed on the cheeks and shook hands sincerely and Michael turned to

Sam proclaiming, so that everyone could hear.

'You know what the Orientals say, don't you Sam, when you save someone's life, which is what you did for me, you are responsible for that life forever.'

Sam walked over and stood in between Michael and Lucila, wrapping his arms around them both affectionately.

'Well in that case.' Michael continued. 'I'll be back for another fantastic lunch like that, every weekend from now on!' Everyone laughed and the attractive couple left, Sam couldn't resist looking at Lucila's rhythmic rear, when she Samba'd towards the front door, arm in arm with Michael.

'I'll just take them across darling.' He called over his shoulder to Phaedra, who made a sign of a throat being cut with her long painted thumbnail. 'Don't be long darling...' She called back, with a fake smile and a warning in her dark Mediterranean eyes.

Back in the tent, Justin found himself alone with Harold, because all of the females were gathered in the house chatting with Phaedra.

'Well it's a wonderful home, isn't?' Justin said to the parking warden, searching for a suitable subject, while sitting back on the cushions with a balloon glass of Champagne cognac.

'This is not a home comrade, it's a fortress, a kind of Colditz Castle.' The Welshman said, with amused devilment in his bloodshot eyes, for the first time that day.

Justin looked around the grounds and said. 'I don't understand Harold, what do you mean, it's beautiful here.'

'Yes, a beautiful concentration camp.' He chuckled, enjoying Justin's surprise.

'I'm sorry Harold, I'm still not with you?' Justin answered irritably. Young hairdressers were used to having conversations for fun, with a little flirting, and trendy banter about the latest hairstyles, fashions and what one should or shouldn't wear.

This guy Harold was some kind of manic-depressive. Justin thought, remembering that he'd read about people like this in one of the fashion magazines; Nova, that was it.

90

'Well, what did the Germans have in the war? He paused for effect. 'Vicious Alsatian guard dogs? Well they have them here. Barbed wire fences, they have those too.'

'I haven't seen any barbed wire, you're crazy man.' Justin argued, putting down his empty glass, feeling a little drunk.

'You look closely when you leave; they're camouflaged with two feet deep of spiky roses, clematis and hawthorns, this place is still impenetrable. Then there's the moat, whose little rowing boats aren't always there you know. What's more they have cameras all over the place, it wouldn't surprise me if they weren't monitoring us right now.' Harold continued his plot looking dramatically left and right for effect.

'You're exaggerating Harold.' Justin chuckled.

'They were more than likely watching you, when you were crossing the river you know, and have you seen the motor launch, with the specially ordered extra engine, I mean, how fast do an old retired couple need to go, just to visit a few friends up river?' Harold asked with glee.

'Listen Harold, this isn't an Agatha Christie novel, everyone has a high fence if they have a nice house, I was only reading the other day in the Daily Mirror, burglaries are up!' Justin replied.

'Have you ever been to the local shops with granny? It's as though you're taking part in the Monte Carlo Rally!' Harold persisted.

'Well - most Italians and Greeks drive quicker than us,' Justin said coolly. 'It's all part of their culture.'

'Yes? And what about the dog's names?'

'They mean something in Greek?'

'Yes, revenge! Come with me my naïve young conspirator.' Harold got up and gestured for Justin to follow him. They walked across the substantial lawn, down to the mooring in front of the magnificent, gleaming boat.

'This is an ocean-going Dommel power cruiser, built by Lürssen Yachts. It's called Scylla, also from Greek Mythology.

She was a beautiful nymph, but turns into a deadly sea monster if anyone upsets her. Look at the size of those engines!' He indicated. 'Listen to me, I've researched this boat and the story is incredible. There're only two in the whole world, both built by the German navy as military craft, yes, not for your average old-age-pensioners.

The sister ship was called El Chris and was much bigger, but this one is smaller and faster, nearly forty knots, most fast boats do about twenty knots. They're called, Type 140, Jaguar class, Fast Attack Craft. How many people have attack crafts at the back of their houses?'

'It doesn't look like a warship, it just looks like a luxury holiday boat, that you see in expensive ports.' Justin said. I saw loads like this last year went I went on holiday to Málaga.

'Yes, of course it does now, but it was built by specialist who build military boats. They bought it four years ago, this one is made of mahogany on a titanium frame, and do you know how many boats in the world have lightweight titanium frames? Hardly any, the stuff was top secret a few years ago. It wouldn't surprise me if it didn't have a missile launcher that could pop out of the top any minute.' He smirked.

'Harold you really do have an incredible imagination you know.'

Justin shook his head thinking that Charlotte was right, what an idiot.

Then surprisingly the boat started to rock gently from side to side and bounced against the tyres protecting the little private dock, almost imperceptibly at first, however, after a minute or so, it seemed to be moving excessively on such still water.

All of a sudden Justin heard a deep bass noise, similar to a motor engine beginning to roar, from somewhere inside the hull.

'Wow! Justin gasped, turning to Harold. 'Is the boat starting up? It sounds like the engines are growling.'

For some reason unbeknown to Justin, Harold couldn't answer; he looked frozen to the spot.

'What's wrong Harold? You look like you've seen a ghost.' Justin chided, a little inebriated.

Harold now turned an even paler shade of grey than

usual; Justin glanced at him again, he looked as ridged as a stone statue in the park; the hairdresser mused that he might never speak again; until Harold stuttered quietly.

'That...that noise, is not the engine's.' He paused. 'It's the dogs, somehow they've got out.'

At that moment, the movement of the boat became more violent and the force of the rocking noisily slammed a door twice:

Bang! - *Bang*! Resembling shots from a double-barrelled shotgun, the two boys almost jumped in the river.

'I thought the dogs were locked in?' Justin said, more than a little apprehensively.

'Whatever you do, don't budge an inch.' Harold whispered nervously, barely moving his lips, like a bad ventriloquist. 'Old Nanny J must have forgotten and left the door open when she fed the Alsatians - before she came over to the lunch.'

'Why aren't they barking or anything?' Justin said with false bravado.

'They don't.' He said knowledgably. 'Dogs bark when they are afraid or to warn you off, these two have been trained to surprise and kill you, they're not at all scared.'

At that instant Nemesis and Helius, appeared on the upper deck.

'Oh my God!' Justin gulped in horror. 'They're gigantic.'

The two dogs peeled back their lips exposing massive canines; purposefully they lowered their heads in attack mode. Justin couldn't remember when he was more frightened. And then he did.

When Justin was five years old, his parents took the young family in their grey Ford Anglia on a caravanning holiday to Canvey Island, which wasn't too far from where he was brought up in Gant's Hill, Essex.

After a few days of intermittent sun and rain, they were all playing football on the grass recreation area near the snack bar, which wasn't much more than a garden shed, when Justin's dad fell over and twisted his ankle.

He limped complaining fervently into the caravan, because his ankle had blown up like a balloon.

The whole family were making a fuss over dad, getting bandages, warm water for bathing and of course, following the British tradition of solving all ills, physical or mental; Justin's mum made, 'A nice cup of tea.'

Young Justin wandered around the caravan site kicking stones and throwing sticks, totally bored by all of the fuss over his father's ankle, when suddenly, he saw a large black Alsatian dog, whose massive head towered over the young lad.

Living in a council flat all his life, where pets were not allowed, Justin suffered no fear or come to that, any other feeling towards these four-legged creatures, in fact he had never seen a dog close-up in real life. However, when the Alsatian, just as bored as the little boy, stooped down into play position to attract the five year old, Justin became nervous and ran off. The Alsatian thought that was a signal for a good chase and catch game, ran after him and pulled the boy to the ground, pinning down his little shoulders with big furry paws, while he panted and dribbled expectantly on his captive's face. Justin started to cry and faintly called out for his mother. *'Mum! - Mum!'* Unfortunately, the family hadn't noticed that he'd gone off; therefore no one answered his pleas for help. The Alsatian flopped down on top of Justin and licked his face, giving an occasional bark. It was about twenty minutes before the dog became bored with his new friend and went back into one of the caravans. Therefore, from that day forward, Justin was a little frightened of all dogs. Accordingly, he was absolutely terrified of Alsatians.

'Listen Harold...' Justin said quietly, without moving his head or taking his eyes off the two enormous animals. 'Why don't we just jump into the water, we might be able to out-swim them.' Justin reasoned optimistically.

'Are you a powerful swimmer in that strong Thames current?' Harold questioned. 'Because they are!' He cried almost in tears, surrendering to the inevitable outcome of being mauled to death.

Justin slowly turned his head towards the house hoping to see some help; unfortunately, the garden and marquee were empty.

He saw some movement out of the corner of his eye to witness Nemesis and Helius, both skipping casually down the steps onto the lower deck in less than two seconds, until their massive, panting, open jaws were level with the two young men's eyes, there wasn't more than ten inches between them. Justin could actually feel their warm breaths on his face, which was now sweating profusely. The horrible memory of his last Alsatian experience, which had melted into the recesses of his mind for the last seventeen years, now came rushing forward in horrific reality.

'I'm going to run.' Justin whispered in desperation to Harold, who was still glued to the spot.

In sheer panic he turned with every once of energy and threw himself towards the house.

It was at least fifty feet up a steep slope to the marquee. At that moment, with a mixture of tears and sweat in his eyes, he couldn't even see the cottage. His trendy pointed shoes found it hard to get a grip. The Carnaby Street hipster trousers started to slip down over his skinny hips, with the weight of the oversized belt. Moreover, the deep pointed collar on his psychedelic shirt was cutting into his neck. He believed that he had no choice; except to run for his life,

Both dogs leapt off the boat at the same moment, rushing towards Justin at full speed. After less than four strides the dogs were level with him, one on each side, he knew he didn't stand a chance.

Justin took another two strides, by now the dogs were way ahead, he called on all of his strength; the huge animals profited from a leaping gait, three times the length of any man's, the hairdresser, who smoked twenty a day, looked up and the dogs were now way ahead.

Then, with a final huge bound they turned, jumped on two black and white footballs that Charlotte kicked into the garden, about ten feet in front of her. The young girl bent over and started to whistle, Heli and Neme picked up the balls and ran over to her with their tails wagging furiously.

Justin collapsed on his back. He wasn't sure how long he had been out; incredibly it felt like an eternity.

Justin's body was cold and wet, his essence appeared to be light and floating, his long hair swished from side to side. He thought that he should open his eyes, yet he felt so peaceful, any effort seemed almost impossible. Then he did it.

The hairdresser stared into the open space and experienced for the first time in his life a bizarre kind of tranquillity; he was definitely lying down, while everything around him appeared so different and he couldn't really feel his body.

A large fish swam closely over his head, it looked like a salmon, however, he wasn't sure, because usually he'd only seen them when they were smoked or in a frying pan. 'Oops! There's another one,' he thought, 'or was that a trout?'

It was difficult to see clearly, because the Thames water appeared to be so many different shades of dark green and muddy blue. Justin was experiencing a strange peace, lying there on the bottom of the great river.

There were hundreds of plants blowing in the tidal wind, up and down stream, just like his hair, even his psychedelic shirt floated and bulged on the watery breeze.

The hairdresser looked up towards the surface, a school of tiny fish created a smoky cloud, blocking out the light momentarily; after a few seconds, the bubbling stream was clear again.

Golden shafts of sunlight crashed through the surface of the blue - green liquid, although Justin felt uneasy now.

He thought he heard shouting, panting, breathing. 'Breathing! Oh my God!'

His mind screamed, yet no sound came out of his mouth.

Then he saw them, two enormous Alsatians with massive heads and open jaws. They were diving at high speed straight for him. He tried to lift his arms, they wouldn't listen to him; they just floated there like aimless underwater debris. He screamed at his legs to run, to swim, or to move, regrettably, they too ignored him.

The dogs were getting closer now, their long fur

floating as soft as silk behind them moving with the force of the water. Their bodies were really long, moving swiftly from side to side, completely smooth now, like predatory fish.

'Wow! They are so weird…' He thought. 'Heads of killer dogs, yet the bodies of furry sharks!'

They raced towards him at speed, the sun was stronger, so much brighter, and he needed to squeeze his eyelids as tight as he could, to keep out the blinding light, to stop the pain of the death he was about to endure.

Now they were shouting and he was so cold and wet, he was surely going to drown, before the dogfish killed him.

'Justin, Justin…' Charlotte said, pouring more water over his head from an old watering can.

'You'll drown him darling, if you pour any more water on his face.' Phaedra said concerned.

'He'll be alright in a minute, this hot Indian summer we're having has made a lot of people feel faint.' Sam assured the small group, standing over Justin.

'I think he drank too much.' Charlotte chipped in. 'Oh look he's opening his eyes, are you okay darling? You fainted about five minutes ago.'

Justin could now see the school of fish were more like a group of bystanders, he touched his soaking wet shirt and knew it would be ruined with all this water. And why did Harold's viscous attack dogs, run past him?

'Oh my head…' He groaned sitting up.

'Hello Justin, you know you've got to do more exercise…'

His girlfriend reprimanded. 'I mean all that champagne, wine and brandy and then playing with the dogs in this heat, it's not good for anyone, especially when you're out every night till late, and only get a little sleep at the weekends.'

'Why don't we all go into the house and have some coffee.' Phaedra said comfortingly.

Charlotte helped her wet boyfriend up from the swamped grass and Pippa and Harold made their apologises, leaving with a cursory wave to Justin, who was pleased to sit in a comfortable upright chair in the living room, where they were playing some classical music on the Phillips record player. Phaedra brought coffee, Greek and Italian on a tray with some cakes and biscuits. Charlotte squeezed on the wet chair with Justin, plonking her bare legs on his lap, asking for a cuddle.

'How are you feeling now Justin?' Sam asked concerned.

'I'm so sorry Sam.' Justin said, more embarrassed than he could ever remember feeling. 'Harold started telling me stories and…'

'Oh don't worry…' Phaedra comforted him. 'Harold is a very special young man, and Pippa is in love with him, therefore we must accept her decision. We have always said that whoever our kids pick, and are happy with, will be part of our family.'

'Oh, thanks so much Phaedra, it's been quite a day one way or another, though life's always interesting when you have Charlotte as your girlfriend.' He started to laugh heartedly, the others joined in.

'And expensive I would imagine.' Sam said, placing his wallet back in a drawer against the wall.

'Thanks grandpapa, so much, you're a life saver, you really are.' Charlotte said in a spoiled baby voice, having jumped up and kissed Sam, after stuffing his money into her bag.

Charlotte and Justin left the house at half past seven, reiterating all of their apologies and thanks. Phaedra had previously made up a hamper of food to help Charlotte through the week, including one of Nanny J's famous fruit cakes, each piece was guaranteed to fill any stomach for a day or two. Sam said he would drop them with the outboard because he thought that Justin had experienced enough excitement for one day.

When the young ones drove off, Sam attached the rowing boat to the back of the outboard and towed it around to the other side of the island, leaving them moored with the power boat and the house with its mote was completely cut off again from the nearby banks.

Chapter 7
Otford Village, June 1907

St Bartholomew's church covered one side of Otford village green, and albeit rather small, its square tower and spire still looked striking, following its much-needed restoration a few years earlier. The interior of the cosy building was unusually wide and squat, yet easily held the twenty-one people who were attending the Memorial Service for Peter Trubshaw Junior: who had died at the age of fifteen on the anniversary date two years before. Little wooden doors, closed off the long box-pews, and the overhead light infiltrated the petit seventeenth-century glass panes that added to the warm atmosphere in the church.

Towards the end of the service, after the Anglican Vicar clutching his missal, finished declaiming from the pulpit in sepulchral tones; Peter junior's former head-teacher Mr Rochester, gave a long-winded eulogy that started eyelids drooping. The village doctor, John Gale, who was a close friend to Peter's family, spoke briefly, yet with a great understanding of the boy's long-standing illness and his enormous courage throughout. General Trubshaw, the boy's father gave a wonderful tribute, explaining the love he and his wife Lady Margaret had for their only child. And how, for many years they thought that they would never be blessed with this single offspring.

However, when the baby announced his arrival with a hearty cry, they knew that Peter junior was worth the wait. Unfortunately, his time with the family was so short; Harley Street doctors, quite early in his life confirmed that he would die young, therefore they decided to celebrate and love every hour of his short existence.

The organist played them out tonelessly; the Vicar stood at the open doors and gave comfort to his congregation while they dispersed onto the village square.

The General shook hands with his friends and fellow parishioners, after the last one left he turned to his wife Margaret and said as cheerfully as he could. 'Shall we go into the village my dear?'

'No Peter, I couldn't cope with seeing any more people, I just want to go home, I am too upset, and have had some palpitations this morning, we could have a drink in the garden if you wish, it's such a lovely afternoon.'

'Of course Margaret, I'm so sorry, I was being insensitive. Jarvis is just over there, we will be home in a few minutes.'

When the Trubshaws arrived on the green, Doctor John Gale was trying to get his motorbike started, without much success.

'Having some bother John?' Peter Trubshaw enquired.

'He's a strange creature Peter.' John joked. 'I've listened to his heart with my stethoscope and it seems to beat surprising well, and yet he does not enjoy this warm weather we're having, and so I think that I might have to allow the beast...' He paused, searching for the appropriate word. '...What do the Spanish call it?

'A siesta?' Peter enquired laughing.

'Ah yes, that's it or perhaps a nice holiday somewhere damp, that's when the monster's at his best.'

The three friends laughed, they needed to lift their spirits, even though the couple's son had died two years previously, the Memorial Service had opened emotional wounds. Peter junior had caught pneumonia when he was a baby; he never fully recovered, and was a valetudinarian throughout his life. He had asthma as well as eczema, and found it difficult to play with friends of his own age for more than an hour or so. Unfortunately, he was also unable to take part in any of the country events, school outings or the usual social activities that the other upper class children of rural Kent enjoyed, because inevitably some illness occurred that incapacitated him. The Vicar walked over to the group to examine the motorbike. 'I must say Doctor Gale, I really do not understand this new desire to ride machines.'

The Vicar spoke through his nasal passage as if he had a cold; the small silver, pebble-thick lorgnettes that squeezed his already pinched nose seemed to make it worse. In consequence the doctor didn't comment, because he thought that it was more than likely a sinus problem. The Vicar apparently had the same affliction for as long as the young doctor had been in the village, which was now nearly eight years. The Anglican clergy had not chosen to marry.

A small, thin, balding man with tiny, agitated black eyes, pale lips as thin as cigarette paper and an unhealthy blotchy skin, the colour and texture of unripe turnip; may not have attracted him to the typical Edwardian women.

If he'd been the recipient of thirty thousand a year, he may have been a better candidate for a successful union, perhaps with a family harbouring several daughters, he could conceivably get the one with a difficult disposition or almost past the marrying age.

Certainly, the low paid Vicar, albeit with a pleasant house attached to the church, wouldn't have been in a position to offer the luxurious lifestyle that so many of the upper classes desired at that epoch.

'Luckily I did not give up on my faithful old horse Mary, she just gets a rest now and then.' The Doctor admitted.

'Would you both care to take tea at the Manor? I would be delighted to show off my latest acquisition.' Peter Trubshaw said enthusiastically.

'General Trubshaw, pray do not tell me that you have also followed the Devil and bought one of these awful, noxious contraptions?' The Vicar lamented.

'Oh no Vicar, my purchase has four legs.' He said delightedly. 'Although he might have a little of the Devil in him, as soon as one enters the stables, he starts to demolish the stall and anyone who is unfortunate enough to be standing within range! In fact, he is a Selle Français thoroughbred stallion, called Black Silk, yet due to his temperament, the staff are calling him Black Satan!

'Perhaps I should bless him when we get there.' The Vicar said seriously, sensing no humour.

'You might be better blessing the staff!' The Doctor joked.

Chapter 8
The Stable Boy

Somerleyton Manor was a substantial Elizabethan hall, steeped in history that languished in approximately ninety acres of forest and farmland that was mostly worked by tenants. At the back of the impressive residence, outbuildings included a coach house and yard, a substantial stable block, a generous tack room and stalls for forty horses, backing onto a four-acre dressage paddock.

On the other side of the cobbled-stone courtyard, sat a trio of matching cottages. Mr and Mrs Jarvis had one dwelling; Mrs Jarvis did all of the ordering of provisions, the cooking and was in charge of the housekeeping.

Maisy and Florence, who both lived in the village, came everyday to do the beds, fires and cleaning. Maisy also doubled up as lady's maid when it was necessary. Agnes was the young scullery-maid and lived in the cramped mansard.

Twenty-seven years had Mr Joe Jarvis been with General Trubshaw, firstly in the role of valet, when they were still in the Guards and the last twenty years at the Manor with the General's household. The former sergeant was responsible for all of the staff and the estate. He dealt with the tenants on a daily basis. Liaised between the groom and his master, drove the carriages and acted as a butler, when there were guests or on special occasions. Unfortunately, he never enjoyed this role; he used to tell his wife 'It's all a bit fancy for me.' Like most servants at that time he usually worked fifteen hours a day, seven days a week, usually he had a rest day once a month; his salary was thirty pounds a year, plus food, livery and accommodation.

The second cottage was very small and only had two occupants. Bill, a prole, who had worked the land close to the house all of his life, and his dog, Shep, a border collie mix. Bill's wife had died of pneumonia five years earlier; he earned twenty pounds a year, plus food and accommodation.

He was a quiet man, who had taken the death of his wife badly, they had been children together and she was the only person he was able to talk to. Bill barely uttered two sentences to anyone, nevertheless, he was liked and trusted by the whole village and surrounding farms. Mr Jarvis often said to his wife, 'If we'd had a regiment of Bills in the last conflict we could have beaten the world.'

The third stone dwelling was almost derelict and mostly used for the storage of tools, for the two gardeners, Big George and his equally tall son Young George, who lived just outside the village, their earnings were lower and they didn't have the advantage of a tied cottage. When the Trubshaws and their guests arrived at the Manor, all of the staff was there to meet them.

Peter led the way and entered the massive black and white marble hallway with its imposing circular staircase that took up half of the ground floor. He escorted the guests into the library where he had a painting on an easel of his new stallion.

After Jarvis had taken the Sociable and horses to the groom at the coach house, he quickly ran across the yard to the back door of the manor, greeted his wife fleetingly in the kitchen, changed his jacket and went in the library to serve the guests.

When he opened the double doors into the room, wallpapered with thousands of books from floor to ceiling, he saw the three familiar faces from the village church looking at the immaculate oil of the Black Devil in an uncharacteristically sedate portrait, on the pristine lawn in front of the great house.

'I can tell you gentlemen you have never seen anything like it, he is a massive nineteen hands – that is seventy seven inches high or six feet, five inches at the withers.' Peter boasted proudly.

'Excuse me General, Mrs Jarvis has prepared a light luncheon, will you be eating in the dinning room or would you rather we set up here?'

'Her Ladyship has a headache and has gone to her room, therefore would you ask Mrs Jarvis to send up a tray please? I think we men will be happy here.

However, Jarvis, after the food and drinks we are going to pop down to have a peep at the new stallion, so ask

Victor to take him out into the paddock, will you?'

'I am sure he will *try* Sir.' Jarvis replied facetiously.

The General had an exasperated glint in his eyes when he looked at his former sergeant. They had shared many experiences together in India and knew each other very well. They were both in the European Light Cavalry Regiment. The General recognized that Jarvis didn't enjoy the role of butler; even so, he couldn't cope with someone new in the house. Especially a formal butler, with all of the snobbery and pomp that affords such a person; assuming they would be similar to the butlers on most of the large estates owned by his friends and acquaintances. They also enjoyed a higher salary than other servants, and so, as he always explained to Margaret, 'One had to keep an eye on expenses.'

'Thank you Jarvis, oh bring a bottle of vintage Krug from the cellar, will you?' Speaking with a reprimanding voice.

'Yes Sir.' Jarvis said without moving.

'Was there something else Jarvis?' The General asked irritably.

'Just a small matter Sir, Bill found a gypo boy running around the estate this morning, quite young, don't speak no English that we can understand; shall I throw him out Sir?'

'Oh yes, I shall leave these minor matters to you Jarvis, do not bother me with this trivia.' The General said, wanting to get on with his lunch and talk about his new gift, to himself.

'Yes Sir.' Jarvis turned on his heels and walked to the door.

'Jarvis!' The General called.

'Yes Sir.'

'Do it gently man and give him a farthing.' The General advised more sympathetically.

'Yes Sir.' Jarvis replied, with a disapproving sigh and shake of the head.

Peter went back to his friends apologising for the interruption and they sat on the large French Belle Époque style, dark yellow, chintz sofa and Chesterfield leather chairs that Margaret said was so fashionable. Vicar Smallbouys and the doctor had observed the instructions from the General to his 'man' with some interest.

'I am not certain Peter, if you should allow the servants so much scope.' The conservative Vicar preached, holding his fingers together while pacing in front of the majestic fireplace. 'Ever since the general election last year, I have noticed a distinct lack of respect from the servants and the working classes in general. These Liberals may have won a landslide victory, notwithstanding which, I am quite sure that the House of Lords will keep them in their place, and none of these ridiculous equality laws will be passed.'

'Times are changing Vicar.' The young doctor alleged. 'We cannot keep putting young children down coal mines and killing them off, before they have had a chance at life.'

'I am sorry Doctor, I must say, that is poppycock! Soon you will be telling me that these new unions are a good idea, before long we shall see mad suffragettes and East End cockneys revolting and taking over the Government!' The Vicar lectured excitedly.

'Well gentlemen, we should not worry about these matters.' The General bellowed.

'This is after all the Golden Age. Our dear Queen Victoria is dead and we now have the world's most gracious socialite as our king. England is the greatest nation on earth and the most prosperous, therefore we should all be grateful for our comfortable circumstances.'

'Speaking of money…' The vicar asked, looking at the expensive, gold-framed painting of Black Silk. 'May I ask if you paid a handsome sum for your new prize Peter?'

'Actually, just between the three of us, he was the most expensive thoroughbred ever sold in England, in fact, even this painting cost a fortune, done by an old chap called John Frederick Herring, great artist. Mind you, he looked as though he was on his last legs when he came to the manor.'

'And the thoroughbred, Peter?' The Vicar asked avariciously.

'Ah well, not a word to Lady Margaret…'

The two men leaned forward expectantly, when they

were interrupted by Jarvis who came in with an ornate gold and silver tray with a matching terrine, containing goose pâté, he took a cloth and opened the Champagne skilfully with an exaggerated *pop*!

'Oh bravo!' Applauded the Vicar, guzzling the first mouthful of the expensive bubbly liquid, before Jarvis had finished pouring for the others.

'May I propose a toast gentlemen? To our great King of England; to Edward VII.' The General said light-heartedly.

The three men lifted their crystal flute glasses and repeated the toast in unison.

'Edward VII!'

They ate a hearty lunch of game pie, lobster, trout, caught from the estate's vast lake, home-made bread, cheddar cheese from one of the tenant farms and a wonderful apple pie with rich cream that was the speciality of Mrs Jarvis. They emptied two bottles of Claret and one of Napoleon brandy. By the time Peter Trubshaw got up to show off his new stallion, the three men were rather inebriated. The General pulled the maroon coloured cord with its gold fringe next to the marble fireplace, to alert the servants, and they made their way down to the paddock, with a disapproving Jarvis catching up behind them. They could see the magnificent stallion ahead, tied to a pole that was in turn fixed to the study paddock fence. As soon as the Black stallion saw them, he went into a nervous frenzy. When they arrived a couple of feet in front of him, his nostrils flared, his perfect, white teeth flashed and he reared up on his glossy flanks neighing a devilish bay. Victor the groom had armed himself with a whip and a broomstick, yet kept out of range of the powerful hoofs, seeking any target within striking distance.

'Oh my Lord...' Exclaimed the vicar, 'He is the tallest horse I have ever seen.'

'Well done Peter, he is absolutely stunning.' Added the doctor.

'One hundred guineas.' Peter whispered proudly. 'Notwithstanding, I had to have him.

At that moment, Black Satan reared up again and

snapped the knot previously holding him down, in panic Victor cracked his whip in front of the horse's head to push him back, unfortunately for the groom, Satan wasn't afraid and pranced into the air as swiftly as Pegasus, flying straight over a petrified Victor, knocking him to the ground unconscious.

Alas, the black stallion had not finished with the stick-waving – whip-cracking groom yet. Braying and snorting he turned on the ostler again, he reared up with his massive hoofs flaying, his long, thick tail sweeping from side to side like a young tree in the wind, his beautiful dark coat glistening in the sunlight. The doctor observed the scene with a sense of horror and owe.

He remembered an incredibly beautiful oil painting by Rosa Bonheur, depicting a great black horse, rearing up just as Satan was doing now. The work was called *The Horse Fair;* he had seen it at an exhibition the last time he was in London. Suddenly, Jarvis, who had slipped under the fence unnoticed, made a courageous dive and gripped Victor's ankles firmly, pulling the comatose groom under the paddock's fence to safety. Satan lashed out into the air with his hind legs, flicked his mane in the breeze and galloped as rapidly as a whirlwind, towards the other side of the paddock.

Several members of staff rushed over and carried Victor into the Jarvis's cottage laying him on the kitchen table; he was so pale, resembling a grey marble sarcophagus.

The Doctor examined him closely moving all of his limbs in search of breakages. After a few minutes, the cold-water cloth on the groom's head seemed to revive him. Doctor John Gale MD confirmed that the patient had no broken bones or concussion. As usual, he did prescribed a glass of brandy and the rest of the day off. He was always trying to get a better life for the poor villages and farmhands within his practice. Because a groom only earned fifteen pounds a year and often slept in the stables.

The upper class Edwardians returned to the house somewhat distraught. Recuperating in the salon, Vicar Smallbouys, after another couple of drinks decided to leave as he felt a headache coming on and made his apologises. Bill and Mike Jarvis were asked to escort the unstable clergyman to a waiting trap; after a few yards, his legs gave way and his head swivelled. Without hesitation, Bill tossed the flimsy body over his ample shoulder like a rag doll, and dumped the feeble clergyman in the two-wheeled vehicle. Margaret came down refreshed after an afternoon nap, having heard the commotion. When she entered the salon, John Gale and her husband Peter recounted their experience with the infamous horse and the injured groom.

'I must say Peter that you seem to have gained a certain satisfaction from the narrow escape of poor Victor.' Margaret chastised.

'No-no Margaret, it's just that seeing Black Silk leaping through the air like a mythical winged-horse, was so – so spectacular! What did you think John?'

'I must admit that I have never seen a horse so beautiful and yet so wild.' John commented with a certain admiration.

'Well you must stay for dinner John and we shall put you in the blue room, tomorrow morning we can all go out for an invigorating ride, on the more sedate horses of course.' Margaret suggested.

The Sunday morning sunrise promised a beautiful day, the acres of emerald grassland near the Manor glistened with early due, cocks were crowing on the tenant's farms and the air still had the fragrance of fresh damp grass from the past cool night.

Lady Margaret, Peter and John convened in the dinning room for breakfast, at eight o'clock, which was laid out along the long mahogany table designed for the breakfast buffet.

Maisy and Florence served their employers and their guest, having arrived two hours earlier, with an array of culinary delights from the local tenant's farms. In more conservative houses of this standing, the maids wouldn't have been allowed to serve in the dining room, but the General was relaxed about the protocol, and it was much cheaper.

Lady Margaret was brought up with an enormous

staff, but she had married a gallant soldier for love and accepted his informal manner and parsimonious ways. Margaret chose some bread, fried eggs and a small portion of grilled mushrooms. Peter helped himself to the grilled tomatoes, black pudding, scrambled eggs and all of the toasted bread. John only drank coffee, as a bachelor, he wasn't used to such a prepared feast first thing in the morning. Jarvis opened the dining room doors and stood in front of his Master.

'Excuse me Sir.' Jarvis said, with some trepidation.

'What is it Jarvis? We need some more toast here.'

The General voiced impatiently, nursing a throbbing hangover. Margaret lifted the silver toast rack and waved it at Jarvis playfully, yet he didn't budge, and gave an embarrassed cough saying. 'There appears to be a problem Sir...'

The doctor, helping himself to a second coffee from a solid silver pot, looked up at Jarvis with a puzzled expression, and the General asked tetchily.

'Please do not tell me we have no bread Jarvis, like last Sunday, you know her Ladyship is very fussy about her bread, and of course we have a guest this morning, what's more you should be in no doubt by now how *I* feel about running out of supplies.'

'No Sir, it's not the food that's *run out.*' Jarvis's voice now acquired an ironic tone.

The General noticed it and walked over to the serving table and started to lift the heavy ornate silver lids irritably, taking random portions of eggs, bacon, mushrooms and cold meets.

'Jarvis you are really annoying this morning, more so than I am accustomed.' The General mumbled, filling his mouth with bacon. 'We shall just make do with what we have - that will be all.'

Jarvis still didn't stir.

'What are you doing standing there man? Can you not see we are trying to have our breakfast!'

'The gipo boy Sir...' he said languorously.

'I thought that I asked you not to bother me with such matters, did you not get rid of him yesterday?'

'I did Sir, with a good clip around the ear to boot, barring that, he came back last night and slept on the stable floor...'

'What! Do I really have to do these things myself Jarvis? The General growled, pouring some freshly squeezed orange juice from a Viennese cut crystal jug.

'Well he's gone now...' The former sergeant continued playfully.

'Then why are you bothering us Jarvis?' Lady Margaret joined in, contracting her husband's stress.

'Because he has stolen the new stallion Milady.' Jarvis explained in a monotone.

'*WHAT!*' The General leapt out of his seat as springy as a Jack-in-the-box, the orange juice splashed across the table, the doctor stood up aghast and Margaret patted her mouth nervously with a gold monogrammed, Irish linen serviette.

'Are you telling me that you have let some gypsy child, come onto my land and steal my hundred guinea stallion?' The General raged, his fists clenched and his face glowing redder by the minute. The doctor took his friend's arm in an attempt to calm him; yet, he was livid.

'Please do not vex yourself so, Peter...' John counselled reasonably. 'The boy cannot have gone a long way with that stallion, he is far too unmanageable, too feral, perhaps the lad just opened the stall and the horse bolted, and now he has run off because he is frightened.'

'Peter, I thought you said that the horse cost twenty guineas?' Margaret asked, annoyed by the lie.

Peter looked embarrassed; he didn't want to tell Margaret how much he had really paid for the rare stallion, in fact, even he was shocked by his own extravagance. He ignored his wife and blustered on.

'Well do not just stand there Sergeant, saddle the horses, get the shotguns and rouse every able-bodied man into the field!'

The General's years of training sprang him into action, just as though he was ousting a group of Indian nationalists, who had rebelled against British rule in the Punjab.

Chapter 9
The Chase, June 1907

In the cobblestone yard of Somerleyton Manor, a band of men, including a group from the tenant farms, were saddling horses, checking guns, unpacking boxes of ammunition and filling ammunition belts. One man, known as Old Ned, who held a certain reputation for hunting and tracking, brought his two large bloodhounds with him, attached to long leather leads that he had wrapped around his right fist. He steered the animals into the stables and examined the Devil's stall carefully, the dog's forensic noses automatically analysing the recent history. On returning, he approached the General and explained loudly for the benefit of all present.

'I've looked at the thoroughbred's stall General and the boy slept there last night and has not been long gone.'

'What? Are you telling me that this boy actually slept in the stall, on the straw beneath the stallion?' The General exclaimed, looking around the whole group incredulously.

'I am.' Old Ned clarified, with the confidence of a tracker of fifty-five years experience.

An audible rumble of muted conversation rose up from the assemblage of hunters.

'Ned, we are talking about a stallion that is virtually impossible to approach single-handedly.' The General explained pedantically, trying to take control of the situation. 'A stallion that nearly killed the groom, ah-ah, Victor yesterday: a stallion that nobody can even get a saddle on! And you are saying that this little gypsy boy slept with this dangerous animal all night, and not a soul near the stables heard a peep out of either of them?

'I am.' Ned said unquestionably.

The Doctor had strict instructions from Margaret, when she pleaded earlier. 'John, do please look after Peter, you know he can be so unreasonable where his horses are concerned.' Therefore, he sidled up to his friend to give moral support in front of the assembled men.

Despite the Doctor's backing, the General totally

occupied, ignored him, mounted his thoroughbred and spoke to the gathering, standing straight-legged in his stirrups, inspiring them to launch into the battle.

'Now listen here gentlemen, my horse, Black Silk has been stolen...' A few of the men whispered under their breaths, about it not being such a bad idea, if the Devil never came back.

'He has been taken by a young boy, I do not know how he has done this, because we all know the horse is rather temperamental...'

One of the men said to Bill softly, 'More like mental I'd say.'

'It would seem obvious to me, that the boy was just a bait, and that he is part of a large gang of horse-thieves who knew about my valuable livestock. Therefore, it is very likely that there will be quite a few of them, possibly armed!

We shall of course try not to harm these ruffians when we find them, yet should they resist, we shall have no choice except to shoot them down. Do you all understand gentlemen?'

The men touched their caps mumbling in a gesture of servility and obedience.

The tenant farmers were not actually employed by the General; they merely paid him a rent so that they could work the land. Nevertheless, Edwardian villagers and farmers still followed the tradition of obeying the Lord of the Manor - particularly against outsiders and gypsies.

'Let me be clear, under no circumstances must there be firing anywhere near the horse, he is a very valuable animal. All right then, let's be off!' A couple of men had brought their hunting horns and blasted their haunting cry.

Lady Margaret watched the huntsmen canter across the drive, at the front of the great house; she had a perfect view of the countryside from the vantage point of the master bedroom suit. It had been designed to centre the Manor's façade, to emphasize the balance and style; the room had a massive window and a substantial, elaborate balcony, covering the pillared porch that surrounded the front door.

Margaret Henrietta Trubshaw, nee Weymouth, was the daughter of Baronet George Henry Weymouth and Lady

Emma Jane of Somerleyton Manor. To her amazement at three years old, she acquired a baby sister, who everyone seemed to be fascinated by and called her Georgina Jane.

The young ladies' education, upbringing, in fact the sibling's entire existence, was based on the sole intention of acquiring a titled husband with a substantial income, because the Baronet had failed to produce any sons.

Her father seemed possessed by the task and would often say. 'Upon my word, marriage is a business arrangement between gentlemen, women play no part in this matter, until the honeymoon night!'

This philosophy was not only founded on family tradition, but necessity, because the aging Baronet had squandered his fortune and only had the house in Eaton Square, south west of London, and the country estate including contents, to leave in his will for his wife and the girls.

Margaret's mother and three aunts trawled the two attractive marriage prospects around to every appropriate occasion, for the seasons in London, Bath and for that matter, even provincial Kent.

Following a meticulous, military style campaign over an exhausting eighteen-month period that would have made any Boar War general proud: young Georgina Jane's engagement was finally announced to the Right Honourable James Babcock MP, who had been confirmed as the Conservative representative for the constituency of Norfolk East at the last election.

He had twenty thousand a year and a substantial pile near Norwich.

Certainly, it was not a perfect arrangement; Members of Parliament were starting to be considered respectable members of society, well, only those from the Conservative party, however, to many of the upper classes, politicians were not much better than trade's people.

The second problem with this union was that Lady Margaret, as the elder sister should have been married off first.

Another year past painstakingly slowly and despite the best efforts of the extended Weymouth family and their friends, Margaret was turning out to be rather pernickety.

Lord Wakefield would have been a perfect candidate, according to the Baronet, with forty thousand a year and a decent estate, though at sixty-two years old, Margaret felt that he was, '*A little too old.*'

Her mother Emma was very enthusiastic about Mr Goodbody, he was the heir to an American grain fortune, only thirty-one years old, he already had twenty-five thousand a year, unfortunately some said he looked like a stuffed pig and Margaret felt that he was, '*A little too fat.*'

The family had high hopes for young Angus MacDuffer, he wasn't old or fat, actually, he was younger than Margaret at nineteen, he didn't seem particularly bright, yet with a substantial fortune from his uncle and over fifty thousand a year, why consider his intellect? The uncle apparently owned half of Scotland; therefore, he was surely a good nominee for the attractive Margaret. Unfortunately after meeting him on two separate occasions. The first, at a country house party at Knightly Hall, when to the amusement of most of the guests, he misplaced his breeches whilst climbing a tree. The second time, was when he lost his front incisor falling from the first floor window of a stately home. Margaret said. '*A little too stupid.*'

The evening before her twenty-fourth Birthday Margaret announced to her parents that they need look no further, because she had found the man she wished to marry, whilst out riding in Hyde Park, on her last season in London. It was truly wonderful that he wasn't fat, old or stupid, unfortunately though, he was not titled or very rich.

Captain Peter Trubshaw had his modest salary from the army and a small trust that jointly provided fifteen thousand a year, he also had a fifty per cent interest in a small stud farm in Kent. Other than that, he was virtually a pauper. Lady Margaret's parents did not approve of his curriculum vitae or his lack of annual income. However, after meeting the tall, gallant and handsome soldier, Margaret's mother was enthralled.

The Baronet on the other hand after an extensive interview, did not like him at all from the day that they had first met, until the Baronet's last day on this earth. Lady

Emma Jane Weymouth understood and told her daughter that marriage should be as paradisal as possible and that she should be terribly modern and break the mould by marrying for love

Margaret sat in front of the gold-framed mirror combing her long hair with a bone and silver comb, while the hunt performed its exercise to the cry of horns and barking bloodhounds.

She considered the events of the last two days at length, then reached over pulling the cord next to her bed for a servant, and was surprised after a few minutes to see Mrs Jarvis knock and enter.

'Sorry Milady, with the hunt on everyone is so busy preparing lunch, I thought that I would see to you myself.'

'Thank you Mrs Jarvis, actually it was with you that I wished to speak.'

'How may I help you Milady?'

'In regard to the hunt for the gang of gypsy horse thieves, are you not the only person who has actually met this boy?'

'Well not quite Milady. He approached Bill when he was working on the new ditch, he didn't seem to speak much English, well nothing really, mind you, he was very polite in his manner and thought that he might have a job here as stable boy.

'I was told that he is very young?'

'Yes Milady, he was unusually muscularly, but he was only a child.'

'I believe that we had corresponded with someone abroad about the position, although I thought it was for a French adult. This gypsy boy, Mrs Jarvis, what was your impression of him?'

'Well Milady, firstly I don't think he's a gypsy, you see Milady, we offered him something to eat and he got all his money out to pay for it.

I never heard of no gypsies doing that, he seemed to be, well, nicely brought up, he was very dirty, he smelled like a horse, and he had grown out of his old clothes. In fact, I've never seen a boy like him before. And Bill liked the boy; he's a simple man but a very good judge of character.'

Ah yes Bill, he's the land-worker is he not? I remember him from the servant's ball last year, a widower I believe.'

'Yes Milady, he's a quiet man, but everyone likes him, been here from a boy.'

'And what about my husband's theory, that the lad is part of some sort of gypsy gang?'

'I wouldn't want to criticise the Master, Milady, but...'

'Excuse me Milady.' Maisy cried running into the room curtsying clumsily.

'Maisy!' Mrs Jarvis said, shocked by her rudeness.

'Excuse me Mrs Jarvis, Milady.' Maisy kept curtsying. 'I think you had better look out of the window quickly.'

Margaret and the two servants ran over to the large window and to their amazement, they saw in the distance Zamo riding Black Satan bareback, at incredible galloping speed across the top of the knoll over looking the Manor.

'Goodness gracious me.' Margaret said holding her fingertips to her mouth. 'I assume that is the young boy, Mrs Jarvis?

'Yes Milady.' Mrs Jarvis said with a hint of admiration.

'I thought nobody could ride that 'orse, he hasn't even got a saddle.' Maisy added with surprise in her high-pitched voice.

Zamo's knees were held high like a jockey's, his head was low and close to the stallion's ears, he rode with ease and grace, completely moulded to the shape of the horse, like the best racing saddles; then they heard the horns and the dogs barking in the distance.

'Oh dear.' Margaret cried. 'Open the balcony doors Maisy, quickly!'

The three women walked to the edge of the grand balcony to see Zamo riding straight for the house.

Almost immediately the pack of hunters appeared on top of the knoll clearly chasing after the boy, somewhat fruitlessly as Black Silk was far too quick for the best of them.

'My goodness…' Margaret said. 'Look at the speed of that horse!' When Zamo reached the gravel driveway he was way ahead of his pursuers, recognising his new friend Mrs Jarvis on the balcony, he slowed the horse to a trot, pulled his bare feet onto the horses back and stood up, as though he was surfing a rough sea, waving both hands triumphantly and grinning from ear to ear. As he reached the coach-house gates, he expertly slid back down to a sitting position and steered the great stallion into the yard. The three women were in shock, they had never seen anything like it; and were suddenly very worried.

'Mrs Jarvis…' Margaret said urgently. 'To the stables as quickly as possible, before those hounds get there.'

The three women, ankle-length dresses and aprons flowing, rushed down the long winding staircase and through the massive hall. Margaret aimed for the library door, when Mrs Jarvis said. 'This way Milady, through the kitchen, it's quicker.'

The Mistress of the house appeared confused for a moment and hesitated. She hadn't been to the kitchen since the fire five years ago. Finally, the lady of the house turned towards the servant's door and stepped gingerly over the threshold of the social frontier into the world of working-class domesticity. In single file at the pace of prancing deer, they ran past the pots and pans, the hanging meats, the sugars and preserves, the huge range and out the back door. By the time they crossed the yard, the barking of the bloodhounds could be clearly heard jubilantly close to the Manor. When Maisy arrived at the stable block panting, a little ahead of the other women, she opened the tall oak door and stopped in her tracks. The others caught her up and the three nervous women now stood together in silence, gazing at the most amazing sight they could possibly imagine.

Satan was calmly drinking some fresh water from a bucket and Zamo was brushing his beautiful long mane and whispering in some strange tongue, close to the stallion's ear. When Zamo noticed the women, he gave a curt, performer's bow and said with a huge grin.

'Bonjour Mesdames!'

Perhaps it was the relief of seeing the horse safely returned, or it could have been the worry that something would have happened to her dear husband if he had fought with a gang of gypsies.

Finally, Margaret couldn't help herself and she started to laugh uncontrollably. The two other women caught the affliction and they all laughed hysterically together, as the posse raced up behind them.

The huntsmen could not believe their eyes, the lady of the house in her dressing gown, not only outside of her boudoir, not only outside the house, but standing in the stable doorway!

Furthermore, beyond the three laughing women a small boy, calmly brushing the mane of the most dangerous animal they've ever had on the estate.

In the drawing room an hour later with three brandies swallowed in quick succession, Margaret, Peter and John were still astonished by the description of Zamo's dramatic arrival that Margaret had portrayed in graphic detail, several times over. The Doctor suggested that they have the boy brought up so that the trio could examine him and try to find out what he wanted and who he was.

The General rang the bell and a few minutes later Jarvis brought Zamo in, roughly holding his jacket collar, shoving him forward as though he was sweeping out the horse manure from the stables.

'Here he is Sir.' Jarvis said with instinctive dislike.

Zamo pulled his shoulder away from the large man's grip and poked his tongue out at him. Jarvis' body moved towards the child as though he was going to clip his ear again, when Margaret said quickly.

'Jarvis, would you ask Mrs Jarvis to come up please?'

With a, *'I'll sort you out later.'* look to Zamo, Jarvis answered. 'Yes Milady.' And turned on his heels.

John turned to his friends and asked. 'May I question him Peter?'

'Of course dear boy, carry on, should be interesting I'd say.'

John looked kindly at the young boy, pulled a

footstool over and sat in front of him.

'Do you speak English? The Doctor said gently with a huge smile.

Zamo thought that this English one is smiling like François said they all do and yet he looks a little better than the rough man who hit him last night.

'Perhaps he is a mute.' The General added when Zamo didn't reply.

'I do not think so Peter...' Margaret said. 'Because this morning I think he spoke in French to us.'

'Well, does anyone speak French?' The General asked.

'I do not speak French, but I do know one phrase to ask if he speaks French.

'What did he say?' Peter asked his wife. 'This is worse than trying to get a gin and tonic when I was in India.'

'Parlez vous Français?' The Doctor said looking at the boy smiling.

At last, Zamo's face lit up and he replied relaxing his shoulders for the first time. 'Oui je parle Français.' He replied, lifting his arms with a Gallic gesture.

'Ah success!' Said the Doctor excitedly, he is French.'

The Doctor closed on the apprehensive boy, felt the muscles in his arms and legs, and said. 'I have never seen such a young child with well-developed muscles like this; he could have been working in a coalmine, although normally those children rarely look as healthy.'

'Surely he is too young to work in a mine.' Margaret asked.

'Unfortunately not, they often start at the age of five years old.' Peter replied, disgusted by the thought. 'No, I think we have a young French boy who has worked vigorously and fallen on hard times.'

Margaret and John breathed a sigh of relief as though they had past the first part of a complicated exam, when the General said. 'Well now all we need is a French wallah to translate for us.'

'Yes, there must be someone in Kent who speaks

French, after all they are not that far across the channel, does Lady Harcourt not have a French maid Peter?

'I couldn't say Margaret…' He said embarrassed by the thought. 'I do not make it a habit to go around looking in our neighbour's boudoirs searching for their foreign servants.' He scoffed. At that moment, there was a knock on the door and Mr and Mrs Jarvis entered, Zamo stared at Mr Jarvis anxiously.

'Thank you Jarvis, it is just Mrs Jarvis we need.' Margaret said dismissively. Jarvis walked out without speaking. 'Mrs Jarvis, firstly thank you very much for all of your kind help this morning, the Doctor has established that this young man is French, tell me, do you know any servants who are French on the other estates?

'I can't think of any Milady.' Mrs Jarvis replied.'

'I have it!' The General said. 'What about the headmaster, Mr Rochester?'

The Doctor and Mrs Jarvis both cringed in unison at the thought of anyone they knew being questioned by the *'Hand of God'* canning headmaster, as he was unhappily known in the village school.

Margaret said. 'I have never been fond of him; he is a man full of unwarranted pride and importance.'

'I know!' The doctor said enthusiastically. 'I shall ask Miss Wodehouse, the new schoolteacher at Chatsworth, she teaches languages and may be willing to help.'

'That would not be the mad woman who looks like a man and rides across my land every morning?' The General said.

'Actually, close up she is a very handsome young woman indeed, who prefers to ride astride like a man, she is an excellent horsewomen and has a wonderful, rather unusual chestnut mount.'

Margaret thought with amusement that the doctor had noticed rather a lot of details about the young schoolmistress.

Mrs Jarvis…' Margaret said. 'Would you kindly give this young man a good bath, and I think that we have some nice clothes from young Peter's wardrobe that will fit him. Then give him some dinner and find him a better place to sleep than under the stallion. Tomorrow we shall try to find someone who can communicate with him and we shall see what will happen next.'

'Margaret...' Peter whispered to his wife. 'I do not think that we should give our dear son's clothes to this-this boy.'

'That will be all Mrs Jarvis.' Margaret said, waiting for the servant to leave with Zamo, before tuning to her husband saying.

'Peter I have been meaning to throw away many of those clothes for a long time, yet, I could not bring myself to do so, therefore he might as well have them, he cannot walk around the estate in those awful rags.'

'Actually Peter.' The Doctor added encouragingly. 'You now have someone who can exercise your new stallion, it might be worth it to have him on the staff?'

'John, do you think that you could ask Miss Wodehouse to visit us here for tea tomorrow and try to communicate with the boy? We would be most grateful to you.' Margaret flirted subtlety.

'Of course Margaret...' He said smiling at the attractive woman. 'I shall visit her cottage this afternoon.'
Peter looked over at his dear wife who he loved more than life itself, he saw the excellent way she managed the household servants, his friends and business partners and actually she was pretty good at controlling him as well. He remembered the first time she took control over their future.

When Captain Peter Trubshaw married the great love of his life, Margaret Henrietta Weymouth, he had little money, and his other great passion, the stud farm and stables didn't provide him with much of an income. The newly married couple rented a pretty cottage in Sittingbourne, Kent and had one servant, a widow called Mrs Albright, who lived in the village and worked for them five days a week as they couldn't afford more. After fourteen months, Peter's partner wanted to retire from the army and sell his half of the business, and so the young captain was obliged to buy the other half or close down.

Unfortunately, the business deteriorated and the newly wedded couple feared that they might have to close the stables and sell the horses, because Peter had used most of his savings to purchase all of the shares and now he had virtually no capital left. The soldier was devastated by this problem, not only because they desperately needed the money, he also didn't want his father-in-law's warning to Margaret to come true.

'If you marry that army fellow, you'll both be in the workhouse within two years!' He predicted.

Peter couldn't imagine the love of his life, Lady Margaret, daughter to Baronet Weymouth in a workhouse or come to that, himself in a debtor's prison. Furthermore he had an insatiable passion for the equine business and couldn't contemplate a different lifestyle. Having been a captain in the cavalry, he knew a great deal about thoroughbreds and not much about anything else, unless you include killing people, as he was often obliged to do in the army.

One cloudy day in the summer of 1878, Peter met Colonel Ridge at his London club, who he was slightly acquainted with during his service in India. The Colonel had more than a few drinks and was reading the latest copy of Punch. He invited his ex-army colleague for a drink and explained that he was assigned as Lord Curzon's secretary, who was the Under-Secretary of State at the Foreign Office.

After another couple of brandies, he whispered to Peter.

'In utmost secrecy old boy.' That Britain was going to war against the Boers, or Afrikaners as they were called locally in South Africa. He went on to disclose that he would be working with the quartermasters and was responsible for finding a vast array of supplies for the expedition - including some horses.

Peter explained excitedly that he owned a stud farm and could supply the horses; in fact, he had six wonderful thoroughbreds that were ready straight away.

'You do not understand dear chap.' laughed the drunken Colonel. 'They might do for a few of the officers, but I need to buy thousands!'

After weeks of drawn-out negotiations with the war department and endless expensive dinners and gifts bought for Colonel Ridge. Peter managed to secure the contract to supply all of the necessary horses for the entire campaign. The only problem was, he couldn't afford to buy the livestock from his contacts in the first place. Following exhaustive, unproductive discussions with numerous financiers, Peter was desperate, he had little money left and didn't know which way to turn. Margaret listened to Peter's anguish over a long dinner and eventually said. 'What you need my darling is a partner with a large sum of money.' Peter cuddled his love and replied that it was easier said than done, because the banks and money lenders were not fond of investing in horseflesh, they preferred more substantial commodities like gold, silver or share certificates in major businesses, such as the East India Company.

Nothing could hold Margaret back; despite her upbringing, she was a strong and determined woman and said that she knew someone who would put up the money, without any security for a half share in the venture. 'My Darling,' Her husband said affectionately. 'You do not understand the world of business. No one will do that, particularly as they are not acquainted with me, and as a former army officer I have no previous record in this kind of big business.'

'This person will definitely do it.' She said confidently.'

'Who is this fool?' Peter pleaded exhaustedly.

'Me!' She said.

Margaret had secretly sold and pawned all of the family jewellery that she had inherited from her grandmother and mother. She also borrowed some money from her sister, who was under '*pain of death*' secrecy not to say one word to their father. Eventually she had enough money to keep the stud farm going, pay the house bills and most important, buy the first batch of horses. Peter was virtually in tears when he accepted the money, feeling that he had failed his dear wife as a husband and provider.

'Well if there is one thing that the British have been good at over the years, it was attacking other countries.'

Peter explained one night to a group of close friends over a dinner party.

'We supplied horses for the first Boer War, the campaign in India and then the second Boer War, where of course we were somewhat more successful.'

By the time Margaret's parents had passed away, the Trubshaw's company had sold thousands of horses and they were incredibly rich. They inherited the Manor house, as Margaret was the eldest child, not that her sister wanted it. The whole place had been run down and needed a fortune to bring the estate back to its original glory. Luckily, by then the Trubshaws had a fortune, sufficient to restore a whole town. Nevertheless, Peter never forgot the day he was nearly on the road to the debtor's prison and the painful embarrassment of his wife saving him, by selling everything, she owned, and so he was always rather careful with his money from that day onwards. Well, except for anything to do with life's little luxuries and the horses of course.

Peter walked his friend the Doctor, down to his aging horse that had been brought from the stables by Victor.

'I'm terribly grateful to you John...' Peter said sincerely. 'I think that Margaret has some special feeling for this young lad, could be something to do with the memorial service, our lives have been in a vacuum since our little son died.'

'I understand Peter, grieving is a strange process, sometimes you think that it has past and then something happens in your life and the feelings come back.' John said with a wisdom gained from the many deaths he had presided over.

'Thank you so much John, we look forward to seeing tomorrow.'

Peter returned to the house and searched for his wife, eventually he found Margaret in their deceased son's bedroom looking at his old schoolbooks.

'Are you all right Margaret, I hope this young lad has not upset you in some way?'

Margaret placed the books on young Peter's desk by the window and wrapped some ribbon around them.

'You know Peter...' She said dreamily. 'I think our

dear friend John is rather lonely.'

'He looks all right to me, rides well for a doctor. Dam nice of him to speak to the teacher woman for us.'

'I think he may have an ulterior motive.' Margaret said smiling, closing her son's desk drawer and her memory of him.'

Dr John Gale MD had met many attractive women since he started his practice in Otford. He had asked permission of several fathers, if he could speak to or ride with their daughters, yet few had agreed, due to his low income. Even those who did allow him some heavily chaperoned contact with their young daughters; saw it only as practise for some better prospect with a proper income and land.

John found it difficult to find the right kind of girl; many were wed, some, if not most, were empty-headed teenagers, who had been educated in the Victorian art of being a suitable wife for a rich man.

They were all youthful and perfectly presented. This usually involved being able to sing reasonably well, play the piano or some other musical instrument competently.
Perhaps they could recite a little poetry. Certainly they would be adept at riding side-saddle, the more advanced would take part in local dressage events.

The female subjects of Edward VII were upper and upper middle-class young women, who were proficient at needlepoint and gentile flirting with prospective husbands, though not much more beyond that. One of the problems for these young Edwardian females, was they weren't given the same level of education as their fathers and brothers, the older generation saw it as a complete waste of money.

When John heard that the Liberal Party had won the General Election the previous year he was delighted.

The last few elections under the Conservatives, supported by the wealthy upper classes and to a lesser extent, the middle and upper-middle classes, had made their fortunes on the backs of impoverished women, children and low paid, uneducated male workers, who were not much better off than serfs. The factories were crammed packed with young, sick children and frail women, working their fingers to the bone sixteen hours a day; in badly lit, freezing cold or boiling hot, filthy, rat-infested factories. These poor people were paid miniscule wages of less than ten pounds a year. Away from the inner cities, farm workers and crop-pickers were also badly treated and underpaid. Often sleeping in the fields without food, water or shelter, summer and winter, next to where they worked.

On the grand estates like Somerleyton Manor, the servants had a slightly easier life. They usually had a warmish, dry place to sleep. Often squeezed in the loft or mansard of the great houses, two or three to a bed. Sometimes they were put in run-down cottages, without kitchens, bathrooms or toilets.

These workers were given clean uniforms with white gloves, so that they could enter the luxurious houses of their masters, prepare their clothes and serve their food. The upper classes were worried by their servants' cleanliness; they were accused of having dirty hands. Accordingly, unlike the field workers they enjoyed the dubious advantage of being able to eat the luxurious leftovers from their employers.

However, often the best parts were given to the aristocracy's dogs first.

Life for the servants at Somerleyton Manor was one of the best that John had seen; yet it was still a long way from the sheer luxury and extravagant behaviour of their employers. Which is why after the death of Queen Victoria and the subdued manners she epitomised, the masses were now looking for a better life, away from the persecution and servitude of the rich and titled few.

Dr John Gale was a Socialist, who believed that everyone should be given an equal chance in life. That everyman should have the vote, even if he wasn't a landowner. He wanted to see an end to young children under eleven years old working, so that they could have the chances that he had enjoyed and to be well educated.

He was still unsure about women having the vote. Having met so many brainless girls from all levels of society, the doctor wondered if they would ever vote against the wishes of their fathers, if at all. In his practice a large number of the wealthy young girls were so fragile and weak willed, they often fainted trying to get their corsets tighter, just to impress a visiting suitor. John thought that if they acquired the vote it would just give extra votes, as well as greater power and influence to the men of the house, who would tell the women who to vote for and prolong the status quo.

Dr John Gale wanted to find a girl with a mind of her own within his endogamy, someone who would stand up to her father.

If she wanted to marry a country doctor with a low income, who believed in socialism and equality, she would. A man who helped the sick, but had no prospects of any kind of real wealth; except a modest cottage, ten times smaller and a lot less luxurious than his friend Peter Trubshaw's stable. Well they should allow their daughter or daughters to open their hearts to such a man, shouldn't they?

John pulled up his horse, she looked tired, whilst he was dreaming, he hadn't noticed that he had pushed her to a gallop and at her age, she couldn't keep that up for long.

He dismounted, took her bridle and walked the last two hundred yards to his cottage. Perhaps he was being foolish, what girl, let alone an attractive, intelligent girl would fall for someone like him, except perhaps, someone unique like Miss Wodehouse?

Chapter 10
London, February 1964

London's bright red, double-decker buses were having their usual gladiatorial combat with the pushy, black London taxis. And recently, due to a change in transport laws, the new Mini-Taxis outdid the blacks and reds using their agility and speed. The mechanical combatants spread out all over London and particularly in front of the city's most iconic storefront on Knightsbridge's Brompton Road, where they joined the lucrative race for paying passengers.

Phaedra, Charlotte and Pippa were excitedly shopping in Harrods. The step-grandmother looked 'Fab!' According to her granddaughters, when she bought an Yves St Laurent hat on the first floor. Pippa carried a green Harrods' bag accommodating a new pair of shoes and Charlotte wore a fine noose of gold with a matching heart from Tiffany & Co, cherishing the renowned turquoise box it came in as much as the jewellery inside.

'Mwah! Charlotte gave Phaedra a huge lip-sticky kiss. 'Thank you so much Ya-Ya, I love it.'

Pippa followed suit and took Phaedra's arm turning into the dark green and gold coloured lift. The disabled liftman that was just starting his shift followed them inside to operate the brass handle. He politely asked where they wished to go. Phaedra had claustrophobia and acrophobia, therefore she hated lifts and so she clung on to the girls tightly and squeezed her eyes shut.

'May we go to the pet shop Ya-Ya, I've heard that they've got a real lion cub and some chimps in there.'

'No darling! I hate to see animals in cages, especially wild creatures, down to the food hall please.' She answered the lift-operator.

Charlotte looked sulky and pleaded. 'If we are going to buy food I've got to have some of those super chocolate thingies Pip…'

'You're such a brat Lotte, what are they?'

'You should know Pip, your horrid parking warden ate the whole bag last time you both came over.'

'Do you mean the chocolate covered dried fruit, at a Guinea for about four ounces?' Pippa teased.

'Yes my Caviar-Eating-Commie sister.' Charlotte said, cuddling her sibling.

The three women entered the expansive food hall selling chocolates and cakes, filling several bags.

After Phaedra picked up two bottles of Vintage, Louis Roederer's Cristal Champagne, in the wine hall, they went on to the crowded delicatessen department. Phaedra had turned off to her bickering girls and ordered some pâté, when Harold came over to them wearing his warden's uniform with the hat tucked under his arm.

'Hello everyone, I thought I'd find you here.' He said, surprisingly cheerfully with his best Sunday-chapel accent. Phaedra and Pippa kissed him hello, but Charlotte held back.

'Come on Lotte, be nice, you're not still angry with Harold over the dog story are you?' Pippa said touching her arm.

'You almost frightened poor Justin to death Harold, he's afraid of dogs because he was attacked when little.' She said about to stamp her foot.

'Oh, it was lovely was isn't?' Harold giggled. 'When the dogs leaped off the boat, I thought his heart was going to stop, you know.' He shook his head thinking about it with a grin from ear to ear.

'Are you coming for lunch Harold?' Phaedra asked kindly, despite hoping that she would receive a negative response.

'No – no thank you very much Mrs Trubshaw, actually I've just got to pop out and put a ticket on your car at the back of the store.' He said with a straight face.

Charlotte thought about hitting him over the head using her beautiful Tiffany bag, when he said. 'Just joking ladies, just joking.' At that moment Harold turned around and said quietly to Pippa. 'Have you noticed that man following us?'

'What man?' She asked.

Phaedra had detected him a few minutes before and looked around recognising the disabled liftman, standing a few yards back pretending to examine some fruit. He became aware of them watching and walked over to Phaedra saying. 'Sorry Madam, I think you dropped this in the lift.' He smiled holding out a bulky, brass-locked leather folder. Charlotte turned to tell him that he was mistaken, as Phaedra would never be seen dead with anything as naff as that. 'Who would want one?' She thought, when Phaedra said to her surprise, 'Oh yes thank you.' And put it in her shopping bag.

The three twenty-year olds looked at each other and then at Phaedra in disbelief, although she ignored all of them. Harold whispered under his breath to Pippa. 'See what I mean.' Phaedra paid and picked up her food from the green, apron-wrapped server and asked the others cheerfully if they were ready for lunch.

Harold made his apologises and the three women took the lift to the fourth floor restaurant. The large room seemed crowded with a noisy batch of locals and tourists, consuming the expensive food and wine with the urgency of starving dogs. Once they were seated next to a window Pippa asked her step-grandmother. 'I didn't see that folder this morning Ya–Ya, how did he know it was yours?'

'Oh I don't know darling…' She said casually. 'I've been coming here for years, they're very good at remembering the regulars you know.' The waiter came over interrupting them and the greedy sisters ordered everything they loved, yet couldn't usually afford, grace of their dear, Greek step-grandmother.

'Ya-Ya, could I borrow one of your cocktail ciggy's, I've left mine at home.' Charlotte pleaded.

'Why don't you keep the packet darling, I've lots in my car.' Phaedra said kindly.

When the Trubshaws finished the long luxurious lunch and had a quick look around the sport's department, where Phaedra and Pippa bought new tennis outfits, they spent another twenty minutes meandering through the layers of extravagant clothes and gifts and left the famous store by the main entrance. The girls turned left down Brompton Road and walked into trendy Beauchamp Place to see the shops' new spring collections, after a couple of small purchases Phaedra said.

'Darlings, I know I suggested that you stay the night in Ham, but I'm sorry, I need to cancel as I've an awful headache after that Chardonnay. Would you mind if I left you two to carry on without me?' The girls protested, nevertheless, said that they would call her tomorrow to see if she felt better, and decided to go off to Kensington Church Street and do some more shopping.

'Oh, by the way will you phone Sam from a call box and ask him to meet me at the usual pier? I should be there in about twenty minutes.' The girls agreed and kissed her goodbye.

Phaedra jumped into her souped-up Mini and zoomed off, leaving ten per cent of the tyres' rubber in the kerb.

In the distance, the young sisters saw the black Mini barely make the red light, when it screeched to the left towards Fulham Road. Pippa tuned to Charlotte and said curiously. 'Harold thinks something's going on between that Harrods chappie and Ya-Ya.'

'Oh don't start again Pip, it's becoming really annoying; ever since he heard that he wasn't tall enough to go into the police, he's trying to prove that he's not a dumb parking warden and some kind of Sherlock Holmes.

Justin said he had a whole list of reasons why our grandparents are international crooks!' Charlotte said exasperated.

'Talking about crooks, I hope you're not going to steal another dress from Biba when we get there.' Pippa admonished. They arrived at the end of the fashionable street and turned left into Brompton Road.

'I don't pinch stuff, I'm not a crook, I just change the dress I bought last week for a new one. I really look after them; they're just like new! Besides, I can't today, not dressed like this, it only works if you go in virtually naked except for last weeks dress, you can't have a bag or anything. You try the new one on in the cubicle and return the old one to the rail and walk out.' She said conspiratorially.

'I don't understand, don't they notice?'

'Usually not, it's so packed inside, they're taking a fortune, mind you, once they had an old woman working at the till, at least thirty, and she stopped me, so I just said, *do you think I came in naked!*' Charlotte giggled.

'Charlotte, that's still stealing.'

'It's not silly, because I paid for the first one, I mean if you got home with a dress and it's too small, you could change it for another one, couldn't you?'

'Lotte you've changed that dress every week for the last six months!'

'Well I'm still growing up!' She giggled.

Two women in their forties walked passed the young girls with armfuls of carrier bags from most of Knightsbridge's designer stores, they also wore three-quarter length fur coats.

Charlotte looked at them admiringly and tried to count how many bags they had between them, when Pippa grabbed one of the women by her arm and screamed.

'Do you know how many animals had to give up their lives so that you two could walk along here showing off how rich you are, with these tortured animal coats?' Charlotte looked embarrassed, one of the women blushed and walked ahead, but the second woman looked like she had been challenged before in the Harrods's area and replied:

'They're just like rats young lady, like the man who bought it for me!' The tall woman smiled at the girls as she walked off with a wiggle. Pippa looked shocked.

'I can't believe that awful woman, she felt proud of killing defenceless animals, no wonder she goes out with a rat, they're obviously made for each other. Dam! I wish I'd thought of something clever to say before she left.'

'Oh shut up Pippa, what do you think of my new watch?' Charlotte asked, flashing her wrist wrapped in gold with a ruby studded winder.

'Lotte please don't tell me Biba are doing Cartier watches now?'

'No silly, Count Sergei gave it to me.' She said in that spoilt, puerile voice she put on when she got presents.

132

'Isn't that the old guy you crashed into, with the Rolls?'

'Yes - he likes me - keeps sending flowers and chocolates - he also got me that photo session with Ossie Clark and Alice Pollock, he knows everyone and is so nice.'

'You're not shagging him are you?'

'Don't be so disgusting Pippa, he's older than granddaddy, he just likes to take beautiful young models out for lunch and buy them presents.' She giggled looking at her own reflection in a shop window.

'You're incredible Lotte, you've made being spoilt an art form, come on let's try and get a cab, before those furry monsters up there.'

Charlotte put four fingers in her mouth and gave a deafening whistle, a taxi and the whole of Knightsbridge turned towards the attractive girls. They jumped in the back and Charlotte said:

'Bus Stop please.'

'Which one love? There're a lot you know…'

'Don't be silly.' Charlotte said looking at her sister and making faces as though the driver was an idiot. 'The shop with the great hats, next to Biba? In Church Street? Hello, I mean everyone knows Bus Stop, don't tell me you've never bought anything there?'

'No luv, I'm more your Petticoat Lane type meself.' He laughed.

Chapter 11
Doctor John Gale, Otford, 1907

After retuning to his little cottage, bathing quickly and pressing a shirt with the iron from the hot range, wearing his best tweed jacket and using too much Eau de Cologne, John made his way over to Miss Wodehouse's cottage. This would be his first visit to the teacher's home; he'd only met her once the previous year when the headmaster's wife, Mrs Garood, formally introduced them at the school fete. Her beauty, not forgetting her forthright manner immediately struck the young Doctor. Few women had been educated to her standard and John assumed that she would have worked incredibly hard. No doubt she found it an enormous struggle to get such a teaching post as a young women, even at this famously modern-thinking school, originally founded in 1432, with scattered classrooms in several houses around the Sevenoaks area. John had deliberated over his fellow villager lengthily. Miss Megan Wodehouse would be considered tall for a girl, about five feet seven inches, her thick mane of auburn hair, the colour of mink, was usually brushed into a natural ponytail, quite unlike most of her contemporaries who fashioned elaborate coiffures. Her almond shaped eyes were the dark, golden chocolate colour of a brown bear. She didn't appear at all fat nor fragile, clearly strong and fit; normally exercised her horse daily, and started refurbishing her own small cottage without help. John often sneaked past at a discreet distance and could see her replacing roof tiles, painting windows, chopping and sawing wood; she also changed the nameplate from Lavender Cottage to Marx Cottage. Miss Wodehouse certainly wasn't afraid of physical work and actually seemed to thrive on it. John had seen her on several occasions, always wearing jodhpurs or working trousers, with jackets, shirts or jumpers. He wondered if she even owned any dresses or skirts.

The teacher had taught at Chatsworth School for Young Ladies, for the last year or so. Evidently making quite an impression on the staff, children and their parents from the first moment, although well liked and admired for her modern teaching abilities, she was said to be a young woman who would not to be quarrelled with.

In fact, she became the talk of the village and surrounding pubs and farms, when she recently kicked a rude farmer into a muddy ditch, after he protested that, she illegally trespassed, whilst ridding across his land.

The Doctor had tried to make discreet enquiries about her social life; however, the only information he obtained was that she occasionally received her cousin, Elijah Wodehouse, who practiced law at the firm Birkett, Burlington and Benton at Lincoln's Inn in London. When he reached Upper Lane, a cold wind blew and the trees cried their last leaves. About a hundred yards from her residence, he quickly pulled up old Mary, chancing upon a large number of horses and carriages outside her cottage, extending some way along the lane.

When he stared more closely, he saw that many of the carriages carried posters and placards. The Doctor steered his horse cautiously towards Miss Wodehouse's cottage. Where he saw a long banner hung like a hammock between two naked trees, right across the width of her home, it read:

Today's Speaker Dame Millicent Garrett

There were more signs attached to the fences and trees, they read in different handwritings and colours:

Women's Suffrage
Support Mary Wollstonecraft
Suffragist Movement
WSPU
The Women's Social and Political Union
Support Emmerline and Christabel Pankhurst
Suffragettes Will Win
Women Refuse Taxes
Men and Women are Politically Equal
Thomas Hardy Appreciation Society

John dismounted slowly and led his mare towards the cottage somewhat apprehensively, at the gate a small rotund man with short spiky hair in a badly fitting, grey tweed suit, maroon Brogue shoes and small, round, tortoiseshell glasses, balanced on a spindly nose, came over to him and shook his hand furiously saying:

'Hello! I'm helping out with the horses until Dame Millicent speaks, go right in.' The temporary groom smiled, pointing to the door with hearty enthusiasm. After the greeting, John realised to his astonishment, that this person was in fact, a women.

The Doctor could hear a dissonance of sounds and activity from inside, reaching the door he observed that the small stone house appeared to be packed with men and women of all ages, shapes and sizes. Judging by their appearance, they were also from different classes and varying incomes. A few people dressed as men turned out to be women, yet most of the assembly looked like the average patient that the doctor saw everyday when practicing his profession. However, he had never seen these various classes mix on an equal footing before, in the same room. Some of the women were dressed in long feminine dresses with elaborate hats; carrying umbrellas, others were wearing service clothes. The group seemed mostly upper-class women, the few men wearing labourer or tradesmen's clothes, a minority dressed as middle-class professionals.

John became overwhelmed and pushed his back to a solid wall, took a deep breath and watched fascinated, while the crowd argued and discussed the rights of women, and the political changes needed to bring about equality to all workers, rich or poor, landowners and tenants.

He noticed that around the walls were banners in green, purple and white, one such banner had the words 'Hope', 'Dignity' and 'Purity' in each of the colours. He then noticed that some women wore scarves and a couple had jewellery in the three corporate colours.

After eavesdropping on the various arguments, he discovered that many people had similar views to his own, even though he had rarely, if ever, expressed them, as most of his acquaintances in the rural setting were right-wing Conservatives. The thought of asking someone like General Trubshaw to give his staff the weekend off, let alone join them in the kitchen as equals for lunch, would have been unheard of.

The meeting started with Miss Wodehouse welcoming everyone to her cramped parlour and apologising for the lack of amenities. When she spoke, John thought that she looked incredibly beautiful and had the voice of an angel. This would be his first opportunity of studying her closely without her realising, as the whole room looked at her, hanging on to their host every word. She then went on to introduce a man called Mr James Keir Hardie who the year before, had formed a third political group that he called *The Labour Party*.

The Doctor did read newspapers occasionally, although he had never heard of this man or his alliance.

Everyone, including Doctor John was appalled after he explained eloquently, in a working class accent, the awful conditions in which men and young boys worked in mines and factories. He elucidated that his members were seeking a classless society, free of exploitation and an end to children as young as six working underground. He went on to describe the enlightened work of Robert Owen, a Welsh industrialist, who'd built a development in Lanark, Scotland, where employees had excellent working conditions, quality housing nearby and the company still made outstanding profits. The audience warmly applauded him.

The next speaker, a plump upper middle-class woman suggested withholding taxes from the Government as a protest, another who wasn't much taller than a twelve year old, talked about her plans to break all of the windows in Downing Street and then chaining herself to the railings. A rather effeminate looking man with a breast-pocket handkerchief folded like a pink peony, and an elaborate costume, discussed at length the greatness and understanding of playwright W. Somerset Maugham.

John really enjoyed the meeting and as the afternoon darkened to evening, forgot the initial reason for his visit, then the young woman that he'd come to call upon, and with some verisimilitude, had been thinking about constantly for the last year, stepped up onto the box used as a dais.

'Ladies and gentlemen.' Miss Wodehouse announced. 'It is with great pleasure that I now introduce our last speaker and guest of honour:

Dame Millicent Garrett!'

The audience was ecstatic, clapping and cheering as the fifty-eight year old icon of the women's movement reached the little elevated crate.

She spoke modestly about the school that she'd founded and described her work with the National Union of Women's Suffrage Societies. The audience were truly moved by her description of the horrendous prisoner of war camps in South Africa that had been created in the wake of the Boer Wars; explaining in detail that men, women and children were being starved and beaten in appalling conditions, by their English overseers. She had reported to the government and attempted to persuade them to close these British concentration camps. Dame Millicent Garrett gave a clear impression of her intelligence, unwearied energy and reasonableness. After an hour, the audience became enthralled, emotionally exhausted and clapped constantly for ten minutes after she left the makeshift podium.

Miss Wodehouse then returned to the dais looking radiant.

'Now, ladies and gentlemen, I wish to ask you for a show of hands on the subject of this meeting: will everyone who believes that all men and women over the age of twenty-one, should be treated equally and take part in the next election! Please vote by raising your hand now.'

John Gale had become so absorbed by the powerful and persuasive views of the various speakers that he'd almost forgotten that his presence was no longer merely that of an observer. He was actually part of the meeting that surrounded him, and yet when the question had been raised, he could not after one afternoon, reverse the opinion he retained for years. He believed that most young women that he had met through his practice or socially were just not ready or capable of voting on such an important subject. They seemed to be more interested in their appearance and finding a husband with several thousand a year, so he assumed that no one would notice him and therefore he just kept his hand and head down.

The gathering couldn't wait to be asked and unreservedly threw their voting arm in the air; all of them; in fact some people actually put both arms up as though they wanted an extra vote. All of the protagonists were delighted as they looked around the room gleefully, to see the one hundred per cent support of like-minded people. Someone started to break into spontaneous applause, when Miss Wodehouse raised her hands for silence, pointed to the Doctor and said loudly.

'One moment ladies and gentlemen, it would seem that I must now ask for a show of hands for those of you who are *against* the proposal?'

It was so silent you could hear someone folding a ballot paper, had there been one. John looked up slowly, he saw to his dismay hundreds of piercing eyes shining on him with the same menace as searchlights in a South African concentration camp. His mouth refused to form any words, he couldn't think clearly, he wanted to throw his arm up and say:

'Yes, I agree, all of you intellectual, powerful women should have the vote.'

Nonetheless, he knew that the moment had past, and should he be so weak and just follow the crowd to avoid this awful embarrassment? Or just to carry favour with a woman, that he now realised he cared for immensely, a woman for whom he had strong feelings, infatuation or possibly true love? The painful silence seemed to extend for an eternity, the people who were standing near the stranger slowly moved away, forming a circle around him as tight and threatening as any hangman's noose.

'Well Doctor?' Megan questioned. 'Do you now wish to explain to all of these people, why you, a young country doctor and property owner, should have the intelligence, the experience and the right to vote, whereas Dame Millicent Garret a representative of the British government or Mr James Keir Hardie, the president of the Labour Party or I, should not?'

As a doctor, John knew that his reddening face and ears and the furnace like temperature running through his entire body, were merely a reaction of the brain pushing blood around his head, however, he also knew, that there was nothing he could do about it. Unfortunately, his medical training didn't help, his throat became completely dry and even if he knew what to say, his voice had left him. For some bizarre reason that he regretted for weeks afterwards, he gave a small jerky bow before walking straight out of the cottage door. When he found his horse, he heard Miss Wodehouse speaking as loudly as she could to the attentive audience:

'That, ladies and gentlemen is the kind of stupidity that we are up against.'

This rallying call to the crowd ignited, unanimous and vigorous applause. A sound that pealed around his head for days afterwards. When John arrived home, his head started spinning while he interrogated himself, why did he go into the meeting? Why did he not just go over to Miss Wodehouse, quickly ask her to help with the French boy and leave? Why did he not leave before the vote? Why did he do that stupid nervous bow like a popinjay?

Why? - Why? - Why? He bowled the whiskey glass that he'd already refilled three times into the fireplace with a *smash!*

The following morning after a restless, sleepless night, he awakened determined to ride straight over and explain everything to Miss Wodehouse. He then drank some sweet tea and considered that it might be better to wait until the end of the day. Perhaps she would think about the meeting and be more sympathetic after say, twenty-four hours. Her reputation suggested that she might need a couple of years to recover; actually, she might just burn his house down while he slept.

'Stop!' He told himself aloud, it wasn't that bad,

except for the stupid bow, 'Oh God, it was that bad.' He worried.

Throughout the day, he conjured up several plans of action, each one worse than the one before. 'I'm an idiot!' He screamed aloud. The Doctor found it difficult to concentrate on the patients.

By the afternoon, he knew he needed the advice of a woman, he looked at his watch; again. Peter Trubshaw would be out on the estate, and therefore it would be an appropriate moment to find Margaret alone at home.

Half an hour later, he found himself in front of the Manor and was amazed to see an impeccably dressed young lad skip down the stairs from the house and take the head of his horse.

'Bonjour Monsieur.' The elegant miniature gentleman said, with a huge relaxed smile.

'Oh, ah, bonjour.' The Doctor stuttered, trying to remember any French word to complete a sentence.

He pointed and mimed his way up the steps and walked into the opening doorframe. Zamo leapt onto Mary without using the stirrups and rode the horse at a gallop towards the stables.

'Good afternoon Doctor.' Jarvis said, escorting him toward the drawing room.   'Are you expected Sir?' Jarvis said in a tone that confirmed that he wasn't.

'No Jarvis, I am hoping that her Ladyship and the General will have a moment, as I have some news regarding the young man, I must say I did not recognise him today.' John said nervously, looking over his shoulder to the front door of the house.

'He's still the same gip...' He stopped himself. 'Same boy, underneath the clothes Doctor.' Jarvis said sceptically. 'Unfortunately the General is on the estate at this time.' Again the inference was, you know he is, don't you. 'I shall see if her Ladyship is at home Sir.'

John paced up and down wondering how he would explain the last twenty-four hours to Margaret and how much of his true feelings towards Miss Wodehouse he should declare, if any, when she now hates him more than she hates the guards running the South African concentration camps. Lady Margaret entered the room with Maisy; she looked stunning in a pale blue, long dress, a similar colour to her ocean azure eyes. Tied at her tiny waist, a dark blue silk sash held her tightly.

'Doctor Gale?' She said formally. 'I am terribly sorry, my husband is not at home at the moment, would you care to wait for him?'

'Actually Lady Margaret, it was you that I needed to speak to, for a few moments if possible?'

'Certainly, may I offer you some tea perhaps?'

'Thank you.'

'Maisy would you bring some Darjeeling and some tea cakes please.'

Maisy rushed out of the door in her usual uncomfortable fashion and Margaret floated over to an ice coloured, silk chair; the Lady sat and gestured towards the twin on the other side of the fireplace.

'Thank you Margaret.' He said less formally, relieved to speak to a friendly face.

'How are you John? You look a little tired' She said concerned.

'Well it has been an interesting couple of days, I have come to report back having spoken to Miss Wodehouse.' He exaggerated. 'Firstly tell me, how is the boy?

'Well, Mrs Jarvis has found him some clothes from my son's wardrobe and cleaned him up and you may not recognise him!' She said delightedly.

'Actually he took my horse and looked a proper gentleman.'

'It has been so pleasant to have a boy on the estate, even though I cannot communicate with him, he is wonderful at mime and runs around like a monkey. Peter is delighted and they have been out riding together. At last, Black Silk is being exercised, he is a wonderful mount, notwithstanding, he will still only allow Zamo, which appears to be the young man's name, to ride and groom him. After all, if we hadn't taken him in, it would have been rather cruel to send him back to France. So prey tell me John, when is Miss Wodehouse coming over to help us

142

question the young man?'

Maisy entered with a silver tray overflowing with an array of cakes and biscuits as well as the Indian tea. Margaret said she would pour and told Maisy to leave. Peter gave a shorthand, edited version, of his meeting with Miss Wodehouse and her associates, leaving out the most embarrassing parts and asked Margaret's advice on what he should do next.

'I have heard that she is a most determined young woman, which is something most admirable in these modern times. Women do need to guide their husbands and male relatives, even if men do not realise that they have come to the correct decision, because of feminine direction.'

'Margaret, you are truly wonderful, I doubt if Miss Wodehouse has realised the subtlety of a wise woman, I think that she is a little more, how shall I put it, black and white?' The Doctor said looking for a way of explaining the forthright teacher.

'I understand that the awful Farmer Giles saw the black in his eye, when he met her.' Margaret laughed.

'Margaret, if I did not know better, I would think that you approve of this young woman's behaviour.'

'If I were her age and had not had such strict parents, I may well be very similar to the Marxist, suffragist Miss Wodehouse.'

'So, I was right, you are the best person to advise me. I have tried to explained the misunderstanding with her, and yet she is so unreasonable, what shall I do?'

'Write her a nice letter John and apologise for everything you have done, even if you do not think you have done anything wrong.' Margaret counselled.

'I did not want to appear weak; she is so forthright!'

'My dear friend, sometimes you need to apologise, even if you believe that you were following your conscience, having admitted that you were at fault, some people will often concede that they were partly to blame as well, but not until you have grovelled a little, it's all part of courting John.'

'But Margaret, we are not courting, I have barely managed to pass a simple, 'Good morning,' and I have already made her an enemy! What will she be like if we actually start a conversation?'

Margaret laughed, 'John you are such a wonderful doctor and truly wise for your years in so many ways, however, you are certainly a child when it comes to young women.'

John thanked his wise friend and couldn't help thinking that if she weren't in love with his friend Peter, she would make him a wonderful wife, even though he was younger than her. He went home, poured himself a drink and wrote the apology. Nine times, before he sent it.

Doctor J Gale MD
The Old Mill
Lower Lane
Otford

28th July 1907

Dear Miss Wodehouse

Firstly, I would like to send my sincere apologises for entering your home uninvited. I had no prior knowledge that you were having your meeting and originally intended to simply convey a brief message from General Peter Trubshaw and Lady Margaret, who were hoping to ask for your assistance in a private matter.

Furthermore, I should say that I was full of admiration for numerous speakers at the meeting and had a proclivity with many of the opinions expressed. Quite frankly, I have never heard people speak in that manner and I was taken aback when asked to vote.

Therefore, I would be most grateful, if you would allow me to call upon you again, so that I may have a chance to apologise in person and explain my mission, concerning Somerleyton Manor.

Your humble servant

Dr John Gale

Miss M Wodehouse
Marx Cottage
Upper Lane
Otford

30th July 1907

Dear Dr Gale

Further to your obliging letter of the 28th instant. Despite the fact that I accept your apology out of good grace, I cannot in all honesty understand why you were so taken aback.

Concerning giving my assistance to a Lady, I would say that I am a supporter of a Republic and have no desire to meet people who carry egotistical and meaningless titles.

Concerning giving assistance to a General, I would say that I am a pacifist and have no desire to meet warmongers.

Concerning meeting you again, I am a Suffragist and have no desire to meet with people who do not support this cause.

Sincerely
Miss M Wodehouse

Doctor J Gale MD
The Old Mill
Lower Lane
Otford

1st August 1907

Dear Miss Wodehouse

Thank you for responding so promptly to my letter. I understand your reluctance to help the Trubshaws and me.

Therefore may I plead for your help on behalf of a poor young boy, who the Trubshaws have taken in, off the street?

Apparently he has no family and is unable to speak English, the Trubshaws need to communicate with the young lad to enable them to find a place for him. May I therefore ask on his behalf, if you would be able to assist, as he does not speak English?

Your obedient servant
Dr John Gale

Miss M Wodehouse
Marx Cottage
Upper Lane
Otford

3rd August 1907

Dear Dr Gale

Further to your pleading letter. It would seem that you would stoop to any depth to appeal to my conscience. I only speak French and Spanish and have a cursory knowledge of Italian and Latin.

I will be able to interview the boy on Saturday morning next at eleven o'clock. I will attend the Manor, and I shall see the boy alone.

Sincerely
Miss M Wodehouse

Megan Wodehouse arrived promptly on the hour, riding astride in white jodhpurs, a white shirt with a matching neck-scarf and a waisted, black jacket. Her magnificent horse was a rare Przewaiski stallion; he had a sturdy, large head, with a short, erect, chestnut, brown mane and looked a least 15 hands. John thought as he looked through the Manor's drawing room window that the horse was a perfect complement to the rider. Victor took her horse at the steps and Florence showed her into the drawing room, where the three adults were waiting with the perfectly groomed young boy.

Peter and John stood as Megan entered the room with her confident boyish gate, John did the introductions, the teacher greeted and shook hands casually with the three adults, leaving out their titles and turned to the boy.

'Tu est Français toi?' She said fluently.

'No, mais je parle Français.' He replied excitedly.

Megan looked up at the adults as she kneeled on the floor with Zamo to disperse any fear he may have had, despite the fact that Megan soon realised the boy seemed to be amazingly confident for such a young child.

'He says that he is not French, he just speaks the language, I shall take him for a walk and question him further.'

Without waiting for a response, she took Zamo's hand and walked into the great hall and purposely through the servants' area continuing into the stable yard. The three friends were silent for a few moments until the teacher had disappeared from sight.

'Well!' Said Peter, 'I see what you mean John, she is a very confident young woman, I dare say if she had some proper girl's clothes she would be quite attractive, what?'

'Peter you are so old fashioned, she is an educated woman, and is dressing for herself, not to find a rich husband.' Margaret explained.

'I would say that she will have to get one soon, she will not be a filly for long.' Peter laughed looking at John for encouragement.

The servants set the dinning room table for an elaborate lunch and waited for their new guest to return with Zamo, after an hour of Peter of pacing up and down, he could wait no longer and ordered champagne and canapés to keep him going.

'John, let me tell you about my new project!' He said, with his usual enthusiasm for new ideas. 'Aircraft!'

'Oh my God Peter do you mean these new flying machines?'

'Exactly, you know a few years back when we were quite young; we started supplying the army with horses, as you may have heard. Now imagine if there were to be another war, one side had thousands of horses and yet the other side had a few flying machines: Dropping bombs! Who would win?'

'Well' John said. 'I doubt if there will be any more wars and these machines sound very dangerous, I understand they crash all the time.'

'Everyone here crashed when they tried to get on Black Silk, yet little Zamo knew the trick. Now if I can find the trick with these motorised flying kites, I could supply the whole of Europe and maybe even these American fellows.'

'There is no point in arguing with him John, he has already ordered one.' Margaret said as a fait accompli.

Florence opened the door and curtsied, she was about to announce Miss Wodehouse, when she strode into the centre of the room with young Zamo on her arm, before the maid could speak. Peter walked over to her ingratiatingly and asked if she wanted some champagne before lunch.

'No thank you.' She said firmly. 'I do not have time for lunch.' Peter started to turn on the charm saying... 'We would be delighted to have such a charming young lady for lunch, especially as they have wild boar from the estate and...'

Miss Wodehouse interrupted forcefully, saying that she was a Vegetarian and nothing could be less appetising to her.

'Allow me to explain what I have learnt from Zamo.' The General sat reluctantly at Margaret's request and listened carefully, Margaret and John said how grateful they were and positioned themselves attentively in silence.

'It has transpired that Zamo entered this world in the Grimaldi touring circus while it visited Prague and has toured with them ever since. He has never been to school, he cannot read or write in any language, he has no knowledge of maths or any of the usual subjects one learns at a conventional school.'

'That is really strange...' Said the General interrupting, to the annoyance of his wife. 'He appeared to be quite bright really, wonderful with the horses.'

'I did not say he lacked intelligence, quite the opposite, I said he had not enjoyed a conventional education by your standards.' She said casually waving her hand around the luxurious room.

'Zamo is polyglot...'

'What?' The General asked.

'The boy speaks numerous languages, he certainly speaks, French, Spanish and Italian, he told me that he spoke to his mother in Czech and Russian. The young man has never known a father, and something has happened to his mother, yet he is reluctant to talk about it, he just says that she was an *Uccella Che Volano.*

I think it means a flying bird; it may be that he is referring to the trapeze that he says he can use. He proudly said that he could perform most of the circus acts to some degree. You may have already noticed the boy has a special way with animals. Incidentally, he asked me to tell Peter that the horse is not happy with its stall?' She said smiling for the first time.

'What?' The General said aghast. 'I like this young lad and he is quite extraordinarily gifted with horses, beyond that are you telling me he talks to them? Perhaps they have mentioned what they would like for lunch?' Peter said standing up and looking for support from John.

'Peter I am not here to make judgements, you have asked me to translate for you and that is what I am doing, despite his extraordinary abilities, he is only a child with a vivid imagination.' She said defiantly.

'Please Megan, this has been so helpful, do go on.' Margaret said kindly.

'Somehow he has been told that you were looking for a stable boy and that is why he was brought here by his brother.'

'Yes we received a letter from some people in France or Italy a few weeks ago, but we thought it was an adult and they didn't mention any family we knew and so ignored it.' Peter said dismissively.

149

'I now understand why he is so muscular.' The Doctor said. 'In a circus he must have been exercising everyday.'

Peter had his head down reflecting on what Zamo had said about his stallion, suddenly he looked up and pronounced. 'Miss Wodehouse, Zamo might be right actually, that is the largest horse we have ever seen, the stall could be too small for him, will you tell the boy that I shall build a bigger one.' He smiled a little embarrassed.

Margaret took Peter to one side while Megan had a long conversation with Zamo, John noticed that Margaret was getting her own way as usual, he couldn't help admire her. They all turned back into the centre of the room at the same moment. Megan spoke first. 'He says that he would like to work here looking after the horses, he says he can sleep in the stable.'

'Well, Zamo, I think we can do better than that, he will move in with Bob, I think he will be very welcome there.' The General said, appeasing Margaret.

'Megan, am I right in thinking that you like the boy? Has he found a connection with you?' Margaret said in a sisterly manner.

'Well Margaret, an anthropologist would be in heaven if he could study this young man, nevertheless, unusual as he is in this society, in the end, he is just a seven year old boy, and needs somewhere to live and an education.' Megan lectured.

'Megan would you help us educate him by teaching him English?' Margaret asked hopefully.

'I am not sure, I have commitments to the movement and my job...'

'Megan, there is no one else, we cannot send him to Mr Rochester's school, he would die there, he is as wild as a cat.'

'I shall consider it.' Megan used words economically; she turned and left as speedily as she arrived.

On the steps in front of the great house Megan reflected on the events she had experienced, realising that Doctor John Gale had made an impression on her.

He was quite good looking, she thought, not as

pompous as Peter Trubshaw and the rest of the Conservative snobs. Although somewhat weak, he didn't look like he could chop enough wood for an evening's fire, she smiled to herself. He did have devastatingly blue eyes, Megan wondered if she would enjoy kissing him, he was rather short, but he did seem to be kind and intelligent, even though every time she saw him he dropped everything and stuttered constantly...

'Your horse Miss?' Victor said, after standing there for several minutes.

'Oh I am sorry, thank you Victor, it was kind of you.' She said speaking to him as an equal. Victor noted her friendly tone and blushed as she smiled and looked directly into his face.

She rode off at a gallop and Victor was still staring at her departure more than a little conscious of her tight jodhpurs bouncing on the saddle.

He gave a slow whistle as he returned to the stable.

Chapter 12
Marx Cottage, Early December 1907

John looked down onto the beautiful village of Otford and the surrounding crisp white blanket that had covered the hills, trees and stone edifices for the last week. The cold air encircled his horse's breath evaporating the steamy clouds as quickly as they were expelled. The distant church was smaller than his fist, he felt as though he could reach out, pick it up, shake a surrounding globe and see snowflakes swirl around the spire. The view had never looked more beautiful, he had never felt so exhilarated, so much *joie de vie*, because as he touched his thick, coat's pocket, he could feel his revered piece of paper, the letter that had been given to him from his seven-year old friend, acting the go-between. He had received a few notes from Megan over the last four months or so, mostly apropos to the progress that Zamo had made, sometimes instructions about books he needed, or last minute changes to his lesson's timetable.

Originally when Megan agreed to teach Zamo, she insisted that the curriculum could only be two to three days a week, she was decorating her rented cottage, teaching at the school, exercising her horse and most important to her, fighting the suffragist campaign, which according to newspapers had spread like butter on hot toast across the country. One of her conditions stipulated that she would only teach Zamo alone in her home. She would not go to the manor and be seen as a governess or servant.

The Trubshaws found this inconvenient; therefore, John took the opportunity and rushed to avail himself to the task of delivering and returning the student. Each time John arrived at the makeshift school with Zamo, he managed to get a few moments with Megan, when he ushered the boy inside, even though she often closed the door in his face halfway through his rehearsed script. Certainly, Doctor Gale was a determined man, hoping that if Megan could only get to know his character, she may learn to care for him.

The real John Gale, as he thought of himself, a doctor, a healer of the sick, a Socialist and campaigner for better conditions for the working classes, and now, albeit with some reservations, a supporter of votes for all men and women. And not the idiot, who months previously had stuttered and bowed out of her parlour during her convention, having failed to support the suffragist on her life's quest.

Recently, he'd been allowed to enter the parlour for a few minutes, to warm against the snapping fire amid the metal dogs, he used the opportunity to look at her books, discuss Zamo's incredible advancement, not only with English, spoken, written and read, but also with his general education that she'd not originally been employed to undertake.

The Doctor felt that Zamo's progress had in turn helped his own relationship develop with the wonderful, yet aloof Miss Wodehouse. John checked the silver pocket watch in his waistcoat for the umpteenth time, he still had a few more minutes to wait, because he'd discovered that she didn't care for him to be unpunctual. John removed one of his warm leather gloves, searched yet again for her letter and enjoyed analysing every word for some kind of romantic nuance.

Miss M Wodehouse
Marx Cottage
Upper Lane
Otford

2ⁿᵈ December 1907

Dear John

I wonder if you could kindly come to my cottage for tea at four o'clock on Sunday afternoon next, when I would like to request your assistance on a personal matter unrelated to my teaching Zamo.

With kind regards

Megan

John mounted his senile horse Mary and they walked down to the village square, her hooves crunching on the hardening snow, making slow progress to the beginning of Upper Lane towards Miss Wodehouse's renamed and redecorated cottage. The young doctor knew every word of her letter off by heart, analysing it for days as closely as The Times crossword.

'Dear John.' Well that was a wonderful beginning because her previous notes were always addressed, 'Doctor Gale.' Actually he remembered the last one said, 'Doctor John Gale.' Therefore, the rather personal 'Dear John' delighted him, as it was really a huge step forward.

The next line had a lot of charm, not only was it an invitation to tea, he'd never been offered anything liquid before, not even water, then the word 'kindly' popped up, normally he would at best get a 'take this or take that.' Recently a few pleases and an occasional thank-you were slotted in, yet this was the first 'kindly'.

Then there was the uncharacteristic 'request your assistance' she was always so overpoweringly in control, the idea that she would request anyone's assistance was a miracle in itself, actually asking for assistance was almost politely servile.

All of the above was an enormous progression, however, the words that drove him to the current excitement were 'personal matter.' Surely, these words could only refer to their relationship. Perhaps she had been harbouring fledgling embers of love for him, from the first moment they'd met at the school fete?

Her coldness and sometimes outright aggression were perhaps, just symptoms of frustration as she could not express her true feelings. Then the Pièce de résistance; 'Megan' She actually wrote her Christian name for the first time in nineteen months!

The horse brayed as they reached Megan's cottage, John was surprised to see a carriage outside; he naturally assumed that this 'Personal matter' would be discussed alone.

He lifted the lion's head knocker and within seconds of it closing its mouth with a thump, Emmeline Pankhurst opened the door.

'Good afternoon Doctor Gale, please come into the parlour, Megan is making some tea.' The campaigner said graciously. 'You will remember my daughter Christabel from the last time we saw you here.' She continued without any sign of malice towards his previous pathetic exit.

'Yes-yes, of course it's a pleasure to meet you again.' 'He said recovering from the embarrassing memory; he noticed that they were both wearing the campaign's tri-coloured scarves.

Megan entered in her usual uniform of blouse and trousers and placed a tray of tea and cakes on a small oak table saying. 'Hello John, thank you for coming, you know my friends I believe?' She poured the tea and served the cakes to her two friends and then as John appeared to be frozen on the spot she encouraged him to sit and gave him a cup of Darjeeling.

After a brief conversation about the cold weather, Megan looked at her admirer and said directly. 'I assume that you are aware of the Government's actions that have recently caused the death of some comrades?'

The Doctor was determined not to make a fool of himself this time and so he answered cautiously. 'Well I have of course been following your – eh - the campaign very carefully, I know that a lot of women – eh - campaigners, have been arrested for breaking windows etcetera.'

'As you may know Doctor.' Christobel explained. The women in the movement have been characterized in the press and by the government as hysterical harridans.'

'How a-awful.' He stuttered.

Emmeline asked. 'Have you heard about the 'Cat and Mouse' that the police and authorities have started to play, Doctor?'

John thought that this might be a trick question and was racking his brain for the correct answer. If he said no, would they see through his lie about following every detail of their campaign, and if he answered yes, he could get into further trouble if he's questioned about it.

'I did hear something, although I was not entirely

sure what has happened.' He lied convincingly.

Megan turned to him with what he thought was a pleasant smile, but instantly wondered if it was a smile of sarcasm.

She began to explain. 'Every time one of the activist is arrested and jailed she automatically goes on a hunger strike...' As she spoke John found himself staring at her generous mouth and dark eyes, he started to imagine kissing her moist lips.

When she talked fervently, her small nose moved slightly up and down and the creases between her nose and top lip tightened, he found himself mesmerised.

'They used to try and force-feed our sisters, however, so many people, men and women complained, as this is the rough treatment they normally give to the insane.

They have now been told to let the poor women starve almost to death, and then they release them at the last minute, hoping they will die somewhere outside of the prison.' She declaimed, from her velvet, spoon-back chair.

'We rush them to hospital, unfortunately many have died within a day or two because the doctors are not always trying their best to save them; many feel that they have brought it on themselves and concentrate on other patients.'

John thought, 'Oh my goodness when she speaks so passionately and stands close to me, it is as though we are totally alone, if I could just have the courage to lean forward a little more, our lips could almost touch...'

Crash!

John's teacup smashed on the floor, the Indian infusion went all over the carpet and he fell forward on his knees in front of the schoolteacher.

'Are you alright Doctor?' Emmeline and Christabel cried in unison. 'I thought you were going to faint on top of Megan.' Christabel worried.

John jumped up and stood on the saucer that hadn't broken, until that moment, saying. 'Oh, I am so sorry Megan, I – I am just incredibly shocked by what you have said, what could I do to help?'

Totally infatuated, John couldn't remember what she'd said after the part about the hunger-strike, he just wished that she hadn't sat so close to him The young doctor couldn't concentrate on the meaning of her words, only the ardent way she expressed them, the fragrance of her perfume and the look on her beautiful face.

'Well Doctor, thank you very much that was exactly the reaction we were hoping for, because we need you to help set up a small hospital in London to save these dying women.' Emmerline explained.

'A hospital?' He said, trying to keep the shock out of his voice.

'Yes we, the *WSPU* have rented some rooms in the East End of London, John Fisher Street near the Tower. We have some nurses and equipment, all we need now are several doctors, regrettably, few women have been allowed to train as anything more than midwives or nurses, therefore we shall have to find sympathetic male doctors, Megan tells us that you are keen to help the Movement.'

'Help the movement?'

Megan stood near to the young doctor and looked straight into his eyes, as she was nearly the same height; he'd never been so close to her, he could feel the warmth of her body, when he spoke he noticed that his breath blew little strands of her hair that fell around her soft cheeks.

'Well of course, I-I ah, I would be delighted to help – ah – the Movement, certainly I must continue with my patients here in the village and surrounding area and I have a commitment to Zamo...

But after that – yes – I will help all I can, will you be going to the bedrooms – ah – I mean hospital rooms, Megan?' He asked nervously.

'Yes I will, there is a meeting next Wednesday evening, I thought that it would be good for Zamo to see democracy at work, his English is much improved and so he should be able to understand the speakers, would you care to join us, John? We need all the help we can get and you could look at the makeshift clinic while we are there.'

Going to London with Megan in the evening, was more than he could have dreamed of, they made the arrangements and he left without his feet touching the ground.

Chapter 13
The Ides of March, 1964

Phaedra pulled her Mini into the Trubshaw's mainland garage behind some boathouses in Richmond; she exited the door on the riverside with armfuls of bags from her shopping spree, where Patrick O'Higgins, a hefty, middle-aged Irish bachelor was sanding down a blue, fourteen foot, Flattie skiff. He had a tin of Old Holborn tobacco and a packet of Rizla cigarette papers on the bench, next to a half-empty pint glass of Guinness. A dying cigarette appeared to be glued to his bottom lip.

Clearly Popoloposis loved her homeland; nevertheless she never tired of looking at the sensual curve of that part of the Thames. The silky flow of diluted greens and blues, painting a kinetic, reflected watercolour of the upside-down bridge, which was framed by Richmond Hill on one side and the tall trees of Twickenham on the opposite bank.

'Hello Phaedra.' Patrick chirped, with his County Cork accent.

'How's your love life? My Irish Don Juan.' Phaedra joked.

'Now would you be offering something, you golden-headed Greek?' He flirted.

'You don't want an old lady like me, I thought you were in love with that Swedish tourist in the boat last week?'

'When you have someone who drinks as much as I do, a week is more than enough for most girls, not that she was a teetotaller you know.' He said taking a swig from his glass with a golden harp emblem.

'What happened to your face Patrick, did she beat you up before leaving?

Patrick ran a finger over a black eye and a congealed cut over his left eyebrow.

'Oh, it's nothing really, I came out of O'Flaherty's last night, you know, the Irish pub near Hammersmith bridge, and I was just getting on me Harley when these lads came up on those little Vespers you know, with all the mirrors and foxes' tails hanging all over the place, 'Mods' they said they were. And before you know it they were stupid enough to start kicking me Harley calling me 'A Rocker' and such like.'

'So did they attack you Patrick?'

'Well you could call it that, one of them had a bike chain hidden up his sleeve, one pulled out a wee knife and the other had those funny things, what do you call them? Knuckle dusters, so it wasn't really a fair fight as there were just the three of them like.'

'Patrick, tell me the truth, did you get hurt?'

'Not really, I didn't see the first one with the chain, which is how I got the cut and the black eye, but after that it was pretty much like an average night in Dublin.

The lads went in the Thames and I thought that the scooters could do with a wee wash, so they went in after them.'

He laughed remembering the three boys choking in the water.

'I suppose it keeps you fit Patrick.' The friends laughed together. 'See you later Romeo!'

Phaedra walked west along the riverbank past a stream of tourists with ice creams and a few cyclists going almost too slowly to stay up, not forgetting that she promised Patrick to look out for a nice young Catholic girl en route. She past the houseboats and the beautiful op-art Friesians, grazing on London's inner-city farm, and took the towpath to the ferry crossing for the little Twickenham ferryboat, where Phaedra saw Sam waiting for her in their motorised dinghy.

'Ahoy there young lass!' Sam Joked. 'Are you all right darling? The girls phoned saying you have a headache?'

Phaedra tossed her shopping bags and shoes into the boat, hiked up her knee-length Channel skirt and jumped into the craft, almost falling on Sam's lap.

'Steady on my love, I know you've missed me the last five hours.' He laughed as he helped her up. Phaedra kissed him and said. 'Let's go Capitano!'

159

'Is everything OK? I thought you were out for one of those girl's marathons?' He called out above the noise of the outboard.

Phaedra put her thumbs up and gave the diving hand-signal to go forward. When they arrived at Duck's Island, they threw all of the shopping bags onshore, jumped out of the craft, and Phaedra clutched her heels walking on the lawn barefoot. Sam came up behind her with the designer bags and offered: 'Feel like a nice glass of bubbly?' Thinking she might be in a bad mood.

She looked up at him seriously and declared. 'I had a contact. We've got a new job.'

They walked into the house purposefully, put the food in the fridge without speaking; Phaedra took out the leather document case she'd been given, Sam grabbed a packet of biscuits and closed all of the outside doors. The couple strode over to the large stone fireplace in the drawing room.

Sam took the right side and Phaedra the left; they simultaneously grabbed the rusty metal horse heads on the buttresses of the chimney and turned each operculum twice. The back stone wall of the hearth slowly grated open into a concealed stairwell, they entered and Sam pressed another horse's head forcing the stone wall to close, the noise of an airlock hissing behind them.

The large basement opened into a single room covering the same space as the entire house above, there were no windows although several office lights on four desks facing a pin-board wall illuminated the room. A large projector screen and rows of files decorated one side. Phaedra went over to a keyboard and pressed the escape key.

A piece of the wall moved up with a swish revealing ten small television screens. She tapped the keyboard code to enliven the screens, when a three-dimensional plan of the island appeared.

As she typed, the screens showed graphically metal blinds closing off the house's windows and doors, the outside images of ten secreted cameras showed the island's boundaries.

Sam placed the case onto a metal table closing a heavy lead covered lid over it, six feet away he pressed a button and the metal box scanned the contents, a green light flashed 'OK.'

Sam went to a safe and took out two keys. Phaedra lifted the case out of the box and placed it on one of the desk, Sam put the two keys in the locks. He only turned the one on the right, the locks flipped open and he emptied the contents out.

'If I ever get Alzheimer's I might forget and turn both those keys one day, *Boom!* What a way to go!' He gestured an explosion with his hands. 'So, what do we have here?' He asked rhetorically. Leaning back in a chair, he started to look at photographs, maps, diagrams, and read a thick printed tome. Phaedra went to a large fridge, packed with enough food for a long stay, grabbed a bottle of sparkling water and two glasses from the cupboard above and sat next to her husband.

'The hit's a woman.' Sam said with surprise.

'That's unusual, I thought we don't like to do women?'

Sam kept reading and then said. 'You'll want this one; everyone wants this one!'

'It's not a German is it?' Phaedra said with a slightly stronger Greek accent.

'Now my dear, I want you to stay really professional on this assignment, because it will be a very difficult, according to this the Israelis are looking for her as well.'

'A Nazi?'

'Yes. I'll read the summary to you. The hit is an Ilsa Klup, she married a German concentration camp commander during the war, evidently, she used to enjoy having the prisoners tortured and killed for looking at her. Her husband was very jealous and shot loads of prisoners who stared at his wife, so she would walk around lubriciously, in sexually provocative clothing as an enticement for the poor starving men. She also had a fetish for tattoos. Evidently, they caught Klup after the war and she went on trial in Nuremburg; they sentenced her to death, the Germans had hanged her husband earlier, but she

161

managed to escape.

'I don't understand, how could she get away?' Phaedra asked in amazement.

'Well in this story, it's germane to know that the Vatican Bishop Alois Hudal helped her flee. You remember him; he set up an underground movement called 'Ratlines'. Some say she tried to commit suicide, others said she got out of the prison in a laundry basket, anyway it says here that she hid in a Vatican car with some priests, who had an official Vatican CD number plate '*Corpo Diplomatico*' they sneaked her through the borders of Switzerland to the Vatican City in Rome.

Then the so-called Vatican Refugee Organisation (*Commissione Pontificia d'Assistenza*) contacted Franco's Fascist in Spain, so that she could obtain a Spanish passport, move to Argentina and live happily every after.

Just like loads of Nazis that the Catholic Bishop and his friends have smuggled out of Germany and Italy since the end of the war.'

'So where is she now, this wonderful woman?' Phaedra asked.

'Well, according to the file, before Klup left for South America, she met with one of Franco's hatchet men, a fellow called Colonel José Valles-Carrera, one of the leaders of the Falange Party, and fell in love. They are now living in Barcelona and are the toasts of Nazis from Italy, Germany and Franco's Spain. She has a new identity and owns a famous art gallery and jewellery shop, that the Israelis say is full of stolen Jewish paintings and antique gems.

'I don't understand why no one has hit her before?' Phaedra questioned.

'Have a look at these photos, the first one is Ilsa Klup at her trial.' Sam explained.

'Wow! Phaedra whistled. 'A real buxom, blonde bombshell, she looks like Marilyn Monroe's ugly, fat sister with piggy eyes, if she had any more eye-shadow and lipstick she could be a Dame in a pantomime.'

'Yes my love...' Sam said pacifying his loved-one stroking her shoulders. 'Now look at this older woman with her husband, Señora Suzanna Valles-Carrera.'

162

'Oh gosh, this one has class! Black hair in a discreet chignon, slim, tall, elegant with a beautiful black suit, could be Dior, subtle make-up. This can't be the same woman?'

It is, according to this file, cosmetic surgery has given her higher cheekbones and stretching back the facial skin gave her almond shaped eyes. She's even lost her German accent and tells everyone she is old Scandinavian royal family. She likes her friends and socialites to call her *'The Duchesse'*, spelt the French way. Evidently that's mostly related to the power and money of Colonel José Valles-Carrera and the high society parties she throws for the bigwigs from the Catholic Church, the South American Embassies and the leftover fascists from northern Europe. It says here that Franco really likes her.'

'Lucky woman, that's a good recommendation.' Phaedra said, with loathing in her darkening eyes. 'They sound like a Faustian couple. It's incredible that in 1964 with Europe coming together, a former, badly educated Nazi guard, who tortured and killed innocent people, can be sentenced to death at Nuremberg and then a few years later, pop up in another country as a rich Duchesse living the life of an aristocrat!' Phaedra got up, lit another cigarette, and puffed the smoke with the energy of a steam engine. 'When do we go?'

'Well my dear.' Sam said with an exaggerated posh accent. 'We have two, very exclusive, gold-tooled invitations, to a new art and jewellery auction. We will have dinner and cocktails at *El Restaurante La Torre d'Altamar*, on the roof of the cable-car tower in the old port of Barcelona, for Saturday night the 25th April. We have a personally signed invitation by the *'Duchesse'*. I'm a right wing, supremacist Italian millionaire and art lover, Ricardo Colaneri, and you are my dear extravagant wife Paola Colaneri. The party is in six weeks time. We should go early as there will be lots of security, we don't want any surprises in a fascist country.' Sam explained thoughtfully.

'I don't think that I could pretend to be a fascist sympathiser Sam, even for a few minutes.'

'We might have to pretend, we did it during the war, when I had to get you out of Greece.'

'I don't understand, I always believed that once the war was over and the whole world saw what Hitler and his people did, no one would ever want to go back to those dark days.'

Sam thought for a few moments and then replied with a slightly croaky voice. 'During the second war, I was too young and foolhardy in the first one. I noticed the locust's filled winds of Nazism waft across Europe; individuals were caught up in a swarm of evil that made countless people feel powerful and superior. Many were afraid to be downtrodden and preferred to be the ones doing all of the treading. It's some kind of insatiable force that carries a certain type of person on a kind of unstoppable, malevolent tidal wave.'

'Are you worried Sam darling?'

'We'll need to be very careful on this contract Phaedra, the report has a great deal of background intelligence.' He said scanning the huge folder. 'Apart from the normal heavy handed Spanish National Police, the Local Police have their own agenda, there'll be the Guardia Civil, a law unto themselves, many of whom were Franco's soldiers in the civil war, the Spanish Secret Police, controlled by the Colonel, he might also have his own people, maybe a few bodyguards, could be ex-special forces, it says in the report that he's a director of something called the, Fondazione Nazionale di Cristo.'

'What's that?'

'I don't know. It's an Italian name, sounds slightly religious and a little fascist, could be a front for some kind of business. On the other side of the fence, yet equally dangerous, are the Republican freedom fighters, with sub-groups from the Basques and the Catalans, the Socialists, the Communists, the Anarchists, they all have armed factions. Then there're the foreign units, secret Nazi representatives from Germany, Italy, also the Vatican agents and God knows whom else. The report says that some Israeli agents might be there due to the stolen paintings and jewels, because of the cold war the Russians might be interested, they don't tolerate the extreme right. Particularly since the Americans have become friendly with Franco, they don't like him, but will take anyone except the Communists, just as they've done in South America. And anyone else who would like to get the stolen goods, kill these guys or us, if they know who we are or if we get in their way.'

'Are you sure you want to do this one Sam it sounds so dangerous?' Phaedra put her arms around her husband, resting her head on his chest, concerned for the man she had loved everyday; every moment, from the night, he saved her life in Greece, more than twenty years before.

'Well.' He chuckled. 'We could go to the Old-Timers Tea Dance next week, at The Royal Star and Garter old soldiers home on Richmond Hill instead.

Or we could take the Bristol, stop at a couple of Châteaux in France, I'll give Stuart a call, you love staying in his house.

Then pop down to Barcelona and get rid of someone who has escaped the death penalty, having murdered and tortured hundreds of innocent prisoners of war, before she and her fascists friends kill anyone else?'

'I'll start packing then!' Phaedra said excitedly.

The following morning Sam went to see Nanny J at her little flower-covered cottage and explained that they were going away for a few weeks. He then went over to the dock and started the power cruiser that he'd been equipping all morning. He circled the island and slowly cut through the dark green water towards Richmond's boathouses using little of the massive engines' power. The riverbank was quiet for a change, too early for the pub-crawlers, tourists and peddlers. However, he recognised and waved to the old man with an artist's long grey hair and pointed beard, painting the famous bridge; as usual the artist barely gave a nod in response. A couple of the boathouses had opened, with someone invariably rubbing down the underside of a particular craft. Patrick O'Higgins looked up from his sanding when he recognised the deep growl of Sam's powerboat even at low speed, and popped his head out of the yard, holding a large mug of milky tea.

'Are you visiting Sam?' He called out over the water, grabbing the line Sam chucked onto the dock. Patrick moved quickly to the bow and secured the expensive launch, while Sam pressed a button and an aluminium, telescopic gangplank slid out, with the whine of an electric motor taking the strain.

'Aye, you've got a lot of gadgets on this beauty, the Scylla, what a fantastic name for a thing like that.' The Irishman said admiringly, looking at Sam using the remote control to slot the gangplank back. 'Will you be having a pint of the black stuff, me ol' friend?'

'Oh no, the last time we started that, it took me a week to get over it and Phaedra didn't speak to me for a month!' He joked, putting his arm around the shoulders of his friend and business partner. 'So how's the boating business? Are we making any money?'

'Now don't be stupid Sam, if it was money we wanted, we would never start messing around with boats, would we now?' Patrick laughed.

'I seem to remember a young innocent Irish lad saying to me about twenty years ago; that with tourism, fishing and boat repairs, a little business like this could make a fortune so close to Richmond Bridge, if I only had £500.00 to invest.'

'Are you frigging crazy, the building is worth ten times more than we paid for it alone!' Patrick said, starting to get heated.

'That's true my leprechaun friend, and I do have the advantage of a two car garage on the mainland and a lifetime drinking partner!' Sam laughed to show that he'd given up years ago, when it came to getting any money out of his half of the business.

'Actually I wanted to ask you a favour, if you're not too busy.'

'Let's go down to the pub and discuss it there.' Patrick said enthusiastically.

'Oh no, if you like the idea, I need your help straight away, besides the pubs haven't opened yet.'

'Are you mad Sam? I've me own key for the lock-ins!'

'The last time I had a lock-in with you, I didn't leave till five in the morning.'

'Come in then, at least I can finish me tea, I hope?'

The old friends walked into the boat yard, Sam finding a narrow wooden bench to half sit on.

'You're always saying that you admire my boat, would you like to take her on a long trip?'

'Actually Sam that would be wonderful, because I've got two Swedish girls coming over next week, and well - with a boat like that I won't get off the bunks for a few days!' Patrick could not have been more excited.

'Sounds great, but I mentioned the word 'favour' I need you to leave this afternoon, your passport's up to date?

'Of course it is, I'm over to the Emerald Isle every month to be sure. But what's the rush, are we smuggling?'

'No nothing sinister, Phaedra and I are having a little holiday in Barcelona and we thought that it would be nice to have the Scylla down there for a few day trips, so we could see some friends along the coast. We're driving down and we need you to go ahead as it takes longer by sea.'

'Barcelona?' He paused stroking his chin. 'Well now, I'm not sure Sam, do I want to go on a luxury powerboat to the Mediterranean, all expenses paid, of course.' He smiled.

'And tell me, that's not the Barcelona with all those young, sexy, Flamenco-dancing girls, who love Irish lovers, is it now?' He paused again until a huge grin crossed his face. 'When do I leave?'

'Here are the keys, the fridge is full, and the cupboard has Irish whisky and the black stuff, there's a folder on the bridge with the manual, charts and instructions of where and when to call me when you get there. I've booked a berth in the old port and I'll buy you a drink on the beach.' Sam smiled and walked into the garage to check his Bristol.

'Hey Sam, I've got a mate staying with me, can I take him?'

'Did you say him?' Sam called back from the garage.

'Yes it's Freddie you remember him, English, black hair, boxes sometimes.'

'Isn't he the British champion, Freddie Mills?

'He was crowned light-heavyweight champion of

the world in 1948. Mind you he's a bit past it now, he mightn't be alright for an Englishman with the Queensbury rules these days...' He joked, 'he fights more like an Irish drunk in a Dublin pub.'

'I heard he was more of a street fighter than a boxer, isn't he the chap they say works with the Cray twins and other crooks?'

'You know Sam, he's always been a decent fellow with me, never slow to put his hand in his pocket at the bar like, but there're a few rumours about him going around.

I'll tell you something, some people on the river even say you and Phaedra are crooked, not everyone has a private island and these beauties.' Patrick said, pointing to the boat and the cars.

'In my case it was all inherited from rich parents Patrick, I'm useless at business as you know, when you see how much I've made from you.' Sam joked, patting his old partner on the back. 'I'll see you and Freddie in Barcelona then?' Sam waved and walked towards his home along the towpath. He realised how lucky he was to have a friend such as Patrick, he wouldn't be able to trust anyone else with his powerful boat, and who else would be mad enough to go off at a minute's notice.

'I'll be the one doing the Flamenco with a few of those Spanish girls in the long dresses.' He called after Sam excitedly, rubbing his rough hands together at the thought of the adventure.

Further, along the path the old painter looked up with hooded chameleon eyes and picked up his multi-coloured palette. When he casually turned around towards Sam and Patrick, a camera under the palette made several clicking sounds. He then packed up and walked slowly towards Richmond's town centre. Sam pretended not to notice.

The old Polish man scraped a living together by selling information to the Eastern Block. Most of it was useless as he was more of a snoop than a spy, even Sam had paid him a few times, for keeping an eye on Duck's Island and running a few errands for Nanny J.

Nevertheless, the crazy old man found it hard to

make friends or even mix with people. Sam had tried to befriend him for over fifty years, yet he preferred his paintings and his six, tiny Chihuahuas, to human company.

Chapter 14
London, 12th December 1907

The sun was bruised by dark clouds, yet cleverly aimed its fading golden rays above the pedestrian gantry of Tower Bridge, and steered a path over Hyde Park in the west of London. The weather was bitterly cold that afternoon with a blackening eastern sky. In the centre of London, the thirteen-year-old structure looked incredibly handsome to the occupants of the black Landau, which wobbled over the cobblestone road, leading to the magnificent twin-brick towers. His gantries stood like chess pieces on opposite banks of the river, housing the teenage building's massive steam engines that lifted his metal wings.

The four Kentish visitors were very excited from the time they boarded the train in the garden of England. Lady Margaret was looking forward to the Suffragist's meeting. Ever since she'd met Megan, despite their different backgrounds and life-styles, they'd become close friends. Margaret was now a financial supporter of the movement, despite the fact that she'd never been to any of its meetings. Zamo's face was alight with the sights and sounds of the Thames and the bustling centre of the city. Doctor John Gale's face was also rather animated for a different reason, he was sitting next to Miss Megan Wodehouse and was about to spend the evening with her, albeit whilst inspecting and possibly helping with the new hospital, set up by the Women's Movement. They'd arrived at London Bridge train station at three o'clock, where they were met by the uniformed driver and carriage from the Pankhurst family, and gazed at the tourist's sights on either side of the great river Thames.

After they passed St. Katherine's Dock, the area deteriorated dramatically and they soon stopped outside 103 John Fisher Street. Zamo leapt out of the coach excitedly before it had halted, while John was delighted to take Megan's gloved hand for the first time since he'd met her, she stepped onto the pavement.

Zamo helped Lady Margaret down and Emmeline

and Christobel Pankhurst immediately opened the door at the top of the three York-stone steps.

'We are so pleased to welcome you all on this freezing London afternoon.' Emmeline said, wrapped in a thick cape.

Megan introduced Lady Margaret; Doctor Gale shook hands with the famous campaigners and Zamo bowed, saying in excellent English, that he was very pleased to meet them all, which delighted everyone present.

They reached the first floor where a plaque proclaimed the first '*WSPU Women's Hospital*'.

They entered the rooms on the first floor that were clouded by the damp wood, burning in a small grate, housing a unproductive, smoky fire. The cold clinic was simply furnished with closed large windows. There were ten made-up beds with china bedpans under the iron bedsteads, a few side tables, a metal medical cabinet and some mosquito nets hanging in the corner of the long room.

However, it didn't really look much like a modern hospital, merely a large room, although it was scrupulously clean and smelt strongly of disinfectant.

Emmeline turned to the Doctor and said. 'This is Nurse Updight Doctor, she has worked tirelessly to make the hospital ready over the last few weeks.' The nurse stood proudly in a sheet-metal-strength, starched, cotton uniform and looked around the room with a sense of ownership.

'Good afternoon Doctor.' She said cheerfully. 'I have *my* first patient here, Mrs Bancoat, straight from the prison this morning, the poor woman has been nearly starved to death.' She explained with a kind of admiration.

Without any of the usual niceties, John walked quickly over to the dying woman and opened his Gladstone bag urgently. He pushed Mrs Bancoat's long lace sleeve back and took her pulse. Immediately he tried to undo her elaborate high-necked collar without success and so he turned to Nurse Updight and commanded. 'Nurse, remove this woman's blouse.'

'I beg your pardon Doctor, this poor woman's unconscious, it would be improper to remove her garments in front of a gentleman without her permission, even a doctor.' She said stubbornly.

John silently reached into his Gladstone and pulled out a scalpel, he inserted it into the neck of Mrs Bancoat's blouse and cut it open to her waist. Nurse Updight rushed forward and grabbed the patient's hand protectively, before she could speak the Doctor said in a tone not to be argued with. 'Open that window quickly.' He then shoved the nurse out of the way and cut the rest of the woman's blouse and corset off, using a stethoscope on her exposed breast. He looked around the room fleetingly and said to the women who had now moved in closely to the bed.

'Do you have something to hang a drip from?' They all looked puzzled. 'Quickly get me some string or cord.' He pushed the patient's bed under a wall-fitted gas lamp and grabbed a bottle of clear liquid from his bag. 'Come on!' 'He shouted.'

'We do not seem to have any.' Emmeline said searching aguishly.

John walked into the room at the end of the ward that was being used as an office and staff room for the nurse, judging by the evidence of the teacup and handbag on the small table. He grabbed a long half knitted scarf with the needles attached and brought it to the patient's bed.

'That's my knitting!' Nurse Updight complained as he ripped the top open and tied one end to the gas-lamp, the other end he attached to the saline and glucose drip, John pulled gauze from his Gladstone, dappled a clear liquid from a long bottle and used it to disinfect the patient's arm. At speed, he attached a tube with a needle to the end of the bottle and pushed it into the patient's vein. He then removed the high stack of pillows the nurse had built under the suffragist's head and put them under her feet.

Finally, he removed her leather ankle boots and put his stethoscope back onto her bare breast listening to her heart again. The room was completely silent for the next few minutes, when suddenly, colour started to appear in the woman's cheeks and she gave a huge sigh. Nurse Updight gasped and put her hands over her mouth, thinking the worst, and then the patient's eyes opened. The feeling of euphoria was palpable, as the small group gathered around the bed, Mrs Bancoat tried to speak, yet her voice was silenced by the weakness of starvation, dehydration and a lack of salt, yet she smiled at John, which was enough for all of them. The Doctor pulled a blanket over the patient and spoke passionately.

'Mrs Pankhurst, this is not a field hospital in Africa, we do not need mosquito nets, if the main problem is going to be starvation, the patients will need liquids similar to the ones I have brought today. The air must be fresh and smokeless and the patients should have loose comfortable clothing and plenty of blankets. Nurse, take these bottles. Here is a list of what will be necessary, I suggest that you send the nurse to get these as soon as possible. Oh, I am sorry about your knitting nurse, you will need proper drip trolleys for every bed.'

Lady Margaret and Miss Wodehouse were most impressed; whenever Megan had seen John, he'd always been a bungling, stuttering idiot, unlike Doctor John Gale at work; he was undeniably a man of action, confident, forthright and very professional indeed.

'There is one thing more Mrs Pankhurst.' He said turning around to include everyone in the ward.

'If you want to be treated as equals, you must allow me the same courtesy. If a man or woman is dying or very ill, one cannot give consideration to their attire, a doctor must have the confidence of his team.' He said looking purposefully at the nurse. 'I am quite sure that one day it will be normal practice to have women doctors, and if such a doctor is in a hospital or in the field of battle, she may have to rip off the clothes of a wounded soldier to treat his wounds, wherever they are!'

'Doctor Gale, I think that we all owe you an apology and our gratitude.' Emmeline said. 'We are so used to working against men; we perhaps sometimes forget what it would be like to work with men, on an equal footing. I have often said that male society has a long way to go, I now realise that we will all have to adapt to the new world.'

After a short pause, Christobel said. 'Mother we must go, our comrades will be on their way.'

'Yes, onwards and upwards!' She said smiling to

Margaret, who looked slightly apprehensive. The women picked up their green (hope), purple (dignity), white (purity), banners, flags and scarves and headed for the door, with Zamo and John following them excitedly.

'Bring your Gladstone bag John.' Megan said, with more warmth and admiration than he'd ever heard from her in two years.

'Why Megan! Are you expecting some of the male followers at this meeting to faint?' He teased.

She gave a half smile and said seriously. 'It is always better to be prepared John.'

He was so delighted when she used his name so. The four women stepped on to the icy street with John closing the door behind them. They could hear a marching band filling the air with its brass and thumping drums in the distance.

'May I offer you my arm Miss Wodehouse?' He said, exaggeratedly raising his elbow, as though they were going to dance the Gay Gordon.

'You may Doctor Gale - anything to keep warm.' She teased. Megan picked up his mood and felt so proud of his professionalism in the ward. The suffragist held John's arm looking into his blue eyes, anointing him with that brilliant smile that he'd only seen once before. Beautiful as she was with her usual business-only expression, when she smiled, a tsunami of joy flooded her face and splashed everyone around her.

'I have been trying to ask you something for the last few months.' John said shyly, walking on the outside of the narrow pavement.

'I thought you were trying to ask me something ever since we first met at the school fete, and when you frequently passed my cottage in the distance!' She taunted.

'Do you mean to tell me that you've seen me passing, and knew that I have cared for you these last two years?' He said naïvely.

'My dear John, I may not dress like most females you know, and my opinions may be rather modern for a country doctor, yet I am still a woman.'

'You are?' He questioned foolishly.

Megan laughed more than he'd ever seen before and the doctor said.

'Oh yes, I am sorry, of course you are, and such a beautiful woman at that.'

When they reached the end of John Fisher Street, they heard chanting from a large number of protesters marching down Dock Street.

'Are they our people?'

'Yes.' She smiled at his new commitment. 'They are *ours*.'

'It would seem like a big meeting, I thought it was going to be similar to the one at your home.' He queried.

'John.' She said sincerely, holding his arm closely. 'I am going to tell you something that I have never told anyone before; a secret, my secret, can I trust you to keep it to yourself; cross your heart and hope to die?'

'You know you can, I would never do anything to hurt you Megan.'

The girl searched his face for a trust that she had hoped to find in a man for many years. She sighed silently and her shoulders visibly fell with the relief one feels after dropping a heavy load, which had been carried for a long time.

'John, I had an unhappy and difficult childhood.' She said reflectively.

'My dear Megan, I am so dreadfully sorry.' John exclaimed, truly upset at the thought of anyone hurting the only love of his life.

They turned right onto East Smithfield and walked slowly arm in arm towards Tower Bridge now submerged in spasmodic fog. Megan's eyes glazed over; she became silent, unseeing the reality in front of her and reflected back to a time that she had trained herself to forget.

Megan's father died when she was a small baby, there followed a difficult period for her mother Delrina. She had never been a robust woman and after Megan's birth, doctors confirmed that her child-baring days were over. Delrina was a well-educated, delicate, middle class woman, who had been attractive when she was a young girl.

Unfortunately, at that time she didn't have the money or the strength of character to survive for long on her own. She married below her, quickly and foolishly, her new husband Arnold was a widower and worked as an independent, agricultural grain supplier, he travelled often and soon spent her meagre inheritance. He drank a great deal and thrashed her regularly. Megan tried to stop him on many occasions from an early age, unfortunately it usually just ended with her being beaten brutally as well.'

When Megan past her thirteenth birthday the beatings started to become, more sexually orientated. The stepfather would throw the teenager on the bed, lift her skirts and spank her bare bottom with his hands and he started to pinch and squeeze her breast sadistically. Megan feverishly complained to her mother, regrettably due to timidity and fear she had for her husband, she couldn't help her only daughter; in fact, she couldn't help herself. Over several years Delrina became poorly, Megan was terrified that if her mother died she would be trapped and alone with her stepfather, and so she did everything possible to look after her rapidly ailing parent. Lamentably, at only forty years old Delrina grew weaker and weaker, some kind of inner light left her eyes and she was reduced to a crumbling shell, encasing her former self.

One early morning before the sun awoke, Arnold came into the house stinking drunk, he had been out all week and returned in a filthy mood. Megan heard the front door slam and suspected the worst. She jumped up and wedged a small chair under her lockless door, sat on its seat and listened nervously, eyes closed with her head against the wall, holding her breath. The drunk passed her room slowly and bumped into the hall sideboard, knocking a glass vase to the floor. Megan's heart missed a beat when she heard the crash of a hundred pieces, scattered across the surface. The teenager jumped back into her bed and pulled the eiderdown over her head, hoping the drunkard would melt away.

The instant Arnold entered her mother's room the screaming started. For a moment Megan couldn't move, her body felt as heavy as lead, the thought of facing another battle and receiving one more beating frightened her. Over time she had become psychologically abused and vulnerable, so that her resolve had crumbled like the spirit of a captured and broken wild horse. Delrina screamed again, an awful pleading scream followed by beseeching sobbing, and so Megan couldn't stand it any longer. She leapt out of bed wearing only her nightdress, tossed the chair to one side and ran across the hall into her mother's bedroom. Delrina was curled on the floor in a foetus position and the heavy man was kicking her in the stomach with his work boots, blood poured from her mouth and ears.

Megan was fifteen by then, nearly her final height and had the mature body of a young woman; she jumped on her stepfather's back pummelling his neck and shoulders with her fists, unfortunately her efforts made little difference. He grabbed her by her nightdress and threw the lightweight girl on the bed, ripping her froufrou neckline as she fell. She tried to bounce up, however, he smashed the palm of his right hand across her cheek and she fell backwards, her head hitting the brass bedstead with the force. For a few moments she was dazed, a painful bump swelled above the nape of her neck and her reddening cheek throbbed. Before she realised what was happening the brut was on top of her and ripped her nightdress in two, revealing her nubile naked body. Again, she punched his chest and face to no avail. He clenched his left hand around her throat choking her, pining her body against the mattress of the matrimonial bed. Megan saw his eyes flash with a dark desire she'd never seen before. Unfastening his breeches' belt with his other hand, his full weight on top of her, she soon felt his exposed flesh against her own. Megan kicked wildly with her bare feet, nevertheless he easily pulled her naked legs apart, she felt sick as his brutish, bearded face came close to hers, he reeked of horse-sweat, tobacco and beer. When she felt his weight on her soft stomach, she screamed for her mother at the top of her voice:

'Mother – Mother, help me!'

By some miracle of inner strength, perhaps it was a mother's primordial urge to protect her young. Delrina managed to urge her weak, trembling body to get up from the floor and with unknown strength. She smashed the drunk repeatedly on his back with a brass poker from the small fireplace. He snarled like a wild beast and turned on her, the first blow hurled the frail woman across the room.

The poker fell on the floor. The following punches and kicks seemed to turn Delrina's frail body into a rag doll that had lost its stuffing. She couldn't even cry-out any more.

Megan flew up, now completely unaware of her defenceless nakedness, dived to the floor and grabbed the poker's handle with both hands, she swung her arms back like a tennis player. Arnold saw the young girl out of the corner of his eye and swivelled to face her, just in time for the hooked end of the poker to catch him in the right eye and pluck it out, like a fish from a lake. The drunk screamed in agony holding his empty socket, and stumbled towards her in a blind rage.

Megan swung the brass rod back to the other side of her shoulders and with all the force she could muster caught him in the left temple; he pitched forward and collapsed on top of Delrina.

For a moment Megan couldn't believe the reality. She was experiencing a dreadful nightmare, her spent arms dropped by her sides, and her raged-inspired strength ebbed away from her whole body as she fell on her knees.

Notwithstanding his injuries, to Megan's horror, the now one-eyed monster started to slowly get up. She couldn't move, she felt inert; her only feeling was that of resignation. She had a strong desire just to lie down and let this now distorted fiend have his way with her. Suddenly his fat, bloodstained hand grabbed her slim milk-white leg. She gasped as he got up onto his knees turning towards her. The fading candlelight flickered on his grotesque twisted mask. At once, she saw her mother unmoving beneath him, the weak woman she loved and cared for, ever since she could understand her pain. The mother who had lived in fear most of her existence was now lifeless.

The bloody aggressor now tried to pull himself up and put his hand on the teenager's soft shoulder. She struggled to her feet, searching for the strength to move, to run. For a moment she looked down at him on the floor.

Megan stood as still and cold as a Greek marble nude, frozen on a pedestal, when she relived these moments in her nightmares and during so many sleepless hours, the instant past eternally. Finally, she stood with her knees bent and her legs apart with the metal poker in both hands. Remembering the county fair striker, where she'd once used a sledgehammer to hit a disk of metal, that shot up a track of six feet to ring a bell, and win a prize.

Megan used the poker on her stepfather's head repeatedly, until a kind of bell went off somewhere in the recesses of her mind, the prize this time was his final collapse.

Absolutely exhausted she fell on her knees, tears in her eyes, the blood from her mother and stepfather ebbed across the wooden floor through her toes, deep crimson, like a high-summer's tide at sunset, she couldn't move for half an hour.

Eventually, her head cleared somewhat; she crawled over to the bodies and pulled the mutilated man off his estranged wife. The young girl shook her mother gently, however, the body, resembling a half empty grain sack, had no life in it.

Megan dressed quickly in a blouse and trousers, saddled and mounted her horse, arriving at the veterinary, Mr Kinly's house, in a few minutes. There were no doctors in the hamlet and so most of the locals consulted the caring medic for both man and beast. He didn't appear to be shocked when she stood in front of him. Her long hair a tangled mess, her hands and face covered in dried blood. The whole valley knew about the violence in Arnold's black heart. After a moment, she said simply.

'My mother has been hurt.'

He returned with her immediately, entered the house, and followed the blood trail to the bedroom, while the young girl waited in the kitchen. Professionally, he took the pulses of Delrina and the stepfather; they were both dead. Silently the vet looked at Megan's torn, bloody nightdress on the ruffled bed, the bloodstained poker on the floor and he examined Arnold's head.

He walked downstairs and calmly asked Megan if

she had any relatives nearby, armed with her response he took her to an aunt's house in Lewes. Megan lived there until she went to teacher's college. She discovered later that Veterinarian Mr Kinly, had told the police that Darlina admitted to killing her husband as she lay on her deathbed.

Miss Wodehouse has never returned to the house or seen Mr Kinly since.

Megan looked up at their lofty destination, now a sharper image, and turned towards the young doctor. 'My father died when I was a baby and mother died when I was fifteen. She remarried to a bad man and my life was so difficult at home.' She glanced at John reflectively. 'John. Throughout my life, I have not had any reason to trust men.' Megan said with untold pain reflected in her eyes.

'You can trust me Megan.' He said, holding her arm tightly. 'I want to marry you and if you agree, I shall look after you for every moment from now on.'

Miss Wodehouse stared into the doctor's face, she wished her mother were alive, so that she could ask her what to do, 'How do you know if you are in love?' She asked herself, 'and how do you know if it will last?' Her handsome face broke into that rare smile again and she spoke light-heartedly.

'I think that Megan Jessica Gale sounds quite nice.' She laughed.

'Do you mean you will have me?' He pleaded optimistically, turning to look into her mahogany brown eyes, his knees weakening.

At that moment, there was a cacophony of noise from Mansell Street emanating from a massive march, fronted by eight women of varying sizes, filling the width of the street resembling a moving reed pipe. They wore long coats, scarves and large hats. The outside ladies were carrying the banner's poles in the movement's colours. The band they heard earlier now came close behind them, with hundreds of women following. Another group snaked down Minories Hill and when the couple looked at the bridge, it was filling up with swarms of women, dressed in their Sunday best, from the south side of the Thames. On their right, sat the thousand-year-old Tower of London, shiny, black Ravens noisily guarding its walls and destiny with their presence. The marcher's breaths filled the atmosphere above their heads with damp fog, which mixed with the cold air rising up from the slowly freezing Thames, fifty feet below. A Brigadoon mist crept over the surface of the water concealing its deep secrets.

'Oh my gosh!' John said excitedly, as they walked passed the Tower, snapping out of the mesmerising spotlight of his love's stare. 'I have never seen so many women or come to that, so many people in one place.' John kept tuning around looking at the marchers coming from all directions and converging onto the bridge. 'I do not understand Megan, where are we all meeting?'

'We are going to the bridge to stop a Royal Navy battle ship getting through, if it is possible, to obstruct the bridge from opening, we can ground the warship when the high tide goes out at about six o'clock and block the whole of London for months.'

'Oh no Megan, that will be in less than an hour!' He checked his pocket watch. 'We cannot do this, it will cause chaos!'

'Exactly!' Megan shouted above the deafening noise with a wicked smile.

John glanced anxiously at her as the determined marchers carried them forward.

Emmeline and Christobel Pankhurst joined the couple, opening a banner for two. The crowd recognised the matriarch and parted like waves in front of a powerful ship, they advanced towards the centre of the bridge with Megan, John, Margaret and Zamo in tow, as obedient as the tender of a steam train.

In the distant haze hanging over the great river, a haunting foghorn resonated from the warship, announcing its arrival.

Chapter 15
The HMS Aboukir, 12th December 1907

The magnificent bridge stood on his waterlogged brick hoofs, spanning two hundred feet over the centre of the Thames's deepest and most turbulent section of polluted water in central London. When raised, the metal wings peaked at one hundred and thirty-feet above the liquid floor. Once the bridge committee had chosen the design by Horace Jones in 1884, it was acclaimed a revolution in design history and certainly the only solution for the busy marine thoroughfare.

The bridge was obliged to open his doors hundreds of times a day for the passing maritime traffic, which needed to offload at the world's largest warehouse. When Sir Horace died working on the project, John Wolfe Barry took over the design and construction, some say for the better as the new stone façade and brown painted steel, blended well with the ancient Tower of London on the south bank. Tower bridge had lifted his road above the waterway thirty-five times that day and the next occasion he needed to expose his undercarriage was forty-five minutes after the suffragists had arrived at the entrance towers, at five thirty, to allow the HMS Aboukir, to enter the pool of London before the strike of six.

The heavily armoured warship had been built by Fairfield Shipbuilding & Engineering in Govan, and launched seven and half years earlier on the 16 May 1900. The floating warmonger weighed in at a hefty twelve thousand tons, due in part to its battle armour, it had a length of four hundred and seventy-two-feet. The twin lofty masts and four chimneys could just squeeze under the open gateway of the Tower's pedestrian gantry.

Michael Renshaw always wanted to be a harbour pilot, well actually, as a child, he really wanted to be a naval captain and walk in his father's famous footsteps. Captain George Renshaw, who had retired the year before on the 25 September 1906, after forty years in the Royal Navy. The notably strident officer worked his way to captain of a Royal

Navy destroyer, from being a cabin boy at the age of twelve on a merchant freighter, a fact he never let anyone forget, including his two sons Michael and Charles.

The elder Charles, had followed his father's illustrious career and qualified as one of the Royal Navy's youngest warship captains, unfortunately; 'Michael just couldn't cut the mustard,' according to his perfectionist parent.

Therefore, as a second choice to being a naval officer, Michael managed to get a licence as a harbour pilot, even though it took three attempts at the complicated examinations. It was a difficult and responsible career, steering a vast array of large ships into and out of comparatively small births. His father wasn't impressed and commented to his wife Pearl, rather condescendingly, she thought, while Michael was training, that…

'It was a job not much more difficult than playing with a boat in the bath!'

Michael respected and disliked the gruff captain; on the other hand, he adored his dear mother.

Pearl was one of the few people who really understood his feelings. He hadn't done well at school or at sports, he didn't enjoy fighting and wasn't very good at it and often came home with a black eye or a cut lip.

Pearl never asked him the circumstances; she just bathed his wounds and held him close. They had an instinctive understanding, often sitting before the small fire that crackled in the kitchen stove for hours, over milky tea and home-made fruitcake, talking companionably about everything and nothing as only mother and son could.

Michael was a handsome young man, of slight build, not as tall as his brother Charles or his father. He had a shock of gunmetal black hair, a ready smile and expressive mannerisms; women felt comfortable with the gentle young man and enjoyed his conversation and enthusiasm for literature and the arts. He was incredibly observant, spotting the fine details of architecture and design, and even though he rarely accumulated much money to spend, he managed to collect a small number of pocket watches, having learnt how to dismantle and restore them.

He loved writing and his letters had the sempiternal youth of poetry. Michael couldn't have been more excited on the day he started his apprenticeship at the Port of London Authority five years earlier. The long hours and incessant study was an arduous task, followed by endless assessments and practical training. Firstly, the pilots had to know their river intimately and every inch of the ports.

This was incredibly complicated because the Port of London was one of the largest in the world, encompassing a most temperamental river, fed through its large gaping mouth at the English Channel. Pilots also needed knowledge of the direct courses and speeds of many ships; they needed specialized information of local winds, weather, water depths, tides, currents, and underwater hazards.

When Michael Renshaw was told yesterday that his very first *proper* job as a qualified pilot would be parking the warship HMS Aboukir, he was delighted and immediately told his father whom he'd been trying to live up to and impress since he was a child.

That morning, Michael awoke with the barrow boys at four o'clock, working on his already impeccable, brand new uniform. It didn't fit him as well as his father's uniforms as they were bespoke, except this new idea of ready-made suits was wonderful and allowed the new pilot to look nearly as well presented as his ancestor at a fraction of the costs.

He started polishing the brass buttons, re-sharpening the razor-sharp creases in his trousers, as well as sponging and pressing every inch of the thick wool cloth. The starch in the shiny collar and cuffs that he attached with gold studs to his new shirt, made it difficult to move and his brand new leather boots were killing him, even with the cotton-wool, his mother had fixed to cover his painful blisters.

Nevertheless, standing there in front of the three-quarter-length, bedroom mirror in the pool of soft candle-light, albeit amid the frayed edges where the silver had left the glass some thirty years previously, he saw a very handsome young pilot officer.

He really looked the part as the official representative of the Port of London Authority, and a member of the United Kingdom Maritime Pilots' Association that had been founded by Captain George Cawley in 1884.

Once dressed, he presented himself to his greatest admirer and she straightened his tie lovingly, and even though he had fiddled with his appearance for the last hour, she managed to find a tiny hair on his shoulder that her favourite son had missed.

'Put this scarf on it's really cold today Mikey.' Pearl said caringly.

'Mother please, don't start wizening, I'm a harbour pilot now, you shouldn't call me Mikey, it's for children!'

'You're still my Mikey, even if you become the Harbour Master himself.' She said, tying his scarf tightly around his slim neck.'

Under protest, Michael left his parent's house in Parsonage Street, thirty minutes early with an ever-caring mother on his arm. They said good morning to the cheerful, whistling milkman, his bottles rattling a tune on the cart. Mother and son walked through Stebondale Street that ran along Millwall Park, where the boy did most of his growing up, playing football with his friends, and they soon fell onto the river's edge on Ferry Street.

'Let's go around the other side Mikey, because there's always a black cat on this corner.' His superstitious mother said.

'Mum you're mad, there're millions of black cats running all over London, we can't miss them all!'

'Yes but, this one is a big Tom and Mrs Wainright said he ran in front of her last week and then she lost her purse in the market.'

'If I followed all of your superstitious advice Mum, I'd never go out!'

The view across the horseshoe curve in the river was breathtaking, with what must be, the locals thought, the most stunning backdrop of any stretch of water in the world. The Royal Navy College opposite was one of the icons of East London, built in two halves by Sir Christopher Wren, so that the Palladian Queen's house, erected by Inigo Jones earlier, looking down from the hill in the distance, could keep its incredible view of the river and vice versa.

'Thanks mum, but that's far enough...' Michael said firmly coming to a stop. 'If I let you cross the river, I won't get rid of you until you've tucked me in at my desk.' He laughed, putting his arms around his best friend affectionately, using a tone that was emphatically final.

'Alright Mikey, you know how proud of you we all are, just do your best son and I'll see you for tea tonight.' She said cheerfully, waving and smiling as her son walked away, more enthusiastically, than if he was leaving to emigrate to Australia.

Michael walked down to the Greenwich foot tunnel that had been conveniently opened five years earlier, because there were so few crossings over the river for the dockworkers in that area.

He entered the first of the twined, red brick, glass-domed entrances to the lift shaft; to Michael they seemed like mini versions of Saint Paul's Cathedral, balanced on either side of the watery road into London.

He never risked the cranky lift that cut quickly through the shaft; it was far too claustrophobic; he preferred the wide spiral staircase. When he stepped off the last metal plate step, he paused for a moment before entering the wormhole passage. Unconsciously Michael took a deep breath, lowered his head and quickened his pace on the large slabs of York stone pavement that descended into the depths of the sub-riverian tunnel. He mentally counted out the one thousand, two hundred feet, along the dim tube and tried to ignore his nagging thought of thousands of gallons of water flowing overhead.

The echo of his boots bounced around the spooky passageway, when he reached the lowest part of the walk, the novice pilot was delighted to start the steep slope up to the exit. Michael quickened his pace until he reached the glorious ice-blue daylight streaming through the glass dome at the other end; no matter how many times he faced this journey, the burrow with its thousands of white tiles always made him feel nauseous.

Pearl looked out for her favourite son across the wide Thames from Ferry Street, she felt nervous for the boy, he was kind and sensitive and so keen to impress his father, yet she worried that he wasn't cut out for such a difficult and responsible job. His poems were beautiful, his sketches of the river and its passing ships outstanding, though her dear second son seemed too frail physically and mentally for the demanding life of a Harbour Pilot.

Out of the dome on the south side of the Thames, the young navigator breathed deeply and turned onto Greenwich Church Street, named after the ancient Saint Alfege church at the other end of the thoroughfare. Then he turned east onto the towpath, walked past Greenwich Pier, which was one of the busiest landing points on the river. He skipped through the beautiful gardens on the water's edge, happier than he could remember, Michael's feet barely touched the ground as he gave a friendly salute to George II, who John Rysback had chiselled into a stone Roman Emperor in the centre of four crossed paths. He walked at speed, the crisp and sunny December day began to deteriorate, due to the arrival of dark clouds staining the horizon, over the distant English Channel. The young man sauntered past the width of the Naval College, where his elder brother Charles had qualified ten years earlier. He passed a group of noisy cadets walking through the vast gardens, but he didn't care anymore about the navy, or his inability to join it, he had his uniform now and one of the most responsible jobs on London's waterway. Michael looked along the river to the east, its banks ever wider until it opened its mouth completely and joined the English Channel.

'Hello Renshaw.' The skipper of the pilot vessel called out happily, when he sidled next to his new young colleague.

'Oh hello Norman, I didn't see you coming, I was thinking about the job today.'

'Better keep your wits about you Matey, I heard the HMS Aboukir's skipper is a right bastard!'

'Oh really.' Michael gulped. 'Well I'm sure the crew will be helpful.' Michael suggested with false confidence.

'I wouldn't count on them lot Mike, them sailors are

a load of *Yes-Men*, scared shitless of the officers, they're not like the crew of a proper merchant boat, we all look after each other, don't we?'

'Yes, of course, I'm sure it will be fine, it's only a couple of miles up river and it's a clear day, good visibility.'

'No mate, looks like a demanding tide to me.'

Norman Roughan was forty-two-years old, but looked sixty. His thick short hair and beard as bright as copper with a face and arms covered in freckles to match. A rugged tugboat skipper since he was a teenager, he worked the Thames without paper qualifications, and learnt everything there was to know about boats and London's river from his uncle. Somehow he just meandered from job to job and boat to boat, until he got the captaincy on the harbour pilot's vessel seven years ago. Michael would be the third pilot he had ferried around since he started. There was nothing he liked more than winding up the *new boys* with his stories of disasters and evil captains, one of whom he said. 'Actually chucked a pilot overboard in a raging temper!'

After passing the college, they took the short walk down-stream and saw their destination, number 18 Ballast Quay. The endless line of Victorian warehouses and the Lowly factory's large sign was a beacon from half a mile back. When Michael arrived in front of his new place of work, built twelve years previously by George Smith, he couldn't help gaze at the façade of the Victorian, brick house in awe, just as he had done every morning since his appointment last week. Michael loved to read the inscription in incised sans-serif capitals in the stucco:

'HARBOUR MASTER'S OFFICE'

The feeling of pride he felt was indescribable. After greeting Captain Harris, the Harbour Master for the last thirty-seven years, Michael went to his desk and rechecked all of his charts and paperwork, for the hundredth time, so that he was ready for his first charge. After half an hour the Master sent him out, to check on a small fishing vessel that looked too low in the water and when he got back, the temperature had dropped and the morning had come to a peaceful end without incident. Pilot Renshaw took an early lunch of eel pie and mash potatoes with green parsley sauce, at Goddard's restaurant, with a large group of Dockers that were all complaining about the icy weather over the water and the lack of work.

At four o'clock, the Harbour Master told Michael and Norman that the ship-to-shore lights had informed them that the Warship HMS Aboukir was coming up the Thames.

Michael nervously checked yet again that all his charts and the appropriate permissions were in his official pouch for the ship's captain to sign, and the two men fell out of the front door and braved the cold air that was getting increasingly foggy over the fast moving metal-grey water.

The novice captain checked his watch as he boarded the Pilot's vessel, it was four-thirty. He considered that he should have plenty of time to get the warship into its berth before the low tide at six o'clock, as the journey should only take half an hour.

Norman walked ahead and jumped onto his tug with the confidence of a man whose job was an extension of his personality. At first, Michael couldn't see anything outside the little wheelhouse of the Mary-Beth; it was as though the cabin had frosted glass. To the fledgling pilot's annoyance, Norman started to recall in detail the last time the fog had come down to cloak the Thames so dramatically. Unsurprisingly the pilot came out of the story badly and... 'All of his documents ended up in Davy Jones's locker.'

Michael realised that the craggy tug-boat captain was just as superstitious as his dear mother, he doubted the existence of Davy Jones or his locker and the chance that it was in the comparatively shallow Thames; therefore, he just laughed off the stupid story, but tied the string around his leather portfolio somewhat tighter, just in case.

Without taking a breath from his next story of woe, Norman pulled hard on the fog warning rope in the cramped wheelhouse, and the eerie horn played its warning chord like a solo trumpet boy. The HMS Aboukir cried back immediately, its hearty horns using the power of a full orchestra.

Despite Norman's diminutive statue, the constant

annoying banter and his total lack of any recognised qualifications, he was clearly a master of the river. He pitched the stout, clumsy looking tug from one side of the waterway to the other, spinning the large wooden-spoked wheel with the fluidity of a croupier's flick on a casino's roulette wheel. The visibility was deteriorating fast, but little Norman had a sixth sense and he soon had the Pilot's vessel gently bouncing next to the metal steps that ran down to the tug's deck from the massive fighting craft towering above them, as solid as a five story building. Norman secured a line stabilising the craft with the casualness of a London taxi driver.

'Here we are Pilot, try not to kill more than four people, the fifth one's meant to be unlucky!' Norman just couldn't help himself and chuckled until Michael leapt onto the violently seesawing, metal staircase that clung precariously to the armoured ship's hull. At the top of the steps, Michael fell onto the slippery deck and was immediately supported by a young able seaman. He jumped to attention and saluted the pilot who had Captain's status aboard ship, after HMS Aboukir was signed over to him and throughout the whole period he navigated the craft until it arrived safely in its berth.

'AS Fowler, *Sir!*' The chirpy sailor announced. 'Known as Clucky to the crew, *Sir!*' He clarified without humour.

Michael smiled as the seaman kept a straight face and was about to answer when Norman gave another tug on his foghorn to say he had cleared the ship's immediate path.

'Take me to the bridge seaman!' A line Michael articulated in the style of a Shakespearian actor and had practised in front of the mirror a thousand times since he'd started his training.

'The Captain has requested you meet him in the conning tower, *Sir!* Due to the bad weather, *Sir!*'

'Alright, carry on Clucky, I'll follow you.'

In modern warships built at the beginning of the twentieth century, a heavily armoured conning tower was built where the vital command staff could be housed in safety, to ensure that the ship could be commanded in battle or in bad visibility. This tower was often built higher than the bridge in a place where the captain could see most of the ship. Clucky, standing as straight as a plank of newly cut wood, presented the Pilot to his ship's Commanding Officer, Captain Edgar Pritchett. Everyone saluted formally and the young pilot opened his document case asking the Captain to hand over control of his ship by signing six copies of the appropriate certification, that gave the pilot from the Port of London Authority the responsibility for the great ship, until it was safely in dock. Captain Edgar Pritchett accompanied by his officer of the watch, Henry Death carefully read all of the papers.

'Before I sign these documents Renshaw...' He said arrogantly. '...Do you mind if I ask you how long you've had this position, because you look dam young to me and I do not intend to hand over my ship to just anyone, it's only a few years old you know!'

'I've been a member of the United Kingdom Maritime Pilots' Association and attending the Port of London Authority for the last five years Captain.' He answered confidently, without qualifying the answer with the detail that, despite the fact that he attended the Port of London Authority during this time, it was as a trainee.

Captain Edgar Pritchett mumbled under his breath in the direction of his OOW that pilots and policemen were all looking like children these days, and with a theatrical show of reluctance signed over the HMS Aboukir legally to the young Pilot.

'Thank you Captain.' Michael said saluting.

'Thank you Captain.' The two officers answered, using Michael's new, temporary, legally binding title.

'Leaving the bridge!' Captain Edgar Pritchett confirmed formally.

'Taking the helm.' Michael replied with another one of his endlessly practised commands.

'Mr Death, send a seaman to the bow to keep watch in this fog, will you please?' Michael commanded.

'Aye – aye! Sir! The officer of the watch confirmed, leaving the tower.'

A couple of minutes later the tower door opened and

AS Fowler entered.

'Cup of tea Captain?' The seaman asked, entering with two steaming mugs.

'Thank you Clucky.' Michael said, noting that they were alone. 'How long have you been in the navy?'

'Three years Sir, I had to get away from me Pa, he was a real terror on a Saturday night, if you know what I mean Sir, drove me poor mum to drink he did.'

'And what's it like on this ship?'

'I love it, we got a great galley, always plenty to eat, we didn't get that at home, when Pa came up from the mines he had a terrible thirst he did. There was never any money left over for grub for the kids, see.'

'What about your mother, don't you miss her?'

'Well that's how I got here Sir, she went off with a sailor, so, and it was just me and me five younger brothers and sisters at home.'

Michael realised that not every man had a good relationship with his mother; he thought that he must be one of the lucky ones.

'All ahead slow!' He commanded.

The seaman grabbed the brass control handle on the telegraph, rang it forward and then rang it back to 'Ahead Slow'.

Michael always thought that the telegraph controls on ships were very beautiful. The ship's mechanism had many similarities to timepieces. He loved his own collection of pocket watches and even had one of the new wristwatches, although most people thought they wouldn't catch on. The Aboukir used the illuminated, brass Chadburn Telegraph, a single sided command handle that stood forty-three inches on its egg timer shaped base with a white clock-face nearly a foot across. The Liverpool Company who made these fine instruments, had gained a reputation of excellence, in fact, most Royal Navy and British commercial ships used them.

'And how do you get on with the Captain and the OOW?'

'Well Sir, Captains are so far above us crew, we don't get to see them much, but Doctor-Death is always on our backs, they say he's ambitious and doesn't want any mishaps that might upset his career.'

'I thought his name was pronounced, 'De-Arth?''

'Ah yes Sir, it is if he's in ear-shot, but we all call him Doctor-Death, it seems to suit his personality, if you pardon the frankness Sir.' Clucky said, grinning mischievously.

'Have you a timepiece Clucky?

'Yes Sir, got it in the Old Kent Road for Christmas last year, from a geezer in a pub.'

'Alright, let's synchronise our watches, it's now exactly five o'clock.'

'Uh… I make it five ten Sir.'

'Do you understand synchronizing, seaman?'

'No Sir.'

'Give me your watch, I'll put it right.'

Clucky hesitated. 'You'll get it back man, hand it over.'

Fowler reluctantly gave his pocket watch to the Pilot who matched the time with his own. The seaman looked relieved to get it back.

'Now listen to me carefully Fowler, every ten minutes tell me what time it is, do you understand?'

'Yes Sir!' Fowler answered positively, although his face looked confused.

'What is it?'

'Well Sir, you said we both had our watches *sink-sinked?* And so I don't know why you want to know what mine says?'

'This weather is really bad and we have to be past the Tower of London and into the ship's berth by five forty five, we have a window of between fifteen and thirty minutes at the most, after that the tide will be out and the water will be too low for this heavily armoured ship to pass under the bridge.'

'What. We'll go to ground Sir?'

'No we won't, the steaming time is only half an hour at most, we should pass under Tower Bridge in fifteen minutes, but as the weather's so bad with visibility less than one hundred feet, I want to keep track of every minute.

Got it?'

Fowler nodded. Michael opened his case and checked the charts again; he looked around the small tower and ran his hands over all of the equipment ensuring everything worked properly. Fowler saluted when the officer of the watch returned and said.

'Visibility is down to fifty feet Captain, and the rain is getting heavier, Captain Pritchett has just spoken to me and has asked if you can confirm that we shall reach our birth before low tide, Sir?'

'Please reassure Captain Pritchett that everything is under control Mr Death.'

The OOW turned to the young seaman and barked, 'Fowler, jump to it man, tell the Captain what the Pilot said…Excuse me Sir, what the Captain said.'

'Wait Fowler! Actually, I need the seaman here Mr Death, I shall require constant reports from all sides of the ship, unless you wish to keep running around the port and starboard sides yourself, Mr Death?'

'No Sir, I'll blow down and get another AS up here.'

'Mr Death went over to the brass topped voice pipe, lifted its cap and blew into the horn, which created a whistle. 'Send an AS to the conning tower immediately sergeant.' The OOW commanded and closed the bell-shaped speaker.

'Permission to speak, Sir.' Fowler said loudly.

'Carry on seaman.' Michael said pleased with the way he had handled the crew so far.

'Twelve minutes past five, Sir.'

Michael peered into the fog and moved the steering two notches toward starboard.

Chapter 16
Tower Bridge, December 1907

Lady Margaret and Zamo were huddled under the flimsy umbrella they had brought from Kent; it was becoming a filthy night, suffering heavy globules of rain moving sideways over the freezing water. The visibility was so poor in the fog; the hundreds of drenched protesters could barely see the top of the bridge's four towers or even the riverbanks. Those who stood right in the middle of the bridge, where the road was mechanically torn apart, only saw abstract shapes of the crowd close to them, and that was exactly where the two residents from the rather comfortable Somerleyton Manor were now waiting.

'Zamo I want you to hold my hand.' Lady Margaret commanded. 'If any policemen tell us to move on, we must do so, we are not going to break the law, do you understand?'

'Yes Lady Margaret, it's very exciting, non?' He said, with his cute accent and a huge smile.

'Yes Zamo it is, the last time I came here was for the Royal opening, it was very similar, there were thousands of people, hundreds of boats, everything was draped in crimson cloth and I saw his Majesty the Prince of Wales turn a silver cup, placed on the road here to open the bascules…'

'What is bascules, Lady Margaret?'

'They are the part of the bridge that opens in the middle of the these large towers, underneath us Zamo, look!' She explained pointing to the bitumen crack.

Near the centre of the bridge Emmeline and Christobel Pankhurst turned their banner to face the crowd, the black ink spelled out their simple yet powerful message:

Deeds Not Words

Emmeline stood on her soap box and the crowd, now in their thousands cheered enthusiastically.

'Fellow suffragists…' She called through a loud

hailer. 'We have asked the Liberal Government and directly Mr Lloyd George, who has promised his support, to start the process for women to have the democratic vote!' The crowd went wild with excitement; just the word 'vote' seemed to act as political aphrodisiac.

'Whether or not the physical size of our brains is smaller than the average man's...' The crowd laughed at the newspapers' jibe and screamed at the top of their voices every derogative remark they could think of about men.

'We are still smarter than most of them and capable of voting-out the idiots in Parliament, who we don't want!'

Again, the nice, respectable Edwardian ladies shouted abuse and cheered their messiah. Megan held onto John's arm tightly, looking closely at his face she asked. 'Are you all right John? I was a little naughty not telling you the reason for our meeting today, I thought that you wouldn't have come if we told you about the obstruction.'

'I think I may have stayed at home, except I would not care for you to come here on your own.' He said looking around concerned.

'Kill all men!' A blubbery lady screamed at the top of her recitative voice next to the couple. When John and Megan looked around, the woman smiled and said to John. 'Not you Sir, just the bad ones.' They all laughed.

At that moment, a surge in the crowd at the South Tower moved as rapidly as a wind through a cornfield. 'What is happening John?' Megan asked.

'I cannot see, I shall climb up on the balustrade and have a look.' John said putting a foot in between the slippery ornate ironwork.

'Be careful John!' Megan cautioned, looking over the edge into the black hole beneath the bridge. The rain and near freezing conditions made the ornate stone and wooden balustrade as slippery as an ice rink.'

'There are men in navy blue uniforms and hats, pushing their way through the crowds,' John shouted down to Megan and a small group of demonstrators gazing up at the mad man balancing above them. 'They seem to be using long sticks to hit the women and some of the demonstrators are blocking the men from getting into the cabin near the south pillar.' The listening group nearby passed on the news that spread rapidly in all directions. Swiftly as telepathic ants, waves of women pushed their way down to the group of Tower workers, who were trying to enter the control cabin to start up the steam engines and open the bridge. The HMS Aboukir was approaching in the sullied mist.

Aboard the warship, the crew were anxious.

'Five thirty Captain Renshaw!' AS Fowler said.

Renshaw thought that Fowler was a biddable man and if all the crews were going to be so acquiescent, his job would be easy, and the fears that kept him awake over the last few weeks would be quelled.

'By my reckoning we must be about fifty feet from Tower Bridge, are there any sightings from the look-outs Fowler?' 'No Sir, they say it's a right pea-souper, they can't even see the shoreline that can only be about thirty feet off the port side, Sir.'

'Let's have another foghorn warning, a nice long one this time.'

'Aye-aye Sir!'

Mr Death entered the conning tower and saluted the Pilot. 'Excuse me Sir, the Captain, sends his compliments, and asks how long before we pass Tower Bridge?'

'In a few minutes, we have flashed our signal lights to the control cabin on the bridge, mind you I doubt if they can see them yet. They will flash back with two white lights when they do. Mr Death, tell me, do you have any spotlights on board?'

'Just one Sir, on the bridge.'

'Good. Get a man to point it to the forward bow.'

'It won't help much Sir, in this fog it will just bounce the light back.'

'I know Mr Death, but when we get really close I shall need all the help I can get, because the mast and chimneys on this vessel only just clear the bridge when it's fully open.'

'Aye-aye, Sir! The OOW rushed out of the door into the blustering rain and Fowler tugged on the horn releasing its warning cry.

The demonstrators all looked towards the blackening abyss in front of them fearing the foghorn's eerie warning.

'Wow!' Zamo said excitedly to Lady Margaret. 'The warship must be very close to us!'

Margaret put her saturated sleeve around Zamo yet said nothing. She looked at her watch attached to a ribbon on her dress, it said five thirty four. She couldn't see anyone she knew and contemplated trying to fight her way off the bridge. The Lady decided that she had led a sheltered life and if all of these other women could hold their ground and show unity so could she.

On the east side of the South Tower, surrounding the little glass and wood control cabin, contained by a wrought iron railings and lit by a single gas lamp, a group of eight engineers and a very short, chubby policeman, were literally in battle with thirty to fifty women. The men were armed with canes, the policeman with his truncheon and whistle, and the female soldiers carried umbrellas and solid bags. It was a stand off. The stubby Bobby stood at the foot of a sestet of steps that led to the wood and glass door of the cabin and was now chest to chest with Daisy Maynard; she wasn't going anywhere. Her back was firmly pressed against the black railings, carrying her newly bought, very expensive hat from Bond Street, it came in a red, green and gold, stamped top bonnet box. She gripped the ample brass handle, holding the hard-wearing shield in her left hand for protection, and in her right her hand, her best umbrella ready for any onslaught, like a gladiator's sword.

'Madam!' Shouted the superior looking engineer over the shoulder of the policeman. 'If we don't open the bascule for the Aboukir in the next few minutes it will crash into the road crossing and all of you will be killed!'

'We don't give a fig!' Daisy shouted back, her high rosy cheeks glowing.

Sixty feet behind them in the centre of the crossing, a woman shrieked and pointed towards the dark hole over the Thames. 'Look!' She screamed at the top of her voice, pointing her right arm straight out. The crowd turned towards the emptiness to see an eerie corona hovering over the misty water; exactly level with the road they were standing on. Uncharacteristically, the thousands of demonstrators became silent, when, as frightening as a ghost from the deep, the silhouette of the enormous HMS Aboukir began to be sketched on the foggy, grey canvas in front of them.

'Oh my!' Said Daisy Maynard. 'Look at the size of that thing.'

On the south side of the river a howling line of black police vans came winding towards the Thames crossing, only coming to a last-second halt at the edge of the protestors. Captain Ryan was a tall, wiry-haired Irishman, originally trained as a sergeant in the guards in his youth and was always sent to London's most difficult situations. If there were violent strikers, Ryan was there, if there was gunfire and killing, Ryan was there, and now his commanding officer gave the trouble-shooter his instructions precisely.

'Clear the bridge Ryan, even if you have to throw every last one of those dam, stupid women in the Thames!'

Suddenly there was a sharp crack of broken glass, some of the women had gone around the other side of the control cabin, climbed up onto the ornate lookout post and found the glass door. When Dawn Adams entered the control room with her sister Jane they were shocked to see a forest of handles, like those of a train's signal box, growing out of brass edged slits in the floor. A commode sat against the wall and the large windows on all sides gave a magnificent view of the Thames and the deadly warship approaching through the smog.

Ryan brought a team of thirty policemen and ten ruffians from the docks that he used in what he called, 'Extreme Situations'. At the same time, Megan and John arrived twenty feet in front of the all-important cabin. Ryan's men easily fought their way through the crowd of demonstrators, leaving a trail of blooded bodies in their wake. The wailing wounded and bleeding women lying in pools of rainwater soon turned the road surface into the colour of a drenched poppy field. Megan, now way ahead of

John, ran to the South Tower cabin at the same moment Ryan and his policemen arrived, their truncheons previously reddened by their violence. Nevertheless, most of the real damage was done by the mercenaries from the docks, they carried iron bars and enjoyed using them on the helpless, mostly middleclass ladies.

The leader, a rough looking mariner known as Jack 'Brixton' Dirk, because he was no stranger to the prison of the same name, went straight over to Daisy and without a word, smashed her over the head with his crow bar, her blood saturated hat floated to the pavement's flowing rainwater and she collapsed on top of it. Megan didn't hesitate and launched herself at him, pulling the tough docker to the ground, other women joined in beating the man over the head with bags and umbrellas. He was a robust type, used to a roughhouse and started to get up, despite the barrage of punches. Megan pulled up her skirts and petticoats and with one perfectly timed kick, smashed her leather heel into his forehead. He fell back on the slippery surface and another half a dozen delicate ankle boots soon smacked his skull in unison. John arrived behind his love and pulled her back urgently, because he spotted another half a dozen dockers effortlessly crashing through the women's blockade.

Megan tried to haul herself away from the Doctor to get into the centre of the fray, but he held her tightly and screamed above the cacophony.

'Megan, please, there are too many of them, you'll get hurt.'

She turned quickly, her eyes drilling into him, her misty breath on his face saying passionately. 'I have been hurt many times before John and for no reason...' She cried with a throaty voice. 'But now there's a good reason, a cause, to stop all women from being hurt, by men, men who have the law on their side, men who think that it's their right to harm their wives and daughters. When women have the vote, and they will one day, we shall put an end to violence and war, and men will no longer be able to stop us, using police, hooligans and the courts!'

John held her close, wrapping his arms around her,

he could see tears flooding her beautiful mahogany eyes and her cheeks were flushed from the cold night air and the passion she felt so strongly. He realised that her feelings were not just based on the events of that evening; they were the result of years of violence against her mother and herself. She had confessed her abusive past, but he guessed that her brief description of her mother and stepfather covered years of maltreatment.

'I understand how you feel and I agree to committing acts of civil disobedience; but it's just not worth risking your *life* for this cause Megan.'

Emmeline and Christobel Pankhurst charged through the crowd in the centre of the road crossing, barking orders to a group of seasoned campaigners who guarded her flanks.

'Angela take six women, go down that little staircase next to the tower, it leads to the worker's entrance and the coalbunkers portal. Try to get in there, you'll find four large boilers and two huge steam engines, do whatever you can to stop them opening the bascules.' The group of women rushed into action. Emmeline then turned to a second well trained group, 'Ladies, there's another control cabin behind the south tower facing into London, if they start to open the bridge, use the handles in there to close it.'

'But Emmeline…' A skinny woman asked. '…How do we know which handle to operate?'

The leader had done her research.

'Jennifer, there's a brass tube on the wall, like a huge thermometer, within the glass front it shows when the bridge is moving, if it starts to go up, just move all of the handles until it stops, now go quickly, they seem to have crashed through our sisters on the other side!'

All of a sudden, a communal cry erupted from the crush, whilst the steam engines signalled their job had begun, with the powerful hiss and thunder of a motor capable of lifting the monsters great wings.

'Oh God!' Megan cried. 'The engineers are going to open the bridge with the women still on it; what time is it John?'

'Five forty five…' He screamed against the noise

and the howling, saturated wind. 'They do not have long, where are Lady Margaret and Zamo?'

The drenched couple looked around the South Tower area, total chaos, there must have been over two thousand women on Tower Bridge and the entrance roads, now joined by police, dockers, newspapermen and spectators.

There was barely room to move, let alone fight. However, the bridge engineers and Captain Ryan managed to secure the South Tower's control-room and were about to lift the roadway.

Another snake of black police vans arrived on the north side of the river boasting a group of thirty policemen carrying a thick ship's rope. The uniformed men pushed their way through the throng of protesters until they reached the centre of the bridge where the road would crack open. The police surrounded the women quickly, trying to herd the suffragists off the bridge using the heavy encircling cordon. Some of the crowd were lassoed away from the central position; however, much of the pushing and shoving seemed to simply turn in circles.

Until the earthquake started.

Lady Margaret and Zamo were literally standing on the join in the road when the thundering noise of the earth parting beneath their feet began, a spasm of horror gripped Margaret's face. Hundreds of women and all of the policemen ran for their lives in panic, searching for the safety of flat, immovable cobblestones on both sides of the erupting road. A rotund policeman fell and was sent rolling down the slippery slope as fluently as a ten-pin bowling ball, when he spun onto flat ground he crashed into a group of uniformed officers who fell as clumsily as skittles.

Several women including Margaret clung to the icy balustrades and ironwork on either side of the lifting road, as it was now rising up ten feet above the gateways.

When the road bridge gained height most people gripping onto the sides slid and tumbled down to the bottom. Zamo grabbed hold of the moving balustrade searching for Lady Margaret, he heard screams coming from the opening tarmac on the other side of the separating roadway. He swiftly made his way to the top of his half of the moving balustrade and at the peak he looked over the edge. Through the mist he could see two women hanging onto the lifting bridge. Somehow they'd fallen over the side of the road as it opened, clinging on to the last girder near the break in the road. Their legs swung wildly over the water, as precariously as a ragged flag in the wind. The pinnacle of the bascules was now climbing to more than forty feet over the forbidding Thames below.

On the conning tower of HMS Aboukir, the three seamen gasped in unison as the huge bridge came into focus since the curtain of fog had slowly began to evaporate in front of them, just enough to view the shape of the brick gateway.

'Jesus Christ!' Mr Death yelled. 'We're on top of the bridge and it's not fully open!'

The men were dumbfounded and then Michael hollered. 'Slow-astern Fowler!'

The warship's bow found itself only a few feet from the edge of the great bridge. If it continued, the masts and funnels would crash through the rising roadway, the chimneys would fall into the boilers below, cause a massive explosion, which would in turn ignite the munitions on the warship and blow away Tower Bridge, all of the people and the surrounding area.

The command to reverse had caused a whirlpool under the armoured war machine's belly, its twelve thousand tons swooned in the water as the mariners and thousands of people on and next to the bridge, held their breaths. Gradually it stopped moving forward, seesawing from side to side. The seamen couldn't believe their eyes; the moving drawbridge was now opening to its full height. Unfortunately, through their Watson binoculars, they could see three women dangling from the highest point of the roadway, one hundred and thirty feet over the icy water. Two on the south side and one on the north side. Other women and some policemen were hurtling down the road like toboggans on an icy mountain slope, crashing into hundreds of people falling onto the flat part of the Thames crossing. In panic, one of the hanging women cried out.

'*H-e-l-p!* I can't hold on any longer!'

Her small fingers slipped from the saturated roadway's edge and she dropped like a stone into the icy black liquid. The multitude of women and men on and around the bridge shrieked in chorus as they heard the water splash, swallowing her whole. Her last scream echoed under the bridge, and the muddy river rippled outwards as she quickly disappeared beneath the surface. Only her pink hat stayed afloat, marking her watery grave, like a silk tombstone.

'Man overboard!' Michael yelled at the top of his voice. 'Fowler, man the life-boats!' Fowler rushed out of the door bumping into Captain Edgar Pritchett, his eyes full of sleep and his voice the worse for too many brandies.

'My God man! What on earth are you doing with *MY* ship?' He slurred angrily.

'There's some problem on the roadway of the bridge Captain, and a woman has just fallen in the water, she won't last long in this temperature...' Michael said calmly.

'And what's worse there're two more clinging on by their finger nails, if the drop doesn't kill them, the icy water will. Mr Death...' He commanded, ignoring the drunken sea Captain. 'Make sure that spotlight's on the water will you please, just in case the woman manages to float up.'

'Look at the time man!' Pritchett garbled. 'If we don't get through the bridge we will go to ground on the lowering tide, you must give the order for 'Ahead-full'.

'Captain, there's a woman overboard and two more hanging from the bridge we can't barrel right over them.' Michael lifted his binoculars again and said. 'Oh no, oh my God, there's a child up there too, clinging on to the top of the balustrade.

'But my ship Pilot, no one person is worth my battle ship!'

'Mr Death! Get that light on those women.'

Michael screamed, without putting down his binoculars trained on the abyss created by the beast's open wings.

In the bowels of the great bridge's engine rooms, six

blackened stokers hovelled coal from the gritty bunkers with swollen muscles. The fuel arrived on a small train track that passed through a closed yard beneath the bridge, hidden from public view. The stable for the horsepower, lay thirty feet along the south side of the river. When Angela and her five colleagues jumped out of the bunkers, nearly as black as the stokers, the men leapt to one side in shock. The screaming women ran in all directions to look for a way of stopping the bridge from moving. On the back wall a long metal rack held forty or more heavy black iron spanners, some as tall and heavy as a ten-year-old child. Angela didn't know what to do, but remembered the expression, 'There was a spanner in the works'. Therefore, she grabbed the largest one and using all of her strength, hurled the metal tool into the massive cogged wheel, which pumped the steam.

The chief engineer had just arrived from his office in the north abutment, but he was too late. The noise in the underground bascule chamber was deafening, as metal crushed metal and the mighty machine hissed to a thunderous halt. Stokers and men from the bridge master's command, descended on the soot-soiled women and dragged them screaming onto the street that lead to the south side of the tower. When the huge, green painted engines were working, they powerfully pumped water and steam to the lifting engines; that could raise each bascule weighing one thousand, two hundred tons to their full height in a seesaw motion, but the comparatively small spanner had done its work and one of the engines grinded to a excruciating stop.

Above on the bridge's roadway, Megan and John were being crushed and battered by the horde, sliding down the asphaltic surface when the bridge rose up to ninety per cent of its full height. John managed to attach one woman's broken leg to a splint made from two umbrellas and a long leather belt, he wrapped several bleeding arms and heads with strips of torn dresses, but it was impossible for one man to cope with the injuries of the hundreds of wounded around him. Megan was climbing over the drenched horizontal protesters looking for Margaret and Zamo; regrettably she couldn't see her new friend or her student in the sea of broken bodies. Abruptly, the huge spotlight of the warship focussed on the women hanging from the roadway girders above. Suddenly, someone gave a frenzied shriek at the top of her voice.

'Look up there!' She pointed.

For the first time since they parted, in the centre of the bridge, Megan saw Lady Margaret; hanging in mid-air as flimsy as a Victorian doll on a Christmas tree, one hundred and thirty feet in the open space over the freezing, poisonous, dark Thames.

'John! John! Where are you?' Megan cried-out rushing back to the place she left the doctor, patching together as many suffragists as he could from his Gladstone bag.

He was standing now with most of the others, gazing up in shock at Margaret and another woman, moments from falling to a certain death. Megan grabbed his arm and pleaded.

'John what can we do? We never thought the authorities would be so aggressive with all of these people here.

Let's break into the steering room or whatever it's called and try to lower the bridge!' Megan cried desperately.

'I don't think we could get in there now, the engineers have locked themselves inside the two control cabins, and besides if they lower the bridge, the force will throw the women off and even if they could hang on, when the bridge closes it will either cut their hands off or trap them under the roadway.'

At the tarmac summit, Zamo looked down at the huge ship and its cone-shaped beam, braking through the fog. He glanced around the crowds on both sides of the open bridge and on Tower beach. The woman hanging from the other half of the roadway was sobbing and talking loudly to someone else.

Then he heard Lady Margaret's voice, he realised that although he couldn't see her, she must be hanging under his side of the elevated roadway.

He called out as loud as he could, at first, she didn't hear him, but then he heard her lovely soft voice.

'Zamo is that you?'

'Yes, is me!' He yelled loudly.

'Zamo listen to me, save yourself, try to slide down the road very slowly and very carefully, do you understand, go now, I shall be all right.'

'No – no - Lady Margaret, I wait for you.'

'No Zamo, I cannot hold on much longer, do something for me, will you? Tell Peter…tell General Trubshaw that I love him, but now you must leave, please Zamo go, you are just a small boy, you have your whole life ahead of you, go quickly, hold on to the balustrades, just pretend it's a normal ladder.'

It was uncannily silent above the maddening scene below. He felt like a bird of prey surveying wetlands from the highest perch. For the first time since he left the circus he felt completely alone. He didn't have Bill or Mrs Jarvis to give their advice. Shep wasn't wagging his tail in support; Black silk didn't prance in front of him with the power to carry him away from danger.

Zamo put a hand in his trouser pocket and felt the little box his brother François had given him the last time he'd seen the great clown, at the gate of Somerleyton Manor. At that moment, the warm summer day seemed like a lifetime ago, he didn't know what was in the box, but thought that this was a good moment to find out.

The young boy opened the cardboard square with one hand while he clung to the balustrade in the howling wind and rain with the other.

Inside there was some tissue paper that came apart in his wet fingers, and there, filling the little box, sat a clown's red nose; François's nose.

The ship below him now made a strange whooping noise three times. When the fog started to lift a little more, he could see a small boat with four sailors rowing to a spot under the bridge; a second spotlight now shone on them from the riverbank and Zamo remembered his half-brother's advice. *'If you have a problem Zamo, you must ask yourself this one thing. What would circus people do now?'*

There was a terrible rasping howl from the lady opposite. She had lost the grip of one hand and swung

207

wildly from the other, after two or three swings as rhythmically as a grandfather clock's pendulum, she turned to Margaret with fear in her eyes. She tried to speak to her suffragist sister, yet she fell to her death as fatally as an acorn from a great oak in an autumn wind.

At that moment, thousands of spectators on both sides of the river as well as the demonstrators, wounded or standing on the edges of the bridge, all screamed in harmony when the woman dived into her watery grave below, no one more ardently than Michael Renshaw's mother, Pearl.

Mrs Renshaw cradled her face in her hands and prayed for the poor woman's soul. She felt helpless, her son was in danger just a few hundred feet away and there was nothing his mother could do to save him. A few minutes later an old Jewish man with a child came up and spoke to her. He had a strange accent, but she understood, there were a large number of Jews in the East End. He seemed to be completely confused by the events unfolding in front of the thousands of people on and around the bridge, as though he was on a strange planet.

'Excuse me, what's happening here?' The small woman looked stressed and said: 'There's a problem today, the Suffragettes are demonstrating and there's a warship coming through.'

'Can the ship still get through?'

'I don't know...' She said, tears filling her eyes, 'I'm so afraid.'

'But my dear lady, you mustn't get so upset, I'm sure either the bridge will open fully or the ship will turn around, it will certainly have an experienced captain, everything will be fine.'

Pearl Renshaw broke into tears and dropped her face into a lace handkerchief.   'He's not experienced, he's only a baby and he's going to die!'

'I don't understand...' Hyman said confused.

Pearl didn't hear him; she could only see her own child in danger. Some people standing behind them spoke to the old man, explaining the crises, but Pearl's head was on the Aboukir.

Mr Liberman was an ascetic, his tiny village in Germany seemed busy to him, and therefore he rarely went out. He'd brought his son to London to visit the engineering feat, not only because he'd dreamed of seeing the bridge even before it was built, but also because he wanted to help his fourteen year boy. Other children were playing games and mixing with kids their own age and were mostly happy.

Moshe had never been happy. He enjoyed his little building blocks when he was a toddler, but only once he had knocked them all down.

As a hermitic engineer, Mr Liberman enjoyed making things, occasionally spending months alone in his workroom, unfortunately he could never convince his little son to do anything other than destroy every creation he saw. Pearl walked away from the mad old man anxiously, she worried about the people on the bridge, but she felt tortured by the danger her son faced. The warship would have been packed with ammunition as it had just returned from exercises in the North Sea. If it collides with the bridge, she thought: her Michael would not only be blown to heaven, but he would be known as the pilot who destroyed the great ship and the world's most famous bridge. Pearl looked up now at the top of the open roadway and prayed that her son would be safe.

An old sailor who stood next to the frightened woman was shaking his head slowly. He said to her or perhaps to himself, without taking his eyes from the expanding, rippling circle of water that marked the suffragist last resting place:

'Some say drowning isn't a bad way to go, an easy passing between life and death.' He looked melancholy, as though he had contemplated his own final hour at length. Just below the bridge's pedestrian gantry the young clown stood up on his feet, to the horror of those below.

'Lady Margaret, not let go...' Zamo shouted urgently, 'I coming for you!'

He slid purposefully down the balustrade with simian instincts. Hand over hand as he'd done so many times in the big top. After ten feet, he found the ship's rope, left behind by the cascading police, who now stared up at

Zamo with the rest of the crowds on both sides of the river. He undid the huge knot and tied it around his waist. The skinny lad then pulled up the rest of the line looping it into a coil, which he put over his right shoulder. The Aboukir's spotlight followed his every movement, as did the thousands of onlookers below, never have so many people been so silent. He climbed back up to the peak and looked over the edge where Margaret had her arms wedged in between two metal girders.

'I come.' He shouted confidently, 'I come!'

Zamo tied the middle of the heavy hemp to the top of the balustrade and stood up on the sharp, metal, triangular edge of the roadway, to the dismay of the pensive spectators below. His arms outstretched, he stepped his right foot out slowly like a tightrope walker, along the slippery edge. Then carefully lifting his other foot from the surface he slid the soles of his feet one in front of the other. After eight steps, a howling wind came up from the river, heavy with rain. He lost his balance, his arms flapped as ungracefully as a floundering bird and he wobbled on one leg.

The crowd below screamed and clasped their faces; Pearl Renshaw put her hands over her eyes. She knew that she just couldn't cope if the little boy fell to his death, as did the two women before him.   It didn't seem that long ago that Mikey was his age, not that her gentle son could've stood up there walking on the road edge, that could only be an inch or so wide.

Zamo swayed to the left and right using his arms and right leg to find his centre of gravity. He remembered the tightrope walkers in the circus, if the cable moved too much they stabilized it, then moved quickly forward, it was just like riding a bike, his mother explained.

'The slower you go, the more difficult it is!' Zamo took quick strides until he was level with the dangling woman from Kent. He crouched down, looped the twine through a girder, dropped the end next to her, and asked:

'You can put rope around?'

'No Zamo,' she said hopelessly, 'My arms are stuck, if I let go I'll fall. Zamo listen to me, please save yourself, go back!'

'*Es no problema.*' He said in Spanish without realising.

He took the end of the cord and leaned over the gaping hole threading it through another cross girder, a foot from the edge.

Way below, John and Megan looked up anxiously in the midst of the growing throng.

'They are both going to fall John!' Megan said with tears and rain rolling down her cheeks. I should never have brought you all here, the movement never dreamed that they would open the bridge with so many people on it.' She cried. 'I am so sorry.'

John, like the rest of the surrounding people just looked up with a dry throat, in deafening silence, no one could take their eyes off the couple in the two misty spotlights, despite its morbidity.

On board the warship the only sound was Captain Pritchett pacing up and down alone on the ship's bridge, with his second bottle of brandy in his sweating palm. He could see the tide begin to ebb away like water down a bath's plughole and the heavy craft slowly sank towards the river's bottom.

Pilot-Captain Michael Renshaw, Officer of the Watch, Mark Death and Able Seaman Fowler, used their Watson's trained on the small boy nearly a hundred and fifty feet above London, trying to attach a line around a woman in a full length dress and coat, still wearing a large brimmed hat, who was dangling like an ape from the rafters of the world's most famous seesaw bridge.

Zamo now slid over the side of the roadway so that he was also dangling off the edge, arriving level to Margaret with a huge smile across his little face. He wrapped the end of the rope around her waist and made a tight double knot, and then he leaned down, put a loop of rope level with her knee, and attached it through the rafter above their heads, hanging on to the metal bones of the bridge with one hand.

'Lady Margaret, put foot in rope and push up.' He said smiling at her.

'I cannot Zamo, I am too afraid to let go!' She said with tears in her eyes.

'You can, is easy.' Zamo said encouragingly.

'Zamo…' Margaret started.

'What is?'

'Zamo, please, if we get back to Kent…' She paused, finding it hard to speak…'Will you, will you become my son?' Lady Margaret said softly with tears cascading over her powdered skin.

Taking into account the bereaved woman had only been hanging under Tower Bridge for a short while, she'd quickly reviewed her whole life.

She loved her husband Peter more than ever and despite enjoying the wealth and comfort of Somerleyton Manor, the wonderful clothes, paintings, antiques and lifestyle, which her money and position afforded her, she realised, hanging as tenuously as a wind charm in the rain, moments before certain death, that after two and a half years, she hadn't recovered from the loss of her beloved son. The pain was still an intricate part of her. Perhaps it was having another child around the house or her secret desire never revealed to her husband, to have more children of her own, yet over the last ten or fifteen minutes Margaret knew that having a family, a child, was the most important thing in her life.

Zamo looked at Margaret, as never before, his eyes were level with hers for the first time since he arrived at the manor. They were swinging from a twine of hemp and facing death together She no longer appeared to be the beautiful tall lady who owned so much and lived in a huge mansion.

She was a woman who loved him like a mother, perhaps he thought, more than his own mother, who always looked on him as an inconvenient error. Zamo looked down at the thousands of people, the huge warship, and spotlights from both ship and shore and said calmly in his best English.

'I be son, please put foot in rope now.'

Lady Margaret Henrietta Trubshaw placed her foot in the loop and kissed Zamo on the cheek. With an enormous effort she pushed herself up onto the roadway summit, pulled her newly adopted son towards her and together, they used the rope attached to the balustrade and slowly made their way across the top of the steep tarmac tor, in the direction of the ornate wall at the edge. The sound of cheers and applause from thousands of relieved Londoners filled their ears. With Zamo's help, Margaret made her way down the slippery balustrade using the rope to slow her decent. When she finally reached level ground to a heroin's welcome, she was still wearing her hat, albeit askew; a photographic record of which, was in almost every newspaper around the world over the following weeks.

The three seamen on the conning tower of HMS Aboukir also breathed a sigh of relief, when the Captain-Pilot broke their silence.

'Full astern! Fowler please.' Michael said with a sense of respite. Alas his lighter mood was short-lived because the heavyweight fighter groaned and creaked yet didn't move more than a few feet.

'Left full rudder Mr Death please, ahead full Fowler.'

The OOW complied by swinging the wheel as fast as he could and Clucky moved the brass telegraph arm back and forward into the correct position, its ringing bell confirming its obedience.

Despite the manoeuvres the former battle champion would not budge, the great ship lurched slowly to the left and Captain Pritchett lurched through the cabin door and almost onto the floor. A huge cheer from the suffragist confirmed their victory, the massive HMS Aboukir was finally aground.

'You bloody fool!' He screamed at Michael his brandy-breath filling the small cabin 'I told you to move my ship before it was too late, you heard me Mr Death, you're my witness...'

He pointed to his officer and swayed more than the ship's movement required.

'And you wouldn't listen, would you?' Captain Pritchett said trying to sound plausibly sober.

'Captain, the Port of London Authority doesn't run over dying women floating in the Thames. Now I suggest that you return to your cabin and let us see if we can get this vessel turned around and off the sandbank.'

'Off the sandbank! Who steered us on the sandbank in the first place? You bloody schoolboy, wait to we get back in port, I'll have your licence, if you've got one, before you can say Jack Robinson!' With that, the drunken Captain fell out of the conning tower door. There was an uneasy silence in the cabin.

Michael opened his case and checked his charts and calendars; they showed him that he was in the deepest part of the Thames. Furthermore as it was now six-forty-five, the tide had sunk too low to move forward or back.

He would become the laughing-stock of every captain and pilot on the river, and most important to Michael, to one retired captain who he had so wanted to impress. The problem he realised was that this heavyweight fighter could settle in the sand, perhaps even list over to one side and be immovable until the late spring. His name would be associated with this monument and tourist's attraction in the middle of London, and the incident would feature in every document and no doubt every newspaper for months. He would be blamed for his inexperience and stupidity. Captain Pritchett would no doubt contact everyone in the navy who owed him a favour, and Michael would be drummed out of the service with his father and brother saying *'I told you so!'* to his mother and anyone who would listen. His career was finished before it even got started. Five years of studying wasted. And now that idiot captain is shouting something from below.

'Ahoy Aboukir! Ahoy there!

'Captain!' Clucky said enthusiastically. 'Look on the Port side.'

Michael looked out of the window through the lifting fog and saw a sight that he couldn't have dreamt of.

'Hello Matey! Want me to tow this bathtub into deep waters?' Norman Roughan laughed through a loud hailer. Michael grabbed the ship's hailer and rushed outside.

'Norman we can't move aft or stern!'

'Leave it to the experts, Right-full rudder, Slow-ahead will do it, get the boys to grab a line.'

'Are you mad? There's no depth near the bank on the starboard side, I've studied all of the charts!'

'Not until three days ago there wasn't, but they just removed an old wreck, been there forever they say. Anyway now there's a big hole and enough room to turn your tin-pot, just follow me Matey and you'll owe me a drink for the next month!'

With that, Norman tugged his horn, and threw a line to the implanted monster. After a few minutes the sailors attached the heavy rope, it soon lost its slack and the massive battle-ship lunged to the starboard side, the noise of the bottom scratching on the river's bed filled the air for a mile up and down the river, and the spectators from the bridge, ran along the Thames path to watch the next unfolding drama.

After the longest thirty minutes of Michael's life, the heavyweight settled into the water and sauntered through the empty grave of the ascended ruin. Once the Aboukir started to turn around, the engineers in the South Tower cabin began to lower Tower Bridge's huge mechanical wings, having cut out the spanner and the crowd on the riverbanks cheered and clapped with relief, except the suffragists who booed disappointedly. Norman flashed Morse to the Captain-Pilot telling him that there was a temporary berth waiting for them further down stream and after half an hour when Michael finally told Clucky to signal All-Stop, the whole crew came on deck and clapped the Pilot as he descended from the temporary bridge.

He signed back the ship to the OOW Mr Death, because Captain Edgar Pritchett refused to see Michael Renshaw again, or as Clucky said when he shook hands with him. 'He's too pissed to get off his bunk!' The pilot walked past the crew on the lower deck who clapped and smiled at him some slapping him on the back, as he swept past. He paused, looked back at the unbeatable fighter and saw Clucky and Mr Death looking down at him, when they saw his face they both gave a sharp formal salute.

Michael Renshaw, Pilot, straightened his cap proudly and walked down the ship's gangplank onto the port, where a press of newspaper reporters and photographers stood with a cheering crowd from the East End who stood alongside the warship. The pilot wondered how he was going to explain the last few hours to his mother, when he looked up to the top of the stairs he saw her standing there, soaking wet, waiting for her son with his Macintosh. The qualified pilot waved, the proudest mother in the world waved back. The following day one of the headlines proclaimed.

Warship Captain Saves London

Chapter 17
France, 1st April 1964

Sam and Phaedra stood on the deck of the slothful boat train that swayed and dipped its way into the port of Calais. It was a clear, cool, April Fool's Day with all of the details of the cluttered metal boat and rail-port looking its usual ugly self, in the harsh cold fluorescent light. Even the beautiful and luxurious Bristol appeared bland, bumping its way over the numerous inlaid railway tracks stretching for miles around the edges of the little town of Calais.

They motored along the narrow, yet empty N1 road, shouldered by its towering poplar trees that always reminded Sam of the cinema advertisement for 'Start-rite' children's shoes. The twin cartoon protagonists holding hands at the beginning of the elongated tree-lined road, suggesting the footwear would last forever. Phaedra was map-reading and keeping an eye on the second rear-view mirror, for any car that kept up with Sam's high speed, which would have been difficult against one of the world's most powerful cars. They did their usual trick of pulling off the road occasionally to see if any familiar cars had pursued them, though the route to Chantilly past without incident or a tail.

'Shall we look out for a restaurant darling, I'm starving.' Sam said.

'You're always hungry, you'll have to wait until dinner, the food is great at the Pavilion.'

Sam drove unhurriedly pass Chantilly's massive forest, with its maze of crisscross roads and extraordinary little White Queen's Castle that reflected and glistened on the Etangs de Commelle. Until they reached the curve in the road Sam knew so well. He slowed to a crawl in anticipation of the magnificent château slowly rising up on the horizon in front of them, as usual; in the spring it was surrounded by a haunting mist that gave the ancient building its fairy-tale appearance.

'Wow, look at that Phaedra, I've seen it so often and yet it still impresses me in the same way it did the first time.' Sam said in awe of the shimmering grey, enchanting château. 'Shall we have a quick look at the horses before we check in at the hotel darling?' He asked rhetorically driving down into the valley.

'When have I ever been able to stop you looking at horses?'

'Thank you Phaedra darling, we won't be long.' He smiled as excitedly as a small boy going to the zoo.

The stables, commissioned by Louis-Henri de Bourbon, 7th Prince of Condé, were nearly as beautiful as the château, albeit smaller. The local villagers said that the prince thought he would be reincarnated as a horse; therefore, he built stables that would be as comfortable as his magnificent house nestling down the hill. Sam spoke to the stable staff at length, expertly examining the vast number of different breeds of horse they kept there, the employees seemed to enjoy speaking to the equestrian, in his near perfect French as he had a vast knowledge of horses, nearly as much as he did.

An hour past before Sam noticed that Phaedra was looking extremely bored, having stamped on four deceased cigarettes.

'Sorry darling let's go to the hotel.' Sam said apologetically, looking back at the equines passionately.

The huge car negotiated the twisting road until they reached the silky river Oise, there were no headlights on the unlit road behind them for miles and so they made their way through the complicated narrow network to Toutevoie and its little hunting Pavilion that bordered the great river. Sam and Phaedra knew the place well, it was at the end of a cul-de-sac, and the car was soon secreted behind a hedge, invisible from the road, yet in sight from their room overlooking the slow moving river.

The whole place was inexpensive and scruffy, although the cuisine was a journey into a gourmet's paradise. The restaurant on the ground floor was positioned to overlook the waterway and the couple sat in front of the massive log fire at the end of the stretched room. They finished their fourth course after three hours, having discussed everything except their next job in Barcelona.

Phaedra complained that she was worried about the grandchildren. Pippa was so well educated and smart, and yet seemed to be wasting her life with her weird parking warden, and Charlotte had no common sense and lived life hedonistically, without any thought for the people around her.

'You know my darling, we have fought our way through two world wars, our friends and family have been killed, and humanity was turned upside-down by fascist. Now we live in fairly, peaceful times, life is more frivolous, the girls know we have enough money and so there's no pressure for them to do anything except enjoy themselves. What would we have given for such peace over the war years?'

'I know Sam, but I don't trust that model agent of Charlotte's, calling her by a boy's name and sending her half-naked all over the place, with weird old men gawping at her!'

'I remember you had many men looking at you, after the war, when we used to go out dancing, and on the Cote d'Azur, in those sexy little dresses *and* lying nude on the beach.'

'Yes, but the beaches were deserted and the dresses I wore in the towns did at least cover my bottom, Charlotte doesn't wear knickers half the time!'

'I don't think she has time to launder them, she seems to be out most evenings...'

'Exactly, that's what I'm saying, she's so hellion, like a child, goes to bed at two o'clock in the morning, sleeps until the afternoon, does a some modelling or at least talking about modelling to the other girls over lunch, and then she's out again at the clubs, what are they called? The Cromwellian or Whiskey something or other, and the last time I went to her flat it looked like the aftermath of an earthquake!'

'I remember the first moment I saw you in Greece, you were so beautiful, you had your dress rolled up in your knickers, with beautiful, bare, brown legs, half submerged in the waves, washing yourself in the sea, while most of the women in the village were wearing long black dresses with their heads covered, like nuns!' Sam laughed.

'Alright, but if it keeps going like this, by the time Pippa and Charlotte have children they will be walking around completely naked in Oxford Street!'

'Come on my love, we have a long drive tomorrow, let's go to bed and make love' He suggested lovingly.

They thanked the waiter and left him a large tip, which he ignored in a blasé fashion, until they left the restaurant.

'I shall never understand men, they don't age or grow up, life is so unfair for women.'

'I know it is my darling, did you pack your new diamond ring I gave you for our anniversary?' He teased smiling, and then he turned and intensely studied the sparkling dark river, like a cat following a ghost that no one else can see.

Mr and Mrs Renault, as they were signed in, walked arm in arm to their room on the first floor, just as a heavily laden barge cruised silently pass in the darkness.

The only passenger on the bridge used binoculars on the hotel windows, he then checked the photographs he had in front of him. Sam and Phaedra looked back from the glossy black and white paper.

Chapter 18
Moscow, April 1964

It was early morning in Moscow, the biting wind from the east encouraging the snowy crevices, dressed in white lace on the buildings and trees to sit tight. The sky was still pitch black and the streets were deserted. Lubyanka Square was empty, when the black Volga Gaz-21 Limousine came to a gentle halt.

'Are you sure you'll be all right here General? It's still very cold' Sergeant Ruska asked his passenger in the back seat. 'I could wait to save you the walk.'

'No Alex, I want to look at the toys and I'll enjoy the crisp air, it's not far, come back for me at twelve-thirty as usual.'

'Yes General.' The driver jumped out of the car and ran around opening the rear door for his boss.

General Fyodor Poluostrovich stepped out onto the pavement in front of Moscow's famous toyshop, Children's World. Glad of the heavy coat bought at Sears the last time he was in the United States and the warm scarf given to him by his younger sister Irina the previous Christmas. He reflected how much he enjoyed his extended family and regretted not having a wife and children of his own, he had calculated many years ago that it was a necessary decision in his profession. Families made you vulnerable.

Throughout his career he had witnessed the problems foreign militants and even his own agents had when their families were put at risk, even the toughest men were weak when someone kidnapped and tortured their wives and children. Then there were the Nancy-boys. We all had our share, he reflected, although the British seemed to have most of them. The French and Italians didn't care who was homosexual, but the homos in Britain would do anything to keep their little secret, which was great for us, he thought. We only had to send our agents to their parks and we would soon catch one of their MP's or Civil Servants, looking for one night of guilty pleasure or even a secret affair, to make the subterfuge of their empty

221

marriages more bearable. He made a mental note to check on his agents in Cambridge, the four remaining needed a little prodding after the first two defected. They were enjoying their cosy double-lives too much recently, since the loss of Anatoly.

The General scoured the massive array of toys in the shop's windows, took out his mini recorder and listed a few things that maybe suitable for his sister's two grandchildren on their birthday. That's the advantage of twins, one birthday, one Christmas, finished.

Finally, the aged Russian made his way across Lubyanka Square to his office building of the same name. He loved the old, yellow stone edifice, originally designed by Alexander V. Ivanov in 1897. In those days the All-Russia Insurance Company occupied it, however, he thought, it was wasted on them.

The beautiful parquet floors and the Baroque style, was perfect for a prestigious government organisation like his and the deep basement made such a convenient prison and persuasion unit.

Fyodor checked his watch against the impressive clock on the façade of the KGB headquarters, 5.30 am, perfect, he enjoyed being the first person there, it kept the lower ranks on their toes.

The lights in General Fyodor Poluostrovich's office on the third floor were low. On his rickety antique desk he had three telephones connected to a scrambler. Each time one of them rang, the new electric, Russian audio version of the Enigma Cipher, originally acquired from German, Polish and British sources during the Second World War, would automatically alter the voices of each party and make it impossible for anyone to record or listen in to the call. He only wished that the Russian scientists could have made it a little less clumsy. 'It looks like a fridge!' He complained when it first arrived.

Fyodor used the opportunity of the empty office to search the desks of his underlings. He had discovered that even trained agents left little clues to their indiscretions: mistresses' phone numbers and black-market contacts. There was always some useful ammunition that Fyodor could store and use one day when he had to. He remembered the drugs he found in comrade Alexei Pulaski's drawers late at night nearly fifteen years ago. There were details of cash withdrawals and then the following week, the testimony from his supplier, albeit extracted with a great deal of bloodshed. He knew that one day this evidence would be useful against such an ambitious young graduate. And what happened? Two months ago after Pulaski was elected into Politburo, he tried to cut the budget of the General's department. Fyodor attempted to talk him out of the stupid policy and all of the grandstanding and the newspaper interviews, yet he wouldn't listen. So, the General's young, sexy, highly trained agent Olga, acquired an invitation to Pulaski's hotel room and just as he pulled his trousers down, she showed him the evidence. Needless to say, Fyodor now had another politician in his pocket and autarchy for his department.

'This job can be so rewarding.' He said to himself, lighting another cigarette.

At seven-thirty, the General's devoted secretary arrived in his office with a cup of hot tea in a glass, no milk, just a splash of Provençal honey; another gift from the French embassy. Alena Arzamasskaia was an attractive, thirty-eight-year-old virgin. She had almond shaped, dark eyes, which slanted upwards in the corners, a prominent nose and full lips. In fact, all of her face and body had a smooth roundness, resembling the rolling hills of Tuscany. She had worked for the General since she celebrated her twenty-second Birthday, fell in love with her boss within a month, and has been waiting for him to notice her ever since. The employees of the building called her Poluo's-Pooch, because they say she follows him around like a puppy. Not that anyone would utter such a thing in front of the General or Alena, unless they wanted to be transferred to Siberia.

One of the Colonels in the French department on the second floor used to whisper to his colleagues, 'It's incredible; the General knows what's happening all around the world, but hasn't noticed the feelings of the girl in the next office.'

A little orange light flashed on top of his black phone. Poluostrovich knew it would be one of his agents; he took a long drag from his cigarette and turned the packet in his fingers. The maroon packet with gold letters spelling CCCP, were a simple design occupying everyone's desk and the only, non-black market brand available. Nevertheless, the spymaster had a supply at home of American Rothmans, not that he would ever smoke them at work. He answered the phone in his strange northern Russian accent. 'Yes?'

'Comrade General? It's Yuri Misezhnikov, from our French embassy…' The young Muscovite agent confirmed. 'We have passed the French hotel on the Belgium barge and the British agents have arrived, it looks like they are staying the night, I shall keep them under surveillance as ordered, comrade General.'

General Poluostrovich took another gulp of smoke from the Soviet tobacco and said in his deep, husky voice. 'Is the Count in Barcelona yet?'

'I believe he has been delayed, his contact is still in London.'

'Do we know who she is yet or if she's going with him?'

'I'm not sure Sir, we tapped her phone, but it was cut off, possibly by herself or by the telephone company.'

'Do you think she's aware of the line being tapped?'

'I'm not sure yet, she's smart and very prudent, having changed vehicles, she started with a small scruffy car, then switched to a very fast Mini, my contact said that the girl's very good at shaking off our people. They say she keeps getting away, seems to disappear into shops for hours coming out in different clothes and they are losing her, I'm told she's very beautiful though!'

'Let me know when they arrive in Barcelona.' The controller barked.

'General; the British agents…'

'Ex-British agents, they are freelancers nowadays.'

'Ah yes Sir, this is a complicated business…'

'Well?'

'You said they were very dangerous – except – well - they just look like little old people having a holiday.'

'Exactly Misezhnikov, that's why they're so dangerous.'

'Yes General, ah, do you want me to keep following them?'

'Agent Misezhnikov, listen to me, I've known that British agent for a long time, the last time we observed him, he shot his mark from a fast moving boat, two kilometres away, right between the eyes, we older people are still very capable you know.'

'Yes General – of course – I wasn't suggesting you were – ah, shall I follow their car when they leave?'

'No! I told you the only way to follow them is on the river, they would spot your car within a few kilometres, and then you might find yourself in that river, wearing concrete shoes!'

'General, at the KGB training centre, I was the top student in my class.'

'At the British Secret Service training centre this agent *taught* the class.'

'Yes General, I don't understand how we can be sure they are going to Barcelona, Sir?'

'We cannot be sure, they could have any one of several jobs, except for one piece of evidence…'

'Sir?' Agent Misezhnikov asked nervously.

'My big toe is itching, and my big toe rarely makes a mistake.' After a brief silence, the agent in France said. 'Yes General.'

The Master took another long drag on his cigarette, 'Now stop asking me stupid questions you college-idiot!'

He said viciously. Without waiting for a reply General Poluostrovich put the phone down and the cipher started to whiz and vibrate noisily, he whacked it with an ashtray, after a few seconds it fell back to sleep.

Agent Misezhnikov was annoyed with himself, this was only his third proper international mission since he qualified from the Soviet Secret Service training centre. General Poluostrovich was a legend at the academy, a chess master and a spymaster. They say that he worked on plans over a period of years, amalgamating the solutions for any new problem with his long-term plans for the Great Soviet.

'Everything he does...' said the lecturer at the military school. 'No matter how casual or unrelated it seems, is part of a complex and intricate plan so vast, that only he understands it.'

The young agent wanted to impress the great game player, except now he felt as though he had just asked too many thoughtless questions. This freelance assassin who looked so old, must be about the same age as the General, no wonder the master became angry when Yuri suggested the Englishman looked too elderly to be an effective killer.

Yuri decided that he must use his initiative and came up with his own plan. He decided to despatch a colleague to London over the next week. The lazy slob never did much work anyway, he could send him to the British agent's house to have a smooch around, he might get confirmation of their true destination and their itinerary.

Tomorrow morning, despite what the General said, he would use two agents and they would do the leapfrog following trick, using three cars. It was almost impossible for targets to realise they were being followed if you used the leap-frog, as each car kept overtaking and pulling over and used parallel routes. On the long roads of France Yuri's men would soon see where they were heading, and what could the little old couple do against three young, fit, highly trained agents?

He did have the list from the Count of the couple's favourite stopovers, but they could still be heading for Switzerland or Italy as they evidently had favourite places all over Europe, according to the contact in London. Unless she knew who the Count really is and was playing him like a violin?

General Fyodor Poluostrovich was the son of a wealthy Landowner who was murdered by his own serfs, born in the small town of Tazovskij in the Zapadno area of the Great Soviet Republic, northwest of Siberia. He became a navel officer during the second war, steering a submarine under the Karkoje More, the icy Kara Sea.

The advancing Germans had killed both of his younger brothers during the invasion of Volgograd. He swore on the day he heard the news, to make the irradiation of as many Germans and Nazis as possible his life's work, which wasn't very difficult these days for the senior controller of the KGB. He wasn't happy with the British and the Israeli's either. They'd made such a mess of Palestine that it would be years before the USSR would have a stronghold on the Eastern Mediterranean. Nevertheless, there was always his long-term plan that could eventually solve all of the geographical problems across the Soviet's borders; it was just a matter of time and patience.

The Russian General remembered the first time he met Captain Sam Trubshaw, it was a freezing day in Budapest. A Swiss-German banker turned out to be one of the scientists who were experimenting on prisoners in the Nazi concentration camps. He also had a side business of running stolen gold bullion into Switzerland.

In 1944 the Nazi amounted a fortune in a numbered Swiss account, saw the end coming, changed his nationality and suddenly became a legitimate private Swiss banker, leaving Germany before the allied forces arrived. The Soviets were the first to track him down after the war, and when he attended a financiers convention in Budapest, they saw their chance to get back some of the stolen gold from the prisoners of war, Russian banks, companies and private dealers.

Fyodor Poluostrovich had the millionaire hanging upside down, like a Serrano ham in a Barcelona delicatessen. He thought that he could *persuade* him to arrange the transfer of gold bullion back to Moscow. Unfortunately, the German was smarter than the General considered, and had two hidden Hungarian mercenaries watching his back. Sam Trubshaw had arrived a week earlier than everyone else and had noted how many protagonists there were, he had the factory under surveillance for several days before anyone else arrived. Just as Fyodor was going to be shot in the back of the head by the female Hungarian mercenary, Sam intervened.

The British got the gold and Fyodor Poluostrovich kept his life. Sam and the General have crossed swords several times since then, which has made the British assassin a challenge for Fyodor, who now has a file on Sam and his wife the size of a trunk. When Poluostrovich received intelligence last month about an Israeli agent going after Ilsa Klup, he thought that the British assassin might be going as well and started general surveillance.

The Russian knew that Sam was a gun for hire, except unlike most of the freelancers in this business; he had a conscience, and only hit the most deserving candidates. Looking at Ilsa Klup's dossier, she definitely came into that category. The General's men had wasted a fortnight having Sam's boat followed down the French coast and through the Canal de Midi. When he heard from a part-time soviet agent, Count Sergei Belevsky-Zhukovsky based in London, that the assassin and his accomplice wife were 'Holidaying' in France.

The Count managed to earn himself a tidy sum when he got a list of places the British agent usually stayed in, which is how they found him last night.

Unfortunately Fyodor doesn't know his adversary's next stop or the final destination, but he has people ubiquitously looking. At the last meeting of the top controllers in the KGB, Fyodor verbalised what many of his colleagues had thought for a long time.

'The biggest problem since the Cold War started, is that we're training agents on a mass production scale as fast as lead soldiers, and like all mass production in the USSR, the final product is usually rubbish!' The General made a call to his American double agent in Spain and told him to look out for the British assassins on the French-Spanish borders. He then made the same call to his agents in Italy and Switzerland.

Chapter 19
Christmas 1907

The Manor glistened beautifully that morning under a rare lucent light, melting the dusting of snow on the surrounding hills, trees, rooftops and across every stone detail of the house, painting white splashes on the perfect, chocolate box picture. Lady Margaret rushed around her home and garden giving orders to the magnified staff that had been expensively employed for the pre-Christmas party, checking the preparations that started two weeks earlier and were coming to fruition for the following day. Since her near-death experience hanging from the top of Tower Bridge, the lady of the house felt rejuvenated. She confessed to Megan, who she found to be a surprising soul mate and confident, that the suffragist cause, the marching, the shouting and even the tousling with police and ruffians, was a truly exhilarating and cathartic experience. With help from Megan and the Pankhurst family, she had already organised her first campaign meeting at Somerleyton Manor that shocked her husband and the conservative servants, particularly when they saw working-class people coming through the front door and sitting, yes, said Mr Jarvis, 'Sitting upstairs!'

When she and Peter inherited the house, their horse business was in its infancy and the magnificent Manor had suffered from long-term neglect and decay. Lady Margaret's father, Baronet Weymouth, came from the old school. He employed a vast number of staff that waited on the family minute by minute. The Baronet's cigar would be rolled and cut by his butler, slightly warmed and lit with a long taper and virtually placed in his mouth. None of the family made any effort to dress or undress themselves, more than slightly raising an arm or foot, and the only exercise they partook was riding, once the grooms had properly seated their posteriors. After the Baronet died, the heiress Lady Margaret and her husband Captain Peter Trubshaw started a refurbishment plan for the estate that took several years. To the staff's shock and horror, he sacked all of the farm workers and then gathered the depressed mob together, asking them if they wanted to rent the land, they'd worked all of their lives. Some of the young ambitious men jumped at the chance, however, many of the older peasants were afraid of the challenge. After all they'd been dominated by their 'Betters' all their lives and found it difficult to make any decisions, let alone take on the business of farming in a new and fast moving competitive world. Others said they had little or no money to eat, let alone rent land from the Lord, yet Peter said he would help them every step of the way. The Trubshaw's wrote a contract; so that the tenants could pay after they sold their crops and helped the new businessmen sell as a co-operative, using the system perfected in France. The General instructed his former sergeant and valet to organise the whole thing, like an army manoeuvre.

After two years, Peter received rents from ninety per cent of the tenant farmers, which amounted to double what the old Baronet had earned by owning and working all of the land himself.

Those who were still struggling were given more time. Peter kept the stables for himself and expanded them, as it became his passion and first business after leaving the army. Accordingly the remainder had been rented off. He kept a small staff including Bill, because Mrs Jarvis explained to Lady Margaret, that since his wife died, Bill would never be able to run any kind of business and just wanted a steady job. Once the horse business was in full flow with climbing profits, Peter started to become more extravagant; he completely refurbished the house, even the servant's quarters. He bought fine wines, paintings and antiques, yet he stayed rather prudent in regard to the costs of his comparatively small workforce. They didn't suffer as such by modern standards, even so in recent years due to the prosperity of Britain, the big estates and fine London houses engaged far more staff, many on larger salaries than Peter usually paid. This fact became a harsh reality for Lady Margaret when she attempted to employ twenty-five extra people for their extravagant Christmas party. The local people were already gainfully employed over the Christmas period at inns, hotels and the new style of factories that were popping-up around the towns and villages. In addition, enquiries to the employment agencies in the large towns of Kent and eventually in London produced polite, yet indignant replies that the offered salaries were just too low for quality staff, for the forthcoming New Year of 1908.

'Peter, I assume that you wish the Christmas party to be a success, do you not?' Margaret asked rhetorically, sitting behind her desk in the library wearing rarely seen lunettes on the end of her nose, a fortnight before the party.

'But of course Margaret my dear,' He replied apprehensively. 'I have ordered some of the finest champagne and wine from Fortnum's in Piccadilly, even caviar and our tenant farmers will bring the best produce in all of Kent!' He exclaimed proudly.

'That may be very well Peter, except we have no one to serve the food or help with the event as you have a reputation of being Kent's version of Mr Dickens's Scrooge!'

The master of the estate stood in shocked silence for a moment and then stuttered. 'Margaret, my dearest wife, pray do not tell me that I have forgotten to buy you a gift for one of our anniversaries or special dates. I have been so busy working on my new aircraft venture with Monsieur Blériot in France, I have not been concentrating on the one thing that is more important to me than anything in the world; my dear wife, and after we make the announcement, our new ward and heir Zamo.'

'Peter,' Margaret fumed. 'I am referring to our staff, Megan tells me that they are underpaid by at least ten per cent and that in this new modern world, they should have more privileges and such like.'

General Trubshaw felt stunned and sat in the chair opposite his business-savvy wife. 'Privileges! Margaret, I know that this young lady has befriended you and is politically completely off the scale like the Bolsheviks, but the staff have a wonderful home here, all they can eat. Observe Jarvis, he acts as though he owns the place most of the time.'

'Peter do you realise how embarrassed I became, when every domestic agency told me that we did not pay enough to get any staff, except kitchen maids!'

'What!' Peter jumped up in a rage and went over to the bell sash that he pulled so violently it came off the wall. He walked over to the drinks cupboard and threw a large Scotch into an antique Venetian crystal glass, swallowing the contents in one gulp.

'May I help you General?' Jarvis asked in his usual flippant tone.

'Yes Jarvis, would kindly ask all of the staff to assemble in the great hall please.'

'When you say *all* of the staff Sir, do you mean the household?'

'No Jarvis, everyone, stables and land workers, everyone who receives a salary from my estate.'

'Yes General, it might take a while Sir.'

'As soon as you can Jarvis and will you ask Master Zamo to come up to the library as well please.'

Jarvis looked somewhat concerned as he walked out of the room, seeing his master strutting in front of the fireplace and lighting a cigar. Margaret continued with her paperwork without looking up. A few minutes later Zamo came skidding into the room at speed and ran over to Margaret, who kissed him enthusiastically, as she had done daily since their death defying walk across the bridge together.

'Zamo, I want you to stand at my side when we speak to the staff...' Peter said putting a thumb in his Westcott. 'It will be a good business experience for you, so that you can understand how a country estate should be run.'

The young man, in an impeccable blue suit stood to attention next to the General, and Margaret looked up over the top of her spectacles without speaking.

After fifteen minutes, Jarvis returned to the door and announced that the staff had been assembled as required. Lady Margaret walked out first, followed by Peter proudly holding Zamo's hand. The staff stood nervously in the great hall, wondering if any of them were being reprimanded or worse, just before the Christmas holiday;

fired! Zamo waved enthusiastically to an awkward Bill, who'd never entered the hallway before, the little boy had become close to him, as he'd shared the man's cottage and dog for the last six months. Peter gave a throaty cough clearing his throat and stood bolt upright in front of his troops in military stance.

'Lady Margaret and I are very grateful to you all, for the hard work you have endured over this last year. As you know we are having a party at the Manor, which is the first occasion for celebration since Master Peter passed away.'

The staff moved uncomfortably from one foot to another and fidgeted with their hands anticipating the second part of the speech that usually started *'However, there will be difficult times ahead...'*

'Now that the refurbishment of the house is finished, there should be a little less work to be done...'

'Here it comes...' Thought Jarvis.

'And so at the suggestion of Lady Margaret, all of you will have two days off each month from now on and from the end of next month...' Margaret coughed loudly. 'Ah, the beginning of *last* month, I meant to say, you shall all receive an increase in you annual salary of fifteen per cent.'

Zamo looked up at Peter with a huge smile as the staff all broke ranks and shook hands and cuddled, then Florence started to cry, Margaret ambled over and comforted her and the household broke into laughter.

Jarvis walked over to Peter formally and said. 'Thank you General, I'm sure I speak on behalf of all the staff when I say that we are very grateful.' The staff broke into spontaneous applause.

'Thank you all, now we have a lot to do before our party, so please go back to work.' Peter took Margaret's arm and led her and Zamo into the library.

'Zamo come and sit here.' Margaret said tapping the couch. 'I looked for you this morning in your new room, but you weren't there, Jarvis tells me that you still sleep in the cottage with Bill.'

'And Shep.' He said with a huge grin.

'Zamo we have something very important to tell you.' Peter said. 'When I heard what happened at the bridge, I felt shocked, and I must admit rather angry.'

'I sorry Sir.'

'No-no Zamo, please understand, I was angry with Lady Margaret for putting herself and you in such danger, if you had not been there, I am quite certain that I would have lost her to the Thames. These articles in the newspapers, have painted a picture that is truly difficult for me to imagine.'

'It very *excitement*.' Zamo said, laughing at Margaret.

'Zamo, listen to me carefully, if you do not understand what I am about to say, I shall ask Miss Wodehouse to explain everything to you.'

Zamo looked intently at the General, who he had grown to respect and love, following their daily cross-country rides together, and the praise he heaped upon the boy constantly. Zamo had been brought up on a strict regime of Practise – Practise – Practise, with little praise or encouragement and even less love and affection; particularly from the one person he really hoped would care for him.

'Because you have a family abroad who we have not been able to contact, we cannot adopt you, as we would need your next of kin's permission, yet from our point of view you are everything that we could hope for in a son...'

Zamo sat on Margaret's settee taking her hand. 'Therefore I have asked our solicitor to draw up the necessary papers so that you will become our ward and heir...' Zamo looked confused. 'This means that you will inherit our estate when we die...' The young heir turned to Margaret concerned. 'Well if Margaret continues with her new cause that may be sooner than we all thought.'

'You die soon?' Zamo quizzed.

'No Zamo, hopefully not until you have grown up.' Margaret added, the General is I believe, joking with us.'

'There are two things that I would like to ask you, firstly, will you take our name?'

The young lad looked puzzled.

'You told Megan that your mother is called

Fratellini, is that so?'

'Yes, Jullietta Fratellini, the best flyer in the world!' He said with almost religious fervour.

'Zamo, we are not trying to replace your family, we just want to add you to ours.' Margaret said kindly.

'And it will be easier for you when you go to school, if you changed your name to something English, perhaps Harold or Arnold. Edwin Trubshaw, for example.' Peter said.

The young boy's face twisted into a mixture of confusion and disgust. 'I must change name to *Harold?*'

'What is your favourite name Zamo?' Margaret asked, sensing an obstacle they hadn't accounted for. After a lot of fidgeting and leg-swinging, he said. 'I be Shep!'

'Is that not the name of the gardener's dog?' Peter asked.

'Is half my dog, Bill say.'

'Zamo please tell me...' Margaret interrupted, 'I saw you waving to Bill in the hall, is he your best friend here?'

'Yes, he no have family, all dead, so have dog and me.'

Peter looked uncomfortable, he hadn't realised that giving away his fortune to this wonderful young man would be quite so difficult. Margaret walked thoughtfully to the newly reattached bell and pulled it gently, Peter poured two glasses of sherry and Jarvis appeared in the doorframe.

'Jarvis would you be kind enough to ask Bill to come here please.'

'I don't understand Milady?'

Peter walked over irritably, about to shout at the impertinent servant, when Margaret took her husband's arm and said gently, I would like to speak with Bill, the field hand, would you call him please Jarvis?'

'What, inside the drawing room Milady?'

'Please Jarvis.'

'Well, I'd better send a maid with a brush and mop as well.'

Jarvis's gratitude for the substantial rise had obviously faded, as quickly as steam from a kettle. A few minutes later, a very embarrassed farmhand, with a cloth cap turning nervously in his hands, self-consciously entered the drawing room, no more than a foot from the hallway.

Margaret smiled at the peon and said. 'Bill, do please come right in.'

Zamo jumped up taking the huge man's massive hand and pulled him into the centre of the room as though he were leading a reluctant mule.

The farmhand looked down and became nervous that a clump of mud on his right boot was going to fall onto the exquisite, Italian marble floor. Jarvis hovered in the doorway with a look of disapproval as though he was about to run in and drag the huge man back to the field.

'Thank you Jarvis that will be all...' Margaret said dismissively, then, she turned to the huge man. 'Bill, the General and I are very grateful that you have given up part of your cottage for this young man, we can see that he has taken to you and your dog.'

'Well, 'e's not a bad young'un Milady.' Bill said looking at the floor, with an emotion in his deep voice that went far beyond his words.

'May I ask your advice Bill?

Bill looked puzzled and embarrassed, standing in his dirty work clothes; not that he had anything else. He glanced at his surroundings, a fairy-tale palace of gold, glass, silk and marble, the titled Lady of the Manor sitting in clothes that cost more than his annual salary, even with the news of a substantial rise; was now asking his advice!

'If Zamo were to have an English name, what do you think it should be?'

Both Peter and Bill looked shocked by Margaret's question, Peter thought, 'Who has ever heard of the Lady of the Manor asking the ploughman, what her ward should be called!'

'Well Milady,' he said hesitantly with ever reddening cheeks, 'I...I don't knows that it's my place to make no suggestions.'

He bowed his head even lower, regretting the mud that had now dried sufficiently to fall from his boots onto the pristine Venetian stone. 'Sometimes though, of an evening, when the three of us is next to a good fire, I call him Sam-boy...' He said smiling at the child: a child who'd brought hope and fresh air into his solitary life, and a child he'd grown to love like a son over the last half year. Peter and Margaret noticed that Zamo looked up at the giant of a man with a respect that only comes with time and childish innocence, not prejudiced by class, education or money.

'Thank you Bill, that is most helpful.' Margaret said with a warm smile. Bill bent down and tried to collect the mud from the floor using his stubby fingers, Zamo scooted across the room, fell on his knees helping the field worker, with the muddy crumbs, and from the uncomfortableness of his palatial confinement.

After Jarvis closed the door and Florence had swept up, Margaret took both of Zamo's hands and said. 'Well, what do you think of the name; Sam Trubshaw?' Margaret asked.

Zamo looked introspective, his eyes stared over at the empty space previously occupied by his close friend Bill as though his essence had stayed behind.

'Actually...' Margaret continued, realising for the first time that the young boy had been influenced by all of the people he'd met in both societies. 'What about Sam – Bill Trubshaw? She added. His face glowed and then he asked enthusiastically.

'Can I be; Sam –Bill – Shep Trubshaw?'

The General coughed and gave Margaret a stare, which spoke a thousand words.

'Well now let me think, that is a very good name, although it may be a little too long for a young man, so we might have to just keep the two names, what do you think; Sam – Bill Trubshaw?'

Zamo's face lit up like a dry bonfire and he skipped around the room chanting:

'Sam-Bill-Trubshaw-Sam-Bill-Trubshaw'. They all laughed together, the adults realising that taking Sam into their lives would be a lengthy and complicated process, which may take several years to complete.

On the day of the party, Margaret hummed around the house and gardens like a bee in a summer field of lavender, checking and fussing over the extravagant decorations gracing every inch of the Manor. The central table, stretching over thirty feet long, had been adorned with the most magnificent silver candelabras. As well as the finest crockery and Georgian silver cutlery that could be found in Europe, in the years leading up to Christmas 1907.

In the centre of the table, a Thomas Germain, French, silver tureen, which turned out to be the most expensive table piece in England.

When it was time for her to dress, Margaret excitedly examined her beautiful oyster pink gown, using extravagant fabric ordered from France and made by London's most famous dressmaker, recommended by Megan Wodehouse.

Lady Brooke, in London's Bond Street. After all, if Princess May of Teck, thereafter called Queen Mary, had her trousseau embroidered by Lady Brooke, she must be the best. She became the perfect dressmaker for Lady Margaret of Somerleyton Manor, being fashionably housed in Bond Street. Furthermore, she was the perfect dressmaker for Margaret Trubshaw, Britain's second most famous Suffragist, due to the fact that Lady Brooke of Eaton, only employed young, working-class women as her seamstresses. As she wanted to help assuage the misery of some poverty stricken village girls, who couldn't find respectable work with a reasonably salary, outside of service or a despicable life in gloomy factories. Therefore, this mixed kudos in the worlds of royalty, fashion and charity couldn't have fitted more adequately.

At six o'clock in the still, cool Kentish air, with hundreds of flickering lanterns running from the front gates up to the Manor's steps, four uniformed footmen ushered the glamorous society into the magnificently decorated mansion. A twelve-piece orchestra filled the air with Wolfgang Amadeus Mozart's piano concertos.

The newly renamed Sam Trubshaw in his posh black velvet outfit, couldn't remember when he felt more excited, peering down onto the great hall through the banisters at the most beautiful ballroom he had ever seen, not that he had ever seen any kind of room except his mother's little caravan before he arrived at the Manor. The Christmas tree glistened and nearly touched the ceiling and three thousand candles flooded the great hall with a golden tungsten glow.

Jarvis took on the role as Master of Ceremonies, announcing the guests as they arrived in finery unseen outside of the royal courts.

'Monsieur and Madam Louis Blériot, The Duke and Duchess of Devonshire, Viscount and Lady Rothermere, Dr John Gale and Miss Megan Wodehouse, Lady Randolph Churchill, Baronet and Lady de Bathe, Captain-Pilot Michael Renshaw and Mrs Pearl Renshaw, The Countess of Warwick, Mr and Mrs Patrick Campbell, Mr Hubert Latham, Mrs Emmeline Pankhurst and Miss Christabel Pankhurst...'

Jarvis started to lose his voice as the house filled up with the fashionable society the Trubshaws had met over the years, the new friends and colleagues Lady Margaret had acquired from the suffragist movement, the business associates from Peter's world of horses and his new venture into the airplane business.

In addition, a group of people who were invited at the request of Mrs Emmeline Pankhurst, who never missed an opportunity to reach people in powerful positions who could further her cause.

Peter looked around the huge hall and said to the Vicar. 'You know Lionel, I have no idea who most of these people are!'

Vicar Smallbouys spoke sympathetically. 'I know how you feel Peter, most of my parishioners look the same to me, I only remember those who have become friends such as yourself and a few who have helped with the church bell-tower fund.' He said resignedly, emptying another glass of champagne.

Florence approached the two men and waited for an appropriate moment to interrupt. 'Excuse me Sir,' she said with a curtsy, 'Lady Margaret says that she's ready for you upstairs.'

'Thank you Florence, will you ask the musicians to stop playing when we come out onto the balcony in about

239

five minutes please.' The master of the house said, also asking the Vicar to excuse him. Peter climbed the circular staircase, walked along the upper balcony and knocked on Margaret's door.

'Is that you darling?' She called out. Before Peter could answer, Maisy opened the door and Peter looked aghast.

'Margaret, you look, well, absolutely sublime.' He said sincerely.

His wife was delighted; she felt spiritually uplifted by her husband's admiration and his obvious love for her. Yes, she knew that she was thought to be beautiful when young, but now the mature, attractive woman experienced a new confidence she'd never known before. The previous two and a half years following her son's death, removed joy from her life, she was completely drained by the terrible period that she believed that she'd never recover from.

Certainly, Margaret had slowly become stronger as time healed her broken heart, nevertheless after the suffragist's meeting and her bonding with little Sam, for the first time she had a new optimism for the future, including an heir to perpetuate the family name. Lady Margaret Henrietta Trubshaw examined the image in her full-length mirror and saw a beautiful, confident and modern woman on the threshold of 1908.

Peter Trubshaw, Lady Margaret and Sam William Trubshaw as he would be known for the rest of his life, appeared on the balcony overlooking their vast number of guests, which prompted the orchestra to silence their instruments, turning the heads of the gathering to the top of the gently sweeping staircase.

'My Lords, Ladies and gentlemen, Margaret and I would just like to say how grateful we are to you all, for coming here this evening, after a gap of over four years due to our tragic loss. We wish to celebrate Christmas with you all, and announce a new business venture...' Peter continued, gesturing to his new partner. 'May I present the rather famous aviator, Monsieur Louis Blériot...' The guests clapped enthusiastically for the pioneer who proudly gave a bow to the congenial British society. 'Furthermore, I am supporting...' He called loudly to interrupt the clapping. 'His attempt to cross the English Channel in his winged aircraft, which we hope to manufacture together in large numbers.' The gathering swooned and clapped at the extraordinary idea. 'Thank you, thank you, I am sure that many of you will deem this feat to be an unobtainable and foolish fantasy, but who among you would have believed a few months ago, that Lady Margaret would have walked across the top of Tower Bridge!'

The gathering stood enthusiastically, applauding and cheering, until Margaret blushed, holding up her gloved hands like a grateful politician. Peter said:

'Thank you, we are most grateful for your support, particularly to our solicitor and for those of you who convinced the authorities that Margaret just strolled out and became lost.' Again, the glittering crowd laughed delightedly and clapped still more.

Peter held up his hands and then continued. 'This now brings Lady Margaret and I to the final and most important announcement we have. You are all aware that my dear wife was not alone on Tower Bridge during that terrible night, and if it were not for this young man...' Peter put his arm around his new ward, tears welling in his eyes. 'We may not have Margaret with us today...' Everyone clapped the beaming little boy sincerely. 'Therefore, it is with enormous pleasure that we officially announce, that Sam William Trubshaw will be our heir and ward!'

The three Trubshaws walked down the stairs and joined their guests who congratulated the new family heartedly. It would be an experience that Peter and Margaret remembered with a warmth and friendship for the rest of their short lives.

Chapter 20
Charlotte's Mini, April 1964

Kings Road started unusually busy that morning; it inchoately developed into one of those rare spring days when the high temperature warmed up London, without the misnomers of weather, called March winds or April showers that often hit Britain anytime between January and August.

The South East's residents and a sprinkling of tourists didn't need any more encouragement, shirtsleeves were rolled up, mini-skirts were pulled up and the usual shopping frenzy started up.

Justin met his friend Alex from Sassoon's outside Sloane Square tube station, because Alex lived with three friends in south London's Wandsworth, while Justin came in from his parent's house in North London. The boys smooched around the tree covered square. Alex asked the price of some flowers at the little stall, scoffing at the elevated Chelsea price, and they crossed the busy road walking past the Peter Jones Department store, when Justin said.

'I've got to get some cigarettes Alex; Charlotte won't have any as usual and even though she doesn't like mine, they aren't trendy enough, she'll polish off the whole packet in a couple of hours.'

'You can get some on the next corner, but I've read recently that they're bad for you!'

'Well they're certainly bad for my wallet, but it's groovy to smoke Alex, you should try it.'

'No, I don't mind the occasional joint, but I don't want to get cancer before I get stoned!' Both boys laughed.

Justin picked up the Evening News; some chewing gum and his cigarettes, he glanced at the headlines.

Beatles Invade America

'Wow these guys must be making a fortune, that's what we should've done Alex instead of being hairdressers.'

'I didn't know you could sing, Justin dear.'

'I can't, nor play the guitar, but neither can Adam Faith and he still gets on the TV. I've seen him in Kings Road, he's always with a different girl, good looking ones too!'

'Well he is gorgeous, kind of short, but I wouldn't say no.' Alex giggled.

The Hairdressers were checking out the new footwear collections in the stylish street that seemed to have more shoe shops than anywhere else in London. The new boutique called Ravel became packed; it had started selling inexpensive Spanish and Italian shoes for men, for four pounds, nineteen shillings and sixpence, in fashionable styles never seen before away from the Mediterranean. The trendy young men stopped to look in the window when Justin caught a glimpse of their reflections. He never really noticed how Gay-looking Alex appeared.

In the salon, he just blended in, and camping it up was fashionable in the world of hairdressing, make-up, models and photography. Justin wasn't against anyone being Gay, although he didn't want anyone to think he was. The cockney lad started to examine his own cool style, that he thought looked great when he went out with his leggy blonde girlfriend, but his appearance seemed somewhat exaggerated, now that he accompanied Alex; who wore Cuban heeled Chelsea boots, skin-tight hipsters and a flower-power shirt. After all you had to be careful, Justin considered, it's illegal to be Gay in Britain.

'What time is it Alex?'

'Well darling, the Rolex that Mrs Granger gave me for my birthday…' He said, lifting his wrist like Margot Fontaine in Swan Lake. 'Says one ruby past twelve!'

'I don't know how you get all these straight women to buy you so many presents.' Justin complained. 'Anyway I must go, Princess Charlotte promised she would be ready by eleven, so I might have a chance of her being dressed by now, I'll see you on Monday!' Alex blew him an exaggerated kiss, because the camp boy knew that the Pink World embarrassed his straight friend.

Justin sauntered along the high street, looking in the shops and at the stylish people, when two beautiful girls in long floral dresses with dirty bare feet, came up to him. One of them kissed his cheek, gave him a flower saying 'Peace and love man.' The hairdresser felt taken aback at first and then realised how much he liked it. He turned around to speak to the hippy girls; however, they were already kissing their next convert. Justin decided that he had to make some money and move to Chelsea, knowing that would never happen in Gants Hill. Somehow the Sixties hadn't travelled that far north yet.

The young hairdresser looked up at the enormous cow's head that sat in between Charlotte's windows, she seemed to be transfixed today on a house in Markham Square, her terracotta eyes in a glazed stare. He crossed the road and entered the street door.

Charlotte heard the doorbell and checked her Cartier watch.

'Could you hang on a moment?' The model said into the new, two-tone green phone. 'There's someone at the door.'

She tiptoed over her clothes that had now flowed from her bedroom and bathroom onto the living room floor like a fabric tidal wave.

'You're early Justin - I'm on the phone.' She said, giving her boyfriend a peck on his lips, having opened the door a few inches to miss her clothes. Radio Caroline blared out the Rolling Stones from a crackly transistor with a wire coat-hanger aerial and Justin's girlfriend made a hop, skip and jump, back to the handset.

'I'm not early Charlotte you're late as usual...' Justin hesitated at the door while he looked around for someway of entering the flat without treading on Charlotte's floating, horizontal wardrobe. 'Oh my God! What's happened here, have you been robbed?' He laughed sarcastically.

Charlotte picked up the handset and shushed Justin by putting a perfectly manicured index finger over her pursed lips.

The hairdresser noticed several tiny stubs in an ashtray that looked and smelt of marihuana.

'Yes that's right it's a black, Mini Cooper, Works-

Special. Yes - yes, that's right… okay I'll hang on,'

'What are you doing?' Justin whispered with a frown.

'Shush! I'm trying to get insurance dopy, have you got a cigarette?'

'But you haven't got a Mini Cooper!'

'Hello, yes I've a pen. What! Are you nuts? I don't want to *buy* the car! I just want to insure it for a month! Yes - yes, well all right then, a year. I know, but I won't be driving it at a hundred and thirty miles per hour, will I? Yes - yes, but listen to me will you? All I do is drive from Kings Road, over to Bond Street to see Gavin. What? Gavin, yes… And then I go to Kensington High Street, and occasionally I go to Ham. Excuse me? No Ham silly, in south London, well listen, you can't go fast because there's too much traffic. I won't be driving it for a year - What? Well it's in my grandparent's name! I'm not that young, you should see the other girls in my agency… A model agency… No thank you, I have a boyfriend… I'm a very good driver… No alright, thank you very much, for nothing!'

Charlotte sulked, like an eight-year-old girl who'd just had her ice cream taken away.

She banged the receiver on the base three times in a temper and dived on the virtually invisible sofa, which also had a blanket of clothes and shoes.

Justin shuffled over to the pile of clothes trying to keep his shoes away from the garments, tossed a few dresses to one side and created a small clothes-free circle to sit on.

'What are you up to Charlotte?' He asked, putting a lit cigarette in her mouth.

'Nothing.' She said in a bratty mood, puffing nicotine through pursed lips.

'Are we going to the Stock Pot or not?' He asked, starting to get annoyed with yet another of the young model's tantrums.

Charlotte, sitting in a black lacy bra with matching knickers; had cotton wool stuffed between all of her toes, large metal rollers in her hair, and white hair-remover on her legs; resembling long, schoolgirl's socks without feet. Justin thought the whole effect looked very sexy, he started to glance around the flat for an empty patch where he could make love to her.

'We'll have to get a taxi.' She complained.

'What are you talking about it's only at the end of Kings Road, we can walk it in...' Justin stopped speaking suddenly and looked at his girlfriend. 'Charlotte? Now just tell me slowly, where's your car and why are you trying to get insurance for a month on some hot Mini?'

'Justin, I promise you...' She said leaning towards him blowing smoke in his face. 'Those fascists bastards have a campaign against me.'

'Parking wardens?' He asked sighing. 'You got another ticket, is that what all this is about?'

Charlotte picked up an emery board, pulled her right knee up to her chin and half-heartedly began to file one of her freshly painted toenails; Justin started to think sexy thoughts again and decided to throw the rest of the clothes off the sofa.

'Did you know that policemen are allowed to break into your car, get in the driver's seat and just drive it away, to some car-pound under Hyde Park?'

'The police have taken your car?'

'No Justin, *stolen* my car and won't give it back!'

'Listen,' He said exasperated. 'I've got a great plan, we'll have a quick shag, which always put you in a good mood, then we'll go to the Stock Pot for a slow, cheap lunch, with a *whole* bottle of wine, after that we'll get a cab over to Hyde park, give them a couple of quid and the problem's solved! So, go and rinse that stuff off your legs...'

'I've already been there Justin...' She said, lengthening his name. 'And they found all of the tickets in the car and now they want three hundred and twenty eight pounds, ten shillings and sixpence, but the car's only worth a hundred and fifty quid!'

'Wow! That's a problem.'

'It's worse than that.' She said, starting to cry.

'Come here.' He replied gently, pulling her close, still thinking about the sex.

'What could be so bad?'

246

The couple sat on the settee and cuddled, Justin trying to avoid the creamy legs on his new trousers, he put his left hand on her back and expertly unclipped her bra with his finger tips.

'I've got Ya-Ya's car and I had a little accident.'

'Your grandmother lent you that souped up Mini?' He said surprised.

'Well - not really; my grandparents are on holiday in France and when I lost my car, I thought I'd borrow theirs, and well, it's so fast! I barely touched the throttle and the whole thing leapt up in the air, then this stupid bus took up the whole road in front of Selfridges and the Mini just went into the back of it! I mean it's not like a car, it's more like a wild animal with a mind of its own.'

'So, what happened, have you told your grandparents?'

Charlotte closed the clip on her bra, looking into Justin's eyes.

'Don't be so stupid Justin, they don't know I have it!'

'Charlotte! Not even you would take someone's car without asking them?'

Charlotte started doing the sexy thing with her lips and began painting her toenails again, this time even Justin's libido started to fade.

'Where's your grandmother's car now?'

'Well the RAC were quite nice and towed the car to some specialist garage, a cockney chappie rang me the other day and said they've never seen anything like this Mini.

Evidently it's of 'rally standard' whatever that means, with loads of gadgets and buttons they couldn't find a use for, and when I told them it belonged to my granny, they all fell about laughing, asking me if I were in the police.'

'So what did you tell them to do with the car?'

They said it's going to cost a fortune to repair and that's why I've been trying to get insurance when you came in.' She mumbled tearfully.

'Charlotte! You're meant to get the insurance *before* you have an accident!'

'I know Justin!' She pouted angrily, searching for something to wear from the floor.

'How did you get the keys anyway?'

'Ya-Ya left a spare set here last time she stayed...' She said still upset. 'So that I could feed the meter, because Sam had picked her up in his car, then when she came back to get them, I must have been out shopping.'

'So you kept the keys?' Justin asked. 'You must tell them Charlotte, or things will only get worse, you said they're really nice, they might be fairly upset at first, but it will be alright.'

'Well now the garage said that some Italian people were looking at the car and asked for my address.'

'Did you bump into anyone else?'

'No, I'm not stupid Justin, besides I only drove it for a few days, I thought my teeth were going to drop out, all that luxury and electric buttons, but they didn't put any suspension on it.'

'So, what are you going to do now?'

'Well you know that Russian Count, Sergei?'

'The other guy you crashed into with the monster chauffeur?'

'Yes, but he's turned out to be really nice and found me a job in Barcelona for £1,500, for just three days work! So if I do that, I can pay for everything and my grandparents won't ever find out what happened.'

'You know that old git fancies you, don't you?' Justin said jealously.

'Yes I know,' she smiled vainly. 'But he's just like a grandfather, he wouldn't harm a fly!'

'I don't trust him, before you know it, he'll be there in Barcelona with an adjoining room in your hotel.'

'Don't be silly he's not even going there...' She lied. 'He just arranged for me to do this art and jewellery show at some posh restaurant and then I'll be back home...'

'And he's staying in London?'

'I think he's going on holiday to France, because he kept asking me for a list of hotels where granddaddy stays, as he didn't know the best places.'

'Come on then, let's go to the restaurant.'

'All right, but I must phone Gavin's in case I've got any castings.'

'It's Saturday and I thought you didn't have to phone-in until the evening?'

'I don't - but I forgot last night, I thought it's Friday, I'll ring Lucy and see if she's got anything.'

'Is she still selling drugs as well as modelling?' Justin asked angrily.

Charlotte picked up the phone and started to bang the handset on the table.

'Now what's wrong?' Justin asked exasperated.

'The bloody phone's been, ah, cu...doesn't work!'

'Charlotte you are the most exhausting girl I've ever met, haven't you paid the bill?'

'It's not that Justin, the red notice only came in a few weeks ago, there's something wrong with the stupid thing, it keeps clicking all of the time, before and after I use it.'

'Ok, so your car's in the pound with a million parking tickets, you've stolen your granny's Mini and crashed it, the phone's been cut off and you can't remember to phone your agent in the evening to see if you have any jobs.'

'Justin stop that...' She hollered, leaning forward. 'You're twisting the story to make it sound like everything's *my* fault!'

'Listen to me...' Justin shouted back angrily. 'I'm going down to the Chelsea Potter for a drink, why don't you come down when you're ready, and Charlotte, try and tidy up a bit, and I see your back on the dope!'

As Justin closed the door, he heard a glass vase crash against the wall and Charlotte scream a muffled barrage of abuse.

Chapter 21
France, April 1964

Yuri Misezhnikov loved his job as a KGB agent for the Soviet Union; it had been his dream ever since his youth. He was brought up in a military orphanage in Kaliningrad with hundreds of Russian and German children from East Prussia, who'd, lost their parents in World War II. He was eight years old when he arrived at the bleak home, wearing a worn-out set of clothes, carrying a small, brown paper bag tied with string; containing a second shirt, an old school tie from his first wonderful school. Where he was enrolled by his beloved parents, in a crisp new uniform at the age of four, a silver pocket watch that was the only souvenir left from his father's battlefield grave and three slightly frayed photographs of his parents, in faded sepia. He was beaten severely on the first day he arrived at the government institution by the self appointed, thirteen year old, head-boy, called Valdas Nazarbayev, with help from his three comrades, who Yuri was told, controlled the orphanage. The new boy lost all of his meagre possessions and his boots within minutes of entering the cold brick dormitory, and cried himself to sleep, without supper. Because the warden said he had arrived too late, following his fifteen-hour train journey. It was nearly six months before he found any proper footwear, albeit two sizes too big, from one of the deceased children, who died of pneumonia in his sleep.

Over the following ten years, Yuri learnt the art of survival under the military regime, in a place where a small piece of stale bread was worth fighting for, even if it meant losing your life, as many children did. These deaths were always documented as accidents during *'Work and educational field trips'*. He robed dead children, pounced on anyone too weak to grip on to their possessions and when food became scarce, the residents looked for dead rats to cook over a secret fire.

By the time Yuri was fifteen he became the unofficial head-boy, following the fatal fall of the vicious Valdes Nazarbayev, who dived from the top of a scaffold five floors up, where he was supervising a group of inmates painting the top floor windows; including Yuri and his four friends. On the day the commanding officer and head administrator read the report of the accident, he noted that Valdes was not wearing any boots and that the little cupboard next to his bunk was completely empty. When Yuri reached the age of eighteen, he applied to join the army where he flourished, after all, it wasn't very different to the institution where he'd grown up and he had the comradeship of his four friends who accompanied him from the orphanage. They soon took over the army barracks just as they had the dormitory.

One year after Yuri's training was finished, the commanding officer of the camp, proposed the three best cadets for a special endurance course to qualify for the KGB. The elite soldiers were told that despite the fact that all three were officially put forward, the KGB had arranged a field test, to see which one would be promoted.

They were taken to a remote area of Kazakhstan and thrown into a survival course that took them through deep water, over high cliffs and in dangerous underground tunnels. On the first day one applicant had a terrible accident underwater, when his tank inexplicably ran out of air and he drowned. Yuri's own climbing rope inadvertently strangled the other applicant, when he lost his footing on a steep climb, only a few metres from the top of the mountain; they'd been ascending all morning. The young man came from a mountainous area of the Soviet and looked so capable, but as Yuri said, 'Accidents can happen to anyone.' Therefore, as corporal Misezhnikov was the only survivor from his group, he was sent to the KGB for further training. The regime at the new camp was Yuri's greatest challenge; the best soldiers from the national army and navy units were proposed to be part of the privileged force. Therefore, despite Yuri's expertise and experiences in the military orphanage, he found it very difficult to keep up with the finest recruits.

Luckily, for Yuri, two out of his four closet friends from the orphanage, also finished their assignments and reached the same level. Over a period of several months, many of the competitors went through a previously unknown number of accidents, and the commanding officer had to report that they'd lost five of their top men, the first phase of six months. At the end of the final course, the commanding officer was pleased to honour the six top candidates for the Secret Service and the star trainee who received special commendation, putting him at the top of his class was, Yuri Misezhnikov. Three years later following many accidents and two suicides, Yuri was delighted that he had been commissioned the youngest Major in the service.

The Russian now sat outside the Café de la Post in the beautiful village of Chantilly with his two colleagues from the Paris embassy, a few steps from their three parked cars.

Vladimir Mordashov wore his usual face of resignation and apprehensiveness and lit another cigarette from the previous one that he'd sucked down to the width of his nicotine-stained index finger and thumb.

The chain-smoker loved the French cigarettes Gauloise. They were smoother than his KGB official issue CCCP's, and went well with the small black coffees laced with Vodka that he'd been knocking back for the last four hours. Vladimir usually liked stakeouts, they gave him a chance to relax, dose off or read spy novels. He was less keen on following people; sometimes you drove for miles and ended up watching the subject eating luxurious meals while he managed with a dry sandwich and a cold drink in a freezing car. Still he thought, at least this posting to France was better than slinking around Stalingrad with snow up to your knees.

The food was delicious, not only in French restaurants, but also in Vladimir's own kitchen, where as a gourmand he ate well and often. The amateur chef studied every cookbook he could find and loved to sit down to one of his own creations that he gorged for hours on end. His speciality was the soufflé, washed down with a wonderful bottle of Meursault, at least seven years old.

He was lucky because he'd been blackmailing a Czechoslovakian wine merchant who had false papers, in the shady area of Paris near the Basilique du Sacré-Cœur, on the rue des Abbesses. Vlad could therefore drink a quality of wine that his meagre salary wouldn't have normally afforded him. Now, he reflected, he was searching for a good pâtissièr with a similar problem. Despite his good taste in food his appearance was meretricious. Mikhail Kalinin had been with Yuri from the first day he arrived at the army camp. Yuri was the perfect leader for Mikhail, completely unscrupulous, always planning, and extremely ambitious. Private Kalinin had helped Yuri eliminate some of the opposition, until they both qualified with full marks and were posted to France. The bureaux had a large number of agents in Europe and there were eight people between them and the chief of French operations, therefore they should be able to work their way up, they schemed, one way or another. Mikhail and Yuri didn't like Vladimir, he was old school, cheap clothes, bad breath that could wipe out insects that flew too near his mouth, and he always did the minimum. He stank of a mixture of cheap vodka and those disgusting French cigarettes that smelt like old socks burning.

Vladimir had used the service to his own advantage, there was a rumour going around the embassy staff that he was responsible for the murder of three prostitutes who worked the Montmartre area of Paris. Vlad' always said he'd never been in that cheap part of town.

Luckily, they would be in three different cars for this leapfrog operation and so Mikhail wouldn't have to put up with his coughing and wheezing much longer. Yuri urgently tapped the table interrupting his thoughts.

'Here they come, heads down comrades.' Yuri commanded.

Sam and Phaedra cruised slowly in their long, silver Bristol toward the château, once they had passed the bend in the road, the three Russians jumped up and rushed over to their cars. Vladimir Mordashov, had a dark brown BMW 700, Berline two-door, purchased in 1959. It had done over a hundred thousand kilometres and was given to his unit after the ambassador's wife in Paris changed it for a new Mercedes. The little German car was messy inside with a torn front seat, a badly stained roof, and an ashtray so full, that the butts had sprawled onto the floor. As the old vehicle pulled away it made flatulent noises from the exhaust. Mordashov liked the little car and its radio, despite its shortcomings, it was real luxury in comparison to the Lada that he had before. Mikhail possessed a spotlessly clean, red, 1956 Fiat 1100 TV, it was a sporty salon that boasted a top speed of eighty three miles per hour, which was considerably faster than the average European car. Yuri drove a black, Citroën Light 15, two door coupe, the three speed gearbox and sports tuning made him the fastest of the three Russians and could reach over ninety miles per hour.

Sam and Phaedra made their way towards the A1 to Paris, past the château and through the Chantilly forest, after a few minutes Sam turned to his wife and said.

'You know Phaedra, I'm not certain, but last night as we left the dinning room, I thought that I saw a flash of the full moon over the river.'

'Sam darling, that's why I love you so much, you're so romantic when we go on trips.'

Sam looked at his wife with a love that he knew was as much alive in him today as it was twenty years ago.

'No darling, the moon was on the other side of the hotel, it looked more like a reflection from binoculars.'

'I know you said we need to be really careful on this job and you are the best there is, but nobody could've followed us last night, there weren't any cars on the road for an hour before we stopped, we didn't have a reservation at the hotel and we didn't tell anyone where we were going to stay.' Phaedra said.

'It could have been a reflection from a boat or a night fisherman with glasses, surely we can relax until we get into Spain?'

'I'm sure you're right darling, nevertheless, when we get on the main road we'll stop and check for small aircraft and start the avoidance procedures, just in case.' Sam said casually.

'You're the boss; I'll get my pad and start taking down car numbers and descriptions until the next stop.'

'Where are we having lunch? I can't believe it, after all of those croissants this morning I'm still hungry.' Sam laughed. There were a few steep hills from Chantilly towards the A1 to Paris and so Sam used the massive power of the Bristol to accelerate up the hills, pushing the monster to over a hundred and twenty miles per hour. When they got to the top of the high ground, they'd pull off to see who would pass, after a few minutes the couple would drive slowly, annoying the French behind them and build up a queue, if there was anyone left in front or behind after thirty minutes, they would go to step two and see if they could lose the car by going back a few miles and start again.

At the top of the first hill they'd overtaken and lost everyone, subsequently they saw a little Peugeot van selling crêpes at the side of the road, and so Sam came to a screeching halt, jumped out of the car and ordered two of the delicious pancakes, while Phaedra listed all of the cars that had past. They greedily scoffed their snack and waited to see if anyone doubled back. After ten minutes, they drove off slowly and kept a close eye on the traffic.

'I don't believe it! You were right, we're being leapfrogged!' Phaedra said sceptically as the red Fiat zoomed past them.

'I wonder where they picked us up, I didn't see anyone after Calais, Patrick doesn't know when we're arriving in Barcelona or our route. I only gave him some call-box numbers in Lyon, where we could turn off for Italy, Switzerland or Spain. You didn't say anything to Cathy, did you darling?'

'Of course not, and she knows better than to ask.'

'It could be one of the big boys with a semi-permanent tail on us, someone with an interest in the hit, who are just wondering if we are going down to join the party.' Sam speculated.

'Who do you mean, your old friend in Moscow?'

'Possibly, yet the leapfrog is too obvious for him, unless the car is being tracked with the new mini-radar systems, maybe the Israelis, the file said they want this hit.'

'What shall we do next Sam?'

He grabbed her pad and wrote in large writing.

'Just in case we're bugged we won't speak until we can scan the car, there's a hotel with an underground garage about an hour from here. Firstly, we'll get rid of these chaps, we don't need to panic yet and we're still a long way from the hit. Don't worry, love you.'

Phaedra wrote down the details of the three cars using the leapfrog and showed the list to Sam, they drove off slowly. Sam calculated that the fastest car was the Citroën, the Bristol could easily out-run it particularly up hill, and so he thought that he could isolate the other two cars. The British agent started to increase his speed as they hit the fast A1 to Paris. After five miles Phaedra wrapped her binoculars in a t-shirt and peered out of the back window, as planned there was no sign of the Fiat or BMW, while they could still see the Citroën trying to keep up about ten cars behind.

'Okay darling read this.'

'We have a small road about one mile ahead, I'll put on some speed and we'll pull off and throw out the tyre busters, get ready.'

Sam accelerated enough to give himself a comfortable distance to stop ahead; nevertheless, he still wanted the tail to see him turn off. The experienced agent made a fast turn, smashed the throttle once he reached the quiet side-road and at the first sharp bend came to a screeching halt. Phaedra jumped out of the car and threw spiky stars across the lane and they both ran into the bushes further up and waited behind a substantial tree with pistols in hand. Within a few minutes Yuri came tearing around the sharp bend in the Citroën and burst three of his tyres in the trap, pouring him into a whirlpool of dust and grass, finally crashing into an irrigation ditch at the side of the narrow lane, his forehead was soon bleeding over the gate-change gear stick on the dashboard.

Sam and Phaedra acted quickly and opened Yuri's front doors. While Phaedra searched the Russian, Sam kept a pistol against his unconscious head. Yuri had nothing on him except a few thousand francs, which was to be expected, although, Phaedra soon found two different sets of identities cached under his leather seat, in a secreted wallet. She then found a pistol and a short nosed automatic. Phaedra went around the car, pulled out the back seats where she discovered a brown plastic folder with documents, and photos of herself with Sam. She looked in the boot and took the spare tyre, the Jack, and the other possessions with her. Yuri started to come around and so the Trubshaws ran back to their car and zoomed off at speed.

A few miles along the road, Phaedra wiped the guns to remove any prints and tossed them into a plastic bag. After twenty minutes, they pulled into a small town that Sam knew well and went into an underground garage. Sam took a scanner from his boot and thoroughly inspected the car, their belongings and each other.

'Nothing!' He said to his wife after ten minutes, 'It was all a little amateurish, I wonder what's going on?' He said puzzled. 'Come on then, let's go.

The British agents slid into the Bristol and took a back road towards Paris; Phaedra unfolded the Russian's papers and read aloud.

'So we have a young man called Yuri Misezhnikov, a Major in the KGB, based in Paris, twenty seven years old, must be one of Fyodor's boys unless there's been a change at the top.'

'I can't believe Fyodor would let him set up a leapfrog on us, he's blown his cover and we're nowhere near the mission!' Sam said in amazement.

'Do you think he's a double, or working freelance?'

'Not under Fyodor, he'd have to be suicidal, no I think he's a young lad recently out of their training school and just making the usual mistakes.'

'Yes that's possible, nevertheless he's a Major, how did he get so high up the ranks, at a young age and be dumb?' Phaedra asked analytically.

'There are two ways, one he's a relative of someone in the bureaux, or he's a successful viscous killer who gets the job done.'

'And so my clever husband, you did see binoculars last night, it might be busy when we get down there, we should have several contingency plans or we could be bumping into assassins on every street corner!'

'I once did a job in Cairo, nasty guy, four different people hit him at the same time, I got there early…'

'As you usually do.'

'Yes, and it was worth it, because I did nothing except keep surveillance on all of the protagonists and I was still paid!'

'You know that we'll have to retire one day Sam.'

'I know, perhaps it's better to keep going until we stop being good at it.'

'I might have to get you one of those walking frames and ask our specialist mechanics to fit it with a couple of jets!' Phaedra laughed, putting her head on Sam's shoulder.

Yuri came around after a few minutes with a nasty gash on his forehead, when he got out of the car he noticed the tyre busters and what was left of his slashed rubber. He picked up one of the little spiky stars and said fervently. 'English bastards!' Suddenly he dashed to the secret pouch beneath his seat, his hand searched the pocket half a dozen times faster and faster, in panic he looked under the carpets, rushed around the car and rummaged everywhere inside the cabin. Then he checked his secret cache behind the rear bench-seat a place he kept his guns; nothing. 'English Bastards!' He screamed aloud. Half an hour past before a reluctant farmer gave him a ride to the nearest village, where he bought three new tyres at an elevated price. He thought. *If I had my gun, I'd shoot this thieving French pig for ripping me off.* He asked for a lift back to his car, but the malevolent garage owner said he was too busy.

'How am I meant to get back to my car?' He asked angrily in broken French. Pierre just shrugged his shoulders and walked back into his office. Yuri felt his leg and his knife was still strapped to his calf, he palmed it and walked casually into the scruffy cabin that served as Pierre's office. The mechanic didn't look up until Yuri had him by the throat. 'I said, how am I meant to get back to my car?' He now had Pierre's attention and with a feeble smile, he said. 'Monsieur, my brother will take you, he has a taxi service across the street.'

'Call him now!'

'Oui Monsieur, tout suite!'

Fifteen minutes later, Yuri arrived at his car, humped the new tyres out of the boot and paid the taxi driver, who left as though he'd just robbed the local bank and was being pursued by Gendarmes. Yuri opened the boot to get his jack out.

'You English shits, the next time I see you, you're dead!' He screamed at the three cows that had walked over to see what all the fuss was about. At two o'clock that night, Yuri finally crashed into his own single bed in northern Paris, on the Rue Marx Domoy, he was so tired, even the noisy trains from the uncomfortably close Gare du Nord couldn't stop him from falling into a dreamless, deep sleep.

The following morning, Yuri telephoned Mikhail and Vladimir telling them to meet him at the usual time and place in Saint Denis.

'What happened to you yesterday?' They both asked.

'I'll tell you at the rendezvous.' He answered brusquely.

Vladimir Mordashov arrived late in the small town north of Paris, as it was such a long drive with so much traffic. He never understood why they needed to meet at the famous Basilica. 'Who cared if three Russian embassy staff met in a bar in central Paris?' He asked himself, whenever this idiot called another discreet meeting at the Memorial to King Louis XVI and Queen Marie Antoinette. It was a beautiful church, full of France's deceased kings and queens, however, once he'd seen it a couple of times, all of those magnificent windows and statues, all looked the same to the middle-aged agent.

He parked his BMW, which he'd washed after driving aimlessly around northern France on one of Yuri's pointless missions, and noticed that the young Major's car had already been parked and looked as though it had been in an accident. The large wings and the chrome bumper that were normally buffed to a perfect showroom shine, now looked like they'd had fifteen rounds with a heavy-weight tree. He entered the empty church, walked around the edges and soon heard his embassy comrades whispering in the nave. The four of them stood there with stony faces. King

Louis XVI standing behind a dais, Yuri equally rigid, and on his left, Queen Marie Antoinette kneeling on a plinth. Just as cold as the dead royalty, Mikhail stood at military ease with his over-developed muscles, busting through his perfectly pressed suit.

'You're late comrade corporal.' Yuri said aggressively.

'What happened to you Major?' Vladimir asked, nodding at the marks on Yuri's face.

'Oh it's nothing, too much vodka last night...' He answered in a throwaway tone. 'And your car, was it drunk as well?' Vladimir teased.

'As I said, I was drunk.'

'We looked for you yesterday, did you find out where they were going?'

'Ah no, their car was too fast, and, as you were both too slow, I drove back to Paris.'

Vladimir searched Mikhail Kalinin's eyes to see if he had the same thought, regarding the veracity of Yuri's story, nevertheless Mikhail's face was an unmoving mask similar to the other statues in the sepulchre.

'What shall we do now? We'll never find them in France.'

'I want you to leave this evening on the night train to London...'

'What? You think they've turned back?'

'No comrade, listen carefully, I want you to go to their place and look around for clues on their whereabouts, tickets, hotel reservations etcetera.'

'If these people are as good as I think they are, they won't leave a map of their route or details of their mission...'

'Don't think comrade, just do as you're told, there's a Polish informant in Richmond, near London, he'll tell you where to find their place, all of the details are in this folder, make sure you're back here in four days, same time, do you understand Vladimir?'

Agent Mordashov snatched the folder without disguising his contempt for the foolish plan, and walked out of the massive church. He'd never been to England and didn't want to go either. He heard it was cold and wet with bad food and strange people.

In the car the Russian decided to take his fur-lined Mackintosh, he had bought last year from an old Mongolian, who farmed Husky dogs for their fur.

The farmer explained that he strangled the dogs by hanging them on a wire in the forest, their back feet barely touching the ground, it took them about three weeks to die and they lost half their weight, so it made it easier to skin them into large pellets. It was the warmest coat he'd ever had and good revenge on those four-legged creatures; he hated animals nearly as much as he hated the cheap prostitutes in the Montmartre area of Paris.

Chapter 22
Duck's Island, April 1964

Vladimir Mordashov looked down from Richmond Bridge, gripping the open neck of his Husky-lined Mackintosh against the gusty wind. The amateur gourmet detested the breakfast offered him at the little hotel that morning. One tepid, slightly grey, greasy sausage, over-cooked fried egg with burnt, black lace edges and what were those sweet beans? He couldn't wait to get back to civilised French restaurants. He looked at his little notebook and read, 'Very tall, thin man, artist, wispy, grey hair and goatee beard, speaks Polish, a little English and Italian'.

Vladimir normally tried to gain a little from his expenses, unfortunately on this trip he had been given a strict budget and so he was stuck in the cheap hotel. He'd heard that there was an area of London called Soho, where he might find some prostitutes. If this stupid assignment went smoothly, he thought he might go over there. He hated women like that, exposing themselves on the street, making men feel as contemptible as they were, but he also knew that he needed them.

There were few people braving the weather, an elderly couple with a dog walking along the riverbank, some tourists in an organised group, following a talking umbrella, a few enthusiastic runners and two cyclists. An old man sat with a mongrel dog on one of the slatted green benches, both at similar times in their lives. Vladimir looked across to the Twickenham side of the increasingly rapid river; it was quiet, except for lights glowing in the Mansion blocks of flats. The Russian felt jealous of the families sitting in their warm homes while he had been sent on a pointless mission. Then the agent saw the man he looked for, sitting on a small folding stool, crouched over an easel. Vladimir walked down the stone steps onto the Thames path, casually looking at the boats bouncing next to him on the restless water. The artist didn't look up even though the rotund Russian's shadow haloed him.

'It's a hot day in Scotland.' He said in broken

262

English.

'Who m-m-makes up these s-st-stupid codes?' The artist asked, stuttering, while he continued to splash a blue wash over the top of his canvas.

Agent Mordashov shrugged his shoulders and studied the stranger, he was so tall his knees came up to his chest as he balanced on the low stool, his long thin face was as gloomy as the English sky and his fingertips were covered in several shades of blue paint.

'So where do they live comrade?' Vladimir quizzed the vulturine profile impatiently.

'Which painting d-d-do you w-wa-want?' The artist asked.

'Painting? I don't want paintings - I want the location.'

'They're one hundred p-pounds each.' The artist stuttered firmly.

'Here!' The Russian said rudely, offering a roll of notes he pulled from inside his furry coat, that he'd already counted that morning. The old man perching on the stool like a wing-clipped bird, took the money without looking up and offered one of his six paintings of Richmond Bridge to the Russian.

'Listen, Aleksander isn't,' He said keeping his hands in his pockets. 'I don't want the stupid painting, just tell me where to find their place, you understand?'

'N-n-no painting, n-n-no directions...' Aleksander said defiantly, with tightening spaghetti-thin lips.

The Russian killer snatched the painting irritably.

'Walk along p-pa-path, sign say Duck's Island, you n-n-need boat, you're a-alone?'

The tired agent walked away contemptuously, without another word and tossed the painting in the River like a skipping stone. When the Russian was out of sight, the artist packed up hurriedly, walked along the towpath and when sure no one followed, entered a pub facing the waterfront, he ordered a pint of German beer and went over to the public telephone. When the ringing stopped, the pips prompted him to push a sixpence into the metal slot; no one spoke at the other end.

263

'Nanny J...' Aleksander said in Polish. 'The Russian has arrived, as I told you, I th-th-think he coming tonight.' There was silence on the line, finally a click told him the phone had returned to rest in its cradle.

Vladimir Mordashov eventually levelled with Duck's Island, it looked deserted. The wind had started to bend the trees and the Thames now swelled more like a raging sea than a city river. The Russian had passed hundreds of small boats along the towpath and decided to return after dark, when he could borrow a craft for the short crossing.

Back at his scruffy hotel, the Russian stared down disappointedly at his cold plate. Roast beef plagiarising leather, two Yorkshire puddings copying tiny boulders, roasted potatoes, raw in the middle with burnt edges and a thick, lumpy, black sauce they called gravy, whose only job seemed to be to soften the hide and stones.

The Russian gourmet couldn't wait to get out of this gastronomic disaster area, before he lost any more weight. He wondered, 'Why are these English so cheerful? With this constant wind and rain, grey skies; plus the worst food he had eaten since finishing with the Russian army.'

It was two o'clock at night, none of the boats on the Thames were locked and so the agent untied a large rowing boat and struggled onto the wet, bench seat. The water continued to be a maelstrom, made worse by the slanting rain. Vladimir rowed as hard as he could, it wasn't far, nevertheless the weather became his enemy and the hundred feet took him twenty minutes. By the time he managed to tie the heavy wooden vessel to a tree branch, he was exhausted and cursed Yuri and his stupid, ambitious ideas.

On the north bank of the Thames in a thick copse, the old artist crouched under a tree with a pair of binoculars. A floppy hat channelled rain onto his caped shoulders.

On the island, the piedmont was steep and difficult to climb, the slippery mud giving no grip, made worse with the drenching rain.

By the time Vladimir reached the fence that circled Duck's Island, his shoes and socks were covered with soupy earth. Furthermore, his dog-lined Mac was twice its normal weight, due to the deluge. To make his task more difficult, the second helping of treacle tart and lumpy custard had started to turn in the sensitive Russian stomach.

The agent looked up at the top of the palisade covered in flowers and vines, about eight-nine feet, he thought, nowhere to get a foothold, he would need to pull himself up. 'Shit!' He said aloud, wrenching two long thorns from his bleeding hand. The soggy agent struggled around the slippery edge of the fence, finding it difficult to keep out of the fast moving water. He searched for an easier access, but changed his mind, as the spiky plants threatened revenge for a few hundred yards in both directions. Vladimir took some wire cutters from his coat pocket and started to cut into the fence and the two-foot-deep bushes behind it. After the third thorn jabbed into his wrist he realised that nearly an hour had past and yet the opening was still far too small to enter. He had emphysematous exhaustion, but kept on hacking his way through the barbed plants.

In Nanny J's cottage, Helius and Nemesis lifted their heads from a light sleep and silently walked over to the front door. The small, shaded table light next to Nanny J's bed started to flash a silent alarm, on and off, waking her from restless dreams. The elderly cripple looked at the dogs that were stretching and yawning, she pressed a button next to the lamp that stopped the flashing. The old woman shuffled across the room, entered the hall and opened the front door, the huge Alsatians padded out into the garden. Nanny J went into her bedroom and wrapped a maroon checked, dressing gown around her frail body and slipped her feet into some fluffy slippers, Charlotte had bought her two years ago for Christmas. She found a torch and her sturdy walking stick and tottered into the garden.

Vladimir had now managed to cut a hole through the wall of spiteful plants, and wire fence, he entered the large lawn-covered interior of the island, albeit covered in bleeding cuts on virtually his whole body. He noticed a jetty on the right and realised that it would've been easier to enter there. However, it was setback in tress and not visible until you were on top of it. He decided that he'd leave from there in one of the little attached dinghies, after he'd broken into the British agent's home.

The whole island was in darkness. Therefore when the Russian saw the house he wondered if he could stay the night. It would surely be more comfortable than his cheap hotel and if they're as rich as the place suggested, he might even find some vodka and caviar. The Russian walked confidently towards the residence and was pleased with what he saw, 'If they're travelling he could even stay a few days, yes why not...' He thought, 'he could tell Yuri he was delayed and...'

Helius and Nemesis stood on two stone plinths that framed a short path up to the back entrance. They were big, even though Vladimir could only see their silhouettes. The stone bases gave them a statuesque height and quality, like some of the French royal family in the Basilica of Saint Denis, but of course the French Louis' didn't move. Unfortunately for the Russian agent, the Greek-god-dogs did, and very quickly indeed.

The Russian was fast. He dived into his furry Macintosh pocket and pulled out his pistol. Nemesis was faster and had her teeth around his shooting arm before he could aim. The force of her running-jump and her weight smashed the agent on the ground as though he had fallen from a first-floor window. A couple of seconds later Helius had him by the throat. The Russian's Husky-lined coat had fallen open and surrounded him on the grass, when Nanny J walked over slowly she thought that, the dogs had caught a huge, silver grey bear. She looked down at the overweight man on his bed of fur.

'Let go!' Nanny J snapped in Hungarian, Helius and Nemesis obeyed and released the slightly, bleeding body, but still stood close by, deterring any fast movement. The Russian glanced at the old woman, squinted his eyes and whispered bravely in Russian. 'Where is Sam going?'

'What?' Nanny J replied; confused by the Russian language, she hadn't heard for years. That was all he needed, a distraction. His training told him that he should get the dogs first. Then he could easily torture the old woman to get all the information he needed. The Russian agent grabbed the gun that had fallen a few inches from his right hand. Pointed it at Nemesis's head and fired. The shot's echo bounced off the house and the rushing water. Nemesis cried out in agony as the bullet went straight through her body. He quickly turned the weapon on Helius and squeezed the trigger again.

David Mark Taylor had been driving an emergency, rescue motorbike for the Royal Automobile Club for the last thirty years. He realised though, if you really added up the number of hours he had actually worked, it might come out that the patrolman only did about fifteen years. Whenever he received a call from dispatch, he calculated how far it was from his house or his sister's place, where he spent a lot of time with her retired husband Tom. David very cleverly managed to fiddle his log so that he could go home early most days of the week. Sometimes he managed a two to three hour lunch break and rarely finished his jobs after four o'clock in the afternoon.

'You see...' He would explain to his closest friends. 'The despatch people have no idea how long it takes to fix a broken-down vehicle or even to drive from one call to another. Often the new patrolmen don't know their way around the streets or a car's engine! And so with all my experience, I do most of the calls in half the time, which is why I'm so good at fly fishing.'

And that was exactly what David was doing on that Friday morning, even though he did get upset when his line snagged. The angler flicked the rod to the right and then to the left, he tried to reel it in. Nevertheless, he thought it must have been caught on an old tyre, there were so many in the Thames around Kingston these days. Suddenly his luck changed, a fairly, fast motorboat passed by and the wake must have disturbed the obstacle, the angler turned his reel with care, rolling in the line slowly.

Suddenly David stopped turning the reel. His wrist just froze, he leaned forward and squinted his eyes, the tyre wasn't a tyre and the large object on his line - that was now floating freely towards him, wasn't a fish. Well, not any kind of fish Patrolman Taylor had seen, and after nearly fifty years of angling he thought that he'd seen everything. Oh no, he decided fretfully, it was an enormous dog.

The RAC patrolman loved dogs, he didn't have one now because Foxy, the family's overweight, ancient, Wire Fox Terrier mix, had died last year and he just couldn't cope with the idea of getting another one yet. Even though he'd visited Battersea Dog's Home twice last month, sadly looking at the strays. The problem was, David was really looking for another Foxy. Most people said you shouldn't do that, just trying to get exactly the same dog; at the refuge, they suggested he should look for something completely different, a Collie or a Spaniel.

Foxy was of course named because she had that lovely golden brown fur, with a pure white chest, well, just like a fox, he reflected, with tears starting to well up in his eyes. The massive floating animal was now almost reeled in to the edge of the water; it was a good place to fish due to the slopping sandy beach that you could usually only find further up river.

'What have you got there then?' His brother-in-law Tom said, sidling next to David.

'Looks like a massive Alsatian or two tied together! Must have fallen off a boat or maybe drowned somewhere along the river.'

'The tide's just going out so it could have floated down from Windsor or even up from Richmond. It was pretty rough last night.' Tom said, staring at the partly submerged fury creature.

'Do you think we should call someone Tom? The dog's home or the cops? There might be someone looking for the poor thing.' David said full of ruth.

Five hours earlier at three-thirty in the morning, Nanny J had less time to think about what she should do, she'd quick reactions when she was young. However, since her accident and over the following years, Jullietta Fratellini had become frail and weak, except in her head.

She felt just as strong in her mind, as she did when she was the world's best, female trapeze artist. She saw the Russian point the gun at the dogs that she had nurtured since they were puppies, lifted her cane with its heavy, solid gold, lion's head, which she stole from a ringmaster in Italy after her accident and smashed it over Vladimir's cranium.

Instantly, his eyes bulged and he stopped breathing. Jullietta went to Nemesis, bent over her carefully and held the huge head.

'Neme, you look like one of Pippa's hippy friends with this little hole in your ear, I'll have to get you an earring.' She said, stroking the dog affectionately that looked very sorry for herself.

Heli padded over and licked her sister's bleeding ear. Jullietta looked down at the Russian, poked him with the end of her stick, then walked slowly towards the water next to the jetty and saw its rage.

'Fetch! - Fetch!' She called to the dogs, pointing to the dead Russian. 'Fetch!'

Helius and Nemesis grabbed the husky-lined Macintosh in their huge jaws and dragged the agent over the slippery lawn towards the river; within a few minutes, the agent in his fur coat was floating rapidly in the violent Thames. Nanny J ambled back slowly to her cottage with the dogs on her heels. Entering the kitchen, she made some milky hot chocolate, gave some digestive biscuits to the dogs and went back to her bed. The old artist heard the front door close, waited five minutes, searched the area for any further activity, packed up his little artist's stool and walked back into the trees towards Twickenham.

The flashing blue lights splashed the river's edge under the grey morning sky; the uniformed driver stopped the black Morris at the water's edge and cut its Police siren.

The CID sergeant opened his passenger door slowly, waiting until the end of his roll-up finally glowed gold, taking a deep drag. Ignoring the waiting uniform, he professionally searched the scene on the river's edge, two anglers, a dead body attached to a fishing line. A bushy tailed young copper with the enthusiastic face of a teenage boy in a fun fair, was running around with a freshly bought notebook. McGregor had seen it all so many times before and asked himself, 'Why can't these buggers die after lunch?'

'Morning Serge.' The police constable said, walking over to the detective, rubbing his cold hands together.

'What's happened here Charlie?' Sergeant

McGregor asked, with his undiluted Glaswegian accent, belying the years he'd spent with the Sassenachs.

'These two men were fishing, illegally on this part of the Thames…'

'Yes-yes, get on with it Charlie, one major crime at a time!'

'Well, one of them *is* in uniform…'

'What a cop?'

'No, RAC Serge…' McGregor flicked his ash and gave Charlie a look of exasperation. '…And they pulled in what they thought was some kind of monster…'

'What?' The CID man gasped. 'Are you having me on Charlie at this time in the morning?'

'No Serge, but when he phoned in on 999, he said they've pulled in some kind of 'Big Foot'. Well we've only just got the whole thing out of the water Serge and it looks like a fat geezer in a fur coat.

'Do you realise that I haven't had my breakfast yet Charlie?'

'Sorry Serge, I've heard you do like your full English, before you hit the road.'

'Do you mind, full Scottish; fried eggs, black pudding, sausages, crispy bacon, a few slices of hot, buttered, white toast, none of this new brown stuff for me and at least three mugs of hot milky tea, you know the one, the chimps drink it on the tele.'

'Yes Serge, about the corpse…'

'Any ID on him?'

'Nothing, not a scrap of paper, no pen, no comb, nothing, except a pair of wire cutters in his pocket.'

Sergeant McGregor walked over to Vladimir's body, his wrinkly skin a pale ivory colour; the Glaswegian took out a pencil from his coat pocket and examined the corpse's hands and head.

'Looks like he hit his head or someone did it for him, loads of small cuts and wounds on his hands and face, torn trousers, could be a burglar, used the wire cutters to break in somewhere, maybe trying to rob one of the posh houses or boats up at Henley. Give him to the lab and we'll see if anyone is reported missing. What's that coat, Mink?'

'I think its fox or dog!' David said angrily, waiting for some questions from the plain-clothes cop.

'Must have been a bloody big dog.' McGregor chuckled, walking to his car, while lighting another roll-up.

'Don't you want to question these two Serge?' The constable asked.

'No, take their details we'll talk to them in a nice warm police station after I've had breakfast and once we know who our furry friend is.'

McGregor's car pulled off, leaving the four men on the riverbank.

Chapter 23
La Plaça Reial, Barcelona, April 1964

The three young girls employed by the Gaudí Hotel, fought their way across the human torrent of Las Ramblas, that was passing and repassing the jugglers, singers and beggars who plied their trade along the shores of the populated street, which divided the old core of the town and ran into the sea. The girls couldn't wait to start their weekly lunch at the Can Cortada restaurant in Barcelona's most famous square, La Plaça Reial. The open space of the plaza, webbed by a labyrinth of spidery streets, caught the Costa Brava's midday sun on one side, which had started to uncover its warm heart, yet hadn't found its wings; therefore long, cool shadows were still painted across Antoni Gaudí's beautiful home town.

Mariesther was the educated one and worked on the reception desk at the distinguished hotel, due to her knowledge of French and Italian. She wore her black uniform of fitted jacket, knee length skirt, flat court shoes and white shirt. For the treasured Friday lunches with her friends, she usually stuffed a few accessories in her handbag before leaving her rented, little studio flat in the morning. She didn't add the complementary pieces until she stepped away from work and the watchful eyes of the Hotel Manager, Señor Anselmo Gomez. Who notoriously noticed the slightest infraction of the hotel's strict rules on dress and behaviour. Women were second-class employees in most of Spain's businesses under Franco's rule. Therefore, the hotel girls paid attention not to upset their alleged 'Superiors'. Mariesther had carefully tied her new Pierre Balmain scarf around her shoulders, that she'd bought in the second-hand market last Sunday, changed into kitten heels, added her tiny, diamond stud earrings, that the young girl thought made her dark brown eyes sparkle and clipped on the nine carat, gold charm bracelet, bought for her birthday four years back by her ex-fiancé, Miguel.

Isabella was the flirty one and at twenty-two, the youngest of the three. Her bust measurement wasn't huge, although her back was narrow and her breast sat prominently in front. Emphasised by the fact that she only wore expensive French bras called Balconette, her only extravagance, which pushed her impressive bosom to its upper limits using a delicate wire frame, like little balconies. A fact that was duly noticed by every red-blooded Spaniard and tourist alike.

She removed her maid's uniform, because Isabella's shift ended at one o'clock on Fridays and she decided to wear her clingy, chocolate-brown dress with tiny pearl buttons. The soft fabric not only showed off her highlighted hair, but also, had the advantage of the long row of closely spaced studs. So that she could reveal as much or as little of her wonderful cleavage as she thought necessary.

Joana was the eldest. Luckily she didn't work in the hotel kitchens on Friday due to her two, twelve-hour shifts over the weekend. Therefore she decided to wear a floral summer dress from last year, hoping no one would remember it. After all, she had changed the belt and added a short matching cardigan in pale blue that the young pauper had knitted herself, due to the pay being so low for kitchen staff. Joana just couldn't afford a new dress until she found a boyfriend to help support her five year old, illegitimate daughter. She also needed to ameliorate her social life and even assist sometimes with the rent, for the small room in her grumpy, widowed aunt's flat.

When Joana's mother was sixteen her baby popped out screaming four weeks early in the small utilitarian hospital in Cordoba. The nurses were nice to her even though her stay was short and without visitors. As soon as they said she could leave, she dressed quickly and hurried down the blue-tiled steps that reeked with the stench of disinfectant. When she hit the fresh air, she quickly looked left and right along the quiet street and not seeing any passers-by, laid her new baby Joana, in a cardboard box next to the dustbins and ran off.

Therefore, baby Joana was taken to Barcelona by her grandmother, where she spent a harsh and loveless life in an orphanage until she was fourteen, when she was thrown out into the world to fend for herself. The next major problem she faced was the absence of paperwork, because she didn't have a father's name on her birth certificate. In fact, she didn't have a birth certificate. Under Franco's regime, this meant that she couldn't get a passport or any other official papers and was considered a 'Non-person'. The young orphan could never get a parcel from the post office or even acquire further education or a decent job, as they all required proof of identity. The one thing that Joana knew with certainty was that her daughter did have a birth certificate, with her father's name emblazoned on it. Whatever happened she would never be put in any kind of home without the love of her mother, even though her father had run off to Portugal and married someone else. Joana knew that the only way to solve her problems was to get a husband.

The three giggly girls counted on several reasons to be close friends: they all worked in the hotel, which allowed them to be united in a campaign of gossip about the managers and guests. The trio were all of a similar age, and most important, they were single and looking for boyfriends, well except Joana, who would happily skip over the courting stage and just get married as quickly as possible. She hated working in the stuffy, basement kitchens under the aggressive head-chef Fernando, she detested living with her three year old in the tiny space her aunt had allotted them, and therefore realised that her two tickets from the Once kiosk for the monthly Lotoria or a husband, were the only way out.

The Can Cortada restaurant spread its twenty tables and seventy-one chairs as far as the waiters dared, into the rent-free space of the public square like a slow moving tsunami. The seats almost touched the beautiful central fountain that the hotel girls liked to think reflected their true eminence.

The beautiful statues that made up the base of the cascading water feature were called 'The Three Graces' and allegedly represented the daughters of Zeus.
They were named, Euphrsyne, Aglaea and Thalia or Beauty, Charm and Joy. The three hotel workers found a good table with a wide view of La Plaça Reial and like most of the

clientele, started their lunch by diving into their handbags for cigarettes. Isabella loved the coloured street posters for Philip Morris cigarettes; the advertisement had realistic artwork of a handsome young man and a beautiful girl, the title said:

'More vintage tobacco makes Philip Morris naturally gentle and mild'

After a few minutes, the waiter took their order for drinks and one plate of mixed tapas that they usually shared between them.

The famous square had been built on the remains of the Santa Madrona Capuchin Monastery, over a hundred years before and the girls were following in the spirit of their stone-carved counterparts, by flaunting in the plaza every Friday for the last four years. Hoping to find love or at the very least, an extravagant and generous date.

Isabella was the first to notice the *'guapo'* on the other side of Zeus's offspring; she thought he looked very handsome, possessing a perfect profile as well as a manly square jaw and black wavy hair. His suit looked expensively Italian and hung beautifully on his broad shoulders, he was sitting at an angle, yet seemed tall and slim even at the table.

'Did you see her jewellery Isabella?' Mariesther asked turning from Joana. 'Isabella wake up, we're talking to you about that young, tarty girl with the rich, old guy in room two-twenty-five.'

'Listen chicas never mind that, look at the Adonis over there...' The girl's heads swivelled at the speed of children's wooden tops and scanned the other occupants of the paved terrace. 'No, not that way, at four o'clock, looks Italian, gorgeous profile, expensive watch, nice hands.'

All three girls zoomed in on the handsome Italian as keenly as ornithologists searching for an extinct species, and started to subtly move their seating positions to get a better view.

'Mamma-Mia...' Joana said laughing. 'Well, I've got *no-chance* with him, he's more than likely here with some model or an actress, besides, since last summer, I've put on these extra kilos, I can barely breath in this dress.' She said patting her tummy chuckling.

Isabella undid some more of her little buttons, until the top two inches of her beautiful bosom started to rise up, resembling twin moons in a late summer sky. The girls sipped their drinks enthusiastically, when Joana started to tap her glass as a warning, saying:

'Hey chicas, look what's walking over to our new boyfriend.'

'Where?' Mariesther asked, looking up too obviously from her glass.

Suddenly the triplets put their heads down and sipped their drinks noisily, due to the two Italian suits that past so closely to their table, they almost knocked the girl's little plate of tapas on the floor.

'Umm! Not bad.' Isabella said into her tall Sangria.

'Yes, mind you, they aren't as stunning as the one at the table, he resembles a god!' Mariesther chirped in giggling.

'Stop being so fussy you two…' Joana said.

'We're three gorgeous girls, they're three really attractive men and so we're evenly matched. I don't mind taking the little chubby one, at least he's male and under forty, they could take us to that new restaurant on the beach, it's open in the evenings on Saturday nights and they've got live music this weekend!'

Giovanni Gibigiano glanced at the three cute girls as he passed by, the short Italian knew that he'd gained some weight and held his stomach in, ever since he joined the *Partito Nazionale Fascista* last year they'd kept him busy. He failed to attend the last three, weekly practise nights for the second greatest love in his life, which was to play football with his cousins, or even the greatest love in his life, to watch the world's best team; Napoli. They were playing at home against Venizia tomorrow and he would miss them: again.

At twenty-three-years old, Giovanni had steadily worked his way up through the Mafia ranks ever since he was a kid, running messages and delivering parcels around Naples for the controlling Family of Marinaio. He enjoyed the power and money he received from the family, therefore he and his cousins never worried about getting front row seats at the stadium or anywhere else they wanted to go. Actually life was good for them. That was after-all the main reason to be in the Italian Mafia and the PNF; you got money, respect, girls and the best of Italy; the food and the football. Giovanni just wished that he didn't have to be in Spain, he couldn't understand one word they were saying and now he was persuaded to meet this crippled guy, because his friend and fellow Fascist Party member had a debt of honour to him from his Sicilian family.

Raffaello was a different kind of guy, Giovanni reflected, he really believed in the Fascist Party and he believed in vendetta, particularly when it involved family. Out of all the people who took their family honour and debts seriously, it was the Sicilians, and of the four, main families in Sicily, the most deadly and vengeful was the Calvino family. They were established for six generations and controlled southern Sicily and parts of Italy. In the nineteen twenties they also moved into some of the biggest cities in America, which was making even more money than their European territories. Therefore, when his best friend Raffaello Massoni said he was on a vendetta, following the assassination of his grandfather last year, Giovanni had no choice but to visit Barcelona and miss some of the most important games in football at the end of the season.

When the Italians arrived at their associate's table, the three girls were staring curiously, the beautiful profile stood up with surprising difficulty, using a black and silver walking stick.

Raffaello and Giovanni stopped to shake hands. However, Marco Sotori couldn't lift his shrivelled right arm. He turned to face the men with a horrifically distorted, chard mask, where there was once a sculptured, perfect face.

Joana gasped, Mariesther hid her eyes with her hands and Isabella turned her head away quickly, closing the buttons of her open neckline.

Marco struggled to his seat, knocking over his coffee cup, Giovanni rushed to pick it up, but Marco's reaction was vicious. 'Leave it!' He screamed. He noticed the girl's reactions and hated them for it. After years of getting any woman he wanted, the now deformed Italian despised all women, for their shallowness, 'Couldn't they love a man who wasn't handsome?' He asked himself daily, since he was discharged from the hospital in Paris last month.

Marco's injuries had reduced him to a half-melted candle. On his left side, he still looked the notorious, striking made-man from Milano, one of the Mafia's finest. A leader in Italy's *Partito Nazionale Fascist.* Last year Marco was on his way to the top, in his Mafia Family and the Fascist Party, feared mutually for his power and influence in the other organisation. Subsequently, there was the simple job in Paris and his life, as he knew it, ended in one night, one car chase and one stupid mistake. His nightmares replayed every second of the last fifteen minutes from his former life. After he tried to squeeze the Alfa Romeo Guilia in between the narrow walls of the Parisian street in hot pursuit, the vehicle was crushed on both sides, and the first explosion blew out the back window of his red sports car. Barely conscious, he climbed across his partner, the dying fat-man and heaved himself over the rear seats and out of the cramped, sloping rear widow frame, slashing his face and arms on the shattered glass. He plummeted onto the cobble-stoned road collapsing on his right side. Still dazed, he peered under his car and saw the British black Mini he had pursued across Paris at the end of the narrow lane. The Rue du Chat-qui-Pêche, he will never forget that name as long as he lives, those English bastards must have planned that route as a getaway, he realised.

The Italian's enemies had stopped about a hundred metres ahead; he could just make out their silhouettes, a tall slim man on the right in black and a shapely female with shoulder-length blonde hair on the left. Marco painfully pulled out his revolver, took aim, stretching out his trembling right arm and fired. It was the kind of shot he'd taken a thousand times before, unfortunately at that moment his head was spinning from the crash and he mistakenly hit the underside of his own car. The moment the bullet left his Benelli B-76 pistol his life went into slow motion. He saw the slug cruise through the air spinning and rebound under the car. He watched the petrol cascade out of the tank in slow motion and settle around his body, creating an explosive puddle an inch deep; saturating his thick, black hair that women loved to touch, down to his handmade, Italian, glove-leather shoes on his perfectly pedicured toes.

In fact, he had a vague memory during those nightmare days when he first arrived at the hospital, that the doctor said his shoes were so perfectly made around his foot, that his skin and the leather had fused together in the conflagration. After they removed the bloody mess, his foot became a sculpture of fleshless bones, deformed like melted volcanic rock.

The bullet ricocheted under the car creating sparks more powerful than any detonator.

The petrol flared up as ferociously as the new American space rocket's tail, he'd seen on television, creating a furnace that engulfed the road and the body lying on it.

'It's amazing!' Said the burn specialist at the hospital, that only one side of Marco was completely burnt, albeit to a cinder. Somehow the rush of air from the ignited petrol, created a vacuum that protected the other side of the Italian's body. Not that these facts were any consolation to the handsome killer. When he regained consciousness after a month in coma, he demanded a mirror. At first the doctors and nurses refused, when he finally saw his reflection he vomited at the horrific sight of pummelled, burnt meat, he wanted to kill himself and asked for his gun. The doctors kept him on suicide watch for months. Then recently, his visitor from Naples told him that 'His people in London with a chain of spaghetti restaurants' had tracked down a blonde girl with shoulder-length hair and a souped up, black Mini. Now for the first time in months Marco wanted to live, he knew what he needed to do, and it involved burning this English bitch piece by piece, over a period of years, she would soon be pleading for him to finish her off. 'But who's in a hurry?'

'So Marco, you look better.' Angelo Massoni's grandson lied.

'Not as bad as the hitter will look when I've finished with her.'

'So where's this girl? We can hit her this afternoon and be back in Italy for the game between Napoli and Marseille next week!' Giovanni said casually.

Marco glared at the frivolous boy, lifted the point of his walking stick next to his chubby face, pressing his twisted and grotesque index finger on the cap and a short, razor-thin blade shot out of the end.

'Hey, be careful with that, we're here to help you.' Giovanni said, holding back the words he swallowed quickly that flashed through his head, '*You ugly freak*'.

'I don't want to kill the woman...' Marco spat. 'I'm going to keep her, and light her up nightly like a church candle, don't you want to see revenge for your grandfather, Raffaello?'

'Of course I do, but I don't have time to keep a pet, if she's young and good looking, I might party with her for a few days and then blow her away, the family in Sicily will be satisfied and life goes on, my grandfather was an old man.' Raffaello said, as though he was talking about going to work in an office. A waiter brought over the coffees the boys had ordered, which they downed in one.

'Listen to me carefully, I'm going to do this my way...' Marco gasped with difficulty as he moved his half-face closer to the Italian boys, the effort causing him excruciating pain throughout his liquefied frame. 'Like my people in the PDF told you.'

Marco was still capable of threatening these young southern, Mafia boys with his fascists friends who ran the Party, as well as his powerful and rich Mafia family from the north of Italy. The Sicilian and Napolitano Mafia families didn't want to upset their northern brothers; they had enough problems with the politicians, police, and at times, each other.

At the other table, the hotel girls paid *la cuenta* and left their vantage point, glancing surreptitiously at the Italians as they rushed away from the restaurant, having decided not to eat lunch after all.

'Okay Marco, you're the boss, just tell us where to get this girl, her name and we'll pick her up for you, no problema.' Raffaello said, resigned to a longer, messier job than he had anticipated.

'At the moment I don't know her name or where she is, I'm told she will be coming to Barcelona soon. I'm speaking to my informer later, the only problem is he's Russian and I don't trust him, so I need to look into his eyes. When he gets here, we'll all go over to see him together and pick up the girl.'

Marco's face cringed in agony as he struggled to his feet; eventually he managed to point himself away from the restaurant, without another word. When Marco hobbled from the table, two men from other parts of the square wearing PDF lapel badges fell in behind him; the two Mafia boys from Italy watched the three leave the famous plaça.

'Holy Mother of God, I've seen some people messed up before, but never anything that bad, he looked as if someone had just dug him up from a grave, put him in a suit and pushed him into the street, I doubt if he'll still be alive by the weekend!' Giovanni said, now that Marco had staggered out of hearing distance, the right side of his body dragging behind the left.

'He will, I know him; he's on a very powerful drug, Giovanni.'

'What morphine?'

'No Giovanni, something much more powerful and dangerous. Hate!'

The Mafia soldiers finished their drinks, tossed some Pesetas on the table and walked towards the throng cruising Las Ramblas.

The camera peering through the first floor, office window continued to make its whiz and snap sound as Moshe 'Mad' Liberman, formally from the Israeli secret service, stared down at the backs of the retreating Italians. Moshe was tired; after all, he was seventy-two-years old and he had been watching several people who were attending the Nazi gala evening for the last three days.

After Moshe escaped from Auschwitz in forty-three, having watched his wife and three children gassed, he worked with the British secret service, until they sent him into the field. He always got his man, yet usually killed half a dozen other people in the vicinity.

Then after 1948, he was a key player during the formation of Israel, working with Aman (Israeli military intelligence) and then Shin Bet (Israeli internal security). It went well for many years until he became the senior hitman for the Israeli secret service, *HaMossad leModi'in uleTafkidim Meyuchadim* (Institute for Intelligence and Special Operations) or as everyone in the business calls it, The Mossad.

During the Six Day War he was invaluable to the Israeli forces, single-handedly taking out huge groups of enemy fighters with his clever explosives.

At that stage, his superiors commended killing twenty or thirty people in one afternoon, but as time went on, politicians started to become nervous. Following the fragile peace the Israelis were struggling with, 'Mad' Moshe's methods were embarrassing. The Americans soon told The Mossad to get rid of him, how could they negotiate with moderate countries, when one of their agents was slaughtering innocent people in large batches, as efficiently as supermarket chickens. These days it was difficult for Moshe to find freelance work; he hadn't had a contract for over a year. Nevertheless, this hit was perfect for him, a radical, very wealthy Israeli group, who didn't mind how many people were exterminated, employed him, so it was a perfect job for the aging killer. Particularly as he was recognised as the world's top explosive's expert. 'If I do my usual job without interference,' He planned, 'I'll blow the whole Tower-top Restaurant into the sea!' Let's face it, he consoled himself, all the guests at the event would be Nazis, Fascists or supporters of one or both, 'Let them all be blown to hell!'

Moshe had been living with a brain tumour for the last fifteen years; he didn't care if he was propelled to his god with the rest of them; if they had one. The doctors at the hospital said two things after his last scan. Firstly, he only had a few months to live, and secondly, that he was completely insane. 'Might as well go out with a bang!' He thought, as he packed away his beloved violin in its famous red case, the camera and other surveillance equipment. All of the electronics slotted perfectly into their spongy cut outs like a jigsaw, and Moshe chanted his favourite entreaty.

"For by wise guidance you can wage your war"
"For by wise guidance you can wage your war"
"For by wise guidance you can wage your war"

Mariesther sneaked through the rear staff door two or three minutes late for her afternoon shift at the Hotel and was about to enter the Ladies staff toilet when she was slapped to a halt by the thundering voice of Señor Gomez.

'Mariesther! You're late! He blasted out in the narrow corridor.

'I'm sorry Señor, but it's only two minutes.' She cried weakly without looking into her manager's eyes.

'There's no *only*, Mariesther, you're either on time or late. The clock doesn't hover in the middle, you stupid girl.' He said, standing so close to her, his bad breath of cheap cigars and Señora Gomez's rabbit and garlic stew, filled her reluctant nostrils.

'I'm sorry Sir, it won't happen again.'

'It will not and you can stay an extra hour this evening as a reminder.'

'But Sir I can't stay this evening, I have a...' Mariesther saw her boss's face and knew that whatever she said would only add to his enjoyment of her impossible position. The rules were simple; she either accepted his bullying or lost her job, it was a post that he could easily fill in an hour from an army of desperate unemployed young women.

'Yes Sir.' The young receptionist answered mildly lowering her head.

'Would you like to earn some extra money Mariesther?'

'Ah... yes Sir... if it's...'

Mariesther had several friends who were always being propositioned by their bosses, a pinched bottom in an office hallway, a feel of their breast on the way home, sometimes even worse, some bosses would insist on some kind of sexual intercourse as part of their unofficial contracts to keep their underpaid jobs.

Señor Gomez brought his face close to the pretty girl's bowed head.

'You know my brother runs El Restaurante La Torre d'Altamar,' He whispered in her ear as though he was sharing a secret. 'At the top of the cable-car tower in the old port?'

'Yes Sir, I've heard it's very nice.' She said slightly relieved.

'Well they're having an important private party soon, some sort of auction and fashion show, he's looking for some extra girls to serve the drinks and canapés, go over and see him after you finish your extra hour here, he'll pay you in cash!'

'Oh thank you Sir!' Mariesther said gratefully, she'd done a few additional jobs like this before and you usually got tips on top of any money the restaurant gave you, particularly if there were foreign tourists there.

'He needs a few girls; it's going to be a posh event. Do you know anyone else who you could take with you?'

'Yes Sir, my friends Joana and Isabella will do it, I'm sure.'

'Alright Mariesther don't waste any more time gossiping here, get up stairs to work!' The manager said storming off, pleased with himself. His elder brother had promised him a bottle of French champagne if he found three good-looking girls who could serve in the restaurant until four o'clock in the morning, and may be willing to be particularly nice to some of his fascist guests; after they'd finished the washing up.

Chapter 24
The Massacre of Kalavryta

Just before the town of Lyon in the south of France, having checked that no one had stayed behind them, Sam turned off the autoroute and took a small D road that snaked through a thin tear in the countryside for twenty miles. He stopped in the forecourt of a closed petrol station, jumped out of the car and stretched his legs, looking in both directions. Once he was satisfied that they hadn't been followed by road, river or air, Sam drove a further five miles and pulled into the tiny village of Mont Tas, near Perouges. It was in a cul-de-sac surrounded by hills, very difficult to find with no reason for anyone to visit, unless you lived in or were visiting one of the eight detached houses or the two arable farms. When Sam drove into the courtyard of the last house that languished at the end of the hamlet, Dr Stuart Gale and his French wife Marie-Ange, came out on to the gravel with their four barking dogs and meowing twin Tabby cats.

They kissed Phaedra and Sam before guiding them into the house leaving the noisy animals outside. The couple soon stood next to a rampant fire burning in the grate of the comfortable living room.

'I love your house Marie-Ange...' Phaedra said, throwing down her bags. 'It's a kind of French Shangri-La an hour away from the bustling autoroute.

'Why don't you take a couple of glasses of wine with you and have a little rest in your room before dinner.' Stuart suggested.

'That would be great Stuart, may I just cache my car in your garage first?' Sam asked.

Marie-Ange and Phaedra went upstairs chatting incessantly and the two men walked out to the Bristol. Sam unloaded a couple of bags, which the doctor carried into the house and once Sam was happy with his alarm, he returned to the house and found Stuart melting next to the fire.

'How's your mother Stuart? Still campaigning?'

'Of course, she's fighting with the Mayor in Perouges at the moment, she wants the council to pay to

285

have all of the feral cats and dogs neutered, as some of the farmers have been shooting a few passing strays.'

'I hope the Mayor knows what he's up against…' Sam laughed, stuffing peanuts in his mouth.

'If he doesn't agree she might have him neutered!' Stuart chuckled. 'I think he's realised that he'd a battle on his hands, when she sent a locksmith to change the locks on the town hall door, the old guy thought that she worked there, until the next morning when the civil servants couldn't get in.'

Sam and Phaedra went to the guest's room and rested on the bed with some homemade tapenade and two glasses of ten-year-old Chablis. Phaedra fell asleep straight away, but Sam was restless. He replayed the incident with the Russians in his mind over and over again, unsure why they'd tried to follow him. He couldn't help wondering; were these men the main Russian team or freelancers? Fyodor never interfered in this type of business when it wasn't against his country's interest and if he were just keeping an eye on the big picture, which was his character, he wouldn't have tried to use close surveillance. The travellers bathed and dressed for dinner and joined their friends for a three hour, gastronomic event. They were united with Irena Sendler, who Sam had known since the war, she was a heroin saving children from the Warsaw Ghetto and a friend of Admiral Michael Renshaw. He brought his long-term partner, Eugene Bertron, who was twenty years younger than the retired Navy supremo.

'Irena!' Sam exclaimed, kissing her on both cheeks. And Michael! How wonderful to see you, it must be more than fifteen years since we last met.' Sam said warmly. 'How wonderful to have the three musketeers together again, thank you Stuart, I don't know how you managed it.'

'Yes my old friend,' Michael remembered with a croaky voice. 'I'm sorry to say that I'm on my last sea legs, it seems like a different lifetime when we were fighting together during the wars.'

'He has been very weak recently, but we're Okay, we've been together for forty-seven years last Christmas, so we'll go to our graves side by side.' Eugene explained, with his Provençal accent.

'He's a stupid boy,' Michael smiled, taking the man's hand affectionately. 'Started as my valet when I first became captain on a Royal Navy frigate in 1917, and hasn't stopped fussing over me ever since.' Looking at his friend with ruth he continued. 'He will more than likely be dead before I will, according to the doctors.'

'Enough of this morbid talk; you two will outlive us all, except my Mother...' Stuart chided, 'She will help bury God!' They all laughed. They were served coffee and little cakes baked by Stuart's mother and the Admiral looked as though he was going to doze off. When the table was cleared, Stuart jumped up to greet his mother who hurried in with her boyish gate using a walking stick.

'I thought you had gone to bed Mother.'

'I couldn't sleep with all this commotion from you noisy youngsters.' She said, with an ironic twinkle in her eyes.

'Is that you Zamo? You little rascal.' She asked, peeking over thick-rimmed glasses.

'Hello Megan, I hear you're still causing chaos.' Sam said, kissing his former schoolteacher and guardian on both cheeks.

'I don't know how you control him Phaedra, he used to be so naughty when he was little, always pulling little girls' pigtails, flying through the air and climbing on the roof. When his guardian started buying airplanes, he frightened all the animals in Kent!'

'He's still just as bad Megan and still flirting with young girls.' Phaedra added. Megan sat with Michael and Eugene chatting for a while and then the old lady struggled to her feet.

'Well I'm off to bed, we're marching on the town hall early tomorrow morning, so we can block that stupid man from getting into his office.'

Megan chuckled at the thought and climbed the stairs humming an unrecognisable tune. Marie-Ange helped her up and said she would retire as well; Michael and Eugene hugged their friends and walked slowly out to a waiting Mercedes Taxi. Stuart offered his guests from

287

Richmond some more dessert and they sat around the crocoite red fire.

'I assume you're on a government job Sam?'

'Not really Stuart, just a some business, you know.' Sam and Phaedra never told Megan's son what they did exactly; he thought they were some kind of unofficial diplomats.

'A little German business.' Phaedra said with mischief in her eyes.

'Phaedra you seem to have a passionate hatred for the Germans; how did this all start?'

'Oh, it's a long story Stuart, I don't want to bore you with it.'

'Please Phaedra, Sam was brought up by my parents since a child, he's like an elder brother to me, you're the Godparents to my only daughter Cathy, who's also your best friend, as we have the whole weekend together; now's the time; you have whet my appetite for a good story.'

'Well, you start us off Sam, you're so good at telling stories.' Phaedra said kicking off her heels and curling into a ball on the comfortable cushions, which filled the big settee.

Sam took a deep breath and a sip of brandy.

'As you know Stuart, I was a captain in the Royal Air force and had been assigned to Bletchley Park, because I was good at chess and knew several languages. The brass was looking for people with different skills to help break the Enigma Cipher. They put me in hut eight, we'd made a good deal of progress and discovered the main fault in the German system.'

'How did it work?' Stuart asked pouring Sam another top-up of cognac.

'They made the machine so that it could never use the original letters of the message…'

'I don't understand, which original letters?' The doctor asked.

'It worked like this, if they typed the word *AND* the Enigma machine would randomly change the terza rima of letters, it would use any letter from the German alphabet, except the letters *A-N-D*, therefore, despite the massive amount of work, we knew that whatever letters weren't used, were the correct ones.'

'I would have thought that still gave you thousands of combinations?' Stuart said, poking the log fire in the mammoth chimney, where he launched another log on top of the pile, before resting back into his favourite winged chair.

'Yes of course, but it was a start, originally discovered by the Poles; our boys also found another machine during the liberation of a Norwegian island, which helped a lot.

After a while, my commanding officer called me into his club for a drink, saying that my language skills weren't needed, but he'd *'Another little job for me'* and introduced an Irish Captain.

There were thousands of Irish helping us at that time even though Ireland was officially neutral. The two men explained that after Mussolini's Fascists had invaded Greece, the average Italian soldier didn't have a taste for the invasion and the Greek Partisans or Andartiko, were doing very well against them. Hitting their camps, blowing up ammunition dumps, stealing jeeps, food, etcetera, and scampering back into the hills that they knew as well as their own back gardens. The various Greek groups were running rings around the invaders, even though they didn't have a proper uniformed army.'

'Yes...' Phaedra interrupted. 'The Italians were no match for us Greeks, even though Hitler gave them loads of arms and air cover.'

'Unfortunately...' Sam continued, smiling at his wife's patriotism. 'The Germans took over the occupation, well as we know from the war crimes trials, they had their own special way of controlling the population, if one German soldier was killed, they would kill ten Greeks or more in retaliation.'

'Usually a lot more!' Phaedra added with Hellenistic hatred in her eyes. 'Including women and children!'

'Yes it's true...' Sam continued. 'They were brutal; they also stole everything that could be moved and sent it back to Germany. All of the gold from the banks, the art, and towards the end of the occupation all the food; the Greeks were literally starving to death on the streets, even in Athens.'

'You know...' Phaedra added. 'As the Germans were leaving, even in the last few days, they would burn all of our food growing in the fields that they couldn't take with them!'

'Oh my God Phaedra I'm so sorry, I didn't realise, your life must have been unbearable.' Stuart said sympathetically with his father's compassion.

Phaedra looked over at Sam and then at Stuart. Their friend had that gaze that most people had once they became familiar with them. Phaedra thought: *Sam wasn't always hugging and kissing her. They didn't hold hands in front of their friends. People just sensed that they had something together that many couples didn't have. Sam was her best friend. They were lovers, even after all of these years. Sometimes when they were on a job together, they were like brother and sister. In danger they worked as conjoined twins, two separate bodies with one mind, with the telepathic sense of ants, defeating an enemy of the nest. In some ways they complemented each other. Sam was strong and calm, always looking at the overall picture. She was hot headed and passionate. She liked to think that when they were in danger, she was the best partner he could have. Because she would never give up. Phaedra loved the idea of being a daughter of Electra, the Greek goddess of retribution, even though Sam always held her back when she became angry. She looked at her love with admiration; she knew that even recounting this story with this close friend, he would underestimate what he had achieved. In all of the war stories he would always be the invisible man. Sam left the medals and praise to others; he found all the satisfaction he needed in his family.*

'My commanding officer and the Irish captain, Conal O'Donnell, briefed me on the situation, saying that the British Government were getting pleas for help from every free-Greek around the world. The problem was that the allied forces weren't ready to attack and liberate Greece.

Therefore, the top brass decided to support the partisans in the mountains with supplies and arms, despite the fact that the Allied Forces didn't have any sites where our planes could land safely.

Conal and I were sent with a few commandos from the Second Special Air Service to find the landing fields and make contact with some of the local commanders. This turned out to be more difficult than London thought, because there were numerous diverse political groups, all of which had their own commanders and allegiances.

After we'd been there for a month or so we decided to separate so that we could cover more ground. One day, I walked around a local market and saw an incident between a young boy of about twelve years old and a market trader. He was selling, as I found out later, his uncle's false leg. He needed some food money for the family; unfortunately the man who bought the limb hadn't paid the boy who was called Dimitris Popoloposis. He tried to fight with the marketer, but it was useless, the lad couldn't match an adult and so he sulked off. About half an hour later, the man left his fruit stall carrying the stolen leg, leaving a sign saying, 'Back in ten minutes'.

Once the stallholder disappeared out of sight Dimitris popped up, removed the tarpaulin from the fruit and started selling the produce at half price. Needless to say, business was brisk. There'd been a great deal hardship and food was comparatively expensive because of the short supply. About fifteen minutes later, I observed the owner of the stall coming back without the leg, no doubt, he'd sold it, yet Dimitris appeared too busy selling the fruit, to notice. The market trader saw the crowd around his pitch and went insane when he realised what was happening. He grabbed a machete that he used to cut watermelons and it looked as though he was going to cut Dimitris' head off. The boy speeded into the market crowd with the grocer's machete swinging like a propeller inches behind him. It was chaos, people were screaming, dogs were barking, the boy rolled under stalls, jumped over barrels and cars and the irate marketer was still close to catching him.

About ten minutes later Dimitris, took a different

route and ran past me, his red-faced pursuer almost caught him with the melon-slicer, so I thought that I should give the boy a chance and stepped in front of the crazy man. He took a swing at me with the long knife, luckily I managed to take it from him...'

'That sounds easy Sam, but I can't imagine how I would've done that myself.' The doctor commented.

'Stuart, don't you remember? Sam used to be the senior instructor at the Special Air Service in counter-espionage before and after the war?' Phaedra said proudly.

'Well he'd tired himself by then...' Sam said modestly. 'So it wasn't too difficult - anyway the young Greek boy ran off with his pockets stuffed with money from the fruit sales.

Then roughly two weeks later, I was surveying a flat field that would've been good for a landing strip, when suddenly the long grass parted and ten armed men jumped up like frogs and surrounded me. I tried to explain that I was a British agent and on their side, nevertheless, these guys were feral and only wanted my equipment and my money etcetera, actually they seemed happy to kill me for it. In fact, I thought that two of the old grisly men were going to finish me where I stood. I started to hand over my stuff while I searched for a handgun; I knew that I couldn't win, though I decided stupidly to take a few with me. Suddenly, we all heard shots, we looked up to see about eighty or ninety heavily armed men coming towards us from the surrounding forest. At first I felt relieved, but the new chaps tied me up with the bandits and took us all to a secluded camp in the mountains. It became a tough trek, as I had my hands tied behind me the whole way, they didn't share their food or water throughout the nine hours, and so by the time we arrived at their hideaway, I wasn't feeling very perky.

In the encampment, they questioned me aggressively. I kept track of the time and I knew after three days without any food or water, I wouldn't last long. I'd lost a lot of blood from the interrogation methods and would've told them anything to get out of there; unfortunately, they thought I worked with the Germans. To make things worse they kept killing the men who first grabbed me one by one.

Most of them looked even worse than I did, with fingers, hands and arms recently hacked off. The people holding me were freedom fighters from the Greek Communist Party (KKE), evidently the fellows at the potential landing field were just thieves, with no political allegiance. They'd killed a few of the KKE comrades and raped some of their family the week before and so the Communist group wanted to mete out revenge, and it looked like I would be thrown into the grave they'd been digging, with the rest of them.

One morning a certain excitement swirled around the camp, I felt really weak by then and couldn't stand up. I saw a group of women with a donkey laden with food and supplies accompanied by some children; one of them resembled Dimitris, the young boy from the market. These were obviously the families of the fighting group. They started a party; eating, drinking heavily, dancing, and some of them went into the tents. By then the thieves were down to three. They appeared to be the leaders and late in the evening were dragged out into the centre of the encampment next to the huge fire. A few of the women and girls started to go crazy and accused them of rape and theft.

The Communists tied them to stakes and burnt them alive. Once the screaming and fires died down, two men came over for me. I didn't resist, actually I could barely stand up by then and found myself tied to a wooden frame ready to be roasted as well.

Several people, including women and children, piled wood onto the fire while a drunken chap with a half empty bottle of ouzo and a burning torch stood over me. He lit the wood, and the flames flared up around my feet. I started to think that it would've been a good moment to have some religious affinity. I remembered my early life and how lucky I'd been until that point.

The smoke started to choke me, and I was getting extremely hot, when suddenly there was a load of screaming and I felt cold and wet. When I opened my eyes two men, a young women and a boy were standing in front of me with dripping buckets.

One of the men lifted my head up and young Dimitris identified me. I was dragged back to the wooden

293

cage and collapsed onto the ground. The next morning when I woke up, I was naked under some clean sheets on a fairly, comfortable bed. An old woman sat next to me and started pouring some soup into my mouth. I tried to thank her, but the lack of food and water, mixed with the choking bonfire from the night before, had closed my voice off for a few days. For about a week Dimitris and his mother came into my makeshift cage with food, drinks and after a few more days, some soap and a bowl of water with some clean clothes. I started doing exercises and running on the spot and despite the fact that I didn't speak Greek, I made some contact with the boy and his mother who were wonderful people.

Two weeks past, I heard horses coming into the camp that created a lot of enthusiasm and saw three men wearing army uniforms. Each one with an impressive, long, highly groomed beard, the likes of which, I hadn't seen since I was a child in the circus and that was on the Bearded Lady!' He joked.

Phaedra and Stuart laughed at the image.

'Within an hour or so, two of the partisans came into my wooden prison and dragged me over to a large tent, where the leader of the Communists sat behind a table with the three beards. There were several other men sitting on chairs behind them including an old gentleman with half a leg. The beard in the centre was a heavy man who wore a Sam Brown belt that seemed to nail his uniform to his body, as tightly as metal rings around a beer barrel, he was the first one to speak and said in English, 'Who are you?'

I explained my mission and that I had no connection with the bandits they'd found me with, saying that their underground could contact my people, who would surely verify who I was. When my long story ended, the four men behind the table and the guards around the room looked at me in silence. I felt much stronger and wondered if I could fight my way out of the camp, because the guard nearest me had a long knife tucked into his belt and a rifle loosely hanging from his left hand. I calculated that unless he was left-handed, I could jump him, use the knife and get the rifle before he had a chance to swap hands and fire. Before I made the decision, the tall beard on the left got up and grabbed me, I was about to throw him at the guard when he said:'

'My friend, on behalf of the Free-Greeks we all welcome you as a brother!'

'Over the next few weeks the Communist group helped me find my way around and I sent several messages to my Irish colleague, Captain Conal O'Donnell, regarding several possible sites for our planes to land. Unfortunately the Germans were really digging in and had by then taken control over most of Greece.

Young Dimitris became my faithful sheepdog, he never left my side, saved me from endless mistakes and translated wherever we went. He was fantastic at finding food, safe houses and even enemy arms. In a short period, we became great friends and I realised that I would've been lost without him. Life in Greece at that time was virtually impossible, because of the different political groups, outlaws and just desperate people like the man who stole the leg, who had lost all of their humanity, because day to day survival was so hopeless.

One day, Dimitris and I found ourselves alone near the little harbour of Diakopto on the north east coast of the island, about twenty miles from his hometown of Kalavryta. The port looked empty except for a couple of fishing boats and a beautiful girl washing herself in the sea. I used my rifle-sight to get a parallactic view of her and I must admit, I was captivated. She appeared like a celestial sea-nymph floating in the variscite crystal water. The port sat about a thousand yards away. A few minutes past and because of the closeness of the lens, I didn't notice three German soldiers walking towards her, until one of them had his helmet blocking my rifle-sight.

I looked up and they seemed to be telling her to get out of the sea, they were out of earshot, but we understood the body language. She refused, her bravery seemed incredible, the Germans were killing groups of people for no reason whatsoever, and so what could she do but obey? She had a mop of black hair and a beautiful tanned body, wearing only a simple floral dress. One of the soldiers walked into the sea and started poking her with his rifle butt. We secreted ourselves in a copse because we couldn't give our position away, I looked around with my binoculars and the three soldiers were apparently alone.

The girl kept arguing with them excitedly, then the one close to her started to walk deeper into the water. As the waves started to cover his Jackboots, she looked as though she was taunting him to come to her, waving her hands in his face while walking back into deeper water. All of a sudden, he lunged at the girl, I pulled my sight up to my eye and they materialized like giants in the lens. She had her back to me; suddenly I noticed that she slipped her hand up her dress, pulling out a vicious looking knife. I took aim at the German soldier, but Dimitris said in his few words of English, 'Wait, it will be alright, she's my sister'.

Suddenly, half a dozen Greek partisans jumped out from some covered boats and machine-gunned the soldiers. The first one crashed into the sea and before the other two hit the beach, the girl put the knife in her mouth and leapt into the water submerging out of sight, barely missing the spray of bullets. It must have been fairly deep there because she just disappeared. As you will have guessed Stuart, that beautiful girl was Phaedra Popoloposis.'

'So where did you go Phaedra?' Stuart asked.

'I'd been swimming along that coast and around that village before I could walk, because my aunty lived there and uncle George worked as a fisherman. The old port wall had been made of stone slabs, several of them had been removed under water or just fallen off and so the local people had hidden food and their possessions in the spaces, so the Germans didn't steal everything. I just swam into the caverns and came out more than five hundred yards away, I walked out of the other side of the village just in case the Germans had back up.'

'My mission was incredibly important and urgent...' Sam continued. 'We had to find ways of supporting the Greek resistance, unfortunately my heart started to shove my head out of the way and I wanted to search for the beautiful mermaid, but she'd disappeared. Dimitris explained that she was like a wild cat and would

296

pop up all over the island. At that time, I hadn't seen my wife for about five years, she wrote to me and said that she was getting a divorce and was going to marry an American farmer from Georgia. I couldn't blame her, I'd been in the intelligence service and the Air force for years, half of the time she had no idea if I was dead or alive. It was no life for a woman or my daughter Audrey, and so in a way, I was pleased for her, she's been a decent friend ever since.'

'Especially as Sam has made her and her lazy husband very rich.' Phaedra added annoyed.

'I've never met a second wife who liked the first.' Sam said to Stuart smiling.

'I now understand why you dislike Germans so much Phaedra.' Stuart said.

'Well up to this point I wasn't fond of them, but things became far worse.' Phaedra answered with tears welling in her eyes. Stuart got up and refuelled the log fire and the glasses of his friends.

'Can you take any more Stuart?' Asked Sam.

'You can't stop now Sam, I've waited years for you to tell to me this story, if I don't get all of the details now, I'll never get it.'

'Have you heard of the 'Massacre of Kalavryta' Stuart?'

Stuart looked puzzled and ran his hand through his hair.

'I'm ashamed to say that I haven't; I'm so sorry Phaedra, living through the war, there were too many terrible stories from various countries. I think that my generation turned off to all of the tales about the Holocaust, the nine million Russians killed, the Japanese prisoner of war camps, each chronicle seemed to be worse than the one before.' Stuart explained apologetically.

'Don't worry Stuart, Greece is a small country and our stories are no more horrible than those from around the world, the difference is that I lived with the Greek tragedy and so it has affected me badly.' Phaedra said sadly. 'Most of the time I don't think about it, and yet because of Sam's job, I'm often reminded that what the young, like Pippa and Charlotte think of as past history; for me, it's still a real, and

297

sometimes recurring nightmare.'

'Then you must go on Sam, you know what they say; a problem shared is a problem halved.' Stuart said kindly.

'Well one of the partisan groups caught a large group of German soldiers in an ambush and held them captive.

Phaedra and Dimitris weren't part of the group, but went up to the hiding place with loads of people from surrounding villages, who'd been raped or plundered, and most of them had relatives who were killed by some of the German soldiers and they wanted to identify them. The German command heard what had happened from a couple of soldiers that'd escaped and the generals went crazy. It wasn't only that their soldiers were caught and could be killed. They knew that the capture of such a large number of men would give the Greek population confidence; that the prodigious war machine could be broken. This might lead to a previously unseen uprising, and if the Greeks succeeded, well, the myth of German invincibility would be broken all over Europe. So, the German army marched from the town of Tripolis to Kalavryta, killing every Greek that they could find on the way, including the women and children.

The Partisans killed all seventy-eight Germans. And then another German force from Aigion executed forty-two men in the village of Kerpini, burning the whole village and all of the surrounding crops. There was a small village on the Vouraikos River called Zachloros, they went in there and killed everyone and tossed the bodies in the river. People living downstream saw their dead countrymen float past for days. Then the Germans attacked the villages of Souvardo and Vrachni; again, they killed the people and burned the villages.

Phaedra and Dimitris came to see me with my little group of British and Irish commandos, she asked us to help attack the Germans who were insidiously surrounding their home village of Kalavryta. Our commanding officer was a charming Irish man with a fantastic reputation for bravery, but he told Phaedra that ten soldiers would be useless against such a huge force and that we were there to land planes, not start a useless battle that we could never win. As usual, Phaedra gave an impassioned speech and pleaded with him to change his mind, and when he finally walked away; Phaedra called him a coward and he had her and her brother thrown out of the camp.

She was hysterical, her parents lived there, with her eighty five year old grandmother, there were aunts, uncles, cousins, and she knew the whole village. I told her that I would go with my long-range Japanese rifle and try to cut down the odds, mind you; we all knew it was an impossible mission. I had Seditious ideas about the British high command, wondering why they couldn't spare a bomber or two. Would it have been so difficult to stop these massacres I asked myself? I suppose I knew in the logical part of my brain, that we were spread too thinly and it wasn't Greece's turn to be saved.

In a small way, the Greek partisans fought back well and killed a lot of Germans. What the invasion force didn't realise was that if you kept wiping everybody out, they had nothing to lose, but to fight or be killed. Therefore with the Greek character being what it is, inculcated in a belief in freedom, they killed as many of the occupiers as they could.

The Germans had three thousand troops and they were all going to Phaedra's village. We had a very difficult journey; little food and the climb would have been impossible for most city-dwellers. Of course I was trained and Phaedra and Dimitris were born near the difficult terrain. We marched over the mountain of Helmos and arrived outside the village on the tenth of December nineteen-forty-three. We saw the German soldiers coming from all directions. Some of the villagers tried to escape, by then the Germans had surrounded the area and they were mostly killed. Phaedra, Dimitris and I were heavily armed, with grenades, pistols and as much ammunition as we could carry, and I had my long-range rifle. Dimitris knew a secreted tor that overlooked most of the village and we camouflaged ourselves there. Some of the younger men bravely went out to meet the invading troops with hunting guns and a few only had kitchen knives. Needless to say, the thousands of troops cut them down mercilessly. I managed to take out a few key people, a couple of officers and a very enthusiastic sergeant on a machinegun, unfortunately it was like trying to kill a swarm of bees with a catapult.'

'I remember...' Phaedra said. 'Dimitris was so impressed with Sam, when he shot a Nazi from such a long distance, my little brother would jump up and down as if Greece had just won the Olympics, he was so brave and full of life.'

'It was December the thirteenth and fairly cold, the three of us were huddled together. Despite the awful circumstances, I remember enjoying putting my arm around this beautiful girl...' Sam said smiling at Phaedra. 'Even if she didn't notice me. It wasn't long before the Germans had taken control of the small town and we watched helplessly as the troops rounded up all of the men and little boys. Suddenly Dimitris and Phaedra jumped up and gasped, I stood and asked them what they had seen, they explained that they could see their grandfather, father and eldest brother. After a few minutes, they saw other male relatives including their cousin Gregorios who had just celebrated his eighth Birthday. Phaedra asked me what the Germans were going to do with them.

'Will they take them to a prisoner of war camp or what?' She asked me, I couldn't form the words in my mouth despite the fact that in my head, I thought the worst. There were just under five hundred Greeks shuffling towards the cemetery, a herd of sheep to the slaughterhouse. A quatrain of Germans shepherded them into a horseshoe shaped hollow and told them to wait there for some army trucks. Unfortunately, just as they lied to the Jews about the extermination showers, they lied about the trucks.

They had already set up concealed machinegun posts, suddenly some flares went off in the village, obviously, a well thought-out plan, the militia debouched from their hiding place, flung off tarpaulins and machinegunners started to fire.

Scores of men hurled their bodies over their wives and children, trying to shield them from the bullets.

Most of them tried to run, some carrying the kids. Some even tried to reach the gunners and fight, but they killed all of them. We stood on the hill in stunned silence for a long time. Then the German officers walked around the corpses looking for anyone alive, sometimes they found children under the dead bodies of their parents, and they finished them off with pistols. I saw one of them was drinking brandy or Schnapps from a flask and seemed to be enjoying himself. Suddenly Phaedra broke the silence and said to me with tears in her eyes. 'Where's Dimitris?'

We looked around the hilltop and couldn't see him. Then, we heard grenades going off. I grabbed my binoculars and there he was, running down the hill towards the hundreds of dead villagers, looking for his family and throwing the grenades at the troops. Phaedra screamed at the top of her voice. A desperate cry, and fell to her knees. A few seconds later, I saw her little brother Dimitris hit the ground with a hundred bullets hitting him from four sides of the field. Without my noticing, she started to run down the hill with her German Lugar handgun. It was a gun she felt proud of, because it had been taken from a German soldier in an earlier battle. I ran after her, caught her about a hundred yards before the killing field and smothered her body in the long grass. She screamed and struggled for ages, pleading with me to let her go to her family and shoot the soldiers, she finally sobbed herself to sleep.'

Stuart got up from his seat and sat next to Phaedra, he put his arm around her and asked. 'I assume Dimitris was dead?'

'Yes, he had countless bullets in him... Phaedra said sadly. 'Therefore it was difficult to recognise any part of his body. I did get away from Sam after a while and went into the village to find my mother; I knew the news would kill her. We thought the bastards had gone; unfortunately they came back into the village. I was with my mum who could barely stand up from the grief and then someone screamed. 'They're coming!' The dark grey uniforms marched towards us filling the width of the street. For a few minutes, I couldn't move. I just stood there on the stone street as they marched closer and closer to me.

They strutted their legs in unison, I began to hear Sergei Prokofiev's Dance of the Knights. The evil soldiers seemed to be marching in slow motion to the music floating around my head, with their bayonets thrust forward. It was a nightmarish ballet, but they weren't dancers, they were murderers. A frightening phalanx that I shall never forget.

The soldiers drove all the women, small kids and babies in arms towards the church; at first, we were relieved that they didn't shoot us. We heard them locking the front doors and running around the outside of the building. We had no lights inside and it was getting dark, the children were crying, as were some of the girls and women.

Then Nina Rapi, who was the wife of one of the Communist leaders, took control. She told us that we were at least safe in the church and when the Germans left, some of our people who survived would come and get us out. We heard the soldiers march off, then it started.'

'What happened Phaedra?' Stuart asked giving her a handkerchief.

'I'm sorry Stuart...' Phaedra said blowing her nose. 'I often think that I've recovered from this part of my life, but talking about it now in such detail has made it seem like yesterday.'

'I'm apologise Phaedra, you must stop, I should never have asked you about your family, I made a terrible mistake...' Stuart said.

'No, no it's alright, the story is nearly over, well this part anyway, I *want* to tell you.

The church went completely quiet, it was eerie, we were interned in shadows, there was no heat or light and the sun had set. Suddenly one of the women screamed, because there was a smell of burning and we saw flames. They had torched the doors and the roof before they left. Smoke started to come into the church and of course, most of the women and children began to panic. The stained glass windows were too high to reach and the heavy wooden doors were shut tight. The wife of the Communist leader stayed calm and some of us tried to smash down the doors with big, metal candelabras and some of the smaller wooden pews. It was getting very smoky in the church because they had lit all four sides. It was a funeral pyre and we were all choking to death. The rafters in the roof flared up quickly and two of the women were killed when a huge piece of blazing wood fell on top of them. They went up in flames almost instantly, it was a horrible sight. Women and children were running around screaming 'We're all going to be burnt alive!'

'You know Stuart the word holocaust...' Sam explained, 'is a Greek word, it means, burnt whole, obviously we now all use it to explain what the Germans did to the Jews.'

'Some people were praying,' Phaedra continued. 'Some were singing a Greek folk song; a few had just given up and were waiting to die. Nina Rapi and I were trying to find an exit or find some way of opening the doors, but they'd been there for hundreds of years and we just couldn't move them. Finally, even Nina gave up and looked at me. I never really got on with her before, she was always showing off as her husband was one of the leaders, yet she put her arms around me, and like sisters we cried together, we knew we were about to be burnt alive.

Subsequently, there was a banging noise outside the door, one woman screamed that it was the Nazis coming back to finish us off. Not that there was much to finish by then, we were all coughing with the smoke, our hair and faces a ghostly white, covered in ash under flaming embers falling down from the roof, most of us were covered in cuts and bruises; most were ready to die. There was a huge crash and the front doors sprung open, some of the women screamed at the thought of a German machine-gunner appearing. As the huge cloud of dust started to clear, we realised that the doors had been completely ripped off their hinges. Suddenly, the ancient wooden entrance raced down the road at speed, we all stood in shock looking at the hole that we'd longed for, over the previous three hours, but were now afraid of. When the dust and smoke completely cleared, we saw a German jeep twenty feet away, with chains attached to the rear bumper, the other end to the church's doors. Standing on the back seat, there was a man. We peered closely at him looking for his weapons, he didn't have any, when he waved, I realised it was Sam. He ran over to the entrance and screamed in Greek, 'Come on girls!' Somehow the hundreds of women, girls and toddlers began to laugh and cry at the same time, all of our men had been murdered, we were at death's door and yet some crazy English guy was standing amongst the flames calling us girls, and waving at the stunned group of women to follow him.' Phaedra paused and smiled at Sam, remembering the image like an old photograph.

'I was certainly very pleased to see Phaedra standing in front of all of those women, with a candelabra in her hand.' Sam also smiled at the memory. 'You know Stuart, the Germans continued with the slaughter and burning, I think it was about eight or nine hundred villages by the time they'd finished. My friend Conal was fantastic and helped as many as he could and tried to get the top brass to assist with some air power. The problem was, just as you and most of the world didn't know the details of the massacres in Greece, the Allied Forces were overrun with stories of disaster from all over Europe.'

Stuart was silent for a while and then he said, 'Well my friends, I now understand so much more about your past Phaedra. I hope though that you won't suffer with the memories and the pain of vengeance. There were a large number of good people in Germany, who tried to help others at the risk of their own lives. I'm sure that at some time in the future, when all of the bad ones are dead, the young generation will be conscious of what happened and will somehow try to make up for their ancestors' actions.'

'For me...' Phaedra said, 'I can't have a Lethean attitude to the war, it's still too fresh in my mind.'

'You may be right Stuart; I know that you were in the medical corps and you must have seen suffering on both sides. I hope we haven't exhausted you with our story. What do you say?' Sam said with his usual excitement for life. 'We'll all get a few hours sleep, and tomorrow, I'll buy everyone an expensive lunch at that posh hotel we went to last time.

The friends all said goodnight and fell exhausted in their beds.

Chapter 25
Risking Lives, Spring 1912

After several days of icy weather and constant snow-blizzard, a freezing, tipexed-out Somerleyton Manor and surrounding woodland, sat in a blank canvas with only the textured grain of the undulating hills and the stone rectangle, to hint at the colours of the secreted house and tor. The chimney's fiery heart in the Manor's huge reception room challenged the cool air with raging, cracking oak and sparking willow. While temperatures outside fell below freezing point, above two feet of virgin snow.

Peter Trubshaw poured more drinks for his wife, Lady Margaret, his ward and heir, Sam Trubshaw, the Vicar, Lionel Smallbouys, his closest friend, Dr John Gale and John's long-term fiancé, Megan Wodehouse. By the end of March, despite the wintry weather, Christmas had been forgotten and the Trubshaws were pleased for another excuse to celebrate.

'Therefore my friends our flying machine company, Blériot-Trubshaw Aéronautique, now has more orders than any other aircraft manufacturer in the world…' Peter said delightedly. 'And we are very excited to tell you that we are going off to New York, where business is booming, to sign an agreement to supply our airplanes, as we now call them, to the Americans!'

'Congratulations Peter, I'm sure I speak for all of us when I say how proud we are of your huge achievement.' John said, holding Megan's hand, sitting closely on the settee. 'Have you bought your tickets? I hear that crossing the Atlantic is very popular these days.'

'Yes indeed, I have contacted the White Star Line and made reservations for the 15 April. Margaret is very excited, she of course will need a completely new wardrobe for the voyage.' He smiled.

They all raised their glasses of champagne, except Sam who had lemonade in a crystal flute glass. Megan asked Margaret about her purchases for New York and the close friends giggled at the details of Margaret's quest, to show-off to their new business partners who seemed very rich, if not rather provincial.

'My dear John, Margaret and I were wondering if you and Megan would be kind enough to keep an eye on Sam whilst we are away. Mrs Jarvis and Bill Smith are looking after him; he gets on with them so well, especially as Bill has a new Collie puppy. Although Sam can be rather a handful sometimes, he still has a wild heart, you know.' Peter said concerned. 'His tutors will be here six days a week, which should keep him busy. He's becoming rather good at fencing now, the French tutor says he could prepare him for the Olympic Games'.

'He seems to be quite dangerous enough for my liking Peter, without arming him with a sword.' The Victor said grumpily.

'He enjoys living dangerously, he was brought up on it.' Megan said.

'And yes Peter, we will of course keep an eye on him, it's great fun to be with the young man, he has taught me a great deal about horses and never stops explaining the art of flying airplanes.'

'I am sorry Peter...' The Vicar interrupted. 'I just do not understand this craze for going faster and faster. Some of these motor cars are now going so swiftly, it's effecting people's brains, I have read in the Illustrated News that if you travel faster than ten miles per hour, you can become insane!'

The friends all laughed at the Vicar's stories of doom, nevertheless as usual Peter's enthusiasm for his new business was relentless.

'Do you know gentlemen that last year some Americans actually landed an airplane on a ship! Do you see what this means? I made my first fortune by supplying horses to the army, now I shall supply the army *and* navy with airplanes. Just as Britain once ruled the waves, she will now rule the skies and rebuild the empire!'

'Peter I have heard from some of the villagers, that you have allowed little Sam in one of these dangerous contraptions, is that true?' The Vicar asked gravely.

'I haven't allowed Sam in the airplanes Vicar, he

flies them!' Sam looked up at the three men, his face almost split into two by his delighted smile.

'Peter I am shocked, how could you risk this small boy's life...' The vicar said, pointing to Sam. 'In a contraption made from paper and glue, when you have already lost one son?'

John, Megan and Margaret looked shocked by the Vicar's outburst and John squeezed Megan's hand to hold her back, though Peter said calmly.

'My dear Lionel, that is exactly why Margaret and I allow Sam to live dangerously, let me explain.' Peter walked over to the Magnum and filled everyone's glass.

'We loved our little boy Peter junior, as much as any parents could. We protected him to such an extent that he did not have the life that most normal, young boys should have had. We, the servants and the school, overprotected him; he never jumped into the lake, never climbed a tree, never had a fight and never reached a gallop on his horse. And why? Because he was so ill and weak. We could not have any more children, therefore we tried to wrap Peter junior up in a protective bubble...' Peter took Margaret's arm and said with tears in his eyes. 'And what happened? He died at fifteen years old, without ever really experiencing life.

In the army, I was forced to risk my life and that of my men constantly, of course many died on the battlefield and in the hospitals afterwards, but the army was a huge adventure, we learnt camaraderie, the thrill of battle, it's something that men often have to do.' Peter put his other arm around his heir, who was listening intently. 'Now we have Sam, for all intents and purposes our only son. We have been given a second chance and whether it is by God's will, destiny, or if we listen to Megan, just by luck, we have been given an exceptional boy.

He has no fear and an incredible ability to fly through the air, even before we had heard of airplanes.

Therefore, we are going to help him to live his life to the full, he still practises his circus skills, he has the fencing lessons, he shoots as well as any landowner in the county and now yes, he is one of the first aviators. Sam saved Lady Margaret's life a few years ago on Tower Bridge, we now see every moment of our lives as a bonus, and who knows, we might all live until we are one hundred years old!' Peter said with a smile.

'I'll toast to that Peter.' Megan said lifting the mood. They gulped down the sparkling wine in silence; Peter then turned to his guests and said cheerfully.

'Actually Sam is the perfect pilot; the biggest problem the industry has at the moment, is the ratio between weight and thrust, therefore the smaller and lighter the pilot, the better. Our engineers believe that the best pilots of the future will start at eighteen years old. At that age, they will be light in weight and have quick minds to cope with the difficulties of flight.'

'Do you think there will still be wars in Europe Peter?' John asked.

'I would like to answer negatively, alas there are groups of wealthy people who are becoming afraid of Marxism and the rise of the common man...'

'They don't need to be Peter, Marx Just wants a more equal society, and it's a beautiful idea that everyone should have the same opportunities, do you not agree?'

'Well we have spoken about these ideas many times Megan and we all know how passionate you are for an equal world. The element that worries me is that human nature works against equality, there will always be some people who are physically stronger than others, there will always be greedy people, who want more for themselves, these people will usually take what they want by force, and I'm afraid that if these people unite, they may persecute, the weak in a Right-Wing revolt.

The Vicar visibly disagreed, yet realised that his earlier outburst was inappropriate, the friends went into dinner and Sam was allowed to try his first glass of champagne, reluctantly served by Jarvis, who still called him 'The lucky gypo-boy upstairs', except these days he only said it quietly to his wife. Because Sam was not only very popular with all of the servants and land workers, but at twelve years old, he'd become every part the young master of the Manor, now speaking English as fluently as most

Englishman, despite a slight indescribable accent and European mannerisms.

At the end of the dinner, Victor the groom and his new assistant Gerald, brought around the trap for the characteristically, inebriated Vicar Smallbouys. They also led Doctor John's new black gelding to the front of the house, as Mary had died last year.

To John's disappointment, his strong willed fiancé still refused to use a trap, and her determination to ride astride her horse had become a fashion among many women. Megan's faithful chestnut stallion, that still had the will to race across the countryside, bounced noisily to the front of the other horses and Megan was the first to mount. The three Trubshaws stood in the warm glow of a close family at the front door holding hands, to see their guests out and wave goodbye. Once the Vicar was safely seated in his trap with the groom's help, he thanked his parishioners for dinner and as the horse started to get a grip in the snow, he tuned over his shoulder and called back.

'By the way Peter, which ship are you two sailing on in April?'

Peter and Margaret answered cheerfully in unison.

'The RMS Titanic!'

Part two

Chapter 26
The Red Dragon, 1964

The picturesque village of Begur was perched on a hilltop a few miles from the unspoilt golden beaches of the Baix Emporda, the *Provence* of Northern Spain.

The native people utilized their strange language, Catalan, secretly, since General Franco had banned its use in all official documents and unofficially on the streets of Catalan.

These measures only increased their hatred of fascism and everything Spanish, including the Guardia Civil, which patrolled the tiny village streets in coveys of two or four, speaking loudly in official Castilian Spanish, provoking and reminding the locals of their occupied status.

The Catalonians were a naturally quiet and secretive people descended from settled Roman soldiers: unlike the their open and noisy neighbours from the west and south of the Iberian Peninsular.

Apart from a certain distain for their Spanish cousins, they also hated the French who lived less than an hour north of Gerona and almost any foreigner who dared to enter one of the most beautiful, lush-green areas of the unspoilt Costa Brava.

Sam and Phaedra rented a newly built house, owned by some wealthy loyalist solicitors in Barcelona, overlooking the deserted little fishing village of Tamariu.

The rocky enclave boasted a yellow beach and a maze of paths through the vast, emerald pine forest that sprawled for miles in all directions, meeting the small, market town of Palafrugell, and then marched on eventually to the Pyrenees Mountains.

They awoke early as usual, drank some squeezed orange juice and walked onto the terrace overlooking the sheer drop to the agitated, spring tide below.

Without speaking they started their daily routine of slow, rhythmic movements in the art of Tai Chi. Once they had warmed-up the couple slid their curved, ornate Thai swords from their sheathes and sliced the air to shreds in a deadly ballet for anyone within range. The exercises took exactly an hour. After showering and dressing, Phaedra squashed her blonde-streaked hair under a brunette short wig and darkened her make-up to match the disguise.

Monsieur and Madam Renault, tourists from France, were ready for their errand, having decided to leave their conspicuous Bristol in the garage, hiking with cached small arms and backpacks equipped for any emergency. They made slow progress for and hour and a half through the dense woodland. A lazy breeze fluttered through the tall pines and disturbed the prickly shrubs, which nature had scattered recklessly across the steep climb. The Renaults kept up a steady pace until they saw the sign for Begur on the narrow road. At the end of another steep hike and fifty stone steps, the walkers entered the tiny central square and made their way to the oasis that was the only bar-restaurant in the village.

A Dalíesque blue sky illuminated the sallow, stone houses and soaring church.

The Begurencs had a historic relationship with Cuba since the nineteenth century and several of the locals wore clothes reflecting the Caribbean Island's colourful style.

Sam wore a false black moustache and some small, round, wire glasses. His wife's long, black, waterproof jacket and beret completed her Latin masquerade. They were well practised in the art of disguise and Sam thought they looked rather impressive, when they'd both laughed hysterically at the odd couple that appeared in their hall mirror on the way out of the house.

The restaurant owner ambled out onto the terrace looking at them suspiciously saying, '*Si?*'

Sam ignored the abruptness and replied in rusty Catalan, '*Hola, bon dia.*'

Avoiding the '*Buenos dias*' used in Franco's Castilian Spain. The slightly softened, yet cautious proprietor relaxed a little and asked if they wanted something to eat.

Sam ordered some red wine and loads of tapas and turned to his wife after the waiter left saying. 'They always say something that's the same in Castilian Spanish and

Catalan Spanish, just in case strangers are baits for the Guardia, who try to trick them into breaking the unwritten law against their language.' Sam explained to Phaedra.

'Sounds like the Germans in Greece.' She spat, at the memory of the occupation.

'Luckily, all those years in Paris have trained us in the art of ordering from difficult waiters…' He chuckled, 'I think we might experience a new level of rudeness when we meet the Chinese again. I haven't seen Mr Chong for many years, he was fairly ancient the last time, according to our French contact, he's still here and hasn't given up his *art.*'

'I've never been fond of the Chinese…' Phaedra said, with a mouth full of anchovies. 'They hate all foreigners, according to the man at the Chinese restaurant in Notting Hill Gate.'

'How can you say you dislike Chinese, when you have a close friend from Hong Kong?'

'Mai-Ling is different, she's my bridge partner and she doesn't like her Chinese relatives either!'

'I don't think I'll ever understand Greek women, or any woman come to that. I guess I'll just love them, buy them loads of presents and not question anything they do.'

'Almost correct Sam, just leave out the plural when you get to the loving and present buying.' Phaedra teased. 'I'm the only one who receives all the loving, n'est pas?'

'Of course my darling.' Sam agreed with ironic obedience.

The couple looked up at the massive stone wall that covered one side of Plaça de Vila. The church built in honour of Sant Pere, was erected originally in the seventeenth century.

When the two bells rang, reminding Sam of their timely task, the three seagulls, which each found a perch on top of the tower, decided to swoop off in the direction of the stainless steel sea, five miles down hill. When they finished at the restaurant, the hikers walked up a steep ally and looked at the incredible view over the Mediterranean.
The Medes Islands in the distance resembled a half submerged rhinoceros, poking his two rocky horns out of the water, waiting for prey. At the top of the hill with a

predominate view over the village and valley, a small stone terraced house left its front door open, with flimsy wooden boxes of Chinese vegetables laid in the hall and spilling out onto the narrow pavement.

'This seems a strange place for people like these Chinese to sell weapons to professionals like us?' Phaedra said, looking at the picturesque scenery.

'What would you do my love, open a shop in Oxford Street, with a sandwich board advertisement outside?'

The couple climbed over the colourful pallet of food, stepping into the hallway, Sam put his head around the sitting room door, adjusting his vision to the dim unlit house, in stark contrast to the brilliant sunny street.

'Hola!' Sam called out. After a two or three minutes of silence, a small Chinese boy of about six years old, dressed as a cowboy, came down the stairs and asked them in impolite Catalan what they wanted.

'Hello cowboy.' Sam joked in Catalan, 'Is Señor Chong here please?' The child's smooth porcelain face showed no sign of cracking into a smile.

'No Señor Chong here.' He switched to heavily accented Castilian Spanish with even less charm, realising that the couple were foreigners.

'I've met your grandfather before, please go and tell him I wish to speak to him again.' Sam said patiently in Castilian.

'You want vegetables or not!' The small boy said angrily, now using disjointed English.

'Listen you little brat...' Phaedra snapped, stepping in front of her husband. 'Go and get an adult before I give you a thick ear!' Before Sam could interrupt, the oriental lad leapt off the third stair, spinning like a top in mid-air, aiming his right foot at Phaedra's head in a perfect kung-Fu move. Phaedra saw it coming when he started his turn and grabbed his ankle with her left hand and his knee with her right. He dangled in mid-air for a couple of seconds swinging as rhythmically as a pendulum in a grandfather clock, and then started to swear profusely in a Chinese dialect. Neither one of the tourists understood the language, but they recognized the sentiment.

'May I help you?' A mezzo-soprano voice said in the shadows, using perfect English. A tiny, Chinese man wearing a face like a shrivelled fig, dressed in a blue and silver, silky tunic with matching trousers and hat, stood at the top of the stairs; his arms folded and hands hidden in the ample sleeves.

Phaedra noticed his shoes that turned up above the toes like a teapot handle, the rest of him stayed in the shadows so she couldn't see him clearly in the dark hall. The boy went limp in her hands and she lowered him to the floor. The old man descended slowly down the steps and said something to the child, who disappeared as fast as a mouse in front of a prowling cat.

'I must apologise for my great-grandson he watches too much television. How may I help you?' He said. Some parts of his face smiled, however, it didn't carry any recognisable emotion.

'We've come to make a purchase, may we come in?' Sam asked from the hallway.

'Which of the vegetables would you like?' The wrinkly old man asked with paper-thin lips, never taking his eyes from Sam or removing his hands tucked into the bell-shaped sleeves.

'Actually last time I was here, I bought a different kind of product.' Sam answered cautiously.

'We only have these few things, we are poor traders.'

Phaedra looked at her husband, her eyes saying that it would be a good moment to get down to business, but Sam had more patience for Chinese customs and responded in a low voice. 'I've come for a Red Dragon.'

The old man didn't react for a few moments and then turned to Phaedra saying.

'You have very fast reactions young lady, have you had any training?'

'No, I practise by regularly beating-up my grandchildren.' She answered flippantly.

The old man turned around and started to mount the stairs saying. 'I'm sorry if you don't want the vegetables, goodbye.'

'Mr Chong, wait!' Sam said urgently, delaying the old man on the staircase. 'I need the bite of a thousand dragons.'

Phaedra looked at her husband as though he was insane; nevertheless his colourful translation had some effect on the gnarled old Chinese, as he floated silently down towards the entrance hall.

When he landed silently on the ground floor with the timing of a seagull, he spun around with an agility he didn't look capable of, to look at the strangers forensically in the strong sunlight.

'Follow me please.' He finally said, after analysing their eyes and turning to the back of the confined sitting room. Mr Chong opened a silky green curtain revealing a wide door, he pulled out a long brass key from his sleeve and his virtually invisible hand opened the lock. The tiny figure gestured to the couple to follow him down the steps.

The room was dark as they entered and an aroma of strong, musky incense filled the air.

He put on a few small lights and moved behind an ebony-black lacquered, oriental style table. Sam and Phaedra cast their professional eyes around the large space.

An ornate screen hid another doorway at the end of the room. Expensive oriental furniture and pieces of art were packed in like Underground commuters during London's rush hour. The dim lights could've hidden half a dozen Chinese warriors in the shadows of the spacious basement.

After a long pregnant silence, Mr Chong whispered. 'Please sit.' They obeyed resting on the edge of the low silky stools. 'What is the purpose of the Red Dragon?'

Sam now dropped his act as an interested tourist and spoke like a man of his profession.

He used his forearm and calves to subtlety check that his two pistols were still in easily accessible places.

'To kill someone.' He replied simply.

'How would you like them to die?' He asked, like a waiter taking an order for lunch.

'It will be in a public place with several enemies nearby, a long delay would help.'

'Is this a simple euthanasia or do you mind if the death is; *painful*?' He asked in a tone that suggested that he preferred the second option.

'Painful would be preferable.' Phaedra interrupted, thinking of the evil Nazi hit.

The wrinkled fig now gave a visible smile, the tiny eyes completely disappearing into his skull for a couple of seconds.

'It is an interesting fact, that most of my female clients intend to inflict long painful deaths on their victims...' Pausing he put his head on one side, looked at Phaedra and asked. 'It is a woman, I presume?'

Sam interrupted the repartee asking seriously. 'Do you have what we need Mr Chong?' If there's something that would give us the delay we need, a certain result, without any pain for the victim, it would be preferable.'

The old Chinese looked disappointed that his psychological game with Phaedra had been cut short, gave a slight sigh and opened one of ten drawers behind his desk. Using both hands with long fingernails that curled like cat claws and were painted with gold leaf, he placed a magnificent, black lacquered box in front of his guests and asked teasingly.

'Can you open it?'

Sam took the smooth shiny rectangle carefully and searched the edges for a space or seam, he pressed the blood-red, inlaid dragon with its ruby eyes, but nothing opened or moved, he turned it over and looked at the inlaid, gold Chinese symbol on the back, but the whole thing seemed to be in one, completely smooth piece.

'I give up.' he said defeated. 'Does it open?'

The frail trembling hands took the objet d'art and passed it to Phaedra.

'I think the lady could open it.' The mischievous old Chinese continued.

Phaedra turned the slippery box several times looking for the key, in the deadly silent, dimly lit room. Suddenly, she pressed the two ruby eyes at the same moment with her thumbs and the dragon's red tail flipped up with the sound of a cork popping from a wine bottle, they flinched and the old man laughed, a rasping sound like fingernails scratching on a blackboard.

'It always makes me jump, no matter how many times I see it.' The Chinese said, getting his composure back.

'Turn the dragon's tail clockwise Señora and the lid will open.'

Phaedra cautiously turned the dragon's vermilion lacquered tail at arms length and the lid sprung open.

The interior was handmade to fit exactly like a puzzle. Phaedra turned the box to the low light, revealing a beautiful black ebony pipe; eight inches long, like a miniature flute. It nestled on a red velvet rack, running along the left-hand side of the box. On the right, six tiny matching darts with needle-sharp points were fitted into the precisely made slots. A small, tinted glass file laid next to the darts, containing a dark red liquid, stuffed with a cork and sealed by thick wax, all of which carried the dragon's emblem in terracotta red and gold inlay.

'A blow pipe?' Sam confirmed.

'Yes, it has a range of two to three metres, depending on the fitness and expertise of the user.' He explained with a sickly grin. 'The pipe and the darts are made from very light bamboo and shark's teeth are used as the needles.

'What happens after the dart hits the mark.' Phaedra quizzed.

'Ah yes, as usual the ladies like to hear the painful details.'

He flicked open an ornate fan using a surprising strength in his wrist and held it over a grinning mouth.

'What's in the bottle?' Sam interjected, not enjoying the old man's game with his wife.

'Two people, two questions, two interests; one answer.' The old man spoke looking at the ceiling, ready to give a philosophical lecture to a class of students. He opened another drawer and grabbed something; Sam and Phaedra both touched their pistols, the old man noticed their reaction, but ignored it, he pulled out an ornate opium pipe, lit it slowly from a burning taper, inhaling the slow-moving, milky-white smoke deeply.

'If we wanted you dead Mr Renault, you wouldn't have made it up the hill.' He snorted, filling his lungs again.

Luckily, his research only went back as far as Sam's contact in Lyon, where he was known by the French alias, he noticed the 'we' and assumed that they weren't alone, so Sam let the old man show off.

'You are very well informed Monsieur Chong.' Sam said in fluent French, to perpetuate the cover.

'Back to the advertising for the product.' He started enjoying the attention like most old people with an audience.

'The Pathogenic liquid is a secret blend handed down to me by my ancestors. It contains the venom of brown-widow spiders, Latrodectus, better than the black ones...' He smiled.

'Because of the extreme potency of their neurotoxic venom; and a special blend from three different snake poisons. The Taipan and the Tiger Snake from Asia, plus the Yellow-Bellied Sea Snake from the South Pacific. This one is very difficult to catch, we often squander a few fishermen during the task...' He chuckled at the thought of some poor seamen being crushed and bitten by the snakes as they struggled to drag them on board a small boat. 'They're well paid; therefore there's no shortage of volunteers for the hunt. We then add an interesting blend of narcotics, which makes it impossible for any antidote to be used.'

The lecturer enjoyed a long pause and a few more puffs on the dream-making pipe.

He appeared to take great pleasure holding back the interesting part of his well-rehearsed fable.

'And now, Madam Renault wishes to know what effect it will have on her enemy, n'est pas!' Another covered smile with the fan and his voice raised an octave.

'The potion causes a type of pemphigus. When the dart touches human skin there's no immediate effect, the recipient usually thinks they've been stung by a mosquito or bee. After a few minutes or so, the area starts to itch; I'm told it's quite pleasant at first, like being tickled with a feather. A red mark appears on the skin and spreads rapidly

319

just under the surface, like the roots from Ginseng. After about ten minutes, when the dragon's tentacles reach out, the itching becomes unbearable, so much so, the victim often tears away the skin and even the flesh of their own body, in an insatiable desire to relieve the burning, excruciating agony. The name comes from the bulging red blisters that creep across the skin and look like a tattoo of a red dragon. Depending on the weight of the individual, death takes about twenty minutes. The worst twenty minutes of their life, before they receive the demise, that they start to plead for.' The silence in the room was palpable; Sam closed the magnificent box and took a brown envelope from his pocket that he pushed across the table. Two shadows came to life from the back wall and twin girls in their twenties moved forward silently, they were dressed in black satin tunic tops and loose fitting trousers, their china-white faces were identical masks of indifference. One opened the envelope examining the contents, while the other lifted the drug filled, floundering old Chinese to his feet, when his knees started to give way. Sam leaned forward politely to help, though the young girls moved swiftly, with the accomplishment of martial arts training, and one said with an American accent. 'No problem we have her.' The buyers looked surprised and then Phaedra asked. 'Her?'

'Our great-grandfather died last year when he was one hundred and three years old, this is his youngest wife; she has taken over the business.'

The old woman looked at them and gave a telling sibylline laugh. The door opened behind them and the three women left arm in arm.

Phaedra put the black, dragon box in her bag checking the zip and the hikers were soon squinting in the welcome afternoon sun, strolling down the hill into the village.

'Wow!' Phaedra exclaimed after a few minutes of silence. 'That was one of the most unusual experiences I've had for a long time, how old do you think she was?'

'I'm not sure, I've seen women in India who looked over a hundred, but were younger than us, and I suppose it depends on their quality of life, exercise and whether or not they are on drugs.'

Just before they reached the central square, they heard a girl's voice crying-out. On the left side of the street down a narrow ally, two young Guardia Civil officers in two-tone green uniforms were standing either side of a pretty, teenage, village girl, dressed in a colourful Caribbean skirt and an off the shoulder white blouse.

She looked like she lived near-by as she wore no shoes.

Franco's guards were questioning her in Castilian Spanish, teasing her when she replied with her Catalan accent. The tall one with a hooked, unattractive nose kept poking her in the chest and leaned against her suggestively. The little one with thick tortoise-shell glasses persisted in pushing her against the wall. She tried to get away unsuccessfully, after a few minutes, the questioning became more heated and then hooked nose put his boot on her bare toes and started to ground them into the cobblestones, she cried-out without tears. Phaedra had seen enough and moved towards them.

'Wait darling.' Sam cautioned, holding her arm firmly. 'We can't risk our cover, we're just wealthy tourists driving to Barcelona for a short holiday, we mustn't take any chances by being questioned by this lot.'

The Guardia were now pulling down her blouse saying she must be searched, Phaedra moved towards them again, but Sam pulled her back resolutely. 'Phaedra, have you forgotten what we have in this rucksack?' He whispered.

'I can't leave her, she's younger than Charlotte.'

'Darling, please listen to me, we are professionals, the hit did far worse things to hundreds of people, we must get down there as quickly as possible and get out of this fascist country. We can't save everyone, this sort of thing happens every day all over Spain.' Phaedra hesitated and looked into Sam's determined eyes.

'You're right darling...' She said in a conciliatory tone. 'I'm sorry, the risk is too great, let's go back to the house.'

The couple turned back down the hill towards the

square, Sam quickened his pace and started to think about the long journey, realising that they should leave straight away. He turned to Phaedra to ask if she could get ready immediately, however, she had disappeared.

Sam raced back up the precipitous hill towards the side turning, and as he guessed, Phaedra was a step away from the two Guardia and the young village girl.

The Greek woman pushed her arm through the four-armed fence of the two men entrapping the teenager against the wall, saying in Castilian Spanish, because she didn't speak any Catalan.

'*Ven aqui guapa.*'

Phaedra pulled her through the gap and shoved her along the narrow alleyway, when the tall Guardia grabbed Phaedra's arm violently swinging her around to face him, saying. 'Hey you, come back here!'

Sam quickened his pace and said to himself, 'You shouldn't have done that young man'. Phaedra turned quickly, put her steel-edged hiking boots just below the tall ones knee and kicked down hard, removing the skin and flesh from the length of his shin. He screamed in agony as he fell to the ground. The little one with the glasses looked shocked, he hadn't seen any action since his training two years before and so he crouched down to comfort his friend, who was rolling on the floor with a blood stained trouser leg. Sam met the females halfway along the ally and said urgently.

'Come on, let's go fast.'

The three ran down the hill towards the square, a few yards from the bottom the young girl directed them into a doorway. Sam and Phaedra followed her through a small ironmonger's shop, the old storekeeper silently unlocked the rear door without being asked, and they found themselves in a flowery back garden. The girl opened a little wooden shed door and entered. Sam hesitated until he saw her open a false panel on the back wall, faced with a rack of garden tools. Beyond the opening was the forest that surrounded the village. The young girl kissed Phaedra's cheek without a word, pushed them through the opening and slammed the door behind them. They moved quickly through the trees until they reached the winding road.

They recognised the area, rushed across the open tarmac, entered a small gap in the wall of pine trees, and ran into the dense forest towards Tamariu. After fifteen minutes, near the winding road to Palafrugell, they heard sirens and ducked into the undergrowth. Behind them, an ambulance, followed by a blue, local police car marked Mosses and an open Guardia Civil green jeep.

The vehicles raced towards Begur with sirens blasting and lights flashing. Once they could see their rented house the couple went in opposite directions with pistols in hand, circling around each side to confirm that it was as deserted as they had left it earlier. The professionals arrived at the front door together and without speaking, they entered and started packing. Within fifteen minutes, Monsieur and Madam Renault in their expensive clothes and designer sunglasses were cruising down the coast road towards Barcelona. When they came to the town of Palamos they saw in the distance a line of cars at a roadblock and slowly glided to a stop at the end of the line behind an old truck, stacked with chickens squashed in small balsa wood cages on their final journey. When they reached the front of the queue a young Guardia Civil officer looked at the beautiful Bristol, and then called his sergeant saying he had 'Foreigners, a man and a woman.'

Sam turned to Phaedra explaining. 'We fit the rough description, they must have noticed your accent and seen the back of me, I think that there'll be loads of tourists coming down for the spring holiday and many of them will be older couples, so it might be okay.'

The young Guardia asked them for their papers, Sam pretended not to understand and spoke to them in French. The boy knew the French word for papers and put out his hand. While he looked at the documents carefully, the sergeant walked over with two others, one with a fierce looking Alsatian dog, all of them armed with holstered pistols.

'You are French Monsieur?' He asked with schoolboy grammar.

'Yes we are.' Sam replied using his clippie Parisian

accent.

'Please get out of the car.' The sergeant commanded.

'We have nothing to declare.' Sam said, suggesting he thought they were customs' officers.

'All of your papers are French, you have a French number-plate, yet the car's British with the steering wheel on the right. Why?'

'Because it's the latest Bristol and they don't make it for export yet, so I bought an English version.' Sam explained calmly.

'I collect these cars.'

'Open the boot please.'

Sam knew they'd need to jack up the car and use an oxygen and acetylene torch on the thick, steel plate before they could find anything interesting and so he opened the boot and said casually.

'That's fine, look wherever you want, it's all open.'

The former British agent looked over at his wife standing a few feet on the other side of the car, who was giving him their secret signal for a problem, which was her turning her diamond ring clockwise around her finger. He walked around to her side of the vehicle casually, making a big show of opening the passenger door and said to her softly in Greek that he hoped no one understood.

'What's wrong?'

'I put everything in the car safe, except I've the black wig in my handbag.' She said in a voice retained for secrets.

'Oh no, that's a shame...' Sam looked around at the roadblock, there were five Guardia uniforms, one with a motorbike, all of them armed, more than likely a rifle or machine-gun in their car boot, the dog sniffing around off the lead, it didn't look very promising.

'Too many innocents for a shootout, too far from the border for a chase, do you think you can slight-of-hand it somewhere?' He whispered.

'I'll try darling, it will be difficult, they're watching us closely, I can't throw it on the ground because of the dog.'

The sergeant looked suspiciously at Sam and spoke to his second in command conspiratorially.

'Listen Pedro, the incident was about two hours ago, the bulletin described them as foreign, one man, one woman, both tall, middle-aged, sounds like them, what do you think?'

Pedro looked at Sam and Phaedra carefully and then at their papers, after a few moments he said. 'They said that the woman had short black hair and they were hippies or hitchhikers, these two look rich, she's blonde, expensive clothes and too old to start fighting with our people in the street.'

'Listen Pedro, during the war, I saw grandfathers fighting for their lives on the streets with knives and sticks, against soldiers with machineguns and tanks, you can still fight when you're old!'

'Yes amigo, but those people were fighting for a cause, why would these two rich people start a fight with the Guardia?'

'Alright let's search them thoroughly, if they don't have anything incriminating, we'll let them go.'

The queue of traffic started to snake back for half a mile with some people hooting and others near the back, turning around dangerously on the narrow road. Only to be stopped by a second patrol further along.

Three cars back from the Renault's Bristol an American couple left their rented Seat and walked up to the front complaining loudly.

One of the Guardia told them to go back to their car and wait.

They didn't understand or didn't want to understand anything he said, even when he tried to speak in English.

They kept shouting that they were from Texas, in fact, the man wore a large white hat to prove it and the woman's second cousin was allegedly a friend of the King of Spain. He was going to hear about this, as they were late for a big dinner in Barcelona.

Phaedra walked over to calm them down and spoke to them kindly like a fellow tourist, at one point Phaedra put her arm around the woman and told her to relax, they would soon be on their way, she said comfortingly. Then two of the Guardia called Phaedra over and asked her to take off her jacket so they could pat her down, another two did the same with Sam, who started to look around for an escape. They found nothing on him, however, his pulse started to rise when he heard one of the officers asking for Phaedra's handbag.

'There's nothing in it.' She said determinedly.

'I must search it.' The Guardia replied equally firmly.

'I've told you there's nothing in it, except my make-up and perfume, now let got!' Phaedra said angrily.

Sam move quickly, jumped into the car, opened the glove box, and pressed the three interior lights in a sequence to make the back panel open, producing an automatic handgun. He clicked the safety as quietly as he could and started the engine. The passenger door was completely open. Phaedra looked over at him and the possible dive into the door. The officer grabbed her handbag, nevertheless she held onto the straps, but he wrenched it out of her hands aggressively.

'Be careful with that.' She snapped. 'It's Chanel!'

Sam was worried that she might hit him, he was willing her to just run and jump in the car, it might be difficult to get away, be not as bad as the Guardia finding the short wig.

They would soon realise it was a disguise and the Renaults with their identical twins the Trubshaws, would be thrown into one of General Franco's famous prisons, never to see daylight again. Sam tried to get Phaedra's attention by putting his right foot on the accelerator, exciting the Bristol's eight cylinders, everyone turned around at the engine's roar.

'*Run Phaedra.*' Sam was yelling telepathically. '*Jump in the car now!*'

Although Phaedra seemed to be concentrating on the man rifling her bag. Suddenly, the police turned around to see someone screaming in panic further up the queue. Four of the Guardia ran along the line of cars, the young officer who was searching Phaedra looked into her small bag without the wig and pushed it back into her hands. As he ran off towards the police dog, which was tearing at the American woman's jacket. Phaedra jumped into the sports car and Sam drove off without looking back.

'What happened?' Sam asked his wife after they hit the open road and high speed.

Phaedra looked pleased with herself.

'I slipped the wig in the American woman's bag with one of those big, smelly dog treats Heli and Neme like so much. She started screaming because the police Alsatian was trying to get the dog treat out of her bag, I slipped another one in her jacket pocket.'

'You know Phaedra, you do get me into a lot of trouble, but you're wonderful at finding a solution.'

The sports car passed a sign that declared '150 kilometres to Barcelona.'

Chapter 27
The Lubyanka, Moscow, April 1964

In the basement of The Lubyanka, agent Yuri Misezhnikov was exhausted, he really needed some sleep. It must have been two days ago, one minute he was drinking a Pastis on the terrace at Les Deux Magots on Boulevard de Saint-Germain-des-Prés in Paris, the next, four burly agents from the KGB dragged him onto an unheated military plane at Orly Airport, and threw him out at Moscow's Vnukovo International. Then, without any explanation from the agents, last night, he reluctantly recognised the famous KGB headquarters from the back of an army truck and almost had a heart attack as he was shuffled down to the infamous basement.

Yuri tried to close his eyes on the throne-like chair, its wooden seat was cold and hard, the back too upright, the metal wires attached to his naked body too threatening. The young Russian's mind raced as quickly as a ball bearing in a pinball machine, bouncing off the walls, and every time his brain rolled down to sleep, someone tapped the flippers and the electric shock launched him back up the pintable with bells ringing and glaring lights flashing around his head. He'd been trained to resist this type of torture; look for signs to estimate the time, was anyone wearing a watch? Do the technicians have beard stubble? Do they smell like they've just had a shower? When the doors open are there any windows? Scratch your hand each time they question you, to keep track of the hours and days. Stay alert, make friends with the technicians, ask questions, and look for clues in their answers. The training was good, very good, although he didn't expect to be interrogated by the same people who instructed him.

In another part of Moscow, General Fyodor Poluostrovich's limo cruised to a gentle halt in front of the magnificent Igumnov House, at 43 Bolshaya Yakimanka Street. The French flag fluttered over the Embassy that oozed splendour and luxury, in fact; it almost became an embarrassment to the original owners, the Igumnov family.

When after more than ten years of building and decorating the flamboyant building, the mansion was still unfinished. The architect, Nikolay Pozdeyev just couldn't stop improving his masterpiece, yet his clients kept complaining that he'd gone over budget and had past the original estimates for finishing the house. The Igumnov family told Nikolay that they'd had enough and refused to pay him another rouble. Pozdeyev became hysterical, saying that he would be bankrupt if they stopped the finance and finally decided to kill himself in October 1893.

Famously, the private house was confiscated during the October Revolution, became a community club and then housed several medical institutions. Ultimately in 1938 it was handed over to the French Government for their embassy and has been celebrated for its cuisine and fine wines by the international diplomatic corps ever since.

Fyodor, as one of the most powerful people in the Soviet Union, albeit unofficially, was a regular invitee. A French soldier jumped to attention when he recognised the General's car stopping at the front entrance, the KGB supremo nodded to his driver, Sergeant Alex Ruska, as he stepped out of the black Volga Limousine, which meant he could be five minutes or all night.

Alex didn't care, he loved his job, it had most of the perks of being a General without any of the responsibility, as long as he didn't upset the great man, he had a cushy job for life.

The head of the Soviet secret service, was escorted through the outstanding hall and up the wide staircase decorated with thousands of ceramic tiles, made at Russia's famous Kuznetsov factory, covering the floor, walls and even the ceiling. At the top of the ornate staircase the General was shown into the main reception room that was buzzing with the upper class, hoi polloi of Moscow, whose lavish clothes and jewellery added to the room's decorations from the Netherlands, the Louis XV-style furniture and the 17th-century French tapestries. When the aide de camp to the French ambassador was told who had arrived, he excused himself from the small group he entertained and rapidly greeted the General at the entrance.

'Good evening General, the ambassador is delighted that you were able to come; please, this way.' The General followed the young man who seemed to float over the antique carpets, dance around the pink, Georgian velvet chairs and land in front of a group of extravagantly dressed diplomats and their bejewelled wives.

'Fyodor Bonsoir!' The new Ambassador, Philippe Baudet said ingratiatingly to the Soviet Union's most well informed spymaster. 'It's so good to see you again...' He continued, whilst snapping his fingers to one of the penguin dressed waiters. 'Champagne General?'

'No, bring me some vodka please.' The General replied in faultless French to the monochrome bird with the tray.

'Allow me to thank you again for your kind help with the custom's office. My wife insisted on having some of her own furniture and paintings from Paris. We don't have the same taste as my predecessor, and she just couldn't live without her own possessions...'

'It was my pleasure Mr Ambassador, I hope that you'll stay here long enough to make all of the moving worthwhile...' Fyodor answered with a slow burning smile that was unable to melt the cold grey steel in his eyes. Philippe Baudet was an experienced diplomat able to keep his face a pleasant mask of vague politeness, regardless of what was said to him.

However, he'd been told on his last day in Paris, to analyse everything General Poluostrovich said. And now as he ushered the devious controller of the KGB towards a docile group of French businessmen, Philippe started to wonder if Fyodor was just teasing him or if had he heard something, what did he mean by, *'I hope that you'll stay long enough to make all of the moving worthwhile...'*

The French Ambassador introduced four of his country's businessmen and their wives to Fyodor Poluostrovich. He was charming and knowledgeable about the enterprises the executives ran, and complimented the women on their clothes and jewellery. He didn't mention that he had an extensive file on all of them. He also knew that one of the group had been taking black money from his

Soviet distributors, which he kept in Switzerland, and that another only had a wife as a showpiece. His real pleasure was in masochistic sexual gratification, that he received from his very tall, young secretary, who was flirting with an American diplomat on the other side of the magnificent room.

The latest arrival in the group smiled at the sixty-year-old man asking naïvely.

'Tell me sir, what do you do for a living?'

'The other three men looked nervously, from one of the most powerful men in the world to their uninformed business associate, when the General answered casually.

'Oh well, I used to be in the military and now I'm a civil servant, the government has kindly given me, what is it they say in England? A pen-pusher's job. Something not too strenuous for my last few years, before I retire to Sukko on the Black Sea.' He said smiling modestly.

After Fyodor had downed another vodka, a distinguished looking, elderly, Swiss man came over to the group. Fyodor smiled warmly and shook hands with Christian Kautz. He was tall, slim and elegant, he wore a slightly dated evening jacket and waistcoat, made from expensive fabrics, his grey-white hair was swept over his ears and a matching moustache was trimmed to perfection.

'Ladies and gentlemen...' He said in perfect French. 'May I poach the General away from you for a few minutes?' Christian smiled, clicking his heels and bowing his head respectfully with old-fashioned Swiss charm.

'How are you my old friend?' Asked Fyodor, ushering Christian away from the group's inquisitive earshot.

'Old is correct, after five minutes at these embassy parties, I want to go home to bed and have some hot chocolate with my little Freda.'

'I hope she is well, I haven't seen her for a long time.'

'Ya, and you won't, she's had enough of these nights as well, anyway don't worry about my wife, it's time you got one of your own Fyodor, people will start to think you like boys, no?'

They both laughed, there weren't many people alive who could speak to the General in this fashion; Christian was one of them. The old man had miraculously avoided making enemies of Hitler, Stalin and Churchill, for one of the world's richest men, a lack of enemies was very unusual.

'I want you to help me get something Fyodor...'

'And I thought you had everything...'

'I have everything money can buy, what I want is Henry de Hartingh...'

'Who or what is that?'

'He's the head chef here at the French embassy, incredible, better than anyone in Paris.

I'm in the last years of my life Fyodor, I want to eat well until I pop off; nothing else gives me more pleasure...' Both men chuckled.

'I've heard that the German Embassy are after him as well, is he really so good?

'I thought you hadn't heard of him? I should have known you're familiar with everyone in the Soviet. Yes, his soufflé is better than sex with a Turkish prostitute!'

'I'm surprised you can remember what that's like...'

'Ah! Touché Mon Général.'

'Are you serious Christian? Can't you offer him something, money, an American car, girls etcetera.'

'I've tried everything dear boy, everything, he's a patriot to France and the Embassy and won't leave, he enjoys being the biggest fish in this small, gastronomic pond...'

Fyodor knew that his old friend could find another great chef anywhere in France or Italy, and yet very rich men often start obsessions for particularly unobtainable items as they have forgotten the sensation of desire. If the chef had started work for him the first time he'd asked, Christian wouldn't have thought much about it, but to refuse all offers, to a man who has the best of everything, becomes a challenge. For old, rich and powerful people, there're so few challenges to be had. Two men with military bearing, wearing thick, grey coats entered the room, showing identity cards to the security staff, before walking towards the

General in unison like conjoined twins. They gave a military salute and asked permission to speak to the Spymaster.

'My dear Christian, it looks as though my entertainment has come to an end, I shall think about your request, give my kind regards to your dear lady.'

'I'm grateful Fyodor, and don't forget my suggestion for those lonely nights!' Christian chuckled to himself as he wandered off stroking his moustache. General Poluostrovich turned and faced the soldiers who flashed their identity cards, which wasn't necessary; he knew them well, as they worked at the Lubyanka a few floors below Fyodor's office.

'General Sir!' The dark haired one started abruptly. 'We have been debriefing the Parisian Embassy comrade Misezhnikov, as instructed, and he doesn't know the whereabouts of Vladimir Mordashov.'

'Did you ask him what happened to his papers?'

'Yes Sir, he said they were stolen from his car.'

'I see, give him a nice dinner and a warm bed, make him comfortable, tell him you're sorry for any inconvenience, then bring him to my office at eleven tomorrow.'

'Is he free to go Sir?'

'No-no, he's just free to have a nice evening.'

General Poluostrovich walked over to the American Ambassador and started to chat casually in English.

They had brought in a few more *'diplomats'* last week, which were in reality all CIA agents.

Fyodor thought he should tease him, as they'd tried to get a bugged wastepaper bin into the Lubyanka a couple of days ago. It looked identical to a Soviet bin, although one of Fyodor's observant security men thought that it looked, 'too well made' to be Soviet issue, then they found the false bottom.

The following morning Alex Ruska drove the General to the Lubyanka at eight o'clock, which was uncharacteristically late, due to the fact that Christian's talk of a wife had kept the lonely Russian awake through the night. In his outer office KGB Colonel Leonid Michelson, head of the French bureaux was waiting for him.

Fyodor entered quickly and the Colonel jumped to attention.

'Come Leonid, show me what you've got.'

Leonid wheeled in a blackboard two metres long, covered with photographs and documents arranged in the style of a family tree.

'General, here's some documentation regarding agent Yuri Misezhnikov, we don't have much information about him until he left an orphanage and joined the army, he worked his way up quickly...'

The Colonel used a short baton to point to the relevant documents and photos. 'Now that we have looked closely, maybe a little too quickly. A few of his comrades were killed in accidents, when they were competing for a place in the service. Looking at it now and having spoken to some of his previous commanding officers, he may have eliminated them himself. One of the commanders said he was sure of it.'

'Did you ask him if he reported his information?'

'Yes General, he replied that he didn't, but thought that Misezhnikov showed the type of initiative that may be useful in the service.'

'Send him a message from me, tell this idiot that killing our own men is not what we're looking for, we're here to protect the Soviet, not reduce its population. We have the Americans for that!'

'Yes Sir.'

'Well go on Colonel, what else have you got.'

'He seems to have kept his nose clean, never volunteers for anything mundane, wants to be a front runner, rather ambitious to make a name for himself, as though he's waiting for something grandiose that will promote him.

We questioned Mikhail Kalinin in Paris who was part of his team. He was very loyal to him at first, then he told us that they'd set up a leap frog on a couple of British agents. Yuri went after them on his own and lost the trail, the next day he looked a bit roughed up and said he'd crashed his car while drunk.

Then he sent the other team member, Vladimir Mordashov to England, to try to find out where the agents were going, he hasn't been seen since.'

The Colonel grabbed a folder and pulled out some papers marked 'Top Secret' in English.

'We do have a report general, from our embassy in London, that a man answering the description of Vladimir Mordashov, has been washed up in their main river just outside of the capital. We have asked them to take fingerprints so we can check our records.

'What part of London was it?' The General asked.

Loenid checked his file and said, 'In the west of London Sir, in the province of Surrey.'

The General took the file and asked, 'Find out how far that is from a place called Richmond.'

Leonid looked slightly confused and said, 'Yes Sir. Furthermore, and this is rather strange, our consulate in Marseille, France had some of agent Misezhnikov's papers. His Russian passport, a second French passport with his photo, but a different name, some bank statements from a Swiss bank account, in the fake French identity and two guns. One of which is his registered issue from us, the other had the serial number filed off.'

'How did they get these papers?' The General asked, slitting his eyes in concentration.

'Well Sir, that's the unusual part: a messenger brought them in, wrapped in this brown paper, addressed to you…' The Colonel pointed to a parcel on the desk. 'I asked the local agent to question him; he said that the messenger service was paid to deliver the package by a Frenchman who telephoned. He had left the bundle and the fee with the bar staff at a café on the old port. No one in the café remembered a man. They said a young local boy delivered the parcel to the bar, evidently he works at the market, we are searching for the lad now.'

'But you won't find him, and if you do he will not have seen the man, because he's the British agent who took the guns and the papers off agent Misezhnikov. He addressed the parcel to me as a message, the message reads, *'Fyodor, don't send these amateur little boys to follow me or they may get hurt.'*

The General screamed. 'This idiot agent

Misezhnikov, has gone against my direct orders and I've now been embarrassed by someone that I would hate to win at tiddlywinks, let alone the great game!' He banged his fist on the desk. The Colonel looked surprised by the reaction, the General was always so calm, although like most people in the Lubyanka, he realised that his boss was playing an international game that few people understood.

'Ah, there's one other thing Sir, we've heard from our American double agent, Tex, he has just got out of prison in Spain, took him a while, the yanks had to give him diplomatic immunity and pull a few strings in Madrid, as Franco's boys take American spies very seriously.'

'What are you talking about Colonel? What has this got to do with agent Misezhnikov and the British assassin?'

'Well Sir, you instructed us to ask our people on the borders of France, Spain and Italy to look out for this agent called Trubshaw. Evidently Tex and a female CIA operative posing as his wife, had one of our pictures of him.

They saw someone who resembled the photo, at a police roadblock near the Franco-Spanish border. They tried to get close to him, he was with a woman with blonde hair, but somehow the British got them arrested by the local police and drove off. Evidently Tex and his accomplice were in jail for three weeks.'

Fyodor started to laugh, it was just a giggle at first and then he lost control of himself and nearly fell off his chair, his protective secretary came running in with a cocked pistol in her hand believing that this unusual noise warranted immediate action.

'Thank you Alena, there's no problem. Would you please get me that informer we have in London on the telephone, the weird one from Poland, I've forgotten his name.'

'Yes Sir. He's called Aleksander Glowacki, I think it will be late at night in England.'

'It doesn't matter, if I remember correctly, all he does is paint and walk his dogs.'

An hour later, at eleven o'clock, agent Yuri Misezhnikov was escorted into the Spymaster's office. He stood to attention in front of the General's desk, desperate to explain his actions, he wasn't sure how much his superior knew, he'd been very careful and had practised his art of story telling since he arrived at the orphanage as a child, and so these interviews usually got him another promotion.

'Yuri, I told you not to follow the British assassins, not to make any kind of contact...'

'General Sir...'

'Do not speak Yuri; then you sent one of our people to his house in London, now we have reason to believe that he's dead!'

Yuri gulped and his eyes nearly fell out of his head.

'Don't you think I know where he lives? If I wanted to get into his house, I would have sent a specialist team there; I've heard the place is similar to Fort Knox with pretty flowers. I've just heard from our local informer, that agent Vladimir Mordashov didn't even get pass the garden, but you wouldn't listen to my orders Yuri, by the information I have, it sounds like the Englishman caught you as well...'

'No Sir, I didn't see him, I...'

'No! You didn't see him, but he saw you and look at this parcel Yuri...' The General pushed the brown paper towards the agent. 'Mr Trubshaw kindly sent me your guns, passports and forged documents, he has made a fool of you Yuri, I don't care, but as you are meant to be one of *my* men, he has also made a fool of me, now that is something that I do care about.'

'But Sir...'

'Shut up Yuri and listen, have you heard of Andreeva Bay, on the Kola Peninsula in north western Russia?'

'No Sir, but...'

The General raised his hand to silence the agent.

'It's the Northern Fleet's largest storage facility for radioactive waste and spent nuclear fuel. I understand that it's rather cold up there. We send all our spent fuel assemblies from the shipyards to that plant.

The main storage facility is known as Building 5. The site was built two years ago and contains two storage pools; there have been a couple of accidents there, you

337

know all about accidents, don't you Yuri? Many of your friends and colleagues have been in accidents I understand. Well this afternoon you are going to go up there and be in charge of the safety of the crew, you will have the new rank of corporal and if anyone is hurt under any circumstances, you will be held responsible.'

'But Sir I...'

'Colonel get him out of here please and take all the emblems of Major from him.'

Yuri was ushered out of the General's office, still protesting his innocence. The General touched his intercom button and said. 'Get me Count Sergei Belevsky-Zhukovsky on the phone please Alena.'

'Yes General.'

'Oh Alena, are you doing anything this evening?'

'No General?' Alena said optimistically.

'Oh good, in that case will you work late and also find the file on that French chef everybody likes...'

'Henry de Hartingh Sir?'

'Yes that's him.'

'Will you be working late this evening General?'

'No Alena, I'm going to leave early...'

'Early Sir?' Alena asked in a surprised tone, the General never left early, he always worked a sixteen-hour day, she wondered if he was ill.

'There's another file as well, what's the name of our mole in Paris, the one who works for that red restaurant guide all the French swear by...'

'Oh yes Sir, Marie Bertron, it's a long time since we used him, he chairs a committee that decides who gets the stars or is it rosettes for cooking...'

'That's the one, they make tyres as well, get me all of his details please.'

The General's yellow phone started to click, he yawned, the scramblers whizzed and he reached for the handset with unusual reluctance.

Part Three

Chapter 28
The Ritz Hotel, Barcelona April 1964

Although Antoni Gaudí's architectural influence on Barcelona was evident in almost every barrio of the beautiful city. On the Gran Via de les Corts Catalanes, a more traditional influence from 1919 dominated the street, with its emblematic and traditional luxury: the fabulous Ritz Hotel.

The impeccably groomed, head concierge, in his black uniform with gold epaulets, was accustomed to the hotel's wealthy clientele. He knew how to offer a five star service and also get the best out of them from his own point of view. Because José Reverte-Gutiérrez was a man with connections throughout the city, whatever his guests wanted, José could find it. A discreet lady of the night, smuggled up the servant's lift? No problem. An invitation to an illegal game of cards? Just knock three times and say, 'José sent me.' A reservation in a fashionable, yet fully booked restaurant? José could get you the best table.

Señor Reverte-Gutiérrez's salary wasn't very significant, although after thirty years of service as headman in the concierge's office of Barcelona's most famous hotel. José had managed to educate all five of his children in the best, private French school in the city and his wife was a regular guest in the hotel's expensive restaurant, wearing designer clothes as fashionable as most of the paying guests, albeit famously froufrou.

One of the reasons José was so successful and popular with the hotel's guests relied on his knack to plan ahead. The last thing he did each evening before going home, having scanned the reservations for the following days, was to create a list of the most import and wealthiest guests and make notes on what he thought their requirements might be. In fact, the middle-aged doorman could often prepare services that even the guests didn't know they would need. Only last week, the wife of a Portuguese politician had phoned in advance to order a particular bottle of vintage French champagne for their second night's stay, as it was their fifteenth wedding anniversary. José made a note in his diary and when he saw the government minister alone in the lobby, asked if he needed anything special for the following day. The Minister looked confused, until the charming concierge politely reminded him of the important event. The flowers and the diamond earrings from his cousin's shop, as well as a dinner reservation for two in one of Barcelona's most lavish restaurants, not only saved the man's marriage, but also increased José's bank balance with tips and commissions from all concerned.

Therefore, when José saw a note in the book that a Señor Ricardo Colaneri and his wife Paola Colaneri from Italy, had booked the Royal Suite for two weeks, the clever doorman knew that he would be their guardian angel for their entire stay.

First thing in the morning, he told the head of Housekeeping, to meet him in the suite with her two best maids.

'José, I don't know why you've asked me here...' The overweight Señora Sanchez said angrily.

'...The whole place was dusted yesterday when we saw the booking, we know our job in Housekeeping you know!'

'Ana, I know you do, it's just that these are very special clients of mine and I just made a few notes of what needs to be done...' José said with a huge smile as he kissed the grumpy old woman on the cheek and stuffed a wad of pesetas in her hand. Her face softened as she gauged the thickness of the money between her fingers.

'That's what I like about you José, you're always willing to invest in your future, now come on you two lazy chicas, I want this place spotless!' Señora Sanchez said irritably. The suite doorbell rang and four bellboys in red uniforms with matching pillar-box hats, walked in with huge bouquets of flowers, which they placed around the suite. José cast his expert eye over every detail, like a butterfly searching for pollen, when his concentration was broken by the telephone ringing.

'Yes!' He said impatiently.

'José?' One of the concierge team asked.

'What is it Miguel?'

'Your special guests are here…'

'Where? In front of the hotel?'

'Yes…'

'Grab their bags and keep them there, I'm coming…'

The senior concierge rushed along the plush corridor to the lift, bobbed up and down impatiently, looking at the gold ornate indicator above the metal doors, willing it to move faster, eventually the doors parted. He pushed the ground floor button and the cabin plodded down the shaft with José tapping his fingers together impatiently. Eventually the doors revealed the lobby and he rushed towards the main entrance, delighted to see the shiny Bristol spread across the front of the hotel. A red fiat cinquecento had parked behind the British icon of speed and luxury that led José to think for a moment, 'Wow you could put one of those in the boot!'

'Señor Ricardo Colaneri?'

'Sí, que tal?' Sam said.

'José Reverte-Gutiérrez, head of concierge Señor, at your service.' He replied with a flurry.

'May I call you José? Sam asked.

'Sir, you may call me day or night for anything you or your wife require, no matter how unusual your requirements may be.' He said with a masculine, knowing smile.

Phaedra walked over to her husband with a small designer make-up bag, while José clicked his fingers at three of his crew and guided the Trubshaws to the reception desk. Sam signed in as Ricardo Colaneri, handing over corresponding passports and they were whisked up to the magnificent suite. José had a waiter wheel in some champagne and said. 'With the compliments of the management, and here is my card Sir, it has my home telephone number as well as the concierge's office, please don't hesitate to call me, twenty four hours a day.'

'I'm a little hungry, may we have some tapas with the drinks José please?

'Of course Señor.'

342

Sam put the equivalent of half a weeks wagers in José's hand and said that he'll keep him in mind. As he closed the suite's door behind him, the concierge smiled broadly, he knew this was going to be a special guest and with a tip as large as this on the first meeting, José almost skipped along the hall as excited as a schoolboy.

Without speaking, Sam and Phaedra took out some equipment from one of their cases and scanned the room. After fifteen minutes, the couple looked satisfied.

'All clear, now let's get our disguises and go over to the other hotel darling.'

When they arrived at the Gaudí Hotel, Mariesther was on duty at the reception. She saw the bellboy meet Sam and Phaedra who jumped out of a taxi with a small bag and a simple disguise of dark sunglasses and a scarf for Phaedra.

'Thank you Monsieur Renault, will you have any other luggage?' Mariesther asked automatically.'

'Yes, thank you …' Sam replied, reading her nametag. 'I'm expecting a taxi with some cases this afternoon, will you send it up to our room please Mariesther?'

The bellboy quickly escorted the Trubshaws to their room on the top floor. They entered, gave the boy a good tip and closed the door. They looked around briefly and then Sam telephoned down to the reception saying he wanted another room. The bellboy came back up with keys for a slightly larger room a few doors along. After giving a second generous tip, the couple collapsed onto the bed, satisfied that it would be unlikely that anyone would know they were there.

'We have plenty of time before the soirée darling, that will give us a chance to do the surveillance and prepare our exit…' Sam said thoughtfully looking at the ceiling with his locked fingers behind his head. 'I'll pop over tomorrow to *El Restaurante La Torre d'Altamar* and have a look around, and get a reservation for the Thursday before the event. Then I'll learn the floor plan and place some arms in the cloakroom, just in case things go wrong. We should check to see where the cable car goes and learn the road to the boat and the area in general for a speedy exit. I've spoken to a chap who has a Porsche 356 B coupe for sale; evidently it ran in the June 1963 'Midnight Sun' rally.

He says it's ex-works and is the fastest car in Spain...'

Sam said enthusiastically turning to Phaedra, who was now sound asleep on the twin bed.

Chapter 29
Moshe's Last Job, April 1964

It was a cool April, the sky an expensive blue, and the wind-god decided to whip up the Mediterranean into a food-mixer's frenzy. The large ferries from Marseilles and the Balearic islands were banned from entering Barcelona's port, as the sea was far too agitated for swaying passenger ships, however, most of the small fishing boats braved the hilly water; they didn't carry any frail passengers, trying to drink coffee.

Moshe 'Mad' Liberman had messed about with boats since he was a teenager, mostly due to an experience he had after his fourteenth birthday. His dad Hyman Liberman was an engineer and adored his job on the railway. He specialised in designing steam pumps and to his wife's dismay, loved taking machines apart to see how it operated, and tried to improve them. This resulted in a garden shed full of mechanical parts with no home, and very few working appliances in their substantial, yet scruffy detached house.

Since the end of the nineteenth century, Hyman had a burning ambition; he wanted to visit, what he called: 'The world's greatest engineering feat,' that had been built in London, England, in 1884, based on a design by Horace Jones.

After Moshe's bar mitzvah, his father took him to the world's most prosperous city to see the magnificent, Tower of London. Hyman had read newspaper articles and engineering reports about the bridge with a childish enthusiasm, which was not shared by his dear wife Rebecca. Who happily stayed at home, while the 'Boys' went off to play with a huge toy. The Libermans stayed in a small hotel in London's East End and after a decent lunch in a Jewish Thames-side restaurant, they made their way pass the famous Greenwich Naval College. Hyman's plan; to see the magnificent bridge from a distance. The morning of the twelfth began well on the crisp clear December day. Nevertheless, as they walked along the river towards

London's latest icon, the bridge looked much nearer than the reality and the short walk Hyman promised his son, turned into a three-hour trek. By the time they reached the road just before the entrance to the north side it was nearly six o'clock. 'Oh my goodness,' cried the elderly Jewish engineer. 'I had no idea that so many tourists would be here to see the bridge. Now hold my hand Moshe and if we become separated, I want you to come back to this spot in front of this warehouse, do you understand my son?'

Moshe was a quiet child, obsessed with his own thoughts and so his father always found it difficult to know how the boy really felt. Hyman stood next to an English woman staring at a great ship in the darkening water and asked her in good English. 'Excuse me, what's happening here?' The small woman looked stressed and said in a cockney accent, Hyman found difficult to understand, something like:

'There's a problem today, the Suffragettes are demonstrating and there's a warship coming through.'

'Can the ship still get through?'

'I don't know...' She said, tears filling her eyes, 'I'm so afraid.'

'But my dear lady, you mustn't get upset, I'm sure either the bridge will open fully or the ship will turn around, it will certainly have an experienced captain, everything will be fine.'

Pearl Renshaw broke into tears and dropped her face into a lace handkerchief.

'He's not experienced, he's only a baby and he's going to die!'

Hyman looked at the woman concerned, took his son's hand and moved further along the embankment closer to the bridge, thinking that the poor English woman was insane. 'Who's ever heard of a baby steering a ship?' Hyman and Moshe never forgot their experience that afternoon, women plunging to their deaths, thousands of people fighting and screaming, a huge warship almost crashing into the world's greatest bridge. The day changed both the Libermans inordinately, albeit completely differently. Hyman realised he was going to retire into a dangerous world and that he would need to protect his small family. Moshe knew from that moment, that he wanted to captain a ship like the HMS Aboukir and shoot down all of his enemies. He realised that the world away from his little village was an exciting place.

Over the years he'd captained submarines, destroyers and small sailing craft for the Israelis, and yet he struggled with the helm of this little fishing boat. There wasn't enough power left in its fatigued engine, the whole craft was on its last sea legs. Diesel kept spilling out of one of the motor's feed pipes, even though Moshe had wrapped a rag around the leak and bundled it with black masking tape. One of the two pumps hadn't worked for years and the other one wanted to retire. An old fisherman from Mataró further up the coast, who was about the same age as Moshe, had owned the Maria Rosa for the last five decades. Arturo felt as much part of his boat as the keel, although, if he had listened to the advice of his doctor and family, he should have been ready for his pension years ago.

After sixty years of sardine fishing along Barcelona's coastline, he still loved the work; finally he reluctantly agreed to leave the trawling business. On the condition that he could keep his old boat and occasionally take out tourists who wanted to fish and visit the bays of the Costa Brava. In certain circumstances, he would hire out the wreck for the day or week. Arturo was worried about this customer who wanted his boat for two weeks fishing, he was some kind of foreigner and looked too tired and weak to operate his best friend; the Maria Rosa.

'Are you sure you can handle this boat on your own Señor?' Arturo asked in Castilian Spanish cautiously, two days earlier. The payment for the two weeks rental, without the usual haggling and the deposit in cash, helped to convince the old fisherman, even though he thought there was something strange about this elderly man.

After two hours of struggling, the geriatric assassin finally steered the fifteen footer into its mooring, he wrestled with the ropes and ultimately secured the wooden boat at both ends. The Israeli looked around the quiet port, with expert, albeit failing eyes; locked himself inside the cramped cabin and checked the explosives in their metal boxes that filled the small space to the roof. The padding around the ammonium sulphate started to break up and the fumes were eye watering. Moshe wore a wide leather belt that he'd buckled through a hole made with a knife; his trousers had been too big for him for several years, the knees as shiny as his old boots. The faded blue-grey shirt was worn and frayed matching his frail body that looked equally tattered. The man's baldhead was lightly dusted with dandelion fluff over a pale pink skin. The only strength in his disintegrating body came from odium, psychosis and a sense of destiny. He chuckled to himself once he'd finished his calculations and said aloud in his depleted voice, 'Enough to wipe out a Nazi concentration camp, let alone their restaurant...' Moshe then went to his brown hide briefcase and pulled out the thick, cream coloured file; he read the title for the fiftieth time and smiled.

HaMossad leModi'in uleTafkidim Meyuchadim
Top Secret
Ilsa Klup AKA
Ilsa Koch, Sister Suzanna, Suzanna Valles-Carrera

Moshe read the files from the Israelis, the German Government, the Nuremberg Trails and the German Administrators of Prisoner of War Camps. However, the files that really interested him were the testimonies from the actual people who knew Klup. There were also testimonies from her childhood neighbours and classmates, her cousins, business people who dealt with her and her first husband. The most recent reports were from Spain, they were mostly complimentary, except for one thing, there was some unsubstantiated evidence from a local police report, that her old fetish of collecting tattooed human skin had resurfaced; except these days it was only from innocent, young girls. The official file had been pulled by the secret police that had taken over the investigation.

On Ilsa's fourteenth birthday, according to her cousin Helga, who was staying with her aunt and uncle for three months while her mother was in hospital. Ilsa watched her young, Jewish neighbour Klara Rosenthal play in the front garden, from the advantage of Klup's first floor, bedroom window. The young Jew wore a floral dress, white socks, strapped sandals and her mother had tied pink ribbons in her bunches. Klara was playing happily with a wooden hoop and although the same age as Ilsa, she still looked like a child.

Ilsa already benefited from an hourglass figure and could have easily pass for seventeen, she enjoyed the power she felt she had over men during the previous couple of years; it was fascinating. If she pulled her dress up or opened her blouse, boys would do almost anything she asked. She thought that it was like having magic powers, which neither she nor the male sex truly understood.

Annoyingly for Ilsa, these techniques didn't seem to work on her female relatives or classmates, therefore the best method of control was to bully them.
Most of the local girls were frightened of her, even the two or three who were as tall and strong. Ilsa realised that controlling people was based on personality as much as force, and it gave the teenager a strange sense of power and pleasure to see her inferior contemporaries, cross the street or put their heads down when she came into view. Ilsa's neighbour, Klara Rosenthal was a constant pleasure; she had given Fräulein Klup almost all her possessions to avoid being bullied, both physiologically and physically over the previous three years. Klara was an excellent violinist, academic student and top of her class; she wore thick glasses and had braces on her prominent teeth. The schoolgirl was clearly bright and worked hard, not only on her homework, but on Ilsa's as well. At first teachers thought that Ilsa was intelligent, because of her arrogant confidence and her near perfect homework, it didn't take long though for her tutors to realise that she never understood her assignments or anything else during the lessons. The class teacher, Miss Steinbeck, questioned some of the students to see who was helping Ilsa; it was soon clear that no one was willing to say anything against the buxom bully.

Ilsa hadn't seen Klara for the last fortnight because

her parents had been keeping her at home since the accident. Ilsa had trapped Klara in the back garden behind the shed as usual. It was a Friday, when the Jewish girl normally got her pocket money, not that she'd been able to keep it for long over the last year or so.

'Here take this…' Ilsa commanded.

'I'm not allowed to smoke.'

'I said take it.'

Klara held the cigarette at arms length as though it was a bomb.

'Well go on Klara, put it in your mouth and smoke it…'

Klara started coughing on the fumes, screwing up her eyes.

'Come on finish it, don't you want to grow up?'

'I can't Ilsa, please don't force me…' She continued coughing. 'It's burning my throat.'

Ilsa grabbed the cigarette from her neighbour's hand, pulled her shoulder length hair and jabbed the glowing tip on the nape of her neck. Klara screamed in agony and tried to run, but the bigger girl twisted her arm and forced her to smoke ten cigarettes having received four burns on her neck by way of encouragement. When the Jewish girl's parents saw her injuries they rushed her to the doctor, yet Klara Rosenthal never explained to anyone how she became injured.

Because Fräulein Klup never gained any academic qualifications, after she left school at fourteen, she found it hard to find work in her home town of Dresden during Germany's recession, until at the age of sixteen, she saw an advertisement for a position as guard in the Sachsenhausen concentration camp in Oranienburg, even though it was about two hundred and thirty kilometres away.

One of her new co-workers, Ingrid, liked the young mousy blonde at first, until she knew more about her character. Ingrid's testimony became the centrepiece of Klup's trial. The position of guard turned out to be the perfect occupation for her. There was little paperwork, no need for any particular skill and the prisoners in the camp were by definition in an inferior position and afraid of her.

Ilsa continued to develop her torturous character; she had a propensity for maleficence, completely unrestrained by any code of decency as none of her victims were in a position to complain. Some of the other guards were decent people, several were irritable and harsh with the inmates, nevertheless, Ilsa was the only one who truly enjoyed hurting and humiliating the prisoners on a daily bases.

Nazi records showed that in June of 1937, Ilsa married fellow guard Claus Koch, and when a short time later, he was appointed Kommandant at the Buchenwald concentration camp. Frau Koch was delighted by his promotion and excited to move away with him and her uneventful lifestyle. Normally, the wife of a camp commander would live in the nearest village and have little or nothing to do with the work of their husbands. Most German villagers tried to ignore the camps and pretend that they didn't exist, unless they were in the business of supplying food or other provisions, as having a second 'village' nearby could be very profitable. Ilsa soon found the life of a camp commander's wife was very boring indeed and so she insisted that her husband, who was besotted by his voluptuous bride, should arrange a job for her at the camp. Within a month, she was appointed SS Aufseherin at Buchenwald.

Ilsa didn't enjoy a good relationship with her fellow overseers, although as the commander's wife she didn't care, because this was the perfect opportunity for her sadistic personality to bloom into its most devilish form. Doctor Maurice Cohen, a surgeon, was one of the few survivors of the camp and gave extensive testimony at the trail of the SS Aufseherin.

Most of the male prisoners were in a frail condition with rags for clothes and little to eat. And yet, it didn't stop Ilsa teasing them with her clinging dresses and a bulging cleavage clearly exposed. One morning during an inspection of a newly arrived group of prisoners, who still had a vague memory of normal times, Kommandant Claus Koch noticed that some of the men ogled his wife as she rode pass on her horse, wearing tight and provocative clothing. He immediately ordered the men beaten and posted a notice that any man found looking at Frau Koch would be severely punished. This proclamation seemed to give Ilsa a new raison d'étra and she started a campaign of sexual provocation, which satisfied her sadistic instinct; to be sexually stimulating and cause extreme suffering. One of her favourite sports was to ride around the camp exposing her legs and breasts while whipping the prisoners as she passed by. In time, Ilsa Koch's behaviour became ever more extreme, she turned out to be fascinated by prisoners with tattoos or even unusual birthmarks.

Ilsa ordered the guards to strip all prisoners and to bring the ones who were tattooed or birth-marked, to a special hut she'd set up to inspect them. Using medical equipment and a magnifying glass, she would have the men and women laid on a wooden table and examine them closely. If she liked their tattoos, she would instruct the camp doctor to slice-off the prisoner's markings, while the inmates screamed in agony at being skinned alive. If the artistic images were particularly large across someone's back or chest, she would have them killed before taking the skin, as it was easier.

These human pelts were then tanned like leather by the other prisoners and made into lampshades and other household items that were proudly shown in the Koch's village house. One of the products that the SS Aufseherin was particularly proud of was her handbag, made entirely of human skin. Her fascination with this sadistic practice also became a form of income and she took orders from other guards and some of the German villagers and supplied them with various fashion items, made from the prisoner's hide.

According to American records, Nazi superiors arrested Claus Koch for his torturous behaviour and complaints of dishonesty. He was finally executed in 1945 before the country was liberated. Ilsa continued with her sadistic pleasures until the camp was deserted at the end of the war. After her arrest, she was charged with atrocities at the Buchenwald camp and sentenced to death for her crimes, but before her execution, official records showed that she committed suicide on the first of February 1947.

This American information has since been refuted

by the Israelis, documents show that the Catholic Ratlines Organisation, faked her suicide and smuggled her out of Germany for a new life in Argentina via Spain, where she temporarily became a nun renamed Sister Suzanna, at the Convento de Santa Isabel la Real in Granada. A few years after the war ended, she left the convent, having learnt the language, and found a place in Franco's Right-Wing society. She became a nursing assistant as a nun at a maternity hospital called the San Ramón Clinic in Madrid. Working with the Catholic Church, she soon became responsible for all adoptions of unwanted children. These babies were processed through a private Foundation, where she met one of the directors. Working together at the Foundation, Suzanna Valles-Carrera as she is now called, quickly rose from her role of adoption administrator and became a wealthy socialite in Barcelona. She Staged fashion shows and sold jewellery from her own shop on Passeig de Gràcia. Ilsa also married her boss, the rich and powerful former soldier and chief of the secret police; Colonel José Valles-Carrera, who is known as one of Franco's closest counsellors.

Moshe's contract will be carried out at a private, clandestine, Nazi auction, organised by the Fondazione Nazionale di Cristo, on the evening of Saturday 25th April 1964 at La Torre d'Alta Mar that has an elevated restaurant above the cable car's entrance.

Dusk crept over the port surreptitiously; Moshe closed the folder as he heard a meow from the stray kitten, which had befriended the frail old man from the first day he'd bought some bocaronies at the little chiringuito near the port.

She smooched down the steps and curled her flexible body around his legs. Moshe picked up the report again with arthritic hands and realised that this assassination would be known as his finest.

The stray jumped on his lap and turned up the meowing, he'd surveyed the tower a few days earlier, which overlooked the port of Barcelona, and knew what he had to do. The kitten kept up the pressure and lay on top of the paperwork cuffing the short piece of green string holding the pages together, as enthusiastically as a boxer, testing his opponent in the first round of a championship fight. The assassin carefully put the kitten on the floor.

Then he cautiously picked up his antique, red violin case, and ran his fingers over the inlaid gold initials.

FM

He opened the red leather case slowly, and as always was in awe of its contents. The Mendelssohn Stradivarius had been lost for years, until Moshe found it in a scruffy Jewish music shop in the old quarter of Berlin in the late thirties. The young boy behind the counter said he was working there since his uncle had died, six months earlier and Moshe realised that he'd no idea what he was selling. The boy hated being trapped in the place and couldn't wait to go on to university in America. When Moshe said he only really wanted the case, although would take the violin for his ten year old nephew to play with, the young shop worker looked delighted. Despite the fact that the asking price was a pittance, Moshe offered even less.

'I'll tell you what...' said the bored young man. 'I can't give it to you for less, but it's part of a pair, if you like, I'll throw the other one in for the same price.'

Moshe knew that Antonio Stradivari did not churn out pairs of violins in his small shop in Cremona, Italy in 1720. Each of his masterpieces took months to make, with devotion never to be seen since, and yet the amateur violinist was fascinated and said he'd be pleased to see the twin.

'There's no case and it only has two strings...' The boy said apologetically. He walked into the storeroom at the rear of the little shop and within a minute returned with a similar violin covered in dust. 'Here it is, just give it a good clean up with some soap and hot water, then your nephew can use them both to amuse his school friends.'

Moshe had dreamed of owning a quality violin since he first started lessons at the age of three. However, even he never imagined that he would ever see such a masterpiece, let alone own one.

'Alright then I'll take them, but I'm doing you a favour you know, they look very old and used.'

The young man counted his money greedily and said, 'Sorry I don't have any brown paper, we've run out and business hasn't been very good these days with the new government.' Moshe had seen the fascist graffiti outside the shop and understood the young man's desire to leave the racist state.

'That's alright; just give me a written receipt, you know, to make it all legal.'

The young man wrote the voucher clearly and used the shop's official stamp. Moshe said his goodbyes and casually walked onto the street.

After scouring national and local newspapers for a month to see if anyone had reported the violins stolen, and searching catalogues for musical instruments, Moshe finally took the now highly polished, second violin with its new strings and red varnish, to Berlin's poshest music shop and asked the owner to examine the instrument.

The scholarly man looked at Moshe suspiciously and then at the violin, he held the womanly wooden shape with the respect of a doctor holding a premature baby.

'And where did you say you bought this...' he asked.

'You've already asked me that question twice, and the answer is still the same, I bought it from a dealer and I have the receipt at home.'

'I see, well I might be interested in buying it, if the price is low enough, how much were you hoping to get?'

'It's not for sale, I just want you to confirm the name of the maker.'

Moshe had a similar conversation at least twenty times over the following years and eventually found a professor of music and musical instruments from the Conservatoire de Paris, who finally said that Moshe owned a magnificent original Stradivarius and also, the best copy of a Stradivarius that he'd ever seen.

In nineteen forty-five the musician sold the copy through a large auction house, claiming it an original, he received a fortune from a New York industrialist, and since then he played his original masterpiece daily.

Now in the boat's little cabin he set up his device, a

355

small battery operated receiver with chrome aerial attached to a tiny detonator similar to a kid's firework.

He sat comfortably on the hard bench and rested his chin on the polished wood, to play the Wieniawski concerto number one. It was a passionate piece that he'd practised many times before and as he came towards the end, his bow caressed the highest notes a violin could reach, playing 4-Octave, A Major. The shrill pitch activated the little receiver and the firework made a loud bang! The kitten jumped in the air and ran under the seat.

Moshe carefully placed his unique instrument and bow back in its case and examined his device, satisfied it will work when he would need it, and he relaxed on the bench. The kitten resumed its cries for food like a hungry baby.

'Alright you win.' He said and walked over to the cupboard, producing some leftover scraps of deep-fried seafood he'd bought late last night. The feline squatted on the deck and ate delicately, its tail signalling the pleasure she could not voice, so the nationalised Israeli returned to his plans for the hit. Using the vast amount of explosives he had on the boat, he thought that it would go up like a giant Olympic torch. Photographs of the spectacle would cover the front pages around the world.

'Where would those Nazi bastards hide after that?' He asked the baby cat, his only companion in the tiny cabin. The aged man studied the feline; what a wonderful life they have, he pondered. No doubts, they knew that the mouse in front of them was there to be taken, the dog was to be avoided, if they could catch a bird, if it was within their reach, they would kill it. For food, for the pleasure of the kill, it didn't matter to a cat; their lives were unambiguous, without remorse or indecision. Enemies had to be killed without hesitation or guilt; it was the life of a predator. When they were loving and affectionate, they were sincere and yet if they had no one to love, they moved on. Moshe had to be a felis catus, he had to move on, at least until his deteriorating body finally gave up. The kitten jumped up on his lap again and started to play with the old man's shirt cuffs.

'Get down now…' He said annoyed, 'I'm tired.'

The kitten continued to play and wrapped her tiny paws around his wrist, he shook his arm and tried to flick the tiny creature onto the deck, but her claws shot out to cling on and scratched his wrist blood red.

'Ouch!' He cried. Grabbing the kitten's head with Freudian id, he squeezed his right hand over her ears and his left around her tiny neck. After the cracking noise the furry cloth fell to the floor, its short life a brief moment in history.

The old man started to cough fiercely, he felt the pain under his skin, beneath his nails, in his veins, groped for a handkerchief in a trouser pocket and held it over the choking mouth. His feeble body folded in agony. The white cloth soon turned as red as wine, the old man fell to his knees. Moshe struggled to open a half empty bottle of vodka and swallowed hard. The pain was excruciating, but the pure alcohol began to do its usual job of calming the cough and destroying his stomach. He looked down at the kitten, no more than a soft rag on the floor, he poked the black fur inquisitively with an index finger, and then he remembered. Moshe clung to the gold Star of David around his neck, pulled himself onto the dilapidated bunk and chanted his entreaty.

"For by wise guidance you can wage your war"
"For by wise guidance you can wage your war"
"For by wise guidance you can wage your war"

His only wish now was to stay alive long enough to destroy these evil enemies of his God, to book his seat in heaven. Moshe opened his small bag; it contained a rusty tin filled with tooth powder, an old, wooden-handled toothbrush, a small bar of soap and a faded photograph of his wife and children.

He fell into a deep sleep, the empty vodka bottle and the family's images, still in his clutched fingers.

Chapter 30
Sergei's Villa, Barceloneta, April 1964

The enormous hairless head, nearly seven feet above the pavement had a scowl on its face. Due to the tiny white dog the chauffeur dragged reluctantly on a pink bejewelled collar and leather lead. Milyi kept barking noisily and snapped constantly at her adversary's heels. People stared as they passed by. Delicate, white fluffy Milyi and the giant in a grey suit, looked incongruous together. Some people laughed, others seeing the monstrous face, quickly crossed the road. Boris Stadnyk arrived at the beautiful villa his boss had rented, overlooking the beach on the east of Barcelona's metropolis, amongst the little fishermen's houses in Barceloneta.

'Is that you Boris?' Count Sergei Belevsky-Zhukovsky called out rudely. 'I told you to take little Milyi for a good, long walk through *zer* park, and you're back after ten minutes.'

'It don't wolk.' Boris said unsteadily.

'It's because she doesn't like you Boris, no one does, you're lucky I found you on *zer* door, at that illegal casino in Istanbul or you could have ended up in some kind of freak show.'

'Yes, I so lucky…' He replied sarcastically.

'Of course, that place was full of drug dealers, human traffickers and prostitutes, like that funny little girlfriend of yours, what was her name, Desiree?'

'No tolk Desiree.'

'All she wanted was your money and when you were broke, what did she do? Uh? I'll tell you what she did; she went off with that Turkish mafia guy from Ankara. You fall in love too easily Boris and give them everything you've got, and anything you don't give them, they steal from you…'

Boris looked up feigning a bored look, he had heard this story so many times,

about the way the old Count had rescued him. In reality, he thought, the sneaky old bastard needed a

358

bodyguard like himself. The leviathan chauffeur mumbled that he was going to the kitchen. He opened the double doors of the fridge and pulled out a Spanish beer in a two-litre bottle. The Ukrainian walked into the formal garden, sat on the marble bench next to the sparkling swimming pool and breathed a sigh of relief as he started to pour the cool, golden liquid down his throat.

'It wasn't a bad job.' He reflected. The Count owned or rented a lot of nice houses, they went to endless parties and events, not that Boris enjoyed that sort of thing. They had wonderful food and plenty of it, nice cars to drive around in; he found the employment mostly easy going. Watching people, snooping in dustbins, sometimes a few people got hurt. Usually the work involved protecting the Count, he didn't really upset people, rather, he annoyed them, especially women.

The old man loved flirting with women, all women, he had a penchant for really tall girls and upper class women.

If he could find a way of humiliating them, it seemed to give him some kind of pleasure.

The Russian managed to sleep with a few, often, the young ones were drugged first or so drunk they couldn't remember where they were. Boris had to carry a few of the girls out of the house unconscious and leave them in train stations or airports, with a roll of notes in their pockets. Although overall it seemed an undemanding existence, apart from walking the little white rat, which ate better food than he did. Boris survived three ankle bites last week.

Count Sergei worked as a KGB mole, a fascist informer, a CIA snitch, and a Mafia grass. In fact, Boris's boss would sell his own children to the highest bidder, if he had any. The chauffeur did have a sneaking admiration for the old man; he seemed to earn an endless stream of money, due to his incredible ability of being in the right place at the right time. His clients paid him for finding people and information, which no one else could uncover, and most important, they were willing to pay him handsomely. The Count always boasted to Boris that he used to be very wealthy when he was a director of a private Swiss bank during the war. Now he was just another small time crook. For the last week the old Russian had spoken to Barcelona's lowlifes, prostitutes, bent policemen, newspaper sellers and concierges. Now the old man's excited, because he thinks that he's tracked down someone that his bosses in Moscow are looking for.

Then there's the other problem or is it an occupation, the young girl he's been trying to sleep with for the last few months in London, is coming to the villa to attend a fashion show. However, he's even sold her out as well, because a group of Italians are looking for her. Boris thought that his boss hoped to sleep with the girl a few times before he turned her over to the Italians. The Count loved Barcelona; there was nothing he enjoyed more than mixing with rich and powerful people at glitzy events. Especially if they thrived on the wrong side of the law, and yet, were at the same time connected to people in authority, so that they were above the law. Boris had seen a white invitation to the big party where the Russian, no doubt, hoped to make even more connections for his 'International Information Business'. This time with underground Nazis, as well as a load of Mafia and Italian Fascists.

'Boris! - Boris! Where are you? Can't you hear *zer* door bell?'

The huge man stood up with a long sigh, swallowed the rest of the beer in one and walked to the hall. When he opened the wide wooden door the top of which came to his chest, he noticed a long, black American car with darkened windows and three small Mediterranean types on the gravel path. The driver didn't move from his seat. Their clothes were well made, too well made, the holstered revolvers under their suits spoiling the cut. Giovanni Gibigiano and Raffaello Massoni took a gulp when they saw the bottom three quarters of the giant standing in the doorway. Giovanni looked up under the frame and made out a wide pair of shoulders supporting a huge, baldhead and a false eye, several feet above.

Hey!' He joked in English, looking back at Raffaello winking,

'What's the weather like up there?' Boris had heard

that joke and many others in several languages; since he was twelve years old, he never found them funny.

'Wot you wont?' He replied in a bass voice that resonated around the stone porch.

The third man with a walking stick slowly swayed up the path arriving next to his colleagues and said with his twisted and deformed mouth, 'Tell the Count we're here, I'm Marco Sotori.'

Boris slammed the door rudely in their faces and walked back into the living room, the Count sat at an antique desk facing the long windows.

'Italian punks at door.'

'Bring them in unarmed Boris.' The Count said seriously.

Boris retuned to the front door, checking the shotgun in its holder, hanging onto the wooden panelled doorframe. He opened the door enough to allow one man through at a time, Giovanni, annoyed, pushed his way in with insulted bravado.

'Hey stupido, you know who we are or what?' He said angrily, speaking with Italian semaphore.

Raffaello followed and looked around the wood panelled and marble clad, oval hallway. Boris, pointing to the central round table supporting a bouquet of flowers in a large vase, boomed, 'Leave guns there...'

Giovanni pulled out his Bernardelli B-76 pistol quickly and pointed it at Boris, saying, 'Nobody takes my gun, capisci?'

Boris snatched the gun at tremendous speed considering his size and bent the barrel into the form of a banana. Raffaello pulled out his pistol and jumped out of Boris' range, the giant pulled himself to his full height and snatched the shotgun from its holder behind the thick door. The twin sawn-off barrels aimed at the Italian boys' head. Raffaello didn't blink and pointed his pistol back at the giant unafraid.

'Put your gun down Raffaello!' Marco said forcefully as his half melted body slithered into the hall.

'But Boss...' Giovanni pleaded. 'This freak just snatched my piece!'

Marco put his good hand over Raffaello's pistol and pushed down gently. 'Relax, put your gun on the table we're with friends here.' He slurred unconvincingly.

Boris didn't lower the shotgun until the Count entered the hall. The cobalt atmosphere felt as electric as a lightening storm in full force.

'My dear friends...' Sergei said extravagantly, hiding his shock at Marco's appearance. 'Please forgive Boris, he's always over excited, I'm *zer* Count Sergei Belevsky-Zhukovsky, welcome to my home. Please come *zis* way and have some champagne, Boris, bring some drinks etcetera-etcetera.' He snapped at his chauffeur with the usual contempt.

Giovanni regained his confidence, straightened his suit jacket and swaggered into the beautiful living room, looking around as though he would buy the place.

Boris smiled to himself when he noticed Giovanni's eyes flash back to his twisted gun on the floor. Marco entered last and spoke confidently in English.

'I'm pleased to meet you Count, my colleagues in Milano speak highly of you...' reminding the assemble of his fascist back up. 'Over the telephone you said you have my package, no?'

'My dear fellow, do have a seat and call me Sergei.' The Italians sat in separate seats conscious that these meetings could always become dangerous. 'Ah! Here is my trusted servant with some refreshments. Boris, put that here and go and get *zer* photographs of our blonde friend.'

'You only have photos, I thought the girl would be here...' Marco said seriously.

'She is here Marco...' He lied. 'Don't worry, not in *zis* house of course, but safely looked-after by my other staff near-by, first of all we must ensure that she's *zer* right person and there is *zer* discussion about *zer* price of course...'

'We have already agreed the price, Count...' Marco said angrily, opening the large, brown envelope Boris had thrown on the table in front of him.

'First of all Marco, we don't know if *zis* is *zer* girl you want, secondly there have been a few; complications...'

Marco looked at the photos carefully and glanced at the Count. 'These are pictures of a model, from a magazine and a fashion show, how do I know she's the one I'm looking for, with all this make-up and big hair?'

'Marco, you told me that your people with *zer* chain of restaurants in London, were looking for a girl with shoulder-length, blonde hair, who owned a rare, black, souped up Mini, *zis* girl fits *zer* bill. I don't know if she's *zer* one, that's for you to decide, although I understand that there are only two other cars like that on British number plates, and they both belong to a racing team based outside of London and were in a race at that time of your...accident...'

'She just seems too young for the job she has, doesn't smell right, you understand?'

'Marco, all I do is sell information and deliver packages, etcetera-etcetera...' Sergei put a blini covered with caviar in Milyi's mouth. 'What my clients do with *zer* product, is none of my concern. However, I must speak to you about *zer* other problem...'

'What is it Count?'

'There seems to be a great deal of, how shall I say it, international interest in Barcelona *zis* week, from several powerful people, who are of course my friends and clients...'

'Get to it Count!' Marco said with a stare of amused hatred in his good eye.

'*Zer* price has doubled Marco.'

'Doubled!' Raffaello said dramatically, jumping up from his seat and throwing his arms around like a practised Italian opera star.

The Count, a master at this game, barely moved from his relaxed position, he looked only at Marco; he knew where the money lay.

'I thought we had a deal Sergei?' Marco said evenly.

'Marco until *zis* afternoon, I didn't know if you were going to look at these, beautiful photographs, and tell me that I had *zer* wrong product, well, I've had a great deal of difficulty bringing her here and since I've arrived in

Barcelona, I've learnt that there may be other people who are interested in her, albeit for different reasons.'

Marco read the scheming, old, Russian's face and decided he wasn't bluffing, he didn't have any other leads on the professional assassins and so he made his decision.

'Okay Sergei, but I want her tonight!'

'Saturday night, it's not possible before, she has a little job to do, for me.'

'Why Saturday?'

'Marco, I hear you're going to *zer* Duchesse's party, no?

'You hear a lot Sergei, we are in business together, so my people from Milano want me to go, it's also a political thing.'

'Of course, I understand, well I shall take *zer* blonde there for you, signed, sealed and delivered etcetera-etcetera. Isn't that what they say in *zer* movies these days?' The Russian said, laughing at his own joke.

'Alright Sergei…' Marco nodded to Raffaello, who put a hand inside his jacket. Boris took two enormous steps towards him, carrying a threatening expression like a powerful weapon. Raffaello stopped, and then theatrically, with his index finger and thumb, slowly pulled out a brown envelope, putting it gently on the low table in front of the Count. Boris picked it up, flipped through the wad of notes inside and gave his boss a stare that said the amount looked correct. The three Italians got up and walked into the hall. The Russian followed them making polite utterances that one would usually hear at the end of a family lunch, while Boris had the door open. Raffaello picked up his gun from the table and walked straight out, although Giovanni ignored his banana shaped pistol on the floor and followed his friend, vowing to himself that he would get even with the 'Freaky giant'. Marco shuffled slowly to the porch, turned with difficulty and said to the Count, 'We'll see you on Saturday.' Boris kept his hand on the shotgun until they drove off.

'Well done Boris! You see, I do praise you sometimes.' The Count said pleased with himself.

'Hopefully, if all goes well we shall have three

clients this trip. *Zer* big man in Russia, who likes to keep an eye on everyone, our Italian friends with all that Mafia vengeance brewing, and *zer* most interesting of all, *zer* Duchesse with her peculiar fetish for live art. Yes our pretty little girlfriend could be very valuable indeed.' He said thoughtfully, walking into his bedroom with Charlotte's photographs held preciously in his hand.

Chapter 31
Casa Batlló, Barcelona, April 1964

The immortal skulls stared out, with an evil glare from their vertical burial ground, decorated with concrete and sandstone, covered in ocean-deep, coloured *trencadis,* their vacant eyes surrounded by skeletal bones: encasing the occupants of La Casa Batlló. George's Dragon lay motionless on the roof of his victim's mausoleum, with the Saint's stone sword firmly stabbed in his undulating back. The clear moon spotlighted the cold, coral blue vertebrae of the immortalized monster, which seemed to shimmer as the binoculars' glare stroked his sinewy spine.

Sam Trubshaw: dragon-slayer, assassin, executioner, had been surveying this six story, terminal body for three days now. He pedantically noted the movements of the occupants, reminiscent of maggots crawling in and out of crevices in a long-dead corpse. The observer hadn't moved for the last five hours; his prey should have left for a regimental dinner an hour earlier, nevertheless, Antoni Gaudí's famous skeletal building hadn't released the two parasites, Sam waited for.

Señor Josep Batlló, a wealthy aristocrat, commissioned Antoni Gaudí at the turn of the twentieth century to convert the old apartment block into a magnificent organic building in Catalan's modernistic style. He asked that the two lower floors with their high ceilings, be a unique home for his large family, and the upper floors were to be constructed into individual apartments, for the rental market. Gaudí designed the balconies as skulls and supporting pillars as bones, using organic forms in coralesque shapes and colours for the interiors, façade and on the creature-shaped roof. Like all of Gaudí's work, the *Casa dels Ossos* caused a storm of awe and controversy when finished in 1906, after two years of painstaking refurbishment.

Sam checked his watch, quarter past ten; the dinner should have begun at nine thirty. He started to think that they weren't going, and then the couple appeared with three edgy bodyguards, blatantly brandishing machine guns, scanning the lifeless street and surrounding buildings. Sam realised that he'd made the right decision when he formulated the plan in London. The hit, was clearly too well protected in her hometown, with a powerful military police husband working in the upper echelons of the fascist government. The only way to assassinate her would be to get close. Dangerously close.

Suzanna Valles-Carrera had her dark hair in a chignon, which showed off her triangle shaped, diamond earrings. Sam couldn't see what else she wore, as the tall Neo-Nazi was covered from head to toe in a full-length, black, mink coat. He couldn't help thinking that if his granddaughter, Pippa were here, she would have sprayed the woman with red paint. Suzanna, nee Ilsa Klup, arm in arm with her Chief of Police husband, Colonel José Valles-Carrera, walked out of the building as though they were claiming an Oscar.

He wore an impeccable dress uniform; a thin moustache and his thick black hair had been smeared back with some sort of oil.

'Good advertisement for Brylcreem.' Sam thought.

An immaculate black Citroën DS19 with tinted windows and white wall tyres, floated across the Passeig de Gràcia, stopping in front of the couple, at number 43; the chauffeur jumping out of the driver's seat before the car had fully stopped bouncing, and ran around to open the rear door for his employers. Sam adjusted the focus on his old Watson's, looked closely at the Colonel's medals and noticed the back of a pin threaded through his left lapel. Obviously one of his medals or insignias had been cached, until he arrived at his destination or perhaps he just flipped it over for a selected few.

Sam had seen people do this many times, before the second World War, when in certain drawing rooms in London, New York and Buenos Aires, Nazi sympathisers gathered to plan their world domination over a few drinks or even an organised dinner. They always seemed normal folks, chitchatting about the servant problem and the traffic, although when they thought they were with like-minded people, the lapels were flipped over, the swastikas glistened and their evil intensions were revealed.

The Colonel's regiment had been an active part of Franco's oppression of the weak, as well as communists, artists, homosexuals and intellectuals, who opposed him and his regime. During the civil war, their flags and emblems were brazened on every street corner. However, these days, with tourists arriving from all over the world, a world that had recently stamped out fascism, with a new atmosphere of European union, Franco's politics had become subtler. Sam's research and the dossier he had on José Valles-Carrera, revealed that he used to run Franco's, beautifully restored, 1756 French-neoclassical edifice in Madrid for several years. Once it housed the regional government, during the civil war it became the headquarters of the secret police known as *La Casa de los Gritos* or The House of Screams. The headquarters kept their furnaces burning all-year long. People said that the continuous coil of silky grey smoke contained the hearts and minds of Franco's enemies. Sam understood the irony; these two people didn't live in Gaudí's masterpiece for its artistic beauty, or the celebrity dragon on the roof, but for its uncanny connection to death.

The potentate passengers safely in their car, the booted and uniformed chauffeur jumped back in his seat and the strange suspension on the Citroën, whooshed up and down, as the car disappeared down the wide Avenue. One of the bodyguards jumped into an old Mercedes and the other two, heavily armed men followed on powerful motorbikes.

'So, there won't be any escaping through narrow streets.' The assassin thought, still planning the fine details of his mission.

Señor Batlló's *Casa dels Badalls*, as the locals called it, had become an icon for the rich and famous residents who lived in the building. Therefore it'd been easy for Sam to acquire a detailed plan of the structure and even some photographs of the interior from some old magazines.

He studied the plans in the attic from the secure, vacant office block opposite, at number forty-eight. The residential work of art in front of him, gave the average cat burglar an easy climb and so he slipped into his work clothes. The thick, matt-black footless tights slid over his soft climbing shoes easily. The matching top covered his neck and the hood with its tiny eye slits, made him no more than a shadow in the low light. He pulled his matching rucksack onto his back, having packed all of his equipment and left the building surreptitiously. The velvet shadow slid behind a parked lorry, checked his watch and waited. When the cleaning van crawled pass as it did nightly at the same time, the silhouette used it to reach number 43, dashing across the wide Passage. He moved in the dim doorways, and scurried to the back of the building.

Suddenly Sam stopped moving and dived into a shadow, he saw a body lying on the ground next to some dustbins, he stood in silence for a few moments, yet he was alone except for the blanket covered carcass against the wall. Then it snored loudly, he left the shadow and crouched over the tramp. He was in bad condition but no worse that others Sam had seen near the tourist's spots in the city. There were better places to sleep rough; he wondered why this drug addict had chosen this building.

Sam scaled the ornate metal balconies, until he reached the top floor, which had a large glass conservatory. The slim figure carefully cut one of the upper glass panels close to the frame, as he intended to replace it with putty before he left, and entered the apartment as softly as a prowling cat.

The conservatory led to a stunning living room overlooking the main road; it didn't have one straight surface. The handmade wooden windows curved and flowed to the floor, the ceiling arched under a fluted dome. Sam could only think of Jules Verne's Twenty Thousand Leagues Under the Sea, because he'd never seen architecture so beautiful and yet unworldly.

The experienced agent expertly searched every inch of the sixth floor, to complete his research into the prey. Strangely, the whole place resembled a perfect showroom, no sign of any private papers, bank accounts or personal possessions. It seemed cold and impersonal, like a museum or stately home, open to the public with nothing to hide except the extraordinary art of Gaudí.

The professional assassin closed his eyes and pictured the elaborate plans of the building; he walked around each room and then said aloud. 'The attic, where's the attic?' He took off his backpack and found the plans that he laid out on the golden brown, marble floor.

Where there was once a staircase, now stood a solid wall, he searched again in the cupboards, examined the walls checked the windows and ceiling. The ceiling? He looked up at the incredible vaulted plasterwork that cascaded into the centre of the room and rested on a wonderful, round, metal and glass moulded light. Sam walked back towards the organic shaped windows and leaned against one of the pillars that formed arches in front of the wall of glass.

Each pillar had an ornate rim and a moulded base above the floor. Sam tapped the stone and metalwork with a small knife, the second pillar made a different noise to the others, 'No it's not the pillar...' He thought and continued his search, after a few more minutes of tapping, like a hungry Woodpecker he heard something. 'It's the rim on the second pillar.' The black shadow grabbed the raised edge, gently turning with both hands, the metal started to move anticlockwise easily. 'Perhaps it's a combination, two to the right, one to the left?' He asked himself. No, it seemed to be on a thread, after three turns he could distinguish the top of a brass handle, like something from a nineteenth century ship. Suddenly the rim came undone and almost fell to the floor. Now Sam could hold the lever made from cloisonné enamel, that had a miniature, black ebony, human skull at the end. Before he tried to open it, he checked the street from the wall of windows and opened the door leading to the conservatory, in case the handle was alarmed or armed and he needed to make a speedy escape.

The huge apartment felt completely still, no noise from the road or anywhere in the building. Sam carefully pushed the handle down and an electric motor began to whine. The central ornamental light in the ceiling started to descend slowly, it appeared to be some kind of brass tube similar to a large periscope, within a minute or so the cylinder gave a comforting clump and landed on the floor. Sam walked over slowly, put his head in and realised that he'd found a secret lift.

He stepped in carefully and pressed one of the two buttons, the tube started to pull away from the floor. When his head reached the vaulted ceiling he could see a small pool of light above. The capsule now stood in the attic.

A small window Sam had seen from his surveillance on the outside pulled the streetlights into the room. He closed a blackout blind for the little window and waited for his eyesight to recover, he flipped a light-switch and when the lights came on, he gasped.

The room, built under the dragon's belly stretched on the roof above, reminded Sam of an illustration he once saw showing the inside of a whale, albeit beautifully finished in pure white plaster. The rib bones of the creature divided the upward facing lights into sections, separating the space into alcoves.

Clearly, the large space had been converted into an art gallery, with matching gold frames along the walls. Sam looked at each frame, read the little white card next to each exhibit, which had a black and white photograph above the text. He walked around the extraordinary gallery and looked at each piece. A miasma of death filled the room; he felt an empty sickness in his stomach. The black and white photographs were horrific, mostly naked young girls.

The gold frames, tombs surrounding their dead tattooed skin. At the end of the gallery, he saw double doors; they weren't locked and revealed an office. The agent went through the filling cabinets carefully, found bank statements, files on victims, dossiers on enemies and company papers for businesses in Switzerland, Europe and America.

The Colonel was extraordinary rich with business tentacles reaching out in all directions. The language of the invoices spoke of merchandise, yet the spy had the impression that this simple word covered a multitude of possibilities, including human beings. Sam realised that it would take an army of accountants and investigators to uncover the true depth of the criminal activity, which seemed to involve thousands of people in numerous organisations. He left the apartment undisturbed closing the doors behind him. His job was to assassinate a Nazi who had escaped the death penalty, now it would seem that she had aligned herself with someone equally deadly and together they were destroying the lives of innocent people for profit and sadistic pleasure.

Yet this assassin is a professional, he mustn't allow his emotions to disturb his mission. He wasn't employed to end this evil business; just to eliminate one escaped Nazi. Besides, he reasoned, it would be difficult to stop this tangled web of illicit pleasures. What was it Emiliano Zapata Salazar said?

'The only way to kill the snake was to cut off its head.' Perhaps he *is* getting too old, as Phaedra said. He knew his feelings have to be controlled and one man cannot change the world. Sam snapped out of his disturbed thoughts, he flicked the light switch up, opened the blind and climbed back into the brass tube.

Within a few minutes the shadowy figure stood in a doorway on the back street, under the ornate balconies. He quickly put his camouflage clothes in his backpack, added a short Mac and walked along the Passeig Gràcia somewhat somnambulistically.

After twenty paces he stopped, took a deep breath, opened his bag and found a handkerchief. He blew his nose and wiped his face, realising his eyes were sated with tears. Sam understood he must evict the evil images from his mind. The assassin knew that older men became sentimental with the years, although his professionalism reminded him his work must be impartial. If he started to hate some of the marks, perhaps one day he would like one of them.

Moshe 'Mad' Liberman looked down from the roof of the building where Sam had been doing his surveillance; he took a swig of vodka and replaced the cap, lifted his rifle and aimed the magnified sight at Sam's forehead.

'So what are you doing here Englishman?' He asked aloud. Moshe had a feeling that someone else occupied the deserted office building, despite the lack of sound, or light, he couldn't even smell anything, nevertheless after all of these years in the great game, he could feel someone else near-by. Now he knew who accompanied him, and also realised that the British assassin may have come for the same hit.

'Hope you don't get in my way English, I can't stop for you or anyone else you know.' He whispered under his breath. Moshe opened his violin case, brought the rare antique to his chin and started to play a haunting cry in the empty building.

The following afternoon, Sam and Phaedra drove down to the Port of Barcelona in their new rally Porsche.
The power of the engine and the bassi profundo voice from the exhaust, turned heads in the crowded tourist area, and Sam couldn't help laughing at Phaedra's constant glee as she practised with the world's fastest rally car.

'You know Sam it hasn't the road-holding of my Mini, the back wheels have a mind of their own, but this engine is a miracle of engineering, did you see the size of the clutch darling?' Phaedra said excitedly.

'Yes Phaedra, I remember, you got the guys to virtually take the whole engine apart so that you could have a good look a it, and you say I go on about horses! At least they can't be dismantled.' He teased.

'I can't wait to put this monster on a good road, it's impossible to move out of second gear in the centre of Barcelona.'

'Let's just hope all of our contingency plans won't be necessary on our special evening.'

The Trubshaws parked the German icon and walked over to the edge of the dock looking for their unique craft, it had given the couple so much pleasure over the last few years. The enclave was now full of powerboats and yachts, large and small. Their masts tittered an agitated tune throughout the port; the clamour gave Sam a contented feeling of security. Looking at the motionless lake, unaffected by the high waves beyond the Port's stonewalls. Then they saw the magnificent Scylla, dancing gracefully on the floating floor. Sam pressed his remote control, the gangplank whined out, they removed their shoes and climbed aboard.

'Ahoy! Anyone aboard?' They called in unison.

'Maybe they're out shopping, did you tell them what time we were coming darling?' Phaedra asked her husband.

'Sure, but you know what Patrick's like, he has no sense of time.'

Sam went ahead and shimmied down the stairs into the large salon, stopping suddenly in his tracks on the last step at the horrific sight on the floor, Phaedra bumped into him from behind and asked. 'What's wrong?'

He looked down at the three comatose bodies spread over the floor, the broken bottles, the ramshackle cushions and drawers strewn across the width of the salon, clothes, presumably from the naked bodies, were thrown in all directions, like the contents of a ship washed up on a shore. A red, sticky liquid made islands around the unmoving flesh, resembling an aerial map of an unknown Martian world.

Sam and Phaedra moved silently into the room with heroic couplet, Sam lifted his trouser leg and grabbed a small pistol from an ankle holster, Phaedra pulled a heavy German Lugar from her bag, without speaking and resembling their morning Tai Chi exercises, they moved around the room in perfect synchronicity.

Phaedra checked the doorway into the staterooms and Sam knelt down next to the body of a young girl with long mahogany coloured tresses.

The slightly older blonde woman on the floor had her legs entwined with the third girl who looked oriental, except for her boyish, red spiky haircut.

Sam gently took Mahogany's wrist, 'She's alive...' Sam said quietly, to his wife. 'What about the other two?' Phaedra whispered. Sam got up, padded around the pile of bare flesh, bent down to check their condition, when suddenly they both heard a noise from the other end of the yacht. Noiselessly, the couple moved to either side of the doorway as footsteps came nearer to the salon, when the shadow arrived at the door, Phaedra gave it a swift whack on the back of the neck with the heavy pistol and as the large man turned towards her, Sam kicked the back of his knee with force, he cried out and before he hit the oak floor, Phaedra jumped on him pulling his right arm behind his back with her knee between his shoulder blades, the Lugar's barrel stabbed the nape of his neck.

The body groaned painfully and said, 'For Christ's sake Phaedra, if I knew you liked this rough stuff I would've had you to all my parties.'

'Patrick! What are you doing? Sam asked.
Phaedra stood up quickly putting her Lugar back in her bag and Sam bent over his friend on the floor.

'You know Sam, I've had a fairly rough night with these lovely ladies from the casino, but I seem to remember you told me to bring this beautiful boat down here to Barcelona...' Patrick said, straining to get up, his head spinning as wildly as a carousel.

Sam quickly cashed his pistol in a pocket and helped a complaining Patrick to his feet.

'Patrick I'm so sorry...' Phaedra said, steering the unsteady Irishman to one of the long bench seats next to the hull. 'Did I hurt you Patrick? Let me get some cotton-wool and I'll bathe your head...'

'It's not cotton wool I need Phaedra, it's a drink from that cabinet over there.' He said jadedly.

'Phaedra, I think coffee might be better...' Sam said calmly as the mahogany headed girl got up on her knees dizzily.

Phaedra walked towards the galley with an eye on the naked girl and asked. 'Patrick I hope that's not blood on the floor.'

'Patrick struggled to focus and said wearily. 'No I think it's that pink wine they have here, it's a real killer after a few bottles that is...'

'Sangria?' Phaedra called out.

'No the other one, Rosado they call it...'

'So nobody has been hurt?

'No one except me, Phaedra darling, what did you hit me with? It felt like heavy metal...' Patrick asked rubbing his neck.

'Sorry Patrick, it must have been my gold bracelets; Sam's always saying they will hurt someone one day.

The naked triplets found a few garments from the floor and struggled towards the bathrooms worse for wear, the oriental redhead looked on the verge of vomiting.

An hour later, Phaedra, having finished a speedy clean up, started to serve a breakfast of eggs, bacon and toast to the three croupiers and their dishevelled escorts, despite the fact her watch read five o'clock in the afternoon.

Refreshed, the mariners started laughing at the thought that there had been a bloody massacre on the boat and the girls were giggling at Phaedra and Sam finding them naked on the floor.

'The Scylla is a fantastic boat Sam...' Freddie said laughing. 'Patrick knows everything about boats and yachts, but he says there're levers and buttons on this thing, he felt too afraid to touch.'

'Yes, I did leave him the manual, although I assume that you chaps didn't have much time for reading.' They all laughed, the girls looked a little embarrassed.

'So are you here to make us walk the plank Sam?'

'I've got an envelope for you both with tickets from Barcelona airport for Saturday morning, so there's no rush, we thought that we would pop up with the boat and see a few friends along the coast on Saturday evening, maybe stay for a few days outside the city.'

Sam took Patrick's arm and they went up on deck, he had also put a wad of Pesetas in with the tickets, but didn't say anything in front of the girls.

They stood on the polished wooden floor and breathed in the sane aroma of the Mediterranean Sea, seagulls added the sound effects and a feeling of tranquillity engulfed the two sailors.

'You know Sam apart from the fantastic girls and the great food, this city has the most incredible churches you know.'

'Yes Barcelona is a wonderful city, beautiful art and buildings.' Sam said reflectively.

'But am I right in thinking that you and Phaedra are not the religious types, I can't see you reading the bible.' Patrick asked, probing seriously for a change.

'Apokruphos!' Phaedra called up the steps

defiantly, in her mother tongue.

'What's that, is she speaking Greek again...'

'It means apocrypha....' You know, an untrue philosophy, Phaedra has been an ardent atheist since the war...'

'You know as the Germans were killing our children...' She said passionately putting her head up at deck level. 'We were all praying to the same God.'

'We love all of the church's architecture and appreciate much of the good work done, although we don't actually follow any one religion or philosophy, we just think we should all try to be nice to each other.' Sam smiled.

'So are we all going out on the town tonight?' Patrick said, changing the subject.

'Unfortunately we have a boring business dinner in a snooty restaurant, but I'm sure you chaps won't want to miss out on your last nights in Barcelona.'

'Tell me Sam...' Patrick whispered, 'Do you never think of having a little fling with some naughty young girl?

Sam laughed. 'When I was young and during the wars, I met a lot of girls, the wars made us feel that we had to grab life and live it for the moment, but I fell in love with Phaedra the moment I saw her, and I've never wanted to be with anyone else. I do flirt with girls, it makes her jealous, which is a good thing. No one wants a wife or husband that others wouldn't want!' He laughed. 'Come on you've got your tickets, let's see how the girls are.'

The oriental looking girl looked at Freddie and Patrick saying. 'We want to have some dinner tonight hombres, apart from Phaedra's breakfast, all we've had for three days, is drinks!' They all laughed and Patrick promised them some food. Sam walked up into the galley and the Irishman followed him.

'I was talking about you the other day to Freddie, he asked me how long we've known each other, you know Sam it's been a long time, but when he asked me what you were like, I said; I don't really know.'

'What do you mean, you know me as well, maybe better, than anyone on the Thames.'

'Well that's it Sam, when I've spoken to the river people, they all say; Sam, oh yes - nice guy, always buys

377

you a drink in the pub, lovely wife. Yet no one really knows anything about you, you don't seem to work, you take loads of holidays, you look very fit for your age, actually any age, I doubt if I could beat you in a race, but you never actually say anything about yourself: about your past.

'What do you want to know Patrick? He smiled. 'I've had a boring life really; you know I served in the air force through three wars, I joined under age, but many kids did that, we were keen for the excitement, although as our friends were killed, it took the fun out of it.

My daughter and her husband died young in a car accident, so we had to bring up their kids, luckily my parents left me some money and we just live the life of a retired couple. I must admit it's been very easy and sometimes boring, but most soldiers find civilian life boring after the war.'

'Well now that all sounds very reasonable, although you both have a passion for speed, we've had half a dozen people asking us about this boat of yours, I've never piloted or seen anything so powerful, and those cars aren't that slow either!'

'Oh that's Phaedra, Greeks are mad about speed, she used to drive in rallies you know.'

'You see, that's something nobody knew, I didn't know, I mean the locals talk about her crazy driving, although I'd no idea she raced professionally, now tell me something about yourself, something no one in Richmond knows about you.'

'Well, let me see, I'm uxorious to my Greek wife, although you know that. Oh, I know, did I ever tell you that I used to be an Auguste clown in a circus?

'What! You a clown, wow that is something...' He laughed. 'You see, I knew there was a secret past, my God, a clown, wait to I tell the river boys, you don't mind do you?'

'No-no Patrick, if it gives them something to gossip about, that's fine by me.'

'A clown! And it was just for August was it?'

'No, Auguste is the type of clown, you know the chap who has a red nose, white make-up and big lips.'

'I would never thought of you as a clown, not that you are very serious, well a bit, but a clown, come on - I must tell Freddie, he thought you were an accountant.'

They went back to find Freddie opening a bottle of wine.

'So are you two looking forward to going back to London?' Sam asked.

'Not really, Freddie and me are thinking of moving down here for a while, it's a fantastic place to live.'

'Warm, sunny resorts always seem good for a few weeks, but I think you would miss the river and your weekends in Ireland, wouldn't you?' Sam asked.

'Maybe you're right…' Patrick smiled. 'Saturday you said?'

'Yes, would you be kind enough to do one more favour for me…'

'Sam your favours are more like winning the football pools, what do want me to do?'

'Oh just give the girls a call and make sure they're OK, it's been a long trip and I don't want them to worry. Charlotte will more than likely need some pocket money, if you don't mind I'll give you a few quid for her.'

'Of course I will, you know if she wasn't your granddaughter, I would be trying to take her out, she's a real scorcher.'

'Yes she is, and when you get pass her looks and the childish scatterbrain chitchat, she has a heart of gold.' He said reflectively. 'I hope in a year or two she will settle down with someone like Justin and find a sensible lifestyle, she's still rather immature for her age, it's our fault, we've spoilt both the girls. Phaedra and I have lived through difficult times during the wars, when life had to be so serious. Hopefully the Sixties will be a period when we can all relax and live hedonistic lives and never again have to worry about anything more serious than which wine to drink. What is it the kids say these days: Make love, not war!'

'Sounds good to me Sam!'
They both laughed together and downed a glass of Spanish Rosado.

Chapter 32
Heathrow Airport, April 1964

Heathrow Airport's workers buzzed around the hive of the Queen's Building in an organised frenzy, the background hum as annoying as the Muzak in the terminal. Unlike the calm days when it was a little farm of the same name. A black, metal wall of taxis blocked the entrance in front of the terminal, vibrating in unison due to the opusculum of tuneless diesel engines.

Charlotte felt sick, due to the smell and discomfort of the dusty seats on the blue and green coach she'd been on for the last hour, from Victoria Coach Station. It felt so airless and bumpy, unfortunately, she couldn't afford a taxi all the way from London, in fact; she really couldn't afford anything; being virtually flat broke.

The young girl always had a quixotic view of life and yet now she had lost her confidence. The gas, electricity and telephone had all been cut off at her flat, in the former Wright's Dairy block on Kings Road. She hadn't paid the rent for two months. '*Those people are so rude,*' she thought, they'd made a fortune from her over the last two years, and as Charlotte said to Pippa:

'I just can't believe their attitude!'

Her agency didn't seem to arrange castings anymore, well, they did get annoyed when her phone became 'unobtainable' according to the snooty telephone operator, who spoke as though she had missed her calling as a BBC radio announcer. Then she was sent home after arriving two hours late for an early morning job.

'Why do they have to start at nine thirty? Surly everyone would be more relaxed at around eleven o'clock?'

The model found it so exhausting to keep trekking up Kings Road to the bank of call boxes in Sloane Square tube station, to call Gavin's nightly, particularly as they usually said: 'Sorry honey nothing tomorrow, why don't you do some more test shots?'

Justin didn't appear to be speaking to her, she hadn't missed the sex, well not much, she had a certain velleity for her possible ex; what was really annoying, is they used to eat in restaurants two or three times a week. Only the inexpensive Stock Pot on a hard pine bench, some kind of basket over the light bulbs, a bowl of pasta with imperceptible sauce and a candle in a Chianti bottle. Sometimes they had a quick drink and snack at the Markham Arms opposite the flat, if Justin became really broke they would end up at the Wimpy. She hated the lighting and the plastic tables, but at least it was free food.

Now they were about to pull into the coach stop in front of the airport terminal. The broke girl wondered how the porter would react if she didn't give him a tip. She did have quite a lot of stuff, she reflected nervously. On the noisy pavement, the driver pulled out everyone's cases from the storage hold, at the bottom of the smoky coach. One of her bags had burst open; the feeble clip had given up, under the strain of her bulging wardrobe.

'Sorry luv, this one looks too full...' The driver said, trying to squash the lid down. 'Are all those yours as well?'

'Yes, ah, do you think you could help me find a porter, please?'

'Don't worry, when they see this lot they'll be on you like flies, the more the cases the more they charge, right?'

'Charge? I thought it would be part of the service...'

'Phew, it might have been in the old days, but now it's sixpence a case *and* they expect a tip on top. Are you emigrating to Australia?'

'No I'm just off to Barcelona for the weekend...'

'Cor-blimey, taken the kitchen sink have ya?' The driver said over his shoulder, climbing back into the coach.

Several friendly porters went over to the tall model, delighted by her mountain of luggage, she told them she was waiting for a friend. The blonde smiled at a few young men and although they smiled back, she couldn't believe that most of them just rushed into the departures area, leaving her and the Everest of luggage on the pavement. After ten minutes of eye pleading, another smelly coach pulled up with a white sign in the front window saying 'Private Hire'.

381

Miss Trubshaw watched a noisy stream of young men fall out of the door chatting loudly and jostling each other. They all had dark looks, were mostly her age and wore matching white slacks, and navy blue jackets, that sported a blue and purple badge on the breast pocket. Two older men were shouting instructions to them like angry parents, in what Charlotte thought sounded Spanish.

Suddenly one of them turned around; looked at the blonde as though he had X-ray eyes and hit his friend in the back.

'Hola c-h-i-c-a!' The first one cried out to both Charlotte and the band of young men behind him, who were looking over his shoulder.

'You wait for boyfriend?' The second one asked, with a row of white teeth that would have looked good as a keyboard.

'No, I need some help with my bags...'

Before she finished the last word, eight boys grabbed her luggage at Olympic speed and the first one said, 'Where you go baby?'

'Barcelona?'

The fifteen young men yelped out a cheer in unison and surrounded the blonde as happy as half a dozen sheepdogs around a lone ewe. They herded her into the airport, following the two older men riding point, to a check-in desk marked 'British European Airways'. As the front men got to the desk with enough tickets for the group, the young boys started shouting and pointing to Charlotte. The older men looked around and as she found herself hustled to the head of the pack, the one who acted like the boss, turned saying:

'Excuse me young lady, are you going to Barcelona with BEA?'

'Oh thank you, I'm not sure which airline I'm booked with, I'll just have a look at the ticket.'
She bent over in her mini dress and the crowd of boys cheered like they'd just won the cup final, she looked up nervously, held her skirt down and bit her bottom lip. She searched her chaotic bag for the ticket, pulling out several bags of almost empty tubes and bottles of make-up, blonde

hair brushes, bottles of Ponds face cream, the last inch of Colgate toothpaste, three flattened toothbrushes, a curling iron, a hairdryer, three bottles of nearly empty shampoo and hair conditioning, a packet of sanitary towels, a bag of hair rollers, and finally, to the relief of the team manager standing over her, her wallet. Other passengers looked over to see why such a large group of young men were pushing and shoving for position, around a small circle on the floor of the busy airport. The experienced airhostess behind the desk seemed to be rather annoyed by the boy's behaviour and finally said.

'Excuse me Miss, you are holding up the check-in and we only have fifteen minutes to process this group...'

'Oh I'm sorry, I did have the ticket this morning, I think it's in this wallet...'

'And do you have any luggage?'

Eight of the uniformed boys rushed forward with Charlotte's superfluity of bags and boxes like African bearers on safari, and started to pile it on the luggage platform next to the rather matronly BEA airhostess.

'One moment please, are these all yours Miss?'

Miss Trubshaw's face broke into a huge smile as she turned towards her male audience and said excitedly.

'I've got it!'

The audience clapped as though she had just scored a winning penalty and the airhostess put out her hand to receive the ticket.

'This is just a single Miss, are you moving to Barcelona?' She asked looking at the vast array of bags, brown paper boxes and suitcases the boys had piled up.

'Oh no, it can't be, I was told it's a return, I'm coming back on Monday...'

'Not with this ticket Miss, look...' She leaned forward and turned the ticket towards the young girl. 'It has an 'S' in this box at the bottom, that means single.' She explained with a certain satisfaction.

One of the young men moved next to her and said. 'Listen Guapa, pasa nada, you stay in España, we all look after you...' The boys cheered and clapped in unison and agreement.

The older Spaniard took over.

'Could you please tell this young woman if her ticket is valid to fly, if yes, why don't you stamp it and we can all move forward so that we don't miss our flight, we have an important match in a couple of days and we can't miss this plane.'

'Well, yes Sir...' The hostess said, realising this man had an air of being obeyed, and he was after all a valuable customer with a large group.

'Your ticket *is* valid Miss, ah, Trubshaw, but you have far too much luggage for one second class seat...'

'Second class?' The Roedean graduate said shocked. 'He told me I had a first class return, with a window seat.'

The English girl's supporting team went silent after the word 'He' giving each other speculative looks.

'I'm sorry Miss, you will have to pay some excess luggage fees...' The hostess said, with what Charlotte thought was a hint of glee in her eyes.

'But I haven't got enough money to pay any fees...' She uttered sulkily.

'Well I'm sorry Miss, BEA has strict regulations and quite frankly, I've never seen so many cases for such a short trip and as you're second class...' She said with pleasure. The young insolvent girl didn't get the double entendre, be the manager did.

'Excuse me!' The elderly Spanish man interrupted. 'How many cases are my group allowed?'

'Well, as a group of seventeen Sir, we could accept at least, say, thirty four cases, maybe a few more...'

'Alright then...' He said, in front of the now silent audience. 'Put this young lady's cases in with our group, because we only have a small bag each...'

'Oh! I'm not sure Sir...'

'Señora, do as I ask you please...' He said putting his group's tickets in front of the woman, 'or the thousands of our supporters who are waiting for us at El Prat will tear your airplane apart, if we are not on it!'

Without another word the airline employee put her head down and processed all of the luggage and tickets at

384

the rhythmic pace of a conveyer belt. Charlotte thanked the football manager and walked towards the departure gate with the team of fifteen young men around her. Charlotte felt exhausted, but relieved and searched her new Courrèges bag for a cigarette.

'I don't suppose you boys have any ciggy's do you?'

To her delight, six packets were held under her nose by the excited team. She pouted her lips as she gripped the Benson and Hedges 100s and a forest-fire of matches lit up in front of her face.

'So what are you boys doing here?' She asked, getting into her relaxed chat-up mode.

'We are Barça...'

'What's a Barça?'

'No, you no understand, we are the best footballers in España, we are the team from Barcelona, in Catalan.'

'Oh! You mean like Chelsea?' The boys all booed and jeered. 'No like Chelsea, we much better!' The whole team clapped and chanted.

'Barça-Barça-Barça-Barça...'

'I am called Josep Fusté and this is my friend Carles Rexach, you have heard of us, no?'

She put her toes together, shaking her head slowly.

'I'm sorry...' She said. 'I don't know much about football. I only know Chelsea because when they play on Saturdays, the spectators block all of the shops around my flat, it's so annoying.'

'What are you called?'

'My name? I'm Charlotte.'

'You know Charlotte, we won the King's Cup last year, and we're champions!' Carles said proudly.

'Why you go Barcelona, you have boyfriend there?' Josep asked.

'No, I'm a model...' The boys, all listening carefully cheered, whistled and clapped again. 'And I'm going to do a fashion show...' She added more enthusiastically than she really felt.

'Where is this, we come and see you, you have lots of model girlfriends there?' Carles chipped in.

'Yes, I think there'll be other models there, but I'm not sure where it is,' She said. 'There's a restaurant next to a cable car, with a view of the sea?'

The boys looked at each other at a loss, when one of them said.

'I know it, opened last year on the port, new decorations, El Restaurante La Torre d'Altamar, *pero, muy caro amigos.*'

'My friend says it expensive, maybe you come and see us play at the stadium, is called Camp Nou.'

She looked at the boys as they all approached the airplane, she thought that some of them were really cute, although none of them stood much above her shoulders, however, she liked them and for the first time in weeks, she felt safe.

'Who is this... 'He' who book you second class?' Josep asked.

'Sergei?' Well, he's a kind of agent, he knows a lot of people and he arranged this fashion show for a really good fee, you see I'm rather short of money at the moment.'

'Where is, um, tu madre y padre? The English girl looked blank; Josep turned to Carles and said. ¿Cómo se dice madre y padre en Inglés?

Carles turned to her saying. 'Where is your mummy?'

'Oh, my parents are dead...' Before she could explain to them that she had been brought up by her grandparents, Carles turned to the team who were now on the steps leading up to the plane and called out. 'Ella es una huérfana.' The whole team sighed loudly and decided they were going to communally adopt the beautiful orphan, at least until the next game in Milan.

The BEA Herald's propellers started to sing and the smartly dressed airhostesses flew around the cabin as rapidly as sparrows in an aviary, checking the little tables, seats and their belts as well as flirting gently with the young footballers. After take-off, Charlotte finished another cigarette and went into the toilet.

She sat on the seat and counted her money, it totalled three pounds, fifteen shillings and tuppence.

The Count said he'd meet her at the airport and so she hoped to get a sub from him and survive until she was paid her fee on Saturday night, as Sergei promised. She had calculated that she could pay all her bills at the flat, the garage for Ya-Ya's car and still have about a hundred pounds left over for a little shopping in Barcelona and a taxi back from the airport in London.

The broke girl planned to get as much food as possible from the hotel's room service and hopefully cigarettes and other goodies from their shop, if they have one. If it's a five star posh hotel, they might even have a designer shop, so she could put a few things on the Count's bill. Looking in the small plastic surrounded mirror, she breathed a sigh of relief. Yes, she mused, a little more lipstick, a splash of Jolie Madame perfume by Balmain, which had been liberated from an advertising shoot she did last year. There wasn't much left in the bottle, but she was feeling much better.

Before the flight ended, Charlotte worked her way through two airplane lunches, four miniature bottles of Spanish Rioja and a cloud of cigarettes from the boys. All fifteen players gave her their telephone numbers on various scraps of paper and she promised to ring them all, when she knew which hotel she was staying in.

When the plane touched down at the airport, hundreds of Barcelona fans were waving flags, clapping and cheering the victorious footballers. A regiment of police came up the steps ushering the famous team to a special coach and she soon felt alone again in the virtually empty airport. The customs' agents were nearly as pleased to see the tall blonde as the footballers and insisted on searching all her luggage before chalking a white, approval-cross on each. One of them, about the same age as her grandfather offered to take her out for dinner that evening, but she declined. The slightly tipsy girl felt in a good mood again and had seven, officially free, smiling porters, following her with a leaning tower of luggage on each trolley. When she turned into the airport lounge, her elated mood sank rapidly, at the sight of a leviathan, bald man, holding a white card that said in thick black ink: 'Miss Trubshaw'.

The namesake took a deep breath, lifted her chin and walked straight towards the lofty chauffeur.

'Hello Boris, how nice to see you again.' She offered as cheerfully as she could. 'Where's the Count?'

Boris' only answer in a voice as deep as hell was, 'Come.' He turned around towards the exit, his long strides made Charlotte and her caravan, follow like Snow White and her seven baggage handlers. The behemoth chauffeur opened the rear door of a long wheelbase, Mercedes 600, which the young model jumped into; he started to close her door when he noticed the entourage.

'*Whot* all this?' He asked aggressively, in his usual tachygraphic English.

'It's my luggage, you'll need to give them a tip.' She said in her best Roedean accent.

'All is for two days?'

'It's not for two days, I'm here until Monday!' She said, as confidently as she could.

'Huh! Maybe.'

The dwarfs, everyone looked like a dwarf next to Boris, stuffed the young passenger's wardrobe into the black limo's boot and looked disappointed at their small tip in copper change. Boris climbed into the driver's seat and pulled away with a whoosh. Charlotte liked the comfortable, cream-leather seats; the massive legroom and she'd never seen curtains on a car window before. After looking at the suburbs of Barcelona and the blazing vermillion sun for ten minutes, she asked Boris:

'Which hotel am I staying in?'

Boris glanced in the rear-view mirror and without a word, pressed a button on the central consul; a thick glass screen divided the rear seats from the front, with a hum and a clunk.

The passenger tapped on the glass irritably. 'Excuse me - I asked you a question...'

Boris ignored her. Charlotte fuming, rummaged in her bag for the mix of borrowed cigarettes she took from the footballers and filled the large limo with a nicotine fog. She could soon see the pellucid Mediterranean with its matching sky; Charlotte gazed at silent airplanes that scratched the blue surface like loose chalk across a navy blue board. After an hour, the long car came to a halt on the beach road in front of the Count's rented villa; Boris jumped out and opened the metal gates leading into the driveway. The young girl looked around at the deserted road and the single storey villa and called out to Boris:

'I say; this doesn't look like an hotel…'

Boris ignored her. She grabbed the car door handle and pulled, then pushed, rattled it up and down and then realised as Boris looked over and grinned, as content as a hungry dog who had just found a bone, that the doors were controlled from the driver's cockpit. The grey suited chauffeur climbed back into the front seat and pulled the Mercedes into the driveway with the tyres crackling on the stony surface. When the car came to a halt the giant jumped out and opened the rear door. Charlotte climbed out suspiciously and asked rudely.

'Where's the Count?'

The chauffeur silently went over to the front door and pushed it open, the smell of cigar smoke and the sound of Maria Callas singing an aria from Puccini's Tosca, narcotized the warm air in the attractive hallway. She hesitated on the porch when the chauffeur came behind her with two of her suitcases; he used them on her backside to shove her into the hall saying. *'Mauve!'*

The young girl turned with a mixture of hatred and fear on her face, she looked back at the car and the locked metal gates, tears started to well in her green eyes.

Charlotte Trubshaw had reached five years old when she heard that her parents were killed in a car accident. She remembered that her mother always had a wonderful perfume in her hair, although she has never found the same scent since. A tall, athletic woman, who was always smiling was the only image she remembered. Pippa said that their mother used to allow the elder sibling to brush her long hair when she sat at the kidney shaped dressing table. Their father had fair hair and glasses, the two girls remembered him as slim and shy, always reading books and writing at his desk. Occasionally at the weekends, he would throw them in the air or push them on the swings in the garden. When the sisters talked about their parents, the one overriding memory they both had, focused on suitcases, they were always packing and going off on holiday. The girls received presents when they left and when they came back. They received gifts when the adults were busy on the phone or busy going out, which seemed to be almost constantly. In fact, Charlotte soon learnt that if she screamed and stamped her foot, she could get anything she wanted, except she couldn't stop them from leaving the house. Young Charlotte had also managed to get her own way with her doting grandparents and most men she'd met since she was a child. At first she looked cute and adorable, then she grew nubile and leggy and since her seventeenth Birthday, she became beautiful and sexy. Most people did what she wanted for a while, she even managed to convince some parking wardens not to give her a ticket; but unfortunately things were just not working out for her recently. Her looks didn't help her with the utilities or the horrible old bank manager. Gavin was surrounded by beautiful models and seemed immune to her usual tactics that she had perfected to get her own way. Even Justin no longer melted when she sat on his lap in her underwear. Although this awful giant was the rudest person she'd ever met and now all her plans for shopping and room service at a nice hotel, had evaporated, as she seems to be trapped in the lecherous Count's private house. Maybe Ya-Ya was right about him, he seemed nice at first and yet she felt nervous now: she didn't even have enough money to get a taxi or a return ticket to London. Tears started to fall more abundantly down her cheeks, and she felt truly frightened.

Giovanni Gibigiano sat in the Fiat rent-a-car two hundred yards from the Count's house. Once he felt confident the young girl was staying in the place, he drove down to the village restaurant and made a call. The crazy freak Marco seemed to be happy and told him to go back to the Count's villa, he would send some of his fascist soldiers from his boat. On the other hand, he wanted Raffaello at the castle. 'You can set up, round the clock surveillance, but be careful Giovanni, that Russian *bastardo* can be tricky.' Giovanni didn't enjoy this type of job; the freak spoke to him like a kid just starting out.

'Charlotte Darling!' The Count said entering the hallway, with Milyi under his arm. 'What are you doing standing there? Has Boris shown you your suite?'

'No!' She uttered with tears in her voice, wringing her hands. 'I hate him, he so rude.'

'My dear girl, you're upset, come here...' Sergei purred as gently as a kindly uncle.

He put the dog on the floor, his arms around her and his head on her chest, as though he was a doctor listening for her heartbeat.

'I'm not staying here Sergei, I want to go to a proper hotel with room service.' She said as insistently as she could.

'My darling *zis* is far better than a crowded hotel, you will have every luxury here, come and look at your room, I've made *zer* whole thing perfect for you, come-come, look-look.' The Count said enthusiastically, guiding her to the back of the house; still pouting, she reluctantly followed the old Russian. He opened double doors into a magnificent bedroom with French windows leading to an impeccable garden, surrounding a glistening swimming pool.

'Look my dear girl, all *zis* wonderfulness etcetera-etcetera, is for you...' He opened another door exposing a sitting room, her tears started to dry.

'And look here...' He continued, waving his arms extravagantly like a drowning swimmer. He pushed a door leading to a massive bathroom. 'There's a Jacuzzi, a shower and look at *zis*, my favourite girlfriend, a film star's dressing table etcetera-etcetera...' He said proudly pointing to an area with a huge mirror surrounded by little light bulbs.

'I had a second class ticket *and* it's a single!' She pouted.

'Second class! Second class! I'm shocked – shocked. That Boris is an idiot, I bet he kept *zer* change from *zer* money I gave him, and I insisted that you have *zer* absolute best seat on *zer* plane, he's such an idiot, and you know Milyi hates him! Everybody does.'

You promised me an hotel, with room service.' She said, starting to feel better, looking at the deep, blue pool, sparkling in the warm sunlight.

'Listen to me, why don't you jump in *zer* Jacuzzi, there's a brand new Chanel dressing gown, Chanel cream and a bottle of Chanel perfume waiting for you, and I'll meet you next to *zer* pool in an hour with some champagne and Russian caviar. Then you can swim and we shall go into Barcelona *zis* evening for a wonderful dinner and even have a little look at *zer* girl's shops, ah! What do you say?'

The mere mention of shops acted like an adrenalin shot to the greedy model, her face lit up as brightly as the Christmas lights in Oxford Street, as she padded into the bathroom and started to think that Sergei wasn't that bad. She closed the door, turned on the ornate, swan headed taps and started to get undressed, as an afterthought she went over to the door, but couldn't see a lock.

Count Sergei Belevsky-Zhukovsky, walked into the hall with a huge smile on his face, he checked his reflection in the hall's gold-framed mirror, straightened his bow tie and smoothed his goatee beard.

He went into the kitchen and saw Boris eating some cold paella from yesterday's lunch. His eyes squinted with rage.

'What are you doing you idiot? Where's her luggage, how did she get so upset, you know we have to keep her happy until *zer* auction on Saturday night!'

'No *loggage,* she whole house in *cor.*' He mumbled, still stuffing rice onto his fork.

'What? I don't care what she has, go and get all her things and put it in *zer* guest's suite, and no peaking through *zer* spy hole! We have two wonderful bidders for *zis* beauty, enough to keep you in food for months, so stop eating and try to smile.'

Boris stood up and gave the Count a horrific, paella speckled smile, before turning reluctantly towards the front door. Sergei looked at him with loathing and called out, 'Boris, maybe better not to smile, put your hat on and call her Miss and then keep away from her until Saturday, you understand?'

Boris didn't look through the spy hole between the hall and Charlotte's enormous bathroom, but Sergei did.

Charlotte eased herself into the bubbling warm water and the whirling liquid caressed her body, she sunk beneath the surface enjoying the soothing luxury. After twenty minutes she crawled out completely relaxed, onto the marble floor, and found her perfume and body lotion in the distinctive box. She sat on a small stall and covered her naked body in the moisturising cream, enjoying the feeling of luxury. Sergei stared forensically through the peephole also enjoying the young girl massaging the cream, he thought.

'It's such a waste, she's so beautiful, and *zer* face without any make-up is like a child's, so smooth with pale pink lips, always mobile, almost too big, and yet somehow just right. Those bosoms so beautiful...' He swooned. 'With nipples as delicate as tiny, pink, flowers, looking up at *zer* sun. How can people get pleasure from damaging such pulchritude? *Zer* Duchesse and her sadistic husband were made for each other, but why do these weird people want to take something so beautiful and destroy it?'

The unbidden vision of the young girl having her tattoo removed brutally by the Duchesse or being tortured daily by Marco entered his consciousness. The Count shook his head and shuddered at the idea. 'Marco is also a little crazy,' he thought, 'although it's understandable, looking down at a body like that on a daily basis would make most people suicidal. Although he's surely made a mistake about Charlotte, she's too stupid to have been part of any hit. It would be so nice to keep her for a while, and yet with two people offering five thousand dollars, maybe a little more, yes, I'm sorry my dear, it's just too much money to give up, perhaps...'

'Boxes in room. Is else?' Boris said, smiling at the old man with his eye screwed into the wall. 'Boris, stop creeping up on me!' You know I told you to knock or cough, like they do in *zer* movies, etcetera-etcetera.'

Boris walked away triumphantly, happy that he had won a small battle.

Chapter 33
Castell de Plegamans, April 1964

Marco cradled the telephone and smiled in his mind, his face couldn't oblige, incapable of much movement or emotion, even speech could be problematical, he couldn't hear very well either, since his eardrum had burnt with the rest of the right side of his body. Marco knew since he was a child that he wasn't like most people; he didn't feel the emotions or weaknesses that others felt. He'd known a quantity of tough men, when he was a kid during the Second World War, working with the Italian Fascist under El Duce. He encountered many who had no humanity or feelings, then fighting with the Fascist Partisans in the mountains, often slitting the throats of young women and boys, he became completely anaesthetized to any feeling of remorse or compunction. Then the young killer waged a campaign against the British and Americans, machine-gunning the young Tommie's and GI's, he could see their adolescent eyes, yet it meant nothing to him. Following that, the Italians change their allegiance and he was taking pot shots at his former comrades, the retreating Germans.

After 1945, working with mafia families in the North of Italy, seemed like a good idea at first, they needed him, he had been an experienced killer from the age of thirteen, the muscular Italian had also become an expert at torture. There were a few other men in the *Partito Nazionale Fascista* who were as knowledgeable in these fields. However, Marco had something that they did not have; he was persuasive. Since the accident, no, not the accident, the ambush, he reasoned, Marco had lost his dominance, his natural attributes, no longer fit and strong, he could barely see, let alone hurt anyone without a weapon. Nowadays, instead of people trusting him, they cringed when they saw his grotesque, twisted and repulsive body, even from a distance!

When Doctor Pierre Tailladat showed the patient a little mirror in the hospital last January, Signóre Sotori wanted to die. To remove the unsightly mess he had become from this world. As the months went by, nothing changed, Marco had lost the will to live. As an influential mafia made-man and a key commander in the FNP, he had always hated weak men and felt repulsion for the handicapped or injured. Marco Sotori hated himself in the hospital ward and he thought that he would be a useless cripple that many would pity. Due to his position in the Mafia, the Fondazione Nazionale di Cristo and the FNP, the clever killer had amounted a vast fortune, except what use would it be, aside from keeping him alive! He knew even prostitutes wouldn't want to have sex with such a monster, not that he was capable, and how would he ever have any kind of relationship?

Marco always thought he didn't need women, which was easy when he could obtain as many as he wished. Since the explosion, every aspect of his existence had been expulsed.

Until a month ago, when Raffaello Massoni came to see him saying that their people in London had found a lead on one of the two assassins from Paris, who was responsible for the daily nightmare he faced. And now, after weeks of waiting, he just received a telephone call confirming that his adversary had arrived in Barcelona. Marco dragged the right side of his body to the window, for the first time in ages he felt alive again. The beautiful view down to the village of Palau-Solita y Plegamans that sat on the northern side of Barcelona looked so green and alive. Marco Sotori twisted slowly and folded his broken body under the desk; at last, the room he had prepared in the dungeons of the castle below, would receive its first guest. They say she's young and attractive; she must have started in the assassination business early as he did. It shouldn't take long to find out the name of her partner; it was only a split second, and yet Marco thought that he identified an older guy, maybe the client who wanted to go along with back up. 'Ah, so much to look forward to, not the life he had, nevertheless, at least it's a life!' He reflected.

Due to the recommendation from the Italian Catholic Church, Marco Sotori became general secretary of the Fondazione Nazionale di Cristo five years ago, the organisation owned the building housing his office. The Foundation had served him well over the years. It was formed in 1941, from an extreme-right-wing Christian group, in conjunction with the breakaway Italian Fascist Union and one of the leaders from the Falange Movement. They had the money of their religious followers, the political muscle of the fascist, and in the last ten years, the acceptable face of the Spanish Fascist Government, supported by Franco using the party's power and wealth.

The Castell de Plegamans developed into perfect headquarters, a walled fort with vast lands, all the convenience of the local village, yet less than an hour to Catalan's capital city. The fortress was a perfect place to keep the girl and her associate for years, in complete secrecy. The walls were ten feet deep; you couldn't hear a ship's foghorn through the stone, let alone a screaming, burning girl.

The Foundation had organised a dinner that evening when Marco Sotori was going to propose an agreement with a conservative Catholic group in the United States. They were perfect partners for their purposes. An all male organising committee; anti-abortion, anti-homosexual, anti-coloured emancipation. Their distribution networks throughout America, would allow Marco's Mafia brothers to sell their products and set up their casinos, because luckily gambling was one of the few vices they enjoyed and approved of. However, the most profitable part of the company that Marco wanted to develop in the United States, and particularly in Mexico and the rest of South America, was the adoption business. He had invited an American priest to dinner for the following Saturday to try and seal the deal. During the Spanish Civil War and after 1939 when it was officially finished, prison governor, José Valles-Carrera, discovered that the practice of stealing babies from female prisoners could develop into a very rewarding business.

At first, the procedure came from an ideological and political standpoint; originating with an obsession for taking children away from families deemed politically dangerous to the regime of General Franco, and given to his supporters.

Unfortunately, the stock of babies diminished once the fighting had stopped, with fewer female prisoners, and it became more difficult to cover up such blatant injustices.

Then Valles-Carrera approached a Catholic maternity hospital that had a large number of poverty stricken young girls, who were pregnant to missing or dead shoulders, suggesting that they could place the children in good Catholic homes. The nuns convinced the young women that their lives, and that of their babies, would be unbearable without the support of a husband. They easily persuaded them to sign the newly born children over to the Catholic adoption society.

When José Valles-Carrera met former Nazi, Ilsa Klup, incognito as Sister Suzanna, he realised that she would be the perfect assistant for his developing business, because the Catholic Church continued to retain a powerful influence on public life, particularly in social services.

In conjunction with doctors, nurses, priests and nuns, working in hospitals and orphanages, the Fondazione Nazionale di Cristo set up the largest adoption system in Spain, selling new born babies to wealthy couples for as much as 200,000 pesetas, which amounted to more than the price of a small apartment.

The first week of June in 1962, became exceptionally hot and uncomfortable for most people in the airless Spanish capital, although for twenty-eight-year old Paloma Perez, the oppressive weather seemed unbearable, finding herself two days past her pregnancy term. The ballooned girl left her flat for the San Ramón Clinic in Madrid within an hour of her waters braking, having rushed to the hospital on the bus with her closest friend Henriqua. The girls were giggling about Sylvie Vartan singing her new hit record, Le Locomotion, they had learnt the words and were singing while walking along the pavement. Henriqua twisted to the song on the balls of her feet, in time to the crackly sound blasting from her new transistor radio and Paloma could still manage the arm movements, until a Guardia Civil uniform passed by and told them to stop disturbing the peace and turn off their radio. When he turned his back, the girls put their tongues out and started laughing.

'He reminds me of my ex-husband, he was miserable as well.'

Paloma had separated from her brutal husband four years earlier and the father of the baby was another man, a good man, an electrician, called Jorge. They were happy together, albeit broke, and so she was grateful to the Sisters of Charity for their kind offer of help with her first child - free of charge. Within a few minutes of arriving, the young women were sent to a cubicle with a high narrow bed where Paloma was given a flimsy cotton gown and instructed to undress. They both smoked furiously and chatted excitedly about the unborn child while they waited for the doctor.

'You know Jorge is so happy about the baby, we don't have much, but he's made a wonderful cot from a wooden drawer he found in his brother's attic and my old neighbour Señora Ruiz, gave us some clothes she'd kept since her daughter was a baby. She's really kind to Jorge and me; her daughter had reached my age when she went missing in the war. I suppose she can see something of her in me. She's so generous towards us, even though the old girl doesn't have much herself.' Paloma said, finishing her cigarette.

'Well, I've got a little present for you when you come out, it's only from the market, it looks new though, I don't...'

'Are you Paloma Perez?' The severe nun asked, swishing the pink curtain to one side.

'Yes and this is my friend Hen...'

'You will have to leave now, we have no room for friends here and there's lots to do.'

Paloma started to protest, she needed a friendly face, not really knowing what to expect, as it was her first baby; despite the fact that she'd tried for several years with her drunken husband, although the stern nun ushered Henriqua into the corridor pointing to the exit.

'I'll come back after the baby's born Paloma, don't worry everything will be alright...'

'I'm Sister Carmen Gomez-Valbuena, now listen to me,' the small woman said blandly. 'If you do exactly as I tell you, the birth will go smoothly, now put your legs up here in the metal stirrups and we'll check the baby.'

The nun prodded the young woman with rubber-coated fingers and a cold piece of metal, Paloma started to wish Jorge could've been with her.

'How far apart are your contractions?' The spectacled woman asked coldly.

'About three minutes apart – is that normal Sister?

'Yes that's fine, but there're often complications with the first child, especially if the birth is not blessed in heaven.'

'What do you mean?'

'I understand that the child is not from your real husband, all good Catholics know how the church feels about unmarried mothers and babies conceived in sin; don't you?' The nun said scolding.

'You don't understand, I'm separated from my husband and Jorge loves me and is looking forward to having our baby.'

'There's no such thing as separation, divorce and fornication with men for good Catholics, and it's against the law! You should go back to your husband or this baby will not be baptised and will surely go to hell.' The Sister said vehemently.

As the nun turned her back to leave, tears percolated from Paloma's eyes and she wished that she didn't feel so alone. When Sister Carmen arrived at the clinic's office on the fourth floor, Señora Suzanna Valles-Carrera sat at the administrator's desk in a business-like grey suit with a tight, pleated skirt and a waisted jacket. She penned a death certificate for Paloma's baby.

'Well Sister,' she said, without looking up from the hortative folder. 'Can we expect the birth soon? Because the new parents want to leave for Geneva before the weekend and I promised them the baby would be ready, with all of the paperwork properly stamped.'

'She looks ready, within a few hours I would think, although I'm a little concerned by her attitude, she seems quite feisty, not as young as they normally are, there might be trouble.'

'Don't concern yourself with the adoption Sister

Carmen, that's my department; just see that we get a healthy baby. If there're difficulties with the birth you can always cut her open, it makes access to the child a lot easier.'

'As I've mentioned before Sister Suzanna, we only do this if there's a danger of the child being still-born, it's a very painful procedure for the mother and the stitches often turn septic, we must act responsible for the good of both mother and child.' She said piously.

The Director stood up from her desk determinedly, and violently grabbed the diminutive nun's arm pushing her against the wall. 'Listen to me you hypocritical old bag, you take the money each month without blinking, so don't start pretending that you care for these stupid girls or there offspring, they are simply cash cows, so just rip her open and get the baby out, do you understand?'

'You're hurting my arm Sister Suzanna - I must go back to my patients.' The nun said nervously looking at the floor, afraid of the strange, foreign Foundation Director, who had taken control of the adoptions with the bishop's authority and a warning that 'She must be obeyed!'

Suzanna Valles-Carrera had married her husband earlier in the year, although they decided that she should continue to be called Sister Suzanna at work, as it gave her, a certain kudos with the religious factions, and fitted with the image of the Fondazione Nazionale di Cristo.

Raffaello Massoni arrived at the Castell de Plegamans, just as dark clouds smudged the sun that decided to end its day on the Costa Brava by plunging into the distant hills.

The Sicilian's natural temper grew into a fury when Marco summoned him to the huge castle, miles away from the centre on Barcelona, where he was enjoying a fantastic lunch.

The black Cadillac pulled in front of the massive walls and Raffaello Massoni sauntered up to a solid gate.

The young nun, who opened the ancient door at the Foundation's headquarters, had an exquisite face with dark brown eyebrows and matching eyes, over naturally deep-red lips that contrasted with the white starched wimple stretched tightly around her face and the cotton cornette, covering her beautiful long neck.

'I am Raffaello Massoni, I've come to see Marco Sotori.'

He said in Italian with a growing grin as the young girl's face smiled bashfully and her eyes descended to the gravel under a canopy of thick lashes. She didn't speak, yet seemed to understand his language and opened the door just wide enough for the Italian to squeeze through. Her black habit swished as rhythmically as a pendulum in front of him. She mounted the stairs with her arms crossed, hands tucked into wide sleeves. Despite the loose cloth, Raffaello studied her rear as her slim body moved beneath the black habit, he couldn't help wondering what a night of love with the nubile, would be like. When she reached the first floor, she tapped an antediluvian wooden door with her knuckles. After a couple of seconds Marco's crackling, damaged voice answered, she gestured towards the entrance and disappeared along the dim walled corridor.

'Come in Raffaello.' He said without looking up. 'I have some business for you and your family in Sicily, sit down.' He said hoarsely, waving his good arm to an upright chair.

'What sort of business Marco, couldn't you have told me yesterday instead of dragging me out here?'

'Listen to me, this isn't for your hot-headed friend Giovanni, this is the type of business that needs a lot of organising, once it's set up with good customers, we have an endless supply of product and each piece is worth anything from 100,000 to 200,000 pesetas. And you know something, the customers even think you're doing them a favour!'

'Sounds good, what are we selling?'

'Babies!'

'What! No one in Sicily is going to buy babies, we make our own, free...' The Sicilian said with annoyed irony in his voice.

'Listen to me Raffaello, there're thousands of couples who want to adopt babies; cute, white, Catholic, European babies, less than three month's old. They pretend to themselves after a couple of weeks they had it naturally, within a couple of years they forget it was adopted, assuming they've paid for the kid, because we also do a kind of hire-purchase agreement, that's good money, they end up paying double.'

'Okay, I can see how it could make money, but I don't have time to look after a load of screaming kids, they need milk and stuff every five minutes, how are we going to transport them; in crates like sheep?'

'No-no Raffaello, listen to me, this can be arranged, do you know that fifteen per cent of all Spanish adoptions last year went through our Foundation, fifteen per cent! This weekend I'm doing a deal with some people in the States and Mexico, anywhere that has many religious people and a strong church, has a ready-made market. You see, these donors are told by their priests that the babies are better off in a wealthy, God-fearing home, than with some teenage kid who's not religious and has no money. We get most of the babies free from hookers and unmarried kids, who don't want them anyway.'

'Alright that all sounds fine, just tell me Marco, who looks after them from the time they leave the mother until they get to the new parents, not me?'

'Nuns.'

'What?'

'Who opened the door for you? A nun.'

'Actually she was really something, if she's not legit, do you think she might want to marry me for a week or two?' Raffaello said excitedly.

'Raffaello, listen to me, they are real nuns, she's called Sister Virginia, many of them think it's the correct thing to do. Finding homes for the babies, that one has just come out of an orphanage herself, so she's still innocent...'

'Perfect for me Marco...'

'Yes I'm sure, nevertheless, through the Foundation we have thousands of medical and religious people who help collect and transport the babies.

Some do it for their own reasons, but all of them are on the payroll. No one has refused the money from top to bottom, we've got bishops, doctors, government officials, a whole pack.'

'So are you telling me Marco, that you can send a package of babies with a load of sexy teenage nuns to look after them?'

'Sure, all you need to do is find rich couples in your territories who will buy them, then we all make good money?'

'It sounds almost too easy.'

'That's roughly the system Raffaello, for the most part, it's not even illegal and worth over one hundred thousand dollars a year for you and your family!'

'Marco, I heard you were smart, but this is genius! I'll have to check with my father, but I'm sure that we're in, so where are the products, do you have to keep them fresh or what?'

'We have a nursery here and others all over the country, some of the new parents are Spanish, but mostly they go abroad, it solves any problems with the original parents changing their minds.'

'Alright, I'm in, any possibility of sexy Sister Virginia taking me back to my hotel in Barcelona?' He asked as he walked out laughing at the prospect.

The third floor room in the San Ramón Clinic was set away from the main maternity wards on the first and second floors and shared the level with another similar birthing room and the storerooms.

The evening continued to be stuffy and by nine o'clock in the evening, Paloma thought she would explode. She'd a bad case of constipation once, yet labour was worse, not that the midwife or the Sister seemed to care, all they could say by way of comfort to the young girl in agony was, 'The reason you're uncomfortable is possibly because the cervix hasn't thinned enough yet and needs more time...'

The bulging mother took huge breaths and pushed and breathed and pushed and breathed.

The pain became worse as the evening wore on.

'Can't you do something?' She cried.

'If you try to push too soon, it may cause swelling and that will instigate a more painful delivery.' Sister Carmen said admonishingly.

In front of the clinic, Jorge didn't feel much better;

he'd been pacing the pavement endlessly, as mindlessly as a palace guard, having been refused entry to the clinic, because he wasn't the next of kin.

'You don't understand, it's my baby, Paloma's my fiancé!' He screamed for hours on end. The three nuns in front of him formed an impenetrable, monochrome wall, with arms crossed and faces of steely determination framed in their white wimples. Therefore Jorge and three packets of cigarettes pounded the street together for the last four hours.

His only company a band of cicadas with their own maracas.

Then at ten thirty in the evening, he heard a wonderful sound, a baby bursting into life, the cries flying through the open window on the third floor; he knew it was Paloma's baby, his baby, their baby.

He collapsed on the kerb and sobbed, the emotion of the day overcame him, his tears of relief and joy were the strongest feelings he'd ever experienced. Paloma felt the same, delight and liberation, a feeling of lightness as well as the excitement of giving birth, she couldn't wait to see her offspring, a small angel gifted from her body and the essence of the man she loved. The baby must be healthy, she thought, the cry seemed so loud, so strong, surely a boy with lungs like that. Her eyes closed sleepily, it had been an endless pregnancy, a long day, and a terrible few hours. The new mother could imagine her love's face, he will be so happy, a perfect family, just the three of them in Jorge's small flat, they would manage somehow, her mother will look after the little one and she'll be able to go back to work. Sister Carmen injected a sedative in her arm and Paloma fell into a deep, exhausted sleep. Jorge tried to break into the clinic twice more, he was told that the birth was delayed and he should return in the morning after 12 o'clock.

'No!' He pleaded for the third time. 'I heard my son wail, he's been born, I know it was him, I heard him cry from the street.'

'Just come back tomorrow, okay?' He was told with finality.

Jorge walked home slowly, his hands deep in his

pockets, his head drooped in reflection, then just in front of his home, he saw his brother Felipe, waiting on the steps.

'Well, any news?'

'Felipe, the dam nuns won't let me in, I'm sure I heard my son cry, I sat outside the hospital and all of the windows were open, then at about ten-thirty I heard him, the sound seemed to bounce around the street. I ran in and they said it wasn't my baby, they were still waiting, and because we're not married, they wouldn't let me near Paloma. She shouldn't be in that place all alone, those people have no hearts!'

'Well, I don't want to take their side, I mean it is a maternity clinic, there must be other births in there, so it could have been someone else's baby you heard, they all sound the same until they reach two or three.' Felipe laughed, putting his arm around his younger brother.

'No, I could feel the birth, as though I wanted to go to the toilet, then after the crying, I didn't need it any more. I should've just pushed those stupid nuns out of the way and gone up to my chica.'

'Human nature is a strange thing,' Felipe said reflectively.

'No matter how determined a man, he always seems to obey doctors, nurses, nuns and priests. Even more than the police, I don't really understand it, I suppose it's because we believe they are better than us, all that praying to God, and since we were children, we've always obeyed them. I mean; they wouldn't lie to you, they're holy.'

'Yeah, I know, but I'm sure it was my boy.' He returned reflectively.

'Let's go to Can José's bar and get drunk, then tomorrow morning you can go and get both of them, huh? What do you say?'

'Let's go brother...'

Felipe crossed himself and kissed the gold crucifix around his neck, the young men jumped up and skipped down the street excitedly.

Chapter 34
Barcelona, Thursday, 23rd April 1964

The head concierge from the Ritz hotel was delighted when he noticed a reservation for one of his best clients in the large maroon reservations book, which swivelled on a wooden turntable at the luxurious reception desk.

'Do you know exactly what time he's arriving Carlos?'

'Sorry José, he's coming in his private plane directly from Moscow, so he could land anytime.'

'And what's happened to my rich Italians in the Royal Suite? I had high hopes for them; no one has seen them since they checked in. Even their huge car hasn't moved, they've had no room service, they didn't eat in the restaurant last night, this morning I checked their room and all of their cases and clothes are there, but they're invisible.'

'What can I tell you José, I haven't seen them, not that they're as important to me as they are to you.' He teased.

'Carlos don't be like that, I always look after you, no?'

'Yes I know you do, I'm just joking, but wait, isn't that your bonus couple coming through the swing doors now!'

José Reverte-Gutiérrez, the smooth talking, premier league fixer of Barcelona's leading hotel, almost leapt in the air, when he turned to see the couple that he'd hoped would need his services on an hourly basis and increase this month's income considerably. Before Sam and Phaedra started to glide over the luxurious carpet, the concierge appeared in front of them magically.

'My dear Señor and Señora Colaneri, I'm so pleased to see you both, are you enjoying your holiday?'

'Thank you José, yes we've had a wonderful time, although we needed to visit some friends and so we haven't had time to enjoy the hotel, do you have a table in the terrace restaurant for us? I'm starving.' 'Of course Sir, please come this way.' The concierge said guiding them towards the luxurious eatery. The restaurant manger walked over swiftly, if José brought clients into the saloon personally, it meant big tips would be flowing freely; he also had a family to look after.

'Sancho, may I introduce you to Señor and Señora Colaneri, they will have the best table please on the terrace and a bottle of vintage champagne on my account...' He said with a flourish.

'Certainly José, your special guests, are my special guests.' Sancho Pança said ingratiatingly, with a little bow towards the Italian millionaires from the Royal Suit. He knew that if José were buying the champagne, he'd have already received a tip many times the value of the bubbly wine.

'Thank you gentlemen...' Sam said smiling, playing the role of his alias. Sancho, who was nearly as wide as he was tall, rolled ahead of the couple like a bowling ball in his tight fitting black suit, to a large round table.

It was beautifully decorated with a crisp white tablecloth and flourishing pink Peonies. He pulled out a chair for Señora Colaneri, who hated all of this false politeness and would have preferred a rickety wooden table with a glass of Ouzo, overlooking a sunset on the Aegean Sea. Sancho bowled over to his workstation to warn the headwaiter of their good fortune, while José asked his favourite clients, of the moment, if they needed anything else.

'Actually José, I do need your help...'

José's face lit up as bright as a firework display on the fiesta of Saint Juan.

'Firstly, just a small thing, I need about one hundred balloons...'

'Balloons Sir?' José said curiously. 'Would you like them with helium or ordinary air...

'Neither, just flat, I'll put the air in myself, and about two kilos of black-eyed beans.'

'How would you like them cooked sir?' He asked confused by the unusual requirement.

'Not cooked, just dry in the packet.

'Yes Señor that's no problem, I'll have them in your

room within the hour.'

'Thank you, secondly, we made a reservation for this evening at a restaurant called the Torre d'Altamar, do you know it?'

'Yes Sir and may I say it's a very good choice, you know the manager is a friend of mine and has the same name as the tower, just a coincidence, he doesn't own the place, that belongs to our great leader of course. Will you need a car?'

'No José, I made the reservation a couple of weeks ago and I'm rather disappointed, because this morning they've cancelled my table, due to a double booking, they said. Could you help?'

The concierge smiled as though his favourite child had asked innocently for a second helping of cake, saying, 'Don't worry Sir, this is what I do, I shall get you a first class table, it has a wonderful view and you shall have the best seats...' He walked away excitedly, 'Just the two of you Sir?' He asked on his way out. Sam put his thumb up positively.

José couldn't wait to speak to the manager of the Torre d'Altamar restaurant; it was a real tourists trap, with over-priced food and ridiculous mark-ups on the wines. These margins allowed the manager to be particularly generous to the local hotel staff and other employees in Barcelona's tourists' traps, who recommended the rather far-flung restaurant. The only reason to visit the place was for its incredible view over the beach, the sea beyond, the old port and the city of Barcelona. The vistas were truly dramatic, even for experienced travellers like the rich Colaneris.

Señor Gomez, the restaurant manager, was an altogether different character to his brother, the severe boss of the Gaudí Hotel. He always saw himself as a music hall entertainer and believed that his rendition of La Boehm was unsurpassed. He loved the ballet, art and believed himself an aesthete. Unfortunately the entertainment business had past him by many years before. Therefore, he currently saw his role as the manager of this famous, landmark restaurant as his theatre, and he was determined to entertain his guests and staff with his perpetual cabaret; whether they wanted it or not.

'Sebastian, you old fool, what are you trying to do to our business?' José asked over the telephone.

'Is that the semi-retired crook from the Ritz Hotel?' He laughed playfully into the mouthpiece of the gaudy gold telephone.

'Listen to me, you crazy soprano; you just cancelled my Royal Suite guests from that cheap cafeteria of yours. I want their table back, and it better be a large one by the window!'

'No problema amigo, when do they want to come?'

'Señor and Señora Colaneri, nine o'clock tonight...'

'Tonight! Colaneri! I can't guapo, not tonight...'

'Don't you dare do this to me, get rid of some stupid couple from Barcelona, but I must have that table, my children's teeth depend on it!'

'Normally you can have whatever you want - you know that, look how well we've worked together over the years. Except tonight is the one evening, well apart from the private party on Saturday, that no one can have.' Sebastian grabbed his little ornate fan and flapped it furiously in front of his moist face. 'I promise you, listen to me, tomorrow they can come free of charge - what more can a friend do?

'I'll tell you what a friend can do, give them the table tonight!'

'I can't.'

'Why?'

'Because on Saturday night we have a private party for the Duchesse and the Colonel, they have some special guests coming in from Italy and Germany. You know the type of people I'm talking about, we can't discuss them on the phone, can we? So they've booked huge tables for the whole restaurant, I can't squeeze a couple of mice in here, do you understand?'

Sebastian squinted at the phone, as he heard nothing from his old sparing partner. 'Hello José, are you still there? José?' Are you there? Hello...'

José Reverte-Gutiérrez had to think quickly. He knew that if he did this terrible thing, it would be his last trump card, his last form of blackmail. If he did it, if he says the words, his relationship with the restaurant manager would be over forever; completely destroyed. It would be like the old days, a deathblow. Unfortunately José was in trouble, he had bought another apartment, his third in five years and he was short. If he didn't get another one hundred thousand pesetas by next week, his whole house of cards, which he'd built up from nothing, over the last thirty years, would collapse.

What is he going to say to his naïve wife and children; they think he's rich and smart.

Sure he'd showed off too much, the Mercedes last year, the holiday in Rome, the diamond earrings for his dear wife, who eats in the Ritz hotel restaurant, like a tourist.

The whole family were so proud of him, not just the immediate family, the hundreds of aunts, uncles and cousins and their wives and husbands, which made up a typical Spanish family.

José Reverte-Gutiérrez was an icon of the Spanish self-made man, who had survived through the civil war unscathed, with his whole family intact and during the difficult times that followed. He was one of the few people, not in government, the police or a high-ranking army officer, who had made a success of his life. He could make a lot of money from these Royal Suite Italians. He couldn't afford the bathos in front of his friends and family, if he failed now.

'Hello –José are you still there?'

'I'll phone you back in a few minutes.' José said annoyed. He rushed into the restaurant and approached the rich Italians.

'How is your meal Señor Colaneri?' He smiled.

'Excellent José, and how is our table?' Sam asked arrogantly in Royal Suite fashion.

'Tell me Sir, I have arranged for you to be welcomed there, completely free of charge, tomorrow night, how would that suit you.' He smiled hopefully.

'That's very kind of you, however we had a reservation for this evening and that's what we need, you did say José that you could fix anything, and so I don't understand the problem. I was hoping that we would become friends, and business partners in some way...' Sam said poignantly, appealing to the concierge's obvious greed.

The uniformed man stood erect, holding Sam's stare for a few moments, his eyes shielding tormented thoughts.

'Of course Sir, I shall need to make another call.' He took the bottle of champagne from the ice bucket and topped up their glasses, carefully replacing the white serviette and rushed out of the door.

'I get the feeling he's having trouble, couldn't we go tomorrow darling?' Phaedra asked.

'No it's too risky, I need to check the whole place thoroughly, we should know all the exits and I'll have to plant a weapon somewhere. The security I saw with the Colonel seemed very professional, they might go in twenty-four hours in advance to set up the security. This is one of the most dangerous projects we've ever had, a confined space, a top army cum police officer all surrounded by armed fascists. And us only armed with a blow pipe and six darts, I don't like the odds if anything goes wrong.'

'You're making me nervous...' Phaedra whispered softly. 'Are you sure you want to do this one darling?'

'We've already had that conversation in Richmond, remember?'

'We'll keep going then.' Phaedra said, clasping her husband's hands on the table, searching his eyes for his usual calm strength.

José went back to the phone and connected with the Torre d'Altamar restaurant. 'Sebastian I'm sorry, he won't take a table tomorrow. I didn't want to do this, you are forcing me, and it will be your fault. Don't make me say these words Sebastian, but I need this client, I need his money. Are you going to give him a table tonight or not?'

'I told you José I can't, they won't like it, just bring them another night for God's sake, these people are frightening.

'Sebastian. If you don't give my clients a table by the widow tonight...' He paused and swallowed hard. 'I shall denounce you to the police for being a homosexual, I have the photos from Enrique.'

The phone line stayed silent for a long time; finally Sebastian Gomez spoke.

'José, you would do something like that to me, to anyone, just for a few pesetas?' His voice was thick with emotion. 'Do you know what they do to people like me in a prison? Particularly El Modelo, most people I know who were sent there, used a garrotte on themselves.'

'Sebastian, I'm sorry, but I'm desperate, I need these people, we haven't had anyone in the Royal Suite for ages, really rich foreigners like this are rare. For some reason they want to go this evening, they're rich; they want to get their own way. I've just tried to talk them out of it. You know how spoilt they can be, and I promised them I could get them a table, if I don't, they won't ask me for anything else. I didn't want to threaten you, but you must help me.'

Sebastian paused. 'You don't leave me any choice José, so they will have their table, although I hope I never hear from you again.' He said tearfully, cutting the line.

José rushed back to his guests and apologised for the delay.

'Is everything alright José, you look flushed.' Sam asked

'I'm very sorry Sir, it would seem that the restaurant is very busy tonight as there is a large party of foreigners there, but of course the best table is reserved for you and your charming wife. I just hope that you won't be disappointed with the big noisy crowd. Do you still wish to go?' José asked hopefully, hating what he did to Sebastian.

'Thank you, I understand, it must be a place tourists enjoy because of the view, we can cope with the crowd.'

José cruised from the restaurant, entered the bar and poured himself a large brandy, which he gulped in one. He then made his way back to the concierge's office at the front of the hotel when one of the bellboys rushed up to him.

'Señor, one of the guest is asking for you.'

'What do they want, I am just going for lunch.'

'I don't know, I've just taken him up to his room.'

'Okay I'll go before I eat, which room is it?'

'He's in the Grand Suite, Señor.'

412

'What! Do you mean Señor Kautz?'

'Ah yes, I think that was his name, German or Russian.'

'You idiot, I left strict instructions to tell me the moment he arrived.' José shouted angrily, running towards the lift.

'I just told you…' The young boy called out with a gesture of reassignment.

José fell out of the lift and ran over to the Grand Suite, pausing to get his composure and straightening his tie and jacket. He tapped on the door and prepared his smile for the old gentleman, who he called the Silver Fox. He had known the wealthy Swiss since he first started at the hotel.

'Señor Kautz…' José said, gesturing widely as though he was guiding an airplane to its stand. 'I'm so sorry that I wasn't at the front door to meet you Sir. Welcome to the Ritz.'

'You're getting old José, I notice a few more grey hairs and that waist of yours doesn't seem as trim as I remember…' The millionaire joked.

'Yes Sir, but may I say that you have not changed in the least.'

'Oh dear José, even your compliments are sounding older.' He laughed.

'I'm sorry Sir, I have arranged for some more flowers for your room and some champagne with my compliments. Is there anything else I can get you?'

'Come in you rascal, I have something for you.'

Christian Kautz strolled into the bedroom and opened a small leather case. He riffled through ten boxes of various sizes that were all gift-wrapped.

His secretary had done her usual job of buying a selection of offerings for all occasions, so that her boss would never be embarrassed, if he were given a surprise present or if he needed to show that he had been thoughtful to an old, yet forgotten friend. Christian removed the small label indicating the appropriate gender and level of gratefulness.

'Here José…' He said, offering the beautifully wrapped box. 'I was thinking about you last month and

413

found this.'

'Sir...' José said looking surprised and touched. 'This is so thoughtful of you, please tell me how I can repay you.'

'I don't need anything yet, except a nice car for Saturday night, I'm going to that restaurant above the cable car on the port, some sort of art show I'm told.'

'Of course Señor Kautz, I'll get the best car available in Barcelona, and La Señora, she's not with you on this trip?

'No, she's staying with my granddaughter in Cannes.'

'Shall I order some flowers in your name, to say that you've arrived safely?'

'Ah! Yes, that's very clever of you José, I shall write the card; she's at the Carlton.'

'I will send someone to help you unpack, don't hesitate to call me Sir.'

José walked into the hallway and as he turned around to close the door, the old millionaire said.

'Just one thing José, a friend of mine has asked me to look up someone, but I've forgotten his name, one of the disadvantages of old age.

He's a tall man, my wife said he's handsome, about sixty years old, has a beautiful wife with blonde hair.

Ah! I've got a photo here somewhere...' Christian went to his wallet, found a black and white photograph and showed it to the concierge.

'Oh yes Sir, this is the Italian couple in the Royal Suite, Señor and Señora Colaneri, excellent clients of mine, almost friends, do you wish me to contact them for you?'

'Italians? Yes of course, I remember now. No not at the moment, I have a little invitation for them, would you give them this envelope please, in their hands, not at the desk.' He confirmed seriously.

'Certainly Sir.' The concierge said, taking the sealed envelope, closing the door and giving a slight bow.

In the lift José excitedly opened his little box, a pink gold, Rolex Prince stared back at him, he clutched it to his chest, looked into the lift's gold mirror and gave himself a congratulatory smile.

At the reception desk he asked Carlos if he knew where the rich Italians were.

'I think that they are finishing their lunch in the restaurant, I didn't see them leave, but they never seem to pass the desk.'

The concierge walked to the restaurant fascinated that one of his oldest and most valuable clients, seems to have mutual friends with these new rich Italians, who he is hoping to develop into needy patrons. The restaurant manager said that they'd just left and palmed a roll of pesetas in José's hand. They evidently gave him a huge tip. José ran towards the lift when he saw the couple taking the stairs.

'Señor Colaneri!' Señor Colaneri!' The concierge called urgently. Sam and Phaedra stopped and turned on the second flight. 'Señor Colaneri! Señora Colaneri!' He said panting. 'Why are you walking up all these stairs, when we have a wonderful lift for you?'

Sam smiled. 'Hello José how are you?'

'I'm exhausted Sir, I never use the stairs, certainly not to the top floor!' He smiled panting. 'I hope your lunch was satisfactory Señora?'

'Yes it was fine thank you.' Phaedra said politely as she turned and started to take two stairs at a time.

'No Señor please wait a moment, I have a message for you from one of my favourite clients…' Sam looked at Phaedra with a certain insecurity in his eyes. 'I didn't know that you were acquainted with Monsieur Christian Kautz, he's in the Grand Suite…' José said between deep breaths. 'He usually has the Royal Suite of course, but as he contacted us so late, you were already booked and…'

'Is there a problem José?'

Sam said pleasantly, now studying the Spaniard's face carefully. 'Problem – problem! No - no Sir, Señor Colaneri, forgive me, there's never a problem when José is here, it's just that my dear client and well my friend, Monsieur Kautz gave me this invitation for you.'

'Are you sure it's for me José?' Sam asked smiling casually.

'Oh yes Sir.'

Phaedra quickly slipped on some leather gloves from her bag and walked down the stairs saying, 'Yes darling you remember the Kautz's...' And took the offered envelope from the concierge. 'Thank you so much José, men are never good at socialising, that's why they have to get married...' Phaedra smiled. 'Come on darling I have to get ready for this evening.'

The Colaneris went back to their run up the stairs to their suite. When they entered Sam saw a box of balloons in the hall and several packets of black-eyed beans, they cleared the beautiful antique desk by the window and Sam pointed to Phaedra, who responded by putting the envelope on the leather, gold-tooled top. Sam took his car keys and a remote control, silently leaving the room for his Bristol in the underground garage. He returned after a few minutes with a metal briefcase, which he opened to reveal an array of high-tech tools. They both put on rubber cloves and surgical masks. Sam scanned the envelope for metal, nothing. Using a tiny brush he painted the envelope with a fine chemical, turned it over with tweezers and repeated the operation; scanned it with an ultraviolet light, nothing. Then he took a knife, cut open the fold, and pulled out a high quality card. They read the blue ink from an expensive fountain pen.

> *There is a Reaper whose name is Death,*
> *And, with his sickle keen,*
> *He reaps the bearded grain at a breath,*
> *And the flowers that grow between.*

> *Please look after Christian.*
> *FP*

Sam and Phaedra looked at each other curiously in silence for a few minutes. Phaedra lit a cigarette and Sam poured two glasses of wine.

'Well this little note throws up as many questions as it answers...' Sam said.

'Fyodor has been watching us, I don't know how he

knew we were here.' Phaedra added.

'He would have someone in most of the big towns, the incident at the border could have alerted someone to our car.'

'Yes but it's spent most of the time in the garage.'

He could have a copy of the invitation list for the show on Saturday night and traced the hotel's guest's list from that. I'm sure our new friend José would sell his grandmother for a small sum, let alone the who's who from this hotel. Anyway that's why we have the Gaudí as well.

'And who's *The Reaper*?' Phaedra asked: 'what does it mean?

'Well the cunning old man doesn't want anyone except me, to understand the message. However he might think I'm smarter than I am.'

'Don't be so modest darling, you're usually good at crosswords.'

'Well I know it's a poem from Longfellow,' He said sitting at the table taking a pen. '*There is a Reaper whose name is Death*' Sam paused and said, 'Could mean an assassin.' Phaedra waited for further explanation. 'I'll have to think about it for a while.' Sam looked reflective.

'Do you know the man who gave the concierge the note?' Phaedra asked.

'No, I imagine he's someone Fyodor trusts, perhaps a part-time agent, I doubt he's important, just a messenger. Let's have a little siesta and we'll go half an hour early and not only look around for our own set-up, but for anyone else's.'

The Colaneris arrived in front of the tower at eight-twenty-five. Sam wore a dark grey wool suit with a hint of blue in the thread. A silk blue tie in a small knot fronted his white shirt. Phaedra wore a simple black crepe de chine Givenchy dress, splattered with a little extra gold and diamonds to perpetuate the millionaire image.

When the Bristol pulled up in front of the lift entrance, a concierge in a cheap black suit, standing behind a pedestal stand, holding a reservation book, looked up notionally.

Sam rolled down his window and spoke in Castilian

Spanish. 'I have a reservation, is there someone to park the car?'

'I'm sorry Señor, we are understaffed as everyone is working on Saturday night, for a big party, but you can park just across the street it's not busy.'

The rich Colaneris looked annoyed and parked opposite. When they crossed the road and approached the pedestal desk, a skeleton with bare dirty feet and ragged clothes rushed over to them. The carrion stench and the virtually dead individual took the three aback. His face gaunt so that his skin seemed like transparent film over clearly defined bones. His three teeth reduced by cocaine to wooden pegs in an empty mouth. Hooded eyes surrounded by blackened skin appeared to be empty holes in his head. When the virtual corpse spoke, his voice croaked from a dry throat.

'Give me, give, money please...'

'Get away from here!' The concierge shouted at the drugged-filled tramp.

'Just give me, something, anything, please...' He pleaded politely.

The concierge lifted his foot to kick the man away; Sam stopped him with a fast, firm hand on his arm.

'It's alright, I'll deal with him.' Sam said firmly. 'Here, do you have anywhere to go? You need medical help.' Sam took some money from his pocket.

'I just need, need, enough for another two days, only until Saturday night...' He slurred.

'Will you have some help then?' Sam asked.

'After Saturday, I'll be alright, it's all over on Saturday, just help me to stay alive until then...'
Sam stuffed some money in his hand; the drug-addict snatched it and hobbled off as fast as he could.

'There's no point in trying to help them Señor, they just spend it on drugs and alcohol, they're all along the beach, stealing from tourists and sleeping on the sand.

The police beat them up and tell them not to return, but a few days later they come back like boomerangs. This one has been hanging around here for a week now; he keeps saying he's got to stay until Saturday. Maybe he thinks God will save him or it's the end of the world, they all have some kind of crazy story.'

The lift door opened and the concierge ushered the impeccably dressed couple inside. Phaedra held Sam's arm closely afraid of the tiny space and the view as they soared to the top of the tower seventy-five metres above Barcelona's port.

'Wow! Look at that view darling, it all looks so different from here...'

'Yes, I didn't realise it was so high up...' Phaedra said nervously. 'The metal tower looks so flimsy. I thought it would be similar to the Eiffel Tower with huge girders, this looks like a child's Meccano set. If the wind blows it might crash into the port behind us.'

'I seem to remember you were afraid on the Eiffel Tower as well, you'll be okay when we get in the restaurant, it's been here for years.'

'The concierge told me it was new.'

'No, they refurbished it last year, but it was closed during the civil war by Franco.'

Phaedra shivered, and pulled the organza shawl tighter around her shoulders.

The lift doors opened and the atmosphere changed immediately. The lighting was so low; the city's lights sparkled like jewels on the necklace of glass that encircled the octagonal restaurant. In the centre of the suspended room, sat a quadrilateral, black marble cube, which housed the lift-shaft, kitchens and toilets. Muffled jazz filed the platform with the warm tones of Frank Sinatra.

Beyond the small reception area, diners were seated around the outside of the elevated platform, so that all of the patrons had the spectacular three hundred and sixty degree view. The tables were all full; the patrons were engrossed in conversation and the array of plates filling their tables. The receptionist asked the Coláneris if they could wait to be seated. Sam and Phaedra followed the young man's eyes and saw Sebastian telling a joke that involved him in a little Astaire-inspired dance. The German patrons all cheered and clapped enthusiastically. When Sebastian returned to the reception, his broad smile and artistic walk, stayed with him until he heard the name of his new guests. He politely said good evening and with his head bowed, ushered the Colaneris almost in a complete circle to a large window table on the other side of the octagonal. They were guided through a trio of black curtains that completely divided the room, so that there were three distinctive seating areas. After Sebastian left, Sam looked around scrutinising the layout.

'I only had a quick look the first time I came here, as the waiter looked at me suspiciously when I started checking all of the doors.

At night the whole place looks so much smaller than I first thought.

There's nowhere to hide.' Sam said to Phaedra surveying the luxuriously decorated room.

'What about the dividing curtains?' She asked.

'Yes, although it depends what's on the other side, I couldn't stand here with this crowd behind me.'

'Maybe I could just touch her with a dart in my hand.'

'Dangerous, she might feel the prick and could grab you; remember she's a very violent woman. If there was a struggle you might also get pricked, bear in mind what the lady Chong said, there's no antidote.'

'Phaedra, you order for me...' He whispered. 'I'll have two starters; they are usually very small in this type of place. I'm going to the cloakroom to cash the back-up gun in one of the toilet cisterns.' Phaedra ordered several dishes for her hungry husband and non-fattening dishes for herself, starting with a bottle of Krug champagne.

After dinner Sam looked around for Sebastian Gomez and found him coming out of the kitchens.

'Excuse me Señor Gomez, do you have a moment?'

'Yes Señor Colaneri, was the dinner unsatisfactory?'

'No, quite the opposite we enjoyed ourselves. I understand that it was difficult to fit us in this evening...'

'I'm so sorry Señor about the cancellation, this evening has been very hectic, I...'

'No—no don't worry, it's I who should apologise for

being so insistent, you see we are coming here on Saturday for the private party and I just wanted to have a look at the restaurant before.'

'You're coming to the Colonel's party! Oh sir, I am so sorry, I didn't know that you were, well, one of the Colonel's, ah, associates; I do hope you will not tell him about my mistake, I...'

'Sebastian, that is your name I believe, firstly take this...' Sam squeezed the biggest tip the manager had ever had into his palm. 'Now don't worry about anything, I just wondered where we were going to sit on Saturday evening.'

Sebastian rushed over to the reception desk and found the table plan.

'Well Señor Colaneri...' He said looking at the huge wad of notes in his hand. 'You can sit almost wherever you wish, except the top table which is reserved for the Duchesse and the Colonel's small group.'

'I don't understand the table plan, what's this big hashed square in the middle?'

'That's the runway for the models sir, there's a fashion show with the Duchesse's jewellery and then they have the auction of the paintings and antiques. The tables will be around the edges.'

'I see and where will the Duchesse sit?'

'Over here sir on a raised platform. She will have a microphone and arrange the action from up there...'

'And what's this line marked here?'

'That's the curtains sir, the models will be changing behind them and in the middle of the runway there will be a beautiful opaque glass screen, so that the audience will only see shadows of the models changing behind the panel. It will be really wonderful, like a stage show, they're even having a smoke machine. My cousin and my closest friends from the local theatre have helped the Duchesse with the set!' He raved excitedly.

Sam looked at Phaedra who joined the men and asked, 'What do you think darling, shall we sit here on the Duchesse's right it's a table for six, we shall be able to see the show well and the curtain next to us will give us a little more room to breathe.'

'Looks good to me, if Señor Gomez is happy.'

'Certainly Señora, as long as you realise the other seats on the table will be taken by guests of the Duchesse.' The Trubshaws smiled at the manager. He then asked, 'Do you both speak German?'

Phaedra answered before Sam had a chance. 'Yes, I had a lot of German lessons when I was younger, it was obligatory where I lived.'

Sam changed the subject quickly. 'May we have a quick look at the kitchens, my wife is a very enthusiastic cook...'

'Well it's not usual practice Señor, however as you have been so gracious...' Sebastian said stuffing the money in his pocket.

The cooks and waiters looked surprised as the expensively dressed couple entered into the steamy kitchen.

'And is this the only way in and out Sebastian?'

'Yes Sir, the whole place was refitted last year as it had been empty since the war, although the chefs complain that it should been made bigger.'

'That's wonderful, thank you so much for all of your kind help.' Sam said as he ushered Phaedra out of the hot room. 'Is this the way to the cable car?' Sam asked looking at a door next to the reception.

'Yes Señor Colaneri, but it doesn't operate at night, it's just the emergency exit.'

'May we have a quick look?' Sam said halfway down the stairs, not waiting for his response.

Chapter 35
Baby Paloma, Madrid, 1962

At seven o'clock the morning after the baby's birth, Paloma woke up in shock, as a violent thunderstorm filled the furious sky; flashes of lightening shattered the opaque clouds with the ferocity of a drummer's baton, echoing across the capital city and vibrating its ancient architecture.

The hospital patient looked around the strange, bland room, confused; rubbed her eyes with the heels of her hands and couldn't understand what had happened. Her right arm hurt and looked bruised, her womb felt raw and caustic. Wow! She could see her feet! Then the new mother laid back and smiled, she hadn't seen her feet for the last couple of months, yet now, there they were. Maybe Jorge will have a little money left over for a new pair of shoes, she hadn't bought any for six years; Paloma loved shoes. 'Don't be selfish,' she told herself. The baby will need so many things; Francisco, that's a fine name for a boy, after the actor Francisco Rabal, um, he's so good looking. Well Jorge is kind of handsome, not like an actor, he doesn't look rich enough, and he would be too shy to kiss all of those actresses. Yes, it's a good name for a man, Franci when he's little, then he can grow into Francisco. The wonderful feeling of motherhood lifted her mind from the pain.

Paloma's pleasant thoughts were snatched away from her the moment Sister Carmen entered the room, holding a bag of Paloma's clothes under her arm.

'Hello Sister,' the patient said sitting up in the bed excitedly. 'Where's my baby?'

'I'm very sorry Paloma, it didn't make it, so you should get dressed now.' Sister Carmen said, placing the young woman's folded clothes on the bed and averting her eyes.

'I don't understand! What do you mean?'

'The baby was still born, now you should get up, life goes on.'

Paloma jumped out of the bed quickly, regretting the sudden movement immediately, crying out in agony.

'Now what did I tell you, don't go rushing around getting over excited, just stay calm and put your clothes on.'

'Stay calm...' Paloma said in pain. 'I want to see my boy!'

'That's not possible I'm afraid, it's against the clinic's policy.' The nun answered firmly, walking over to the door. Paloma fought against the pain in her stomach and rushed over to the holy woman, grabbing her arm.

'I said, I want to see my boy. I don't care about anyone's policy. I've carried my baby in here...' She cried holding her painful crutch. 'For nine months, he's mine and I want to see him NOW!' She screamed. Sister Carmen hated situations like this, often the young mothers were so shocked by the loss of their babies they usually just left the clinic crying and fell into a reclusive period of morning. Although over the years, the clinic occasionally had a hysterical mother like this one. The staff normally relied on grief to break them into submission and get them away from the building. Following that, it was just a matter of paperwork. The authority of the church would overpower the individuals, particularly as most of them were young girls with illegitimate babies.

'Why don't you get dressed and I shall ask Sister Suzanna to come and see you...' Paloma stared at the nun's bowed head in silence, still gripping the small woman's arm desperately, unwilling to release the wide black sleeve, despite the agony she felt; her legs and arms trembled with pain and emotion.

'She'll be with you in a few minutes.' The nun continued, in a slightly more conciliatory tone. Paloma reluctantly released her hold and the dark habit disappeared through the door into the ink of darkness.

The young woman's head spun frenetically, she remembered pushing the baby out, the warm, wet sensation, the feeling of pain and relief. Paloma could still hear her son's cries as he burst into life. 'Yes!' She said aloud, 'he did burst into life, I heard him, he must be alive!' Despite the pain in her back, arm and womb, the young woman found her underwear and dressed in the blue and brown, floral dress and beige cardigan she arrived in. The weak girl searched in the small cupboard and under the bed yet saw no shoes. Paloma felt drained, she collapsed forward, dropping her spinning head in trembling palms, rubbed her tired face and searched her memory for an image of her child. After the baby was born, she remembered receiving an injection in her arm followed by a deep sleep.

Sister Carmen entered the office on the fourth floor, where she found the Director filling in more paperwork, including a birth certificate for Paloma's son in the new parent's names.

'Sister Suzanna, I told you that this Perez woman would be difficult, she's refusing to leave the clinic saying she remembers the baby, and now she wants to see the body. I don't know what to say to her, will you please do something? I knew there would be trouble with this one…'

'Stop panicking Sister…' Suzanna Valles-Carrera said, getting up from her desk. She opened a wall cupboard using a small key, attached to a gold chain connected to her pocket button. There she found a sachet containing a pale green powder in a small brown box, blackened with an emblem of a beetle on the lid.

'What's that Sister?'

'Spanish fly.' She replied without looking up.

'But Sister Suzanna, isn't that an irritant to sexual organs? She has a bad wound on her vulva that we had to stitch up roughly last night, the pain will be excruciating, and that's surely too much, isn't a poison as well, in large doses?'

'It will keep her mind busy for a while and give me a chance to clear the baby, by the time she feels better, any memory of the birth will have rescinded.

She'll be easier to handle in a couple of weeks, after the drug has done its work and we still have Baby-Frio if any relatives come here.'

'Sister I don't want anything to do with this, I'm not feeling very well, I may have to take a few days off.'

'Yes Sister you may, but you'll still take the money at the end of the month; won't you, you hypocrite.' The Nazi said with a prickly stare.

The door on the third floor flew open, and the German marched into the room with a glass of cloudy water in her hand. When she looked at the bed she found Paloma lying with her knees up, cradling her crutch.

'Take this, you'll feel better.' Sister Suzanna said briskly, pushing the tumbler towards the patient.

'What is it?' She groaned, struggling to sit up.

'It's a pain killer, you must be uncomfortable after your ordeal, take it.' She said convincingly. The administrator had fixed a grey, nun's veil to her head with hairgrips, and her face assumed the suggestion of a smile.

Paloma was in excruciating pain and felt beaten. If only Jorge were here, she thought, she didn't have the strength to fight them on her own. She lifted the glass to her lips and stared at the tall woman standing in front of her. She had a strange glare in her grey eyes. Paloma gazed down at the liquid in her hand, and then suddenly stopped.

'No!' I don't want any medicine, all I want is my baby boy – where is he?' She said with the last of her resolve.

The Director grabbed the frail girl by her long hair and pulled her down violently on the bed, her head anchored to the mattress, the drug splashed on the floor.

'Listen to me you whore, in the eyes of the law you're no more than a prostitute, your baby is dead and gone, do you understand?' Paloma struggled to get up, but she was still very weak and the large woman had the full weight of her body on top of her.

'Now if you don't leave this hospital immediately, I shall denounce you to the authorities for being an adulteress, then you and your lover will go to prison for the next few years. I promise you the church will make sure of it!'

The Director dragged the weak girl onto the lino floor, and kicked her in the stomach three times; Paloma gave a throaty howl of primordial pain as the Nazi stormed out into the corridor. The collapsed girl wasn't sure how long she lay sobbing, although she knew that she needed to get up and leave the clinic, to get help from her Jorge.

Somehow, she stood unsteadily on her bare feet, clenching her painful abdomen and swayed over to the door.

426

She opened it a few inches timidly and saw the empty hallway, blood running down her thighs. Using the walls for support, she found the staircase and struggled to the ground floor, each step more painful than the last. There were two nuns at the reception desk, yet they turned their heads as soon as Paloma came into view.

She almost collapsed onto the slippery pavement outside the clinic, nevertheless managed to walk like a zombie along the empty streets in the torrential rain for twenty minutes, until she reached Jorge's flat.

Jorge and his brother were sound asleep on the sofa in the small living room; they'd been drinking most of the night and imploded in the flat three hours earlier. At first Jorge didn't hear the feeble slapping sound on his door, he thought the noise was part of his dream. He mounted a wild horse without a bridle or saddle and with his brother, was half riding and half flying above the beach in Málaga, where he'd been brought up until he reached eleven years old. His family had moved to Madrid at the start of the civil war due to the lack of work in the little village of Nerja. His father found a good job as an electrician for the local schools' authority and the family's life improved, but the boy's parents often spoke about Málaga fondly, with its simple lifestyle and friendly people. Jorge had wonderful memories of his childhood on the grey stony beaches in Nerja, but what was that banging noise? He jumped up in a daze and ran to the door, it opened easily, because Paloma collapsed through the frame into his arms.

'Oh God!' he cried, 'Felipe wake up, help me!'

Felipe fell off the sofa, half crawled, half dived towards the couple and clutched Paloma in his arms, the brothers carried her into the small bedroom, and laid her on the bed, she seemed delirious. The waif looked as though she had been drowning in a river. The bottom of her dress a palette of blood stains. Her bare feet bleeding and blistered. The two brothers gaped at the young woman in silence; disbelieving that she was the same vivacious girl who left so happily for the hospital two days ago.

'Paloma…' Jorge pleaded, 'What's happened?'

The young girl's head rolled slowly to one side, an inanimate ball. Her breathing faint, a body deflated, resembling a battered doll, limp and concave on the mattress, both boys made the sign of the cross on their chests, and Felipe kissed the gold crucifix hanging around his neck.

'I'm going for help, bathe her head or something...' Felipe said, pulling his shoes on, 'I'll be back as soon as I can!'

Jorge found a towel ran it under the tap and bathed his love's forehead. She made a sighing noise; he stroked her hair and held her head, with tears in his eyes. Suddenly her dry lips parted and she spoke almost inaudibly:

'Jorge...'

'Paloma, what happened to you?'

'Jorge...'

'Paloma, speak to me, darling please...'

'F-Find...our b-baby boy.'

'Where is he? Paloma, speak to me what's happened...'

Her head dropped back to one side and her eyes closed. Jorge held her limp body in his arms and sobbed uncontrollably. Felipe leapt down the staircase, crashed through the street door and ran until he could barely breathe, to his ex-girlfriend's flat on the corner of Calle de Diego de Velázquez.

The former couple weren't on speaking terms, ever since he slept with one of her friends three month's ago, something he had regretted daily, because she was, is, a lovely girl, who he should have stayed with and maybe even married. Felipe knew that he was his own worst enemy, yet he just couldn't stay faithful to any girl for the last seven years. When women showed that they cared for him he panicked, there appeared to be something about the closeness, the familiarity that repulsed him, and yet when he sat unaccompanied in his little studio flat, he felt so lonely. Night after night he had an uncontrollable urge to go out to a club and find a girl, any girl. After a few weeks, he would feel safe again, they would become close and then the whole cycle restarted, faithfulness and security made him nervous;

loneliness made him suicidal. Felipe pressed the doorbell frantically without response, he stepped back and called up to the first floor window, no flicker of curtains, no movement. The young man searched for some small stones in the gutter and started to pelt the glass pane. Eventually the curtains parted and the sleepy face of Vera Garcia-Revuelta appeared. She opened the window and squinted at the pavement, as soon as she saw Felipe, she started to close it.

'Vera – Vera! Please, it's an emergency...'

The thirty-three year old nurse looked down at the dishevelled, unfaithful, lying, cheating, ex-boyfriend; her face a façade of hatred and disgust.

'What do you want now Felipe, you've slept with all of my friends, I haven't found any more since I saw you last.'

'Vera listen to me, Paloma's been hurt, she looks like she's dying, something's happened to the baby.'

'Well take her quickly to the hospital, they have doctors and equipment there!'

'No listen - you don't understand, she's just come back from there, she's unconscious and bleeding from... you know... down there.' He said pointing to his crutch.

Vera closed the window forcefully, Felipe wasn't sure if she'd come down, nevertheless his ex was a dedicated carer and she always liked Paloma, surely, he thought, a girl with her character would put aside his slight indiscretion, for such an important emergency? Felipe didn't know who else he could call, their mother was too old now to help, he didn't know any doctors, he was never ill; as these thoughts spun around his head, the door opened with Vera standing in the shadowy hall.

'Oh Vera thank you, I knew you'd help...' Felipe leaned forward to hold the girl, now fully dressed in her nurse's uniform. She pushed him back coldly with the flat of her hand.

'Don't misunderstand Felipe, I'm helping Paloma because she's a nice girl and its my job, I would do this for any stranger, I still hate you, so don't say another word.'

They rushed towards Jorge's flat; Felipe explained

that Paloma had been in the San Ramón Clinic for two days and then she turned up at the door without the baby, looking half dead.

When Felipe and Vera finally arrived at Jorge's little flat, the brother rushed out of the bedroom, his face a stressed, contorted veil, wet with sweat.

'Vera, I think she's dying, help her, please help her!'

Vera's thirteen years experience as a nurse had prepared her to act swiftly and calmly in all situations, she had witnessed patients with terrible wounds from violence and accidents, and yet the sight of the young woman in front of her, took her back.

'Jorge, go in the kitchen and boil some water and find a clean bowl, close the door behind you, I've got to undress her...'

'But she's my girlfriend, I've seen her naked, we're having a baby together, for God's sake.'

'I know you have, but don't argue now, this might be unpleasant, go and do as I've asked you to do, quickly, and bring some clean towels.' She called out as he hastened away.

The nurse closed the door behind him and pulled back the curtains. She undressed her patient, when it came to her underwear; congealed blood had glued her clothes to her mutilated labia. The nurse opened the medical bag she'd brought and used surgical scissors to remove the cloth from the fleshy wound. It was worse than she could have imagined. Vera took the mutilated body's pulse and temperature; they weren't good. After a few minutes, Jorge tapped on the door and brought in the hot water, when he saw the raw wound he choked. Vera, taking the water pushed him out. After Jorge had circled the living room endlessly like a child's roundabout, the nurse left the bedroom and asked for a phone.

'Is she alright?' Jorge quizzed desperately.

'I hope so, let me make this call first...' She dialled a local number and asked for Professor Gregorio Marañón, she'd assisted the consultant for five years and knew that he would understand immediately.

'Yes Gregorio, the San Ramón Clinic.... No, I don't know what's happened to the baby... Yes, I've heard the rumours, that's why I've phoned you... Yes, she's been butchered... No, just one rough stitch where there should have been eight...Yes, some penicillin and I cleaned the wound, she's unconscious...Ok I will...thank you, I'll wait here for you.'

'What do you mean butchered? What's wrong with her, who is this guy?

'He is a great man, a wonderful doctor, the best, he taught me when I trained at the hospital.'

'Is he rich and famous, does he work at one of the big hospitals?' Felipe asked.

'No, he has a small scruffy surgery and very little money.'

'I thought you said he's something special? Why does he have such a cheap place?'

'Look, he'll be here in a few minutes: he used to be the chief consultant at the University Hospital, although he's always been against Franco and fought secretly with the Brigadas Internacionales during the war. He covertly met with anti-fascist in Italy, Germany and America.

The Brigadas brought together people from all over the world; you know there are good people everywhere. After the fall of Madrid, you know what happened, the fascists rounded up all of the Republicans, Communists and Freedom Fighters they could find, famous people like Hemingway were lucky and went back to America, maybe they could have stopped him as they did with so many others, although Franco's people didn't want to upset such a powerful country.

They suspected that Professor Marañón secretly fought against them, although they couldn't prove anything, so they started a propaganda campaign against him, said his work was unimportant of incorrect, ensured that he couldn't find any top teaching jobs and slowly pushed him into obscurity. We all know what they're like, if you support the regime, no matter how bad you are at your job, you can be at the top of society, with a great position and if you don't, you either disappear or are discredited.' Vera said

431

passionately.

'Well it might have been a little like that during the conflict, although nowadays life's back to normal isn't, we all have work, we are all getting motorbikes and cars, there's law and order throughout the country. The whole country is being overrun with tourists, surely people wouldn't come from England and Germany if it wasn't a free country, would they?' Felipe asked. Last year Felipe saw a street poster advertising a new Enodyne television set. The attractive young woman in the line drawing had stopped her handsome husband from going out of the house, pointing to the advertisement:

¡Futbol!
Barcelona against Madrid
En casa, only 13,500 pesetas
Live the emotion of football in your own home,
¡Sin molestias!

'You know Felipe, you are so inculcated by the propaganda you don't understand anything. At first I thought that I dumped you because your brain was below your waist, now I know you don't have one!'

'Listen Franco's not that bad, our father found a good job before he died, most people are better off now, there's a feeling of respect for the rule of law, the Catholic Church support the government and Spain is now a proud country...'

'You're so stupid Felipe, that feeling isn't respect; it's fear, no one is free to speak their mind and when people do, like Professor Marañón they're crushed or worse!'

'Well everyone I know is happy with Franco...'

'Oh shut up Felipe, who do you know? A couple of electricians who are happy if they can get drunk and laid in the same night! Why don't you go while we wait for the doctor, I'm sure there's some lonely girl out there who's looking for a drip like you.' Vera spoke venomously, turning back into the bedroom.

'Listen Felipe...' Jorge said gently, holding his sibling's shoulders. 'Thanks for bringing her, you'd better go now, I'll call you later brother.'

The bell rang and Vera flung the bedroom door open.

'That's him, go down and let him in Felipe then keep going!' Vera commanded. Felipe was livid, his eyes burnt with anger, he stared at the closed door leading to the bedroom, but didn't see the wooden panel, he saw his ex-girlfriend standing there. At that moment he hated her fervently and knew why he felt like that, it was because he loved her passionately. Finally, with a sulking face, he rushed out slamming the door. He took two stairs at a time to the ground floor, opened the street door and rudely told the Professor to go to the first landing, as he angrily pushed past. Jorge looked surprised when Vera's famous hero entered the scruffy flat. He didn't measure much more than five feet six inches, his head had lost its hair and his thick moustache and owl like glasses, gave him the appearance of a street onion-seller, rather than a campaigning, socialist Professor, who Vera said General Franco feared.

Doctor Gregorio Marañón glanced around the room, kissed Vera on the cheeks and strode into the bedroom, closing the door behind him. After ten minutes, he came out slowly and spoke to the young couple waiting apprehensively.

'She's lost a lot of blood and is very weak, I've brought the ambulance, we can take her to my clinic, although…' He paused and stared at Jorge for the first time. 'Are you the father of the child?

'Yes, but I don't know where the baby is and Paloma walked all the way from the Clinic.'

'First of all we'll try to save her, then we'll see what's happened to the baby…'

'What do you mean try and save her? She's just had a baby; it's not an illness is it? Women have babies everyday!'

Doctor Gregorio Marañón stared seriously at Vera and then at Jorge. He spoke softly. 'She's been treated badly; they have removed the baby crudely, with no concern for her health or welfare. I'll know more when we get her to my clinic, the next twenty four hours will be very

433

important.'

They took Paloma into the old, converted Fiat estate car on a green army stretcher. Vera and Jorge were left on the pavement in shocked silence as the makeshift ambulance shrivelled into a full stop in the distance.

Two days later, the rains had blown to the east over the Mediterranean Sea and the damp air from Portugal, turned into humidity. At six in the evening Vera arrived at Jorge's flat, she was shocked when he opened the door. His beard, several days old and his gaunt dark eyes made him look as feeble as a frightened furry animal.

'You look and smell terrible...' Vera uttered, standing back from his bad breath. 'The professor has called me and we need to go over to his clinic...'

Jorge staggered to the sofa and pulled a shoe on with trembling hands fumbling with the laces.

'Wait, you can't go in this condition, go and have a quick shower and get some clean clothes; you're a mess!'

'But-but I want to see her, she won't ca-care...' He slurred.

'What have you taken Jorge? You can barely stand up!'

'I had to take something Vera, I had to...'

'Ok, go in the shower.'

Jorge tottered unsteadily into the little bathroom, the nurse called out. 'Have a shave and clean your teeth!'

Vera looked around the neglected flat; next to the stove she saw a needle, a tablespoon and several empty paper packets. Jorge hadn't been on drugs for the last two years, Paloma had worked on him and got him straight. He had a good job, saved some money for the baby and if she managed to get divorced, they were going to marry. Vera now worried that he would go back to his old ways, he used to break into apartments and shops, sell anything he could steal in the local market, to buy drugs and had been taken by the police and beaten up on several occasions. They always told him that next time he would go to prison. An hour later they arrived on Camino de Húmera opposite Casa de Campo Park. The scruffy clinic had peeling paint and dark barred windows. Inside it was packed as tightly as the Madrid Metro in rush hour, with noisy women and their children, babies in arms, and old people, coughing and bleeding from minor accidents.

Doctor Gregorio Marañón took anyone and most importantly those who could not afford to pay. Vera knew the receptionist nurse Margarita, who ushered them through the double swing doors into the little ward at the back of the building. The air was thick with the odour of disinfectant. The windows scorned the view of the rear yard, which was stinking from dustbins that had overflowed with rat-infested rubbish, from the Chinese restaurant next door.

Jorge threw himself at his girlfriend, whose face looked smooth and rested on a crisp white pillow. Her eyes were closed and she breathed deeply. Jorge clenched her hand that lay limply on the sheet, yet she didn't move. Her body languished as weakly as an ember fading in the rain. He was on his knees, tears erupting as he mumbled his prayers. Vera turned to her friend Margarita and whispered, 'How is she?' Margarita's eyes and slow moving head, telegraphed the message Vera was hoping not to receive. Doctor Marañón left another patient on the other side of the cramped ward and took Vera by the arm. In his tiny office, where a filing cabinet served as a seat for the little desk covered with tower blocks of papers and files, the professor's face wore an unfamiliar sadness.

'We've all heard the rumours in the medical world about the Sant Ramón Clinic, a load of untrained nuns acting as doctors and nurses, for poor mothers of ill-repute, often with illegitimate and unwanted pregnancies. I've heard that they force many of them to give up the babies for what they call a better life, with so-called quality parents. I've even been told that there's an organisation near Barcelona that's selling the babies, although I really can't believe that the Church could possibly be involved in something like this. That might even be a stretch for Francisco Franco and his corrupt friends.'

'Margarita suggested that Paloma is very ill, will she be alright Professor?'

'Unfortunately I'm not optimistic, when she had the

baby, the midwife or the nuns didn't get all of the afterbirth out, and so it turned septic inside her. We managed to remove the entirety and I had to do a full hysterectomy, there was no choice. As you saw, they should have carefully stitched her virginal labia in operating room conditions, where it had been quite literally torn apart; unfortunately they had just put one stitch and left her with a virtually open wound. Now it all depends on whether or not she was strong enough to survive the terrible treatment she has suffered.

'When she hears that she can't have any more children she will be devastated, they both will.'

'I understand Vera, nevertheless we had no choice, her condition is critical now, without the operation, she would have died in the theatre.'

'Listen Gregorio,' She said with tears in her eyes. 'Please don't say anything about the hysterectomy to Jorge, he's been affected badly by the events of the last few days, I'm afraid he will do something drastic.'

'You'd better take him home now, I shall call you if there's any change.'

Jorge, praying hysterically on his knees, wouldn't let go of Paloma's hand until two nurses helped Vera drag him out of the hospital. Vera made him swear that he wouldn't buy any more cocaine, his mouth made the promise, yet his eyes lied to her.

At eight o'clock that night, Vera received a telephone call from the Professor, to say that Paloma had died.

Chapter 36
Barceloneta, Friday 24ᵗʰ April 1964

Charlotte felt great. Count Sergei had been the perfect gentleman over dinner the previous night, in a great restaurant overlooking the centre of Barcelona. He bought his 'niece' as he described her to the restaurant manager and anyone else who would listen, a fabulous long black dress. Well it was just over her knees, it would have been below the calves on the average Spanish girl, however, by her standards, it did seem fairly long.

Now she was sunbathing by the pool in a new, pale blue bikini, Count Sergei couldn't resist it, or at least it's tiny dimensions. For Charlotte, all presents were ephemeral; she loved them on the first day and couldn't stand them after a month.

A nice Spanish woman called Angelica brought the ivory toned model a wonderful lunch. She had already enjoyed a huge breakfast, although she didn't care, as she thought that she'd lost too much weight recently, due to her poverty-imposed diet.

Charlotte jumped up gratefully to the perfectly laid table under a large umbrella, and salivated over the array of plates, spread on the crisp white tablecloth. There were some tiny fish that Angelica called Boquerones, crushed, tomato covered slices of bread. Some sizzling hot prawns in a garlic sauce, they named something like Pil-Pil, which sounded rather rude to Charlotte; but the young girl was never good with foreign languages, God knows Phaedra had tried. Then Angelica brought a large plate of steaming fried fish on a bed of herbs with garlic mushrooms. She didn't like the way the heads were left on, but the aroma was fantastic. There were also fried potatoes with a spicy pink sauce. She had two glasses of ice-cold, pink champagne, and Angelica said that the Count insisted that she drinks his speciality, called Sangria. It was so fruity and quite alcoholic; she thought that she could finish the whole jug, while sunbathing next to the pool, throughout the afternoon.

The Count had a similar idea, as he'd laced the red

liquid with enough LSD to make Charlotte think she was in heaven. He had planned to spend the night in her bed, before he handed her over to one of the buyers on Saturday. The old Russian was particularly excited, as he'd now pushed the asking price up to a record breaking, ten thousand dollars.

Angelica had given her houseguest three helpings of Flan Catalan and a cafeteria of black coffee. The maid did all of the washing up, tidied up the kitchen and the Count crushed a handful of Pesetas in her hand.

'Shall I come back over the weekend for la Señorita, Señor Count?' The servant asked hopefully.

'No – no don't worry Angelica…' The Count said smiling. '*Zer* young lady will be busy over *zer* next few days, she won't need anything, we shall eat out, etcetera – etcetera.'

Sergei bounced into the garden and gawped at the tall model stretched out on the sun-bed; her milky skin, covered in shiny Ambre Solaire, starting to go the colour of pale Spanish Rosé wine.

'Charlotte my dear; how was your lunch?'

'Oh really super, thank Sergei, can we go into Barcelona later? I've heard that they have so many shops in the centre, I'd love to have another look around, yesterday was so short.'

'Short? We were shopping for two hours!' He gestured with his short chubby arms.

'Oh that's nothing, I usually go out all day in London, it was fun though.' She flirted, biting her full lips.

'Yes–yes, of course it was, you know, I believe that I should buy you some nice diamond earrings. What do you think?'

'I love diamond earrings, but may I get some t-shirts, as I haven't got many things with me.

'Of course my darling, but I did see rather a large number of cases etcetera-etcetera in *zer* bedroom.' The count giggled stroking her painted toes.

'Oh yes, but they're mostly old things, not really suitable for Spain.'

Sergei sat on the end of the sun-bed to have a close

look at the body he'd planned to ravish later. Charlotte looked back, hoping to get as many presents as possible, before she left.

'My darling, I have to go out on business for a few hours, why don't you rest here and enjoy *zer* sun...' He uttered, topping up her drugged Sangria. 'Boris is in his little room if you need anything, and then tonight we shall have lots of fun, etcetera–etcetera.' He said excitedly.

'Actually I do feel a little sleepy...' She giggled, as the LSD started to take effect. 'I'll see you later!'

The acquisitive Count Sergei Belevsky-Zhukovsky was a very happy man. This weekend, he was about to receive the best two things a man of his age and position could get. A large sum of money and sex with a willing, beautiful young girl. Well he consoled himself, she may not be completely willing, but *zer* drugs and alcohol would coerce her into submission, which was almost *zer* same thing.

'Boris! Boris! Where are you! Oh my God are you eating again? Sergei asked rhetorically, finding the pachycephalosaur chauffeur in the kitchen. 'Sometimes I really think you are just too expensive to keep here, you know...'

'Yes. I *spensive*. You could have big *dorg*. Do same job. Like me. You said too many time.' Boris mumbled through the leftover fish stew. '*Dorg* no drive *cor*. *Dorg* no buy *drogs*. *Dorg* no find *gorls* for you.'

'Alright Boris, shut up or I shall...'

'Yes I know. Send me back to Turkey.'

'Listen to me, will you? I'm going out. I shall be home about eight o'clock; it would be nice if you could go out *zis* evening, as I want to have a romantic evening with *zer* girl. Now just stay in *zer* kitchen and your room, leave *zer* girl to sleep in *zer* garden...'

Boris's huge face gave a contorted grin, which said a thousand words that he would've been incapable of verbalising in any language.

His marblesque eye almost left its socket and he started to half laugh and half choke. The Count stopped speaking and stared at him in disgust. Milyi came running in barking at Boris, hearing the altercation. Sergei picked her up preciously, apoplectic with rage and walked out of the kitchen. Through the threshold he turned back and said spitefully, 'Go out before eight o'clock, take *zer* little Fiat and stay out late!'

The old Russian dressed, found his briefcase and walked through the garden, deciding to check on his captive's progress. The light had softened around the pool and the languishing blonde slept deeply on the sun-lounger, like a beautiful marble sarcophagus. The Count stared at her for a few minutes and started to regret his business deals. If I could only keep her for myself, he mused wistfully. He now stood over her, his short round shadow, shading her face that turned towards the sparkling pool.

'Charlotte...' He said gently. 'Charlotte my dear, are you asleep?'

Sergei sat on the sun-bed next to her and slowly put his palm on her flat stomach, she didn't stir. He looked at his podgy, wrinkled hand with its perfectly manicured fingernails and chunky gold signet ring. He thought that it looked so old on her nubile, creamy flesh. The old man ran his hand up her long smooth body to her bosom. He slipped his fingers under her bikini top exposing her breast and gently caressed her nipples with his tongue. His breath deepened and his insatiable desire became stronger. He could feel his own heartbeat quicken, under his damp silk shirt. He stroked her stomach again, following the line of her protruding hipbones. His fingers searched inside her bikini's tiny pants and he pulled the front down lower. Charlotte's legs were slightly apart and he pressed his stubby, cigar-stained fingertips into her silky, blonde triangle and found the luscious crease of her divided soft flesh. The sybaritic sensation made his whole body sweat with desire. The Russian found it difficult to swallow. He pressed his forefinger deeper into her moist soft tissue, clumsily and urgently. His throat was dry, his respiration shallow, his face and neck reddened with lust.

'I'm sorry Ya-Ya! I'm sorry!' Charlotte slurred restlessly.

The Count jumped up in shock panting erratically,

440

as excited as a naughty boy caught with his hand in the biscuit tin. She didn't notice his cacoethes for her body; she just turned on her side in a restless, drug-instigated sleep. The Count looked around the garden nervously, taking deep breathes, no sign of his monster chauffeur spying on him as he often did. He found a handkerchief in his breast pocket and dabbed his clammy face and neck.

Then he relaxed and smiled, straightened his jacket, delighted at the thought of the pleasures he would experience later, when he was completely alone with the drugged body, he had dreamt of for the last few months. Tonight he would be able to do everything he had imagined, and Count Sergei Belevsky-Zhukovsky, was a man with a great deal of imagination.

The sexagenarian left through the garden gate, glancing back momentarily at the cataleptic beauty. As the Mercedes pulled out of the crunchy drive, Giovanni started his engine and followed from a distance.

At six o'clock the Catalan sky had darkened with graffiti shaped clouds painting out the senile sun. A cold wind came down from the Pyrenees, swaying the arms of the palm trees from side to side, like wailing natives. Charlotte's narcotization had laid her unconscious for the last four hours. Her virtually naked body began to tremble in the cool breeze and suddenly she sat up with a shudder. Almost immediately she fell back on the mattress. The garden spun in a hurricane blur. The flowers, plants and pool, now illuminated, swirled together, in a kaleidoscope of colours and shapes that was both exhilarating and frightening. She looked down confused, her breasts were half out of the bikini top and her small blue pants exposed the top of her pubic hair. She got up slowly, staggering against the table. Charlotte sniffed the jug of Sangria and tried to focus on the whirlwind of colours. Without knowing why, she started to giggle. She touched the back of her hair, which was like a baby's matted clump.

Recently she had been buying a lot of Hashish, she thought that she needed it, because her life was falling apart. Sometimes her crazy friend Lucy ran out of Grass and Hash and she had tried a few pills, called Brown Bombers and

Purple Hearts, she didn't like them. She reflected that they were great at the time; you forgot all of your debts and problems with your agency and the troubles with your boyfriend. But wow! The next day you felt ragged.

She realised that there must have been some drugs in the food or drinks, recognising the strange feeling of floating, numbness and dizziness; however, this was the worst she'd ever felt. 'Oh gosh!' She said aloud starting to panic, maybe that monster of a chauffeur had put something in her drink and now he might be somewhere in the house waiting for her to wake up. She staggered across the garden and crashed into a small table.

'Shuuuuush!' She told herself aloud, putting her index finger over her lips. She tried to get up, but her legs wouldn't obey. Therefore, the wobbly girl crawled on her hands and knees towards her bedroom doors. The lights were off and the house seemed eerily empty.

'Where's the phone?' She asked herself trying to concentrate. There wasn't one in her room or the massive living room. The Count had an office; it's bound to be in there.

She found her large handbag, when she peaked inside it looked like a cyclone had dumped the contents of an office and a chemist's shop in it.

She wanted to vomit, her knees were hurting, it must have been the gravel path, she hadn't noticed it at the time. The address book was also a mess.

She flicked through the pages, looked under 'S' for sister. Pippa, no point ringing her, she's too far away. 'B' for boyfriend, three names crossed out.

Justin, he wouldn't come, even if he were in the next house. 'G' for Granddaddy and Ya-Ya, they would swim an ocean to help her, but they're somewhere in France. Then she saw a wad of papers. Who's this? She asked herself in a daze. Josep Fusté, Carles Rexach, Miguel… Oh yes, the footballers, loads of them.

Suddenly there was a noise from the other side of the house, someone was singing. It sounded awful, a high pitch cry, like a cat murdering the lyrics of a Russian lullaby. Then a column of light splashed the hall and she fell back behind her bedroom door. Someone was in the kitchen, sounded as though they were making some food and drinks. Loads of banging of plates and cutlery. The fridge door opening and closing.

Charlotte crawled on all fours along the tiled hall as quietly as possible. When she arrived at the kitchen door, she peeped through the crack made by the hinges and saw Boris, sitting at the kitchen table with piles of food and several bottles of beer. His back was to the open door. She stuffed the Barcelona boys' telephone numbers in her tiny pants and crawled pass the open door with her eyes closed. She was still dizzy and now sweating from fear or drugs, she didn't know which, but she bumped her head on a piece of wood and immediately looked up. It was the Count's office door. Charlotte staggered to her feet. Her head spun and she quickly grabbed the door handle to stabilise herself. The door was open, she fell in, and the door slammed behind her.

Boris heard the noise. Took a vicious looking knife from the kitchen counter and walked into the hall. He peered into the quest's bedroom then the Count's. The leviathan then walked over to the office; knife first, flung open the door and switched on the light. He glanced out of the window into the garden; looked under the old man's desk, yet saw nothing. He flicked the switch bringing back the night, returned to the kitchen and his feast, finally throwing the blade on the wooden table. Charlotte let out a long breath and slowly opened the office cupboard door, stepped down from the cold metal filling cabinet and swayed over to the desk. Unravelling her papers she tried to focus and dialled the first number. After ten rings she realised there was no one there. She touched the cradle and it made a dinging noise that crashed through the silence, as clearly as a cathedral's Sunday call to the faithful. She looked over nervously at the office door expecting the giant to rush in and either kill or rape her. Her head shuddered at the image. The second number rang only twice, a woman answered in Spanish.

'¿Sí?'

'Oh – a – hello…' Charlotte whispered.

443

'¡Háblame!' The old woman shouted.

'Ah – is Josep there please?'

'¡Qué!' The woman said confused. In the background Charlotte heard Josep's voice.

'Madre ¿quién es?' He asked her irritably.

'No sé, una chica estúpida Inglés.' The mother said shrugging her shoulders.

'Niña de Inglés! Dame el teléfono de forma rápida Mama!

'Hola Charlotte es you?' Josep asked excitedly. I thought you call me yesterday, I wait for you, me, my friends, we want to take you out...'

'Listen Josep, I need your help...' She murmured.

'No problema, tomorrow night we go to big party, we have lots of dancing you see all Barça...'

'No Josep listen to me...' She slurred, almost inaudibly.

'What's wrong Charlotte you sound funny, you no drunk on Spanish wine?'

'Josep help me, I've been drugged, I have to get away, do you understand? Someone is going to hurt me...'

'What you say Charlotte, no one hurt you - is just a party, with my friends...'

'No Josep, listen to me, there's someone *here* who is going to kill me!'

'Charlotte I come, speak up, where you are?'

'I can't speak loud, I don't know where I am exactly...'

'Charlotte, how I come if you don't know where, look out of the window, where is?'

'I - I'm opposite the sea, there're lots of small fishing boats and little fisherman's houses, but I'm in the only big modern house...'

'I know this house, my uncle is a fisherman near there, and my Madre say to me, when we are rich from football, I buy this house, it's very famous in Barceloneta, for the rich tourists.'

'Yes that's it, but Josep be careful, there's a tall chappie here, who's not very nice.'

'No problema we are Barça, I bring Carles, when

we are against Germany they are taller than us, nearly six feet, but we beat them, wait outside. Okay?'

'Alright but I haven't got any clothes…'

'Charlotte you crazy, is why I like you, you got more clothes than my whole family, bye–bye, we come.'

She put down the phone as carefully as she could, afraid to pass the kitchen again, with Boris now in the middle of a full folklore concert. She tiptoed into the garden and felt cold, as the temperature had dropped dramatically. She carefully tried the ornate metal gate, but it was locked. The grass was damp now under her toes and so she went around the outside of the house, ducking under all of the windows and re-entered through her bedroom doors. She pulled on a pair of jeans and a t-shirt. It wasn't her favourite. Carefully opening her cupboard door, she slipped on some sandals; grabbed a cardigan and made for the large double gates next to the driveway.

Still dizzy from the LSD, she tried to focus her mind on a switch for the gates, yet saw nothing. The drugged girl could barely stand up now and so she hid under a fig tree next to the gate and in a few moments her eyelids were too heavy to open.

Josep Fusté and Carles Rexach came speeding along the coast road, having changed their clothes and smothered themselves in aftershave. The Italian Autobianchi Stellina bounced at full throttle into the little port of Barceloneta and the extra four spotlights soon shone on the Count's fabulous rented villa. The two footballers got out of their little car and peered through the metal gates.

'Hola!' Charlotte! Are you there?'

She had fallen back into a comatose sleep under the fruit tree and heard nothing.

'Are you sure this the right place Josep.' Carles asked.

'Sure it's the only place like it along the coast, they say they are going to knock down all of the little fisherman's houses and this is going to be a fancy tourists area.'

'Charlotte, where are you - lets go!'

'Maybe she's doing her hair or something.'

Carles added.

'She said she's being drugged and murdered! You think she's doing her hair?'

'Maybe, she's the type of girl that wants to die pretty...' He laughed.

'Carles! Well maybe you're right, she is a crazy English girl, do you remember her luggage?'

'Charlotte, are you coming or what?' Josep called out.

'Listen Josep, maybe she just had a row with a boyfriend, she phoned us to make him jealous and now they're at it in the bedroom, and she doesn't need us.'

'I'm going to ring the bell.' Josep said.

Boris was fairly drunk by now and looked at the buzzing intercom in the kitchen annoyed.

'*Wot*?' He screamed into the little phone on the wall.

'Charlotte is there?' Josep asked. There was silence on the other end. '¡Hola!' Are you there? I want Charlotte.'

'No Charlotte here.' Boris said banging down the intercom.

'Maybe you got the wrong house Josep.'

'I don't think so, I'm going to climb over the fence.'

'Hey be careful, we don't want any trouble with the Guardia, imagine what the manager will say if we are caught breaking into some tourist's house!'

The athletic footballer jumped the fence and looked around the garden. 'Charlotte-Charlotte, are you in here?'

'Ohhhh-Ohhhh! My head...'

'Charlotte, what are you doing under a tree, what happened? Are you hurt.' He asked trying to get her up.

'Hey Josep, someone's coming...' Carles called out.

Josep was crouched over the unsteady blonde, when a black shadow, thirty feet long, created by the light from the house, shot across the front driveway. When Josep turned around the enormous presence of Boris towered above him. Josep looked up in horror, the half-light exposing Boris's marble eye floating in the centre of his massive white globe-head. Boris leaned down, picked the footballer up above the height of his shoulders and threw

446

him across the gravel. Josep rolled like a coin until he hit a bush on the other side of the driveway.

'B-o-r-i-s!' Charlotte screamed with a drug-pitched voice. 'Leave him alone, he's only little…'

Josep started to get up slowly rubbing his head. Boris lifted his size eighteen shoes quickly, after four paces he was on top of the Spaniard before he could find his balance.

Again he lifted the centre forward and flung him as easily as a shopping bag into the house's hallway, slamming his back on the step. Josep cried in agony. Boris grabbed a shovel from the flowerbed, turned it like a knife-blade and lifted it over his head. He aimed for Josep's neck, to decapitate him. As he swung his arms above his enormous cranium with his legs astride, Carles ran towards him and made a move he had practised for the last five years and had become renowned for in the football world. The fans called it 'Rexach's axes'. He famously leapt in the air, swung his right leg back and then at the last moment swept his foot forward, smashing the ball into the goal at a blinding speed; unstoppable for any goalkeeper. This time he aimed for Boris's crutch, and he scored a perfect hit. Boris crashed in agony as heavily as a felled oak tree.

'Oh Holy Mother of God, look at the size of him. Josep said touching his bleeding head. 'Come on let's get out of here before he gets up, next time he might be really annoyed.' Carles laughed.

'Wait, get my bag, it's over there by the pool.' Charlotte garbled from the damp grass.'

The boys found the gate button on the house wall and bundled Charlotte's limp body into the back of Italy's coolest car, for trendy *raggazzi.*

One of Marco's men from his motorboat was on surveillance duty and followed the escapees.

'Josep I don't feel well, where are we going?

'We go my house, you can sleep there.'

'Listen Josep, take me to an hotel, I'm not sleeping with you!'

'No Charlotte, hotel is very expensive, you can sleep in my bed, is no problema.'

447

She wanted to be sick, Josep drove nearly as fast as her grandmother and the car became a spinning top.

'Listen Josep, I don't know what you've heard about English girls…'

'I like English girls, they very nice…' He said, grinning like an Auguste clown with Carles laughing in agreement.

'Josep – Carles, I want to thank you for helping me, but I'm not having sex with you two, do you understand?'

The two footballers laughed hysterically.

'No Charlotte, don't worry, we go to the house of my Madre, she very Spanish lady, in her house no *echar un polvo*, you sleep in my bed, and me, I sleep on the sofa. If I don't sleep and look for some water, my Madre say, 'What you do?' Because when you stay in the house of my Madre, you are her daughter; you understand?

'I think I understand, but let me tell you something…' She slurred with irises the size of a 45 record.

'My grandmother is Greek, and she will kill you if I wake up tomorrow with you two lying next to me.' Charlotte said, as seriously as she could. Both the boys laughed all the way to Josep's little village house in Carrer dels Angels, in the old town of Barcelona.

The tall model half fell out of the little car onto the narrow pavement, desperate to sleep.

The boys gently took her arms and guided her through the front door and directly into the kitchen: where Josep's mother stood at the cooker.

Charlotte wasn't as intellectual or as academic as her sister, and couldn't speak loads of languages like her grandparents. However, the one academic subject where she had the equivalent of a Master's degree was the study and control of men, who were hoping to sleep with her. She had been gawky, like a skinny spider until she was about thirteen. The boys she met tended to tease her, calling her 'Milk-bottle legs' as she was so thin and white. Then one day, almost overnight, the local schoolboys, and then their older brothers, discovered her beauty. By the time she was seventeen even their fathers, started to flirt with her.

Once, when Charlotte was about fifteen, several

rough boys from the local council estate held her down and kissed her. Her grandmother noticed the change in her body and the way men of all ages started to react towards to the young girl. As this was something she had experienced herself, when she was a similar age, Phaedra knew that she had to educate her blossoming granddaughter on how to handle men. She tried to teach her Judo and Marshal-arts, but Charlotte wasn't cutout for fighting. Phaedra discussed it with Sam. They realised that through nature or the fact that they'd over-protected her, she would never be able to fight back, she cried even if she had a broken fingernail. As time went on, Phaedra noticed that her granddaughter soon acquired a natural way of handling men. It wasn't aggressive, quite the opposite. She appeared to melt in front of them, to implode. It had a strange affect on most males. They wanted to protect her against everything, everyone, including themselves. The only unfortunate side effect for her, Phaedra complained to Sam, was that she would always ask other people to help her, and never achieved anything on her own.

'What have you done to this girl Josep?' His mother asked in Catalan.

'She says that she's been drugged and she almost collapsed in the car.'

'Take her into your room Josep.'

The boys guided the tall blonde into the bedroom and laid her like a corpse on the narrow bed. Josep's mother took her shoes off and covered her with a blanket.

'When she wakes up I'll give her some food, she looks as though she's been starved to death…'

'No Madre, she's a model, they're all like that.' Josep said smiling at Carles.

'Well she can stay the night. Don't look excited my son, you're on the sofa, tomorrow we'll phone her parents and get her home…'

'She doesn't have parents she's an orphan.'

'She must live somewhere…'

'She's was going to do a job tomorrow in El Restaurante Torre d'Altamar, the problem is, the man who arranged the work, is the one who drugged her.'

'So what happens when he drugs her again tomorrow night?'

'I don't know what to do. She says she has to go because she needs the money!'

'Listen, do you have this pervert's telephone number?'

'I think Charlotte has it, if not cousin Vincent will get it from his friend the estate agent, the house is just rented for the summer.'

'Alright, when your father gets home he'll ring this man and you two boys will drop her off and pick her up when she finishes. If she doesn't get paid, you can speak to him, so she gets her money.'

'I hope he doesn't have that chauffeur with him...' Carles said. 'We were lucky once, but he'll be ready for us the next time.'

'What have I always taught you boys? You can do anything if you really try hard, you beat Mexico last year, didn't you?'

'Madre you're fantastic, I would never had made the team without you.'

Charlotte slept solidly for fourteen hours; suddenly she sat up, bemused by her surroundings. She looked around the little room full of medals and cups won by Josep since he was a child. The walls were covered in posters of footballers and sexy girls. Abruptly she remembered yesterday, and quickly looked under the blanket, relieved that she was still wearing her jeans and top. She yawned, stretched and felt really rested. She hadn't had two days sleep like that since she was fifteen. There were voices on the other side of the door. Charlotte looked in the little wall mirror and said, 'Wow ugly cow!' She cracked open the door and saw Josep in a tracksuit sitting at the kitchen table, his mother was at the stove making a fantastic aromatic tortilla.

'Hola Guapa!' Josep said delightedly. 'Come and have some breakfast, my Madre is fantastic cooker.'

'Oh! Hello...' Charlotte said. Josep's mother kissed the young girl as though she had known her all her life and guided her to one of the kitchen chairs. She was starving, had three helpings of the omelette as well as chopped tomatoes on toast, coffee and in desperation to satisfy the young girl's hunger, the mother found a piece of yesterday's homemade cake.

Josep's mother chirped away for several minutes as though she was arguing with her son.

'Is everything all right Josep? Is your mother angry with me?'

'No Charlotte, my Madre always speak like this, she very strong woman. She ask me why you so hungry, she thinks the orphanage no feed you.'

'No, you don't understand, I've lived with my grandparents since I was five. I take after my grandfather, he's always hungry as well!' She laughed.

Josep translated for his mother.

'My Madre wants you to phone your grandparents, she thinks you should go home.'

'Josep, listen, don't tell your mother, but I'm in trouble...' she whispered conspiratorially.

'I have to get some money because I have crashed my grandmother's car. That's why I came here for this job. I'm going to phone the Count, to see if I can get my clothes. I'll do the show and then go straight back to London. I'm not going back to his house.'

'Okay, I explain a little to my Madre, you can phone him from there.' He offered, pointing to the phone. Charlotte found her bag and after ten minutes stumbled on Sergei's number.

'Sergei? You drugged me!'

'Charlotte my darling girl, I've been so worried, where are you?' Sergei was waving frantically to Boris pointing to the phone, mouthing the words, 'It's *zer* girl.'

'I'm not telling you, you drugged me!'

'My favourite girlfriend don't be so silly. *Zer* last time I saw you my housekeeper was giving you *zer* wonderful lunch. You must have drunk too much and you know *zer* Spanish sun is very strong, after a few drinks, it feels like being drugged!'

'You promised me an hotel with my *own* room and I've ended up in your house with that horrid monster.'

Josep had his head close to the phone listening and his mother was hovering near to her newly claimed daughter. He kept whispering a translation to his mother, who was standing with her fists on her ample hips, shaking her head in disgust.

'Listen my darling, this is what we are going to do: I shall pick you up myself, without Boris. I'll bring my little friend - you know Milyi is missing you! Then I will take you to a wonderful restaurant. You can eat *zer* best food etcetera–etcetera. Followed by hours of *zer* shopping, for all *zer* naughty things you want, in *zer* best shops of Barcelona…'

Charlotte's face started to soften and she began to think that she did have a lot to drink yesterday and it was true, she isn't used to sunbathing. The thought of a days shopping in the town would be really nice.

After the quick translation, Josep's mother grabbed the phone from her and screamed in Catalan:

'Listen you filthy pervert, she's not going anywhere with you, do you understand! My son and his friends will collect her clothes this morning and then this evening she'll do this show. You pay her the money you owe and then they will collect her. If not you will have me to deal with! Do you understand!' She yelled again, with Josep laughing at his mother's famous temper. The angry woman gave the phone back to Charlotte and pointed her finger admonishingly. The young girl didn't understand the words, but knew that she had to obey this forceful Madre.

'Charlotte–Charlotte? Who was that horrible woman?' The Count asked in amazement.

'She's a friend of mine and she doesn't want me to spend the afternoon with you.'

'Friend? Friend? You have friends in Barcelona? I didn't understand what she said exactly, but as long as you're doing *zer* little job *zis* evening, everything will be fine.'

He recovered quickly and realised that now his plans have changed. He must get the girl to the show, after that he'll leave her to the German and the Italian. Now they can cut her in half for all he cares.

'I went out yesterday to get your money from *zer* bank and as soon as you finish this evening, you will be paid. And if you wish you can go off with these-these friends, etcetera – etcetera.' The Count said looking at Boris angrily, keeping his voice light-hearted.

'Okay Sergei, what time do I have to be there?'

'Well, about six a clock for a little rehearsal, *zer* show starts later. I'll get there at about nine-thirty; I want to introduce you to some nice people who will help your career. *Zer* Duchesse who's putting on the fashion show and a nice Italian man called Marco, who does *zer* fashion shows and business with *zer* models in Milan. They're waiting for you, I told them how beautiful you are, etcetera – etcetera.'

'Okay Sergei.' Charlotte said in a more friendly tone, 'I'll see you later, and you will have my money won't you?'

'Of course my darling girl, don't worry, you know you can trust me, everyone does!'

'Okay Bye!'

'Goodbye my dear... Boris, you see *zer* problems you have given me? How difficult was it to keep an eye on a young girl, who I explained was worth a lot of money. And you told me she just sneaked out quietly on her own?'

Boris didn't dare tell the Count that two little Spaniards beat him up.

'Well, it now seems she has friends here, *zer* little bitch. Tonight when she arrives at *zer* restaurant we have to hand her over quickly and get our fee. This time, don't let her out of your sight. I bet you got drunk last night! Ah! You useless monster!'

Boris walked out embarrassed and started cleaning the car.

Chapter 37
Sant Ramón Clinic, 1962

'I want to see the person in charge!' Jorge screamed at the demure novice nun standing nervously behind the desk at the Sant Ramón Clinic.

A week had past since Paloma died in Doctor Gregorio Marañón's hospital. The Doctor sent Jorge a message advising him to ask the Sant Ramón Clinic if he could see the baby's corpse. Suggesting that he should arrange a funeral for his child at his local church. In that short time, Jorge had already gone back to his old ways, to the existence he had before Paloma stopped his dive into depravity and given him hope. He robbed a petrol station and then a small-time drug dealer, to pay for his habit, stocking up his supply and putting himself in a drug-instigated coma. He was now so thin he resembled the skeleton that Professor Marañón kept in his office, for his unpaid lectures on anatomy. The last time he ate anything was the night before he took his girlfriend and unborn baby to the Sant Ramón Clinic. They splashed out on a restaurant meal; it was to be their last for a while. So that they could finish decorating the little one's nursery, and buying the vast supplies new parent's needed in the first few months after the baby's birth.

Now, the nursery was empty, as was the right side of his double bed. After so much hope and excitement for the future, he had lost two family members within a few days. Jorge knew that Paloma's dying wish was for them to see their son, and the child's father was determined to fulfil that hope. If the clinic refused, he ensured that he was armed with a hunting knife to make them see sense. It had worked on the man in the garage and it also worked on the drug dealer, after Jorge stabbed his left knee. Sister Carmen rustled down the stairs and pulled up at the sight of the trembling carcass that Jorge had become. His trousers were covered in dried vomit, his shirt creased and dirty. The backs of his shoes squashed by his bare heels. The nun stayed back, near enough to smell the disgusting blend of body fluids that covered the young man like a halo.

'Where's my baby!' He screamed wildly with massive pupils in dark, hollow sockets.

'I know who you are, I have explained to the mother that unfortunately the baby was still born, regrettably it happens sometimes, but if you try again we will do everything in our power to help you with the next one.' Sister Carmen Gomez-Valbuena said as calmly as she could before tuning away. Jorge leaped at her and swung her habit around like a large umbrella in a tornado.

'There won't be any more babies...' He half cried, half screamed hysterically. 'Because you killed her!'

'Sister Carmen seemed afraid, her pale, colourless face turned ashen, she tried to recover her composure and said. 'I'm very sorry, I didn't know, she left the clinic without our permission.

We wanted her to stay here and rest, so that we could look after her, yet she refused and ran out without us knowing.' She lied convincingly.

Jorge stood staring at the nun trembling, his head spinning, he was a devote Catholic, like his brother. The religious young man wanted to trust the Sister of Charity, his family believed in the church - in God. Surely these people who did so much good wouldn't have hurt the love of his life. Nevertheless, Paloma's last words to him were clear. 'Find our baby boy.'

'I want to see my son. I must see my son. I promised her I would.' Jorge said gently, loosening his grip on the black habit.

'Wait here, I shall get the Director, Sister Suzanna.'

Sister Carmen walked up to the office where she found Sister Suzanna examining a new pair of diamond earrings in a small velvet box. The Director quickly put them in her handbag and looked at the elderly nun questioningly.

'Sister Suzanna, the father of Paloma Perez's baby is here. He is acting violently; he wants to see the baby. He says Paloma's dead.'

'Well that's half the problem solved, is he alone?' She said, in her usual pachydermatous manner.

'Yes, he looks very ill and on drugs.'

'Go down and get Baby-Frio, wrap it in swaddling and take it to the chapel. Don't put any lights on. I'll bring him down in a few minutes. Hurry! I don't want to spend any more time on this case, all of the files are closed now that the baby's in Switzerland.'

The elderly nun walked into the hallway, opened the hall cupboard and took a pink shawl from a pile of baby clothes, divided into two sections. Blue on the right, pink on the left. Then she continued down to the kitchens in the basement. Some women dressed in white uniforms and a young nun, were working on lunch. Sister Carmen went through to the scullery and opened one of two large chest freezers. A white cloud of freezing air rose up, following the large lid, and the nun waited for the atmosphere to clear. She moved some chickens from one side of the deep freeze and found a large plastic bag, big enough for a Christmas turkey. After pulling off a rubber band the nun slid out the solid contents onto a wall shelf.

It was a dead female baby.

The nun wrapped the pink swaddling around the icy body twice, making a hole for the tiny grey face, smudged with ice. She stood outside the chapel and waited for her boss. Sister Suzanna had called her husband from the office, asking him to send a couple of policemen over to the clinic and then went to the reception to meet Jorge.

She started speaking from the bottom of the stairs; she didn't want to get too close to the druggy. She had covered her hair with a wimple and wore a veil for effect.

'I am Sister Suzanna. You have the sympathy of all of the Sisters of Charity and the Catholic Church. We are all deeply sorry for your loss and suggest you go to your church now and pray for the souls of Paloma and the baby.

Please follow me.' She said walking towards the stairs, with a hand on Jorge's elbow.

'We don't like to show deceased babies to the families as it's so distressing; though as you have insisted, let us walk to the little chapel and pray together.'

Jorge's head lifted from his chin for the first time in days. He followed Sister Suzanna down the steps and

456

entered the windowless room, furnished like a small church. The German walked over to the long metal candelabra and lit two candles reverently genuflecting in front of a painting of the Virgin Mary, barely visible in the darkened basement. She then turned to Sister Carmen and took the frozen corpse, gently pulling back the swaddling from the tiny head. Jorge's face was a sea of tears, saliva dribbled from his nose and mouth, which he wiped with his open sleeve. The drug addict lifted a shaky hand to touch the baby's face, but Sister Suzanna turned away quickly and passed the corpse to the nun, who blew out the dim candles.

'It's Jorge isn't?' She asked, taking a handkerchief from her pocket wiping her invisible tears from dry eyes. He couldn't speak; his throat had completely closed, as had his mind. The man's only vision, that of his dead girlfriend.

'Come with me now...' She said, reluctantly touching his bony shoulder and guiding him up the stairs. 'Jorge, I want you to promise me that you will go directly to your church and see the priest...' Sister Suzanna said, noticing her two policemen standing by the door, talking to the teenage novice. Sister Carmen returned to the kitchens, removed the pink wrap and restored the icy block to the plastic bag and the freezer. In the reception, Sister Suzanna nodded to the policemen as Jorge staggered pass, his feet dragging on the floor like a living corpse. On the street Jorge lit a cigarette and made slow progress, he didn't even know which direction he faced. Grief and drugs had made him incapable of thought, his body a robot, moving aimlessly. Until the teenage novice ran up to him and pressed a piece of paper in his hand, returning to the rear entrance of the clinic hurriedly.

As he dragged his trembling body along the road, he fumbled with the piece of paper that he had clenched like a crushed flower. He opened the note and found it difficult to focus on the childish handwriting. He read the words once, yet didn't understand what it said. Yes he knew the short words, but what did they mean. Who was this young nun, all in white, who rushed out of the back door so nervously?

He found his way into a doorway, took the wrinkly document in both, unsteady hands, smoothing it on his trouser leg. It was clear now, he understood the pencilled words. The young novice was afraid of her superiors, however, she wanted to help him, help Paloma. It was too late for his love; perhaps it was too late for him. Now he read the words again and knew what he had to do, it was just a matter of how and when. He folded the paper carefully; the words were now indelibly tattooed in his memory.

They've sold your baby.

Chapter 38
Raúl Piazzolla Mainetti,
Saturday, 25th April 1964

He lingered for his prey in the empty shop, as expectantly as dawn waiting for the sun.

Two of the three Malvida boys had the dilapidated sofa with its broken springs, and the third one with a cigarette stuck to his lips, had the wooden radio without the dial. They put both items roughly on the pavement outside the musician's fourth floor flat, in the scruffy tenement building at number 23 Carrer dels Flassades, cached in the old centre of Barcelona. There were nine flights of stairs to Raúl's two-roomed flat at the top of the decaying building. The street was so narrow that Lola could pass a loaned cup of sugar to her neighbour and friend Marta who lived technically on the other side of the tiny street.

'Please Señor Malvida, not the radio, it's the children's only pleasure and where are we going to sit if you take the sofa?'

'I don't care Raúl, as you've become so fat on my rent money, they can sit on your lap!'

'But Señor Malvida, I'm fat because we only have bread to eat...'

'Pay me my rent and you can have that disgusting sofa and the broken radio, but I haven't seen a Peseta from you for nearly two months!' He said imperiously.

Raúl Piazzolla Mainetti was born on 2 June 1920 in Mar del Plata, Argentina. He was the sole child of Alberto Piazzolla and Amelita Mainetti. The couple did try for other children, alas, after several years of endeavour, Amelita confessed to her friends and family that; 'God has decided that we put all of our energy into baby Raúl.' And that's exactly what they did. The only music he had ever heard, even before he was born; was the Tango. It was played and danced in every home, restaurant, bar, and café; as well as the little Parque Camet each evening. You could hear the famous rhythm on street corners in the small seaside town, and Tango passion thrived throughout the whole country.

However, Raúl's parents wanted him to be a concert violinist, although Alberto was a Jazz bandleader, he and his wife loved classical music. When Raúl was five years old, the family immigrated to Barcelona; the first thing his father did was to buy him a cheap violin and start him on lessons. Raúl became one with his instrument and the music it produced, before his seventh Birthday.

By the time he reached fifteen years old, he played the piano, guitar and the bandoneon, as well as a professional.

Nevertheless, despite the nagging from his parents, he just didn't have a feeling for the violin, even though he played to a high standard. He composed some astonishing Latino music, according to his parents, and they dragged him around music publishers in Barcelona. Unfortunately the music industry was not as enamoured with Raúl's work as much as his friends and parents. Alberto Piazzolla and Amelita Mainetti didn't have a great deal of money.

Over the years, their son's lessons, his instruments, albeit second-hand, as well as the trips to all of the publishers, had squeezed the couple into poverty. When they had exhausted the phonebook of music companies in Barcelona, they wrote to publishers in Madrid, Paris and London. The only difference between these publishers and the local ones was that the rejections came back in three different languages. Raúl should have been devastated, but he wasn't, because he loved his music and he loved an audience. In the evenings he toured the restaurants and cafés of the city and played to the people of the Calles.

They weren't wealthy theatregoers, they weren't music publishers, and they weren't experts on the subtleness of fine classical music. Nevertheless, when Raúl played the Tango on his bandoneon, red-blooded Spaniards and visiting tourists, jumped up to dance with their wives and girlfriends. A simple meal or tapas in the local restaurant; became a fiesta! Raúl developed into an urban legend and had a huge following, and yet he remained poor.

One night in late October, following his twentieth Birthday, the crowds were few in the cold, windy city. His tips were virtually non-existent, as no one was in the mood to dance in the damp streets, until he heard the rhythmic sound of castanets clicking in time to his bandoneon. He turned to see a skinny teenage girl in a classic red Flamenco dress, gently dancing to his music. He turned and played Flamenco to the chica, whose dark, gypsy beauty fascinated him. She became inspired by his attention and threw her body into the sensuous movements of the Flamenco, stamping her bare, dirty feet onto the stone pavement and used her dress as an extension of her body.

Two became one, their eyes connected by an invisible light. Nearly fifteen minutes past, and when they finally stopped with the young girl's arms and wrists coiled above her head in artistic unison, a previously unseen crowd clapped enthusiastically as they left their tables and emerged out of the warm restaurants. Lola used to dance the Sardana, the national dance of Catalan, but Franco had banned it with a penalty of imprisonment for any offenders. The couple fell in love at first sight and became an item in front of the restaurants of Barcelona: until they married and had their first child fourteen months later. Raúl wasn't an ambitious man. By 1964 he had nine children with Lola, and loved them all. His wife was by then a daily housekeeper for a wealthy banker, who paid her the minimum wage. She had lost the sparkle in her eyes, and the children had reformed her slim body into that of a middle-aged woman, even though she had only just past thirty-six years old. And, her inherited gypsy passion for dance was just a vague memory. Raúl worked the bars and restaurants seven nights a week, looking after the children during the day. He took them to school in the morning, collecting them in the afternoon. The talented musician went to the food markets as they were closing, and having made friends with most of the stall holders, he helped pack up their stalls and collected the fruit and vegetables that had fallen on the road or were too ripe to go back on sale the following day.

He did the same thing with the fishmongers, washing the floors and taking away the scraps for his family's favourite dish of Fidua.

It was more taste than substance, but the kids loved it. Once a month, he even got some meat from the butcher, by saying it was for his dogs. The family did have three, large stray dogs, and a black cat, that were as hungry as the kids. However, the whole family shared the stew, with its hint of meat. The long winter and uncertain spring weather had kept tourists away from Barcelona. Some of the restaurants near the beaches hadn't even opened yet and so Raúl and his ancient Piano accordion hadn't been able to make the rent, on the dilapidated flat. He knew that sophism wouldn't work on Señor Malvida, but said:

'Just give my poor family a little more time Señor, and when the tourists arrive I will pay all my rent...''More time! I'm not going to throw good money after bad, you gave me that story last month, I want you out of here this afternoon!'

'Please, my friend, I have nine children, where will we all go?'

'Did I lay with your wife until she's exhausted with this – this football team of yours,' he snarled licentiously.

'Please Señor...'

'You Latinos are all the same, all you do is make music and babies.' He continued aggressively, looking back at his sneering sons for support.

'Listen to me Señor Malvida, I have a job this evening and all the money will be yours, I promise...'

'What do you want me to do? Stand next to you outside some cheap bar with a hat, hoping to get a few pesetas! Uh! No I've had enough of you Raúl...' He looked at Lola holding the smallest child. 'I'm sorry Lola, you're a lovely woman and I remember you ten years ago, you used to be a real beauty, but you picked the wrong man, this lazy bum will lead you and your children to starvation.'

Lola walked over to her husband and held his arm protectively, noticing the landlord's improper glances.

'You don't understand; I have a good job this evening. Black Tie. I'm playing the violin with a small group at a posh restaurant, and I'm getting a good fee, enough to pay two months rent, well almost. The customers are rich and I'm bound to get some tips...'

'And where is this so-called posh restaurant Raúl?' Señor Malvida asked sarcastically.

462

'It's El Restaurante La Torre d'Altamar - you know, the one they refurbished last year on the port, above the cable car.'

The whole family stood in front of the harsh landlord in their threadbare clothes and matted hair, as still as grey steppingstones, from the youngest to the eldest; only interrupted by the four animals that refused to stand in any order. Raúl looked into the property owners eyes and added, 'It's a private party, invitation only, wealthy foreigners have booked all of the restaurant's tables.'

'Alright.' He said with exaggerated blustering.

'My boys will be here tomorrow morning at nine o'clock. Two month's rent in full or we'll empty the place and change the locks.'

The four Malvida's left without looking back.

'He's such a *pesetero*, this flat isn't worth half the rent he charges.' Raúl said to Lola, who was crying silently into the baby's blanket.

'I must work on your evening clothes, they are mostly torn and the shirt is nearly brown.' Lola said timidly.

At five-thirty in the evening, Raúl polished the ancient violin his parents had bought him when he was a child. He tipped the cat out of the damaged brown leather case and placed the violin carefully inside. Raúl looked in the mirror and saw a tall, fat man in a tattered black evening suit and slightly yellow evening shirt. He couldn't do up the top button and so struggled with the bowtie in an attempt to hold the collar of his shirt together.

'Come here, let me do it,' Lola said lovingly, standing on tiptoe to wrestle with her husband's bowtie around his flabby neck. 'I've tried to stitch most of the holes in the jacket, but those dam moths love this old fabric. You never see this quality in Spain anymore.'

'Well it's not bad for fifty years old, you know, my father thought it looked too old to wear, even when he gave it to me!' Raúl laughed. He looked down at his Lola; her clothes were almost in shreds. If it went well this evening, he might get some more jobs inside restaurants. Who knows, he might even be discovered by one of the rich patrons, then he could get his poor Lola something for herself.

'Señor Piazzolla Mainetti? I am an impresario from the Paris Opera, I love your work, so refined, could you please bring your family to France, all expenses paid and you can star in our new performance at the Opera house. Nine children, oh that's no problem sir, we will arrange everything…'

'Raúl, stop daydreaming and come downstairs, you don't want to be late do you?'

'No - no sorry darling, I was just thinking about the performance this evening, it could be the start of something big you know…'

Lola didn't say anything, she never has. She just kissed him on the lips and guided him to the front door, saying, 'I'll see you later, have you got the special pass they gave you yesterday? Raúl looked back, waving the white security pass, before putting it back in his breast pocket. He smiled at his love standing in the doorway, framed by half of the children and all of the dogs. He was such a lucky man, he thought. The musician walked along the restricted street, in an optimistic mood, three little girls were skipping with some string, and he waited for them to miss a beat before he slipped pass. Then he walked through the Plaça de Comercial, the Mercat del Born was closed in the afternoons and debris from the busy morning's market blew in the growing wind. Raúl loved to walk through the park, even though it was a little out of his way and so he turned left and walked along Carrer de la Ribera. The musician admired the Passeig de Picasso, with its luxurious apartment buildings in a soft sand colour. He thought that the view from the flats overlooking the park must be wonderful. It's strange that such a beautiful area could be so close to his slum street.

He crossed the wide tree-lined road and entered the gates of Parc del la Ciutadella.

It was absolutely packed in the summer, nevertheless the dying sun and the cutting wind had emptied the green space by the early evening. The musician was totally alone. He started to wish that he hadn't sold his coat, scarf and hat in the flea market two weeks ago, although the kids needed some bread with their thin soup that day. Still, if all went well this evening, he might be able to bring home some leftovers from the kitchen. Most people liked him, particularly if they had seen him perform in the street and so he usually managed to get something.

'Good evening.' The strange voice said from nowhere.

'Oh! You surprised me, there aren't many people mad enough to walk through the park on a cold evening like this.' Raúl said jovially to the frail old foreigner.

'Yes that's true, although we are brothers...' The old man said with a strange accent.

'Brothers? Have we met before?'

'No, I've seen you often, you're Raúl aren't you?' The old man asked with a wheezing voice.

'Ah! You've seen me play, were you at one of the restaurants?'

'Yes, I've seen you several times, the public seem to love your work.'

'Thank you, that's very kind, making people happy is a wonderful thing. Seeing them dancing and joyful and then clapping my music; it really fills my heart. Of course it was better in the old days, when I had my Lola dancing with me. The crowds loved her, you should have seen them, she was so beautiful then and such a marvellous dancer.'

'I'm also a musician you know, look!' The old man held up a beautiful red leather violin case with the initials FM tooled in gold. 'It's a Stradivarius you know...'

'You're joking with me, there're only a few in the whole world!'

'Yes that's true and I have one, would you care to see it, my friend?'

'Would I? It's the dream of any musician, particularly a violinist like me.'

'Alright, come over here under this tree next to the bushes, it's a valuable piece, I don't want to be robed.' He said looking around the deserted park. The old man put the case on the ground and bent over it with difficulty. He opened the little lock carefully and revealed one of the most beautiful sights Raúl had set eyes on.

465

'Oh God…' He said, crossing himself.

'This is the most magnificent creation I've ever seen.' Raúl whispered, with a reverence he hadn't felt since his parents died.

The fat musician bent down on his knees and put his face close to the masterpiece, squinting his eyes, afraid to touch its ancient wood.

Then he fell on his side and lay on the ground next to the case. Blood seeped from his jugular vein. His body quivered. Saliva dribbled from his mouth. His corpse released urine into his trousers.

The trembling stopped. Moshe dragged the fat body another two feet under the tree and took the white security pass from his pocket.   Then he turned towards the port and El Restaurante La Torre d'Altamar.

Chapter 39
Teleférico, Saturday, 25th April 1964

At five minutes to six o'clock, Isabella, Joana and Mariesther arrived at the ground floor entrance of the cable car tower and restaurant. The morning's spring weather had faded and fast moving cerussite clouds stained the sky. The noisy crowd of security people dressed in sinister black, made the girls feel apprehensive. The police buzzed around the Teleférico Port Veil, like sinister bees protecting their hive.

There were four Guardia Civil Officers hanging around the lift on the port wall, which went directly up to the cable car. As well as another three green uniforms smoking cigarettes, opposite the staircase that climbed through the latticework of steel girders. On the other elevation of the Torre Sant Sebastià, facing the main road of Passeig Joan de Borbó, security was as thick as a hotel carpet. Eight local policemen from the Mosses station in blue uniforms were spaced evenly across the front of the small entrance as straight as chess pieces, at the start of the game. Their commander, a senior inspector with gold braid, walked over and started talking to the six black suited doormen from the restaurant.

Mingling with the crowd were half a dozen, well-dressed secret policemen from Colonel José Valles-Carrera's own personal team. They scrutinised passing cars and asked any approaching pedestrians, to cross the road. Their demeanour made it clear that this polite request was obligatory. Two short, good-looking Italians represented Marco Sotori. They wore impeccable suits, with smiles to match. The Mafioso walked around the area with cocky gaits looking seductively at the arriving waitresses and cleaners. The three girls from the Gaudí Hotel smiled at the Mafia boys and were giggling over an incident that morning between Señor Gomez, their belligerent boss, and a very difficult guest who didn't like his room. Señor Anselmo Gomez ended up pouring an ice bucket over the irate man's head. Two of the girls were laughing and joking as much as they could, trying to cheer-up their friend Joana, who had received a jolt a few hours earlier and felt terrible. When the Sant José de la Montaña orphanage in Barcelona, told Joana at eleven o'clock on her fourteenth birthday, that it was her time to leave their care, she didn't know what she would do or where to go. Not that the care was very good, most of the meagre rations they received were donations and leftovers from regular churchgoers, sometimes a meal was just a piece of bread. She stood in front of the only home she had known for her entire life, with a scarf wrapped around the few clothes she had been given. She looked back at the orphanage's steps and found it hard to believe that she wasn't allowed to enter her shared bedroom ever again.

After a succession of terrible jobs and slummy places to live, she met a boy four years older than herself and fell hopelessly in love. Vicenç was charming, well dressed and swept her off her feet. After a few months, he expressed his undying love and proposed marriage. One Sunday he took her to see his parents at their beautiful detached house, in an expensive barrio on the eastern side of Barcelona.

Joana realised that her life was about to change forever. The abandonment by her mother, the harsh years in the orphanage, the hopeless period after she'd been thrown onto the street, could all be put behind her. As now, she and her love would be married.

Vicenç's father couldn't have been more charming and ushered her into the drawing room chatting kindly. He said how pretty she was and how happy he felt that Vicenç had found such a lovely girl. He then asked her about her family and she truthfully told her unfortunate story. He was sympathetic and praised her strength of character. He commented that; so many young ladies in these circumstances had become prostitutes, drug addicts or became sickly, due to the harsh treatment and poor food and conditions in many orphanages. Yet he noted that Joana had progressed through this traumatic accident of birth, survived, and presented herself as an attractive, intelligent and respectable young woman. The orphan from Cordoba was delighted by his comments and left the house elated and happy to be alive, with a future that she couldn't have dreamt of during the first ill-fated years of her life. She met Vicenç, excitedly the following week on Saturday night, when he took her to dinner in a nice restaurant on the port. She couldn't wait to tell him of her plans. Although he was older than her, to Joana he still seemed like a young boy. She had to grow up fast, to survive the severe life of an orphan in Franco's post, civil war Spain. However, Vicenç had the advantage of a comfortable home and two loving parents.

They sent him to good schools and gave him all of the love, affection and advantages a young man could have. He seemed subdued over the dinner and after he asked for the bill, told her nervously that his father had not only forbidden him to marry "This waif with no family" but he was not to see her ever again. Joana was in shock. She didn't cry; she was too proud and strong for that, she had lived with rejection from the time that she was a few days old. She'd been beaten down psychologically and physically almost daily in the home. 'Hope.' She had been told, was for fools. The reality was that orphans would be seen as second-class citizens throughout their lives, to be shunned and avoided by polite society.

At first she didn't understand how her love could be so weak. Vicenç was close to tears, but she realised that he was just a child. She reasoned that he wasn't strong enough to stand up to his father. After a difficult couple of months, Joana found a job in a factory. Her strength of character and sheer determination soon saw her rewarded and promoted to the buying office. One day, the boss, a gentle man in his sixties, asked her to go with him to Paris on a buying trip. She understood what he meant, and decided to go anyway. Over the next few years, he was kind to her. He taught her how to order in expensive restaurants, play roulette in casinos, the right clothes to wear. She couldn't have done better in an expensive Swiss finishing school.

One morning several years later, staying at the Hotel Splendid in Cannes, Joana's boss just didn't wake up from his sleep. After the hotel doctor pronounced him dead, she sat on the bed alone and held his cold wrinkled hand.

469

She looked out over the famous Croisette and slowly realised that another chapter of her life had come to an end. She kissed the ashen man's cold forehead and said aloud: 'Thank you old man.'

He had given her a small studio flat in Barcelona; she had built a wardrobe of expensive clothes and was the head buyer at the factory. Her life had improved a great deal from the rainy day she was bounced out of the orphanage, but she was ambitious for more. Unfortunately, the old man's wife and family sold the factory and she was out of work. Then she received a letter from the new estate's solicitors. They said the company owned the flat and she had one month to move out.

The ambitious girl bought a newspaper and started searching for a room and a job. While drinking a café solo on the pavement terrace of Bar Catalan, she noticed a man standing next to her table and he asked if he could buy her a drink. She looked up to say no, and saw Vicenç, smiling down at her. The years had changed him. He looked and spoke like a confident man. He claimed to have a successful business, a wife and a child, although he was unhappy. Her former fiancé begged her to come back to him. Of course he explained, he could never marry her, but he'd thought about her constantly over the last few years.

'I've never stopped loving you Joana.' He pleaded holding her hand.

They started an affair, because Joana knew that she could never really love anyone else. Over the following years, she had his baby, Sandra and three abortions at a private clinic near Bristol, in England. Franco's Spain wouldn't allow the procedure, and the egotistical Vicenç, refused to use a condom. Then as quickly as he appeared, he left her again. His father had found out about their affair and for the second time forbade his weak, vacillating son to see her. That was three years ago, then this afternoon, as she was getting ready for this evening job at the restaurant. Vicenç, came to her room, said he was finished with his wife and wanted her back.

Her friends held her, cried with her, joked with her and yet she was devastated. Her head knew what to say to him, her daughter's father. But her heart…

One of the concierges on the pavement checked their white passes and pressed the lift button to take the girls to their evening job. The girls stamped out their cigarettes noticing a strange, thin, drug addict in rags leaning against a lamppost across the street. He stared at Joana piercingly. They pressed the button for the restaurant, inside the small cabin as quickly as they could; and the lift started its seventy-eight-metre journey towards the sky, Isabella and Mariesther screamed delightedly, watching the incredible vista of Barcelona fall away in front of them.

When the lift doors opened Marco's Italians pushed ahead of the other security guards to search them. After too much peaking, touching and flirting, the girls were met be Sebastian, who dragged them through the restaurant, gave them a pep talk, some black and white uniforms and directions to the kitchen.

'It's going to be a long night girls!' He said theatrically, already looking flustered.

Chapter 40
Quarter-Past-Six

Moshe waited a hundred yards along the road from the restaurant, sheltering from the wind swirling around the Sant Sebastià Tower, until he saw four men carrying musical instrument cases. He walked behind them, preciously holding his red violin case under his right arm, with Raúl Piazzolla's white security pass in his left hand. When the Base player noticed the old man in evening dress following them, he stopped and asked who he was. Moshe managed a smile. The four men thought that he looked strange - his clothes were two sizes too big for him. His scrawny chicken's neck loose inside the large collar of the evening shirt; he appeared ill and had trouble walking.

'My friend Raúl couldn't come, so he asked me to take his place.' He said casually.

'It must be something really serious...' The Base player said, loud enough for the stranger and his fellow band members. 'He was really looking forward to this evening, and God knows, he needs the money.'

'Don't we all!' The sax player added, lighting up a cigarette from the one he had been smoking.

Moshe nodded and copied the pessimistic mood of the band trying to assimilate into the group. The Base player shrugged and led the ensemble towards their engagement. At the lift door the security team, waved the band through after a cursory search and they squeezed into the small lift, fighting for a space next to the bass player's bulky accompaniment.

'Have you ever played here before?' The Guitarist asked Moshe.

'No, but I visited once.' He said truthfully.

'It's a good place for requests, good tippers.' The Saxophonist added.

The Violinist didn't mention that the last time he visited the restaurant tower, was late last night. Moshe 'Mad' Liberman had arrived at midnight. He noticed over the last couple of weeks surveillance that the little, gay

472

manger, usually locked up the restaurant at about one o'clock, after the inebriated Friday night patrons staggered out of the lift noisily. He had to wait until one-thirty that night before Sebastian finally came out of the lift. Moshe slipped into the metal stairwell on the other side of the tower and hid on the first landing against the black shadowy metal. By law, the gate had to be locked, only after the restaurant and cable car had closed, as it was the only exit from the tower in case of fire or one of the two lifts failing.

The old assassin dressed in black and carried a holdall in the same colour. After the manager left, it took him until three o'clock in the morning before he reached the cable car station. He stopped at each flight, barely able to breathe. He was exhausted when he finally peered over the edge of the top floor and looked down at the deserted Lilliputian city below. The old man panted, wiped his sweating face and neck, opened his holdall carefully and pulled out half a bottle of Vodka.

He gulped two mouthfuls and his body folded with the pain. He studied the bottle in his hand knowing he would need more. Having surveyed the structure over the last few weeks, the dying man knew that he would have trouble mounting the hundreds of steps, with the heavy explosives, lifting him nearly three hundred feet above the Port. He'd therefore calculated the minimum amount of Vodka and the minimum amount of explosives he would need for the task. The expert carefully pulled out the detonator wired into the large bag. In principle, a high pitch note from his violin would activate the device; it should therefore be stable in the dark silence.

Nevertheless, Moshe Liberman had a great deal of experience and the one thing he knew certainly about explosives; was that you could never trust these volatile creatures. Above his head the two, large yellow wheels that turned the heavy cables over the parked cabin, were resting. The old assassin knew from his survey that the roof of the Teleffèrico station was the floor of the restaurant. He calculated. 'Blow a hole in that and the entire room would crash into the dock, with a hundred tons of metal girders joining them.' Moshe had always been a perfectionist; he knew exactly how his explosives should react. His work was neat and precise. Unfortunately these days his arteriosclerotic illness and his age had affected him badly. The old man found it difficult to concentrate. It took him over two hours to wedge the bag of explosives in between the massive yellow wheel cog and the roof of the station. He decided to booby-trap the detonator because he had to put it on the outside of the bag, so that it could react to his high-pitched note. Eventually he got back on the floor of the Telefèrico's platform.

He looked up at his work and was disappointed. The contrast between the yellow wheel and the black bag of explosives was a little too obvious. He had hoped that as the roof was dark, the black holdall would blend in, people never looked up, especially as there was nothing to see above the cable car, in contrast to the magnificent view out of the windows. However, he was still dissatisfied with his work; a trained eye might spot the bag with the chrome aerial on the detonator, sticking out next to the handle. He checked his watch, seven-forty-five, too late to go back up, the cleaners would be here in fifteen minutes and the cable car would open at eight thirty. Thirty years ago he could've done this job in two hours and even climbed down on the outside of the latticework metal to the ground. Now he would have to wait until the cleaners opened the fire exit gates downstairs. Then, when the manager put the electricity back on and they took the lift, he could sneak out.

When the lift doors opened into the reception area of the tower top restaurant, the five musicians were thoroughly searched, their instruments were taken out and the cases were explored for false bottoms and hidden weapons. Moshe's weapon was the violin, his bow and his ability to produce the instrument's highest note. No scanner or Nazi punk would be intelligent enough to discover this lethal combination, Moshe mused.

They were ushered into the restaurant and told where to set up. The first thing the regular bandsmen did was search for the kitchen, to ask for some free food and drinks.

Chapter 41
Five-Minutes-To-Seven

Josep and Carles arrived in the Autobianchi with Charlotte. They saw the huge security presence and noticed a group of five young models huddling by the lift.

'Are you sure that you'll be okay Charlotte?' Josep asked concerned, as he gave her a packet of cigarettes.

'Thanks Josep, if there're other models here at least I know that there will be a show, will you come back for me about midnight? It should be finished by then.'

'Listen Charlotte tonight we all go to see Els Setze Jutges…'

'What is it?'

'They are fantastic pop group, ah, how do you say, the Sixteen Judges, they make protest songs against Franco, tonight is a secret concert, but everyone knows about it, all the young people, you'll like it…'

'Okay, I'll see you later.'

To the delight of the two footballers, Charlotte kissed them on their cheeks before jumping out of the car. At the lift door one of the doormen asked for her white security pass.

'I don't have one, I'm meant to be doing a fashion show here!'

The doorman didn't speak English; nevertheless, he put his arms up blocking her entrance.

'Hey Charlotte! Are you doing this show?' Lucila Fernandez-Gonzalez asked.

'Oh hello!' Charlotte said - relieved to see a familiar face. 'I'm sorry I've forgotten your name; you were at my grandfather's house with that actor. Maurice?'

'Well he's changed his name to Michael, but I'm finished with him, I now have an Italian boyfriend. He's the one who got me the job here tonight…'

'This chap won't let me in and I don't speak Spanish.'

'I'll speak to him…' Lucila said confidently, stepping over to the group of doormen. 'Hola! Guapo, why are you not letting my friend in, she's doing the show with all of us.'

'Listen it's high security tonight, loads of rich government people and heavyweight foreigners, she should have been given a pass.'

'Hombre – have you seen what this chica's wearing?'

The concierge looked again at Charlotte, she stood freezing in a pair of earrings and a tiny mini dress that clung to her body. The concierge said, 'Sure very nice…'

'So she's obviously a model for the show and she couldn't hide a toothpick under that dress.'

The concierge looked around and walked over to the kerb saying, 'The lift door is open and I have to check these cars.'

'Let's go Charlotte.'

The six models squeezed into the lift easily, even though the sign said 'Maximum Four People.'

'So how did you get this job? You're a long way from London.'

'Well I'm a bit short this month and the Count found this show for me.'

'Count Sergei?' Lucila asked.

'Do you know him?'

'Yes: are you sleeping with him?

'No way!' He's really old and short.'

'Well you should be careful, he's got the hots for young naïve girls like you.'

'I'm not *that* naïve; I have a boyfriend…' Charlotte said indignantly, hoping it was still true.

The lift door opened onto the small dark reception area and it was pandemonium. Temporary waiters and waitresses were queuing to get in. A few last minute deliveries were stacked in boxes, while the delivery drivers complained because each one had been opened and searched. They had rigged up a metal detector; two Spanish men, with two Italians were searching the guests and staff. Men were taking their jackets off, women were resentfully emptying their handbags and all of the Spanish and Italians were arguing at the top of their voices. The lift doors opened again and another four models joined the queue. There were now four blonde models, twin redheads and four brunettes. Two or three seemed to know each other and they all went into a gossip marathon of fashion shows and photo sessions, model agent's high fees and of course; who is sleeping with whom. Charlotte started to regret not taking the boring language lessons her grandparents had arranged, because all the girls seem to speak several tongues. More staff arrived in the next lift and the cacophony started to drown out the background Muzak.

'Enrico!' Lucila called out to an Italian security man across the metal border of the scanner.

'My bella donna, I tell you come early, but you always late...'

'Yes Enrico I know, but I said I wanted a five-carat diamond ring and you got me this little one... She said giggling and poking him in the ribs with her bejewelled finger. 'Wow! Who's this beautiful blonde, will she be playing with us tonight?'

'Stop it Enrico, she's just a baby, she's new on the circuit...' Lucila said, putting a protective arm around Charlotte.

'I'm twenty!' Charlotte said, wondering why everyone was treating her like a child.

'Come with me girls, take my hand.'

Enrico took Lucila's hand; she in turn grabbed Charlotte's. He pushed his way pass the security and they arrived in the calmer restaurant.

'Wow!' Charlotte said. 'This is fantastic!' On the right-hand side the huge windows looked out at the spectacular view over Barcelona. All along the edges, large round tables were impeccably dressed with white tablecloths, flowers and an array of glasses, plates and sparkling cutlery. The manager, in evening dress and patent shoes, danced around the large room, giving orders to a small army of waiters and waitresses who were putting the finishing touches to the banquet tables.

'Charlotte followed Enrico and Lucila around the octagonal and found a raised catwalk running along the length of the next bank of glass, which looked out to the darkening sea. At the end of the catwalk they'd erected a three-metre square, opaque screen, shouldered by some of the restaurant's black, full-length curtains that usually divided the room into three sections.

'You girls change behind there...'

'Can't the people in the restaurant see us behind that screen?' Charlotte asked.

'You see, I told you she's still a baby.' Lucila said.

'Don't worry baby...' Enrico smiled. 'They only see your shadow, it's a little sexy, no?'

Against the glass wall facing the Telefèrico cables leading to the second tower called Jaume I, a group of five musicians were setting up the temporary bandstand; four of them had a drink in their hands. On their left, a raised table backed onto the curtains. The head-table enjoyed a higher standard of flowers as well as a microphone, a music system and little music stand, holding a folder.

The model girls clambered into the small changing area noisily talking and giggling. Charlotte was pleased to be with young girls again. She loved doing fashion shows and she started to feel as though the trip would work out, as she had hoped before she got on the airplane at Heathrow. Ten clothes rails of beautiful dresses and bikinis were placed in rows. The model's names were handwritten on a piece of cardboard and Cello-taped onto the front. Sebastian pirouetted into the room and clapped his hands to get the noisy model's attention.

'Young ladies – hello – hello – your attention please...' The girls ignored him, so he put four fingers in his mouth and blew a deafening whistle.' The room went silent. 'Thank you darlings!' Now I'm sure you would all like a little champagne and tapas...' The girls started again. 'Silencio por favor!' The girls laughed as Sebastian jumped up in the air.

'Thank you! – Gracias! – Merci!' The girls calmed down again, noticing an attractive waitress stand next to the Manager. 'This is the lovely Mariesther and she will be popping in and out to look after you, but please, it's very busy out there tonight with the most demanding rich people

478

in Spain, so do be patient.

Now the Duchesse, ah – Señora Valles-Carrera, who is running the show and will be paying you all…has asked me to say that she will be here soon, with loads of expensive jewellery…and…I'm told a policeman to keep an eye on the jewels and antiques…'

The girls all 'Wooooed' 'Yes-yes I know, but at the last show it wasn't only the girls who walked out at the end of the evening!'

Another 'Woooo' followed. 'May I just mention that Señora Valles-Carrera's husband is the Chief of Police in Barcelona – yes, you've all gone silent now.

And I wouldn't dream of saying that he is at all unpleasant; I shall leave that up to you to decide, should you have the pleasure of meeting him!'

The room went silent, Joana and Isabella came in with trays of food and sparkling wine and the noisy girls soon forgot their apprehension about the Chief of Police coming backstage. Sebastian waved to the crowd blowing kisses and said; 'Good luck Guapas…' and disappeared. Two hairdressers and make-up artists came into the room and the girls started to get undressed.

When all of the models were down to their underwear in front of the temporary mirrors, the ten girls started to look at each other and giggled. Because they noticed that apart from being tall and beautiful they all had something else in common.

They all sported a tattoo.

Chapter 42
Half-Past-Seven

A noisy procession headed by two police motorbikes came towards the Torre d'Alta Mar restaurant. Their blue lights were blazing and their sirens screamed their arrival, as swiftly as a bird of prey in pursuit of its next meal. The renowned black Citroen DS followed, carrying the Duchesse and the Colonel. The celebrated couple had the help of the Colonel's personal bodyguards, in the form of two motorcyclist, carrying machineguns strapped onto their black leather backs. An armoured van kept close behind. Four men followed in one of the new, specially made, Seat police saloons. The Colonel had ordered the luxury police cars as soon as he came into office in Barcelona; he knew how to get the support of his troops. As soon as all of the security men recognised the now infamous French car, they jumped into position and formed a black-suited wall around the powerful couple.

The Colonel jumped out first. He had reached his sixties, yet he was slim and athletic. His black evening suit tapered into his flat waist and his bowtie sat comfortable under a firm chin. He wore the red Nazi Party badge on the lapel of his open coat, a Falange badge with six spears pointing upward and a gold medal, stamped with Francisco Franco's profile, looking poignantly to the right.

The Colonel was born on the 18 July 1902 in Ambrosero, Cantabria, to a low paid civil servant and his timid wife. He was educated with an equal measure of books and beatings in two Roman Catholic schools in Bilbao. At fourteen he left the teaching brothers, as he hated the strict rules. Nevertheless, he became a devout Catholic. As a teenager he joined the Traditional Party of the Falange. Although they said that they were not on the extreme right, their philosophy was in support of Italian Fascism. The party fought on the Nationalist side during the civil war and José Valles-Carrera soon became an officer and natural leader in the Party. Franco united the Falange with their former enemies the Carlist, but José refused to join and headed his own group. Franco realised that he needed to bring all right wing factions together and so offered Valles-Carrera, the position of Colonel and the job of developing an ideology for his regime.

Valles-Carrera worked with the Catholic Church in Rome and developed the 'Spanish Catholic Authoritarianism Party'.

However, Franco was nervous of the power that this organisation may acquire and declared in September 1943, that it should be called a 'Movement' and not a 'Party'.

Unfortunately for the Colonel over the years the 'Spanish Catholic Authoritarianism Movement' lost its momentum and support, therefore he knew that he had to find another organisation that would allow him keep his power in Madrid, but also maintain his connections with the Catholic Church and the fascists in Italy.

He therefore formed the *Partito Nazionale Fascista* with a group of like-minded people from Italy, Germany and Spain.

This party gave him the political influence of the Falange, the influence and worldwide network of the Catholic Church and the illegal connections and deadly force of the Italian Mafia. He soon realised as Franco aged that his new position would be unchallenged. He controlled the secret police in Madrid for years, and eighteen months ago took over the same position in Barcelona.

The Duchesse stepped out of the car at his side and her attire was rather dramatic; a black and white silk Maharaja's turban and a full-length, black clinging dress that was cut into a low V on her bare tanned back. She clasped the collar of her full-length mink and puffed on a long, ebony cigarette holder to complete the affectation. Nobody asked to see their passes and so they were soon in the reception and through the scanner. Sebastian ran over bowing and scraping and Mariesther stood with a tray of bubbling champagne glasses. They stayed in the entrance area next to the first window with a vista over the city. A long queue soon formed to greet the glamorous hosts.

Fräulein Ilsa Klup, Fräu Ilsa Koch, Sister Suzanna, Señora Suzanna Valles-Carrera; she had to take both her husband's names, which was unusual in Spain as she couldn't use her former German titles. The tall slim woman looked around the beautiful restaurant, puffing on her long cigarette holder. She felt wonderful, although she had enjoyed her journey from the early days in Dresden, when she was a fat German teenager, bullying her classmates, she always felt superior to those around her. She wanted a life where she would be rich and powerful, to have the power to enjoy her sadistic pleasures, and yet also to have a place in society. In a way, she had an elevated kudos by marrying Herr Koch.

After he became Kommandant she felt as though she ruled the concentration camp and to an extent the nearby village. Then after she escaped Germany under the Allies, she found herself on the run and hiding in the convent, she had to take stock of her life, the first few years she was just relieved to have missed the hangman's noose. Then by serendipity she stumbled on the opportunity to take over the adoption clinic. From that moment onwards, she knew where her future lay.

As she breathed in the atmosphere of the magnificent room, full of some of the richest people in Europe, she realized that she had finally arrived. She would be the centre of attention and as always the Bell of the Ball. Ilsa's thoughts were interrupted by the arrival of a Generaloberst who stood in front of her clicking his heels and kissing her gloved hand.

Chapter 43
Five-To-Eight

Marco Sotori pulled up in his black Cadillac sitting in the back seat, with Giovanni Gibigiano driving and Raffaello Massoni sitting next to him.

Raffaello had met Marco when his grandfather, Angelo Massoni called a meeting of the major Mafia families from the north and south of Italy, including some of the richest and most powerful dynasties in Sicily. Angelo Massoni's family had been making a great deal of money in North America and particularly in Las Vegas over the previous years. He was concerned that the many rivalries between the two halves of Italy were using too many resources against each other, which could be used to make more money in other territories.

Marco immediately stood out from his peers. He was physically powerful, aggressive, and yet had a certain charm that made him a born leader. Even some of the old Godfathers listened to him respectfully and afforded him a power and influence that others hadn't achieved until they were over sixty years old. However, Angelo told his immediate family, which included Raffaello, that he didn't trust the man. The Sicilian Godfather controlled his enormous family with an iron fist and a certain perplexing morality.

When Marco's family agreed with his proposal that they should go into the drug business, Angelo refused. Then Marco suggested they go into the kidnap and extortion business, again Angelo refused. When finally Marco said he'd found a good business through his *Partito Nazionale Fascista,* with a group of fascists in Spain; Angelo realised that the south couldn't work with the north.

Marco proposed a compromise. Several families from the north and south would be twinned, and they would work together on several projects in fields of businesses they both agreed upon. Then after a few years when trust between the families had been cemented they could look at other areas of business together.

They set up an exchange. Marco worked with Angelo's family and Raffaello worked with Marco's family. Whenever there was a problem Marco and Raffaello would meet and report back to their families. Unfortunately for Raffaello from the first encounter, the handsome killer from the north always got his own way.

Until that fateful night in Paris when two men died and Marco became a living corpse. Two Italians guarding the entrance to the tower went over and offered to help Marco out of the limo.

He screamed at them to leave him alone and the four Italians waited next to the car for what seemed like an eternity, for Marco to slowly unfold his charred body on to the pavement.

After several minutes trying to cross the fifteen feet to the lift door, most of the security people turned away embarrassed. They blew cigarette nicotine into the wind and looked around the square except towards the decrepit yet deadly Mafioso, dragging one half of his body behind the other.

The two street guards moved the barriers in front of the lift and parked Marco's Caddie as near to the entrance as they could.

At the front of the restaurant the Duchesse and the Colonel were still chatting to the line of guests, when Marco approached slowly with his henchmen close behind. Strangely, Suzanna Valles-Carrera and her husband Colonel José Valles-Carrera were the only two people Marco had met since his accident that didn't seem shocked, embarrassed or distressed by his extraordinary appearance. He had reflected a couple of weeks ago that at times they almost seemed amused by his struggle to appear normal.

Marco stood next the powerful couple and joined in their various conversations with the international guests. While Giovanni Gibigiano and Raffaello Massoni walked into the restaurant to find their table and a drink, delighted that they weren't sitting with Marco and his weird associates.

Chapter 44
Ten-Past-Eight

The Mercedes 600 of Count Sergei cruised to a halt with Boris in a new, impeccable uniform of knee-length, black leather boots, dark grey jodhpurs and Cossack style, double-breasted jacket, topped with a peak cap. Sergei sat in the back with the curtains closed. He wore a button on his lapel that he didn't want passers by to notice. The little red disc had the words; Nation-Sozialistische D.A.P, running around the edges and the white centre sported a black swastika. Since Boris had 'lost' Charlotte he had been on his best behaviour and stood to attention holding the door as the Count exited the rear of the limo. However, the Ukrainian chauffeur gave a disgusted one-eyed look at the Count's Nazi Party badge.

'You don't have to look so shocked Boris,' Sergei whispered while holding Milyi under his arm. 'You know *zer* only party I belong to is my own, its just business!'

Boris made a base groaning noise that the Count assumed meant he understood.

'Go and park *zer* car then show them *zis* pass and wait for me in *zer* reception area, if you stop complaining I might get you a beer.'

By the time Boris found a seat in the reception and Isabella had served him a beer, Count Sergei Belevsky-Zhukovsky was in full swing chatting to the guest's line and then working the rest of the room. He balanced Milyi with a large flute glass of vintage champagne in his other hand and insisted that the waiters feed his dog some of the petit-fours they carried around the room on silver trays. He talked extravagantly in a mix of several languages with various people and then with six Germans. The three men wore the same badge as Sergei, although the women were more interested in each other's diamonds. Slowly the cunning Russian made his way backstage and greeted two models he had met previously. Then he saw Charlotte having her hair done.

'Hello gorgeous girl!' He said kissing her cheek.

'How's my favourite English rose today?'

'I'm not speaking to you Sergei – what did you put in my drinks?'

'Darling I promise you; it was only *zer* strong Spanish wine and *zer* hot sun, etcetera-etcetera. I think you had this new thing that they all have in America, what's it called? Ah yes! *Zer* jets-lags. It makes all *zer* people think they're drugged – even *zer* pilot! He laughed until he choked. 'Oh excuse me...' He said to the group around the models. 'I love *zer* little Jokes, and you Charlotte you've heard of *zis*?'

Charlotte shook her head.

'Yeah,' the English hairdresser chirped in, 'I've heard of that.'

'When do I get paid Sergei?' Charlotte asked, trying to be business like.

'This evening you will meet *zer* lovely Duchesse and *zer* other friend I told you about from Italy. You should be extra nice to them because they will get you lots of *works* etcetera- etcetera.

The Duchesse has arranged *zer* show and she will pay all of *zer* models at *zer* end of *zer* evening, so don't worry my beautiful girl. I have to leave early; but I will take you to lunch and a little of *zer* shopping when we all get back to London.'

Sergei kissed her cheek, waved to half the people backstage and swept out. As he squeezed past the tables in front of the catwalk, he saw Marco Sotori with Raffaello, talking to an American priest at the Duchesse's top table. The Count grabbed another glass of champagne from a floating waitress and walked over. Marco asked the priest to excuse him and beckoned Sergei to come closer.

'Well Marco, did you see *zer* little gift I brought you?'

'Oh, so you don't want the ten thousand dollars now?' Marco teased with more hatred than humour.

Sergei smiled responding quickly; 'At only ten thousand, she is a gift my friend.'

'Raffaello, give him the envelope.' Marco said with contempt.

'Not here dear friends – not here. Come with me to *zer* reception it's quieter there...' The Count said turning towards the exit.

Marco nodded at Raffaello who followed the Count. The shrewd old man wanted Boris to be there so that the payment could be put securely in the monster's hand.

As Sergei and Raffaello entered the reception they saw Boris looking bored, perched on one of the leather chairs like an overgrown teenager on his childhood bike. When he stood up Raffaello still couldn't believe the size of the man. Raffaello passed him the brown envelope and walked away without a word. The Count smiled and said, 'Would you like another beer Boris?'

The Ukrainian looked down at the tiny twenty-five CL bottle he had been given earlier, it wasn't much thicker than his thumb, he replied, 'I *wont* big glass like Germans!'

'Listen you stupid oath, have a small bottle now, when I get *zer* second envelope, you can take me home and drink all you want!' The Count walked away in disgust complaining to Milyi. As he entered the restaurant he saw Marco talking to a couple. The blonde woman looked familiar to him, although his mind was still on business. He searched for the Swiss Millionaire Monsieur Kautz, but couldn't see him. He had tried to make friends with the wily old fox on several occasions, yet only received a polite rebuff. Then he saw Suzanna on her own and rushed over.

'My dear Duchesse, may I say you look marvellous with *zer* turban and *zer* jewels...'

Suzanna Valles-Carrera looked down on the smarmy Russian with repugnance. As she spoke she blew smoke in his face and held his stare.

'I noticed you have popped in to see my little prize. Well, isn't she exactly as I said she was? *Zer* best of *zer* bunch, no?

'Suzanna Valles-Carrera did go backstage and look at all of the girls. She felt as excited as a child in a sweet shop.

They were all beautiful, they all had tattoos and she had a strong urge to take a couple of them there and then and start her torturously erotic game. For some reason unbeknown to her she had always been attracted to pale northern skin, most of the Jews had it, she reflected. The Spanish girls were beautiful, but the twin redheads and the Russian's natural blonde were her favourites. Charlotte was only wearing knickers and a flimsy gown provided by the make-up artist. Suzanna walked through the organised chaos and stood in front of her while she was pursing her lips at the bequest of the make-up girl, for the red wax from Max Factor.

'Hello, it's Charlotte isn't?' The tall German said, smiling kindly.'

'Yes! Hello...'

'I'm Suzanna Valles-Carrera, this is my show.'

'It seems like a really nice place...' Charlotte said as politely as possible, to the woman who the Count said was going to pay her one thousand five hundred pounds this evening.

'You are very pretty-pretty my dear...' Suzanna purred darkly, putting her long fingers under the thin gown at the neck and running the back of her hand along the seam over Charlotte's bust. 'You know I have some precious stones the same colour as your eyes, they are very unusual...'

'I take after my grandfather...' Charlotte explained, which is what she always said when people mentioned the Jade colour.

'I'm told you have a tattoo, may I see it?'

'Oh, ah, yes,' Charlotte said nervously, holding back the gown an inch or so near the top of her right leg. Suzanna put her fingers in between Charlotte's thighs and gently parted her legs, exposing the blue and gold tattoo of a leopard. She ran the long red nail of her index finger around the cat's body and stared at the young girl's crutch for what seemed like an eternity to Charlotte. She became embarrassed and closed the flimsy gown anxiously.

Suzanna snapped out of her evil abstraction saying mischievously, 'Oh that's very beautiful, I'm thinking of getting something like that for myself.'

Suzanna left the backstage area more than satisfied.

'So what did you think of my Charlotte, dear lady?' The Count asked excitedly. She didn't answer, turned her back and walked over to her husband. The Count stood glued to the spot.

Then he noticed the Colonel had spoken to one of his men. The policeman approached the old Russian. He put a hand in his pocket and offered the Count an envelope. Sergei's face lit up and he said in poor Spanish, 'Oh no! I don't take *zer* money you must give it to my servant in *zer* reception.'

The policeman looked down at the little man and threw the envelope on the floor. His face spat a thousand words and he walked off. Sergei quickly picked up the money embarrassed and insulted. Milyi started to struggle, which usually meant she needed the toilet. Sergei put her down and as expected she pee-peed against one of the German's tables. The Count went into the reception and gave Boris the second ten thousand dollars.

'Boris! Don't just sit there, you – you, Ukrainian monster.' The Count said with more than his usual contempt. 'Go down and get *zer* car, I can't wait to get away from these low class people, I'll be down in five minutes.' Sergei went back into the restaurant and picked up his dog. He glanced around the room and noticed the band had stopped playing and were taking a break. One of them looked old and sick, Sergei thought that he wouldn't cope with the usual German singing until three o'clock in the morning. He looked in Marco's direction, but the Italian ignored him and so he took the lift to the street. It was a relief to be outside, the Count saw himself as a respectable businessman, a sophisticated man of the world, who enjoyed the company of women, just as they enjoyed being with such a sophisticated and generous entrepreneur. When these trashy nouveaux riche dare to treat him with such little respect, he was tempted to remind them who his family was before the revolution.

It had started to rain gently, as finely as a translucent net curtain, and the wind pleated its edges. Sergei looked left and right but couldn't see his huge, leased Mercedes 600. He put Milyi on the pavement and they walked together for twenty yards along the road. After five minutes the Count said aloud to Milyi, 'Where is *zat* idiot?' He walked back to the lift area and spoke to the group of doorman.

'Have you seen my chauffeur? You know *zer* very tall, ugly one?

'Yes...' They replied in unison. 'He drove off like he was in a hurry about ten minutes ago!'

Sergei was incensed with rage; he found a taxi and rushed back into his empty house. He searched each room screaming for his servant. He soon discovered that all of Boris's clothes and passport were gone, as was Sergei's best Louis Vuitton suitcase. Milyi started barking and running around in circles.

'Shut up you little rat!' He screamed.

Chapter 45
Seventeen Minutes-Past-Eight

Christian Kautz arrived in a grey, rented Rolls Royce; the little chauffeur who came with it wore a grey suit with matching hair and skin. He could barely see over the steering wheel, yet jumped out urgently to open the door for the elderly millionaire. One of the regular doormen recognised him, pressed the lift button and smoothed him through. At the restaurant reception area some of the guards stopped him, until the Colonel walked over greeting the distinguished gentleman like an old friend, waving the guards to one side.

As they passed the scanner the alarm went off and a blue light flashed above the frame. Several guards rushed over to Christian and the Colonel in panic. Christian slowly put a hand inside his jacket and one of the men pointed a pistol at his head. He smiled calmly ignoring him and said to the Colonel with a smile, 'I'm sorry my friend I have been naughty, I hope you will forgive me?' The armed man froze. A static tension filled the air as people nearby started to look concerned. Christian pulled a long slim box from his inside pocket and walked towards Suzanna Valles-Carrera, kissing her on both cheeks. He put the unwrapped Cartier box in her hand, which she opened greedily to reveal a faultless diamond bracelet. The Colonel turned to the armed security man and said, 'Put that thing away you fool.' He then walked over to his wife and smiled.

'I see our dear friend has spoilt you again my dear.'

The Duchesse kissed the old millionaire and said, 'Yes, doesn't he always.'

'I must apologise for the over-enthusiastic security staff my dear friend.' The Colonel said ingratiatingly.

Christian smiled and spoke charmingly to a small group of people in several languages. After a few minutes he caught the manager's eye. Sebastian came running over companionably, with the respect given to a famously generous tipper. He elegantly floated his old client away from the maddening crowd to a good table at the quiet end

491

of the catwalk.

'Thank you Sebastian... I'm getting too old for these affairs.'

'Your hands are cold Señor, would you care for a brandy?'

'No, do you mind changing my champagne for a German beer, and I won't have the banquet, I'd rather have a cheese and tomato sandwich please, my doctor says no salt.'

'I understand Señor Kautz, I shall send one of our young girls over, she will keep an eye on you.'

'Oh by the way, I saw this in a shop some time ago and thought of you.' Christian said, passing him another one of his secretary's beautifully boxed surprises. When Sebastian ran into the toilet to open his gift, he was delighted to see a Rolex Oyster with tiny diamonds around the face.

'He has such good taste.' Sebastian said aloud to the mirror.

Chapter 46
Eight-Thirty

Sam and Phaedra looked at themselves in the wall of mirrors that graced their magnificent bedroom in the Ritz Hotel. The floor was strewn with Black-eyed beans and burst balloons. Sam looked at his wife and asked, 'Have you got the box from Madam Chong, darling?'

'Yes Sir! Have you had enough target practise?' She joked, looking at the beans.

'Keys to the Scylla, Bristol and Porsche?'

'Aye-aye Capitano.'

'Our invitations and passes?'

'Check.'

'Money for tips and bribes.'

'Check.'

'Machinegun and clip.' Sam asked with a huge smile.

'Great idea boss, one day they may make a miniature version for my make-up bag.'

'Well I suppose we are as ready as we can be. You will stay calm darling if we see any Nazi badges or flags, won't you.'

'Don't forget...' Phaedra said teasingly. 'I am a daughter of Electra, Greek is my name and revenge is my game.'

'I know who you are my darling. Tell me, this evening, are you doing Richard Strauss's version of your Goddess or Eugene O'Neill's version?'

'Now you're showing off, I'm just a peasant Greek girl from a tiny village.'

'So you'll be on your best behaviour?'

'Aren't I always?'

'No, not usually...'

'What's that behind your lapel.' Phaedra asked seriously.

'Just a badge...'

'Listen Sam, I don't care if some stupid fascist wants to wear a badge to make his manhood feel bigger, but

493

I'm not letting you wear one…'

'But darling…'

'I don't care if it's part of the cover, you're not wearing it!'

'Alright, shall I flip it over so that you can look at it?'

'No! I don't want to look at it, I just want you to take it off and throw it out of the window…'

'Bill, my childhood friend from Somerleyton Manor, would be very disappointed, if I threw it away.'

'Was he a fascist?'

'No.' Sam said, flipping over his lapel. He ran the local boy Scouts!'

'It took Phaedra a few seconds to recover from her annoyance to realise that Sam was teasing her, she looked closely at her husband's badge that he had hidden behind his lapel and read:

> Boy Scouts
> Be Prepared
> Kent division

'You sneaky, horrible, trickster…'

Sam pushed her on the bed and kissed her hard on the mouth, she looked up at him and said, 'You did that on purpose to relax me, didn't you?'

'Well we mustn't take life too seriously, these stupid badges are no more real than a clown's sad painted mouth.'

'Talking about a painted mouth, we both need to redo ours.' Phaedra wiped Sam's face and redid her lipstick, and they skipped down the stairs as delighted as kids to their car, which José had had brought to the front. After fifteen minutes, they slowed to see the security crowd and other guests arriving in front of the tower.

Signóre Ricardo Colaneri and his wife Paola Colaneri had driven towards the port. When they arrived at bustling Plaza Francesc Macià, Phaedra looked up shocked.

'Sam look at that monster, it must be four stories high and thirty feet across!'

'I think that's what you call egotistical, I can't

imagine any British politicians putting a poster of themselves of that size in the centre of Trafalgar Square, but our friend Franco, likes to show off.'

Franco's enormous image in his military uniform looked down at the passing cars unworried by any feelings of narcissistic pride. He was celebrating twenty-five-years of dictatorship over Spain and he wanted the population to remember his image. Phaedra looked back at the sky-scraping figure and said:

'I don't understand why the Americans are supporting him…'

'They don't really, although they are obsessed with Communism, they think the extreme Right is better than the extreme Left, besides Coca Cola are opening a factory here next year, you know how Americans think, if people drink cola they can't be that bad!' Sam laughed.

The couple drove through the hive of humming, black and yellow taxis and finally pulled up in their Bristol at the front of the restaurant tower. The air was ignited by a nervous tension evaporating from the tense security staff.

One of the doormen from *El Restaurante La Torre d'Alta Mar,* walked over with a thick scarf around his neck, and an umbrella for the guests. He saluted the image of wealth and possible a big tip. Sam left the engine running. After his friend removed a barrier, the black suit parked the car near the lift door. Sam gave the man a roll of Pesetas and said that he would keep the keys, as he wasn't staying long. At both ends of the lift shaft they were searched and Sam had to remove his car-keys from his jacket pocket to get through the scanner. The Spanish policeman looked casually at Phaedra's little Chinese box, passed it through the scanner silently and waved them through.

On the restaurant side of the security barrier another a Spanish policeman looked at their invitation and steered them towards the meet and greet line.

'Signóre and Signóra Colaneri, how kind of you to come to my little party…' Suzanna Valles-Carrera said ingratiatingly in shaky Italian.

'Your reputation precedes you.' Phaedra said, a little too dangerously for Sam's liking.

'Have you met my husband, Colonel José Valles-Carrera?' Suzanna asked rhetorically in Castilian Spanish.

Sam decided to reply to all of the questions from now on, his Spanish was near perfect, Phaedra's a little rusty. He knew that these people were smart and would soon pick up on his wife's sarcasm.

'It's a great pleasure to meet you both, we are looking forward to the show and I'm hoping to buy a few things in the auction.'

Suzanna turned to the disabled man next to her and said, 'This is our business partner and one of your own countrymen, have you ever met?'

'No I haven't had the pleasure, good evening,' Sam said turning to Italian.

Marco Sotori held out his good left hand unsteadily, which Sam quickly responded to by using *his* left hand. Phaedra's face went white when she realised who he was. Marco recognised her look of shock and disgust, it was the reaction he usually received since he'd left the Parisian hospital. Although when Phaedra mumbled a few niceties he noticed another reaction in her face, which he hadn't seen before: was it guilt?

'Your accent sounds unfamiliar to me, where in Italy were you born, Signóre?' Marco asked suspiciously.

'I was born in Valai, Switzerland, near the Gondo Valley, to Italian parents...' Sam said confidently in the language of his stepbrother Paul. 'My wife is Greek and we have travelled extensively, but wherever I go I always feel Italian.' Sam used his hands with Italian custom, smiled and turned, to get away as quickly as possible; unfortunately Marco had other ideas.

'I have some relatives in the Canton de Valai, the Rosino family, do you know them?' Marco asked, now searching Sam's face with his one eye, for any indication of nervousness. Sam turned back reluctantly and smiled as confidently as he could, noticing that the Colonel had now steered away from a conversation with some Germans and started to listen to Marco's questions.

'I'm sorry I don't. As I said we've travelled so much, I haven't spent much time in my Canton.' Sam gave a curt bow. 'Have a nice evening Signóri. Sam said to Marco and the Colonel, taking Phaedra's hand.

Marco dragged his body over to the Colonel and the Duchesse saying: 'I don't trust them. Her Italian is not very good…'

'She said that she's Greek.' The Colonel answered.

'Yes, but living with an Italian, she should speak better than that.

Although the main doubt is *his* accent, it's from a low class family and not one hundred per cent Italian; he speaks like a lot of cheap labour, which came in from other countries before the war.

They work all their lives in Italy, but they have some other languages or another mother tongue that hovers under the surface. I swear he's not Italian and definitely not Italian aristocracy.' Marco declared defiantly.

The Colonel, who was a naturally suspicious person, called the policeman checking the invitations over.

'Give me the Italian's invitation.'

The former head of the House of Screams had become an expert at spotting a fake identity. He decided to look closer at these so-called millionaires.

'Captain,' He whispered in Catalan. 'Take two men and go over and ask that Italian couple if they would kindly have a drink with us over here. Be very polite, but don't take no for an answer.'

Sam and Phaedra found their seat with the help of Joana from the Gaudí Hotel.

'Oh dear Sam, I didn't recognise him, how did he survive the crash and the fire?'

'Well, he looks as though he didn't survive very well, if I hadn't heard his name, I don't think I would have recognised him, even though we did a few days of surveillance on all three of them in Paris.'

'Why did he seem suspicious about your accent, I thought your Italian was perfect, when we go to Italy they think you're Italian.'

'The problem is we're pretending to be wealthy Italians, old money. I learnt Italian in the circus when I was a child, mostly from my stepbrother. Circus people are working class, they speak slang; I've tried to speak with a posher accent, but real Italians with northern accents have a different way of speaking…'

'So do…'

'Oops! Here comes trouble…'

'Señor, Señora…' The policeman said in Spanish. 'The Colonel would like to invite you both for a drink, please come this way.'

They both stood up, hiding their reluctance and followed the policeman; his two colleagues fell in behind them. Sam quickly retraced his steps from the pavement up to the tower restaurant; he counted all of the secret police, the Mafia boys, the uniformed cops and even the doormen. Without an awful lot of ammunition and a few trained friends, it would be very difficult to get out of the place alive. Phaedra looked at her husband, trying to say something telepathically.

'Do you need the loo darling?' She asked, reminding Sam that two days previously, he'd put a pistol wrapped in a plastic bag in the toilet cistern.

'Signóre and 'Signóra Colaneri, please come and have a proper drink with us, the non-vintage champagne is not so good this year; try this nineteen-fifty-five Dom Pérignon, it's delicious!' The Colonel said with Sebastian pouring at his side.

Sam and Phaedra smiled and drank, noticing that Marco had called in two of his thugs, who leaned menacingly against the kitchen wall in the centre of the room six feet away. Marco slid over as slippery as a snail and started his interrogation.

'So Signóre you were born in Graubünden?'

'No that's quite a long way from my home…' Sam said having done his homework. 'We lived near the Simplon Pass, actually in the centre of Sion, next to the Château de Valére.' Sam continued patiently. Realising they were now surrounded by two Italian Mafia soldiers, three Spanish secret police from the Colonel's own protection force and about a hundred Nazi's in dinner jackets, who were mostly former soldiers. The air had a sinister taste, he glanced at Phaedra, who as usual looked unafraid, but she was edgy.

She changed her position, because she'd realised as Sam had that the best person to attack was Marco. He would be slow and could be disarmed easily. With his gun, if he had one, they might make the toilets without being shot. Then they could get the second gun. Sam was still wondering how they would get out of the toilets and down the stairs. Suddenly, the group turned around to see an elderly man approach waving his arms extravagantly.

'Ricardo Colaneri - my dear friend and the beautiful Paola, how wonderful to see you both again...' Christian Kautz said, kissing Phaedra on both cheeks, and shaking Sam's hand with enough enthusiasm to mix a cocktail.

The Duchesse and the Colonel stepped closer to the three friends who were reuniting so gregariously.

'You know these beautiful people Christian?' The Colonel asked, half looking at Marco.

'Of course, all of high society on the Swiss - Italian border know Ricardo and Paola. The wonderful parties they give are the talk of every gossip column in Switzerland; may I take them away from you? We have so much catching up to do...'

He didn't wait for an answer and ushered the Italian millionaires back to their table. The Duchesse turned to Marco and said spitefully, 'Why don't you take your seat at the table and relax Marco? You nearly ruined my evening and lost me two good clients.'

Christian sat opposite Sam and Phaedra at their table, smiled and spoke softly:

'When Fyodor asked me to come down here and have a look at these naughty people, he said you could be a good friend to have on my side! I didn't want to lose you in the first half an hour!'

'How is the old chess player?' Sam asked with a relieved grin.

'Still difficult to beat, although he did get me a wonderful French chef, so now I have to let him win for the next six months!' Christian's face quickly turned dark. 'Did you manage to bring in any defences?'

'No.' Sam said, not mentioning the gun he left in the toilet on Thursday night.

'Then you had better take this…' He said holding a small pistol under the tablecloth. 'I'm not brave enough to use these things anymore…'

'How did you get it through the security?' Sam asked admiringly.

'I believe your lovely wife is Greek…' He answered, taking Phaedra's hand confidently. 'Well I used a Trojan Horse, or rather a Trojan diamond bracelet.' He smiled at his own joke and got up, Sam slid the small revolver into his jacket pocket. Christian walked over to the Colonel and his wife; Marco stood a few feet away talking to Raffaello and the American priest about their new adoption business.

'My dear Christian, Marco is still unsure of your Italian friends, have you known them long?' Colonel José Valles-Carrera asked.

'Yes, I have known the gentleman's reputation for over twenty years.'

Marco thinks they seemed rather - how shall I say this delicately…'

'You mean they are low class Italians? Is that it Marco?' The old Swiss called over to the disabled Italian.

'You see…' Marco said to the Colonel, having difficulty looking around.

'Listen, his family from two previous generations were trash, they spoke Romansh. The grandparents originally came over to Switzerland from Provence. They were farmers, selling olives. Then his parents started selling Absinthe. It was illegal in those days and they made a fortune. You would have liked them Duchesse: rich, sophisticated and completely unscrupulous.' They all laughed. As usual Christian could say anything to anyone and get away with it.

'You will forgive me if I leave early, I'll soon be past my bedtime.' He joked with a broad smile.

'But Christian, I was hoping that you would buy some of my unique articles from bygone days…' Suzanna purred, avariciously thinking of her nefarious acquisitions.

'My dear Duchesse, if I bought a new tiepin, I would need to buy another house,'

500

'I thought you had enough houses and space to accommodate the Louvre.' She smiled. Yet her white powered face changed quickly into a frightening mask. Christian could imagine the fear she was capable of infusing in others. She touched his arm, and spoke seriously in a low voice, keeping her head close to his, her German accent now heavily cloaking each word. 'I have some rare diamonds and paintings, like Die Windsbraut by Kokoschka and numerous trouvailles that you would love, extraordinary pieces that many thought were lost.'

Christian had heard that the so-called Socialist Party had confiscated this painting in nineteen thirty-seven. For an awful moment he could imagine a Nazi *sturmabteilung* division removing family heirlooms from people's homes, annihilating any foolish resistance.

'It sounds wonderful Suzanna, but somehow I must resist your charms this time, my little Freda would be upset if I didn't consult her.' He paused for the briefest of moments and added, 'She's building a collection from that Russian fellow, Marc Chagall, she loves all of those bright colours...' Christian clicked his heels together and gave a curt bow that ended any further conversation, with more finality than mere words could achieve.

He couldn't resist the subtle gibe about one of the world's most talented Jewish artist.

Christian wore a gold eagle badge on his lapel; it looked like the Nazi version though it didn't have the telltale swastika. Instead, it had a precious Sil-Sinter opal in the centre. These rare opals were mined in Santa Fiora in Tuscany. Christian's opal was a very rare version, given to him by General Fyodor Poluostrovich and was connected to a miniature camera in his jacket lining. He didn't want to risk helping his old friend at this high-security event; however, Fyodor had managed to get Henry de Hartingh away from the French embassy in Moscow. As usual, Christian reflected; Fyodor always knew the right button to press.

The vain chef wasn't interested in money or sex, and the KGB couldn't find any skeletons in his closet. Finally Fyodor used his secret weapon, sending his faithful secretary, Alena Arzamasskaia to discover what this vain master of the kitchen really wanted. His dream turned out to be *Les étoiles de bonne table*, also known as Three Michelin Stars. Therefore, Christian walked around silently snapping everyone he thought the KGB would like to see.

Chapter 47
Ten-Thirty-Five

The food wasn't very good and Phaedra hated sitting with the surrounding medals and badges. She had a Generalfeldmarschall on her left with an Iron Cross glued to his Adam's apple, a Generaloberst next to him and a Reichsführer at the end. Phaedra turned to Sam saying:

'You know the worst part for me is I've started to remember the language and they all sound like a load of old age pensioners at a tea party.'

'They are!' Sam said smiling.

When the meal was finished the lights went down and the five-piece band went off for a break. A handsome young Spanish man climbed up next to the Duchesse's top table, turned the lights down low over the audience and played a trendy mix of French, English and Spanish music. The one thing that all of the tracks had in common, was that the background beat throbbed at the pace of a long-legged model walking. Lights came on behind the opaque screen at the back of the catwalk and the audience could see the sexy silhouettes of the models behind it. A few of the Germans and Italians gave wolf whistles.

When the show started, the catwalk was illuminated so that the girls appeared to float on a cloud above the darkened room. The first two models were brunette beauties from Spain; they wore long black dresses and were covered in dramatic jewellery on almost every part of their bodies. As they stopped to pose in front of the spotlights at the end of the catwalk, the Duchesse spoke into a microphone in what Phaedra thought was a surprisingly sexy voice, explaining the jewellery on sale. As the girls circled the stage like native Indians around a campfire to the rhythm of the music, the audience clapped excitedly. Some of the women were making notes, so that their husbands could 'surprise' them later with a gift from their lists.

'What do you think of our hostess?' Sam asked his wife. 'She reminds me of Cruella de Vil. I thought she looked fairly attractive in the photos we had on file, much better than her days as Ilsa Klup. However, despite the overall expensive style from the distance, when you're close to her she does have an ersatz and evil aura.'

The next two models were the twins, their long red hair cascading loosely over their shoulders; they wore matching navy evening dresses and some beautiful jewellery using vibrant precious stones. Their Scottish looks were a perfect backdrop for the amethyst, aquamarine, peridot, turquoise, topaz and emerald rocks that sat in elaborate gold settings. Phaedra turned to Sam saying: 'I know that I shouldn't, but I'm rather enjoying the show.'

'Well you have always had a passion for jewellery.' Sam said smiling broadly, camouflaging his nervousness for the job ahead. The next group of five girls trotted out as impeccable as dressage ponies and showed off a fabulous range of evening dresses, again they were covered in gold jewellery. The audience was getting quite excited by now, as was Suzanna. She had gauged that the orders would add considerably to her growing fortune. The models finally left the stage and the lights went even lower.

'Damen und Herren! Señoras y Señores! Ladies and Gentlemen! Signori e Signore!' Suzanna Valles-Carrera said in mellow tones. 'Now for the highlight of the fashion show and the beginning of our unique auction, our last model will be wearing Givenchy's famous Duchesse gown in black crepe. Hubert has only made two of these magnificent creations: the original one here this evening was for me. And the second, with my permission, for Audrey Hepburn, which she wore in the film, Breakfast at Tiffany's.'

The audience clapped politely as the Nazi smiled delightedly by her own self-indulgence. 'The model will also be wearing just one, unique piece of jewellery.' Suzanna paused for effect. 'Tonight, I have the enormous pleasure, to offer you a glimpse and if you have a little money...' The millionaire audience chuckled. 'The ownership of the rarest diamond creation the world has ever seen.' Again she paused and looked around at the most unimpressionable wealthy audience in Europe. The musicians filed back onto their little podium, pulled out a new piece of sheet music, and waited for Suzanna Valles-

Carrera to give them their cue. Sam looked over at the performers casually and stared at the violinist, who slipped his red violin case under his seat. Sam thought that the old man was wearing a disguise, as his hair and moustache looked too dark for his skin, but his attention was soon taken away from this distraction as the Duchesse started her speech again.

'This evening, I present to you, for the first time since nineteen forty-eight, when it mysteriously disappeared in India. The original, House of Cartier, Patiala Necklace,' several people swooned. 'It's adorned with two-thousand-nine-hundred and thirty diamonds. Including at its centre, the famously lost Maharaja's, four-hundred and twenty-eight-carat, De Beers diamond!'

The five-piece orchestra broke into the dramatic piece by Carl Orff, called O Fortuna, from Carmina Burana, the striding rhythm being perfect for a dramatic entrance. The verisimilitude of Moshe's performance was enthralling. On either side of the podium two metal cylinders shot red flames and fireworks into the air. The opaque screen disappeared in the haze as smoke filled the stage. The spectators around the catwalk leaned forward in excited anticipation. All of the kitchen staff came running out. Sebastian rushed in from the reception area; even the blasé security guards left their posts and stood in amazement. The smoke cleared and a tall, stunning blonde model stood alone, unmoving in the centre of the stage. A single spotlight pieced the darkness and haloed the girl's porcelain skin. Her tall slim body made even more statuesque by the high chignon, her perfect form wrapped in the famous clinging black dress. The alabaster stature nonchalantly held the Duchesse's long cigarette holder in her left hand; a king-size Rothman releasing its silky plume. Ilsa Klup stared obsessed at her creation, and remembered her youth; when she looked at the Aryan beauty she liked to think she saw a young reincarnation of herself. The whole audience was star-struck by the enormous explosion of sparkling diamonds around the young girl's neck: mimicking the tiny spotlights of the city seen through the surrounding windows. Everyone stood up; many with their mouths open in stunned silence. One person started to clap. Then another, suddenly the entire restaurant were on their feet, applauding and cheering, and some screaming as though Charlotte was a film star. She walked slowly along the catwalk keeping in character, like the Columbia Pictures film studio's 'Lady in a Toga'.

Her head high and her eyes looking straight ahead, holding the long cigarette holder like the icon's torch, until she reached the end of the raised floor. The audience were in shock and awe at the incredible sight. Two members of the posh crowd were suffering even more shock than the rest of the rich diners.

Sam and Phaedra stared speechless at their granddaughter. Not only because Charlotte looked like Hollywood's idea of a princess. Not only because she was in Barcelona and standing in front of them; but because they were about to assassinate the evil woman, who had just walked over and was holding her almost lovingly, like another one of her precious possessions.

Sam tried to clear his mind. *'What was Charlotte doing here? What did the evil Ilsa Klup intend to do with her? Did anyone know her connection with him and his business? Is it all just a coincidence? Is she just doing a modelling job? That music, what's so strange about that music? Think-think! He screamed at himself. That violin player, he's so much better than the others, like a concert violinist. Marco Sotori is in the same room and he should be dead.'*

'Sam-Sam…' Phaedra said.

'What darling!' He said irritably.

'Sam, she's beautiful, magnificent, look at your granddaughter, I've never seen her like this…'

'The note! Fyodor's note, I now understand it!' Sam explained, grabbing Phaedra's shoulders violently. Phaedra looked confused for a moment. She was so delighted by her granddaughter's performance; she had almost forgotten why they were there. The noise around them was deafening as the security people allowed some of the richest of the rich, to climb up on the stage and look closely at the famous Patiala Necklace.

'Phaedra listen to me,' He shouted over the noise, squeezing her arms. 'Mad Moshe is here, in this room! I thought I noticed the red violin case earlier, but it's been so long, I forgot what he looked like. Now I understand. Christian Kautz observing for the KGB - Ilsa Klup - the awful art gallery in their apartment with the tortured young girls...'

'You didn't tell me about that!'

'I know, it was too awful – I felt so sad for them, it made me feel sick...'

'Sam stop! You're hurting me and speaking erratically, it's not like you, I've never seen you so tense before...' Phaedra gasped in a tremulous voice.

'I know, its because I've always put my own life at risk and sometimes even yours, but now Charlotte's life is in danger...'

'What shall we do?'

'Phaedra. Listen to me carefully...' he said lucidly; *"There is a Reaper whose name is Death,"* That means there's an assassin here.'

'Yes, you got that the first day.' Phaedra said concentrating.

'"*And, with his sickle keen,*" That means he's very good at his job, one of the top people in the business. "*He reaps the bearded grain at a breath,*" I think this suggests that the whole lot is destroyed in one stoke, perhaps an explosion...' And then I remembered the name of the poem; it's called 'The Reaper and the Flowers'.

'Sam for God's sake, tell me what's going on!' Phaedra pleaded.

'The last line is; "*And the flowers that grow between.*" The flowers represent innocent people; I've just seen the assassin over there. His name is Moshe; he's a musician and an explosives expert, the best in the world. I'm sure that our granddaughter is in danger of being abducted and killed, by that evil Nazi, so that she can add Charlotte to her deadly art gallery, and I think the rest of us are going to blown to hell in the next few minutes, by Moshe Liberman!'

Suddenly Phaedra realised that if her husband, the

cool professional had become so fearful, it wasn't just an existential anxiety, their granddaughter's life was at risk; all their lives.

'What do you want me to do?' She screamed over the clamour of the excited room. Sam looked around. Ilsa Klup had her arm around Charlotte's waist and was steering her along the catwalk towards backstage. 'Follow me!' Sam shouted. 'And bring the Chinese box.' They pushed and shoved past the excited throng of people and packed chairs, and found the gap in the black curtain that shielded off the temporary changing room. The whole place was buzzing with all the models congratulating Charlotte, the star of the show. The hairdressers, make-up artists and dressers, were swarming around the models as persistently as hungry mosquitoes, trying to jump on the girls and ready them for their next role of modelling some of the pieces for the auction. Charlotte was leaning against the opaque glass smoking. Phaedra called out her name, but she couldn't hear over the cacophony. Then Sam jumped up and wrapped his arms around her.

'Granddaddy!' Charlotte screamed completely stunned. 'What are you doing here?'

Phaedra came up the other side and kissed her granddaughter several times on both cheeks. 'You were magnificent my darling – I'm so proud of you...'

'Oh Ya-Ya, I've got something to tell you, I've been so naughty, you may never forgive me...' Charlotte started to cry and tell her story of the crashed Mini.

On the other side of the opaque glass wall the catwalk had cleared and the spotlights were turned off. Smoke and a few small flames still billowed on either side of the screen giving an eerie light.

Marco Sotori stood staring in a trance at the shadows of Sam and Phaedra against the glass.

His mind told him he had déjà vu. His head started spinning. He remembered his regular nightmare of lying on the ground in Paris, looking under his crashed car. At the end of the road were the assassins. The tall shadow of a man on the right, the vague image of a blonde woman on the left, he fired his gun through the flames and smoke...

'That's them!' He yelled aloud. 'That's them!' Marco turned his broken body and looked for one of his men. 'Raffaello, come here...'

'What's wrong Marco? You look like you've seen a ghost'

'I've seen two. I've found the people who killed your grandfather...'

'What here?' He said in disbelief.

'Yes, they are with the girl we've bought from the old Russian, behind that screen. Quickly go back stage and get a good look at them. Go!'

Raffaello pushed pass the noisy crowd, pulled the black curtain to one side and saw Charlotte with the older Italian man and blonde woman he'd seen Marco talking with earlier. He rushed back and spoke to the disabled man.

'It's the Italians you were talking to. They seem to be rushing the girl out of the fancy fashion show clothes'. Raffaello explained.

'I knew those two were fakes...'

'They look old, we can overpower them before they leave.'

'Leaving! Raffaello listen to me, have we got any machineguns with us?'

'No, your friend the Colonel wouldn't let our people bring any arms, they said they had it covered.'

'Listen to me, these two are professional, I need a substantial weapon.'

'It's okay, I'll get Giovanni and we'll just grab them, I don't know, I'll get a knife from the kitchen and stab them.'

'That's no good, first of all they are specialists and may be armed...'

'How could they get arms past the scanner?'

'Who knows, but they were brave coming in here, so they might have some back-up.'

'I have my Grandfather's old shotgun in the car, I think there's a box of shells as well.' Raffaello said casually.

'Perfect irony...' Marco said smirking. 'Angelo would have liked that, go and get it. Fast - move!'

Raffaello rushed to the lift, he saw Giovanni

chatting up three local Spanish girls working as waitresses; they were all having a cigarette break. 'Hey Giovanni, we've got some work to do, go and see Marco.' Giovanni walked away from the girls reluctantly; he thought that two of them might sleep with him after they'd finished work. The third one seemed to be depressed, but 'Hey' He thought, two out of three's not bad.

Sam turned to Phaedra and whispered.

'Listen my love, you get Charlotte out of here as quickly as possible, we may only have a few minutes.

I'm going to talk to the manager and try to convince him to empty the restaurant. Now that I've put everything together in my mind, I'm sure that Moshe is here for Ilsa Klup and the way he works, there will be nothing left of this place.'

'Okay darling, I'll take the Porsche and you take the Bristol, I'll see you back at the hotel…'

'No Phaedra, if they're on to us it will be too dangerous, go to the Scylla, I'll meet you there, if I'm being followed at least you will have the power to help me.'

Sam kissed Phaedra passionately and stared into her eyes concerned, Charlotte looked embarrassed and giggled.

'Take Christian's gun…' He whispered in her ear, putting the tiny pistol in her hand.

'No darling, I have the Lugar in the Porsche, you keep it.'

'I'm worried about you getting to the car, someone may try to stop you leaving, anyway I've got the gun in the toilet.' He turned to his granddaughter.

'Charlotte, listen to me carefully, we all need to leave immediately, so please do as your grandmother tells you, I'll see you later at the boat.'

Raffaello walked up to Marco and looked exhausted.

'What happened to you? And where's the gun?' Marco asked.

'I couldn't get it past the lift security guys, but there was no one on the stairs, so I walked up, the gun is hidden just behind the emergency stairs going down to the cable car.'

'Raffaello, I want you two to get the young girl and take her to the Castell de Plegamans. When I've finished with the assassin. I'll meet you at my boat, then we can get this other blonde woman and your grandfather will have been avenged. Finally I shall be happy.'

'Where's Giovanni?' Raffaello asked.

'He's keeping an eye on the girl, listen, when I find the guy from Paris, tell a couple of the men to make sure I'm not disturbed: I've dreamt of this moment for months.'

'Don't you want us to help you?'

'No, just make sure I'm alone with him, this is *my* vendetta.'

Sam rushed along the outside edge of the restaurant and ran into the toilet. He closed and locked the third cabin door, stood on the toilet, opening the lid of the ornate cistern. He put his hand in the cold water but the gun was gone. Sam peaked through the door and looked around.

Third Toilet from the right, he remembered. He looked in the first, second and fourth. Someone had removed his gun. Well the Colonel's security team must be good, Sam thought.

He rushed out to see if the orchestra was still playing. He could see Moshe; his appearance was funereal, barely standing up. Suddenly Moshe looked directly at Sam, eye to eye across the room; slowly he opened his oversized evening jacket. Sam saw the hilt of his own gun from the toilet tucked into Moshe's belt.

Of course, he reasoned, Moshe was from the old school, he had more than likely been in the city for weeks, Sam was so wrapped up in his own plan he had missed him, lurking in the shadows of the city. He looked around the room desperately, where would Moshe put a large amount of explosives. With his reputation they could be as big as a coffin. The catwalk. Sam hurried back to the centre of the restaurant; dived onto the floor and lifted the silky fabric that camouflaged the unsightly wooden supports. The floor was clean and the whole area completely empty. Sam crawled a few feet to ensure he could see both ends. Nothing. He popped his head out and an elderly man jumped up from his seat with surprise.

511

'Christian! Listen to me.' Sam explained. 'This whole place is about to blow up! Get out as fast as you can!'

The elderly man hesitated. 'What are you going to do?'

'Don't worry about me, I've told my wife to get my granddaughter out, now I've got to find the explosives.'

'I used to be an engineer, if I wanted to blow this place up I would put the device downstairs in the Teleférico, somewhere near the roof, which is directly under this floor, preferably with some kind of heavy metal underneath, to force the blast upwards.'

Sam thought for a moment and said: 'Thanks Christian, you're right, now get out fast.' He ran towards the reception and saw the restaurant manager.

'Sebastian, listen to me, there's a bomb in the restaurant, get all of the guests out as fast as you can!'

'I don't understand Señor, how do you know?'

'There's no time to argue, your life is in danger, get everyone out!'

Sam rushed down the emergency stairs into the Teleférico station. The whole place was quiet and in darkness. He squinted his eyes to adjust to the low light. The city of Barcelona looked magnificent, sparkling seventy-eight metres below.

Upstairs Sebastian looked for the Colonel; he was standing on the edge of the auction, his secret police staring protectively at the diamond necklace on its black velvet bust.

'Señor Colonel, excuse me, ah, the rich Italian, Señor Colaneri, he told me there was a bomb here in the restaurant and said we should all run outside.'

The Colonel smiled and Sebastian looked confused by his passive reaction.

'I have just heard from my business partner Marco Sotori. He has discovered that the man's a fake and planning some kind of conspiracy. We're all guarding the necklace and the other valuables as he may have accomplices, I've telephoned for some more men.'

'But Sir, he seemed very nice and...'

'You mean he gave you an unusually large tip

Sebastian, that's why you think he's nice. Huh?'

'Yes Sir.' Sebastian said, feeling foolish that the jewel thief had fooled him.

The Colonel looked back possessively at the incunabulum treasures. On the other side of the circular room, Phaedra had lost Charlotte and was frantically running around searching for her. Then she saw Lucila Fernandez-Gonzalez.

'Lucila! I can't believe that I found Charlotte here, now I've found you!'

'Hello Phaedra, I live here in Barcelona and do a bit of modelling, you know, a girl has to live...'

'Lucila, listen to me, have you seen Charlotte in the last few minutes, I just went to get my bag and she's disappeared.'

'No sorry Phaedra, I don't know where she is...'

'Lucila, I know this sounds crazy, but you must get out of here now, there's a bomb in the restaurant, please hurry, that's why I'm looking for Charlotte.'

'A bomb, what do you mean?'

'Look, ah, we have a friend here - he's with the police, and, well, we saw him a few minutes ago, and he told us that they've just had a call, and well, the place, the place...' Phaedra grabbed the young girl's arm: 'For God's sake Lucila, just do as I've told you, the dam place is going to blow up!' She screamed with tears in her eyes.

Lucila didn't believe the grandmother's words, she thought she just wanted to ruin her granddaughter's evening, but she did believe the emotion. She grabbed her bag and made for the reception. After a few feet she turned back saying: 'Phaedra, I lied to you; Charlotte's with Suzanna Valles-Carrera and the Colonel, she wanted to get her money before she left.' Phaedra ran around the circular restaurant looking for her granddaughter. She saw the Colonel and his wife, although Charlotte wasn't with them. The Greek grandmother started to panic.

Sam looked across the ceiling of the cable car station in the darkness. A cold wind blew violently through the open void that led to the next tower. He went towards the back wall and searched for a light switch, but was nervous. Moshe's reputation was fierce; the light switch could be booby-trapped.

Then all of the lights came on and Sam spun around. Marco stood against the door twenty feet away. He closed the heavy metal door and held with some difficulty, the Neumann Brothers, double barrelled, twelve-gauge shotgun, from Belgium. Both of those barrels were staring at Sam's head. Sam calculated that he might be able to dive on the floor, put his right hand in his jacket pocket, pull-out the tiny Fabrique Nationale, Baby browning pistol Christian gave him, aim and shoot Marco before he could pull the twin triggers. Then he remembered he had given the gun to Phaedra. He did have the Chinese box swelling his jacket pocket, although he would be dead before he could open it.

So he said. 'What do you want? I don't have any money.'

'Listen to me old man; you know those old gangster movies where they have a long conversation before one of them gets killed? This isn't going to work like that with me.

Marco pulled both triggers and the massive old gun exploded in his one good hand, the force pushed the barrels up in the air and Marco stumbled back against the door. Sam felt the whoosh of the massive shells pass inches over the top of his head. The energy and his natural reaction pitched him onto the floor. Marco killed the lights to give himself a chance to reload, and so Sam jumped up and ran behind the cable car. His sight started to adjust to the darkness, there was a white triangle near the door, and he thought it could be Marco's shirt. Sam knew it would take Marco several seconds to empty both barrels, reload, close the hilt and re-aim with his one good arm. If he was close enough, after he fired, he could rush the disabled Italian. However, if he were too close that antique monster would blow a hole the size of a medicine ball straight through him. He searched the ceiling and then he saw it. Just above the huge yellow wheel with the cable around it, was a black holdall, a tiny chrome aerial poked out of the top and caught the light.

Sam guessed that it was a radio-activated detonator. Would Moshe have been able to smuggle some kind of remote control pass the security team? Maybe: the crafty old man was very good at this, he thought.

Bang! Crash! Crack! Smash!

Sam ducked; the entire rear, glass side of the cabin shattered into a thousand pieces. Sam considered that if Marco has enough bullets, he could destroy this cabin and he would be standing there with nothing in front of him except the night air. He realised Marco would have trouble pointing the huge gun upwards and so he decided to make a run for the metal ladder against the wall, to try and get the bag of explosives. He just hoped that Phaedra had managed to get herself and Charlotte away from the tower and onto their boat, as he realised that in the next few minutes, he was going to be killed by Marco's huge gun or the explosives.

Chapter 48
Eleven-Fifteen

Phaedra looked everywhere for Charlotte and started to wonder if she had left the restaurant. Maybe she was waiting downstairs? She asked herself, and then she heard the scream. Raffaello and Giovanni were dragging the model through the restaurant's closing lift door. Phaedra looked in all directions for Sam, yet couldn't see him. She rushed through the reception area and found the stairs; on the next floor down she saw the heavy metal entrance door for the cable car. Opposite, there was another lift to the pavement; unfortunately it was also on its way down. The acrophobic Greek looked over the edge of the metal stairs and felt sick, the icy wind cut through her flimsy dress. She saw the Italian's fat, black, dung beetle sitting in front of the restaurant lift door on the street, nearly eighty metres below.

Phaedra hurled herself down the metal fire-stairs and twisted her ankle, falling on the first landing in agony. She grabbed her swelling foot and dabbed her bleeding knee. Then there was a second scream. She looked over the edge again and saw Charlotte, being dragged from the lift into the Cadillac. The Greek grandmother clenched her teeth, threw off her stilettos and ran down the freezing steps in her bare feet; soon finding tap-dancer's rhythm. When she was nearly at the bottom she heard a blast from above. She stopped and looked up. It sounded like a double-barrelled shotgun. She thought; Sam would never forgive me if anything happens to Charlotte and she continued her rush down the stairs. By the time she hit the pavement, the black American icon was shrinking into an inkblot at the end of the road. She sprinted for her car. A phalanx of policemen, chauffeurs and doormen looked at the bruised and bleeding woman in the thin cocktail dress without shoes. Some giggled at another maltreated wife leaving a party early. Adrenalin wiped out any pain or cold; yet her hands trembled, she fumbled with the keys until she heard Sam's voice in her head. 'Stay calm, act with rhythm, not haste'.

Once in the bucket seat, she turned the key and the Porsche screamed its obedience. Within seconds the roaring monster was on its rubber feet and leaping from the kerb. The rev-counter stayed blood red, the dials all leaned to the right and she now glanced at the script on the illuminated dial. 145 MPH.

The coast road was empty. Then in the distance a drunk swayed from the kerb on her right, waving his arms for her to stop. Phaedra pushed hard on the horn and the accelerator. No one was worth Charlotte's life. Then her conscience asked: 'Not even Sam's?' Phaedra wondered if the shotgun was used against him. She shook her head releasing the horrible thought. He'd survived a dangerous life since he was a child, he'll be all right – she hoped. The young tramp saw the Porsche's headlights and the five blazing spotlights attached to a chrome bar on the bonnet. For a moment, he thought it was a heavenly radiance.

He waved his arms again defiantly, tourists always stopped: 'Didn't they?'

However, when the screaming monster accelerated towards him, he suddenly became more sober than he'd been for the last fifteen years and dived behind the row of parked cars. A hurricane of dust and exhaust fumes blew dead leaves in his frozen face.

The Caddie grew in front of Phaedra and she braked hard. To stop the heavyweight car would be easy, when he turns to the left, she could smash into the left rear wing and the car would go into a spin, the other wing for a right turn. Nevertheless, these heavy American cars had over-soft suspension and it could easily flip over and catch fire. The passengers *might* survive; nevertheless she couldn't risk her granddaughter's life. The professional driver could race up next to them and try to swerve the black giant off to one side, which would also be problematic. The rally Porsche had been stripped of everything unnecessary; carpets, radio, rear seats and interior trim. It was far too light for a pushing and shoving match with the American heavyweight.

At the back of the limo Charlotte lay sobbing with dried blood around her nose and mouth. Giovanni had punched her with his closed fist and fractured her nose because she wouldn't stop screaming. She'd never been hit before and was now trembling with fear.

'Hey Raffaello, have you seen that car about a hundred metres back?'

Raffaello checked his mirror and made a noisy left turn. The Porsche followed as if it was being towed, keeping the same distance, its seven lights filling his rear-view mirror. At the next junction he turned left again.

'Yeah your right Giovanni, it's a tail.' The driver said casually, looking in the little interior mirror. 'What sort of car is it? All I can see are loads of lights.'

'I don't know, make another left, when it turns we can see what they've got.'

Raffaello checked his mirrors, Giovanni looked out of the back window, as did Charlotte. She didn't understand their Italian, but prayed that someone was following them. As the streetlights lit the sports car behind them, Charlotte could not believe her eyes, recognising her grandmother's silhouette.

'Ya-Ya! Ya-Ya!' She screamed, frantically banging on the rear glass panel.

Phaedra saw her for a split second as the row of spotlights illuminated the back window of the limo. Charlotte's face mimed Edvard Munch's painting of The Scream, except her palms were beating on the window either side of her head. Phaedra just caught sight of her blooded nose and mouth, her Greek eyes darkened with the hatred of a vengeful goddess. The limo started to accelerate as they turned back to the beach road leading to the Castell de Plegamans. Phaedra's mind went into automatic; she became incredibly calm and determined. There was only one thought in the forefront of her mind: to kill the two men in the car and save the life of her granddaughter.

She attached the four-point rally seatbelt in the middle of her body. Pulled her Lugar out of her bag and checked her spare clip.

She opened a packet of cigarettes and lit up. Her eyes never left the rear of the Cadillac.

Slap! – Slap! – Slap!

'Shut up you stupid!' Giovanni said to Charlotte as

he hit across the face.

'You wait! When Ya-Ya gets here, you'll see what a temper she has!' Charlotte said sobbing uncontrollably.

'Who is this Ya-Ya? Who get so angry?' Giovanni Gibigiano asked with a sneer.

'She's my grandmother and she's very good at sports.'

Giovanni laughed and translated to Raffaello, who joined in the humour.

'Ask her if that's the driver in the Porsche behind us.'

'Yes!' Charlotte replied to Giovanni's translated question. 'And she's a very fast driver.'

'Well if it's only your granny, we'll stop up here and say hello.' Giovanni said cockily, picking up the machinegun stuffed into the pocket next to the back seat and checking the clip.

Charlotte's face suddenly realised that she had said too much, as usual, and she started to bite her fingernails nervously. Raffaello smashed his foot on the accelerator and the huge car leaned back on its rear suspension and whooshed forward. The Italian passed a few side turnings and then made a sudden right turn, causing a fog of burning rubber that filled the air. Then he came to a screeching halt next to a small crossroad. Giovanni knew the manoeuvre well, jumped out of the back seat quickly, crouching next to the rear wing and pointed his machinegun at the corner of the junction. He concentrated on the gap in the road, so that he could spray the sports car and the old lady driving it when she followed them around the corner. Charlotte looked out of the back window nervously. Raffaello waited in the driver's seat and kept an eye on his valuable passenger. A few minutes past and Giovanni started to relax his grip on the heavy metal weapon.

'Hey Raffaello...' He called back to his friend. 'What do you think, we lost the old woman or maybe she just chickened out?' He got up and took a few steps forward, not taking his eyes away from the junction. 'You know that granny of yours...' He laughed, stealing a peek at Charlotte in the back seat. 'She must have gone off to do some sport.'

Bang! Bang! Bang! Bang! Bang! Bang! Bang! Bang! Bang! Bang! Bang!

The machinegun shot erratically into the air with a mind of its own, as Giovanni crashed to the bitumen with two Lugar bullets in his right ear. Phaedra stood in the shadows of the side road, with her legs apart and arms pointed like an arrow, the Lugar formed the deadly metal tip.

She'd used the speed of the Porsche to zoom around the other side of the block and sneaked through the shadows of the side road. The old *'Accelerate - Turn and Fire'* routine was a classic; she'd learnt it in the Greek resistance as a child over twenty-five years ago.

The next three bullets hit the driver's glass window creating a triangle around Raffaello's left temple. He smashed his right foot on the accelerator and the car's tyres burnt black graffiti on the road. He drove the heavy monster as fast as he could, thanks to the bulletproof glass wrapped around the car. When he glanced at the cracked window, he saw the accuracy of the three closely grouped shots. This type of precision of tightly spaced bullets in a snug triangle, told him that the shooter was a pro. Charlotte was now screaming hysterically as the open rear door swung wildly. Almost closing as Raffaello turned to the left and flapping into parked cars when he turned right. Whatever he did, the row of headlights sat firmly in the centre of his rear-view mirror. After three kilometres Raffaello felt calmer, his mind started to piece together the whole story. Marco had described the hit on his grandfather in Paris. The chase through the city, two very professional assassins in a fast car, driving like rally drivers. Now there was a hot looking Porsche behind him and his friend Giovanni surly dead. Who are they? Another Family? Is one of the Godfathers trying to take over?

'I get it now…' He said to Charlotte, not caring that she didn't understand his Italian. 'Our people in London got the wrong woman, uh! The right car, the right hitter, but somehow they got you instead of that bitch behind us. What is this name Granny? She's some kind of Padrino? Maybe it's not even a woman?' He asked rhetorically. 'Is this

Granny the head of a Family?'

Charlotte had her legs up on the back seat in a foetal position, her tears now mixed with blood, sticky on her face. She was too afraid to speak - too afraid to think. Her whole body shuddered like a baby calf, next in line at the slaughterhouse. The Italian men were told to take the girl to Marco's dungeon in the Castell de Plegamans. However, he realised that this professional hitter, calmly driving behind him, would never let him get out of the car alive. Therefore, he decided to drive back to the port and Marco's powerboat. He kept a small crew and couple of soldiers there from the northern Italian Fascist and someone from his Milano Family.

He calculated that if he makes enough noise and keeps the doors closed, they should take out the Porsche driver behind him and he will still be able to deliver the girl. He was nervous yet excited, these adventures always gave him a feeling of exhilaration, it was the familiar sense of danger, killing, and then finally the satisfaction of success. Suddenly his mood changed, he pictured Giovanni Gibigiano, jiggling to the staccato music of his gun out of control, and then he crashed to the ground. No, he'll be okay; he was a professional, he had more experience than his young school-friend. Then he remembered what was left of Marco and knew he had to be very careful, if he wanted to get away from this hitter; whoever he or she was.

The two cars were running south along the sea road of Avinguda d'Edward Maristany, towards the port of Barcelona. It was deserted on the April Saturday night. The Cadillac passed through the Parc de Diagonal-Mar and turned left onto the Avenue Del Litoral, which ran along the beach towards the port. The two cars drove like friends going out for the evening.

There was no rush. Raffaello hoped that he'd find some heavily armed men at the port; Phaedra knew that wherever he went, she would kill him. Only Charlotte sat trembling with fear, because at that moment, she couldn't be sure of anything.

At the Passeig Joan de Borbó, Raffaello lurched to the left and smashed his foot on the accelerator; the

American monster bounced and floated forward, blowing up dust in its wake. The spotlights stayed in his rear view mirror as he sped pass a parade of boats and yachts, bouncing within the calm waters of the cocooned port. When the Italian saw Marco's Chiavari motorboat, with its distinctive dark blue hull, red roof and canopy, he flashed his lights on main beam urgently and leaned on the car's musical horn. The Cadillac gritted its chrome teeth and lurched forward

As he had hoped over the previous fifteen minutes, two soldiers in matching black suits, thin black ties and white shirts, were leaning against the boat's little gangplank, nonchalantly smoking cigarettes. Once they saw and heard the Mafiaesque black limo hurtling towards them, they both pulled out handguns defensively. A man dressed in a Captain's uniform and another in a white towelling dressing gown, rushed out onto the deck with machineguns primed.

The four aimed the weapons at the three tons of black metal and chrome hurtling towards them. Raffaello checked his rear view mirror, the seven blinding headlights were still slotted in the small space as though inside his car. Raffaello saw Marco's men running out in front of him. He grabbed his pistol in his left hand, readying himself for his planned stop. He decided to spin the car sideways, to the right of the dock, just in front of Marco's boat, the bullet-proof car would give him cover from his pursuer when he jumped out. Then he and the other guys protecting the craft could pepper the Porsche until it looked like his grandmother's old colander.

'Okay sweet-thing, this is where your granny or godfather is going to see the angels.' He laughed. Charlotte didn't understand him. She had never been so frightened in all her life. Ya-Ya used to drive fast, although it was never like this. The rear door on her left seemed to be completely broken and was swinging wildly. The Italian driver was very nervous, he sweated profusely and had trouble steering the huge car with his right hand.

On 'Il Ditta,' the Captain shouted down to his men.

'Who is this – it's one of ours?'

The white dressing gown flicked his cigar in the

calm water quickly. 'If he's one of ours, why is he driving so crazy? Roberto, Guido, fire some warning shots!'

Then the bullets came. One hit the windscreen and two or three hit the front grill of the Cadillac. Charlotte screamed at the top of her voice, while clinging on to the handle above her door with both hands. Raffaello swerved to the left and right. The bulletproof glass cracked but held firm. Using his left hand, still grasping the gun, he rolled down the driver's window and screamed at the top of his voice.

'*Stupidi bastardi* …' He yelled waving his pistol. 'Not me, the car behind!'

The men on the boat and the port looked at each other nervously. They could see the black Caddie hurtling towards them on the narrow dock. The driver looked Italian Mafia and was driving with a death wish directly at them. He was pointing his pistol and screaming something like 'You stupid bastards.' The rear door swung wildly open, this could mean there was another shooter in the back ready to open fire. The car seemed to be bulletproof. It was a snap decision when the Captain called out at the top of his voice:

'It's a *h-i-t!*'

All four men opened fire aiming at the open window. Raffaello screamed at the top of his voice, 'The car behind!' He glanced for a split second into the rear view mirror and saw a black hole. The chasing car had vanished, twenty yards before the boat and the barrage of bullets. Raffaello swung the car hard to the right. Charlotte was thrown violently through the open doorway and rolled like a cricket ball to the boundary of the dock's edge. The man in the dressing gown emptied his clip through Raffaello's open window. The bloody corpse slumped on the front bench seat. The head pummelled with uncountable bullets into a bloody steak Tar-Tar against the chrome horn. The huge car spun like a spinning top in a smoke filled tornado and finally crashed into the ancient port wall.

The Italian soldiers were in shock, yet kept their composure whilst they surveyed the area. No one on the port wall. No other boats. No cars or people on the empty, port road. The Captain called out to the men on the dock.

'Hey! Stop that horn and go and check the girl, she looks dead.'

The two young men pulled Raffaello's body away from the steering wheel, releasing the night's silence. Then they walked over to Charlotte's body. They saw the blood on her face, where Giovanni had beaten her. The rest of her body was totally still; limp. She wore one shoe, her head twisted to one side, eyes closed: almost peaceful.

'Well?' The Captain called out.

'I don't know her...' The smaller one said. 'But she looks dead.'

'Don't just stand there. Bring the body on the boat, we'll dump it in the sea, we can't leave it there.'

The young men grabbed an end each, lifting the slender body up the gangplank onto the motor cruiser.

'Where shall we put it?' The bigger one asked, as though he was moving furniture.'

'In the spare crew cabin next to the kitchen, move it quickly! We don't want any Spanish police coming around now.'

The men struggled with the dead weight through the cramped corridor and finally dumped the body on the narrow bunk.

'Hey Guido...' The little Italian said. 'What do you call those guys who make it with dead people?'

'Leave me alone, God forgive you! Your uncle's a priest and you have all of these dirty thoughts...'

'I'm not saying I'm going to do anything to her, but look, she's fantastic...'

'Let's go and when we throw her over the side, I'm going to say a little prayer.'

'Yeah – yeah, me too, it's just you don't see many good looking girls like this one, I didn't even touch her tits...'

'*Marinello!* Will you shut up - for God's sake!'

When the two men arrived back on the deck, the Captain told them to check the Cadillac. Raffaello's body was an unrecognisable mess.

'Take the body and dump it in with the girl...' The Captain commanded. 'Don't forget the gun and anything else that will identify him.'

They struggled again with the second body and eventually dumped it on the narrow bunk on top of the first. They returned to the deck looking for a drink, wiping their bloody hands on a towel.

'Guido, go and phone Marco at the restaurant, explain to him what's happened and that we will have to dump the bodies about five to ten kilometres out at sea. If not they will float back in a few days. We'll take the boat up to the port in Mataró and ring Marco from there, you can stay in town tonight.'

Guido was annoyed at the trivial task, however he liked the idea of a night off in Barcelona. He walked slowly along the empty dock towards a telephone on the main road, and the Captain told Roberto to cast off. The Captain engaged the engine and pulled away slowly, he didn't want to alert the Port Authorities or the Coastguard. Even though they were thin on the ground off-season, they may have been contacted about the crash and the gunfire.

At the end of the dock, a rally, decaled Porsche had parked behind a small green fishmonger's van. As he past a woman's voice said.

'Hey good looking, come over here.'

The Italian smiled at the faint shadow and replied. 'Sorry darling, I have to go to work.'

As he turned away a heavy Lugar crashed into the nape of his neck. A couple of minutes later he opened his eyes. His head hurt and his arms were attached to his thighs with his own belt.

He couldn't get up from the ground, yet lifted his head slowly to see someone standing in front of him.

She had the large port lights behind her, but he made out the silhouette of a slim woman, in a black cocktail dress, bare legs, no shoes and a large gun held threateningly, just out of kicking distance.

'So who are you, the jilted wife? The other girlfriend? Let me go and I'll just walk away, I don't even know who that guy was.'

'Listen carefully, I will ask you some questions and you will answer them. Do you understand?'

'Listen honey, do you really want trouble wi…'

Bang!

'*AAAAAHHHH! Porca puttana, vacca troia!*' Guido rolled over in agony as blood and bits of bone and flesh splattered from his right knee.

'I don't have much time. Listen to me carefully. Is the girl dead?' Phaedra's soft voice asked coldly.

'Oh God, my leg is killing me, you bitch…'

Bang!

'*AAAAAHHHH!* Stop-stop! I'll tell you anything you want…' His other knee exploded like a bloody version of the Trevi fountain.

'Is the girl dead?'

'Yeah – but *I* didn't kill her, get me an ambulance you *vacca*…'

Guido looked up through sweat filled eyes. 'Hey! Where are you, don't leave me like this, I'll bleed to death you bitch!'

Phaedra felt a volcanic fire erupting in her blood cells, the back of her eyes were burning like an eclipsed sun. The roar of the rear engine sports car and a cloud of dust were all Guido heard or saw. The German car tore up to the main road and raced around the other side of the port.

In the cockpit Phaedra's hands trembled violently as she struggled to tear a cigarette from its pack. Her eyelids as leaky as faltering dikes, unable to hold back the flood of tears. She had witnessed her grandfather, father, elder brother, two uncles, her favourite cousin Gregorios and of course, her baby brother Dimitris, who she had mothered like her own child: all murdered in front of her by the Fascist Germans.

Now she had seen her granddaughter murdered on the port. She vowed to Elektra, it was her time to kill. And she had the perfect killing machine at the other end of the harbour.

It was called, The Scylla.

Chapter 49
Midnight

The Duchesse and the Colonel were supervising their staff taking orders for the auction. They were set up on the catwalk with clipboards and money-belts; the models were walking around showing off various pieces of the fabulous jewellery, whilst the sales people were selling paintings, ornaments and small antiques.

They had had interest in the Patiala Necklace, although no one made an offer as high as they'd hoped. Despite the fact that some of the dealers were thinking of working together, breaking the magnificent necklace into hundreds of individual diamond rings, small necklaces, pendants and bracelets. The Colonel hated the Hong Kong owners, known as The Heaven and Earth Society, who had stolen the Patiala Necklace in the first place. They were a tough group of triads and they demanded a high price. He had done some business with their main agent in Spain, although only on the telephone; he lived in a small village in the north of Catalan. A frail, grisly old man, with an annoying high-pitched voice, he had connections with Chinese people in the United States and all over the peninsular, many with a front of selling vegetables or plastic goods in local villages. The Chinese triads had an unspoken agreement with the Spanish authorities: having supplied arms and explosives to various political groups before and during the Civil War, although they kept a low profile. The Chinese rarely did anything that could put them in conflict with Franco's regime. The community only borrowed money amongst themselves, and local, Spanish speaking business owners made any arrangements necessary with Hong Kong's triads.

One of the Colonel's policemen approached him and whispered:

'Colonel, eight more men have arrived and the whole area up here is now completely secure.'

'That's good, but I thought I heard shots a few moments ago – what happened?'

'I'll find out Sir.'

The plain clothes-policeman went into the reception and saw two of Marco's boys guarding the door that led to the Telefèrico below.

'Someone heard shots?'

'Yeah it's just a bit of old business being cleaned up...' Enrico said cockily.

'Listen this is Spain, we're in charge here...'

'Yeah sure, no problema, but you have your hands full upstairs, looking after the merchandise; downstairs is just an old vendetta. It'll be over in a few minutes.'

The Sergeant walked back to the Colonel and whispered in his ear. José Valles-Carrera looked annoyed and approached his wife, who had just made a sale to a dithering old Generalfeldmarschall, wearing numerous WW2 medals.

He said he wanted something from the old days for his younger sister who lived in Argentina. The Duchesse sold him a heavy gold bracelet made from what she called; 'Harvested gold from Germany.'

'Suzanna, listen to me...'' The colonel said annoyed. 'This Marco character is proving difficult to work with. He's downstairs now killing someone. This sort of behaviour is bad for business. Those days are over, it's not Sicily.'

Suzanna smiled sweetly to the old German soldier and kissed him goodbye on both cheeks. Then she turned to her husband. 'The Italians are difficult, but they get results. Marco has this evening secured a deal with a group of fifty Catholic maternity hospitals in the States. They deal with poor Irish immigrants...' She smiled: 'Lovely pale-skinned babies, they'll be worth a fortune in Switzerland and the north of Europe. The priest says they can start shipping next week; so let him have his fun, we've done well this evening.' She said avariciously. Señora Valles-Carrera held her husband's arm and said provocatively in a sultry tone. 'Don't forget darling, we will have a long weekend with the blonde Aryan girl, so it's not all work.'

'Duchesse...' An elderly woman who'd had too many facelifts asked. 'What's the latest bid on this ring, my husband wants me to have it.'

Downstairs in the Telefèrico station, Sam had managed to dislodge the heavy holdall from the top of the yellow metal wheel, which turned the cable, and he missed another round from Marco's old inaccurate shotgun. He slid down the metal ladder with the explosives over one arm, and ran across the platform to the red metal cable car cabin, diving in between the metal railings. The mechanism in the cabin still seemed to be undamaged despite the huge hole in the rear glass. A cleaner had left his equipment inside and Sam saw the driver's lever. He listened carefully yet Marco was silent. He looked at the black bag. It was closed tightly, the outline of rectangle shaped blocks, like flat bricks, poked through the canvas menacingly. Sam examined the lock in the centre of the handles. It had three black wires soldered to the metal clip. Sam knew if he opened the bag breaking the solder, it would activate one of Moshe's famous booby traps. He looked carefully at the small metal device connected on the outside. It was jet black and had a tiny chrome aerial. Again he felt too nervous to dislodge the box, as it also had wires entwined into the bag, as sensitive as a hospital patient on a life-support machine.

Suddenly, he heard two shots fired from somewhere near the door. Sam dived on the floor of the cabin, although he thought that the shots sounded as though they were from a pistol.

If Marco had backup from able-bodied men, he would be dead in a few minutes. Sam heard a faint noise near the entrance, a sliding sound, could it be the door?

Has Marco slid out to get help or more ammunition? Has someone else come in? Sam decided to make a run for it, but he needed to be cautious. It was deadly silent; he couldn't hear anyone breathing or any movement.

Slowly he raised his head to glance through the cabin's side windows; it was still pitch black; the only light came through the station's void for the cabin's journey.

He stood up slowly, his head and shoulders were now level with the glass door that opened on to the platform not far from the exit.

He wished he hadn't.

Marco had managed to drag himself around the other side of the cabin and had the Belgium shotgun securely wedged on the broken window ledge with both barrels four feet away from Sam's head. The black beady eyes of the Belgium stared at Sam menacingly; it was a practised killer with devastating effect, despite its age. He realised that even Marco's dilapidated body couldn't misdirect the deadly shells.

Desperately Sam looked down at the mop and broom and wondered if he could reach them in time.

He couldn't.

The massive blast from the shotgun clanged through his head, and his body crashed to the floor.

Chapter 50
The Scylla

Patrick and Freddie were sitting around a bench-style table under the covered deck of a nice little Rica Motor cruiser, with two attractive middle-aged women and a bottle of vintage Bollinger RD champagne from Sam's cellar. The women were on holiday while their husbands had joined a golf tournament on the Canary Islands. The ladies had three weeks to kill as golf widows and so Patrick and Freddie intended to help them enjoy an Irish holiday, which didn't involve leaving the boat very often, unless the booze ran out.

The identical twin sisters, Margaret Jones and Jackie Jenkins, had both found their husbands in Wales. Now that their kids had grown up and left home, they were fed up with their men, who seemed to prefer going to bed with a six-iron rather than their wives. Patrick and Freddie thought that their newfound friends looked like they belonged in one of Beryl Cook's paintings, but they were fond of wholesome women. Patrick vaguely suggested he owned the luxury Scylla they were staying on, and had asked the ladies if they wanted to go out tomorrow for a high-speed cruise. Both women had buckteeth and couldn't stop giggling at their new friend's jokes. Jackie toped-up the glasses, put on the Phillips' record player and started to swoon to the sound of a new Welsh singer called Tom Jones. After the second bottle had been opened, the four mariners were feeling quite romantic, and started to pair off. Suddenly they all stopped talking, because they heard the shriek of a fast car approaching the narrow edge of the dock.

Jackie said with her Yorkshire accent: 'Now that's the type of selfish Spanish driver I can't stand, this dock is far too narrow for cars, especially at high speed - listen to that noise!'

The Porsche flashed pass their little boat with a deafening, high-pitched scream, followed by the screeching of brakes. Phaedra then used a handbrake turn arriving exactly in front of the gently bouncing Scylla. She leapt out of the car, ran from one end of the boat to the other, slipping the bow and stern lines at speed. She ran up the gangplank, half tripped on the damp surface and made her way onto the deck and then the bridge.

Patrick and Freddie looked at each other concerned, leapt off the girl's boat onto the dock and ran along the edge to catch Phaedra; they needed to explain how they had missed their flight. The massive engines of the Scylla dug a hole four feet deep in the shallow water and Phaedra turned the huge boat away from the dock as quickly as a prancing horse. Patrick and Freddie stood with their hands on their hips in amazement. The marina's rules were strictly imposed. Boats weren't allowed to do more than two knots within the port walls. Phaedra must have been doing ten times that speed.

'Oh Jesus and Mary...' Patrick said in astonishment. 'She's completely mad; that turn almost capsized the Scylla.

'Look at the speed of that thing!' Freddie gasped. 'That woman has turned the harbour into a maelstrom, look!' He said pointing to the other side of the port. 'Some of those small boats are taking in water like they're in the middle of a tornado...'

The middle-aged ladies were in shock, their own boat as well as everyone else's dived and swelled in the wake of the Scylla's rapid exit and they started screaming for their new protectors. Patrick and Freddie ran back to the 'British Open' to see the twins griping onto the gunwale. When the men clambered aboard they held the nervous women closely. Jackie said. 'Has your boat been stolen Patrick?'

'Listen girls that woman is a friend of ours and if she went off like that she must be in trouble, I think we should follow her to make sure she's okay...'

'What; she's your girlfriend?' Margaret asked indignantly.

'No – no, nothing like that ...' Patrick explained. 'She my business partner's wife, she's Greek and has a hot temper, maybe someone has upset her, come on let's go up to the bridge!' The four struggled to the small cockpit, as the

Scylla's wake was only just settling.

Phaedra strapped herself into the control chair as the launch left the protection of the port walls. She pressed two buttons on the instrument panel and a keyboard popped up from the surface; after tapping in a four-digit code, the whole top of the instrument board opened, revealing a second panel, four feet wide, eighteen inches deep. The cabin lights dimmed automatically emphasising the illuminated instruments. The Helmswoman pressed several other buttons and pulled a small switch. A radar screen came alive and showed three vessels on the horizon. Two of the blips were large, slow moving and trawling the Mediterranean about two miles off of the coast. The third was much smaller and moving quickly out to sea. Phaedra made straight for the small blip. They were about fifteen minutes ahead of her. In a normal motor cruiser it would take ages to catch up. However, there was nothing normal about the Scylla. The former military, fast attack craft was capable of a massive forty knots. Marco's Chiavari Riviera enjoyed three hundred horsepower and had been launched only four years earlier. It was quicker than most boats of a similar size, but the Scylla was twice the size and four times faster.

Phaedra pressed another button. Near the bow an array of spotlights lifted their heads, illuminating the roughening sea a hundred feet in front of her. The bridge was silent except for the waves crashing against the hull and the blipping noise of Marco's boat, a small green flashing light on a black screen. The Greek Skipper squinted her eyes, grabbed a pair of Sam's old Wilson binoculars and focussed on the blue and red Italian cruiser. The body language of her prey changed, they turned hard to the starboard side facing north. Phaedra realised they'd seen her powerful lights. She wanted to board the ship to get Charlotte's body. She would never believe that her granddaughter was dead, until she had her in her arms.

On board the 'Il Ditta' The Italian Captain saw the illuminated craft coming at them with a speed that could only be the Police, the Military or the Coastguard. He turned to put the portside, out of sight of the approaching boat, so that his men could throw the bodies overboard with anything else that may incriminate them.

Nevertheless, he misjudged the celerity of the approaching craft, and the Scylla was virtually on top of them.

'Look out!' The dressing gown man screamed as he tumbled onto the deck.

The Scylla's massive engines ploughed a furrow through the restless sea. When the speed increased the attack craft rose up out of the water and flew at the Italian boat planning over the restless Mediterranean. At the last moment Phaedra swerved the helm to the left. The huge launch rose up, almost leaving the water, turned and dived into the Mediterranean as smoothly as a performing Dolphin. The spray washed everything not screwed down on the 'Il Ditta' overboard. The Captain, Roberto and the dressing gown were all thrown onto the deck under three feet of water. The cruiser plunged and rolled, the Captain crawled over the slippery floor and staggered into the wheelhouse.

'What's happening?' Roberto cried out coughing up seawater.

'We're being attacked by that enormous boat...' The Captain shouted above the noise of the waves crashing against the hull. I thought it was the Coastguard, but they would've just stopped us. That monster belongs to someone intent on hurting us!'

'It must be the people with the Cadillac...' Dressing gown said.

'Look out! It's turning. Roberto shouted nervously, pointing at the high-speed monster tearing towards them.

Like a killer whale, the Scylla came at thwartships towards them. Phaedra pulled a lever and a six-foot long, semi automatic machine gun slowly raised up from the front deck. The interior lever, designed like an airplane joystick, allowed the gun operator to lift and point the massive twenty five-calibre weapon using hydraulics. She aimed just below the roofline and fired from right to left. The thousands of bullets acted as sharp as an electric saw. The canvas canopy and the bridge's metal roof were completely sheered off.

The stramash forced the three Italians to dive onto the deck in panic, as thousands of bullets slashed the air above their heads. They tried to make their bodies as flat as they could. The noise was deafening. The roof and canopy were thrown to one side. Both boats came to a virtual standstill, moving slowly with the force of the wind. The Scylla's lights flooded the Italian's shredded vessel. Roberto was the first one to speak.

'Capitano, shall I get up and wave a white flag or something?'

'Do you have a white flag in your pocket, stupido!'

'No - but I could just say we surrender.'

'Listen Roberto...' The dressing gown said. 'If the people on that boat are friends with the guy we shot on the port, I don't think they want to have a chat. Whatever this boat is, it has enough power to blow us out of the water. So just sit tight.

The silence under the powerful lights and deadly weapon scared the Italians to death.

Below decks, Charlotte could see God. She thought He looked nice; she knew He would.

He had long hair and a long flowing, fluffy white beard. A bright Alabaster halo glowed iridescently around His head. Strange she thought - He had no body, just a head and the halo, which now seemed to be moving sideways. The beautiful face started to change, disintegrate, the wispy beard seem to blow away, the round face had a chrome ring and the skin had little craters all around one side.

Her own body was being crushed. She felt cold; she couldn't breathe, as though a great spiritual weight pressed down on her, the spirit was cold and damp. Her eyelids were red, the weight was red, bright red like a dying sun. Her eyes opened slowly, she was rocking from side to side. God was no longer in the porthole.

'*AAAAAHHHH*!'

She screamed, her whole body trembling. The head, a heavy ball of blooded flesh lay on her cheek like a horizontal tango dancer. '*AAAAAHHHH!*' She screamed again. Charlotte slid out from beneath the bleeding corpse of Raffaello. Something heavy fell on the floor next to her feet.

She was only wearing one shoe.

She kicked it off and saw the gun on the floor. Ya-Ya wanted her to have shooting lessons. She went once with her grandparents to a nice country house in Kent. An ex-army type that her grandfather knew from the war, shouted various instructions; about safety catches and firing pins and wind speed and velocity.

The guns were so noisy, when she tried to hit a tiny target miles away. She screamed at the noise and the force of the weapon, dropping it in the grass as though it was a live dangerous creature. After five minutes, she told her grandparents that she'd rather have lunch in the clubhouse.

They never asked her again. Charlotte felt terrible. Her hair, face, mini dress, arms and legs were covered with bits of the Raffaello's red flesh and chips of bones, glued to her with his congealed blood. She looked as though she had crawled out of a muddy pond, but the mud was deep ruby red.

The red, white and blue Chiavari Riviera motor cruiser, bounced over the water urgently; there was that same noise she remembered from the rifle range. She felt sick; she had small cuts all over her arms and legs. As well as the cut lip, fractured nose and black eye she got from Giovanni. Her back was painful; she could feel bruisers all over her body.

Charlotte heard voices coming from above. She quietly cracked open the cabin door and saw a little corridor, the boat slowed and the engine died. She sneaked out carefully, listened at the cabin opposite. Nothing. She opened the door carefully, just another cabin. There were six cabin doors; hers was at the end next to the galley.

She could hear brouhaha from the deck, more Italians. She looked around for a mirror but couldn't find one. She was thirsty. Her bloodstained feet tiptoed unsteadily over the cold wooden deck into the galley. She jumped back in shock. A horrific red monster with stramineous hair stared back at her from the shinny chrome kettle.

'Oh God!' She said aloud. 'I think I'm still dead.'

Charlotte held her throbbing head; she started to

remember what had happened. The horrid Italian boys grabbed her; someone was chasing them, was it Ya-Ya? It was only a quick glimpse as the car turned; she didn't recognise the vehicle. Then they stopped, one of the men started shooting his gun and the next minute he was lying on the floor. Then the car chase again and a crash. How did she get here? The men were all screaming louder now, they sounded panicky. The boat was swaying from side to side, and had stopped moving forward. Charlotte looked out of the galley porthole. The Scylla was bearing down on them. 'The Scylla! Granddaddy!' She screamed.

Phaedra picked up the microphone in the cockpit, pressed a button that altered her voice into a deep mechanical base sound.

'Get off the boat.' She said simply in Italian.

The three Italians looked at each other.

'What are we going to do?' Roberto asked nervously.

'What does he mean, get off?' We're in the middle of the sea...' Dressing gown asked.

'I guess he's saying we jump and die in the sea or we stay here and die.' The Captain said.

The megaphone spoke robotically again. 'Thirty seconds.'

Roberto jumped up waving his hands towards the blazing lights. 'I'm going - I'm going, don't shoot.' As he staggered over the rolling deck the Scylla's machinegun followed him with a deadly stare. He untied one of the lifebuoys that was attached to the inside of the railings, heaved the ring overboard and jumped in after it.

The dressing gown jumped up with his hands in the air, grabbed a wooden folding sun-lounger and they both entered the sea. The small wooden door that led to the cabins below opened. The Captain turned in horror. Some kind of blood soaked zombie put its head out, looked at him and at the wrecked boat-deck saying: 'Where are we?'

The Italian was astonished. The Scylla's foghorn gave a long blast. Phaedra couldn't cope with her emotion, her eyes bled tears, she could barely see. She told herself to stay calm; she had a chance to save one of her last family members. Then she made a mistake. The megaphone spoke again: 'Get the girl on this boat...' As the words left her mouth she realised what she'd done.

The Captain jumped up off the deck and grabbed Charlotte, pulling her viciously to the floor in a rugby tackle, she started screaming, and then she said more calmly: 'Don't hurt me or he'll kill you.' Charlotte had used that word; 'kill' so many times throughout her life. 'I'm going to kill those parking wardens, I'm going to kill my sister if she takes my perfume again, I'm going to kill Justin if he doesn't take the rubbish out.

My grandmother will kill me if she finds out.' Obviously, like most people Charlotte didn't really mean it. It was just an expression. However, when she said that little common phrase to the rough looking Italian Captain, at that moment his face had a strange reaction, his eyes were fearful, it was as though he really believed that he was about to die!

He held her tightly with his arm around her neck. Then he saw a pistol on the other side of the deck and made a dive for it. The machinegun followed him and cut a dotted line across the floor. Charlotte cowed in the corner. The Captain rolled back to Charlotte and checked the gun. It had four bullets left.

About two thousand yards back the 'British Open' was going flat out. They had heard the noise of bullets in the distance and weren't sure if it was thunder because they also saw violent flashes of light over the horizon.

I'm not sure if that's the Scylla or not...' Patrick said to the others. 'But whatever it is, it has a massive amount of lights on it...'

From that distance the Scylla looked like a full moon diving into the horizon.

On the 'Il Ditta' the Captain pulled Charlotte in front of himself as a shield, screaming out across the five yards of water between the boats. 'I'll drop the girl on the port of Barcelona if you let me go...'

Phaedra made a dangerous decision. The barrel of the vicious looking machinegun on the Scylla's deck moved until it was in line with the Captain. The megaphone spoke again: 'I don't want you or the girl; I want something hidden on the boat. Get off or you'll both die now.'

The Captain looked at Charlotte and said in Italian, 'Do you know these people?' She looked confused and shook her head. The machinegun moved again making a whining noise from its electric motors. Then bullets started to pulse out of its barrel with the rapidity of Morse code. The large shells sliced a groove along the back of the boat vertically, as rapidly as a Samurai beheading a slave.

The Captain dived towards the cabin dragging Charlotte with him. The rear end of the 'Il Ditta' started to make a cracking sound. Phaedra knew boats. The heavy engines would be attached to the back of the boat on a metal or wooden frame. The slicing action from the gun would have removed all support and the engines were about to sink into the sea. As a precursor, the boat started to lean stern-most and the bow lifted out of the agitated sea. The Captain realised what was going to happen and dived overboard, he swam towards the distant lights of the Port of Barcelona, not daring to look back.

The Scylla started to move closer to the Italian motor cruiser and came abreast. Charlotte was rolled-up under the dismembered roof of the control cabin, and then she heard a familiar voice. The megaphone was quieter now, without the distorter, her grandmother said softly, 'Charlotte grab the Jacobs-ladder. Charlotte put her head over the railings and saw the rope ladder on the bouncing Scylla that she had used a hundred times.

Her whole body ached. She looked down at the black liquid and remembered how she appeared in the reflection of the kettle; she didn't want her grandmother to see her in such a mess.

Out of all of the lessons her grandparents tried to give her, there was only one that she enjoyed and was good at. Swimming. She dived into the water; it was freezing but felt great, she rubbed her body and face to get the mess off, and swam to the Jacobs-ladder.

Her grandmother pulled her on board sobbing and held her close. Phaedra caressed Charlotte's face and pushed the wet hair away from her eyes. She smiled and said: 'Go in and have a hot shower, you've got some clothes downstairs, get changed.' Phaedra felt exhausted and relieved; her body lost its tension as though she'd put down a heavy bag forgetting she'd carried it for a long time. The Italian's boat shed its last breath, as the heavy engines dragged its dying body to the Mediterranean's floor, a few moments of foamy water and the hungry sea digested its latest meal.

'Ahoy there Scylla!' Need any help?' Patrick barked into a small hand-held megaphone.

Phaedra came to the lower deck and looked down at Patrick, Freddie, Margaret and Jackie. She felt exhausted, but totally relieved to have saved her granddaughter, and to see a friendly face from Richmond.

'I thought you were going to London?'

'I'll have to explain that Phaedra my love... How's Charlotte? Was that her swimming?'

'She's fine, a little boyfriend trouble, but they didn't know she had a Greek grandmother.'

'I saw some fellows swimming back there, shall we pick them up?'

'No they need a swim it's not that far...'

'How's Sam, is he with you?'

Phaedra's face went white. Without a word, she rushed back up to the bridge, forced the engines on full throttle and disappeared in the direction of Barcelona's port; the wake throwing the crew of the 'British Open' onto the bench seats. 'Looks like she's left her husband somewhere.' Margaret said.

All Phaedra could think of now were the gunshots she heard, and The Reaper and the Flowers.

Chapter 51
Wieniawski Concerto Number One

Sam's face contorted with the expectation of death, and his eyes were squeezed tightly together; when he opened them slowly he saw Marco, behind the long Belgium shotgun, the barrels smoking, pointing towards the ceiling. Sam touched his own face and chest searching for a painless wound, then, something strange happened. Marco, who resembled half burnt wax since his accident, imploded inside his eveningwear and melted down to the platform. It seemed as though the force of life had evaporated from within him. Finally the Italian slowly shrivelled on the floor, no more than a deflated balloon. Sam jumped up and saw two bleeding gunshot wounds, one on Marco's shoulder and one in the centre of his back. Not a professional hit he thought, they were too far apart. His curiosity came to an abrupt end as another shot passed close by his ear and shattered the cabin's glass window behind him. His shoulders were splashed with tiny shards of glass, like the beginning of a hailstorm. Again Sam dived on the floor next to the bag of explosives.

'I don't want to kill you English,' 'Mad' Moshe shouted wearily from the shadows. 'But you're getting in my way; go and put the bag back where I left it and I'll let you leave.'

'Moshe, listen to me carefully, if you're here for Ilsa Klup you don't have to worry, leave her to me. She's my contract and no one else will get hurt.'

'That doesn't suit me English, this is my last job, it will be tremendous, in every newspaper around the world. All of those old Nazi's up there that killed my family, these fascists from Spain and Italy with all of their dirty tricks. They all need to be exterminated.'

'Moshe, I understand how you feel about your family, we all lost people; my wife hates them as well. However, there are some innocent, young Spanish girls up there working in the kitchen, the models from all over Europe. Even many of the Germans are not guilty of any war crimes. Most of them are old people like us, who just did as they were told and defended their country.'

'You're going soft in your old age English; Germans weren't commissioned Nazi Generals for nothing. They had to achieve something in that old bastard's eyes. Massacre thousands of innocent people, build concentration camps, furnaces for our women and children...' Moshe started coughing violently and took a swig from his Vodka bottle to quell his unbearable pain, yet make the problem worse.

Sam knew that it was a fallacious hope for Moshe to quit his contract and so while he kept the crazy old man talking, Sam had strapped the holdall to his back by threading his arms through the straps like a waistcoat. He crawled carefully over the shattered glass to the controls in the cabin, reached up and pushed the lever forward. Nothing happened. He realised that the main control panel would be over by the wall; it would have to be activated before the controls in the cabin would work.

'So,' Sam thought, 'It must have been Moshe who fired the two shots earlier, at Marco's Italians, who were presumably guarding the door into the Teleferico.
He then used another two bullets on Marco and the warning shot that just missed.' Sam's gun in the toilet had six bullets, which meant Moshe had one shot left. He seemed very ill and so Sam knew that he wouldn't be able to do any adroit shooting. If he misses on the last shot, he thought, he should be able to overpower the old man fairly easily.

Then he heard the Stradivarius' beautiful tone.

Despite his love of classical music, Sam didn't recognise the Wieniawski concerto number one. It was a passionate piece and Moshe was an incredible violinist. He asked himself, why is the old man playing the violin now? He had heard some time ago that the man was insane; actually someone else said he was dead after his last assassination explosion in Lebanon. Moshe's playing the violin; he has one bullet and a shaky pair of hands. Sam decided to run down the stairs and throw the explosives into the sea. Even if the bag exploded underwater it wouldn't do much harm. Moshe's solo concerto began to reach a very

542

high note and so Sam thought it was a good time to make his move for the emergency exit.

Until he heard the pinging noise.

It sounded like the radar on the Scylla or one of those new electric pub games. However, he asked himself; where was it coming from? Then he saw it. On the little detonator with the chrome aerial, there was a tiny black screen; he hadn't noticed it before in the dark. On the display were two red illuminated numbers. The digits were counting down. Ninety-five, ninety-four, ninety-three...

Sam now realised that the violin's resonance activated the detonator. He looked around quickly, the nearest place to dump the bag was in the sea, but he was too far from the port's boundary. He gaped over the side of the tower. It was a long way down, and at least twenty feet away from the dock's edge, with a soft aquatic landing. He glanced over his shoulder again.

Eighty-five, Eighty-four, Eighty-three...

Sam glanced back into the little station. Moshe was standing on the platform engrossed in his music, the pitch getting higher and higher. Sam wondered if the detonator had two sequences: one activated by a musical note and one on the timer. Would it explode with a certain cadenza, or only when the numbers hit zero?

Seventy-three, Seventy-two, Seventy-one...

The former clown grabbed the mop and broom from the cleaner's bucket and climbed up on top of the Telefèrico cabin, with circus dexterity. He held the cleaning implements with his arms straight out in crucifixion style, to find his balance, and put his right foot on the cable. The thick, black entwined metal was firm and fairly wide, but it was also grimed with grease. His stiff evening shoes had leather soles and an inch of heel.

In the circus they used very soft, flat shoes that allowed your toes to wrap themselves around the curve of the cable.

It had been a long time since he walked a tightrope, although he told himself, it's just like swimming; you don't forget the technique.

He walked quickly under the roof of the station and

543

started to feel pleased by his progress, then he reached the open space and the damp wind blasted him from the right. He swayed, struggling to find his balance. He swapped hands, putting the heavier mop in his right hand like a gibbet, the broom in his left, pointing north. It felt slightly better. It was difficult now as the cable sloped downwards in a long curve towards the next tower, but that was far off. It was less greasy away from the station and he started to find a rhythm. Sam could still hear Moshe despite the biting rain and wind. The violinist had now moved to the edge of the tower so that his detonator could still heed the violin concerto's signal.

'The clock!' Sam said aloud. He stopped on the cable and slowly turned his head, until he could see the red numbers again.

Fifty-one, fifty, forty-nine...

He was worried, he had to get further away from the restaurant, put the broom and mop in one hand, carefully take the bag of explosives off of his back, and throw it with enough force so that it hit the water: not the port, not the boats, not the people...

'Oh no!' He shouted, 'What are all those people doing right underneath?'

A few minutes earlier the security men on the pavement in front of the tower heard the shots and looked up. Then someone screamed 'Look! There's an idiot on the cable with a mop!'

In the restaurant, the other four band members went for a break. The silence allowed people to hear the gunshots. The woman with too many facelifts stared out of the window of the restaurant and saw Sam balancing on the cable. She screamed like a soprano, nearly as pitchy as Moshe's violin, and the whole restaurant ran over to the windows facing the second Tower, Jaume I. One of the Spanish models called out:

'Look down there! There's a man walking on the cable towards the sea!'

The squall became heavier. Sam knew he didn't have long now; he had to throw the bag of explosives as far as he could. He realised that if he fell the eighty metres to

544

the ground, he would surely be splattered like an insect on a fast car's windscreen. He tried to keep track of the red numbers in his head, although another thought pushed the bleeping away from his mind. Didn't someone tell him once that an old frightened man like him would die, falling from a tightrope over a rough sea? Six of the Colonel's men were trying to break down the heavy metal door leading to the Telefèrico. Someone had found Moshe's two Italian victims on the stairs and the police and security men were running around in panic. Most of the guests became concerned by the gunfire and were queuing for the tiny lift. A few of the younger ones braved the windswept, slippery metal stairs.

Balancing on the cable, Sam could still hear the deadly timbre of the violin. He knew he must have been getting close to the end of the countdown.

Looking down, he saw that he'd nearly passed the edge of the dock, although in the howling wind and rain his progress was slow. Just another two or three metres he told himself.

He now put the mop and broom in his left hand to keep his balance, and carefully lowered the heavy bag from his right shoulder. As the bag fell to his wrist the force pulled him off balance. His body swayed to the right and then the left. Sam found it difficult to get his balance, his suit was now soaked to his skin and the rain ran through his hair and into his eyes.

The crowd by the window in the restaurant and the growing group of spectators on the ground, gasped at the same moment. None of them except the man on the cable and the violinist knew the true danger they all faced. Abruptly, Moshe stopped playing. He put the violin and bow carefully on the platform floor, took the pistol from his loose trouser belt and checked his last bullet. The detonator could be activated immediately by Moshe reaching the 4-octave, A-major, or by the clock arriving a zero. However the resourceful Englishman had managed to get out of range. The old assassin had only tested the detonator in the quiet boat cabin of the Maria Rosa. It wasn't sensitive enough for the commotion from the storm. He realise that the sentimental fool was going to try and save the Nazis and throw the holdall into the sea. He had to be stopped. Moshe's hands trembled, he used to be an expert with a pistol, and yet now he could barely see his target, especially as he was moving fairly quickly along the cable. Moshe lifted the gun with both hands, stood with his feet apart. Then he brought the pistol to the same level as his eyes, and fired. The shot rang out across the port, magnified be the metal lace that supported the tower. The crowds in the restaurant and on the pavement went silent. And then they all screamed again. The bullet went in Sam's lower back, just below his coccyx. The force of the shell and the sharp pain pushed him of balance and his feet slipped off the narrow metal cord.

The heavy holdall fell on the right of the cable and his body fell on the left. He clung on to the handles and screamed in agony as his right armpit hit the harsh metal twine. He was like a wooden clothes peg, slung over a washing line. The heavy weight of the explosives balanced his mass on the other side of the cable. He dropped the broom and mop. The ever-growing spectators on the pavement cried out again. For a split second the cleaning implements looked like thin men as they dived to their deaths on the concrete dock. Moshe picked up his violin again and started to play, the music now taking him into a trance of failing memories.

Sam managed to get the crook of his left elbow over the cable. He wanted to swing his leg over as well, as the pain in his arms was agonising when he tried to grip the rough edge of the thick wire. He swung his left leg up, the pain from his wound was excruciating, like a second shot. He missed the slippery cable and his body swung wildly in the wind and rain as weakly as a nubile tree in an autumn gale.

The police, which had tried to open the fire door into the Telefèrico, had stopped after hearing the shot and rushed down one flight of stairs to watch the man on the tightrope.

He had lost a lot of blood, red drops landed on the pavement with a noisy splat. He felt his body weakening, although the fear and pain had given him a burst of adrenalin. He tried again to get his leg over the cable. This time he took several swings, on the third he succeeded. Using the weight of the holdall he sat exhausted on the cable. Most people had left the restaurant, although some were hypnotised by the crazy man on the wire, eighty metres from a certain death.

Slowly he moved into a crouching position, something he had practised a thousand times in the circus, with his mother screaming at him: 'It's easy, you only need confidence, stand up!' He was desperate to please her then. Now he knew that he had to get on his feet for his own sake, it was his last chance. He put the bag on the cable to stabilise his weight and slowly with trembling knees straightened his legs, gingerly balancing on the two-inch cable.

The people in the restaurant and the now massive crowd on the dock all clapped as though he was performing a stage act. Suddenly Sam heard a familiar sound. He searched the sea at the marina entrance and saw a fast moving launch with blazing lights racing across the water, causing the herded craft to recoil in its wake. The skipper with Wilson binoculars in one hand pulled the foghorn three times. He looked down and saw two blonde women; tiny toys on a model boat, waving yellow flares from the upper deck of the Scylla. He smiled; Phaedra and Charlotte were safe. Sam stared at the red numbers at his feet again.

Three, two, one…

The massive explosion filled the air with a fiery ball and rocked the tower, shattering all of the glass windows. The restaurant crowd screamed and cried as they were thrown to the floor by the tremor. Flakes of glass covered their bodies like an icy blanket. One of the twins with red hair screeched at the top of her voice as she saw a triangle shard of glass, four inches long; protrude from her sister's cheek. People rolled around in the cascade of glass, moaning and disorientated. Some of them were unconscious through shock or hitting their heads on furniture. Slowly several people struggled to their feet.

When the little lift returned to the top floor, twenty people who were near the reception, fought with all of their strength to get into the space for four. One blonde woman wrenched the diamond necklace off another's neck; as she turned around to pick up the sparkling jewels, the blonde pushed her to the floor and squeezed into the lift as the doors were closing.

The force of the explosion unbalanced half the people on the pavement as well, they trembled as noisily as bottles on a milk float, before crashing to the ground wondering how they got there. Several burglar alarms were activated on nearby buildings.

The last couple of secret police from the Colonel's private force ran to the lifts on the ground floor. In the distance, the sirens of some emergency vehicles stabbed the moist air.

In the Telefèrico station Moshe lay dead on the platform, the blast had thrown the cable car straight at him. It swayed back and forward hitting him three times.

His right hand lay on the unscathed Stradivari; in his left hand he grasped the faded photograph of his dead wife and children.

A small fire started on the oily cables and was spreading into the Telefèrico station; if it reached the back wall it would blow the oilcans through the roof.

A few people in the restaurant were still staggering up from the floor, several women were sobbing. Suzanna Valles-Carrera was one of the first on her feet, her husband also recovered and jumped up and started barking orders to his disorientated men.

'Are you alright Sir?' His sergeant asked.

'Yes, we're both fine, take all of the men and secure the necklace and all of the other auction items…'

'Shall we help the wounded Sir?'

'No you fool, this could be a robbery, we can sort out a few minor injuries later, get the jewels and other items back in the armoured car downstairs.'

'I'll leave two men to escort you and the Duchesse to your car, Sir.'

'No, we'll be fine, give me your pistol, I'll drive myself.'

The Colonel put the gun in his jacket pocket and

watched the police run around packing all of the valuables in boxes. Suzanna Valles-Carrera stepped over the injured bodies and collected her money from the auction. She saw one of the waitresses holding a serviette against her bleeding head. Close to the explosion, the Generalfeldmarschall lay dead on the floor with a shard of glass in his neck. The Duchesse walked over to him and took his pulse with a concerned expression. Surreptitiously she put her hand in his jacket pocket and removed the gold bracelet she had sold him earlier and slipped it in her bag.

'Are you all right? It's Joana isn't?' The Duchesse asked kindly.

'Yes madam, thank you, I think I'm okay, but I've lost my friends...' She said wearily.

'Good...' She said ignoring her answer. 'Go and get my fur coat from the cloakroom and then you can go home...'

Joana looked confused for a moment, and then she headed towards the cloakroom in the reception area. Suzanna turned to her husband and grabbed his arm.

'Let's go, we have the necklace safe with most of the expensive pieces in the armoured truck, leave the mess to your men...'

'So Marco was right, those Italians were fakes...'

'Yes darling, so let's get out of here. We'll take the lift from the floor below, most of these people don't know there's a second lift.' Joana returned with the mink coat, she helped Suzanna put it on and smiled. Susanna ignored her and made for the reception area.

As they passed the lobby it was chaos. Most of the restaurant guests had minor abrasions and were bleeding from various parts of their bodies.

Any signs of gallantry had disappeared and the lift area was a battlefield.

The Colonel pushed pass the army of guests in their uniforms of evening wear and medals of diamonds holding his wife's arm.

The stairs were much quieter; they stepped over the dead Italians and saw a few people were taking the stairs slowly. On the landing six people waited at the second lift.

When the stainless steel door opened they all rushed to be first in. The Colonel pushed them out of the way and shoved his wife forward. A tall man in a German soldier's uniform grabbed José Valles-Carrera by the neck and pushed him back into the corridor.

'I'm a Reichsführer, you Spanish scum, get out of my way!'

The Colonel's face twisted into a mask of hatred, he pulled out the pistol, shot the old man in the leg and shoved him into the corridor. The women cried out and the other men grabbed the Reichsführer to break his fall. The lift doors closed with only two passengers, rapidly descending the sky-scraping tower to the safety of the street.

Chapter 52
Deadly Endings

'**B**less me father for I have sinned, it has been about three years since my last confession.'

'Ah-ha.' Father Domingo Arenas said, kissing his gold and purple stole.

'Father…I've had impure thoughts…'

'Ah-ha.'

'I've slept with a woman who wasn't my wife…'

'Yes…'

'She was still married to someone else…'

'I see,'

'I loved her so much Father…' The man behind the wooden grill broke down, and fell against the little wooden ledge of the ancient confessional, his knees pressed into the leather-covered, padded step; a small luxury for those with long confessions. The priest was a patient man, understanding how hard it was for some Catholics to confess their sins, to actually verbalise their indiscretions and little dishonesties. He had noticed, since recently returning to Barcelona, that rich people and the upper classes, found it harder to admit their mistakes, than the poorer faction of his congregation. Father Domingo considered that it might be a problem of pride, one of the things priests were supposed to denounce.

He remembered his ordination rites. There were twenty other priests called and presented to the assembly. Firstly, all of the candidates were questioned on their faith. They promised to obey their Ordinary or Bishop. Following these vows they had to prostrate themselves on the cold stone floor, in front of the Cathedral's altar. Their colleagues prayed for them on their knees, and the choir sang the Litany of the Saints, filling the air between the cathedral and heaven. The bishop then laid his hands on Domingo's head, as did the twenty priests following him. The ritual continued with the consecratory prayer when they addressed God the Father, invoking the power of the Holy Spirit upon the entire group. Finally he performed his first act as a minister, concelebrating the Eucharist, uttering the ancient prayer.

Father Domingo Arenas had decided when he was thirteen years old that he would donate his life to the priesthood and charitable works. Once he completed his vows he applied to work in Mali, Africa. He was passionate about helping women and children to lift themselves out of poverty and obtain an education. When the Church instructed him last month to leave the work he'd started years earlier, and return to Spain, he was devastated. He pleaded with his bishop to allow him to continue with the natives he loved. They had learnt to rely upon him for their education and guidance over the nine years that he worked and lived among them, and he claimed they would be lost without him. When he left the village reluctantly, people came from a twenty-mile radius, in cars, trucks, as well as buses and on foot.

They danced, waved goodbye, and sang their songs of sadness for their great loss. Because his spiritual children knew that Father Domingo Arenas was a good priest and a good man. Now the handsome cleric had a different challenge, epitomised by the problems he faced with his parishioner Señora Pepita Ruiz de la Vega-Rato; the beautiful wife of the colourful and infamously corrupt politician, Señor Luis Rodriguez-Rato. The first time he was told by the bishop that he was invited for dinner at the wealthy politician's house, he refused to go. Domingo wanted to visit and help the poor and needy, not the rich and corrupt.

'Listen to me Domingo...' Bishop Alfredo Perez asked seriously. 'This is not the African jungle; we live in a Catholic country with the full support of the Government. The Church and the Government must work together. How do you think the Church paid for all of those years you spent enjoying yourself with those heathen natives?' The bishop asked firmly.

'But Bishop, I was never paid any salary and lived in a mud hut in the village. Most of the food we ate had been gifted, it came from the villager's little farms and their meagre livestock.'

552

'Of course Domingo, but who paid for your training and travel expenses to get you there in the first place? Who paid for you to come back to Barcelona? When you asked for books and medicine, we sent them to you. Someone had to finance all of that.'

'Yes Bishop, although I still don't understand what this has to do with me going to this dinner! I've never been to a dinner before, I won't know which knife and fork to use or what to say to them.'

'Because my son, Señor Luis Rodriguez-Rato is not only a very wealthy politician, but also a generous benefactor of the Church. He and his charming wife are good Catholics and support us. We need to keep in contact with our supporters on a social level, so that we can speak freely to them when we need help; and we will always need help. Your predecessor was very much liked by Señora Pepita and through him the Church received a large number of charitable donations. So much so that he has been made a bishop! The Church rewards those who have the ability to obtain financial assistance. Without people such as these, we would not have any missionaries or even a roof over the cathedral. The work of Our Lord moves in many mysterious ways my son; it's not only a matter of feeding and educating some poor natives. Do you understand now?'

'Yes Bishop, I'm sorry; I was being stubborn and selfish. Just because I enjoyed my work in Africa, it doesn't mean that I can stay there. I realise that, I must help in any way I can. Our Church must survive in Spain, so that it can spread the word of God, and help those who need us around the world.'

'Thank you Domingo, I'm sure they will like you and your...how shall I say this, naïve attitude to life. So go along to the dinner and just be yourself. Be kind to them and who knows, if they are as pleased with you as they were with your predecessor, the Church may be able to do the repairs and building work we so desperately need.
Perhaps one day, we might be able to send you back to your congregation in Africa, as a bishop!'

'Thank you Bishop, I would love to return to my people...'

'*Our* people Domingo, they belong to the Church, our disciples own nothing.'

'Yes Bishop of course.' He said, with unspoken words still reverberating on his lips.

When Domingo arrived at the dinner, he was shocked by the opulence of the Rodriguez-Rato's mansion in Barcelona's richest barrio. He only had his old black suit with its patches on the elbows, a worn-out pair of shoes and frayed dog collar. He felt so completely out of place in the magnificent dinning room, with nine sophisticated diners dressed in clothes and jewellery more expensive than a dozen village's entire wealth, where he had worked in Mali most of his adult life. Domingo was also shocked by the dinner conversation, which was so uncaring towards poor and helpless people, both in Spain and elsewhere. He winced at the sexual innuendos and racial slurs. The conspiratorial laughter about the money gained by land grabs, illegal urbanisations and deposits for off-plan properties. Although the experience that really shocked him was at the end of the first dinner he attended.

'Must you go so soon Father Domingo?' Pepita asked flirting, flicking her long dark hair to one side of her bare, bronzed shoulders.

'Yes, thank you Señor and Señora, it was a most enjoyable evening. I don't think I've eaten this much in years.' He said smiling and patting his hard, flat stomach. 'I must get up early tomorrow, as I need to visit a home for the disabled in Sant Coloma. Some of the elderly there haven't had a confession for some time!'

The other guests looked at the young man smiling at his simple enthusiasm for the futile work.

'I'm looking forward to my first confession with you Father.' Pepita said suggestively, as though the act related more to sexual secrets and penance, than an admission of guilt, repentance and the prospect of God's forgiveness.

When thirty-five-year old Pepita escorted the young man of the cloth, down the huge circular staircase to the entrance hall, holding his arm tightly, Domingo stopped at the door, gave a little bow and offered his hand politely.

However, Pepita planned to continue with this young man as she had with his predecessor and kissed him passionately on the mouth. The priest was shocked. He had never kissed anyone on the lips before, or rather no one had kissed him on the lips before. His face flamed red. He rushed out of the house and didn't stop running until he was back in his little room near the cathedral. Pepita watched him disappear into the darkness with a sense of joy and anticipation that she hadn't experienced since she was a teenager. She said to herself: 'Well, I think that might have been his first kiss; imagine how he's going to feel the first time I make love to him.'

Sixty-nine-year-old Señor Luis Rodriguez-Rato, happily turned a blind eye to the indiscretions off his young and beautiful wife. In fact, her penchant for young naïve priest was the perfect solution. No girlfriends or wives to make a scandal, almost total discretion from the men, and a cheque to the Catholic Church once a month or so kept everyone happy.

The following months became more and more difficult. Pepita came to his confessional each Friday. She told him in graphic detail about her sexual experiences, which included the gardener, her car mechanic and an artist who had been painting her portrait for the last two years. She rarely had any encounters with her husband these days, as he was incapable. Pepita often went into fine detail about the sexual acts that were performed upon her, as well as the bondage games she loved to play on her lovers. The young woman always finished her confession expressing her desire to add the young priest to her list of conquests and at the last dinner, she sat next to him and massaged his crutch under the tablecloth. Father Domingo pleaded with the bishop to stop sending him to their mansion, but he flatly refused, saying that his bishopric needed the young priest's help and compliance.

'Have you finished my son?' Farther Domingo asked, after several minutes of almost silent tears from the confessor.

'No Father…there's more. I've taken drugs…'
'I see.'

'I've robbed innocent people in shops and on the streets...'

'Yes...'

'I attacked a drug dealer and he had to go to the hospital...'

'Ah-ha,'

'Father – I-I...' He stuttered, in immense physical and emotional pain.

'Perhaps you would prefer to tell me in your own words the difficulties you are facing, I may be able to help you...' The priest said kindly, hoping to do some real work in his dioceses.

Jorge paused for a moment; he had walked up jaggedly from the port at a matutinal hour to the magnificent Santa Maria del Mar Basilica. The long Carrer de Montcada was empty; the tiny passage grazed the walls of the lofty church, which was squeezed within the warren of narrow streets. Jorge entered from the west side on Carrer Santa Maria Passeig del Born, through one of the smaller side doors. He looked up at the candle lit, raised altar and made his way around to the back of the church where the twin confessionals lay in wait, sentinels of sin on either side of the long window. The wooden cabins had space for two sinners, one on either side, like guilty scales of justice. Jorge went to the left one because the curved, necromantic wall supporting the back of the church, gave him a secluded, stone womb to wait in. He fell asleep exhausted, until the priest arrived at eight o'clock.

'Well Father...' He started again. 'When my family moved to Madrid from Nerja in Andalusia, we were happy to be in the capital.

My father found work as an electrician, my mother a job at a Catholic dairy, my brother Felipe and I finished our education. Felipe followed in our father's footsteps and worked as an electrician, although I found it hard to get a job I wanted.

I went somewhat loco when young. I got in with the wrong crowd and stole a motorbike. Some older men from the market gave me a job running errands. It turned out that I was delivering drugs. I decided to sell my own drugs, once

I knew the customers, and at first I made a lot of money. After a while, I made the mistake of using my own product. At first it was fun, I had a lot of girls because of the money. By then I drove a Fiat spots car and had some nice clothes. However, I started to fall apart; I was taking more drugs than I sold. I lost my money, my apartment: the whole lot. My brother Felipe introduced me to a lovely girl called Paloma. Wow! She looked so beautiful, she had a few problems of her own. Her husband acted violently towards her, he was an alcoholic and she wanted to get away from him. As you know the laws on divorce make it impossible for women and so somehow we helped each other. Paloma stopped me taking drugs, I helped her get away from her brutal husband and we lived together. Yes Father, we lived in sin.'

'I see.' The priest said.

'She moved in to my place and made it nice, we didn't have much money, but I would steal flowers from the park, yes, I'm sorry Father, that's another confession. I still stole small things. Anyhow, I had stopped stealing from shops and people...the flowers looked nice in the flat, you know, more feminine.

Then one day when I got home from work, Paloma was so happy, singing and dancing around the flat. She loved music, and had the table set out with a white cloth. I think it was the bed sheet; it looked nice and she bought half a chicken, we even had some cava. As soon as I walked in she held me and we danced to a record borrowed from her friend Henriqua. We sat down to this great dinner and then she just erupted in front of me with laughter and tears at the same time. I didn't know what was happening until she said we were going to have a baby.

We cried together, our tears mixed on our faces, as we danced around the room. I know Father we had no right to have a baby, we weren't married and we couldn't marry, because of the law, but we were so happy. I didn't know how we would pay for the baby, although it made me determined to go straight, never again do anything illegal or against our religion. I found a second job and then a third. I was a cleaner in the early mornings, an electrician in the daytime and a barman in the evenings. I worked a hundred hours a week. They weren't good jobs and so we were still broke, but it was honest work and we could see a future: a future for three. When she was seven months pregnant, I came home and Paloma said she had good news, there was a Catholic maternity clinic called Sant Ramón and they had accepted her, saying she could have our baby there, free of charge!'

'So your problems were resolved.' Father Domingo returned encouragingly. Jorge started to cry and choke again and found it difficult to speak.

'That's what we thought Father, however, well, it's a long story. Paloma died giving birth, the doctor we saw afterwards said that the nun's in the clinic had made a mistake and within a few days she was dead.'

'I'm very sorry to hear that.' The priest said softly.

'Yes – after she died, I went to the clinic for my son, our son, and they said the baby had died as well. The Mother Superior or whoever she was, said it was because we weren't married and that it was God's punishment.'

The priest winced.

'I went back to the clinic and a couple of nuns took me to the chapel and showed me my dead baby. It looked horrible, blue in the face so ridged. As solid as the statues in the nativity play at Christmas. My whole body seem to collapse from the inside, I had taken some more drugs after Paloma died and decided to kill myself. As I was leaving the clinic an angel came to me, a beautiful young girl like a nun, dressed in long white robes. She gave me a note; I still have it here in my pocket, saying that the clinic had sold my baby boy!

After a few days I sobered up a little. I went to see my local priest, and told him that the Church was in cahoots with the Sant Ramón Clinic and that they'd stolen my baby. He said that he didn't believe me. I also went to see the bishop. Although when the reception staff saw my clothes and drugged condition, I was shown out. Then I spoke to my brother's ex-girlfriend Vera, she was a nurse and knew a lot of people, including a famous doctor; called Professor Gregorio Marañón. They tried to help me. The Professor wrote to the clinic, he said he wanted to do a blood test on the dead baby, to prove it was mine. They refused, but he applied for a court order. About two months later the Professor contacted a politician he knew from before the war. He complained that the clinic hadn't obeyed a court order to let him exhume the baby's body and do a paternity test. The politician made a few enquiries, and told the Professor to forget the test, as the head of the secret police was now investigating the clinic, and would sort it out.

Three months past with no news and so the Professor went to see a newspaper editor and gave him the story. A few days later, Vera came to my flat in tears, saying that the Professor had been in an accident. He was run over by an army truck while crossing the road in front of his little clinic, and was dead.

My brother Felipe was reluctant to help me, he didn't believe that the Church or the authorities would do anything wrong. After a while he saw how much I had deteriorated and went to the local police, he told them that we had evidence that the clinic had stolen my baby.

They took loads of details from him and said that they would investigate. About two weeks later he was walking home from work and someone hit him over the head in the street.

After he regained consciousness he found himself in a factory that made televisions. When he staggered up from the floor the police came running in and said that he was robbing the place, before we knew what happened, he was sent to prison for five years. Vera was a fabulous girl Father, a nurse and really smart. Too smart for my brother, although she was also very politically active. She was sure that the professor's death was not an accident and that he had been killed deliberately. Even I didn't believe her at first. Vera said that we would be next, and so she left Spain and emigrated to America.

My life had collapsed by then, I started sleeping on the street near to the Sant Ramón clinic. I hoped to see the beautiful nun who gave me the note. After two or three weeks there was no sign of her, then I thought I saw her with another nun walking as though they were glued together. I ran up to them and pulled her arm, the girls seemed shocked. I suppose that I didn't look very presentable by then, because I was using heroin. Anyway, it wasn't her. I asked them what happened to the other nun with the beautiful face and they said she had been sent to a mission in Argentina.

I went back to my old existence, stealing, robbing and buying stronger and stronger drugs. I had found a place to sleep at the back of a newsagent's shop in the centre of Madrid. I used to make yesterday's newspapers into a bed each night. Sometimes, if my head were clear, I would read the papers and magazines.

About a month ago I saw a photograph of the superior nun from the clinic. Strangely, the article said that she was a rich socialite and married to the former commissioner of police in Madrid. It took me a while to understand what this meant. Then all of Vera's theories about corruption and the note about my boy being sold, seemed to come together in my mind. I hitchhiked to Barcelona and found out where this so called nun, who called herself Señora Suzanna Valles-Carrera lived with her husband. This man was the same policeman who was supposed to have investigated the clinic. It wasn't difficult to find out about them, because they seemed to be celebrities in Barcelona. I slept at the back of their building and asked the local people about them. Then I heard that they were giving a huge party for a charity called, Fondazione Nazionale di Cristo. I discovered that the Foundation owned an adoption agency and took children from the Sant Ramón Clinic.'

The priest had now become fascinated by the confession from this poor crazed drug addict with his foolish conspiracy theories, and asked him how he had come to his confessional.

'Well about a week ago, I found the place where these people were having their party and I started to sleep nearby. In fact I had to move further away and sleep on the beach, because they had a restaurant there and the men outside kept moving me on; they even called the police a couple of times. I understood; I could barely stand up most of the time. I lived on the streets; I hadn't had a bath for a while, although a few people helped me with a little money. A few days ago a foreigner, English I think, gave me what used to be equivalent to my two weeks salary, so I managed to survive.

Last Friday night I saw an old man sneak into the restaurant tower late, struggling with a large holdall, as they were closing up. I supposed that he was like me looking for somewhere to sleep, although he didn't act like a tramp. I forgot about him, although last night they had their big party. I saw the head nun from the clinic with her husband. They were dressed up and she certainly wasn't a nun when she arrived. Security people and police surrounded them like a blanket, so I stayed in the shadows. About an hour before that, my heart raced, because three young girls came along and got into the lift, for a moment just before the doors closed, I thought it was Paloma, the girl had the same hair and she looked pretty just like my love. She stared back at me for a second, and then the lift disappeared.

For a couple of hours, maybe longer I fell in and out of sleep, lots of expensive cars arrived and people in eveningwear entered the restaurant. Suddenly there was an enormous explosion and pandemonium broke out. People were running out of the tower, cars were coming up taking people away. It was complete chaos; I even saw a man fall from above the cable car with his clothes on fire, he fell straight into the sea. Then, they were on the pavement, the Suzanna woman with her husband. This time they were alone and rushed towards their French car. I climbed out of the bushes, ran across the road and walked behind them. As I got closer, I could smell her perfume, it's a long time since I smelt a woman's perfume...' Jorge paused, his mind reliving the events from the night before.

'Ah-ha,' Father Domingo said.

'Father – I-I...' He paused again.

'What is it my son?'

'I - I have to confess, that a few hours ago, I murdered the woman.'

Father Domingo Arenas was stunned, he had been trained to never react in the confessional, whatever had been admitted to him; nevertheless, no one had ever confessed to murder before.

'Have you finished your confession?' The priest responded, trying to stay calm, wondering how many prayers a man has to say, to be forgiven for killing another human being.

'I ran up and stabbed her in the neck...' He said coughing violently, 'She looked surprised, almost offended. Her husband broke her fall. I didn't move. I just looked down at her; there was a lot of blood. I thought that I would feel a sense of justice for what she did to Paloma and my son...' He coughed again. 'But, I-I just felt empty.'

'I see...and then you came here?'

'No. I walked away from them, and half way across the road, her husband shot me, twice in the back...'

'Have you been to a hospital?' The priest asked urgently.

He waited again, yet there was only silence.

'Hello? Are you all right? Hello?'

Father Domingo Arenas got up from his hard bench, opened the door of the confessional and stopped at the little adjacent door. He wasn't supposed to look at the parishioners who came to him in the confessional. They should have confidentiality and anonymity. He tapped on the door and said: 'Hello...are you still there?'

There was complete silence, the priest looked around the cathedral, and it was empty. He slowly opened the little door and Jorge's dead body fell onto the stone floor at his feet.

The Beginning

Raymond Russell was born in London and is an award-winning journalist. He wrote the Off Broadway hit, Jack, Nikita and Norma Jeane, and is the author of the London Garden and Terrace Restaurant Guide, The Provençal Diet and numerous television dramas.
Deadly Beginnings by Raymond Russell, is the prequel to the Best Selling Novel, Deadly Endings.

Set in Rome and London in 1947 and looking back to the First World War, the novel develops the characters of the protagonists from the first novel in their earlier years.

The Vatican has survived the Second World War, but its cardinals are being mysteriously murdered one by one. Former escaped Nazis and the Mafia jostle for position in a changing world, where Russian Communism is taking over the vacuum left by a deflated and bankrupt Britain and an exhausted Western Europe.

Sam and Phaedra have been called in by a poverty stricken British Secret Service. Can they find the cardinal killer nicknamed the Purple Assassin? Will they get the upper hand on their old adversary Fyodor Poluostrovich from the KGB and will they discover who wants their daughter dead? It's Deadly and it's only the beginning.

Raymond Russell